AB
FOR THE

Also by Meg Hutchinson

A Handful of Silver
No Place of Angels
A Promise Given
Bitter Seed
Love Forbidden
Pit Bank Wench
Child Of Sin

About the author

Meg Hutchinson left school at fifteen and didn't return to education until she was thirty-three, when she entered Teacher Training College and studied for her degree in the evenings. Ever since she was a child, she has loved telling stories and writing 'compositions'. She lived for sixty years in Wednesbury, where her parents and grandparents spent all their lives, but now has a quiet little cottage in Shropshire where she can indulge her passion for storytelling.

Abel's Daughter
For the Sake of Her Child

Meg Hutchinson

CORONET BOOKS
Hodder & Stoughton

For my husband, whose patient encouragement and faith in this work remained when my own had failed. Thank you, sweetheart.

Chapter One

*'Phoebe Pardoe, I find you guilty of wilful theft. I order you
to be taken to a place of imprisonment where you will serve
a term of fifteen years' hard labour.'*

Phoebe pushed the soiled rags into the hot tub, wincing
as the soda bit into the raw flesh of her hands.

'. . . you be taken to a place of detention . . .'

She scrubbed the rags against the ribbed wooden board,
the menstrual blood of her fellow inmates turning the water
red.

'. . . fifteen years' hard labour . . .'

The words circled endlessly in her brain as they had for
the past eight months.

'. . . guilty of wilful theft . . .'

'Put yer back into it, Pardoe!'

Phoebe gasped as the slim wooden cane sliced across her
shoulders.

'. . . them bleedin' jam rags won't wash themselves – or
p'raps you ain't used to washin'? Yeah, I forgot you once 'ad
a laundry woman to do yer washin' for you. Well, you ain't
got one now, you bloody thief, so get stuck in or you'll be
sorry.'

Phoebe's teeth tightened on her lip; she knew better than to
answer back to Sally Moreton, superintendent of the laundry.
Built like a man, her mouth was twisted up at the side due
to some childhood illness, and her insides were twisted to
match. Beating other women seemed the only source of
pleasure she had, the cane she carried cutting into their

1

flesh on the merest excuse, and often without any at all.

Squeezing the strips of cloth and dropping them into a cane basket, Phoebe pushed against her hair with a hand as bloody as the rags she had just scrubbed, then picking up the basket she carried it to one of the steaming boilers, dropping her load inside. Now she could take a recently removed batch to the yard and peg them on the lines stretched between the buildings. These were the only moments in her long days that she looked forward to. To see the sky, to feel the clean air on her face, to hear a bird sing . . .

'Leave them!' Sally Moreton's cane came down across Phoebe's raw hands, her cruel piggy eyes gleaming at the scream of pain it brought forth. 'Martha can peg them out. We don't want to risk yer delicate constitution by sending you out into the cold air, now do we?'

'But I always do the pegging out!' The thought of not going outside, even for the few minutes it took to peg the strips of torn sheeting to the lines, made Phoebe forget what so many blows of that cane had taught her. 'Martha does . . .'

The stinging cut of the cane across her mouth stilled the rest of the protest, sending Phoebe crashing backward against the cauldron of bubbling soapy water.

'Martha does what I tell 'er.' The cane rose again, swishing downward across Phoebe's legs, cutting through the worn grey calico. 'Same as all the rest of the thievin', murderin' scum in this place – same as you will, Miss High and Mighty Phoebe Pardoe! An' if you answer me back one more time you might find yerself missin' a tongue to answer back with. Now get that lot in.' Lashing out with her foot, she tipped over another basket of soiled cloths, stained crimson against the stone floor. 'An' get 'em clean. I don't want to see no mark on 'em when I come to inspect.'

'You better be ready to play tonight, you stuck up bitch!' Liza Spittle dropped a fresh basket of laundry at Phoebe's feet as the superintendent moved away. 'Or Steel Arsed

Sal might find a bundle of these pushed up a chimney somewhere.'

'She wouldn't . . .'

'Believe me,' Liza cut in, the beetroot birthmark staining the left side of her face seeming to swell suddenly as though about to burst, 'that wouldn't stop 'er usin' that cane if we was to give her a good excuse. Loves to use the cane does Steel Arse. It's 'er only pleasure. Does for 'er what no bloke would – not wi' a face like that.'

'You're disgusting!'

'Am I?' Liza's large hand grabbed the basket Phoebe had lifted and, bundling several stained cloths together, she shoved them beneath the hessian sack tied about her middle. 'So tonight will mek two of us, won't it?'

The rest of the long day stretched out between jibes and advice as to how to please Liza, but there was no sympathy, that was something these women had had removed from them as cleanly as amputation severed a limb. Please God, Phoebe prayed when at nine p.m. the one gaslamp was turned off, leaving the dormitory in darkness, please God don't let her come near me. But instinct told her that God was not listening.

'So, you've decided to be nice to Liza, 'ave you?'

Liza Spittle sat on the side of Phoebe's narrow mattress, her approach from the far end of the line of ten tight-spaced beds lost among the snuffles and coughs of the women who filled them.

The dim light from outside had faded almost to extinction by the time it touched the beds but Phoebe did not need light to tell her who sat beside her; the rancid stale fish smell that always accompanied Liza, despite the compulsory baths with carbolic soap, told her her prayers had gone unheeded.

'I thought as 'ow you'd see sense . . .'

Liza bent forward, one broad hand pulling away the rough woollen blanket, the miasmic stench of her closing Phoebe's throat.

'Leave me alone,' she choked, swallowing the smell of the other woman. 'Please, leave me alone.'

Liza snatched the blanket further down, revealing white calico a pale shadow in the darkness. 'Is that what you said to the bobbies when they come fer you, or did you let 'em do this?' One hand undid the row of flat calico-covered buttons while the other pressed heavily on Phoebe's shoulder, the snores and moans from the other beds indicating that none of the other women cared what was happening. 'In fer thievin', ain't you?' The nightgown opened to the waist, the older woman pulled it wide. 'A necklace so I 'ear, a very valible necklace . . . Look good over these pretty tits I've no doubt. Did the bobbies tell you you've got pretty tits? Did they feel 'em like Liza's doin'?' A scaly-skinned hand closed over Phoebe's breast.

'Stop . . . please!' Tears poured down Phoebe's cheeks, salting her lips. 'Please stop.'

Liza bent forward, the stale fish smell of her gagging the girl beneath her. 'You'll be a-sayin' please again soon enough but you won't be a-sayin' stop. You'll be begging Liza to go on . . .'

'Somebody'll be beggin' but it won't be 'er.'

The voice was a hiss in the darkness as Liza was jerked from the bed and flung face down on the floor.

'I told you to leave the kid be, keep yer filthy paws off 'er!'

One hand pressed to her mouth to stop the vomit spilling out, the other holding the edges of her nightgown together, Phoebe recognised the tones of Tilly Wood; serving a life sentence, the gaunt-featured woman was the only soul in the whole prison who had shown her the faintest semblance of kindness in all of the eight months she had spent in this hell hole.

'Seems as 'ow you don't understand plain English . . .'

Suddenly there were no snores, no groans. The silence from the other beds announced that each woman was awake and listening though none moved.

'. . . well, Liza Spittle, I can mek it plainer fer you . . .'

Lifting herself on one elbow, Phoebe peered through the gloom. Tilly Wood had one knee between Liza's shoulder blades with both hands cupped beneath the woman's chin, forcing her head back.

'Play yer dirty bloody games wi' any other of the pissants you fancies but this one you leaves be, an' if you doesn't then you's goin' to be found behind one o' them bilers wi' a jam rag stuck in yer gob!

'Y'see, Liza, I ain't got nuthin' to lose – I'm already behind these bars fer life an' there ain't nuthin' Steel Arse or the likes of 'er can do to me they ain't already done in ten years. That's a long time, Liza, but you put one more finger on that wench, just one finger, and *you'll* be 'ere for eternity.

'Oh, you knows I pushed my swine of a man down the stairs, they told you that did the wardresses, but what they didn't tell you was I broke 'is neck fust. It didn't tek much . . .'

Pressing her knee further into Liza's back, she pulled the chin upward, bringing a strangled cry from the woman on the floor. 'Just a quick jerk and the spine was broke at the base of the neck. You don't 'ave to be no big bloke to do that, Liza, you just need to spend yer life fightin' off ten brothers an' a bloke you wus never married to in fust place.' The cupped hands jerked again. 'It would be easy, Liza, an' pleasurable, an' you would never know when it was comin', so if you wants to live long enough to get out of 'ere, you'll think on what I says . . . leave this 'un be!'

Rising, Tilly waited while Liza picked herself up and slunk back to bed, hearing the disappointed grunts coming from the shadows; there were many in the room who would have welcomed the snapping of Liza Spittle's neck.

''Er won't mess wi' you any more,' Tilly said, covering Phoebe with the blanket, then louder, ''cos Tilly Wood don't tell the Good Lord 'isself more'n twice.'

*I order you be taken to a place of imprisonment where
you will serve a term of fifteen years.*

Lying in the darkness, Phoebe knew her life would not
stretch that far.

How had this happened to her? Phoebe closed her eyes,
letting the darkness press against her lids, and in that darkness
saw again the summer ball and herself in a pink rose-trimmed
gown dancing with Montrose. Montrose Wheeler, son of
Gaskell Wheeler, owner of the Monway Iron Foundry, had
asked for her hand in marriage and her father had agreed.
The ceremony had been planned to take place at Christmas,
Montrose vowing he could hardly bear to wait until then. He
was so handsome and tall, his sandy hair and light blue eyes
so different from the coarse overfed features of his father or
his thin, sharp-faced mother. Who would have dreamed that
an evening so warm with music and moonlight, so soft with
the promise of love, would be the last time she would see
her fiancé, for in the space of weeks her own father lay dead
and with his death all her own hopes were extinguished.

'It's bad news I'm afraid, my dear.' Alfred Dingley, her
father's doctor and friend, had come to Brunswick House to
tell her himself of the accident in which her father's chaise
fell to the bottom of a vertical pit. Old mine workings, the
coroner had said. Wednesbury was riddled with them and
dangerous shafts regularly opened without warning.

The funeral had been a week later, a family affair with just
her father's brother Samuel and sister Annie, no one being
left of her dead mother's family.

Against the darkness of her lids, Phoebe saw again the
finely drawn face of Uncle Samuel, a carbon copy of her
own father, and the sad blue eyes that seemed to know
more than they revealed. Phoebe realised it was the only
time she had ever seen her uncle outside the house he
shared with his sister, and even on her rare visits to them
she was never left alone with him: 'Because of his stone

deafness, dear,' was what she was always told when she had asked the reason he never went out, an answer that even as a child she'd found unconvincing. Her Aunt Annie in her customary black, shrouded in the perennial air of bitterness Phoebe had recognised from an early age, sat straight-backed in the carriage that followed the hearse, black-plumed horses walking slowly to St Bartholomew's Church and her father's final resting place.

His death had been a blow but there had been worse in store for her, much worse. The reading of Abel Pardoe's will took place in the drawing room of his home, Brunswick House, the following afternoon. James Siveter, her father's lawyer, in a long old-fashioned tail coat that gave him the appearance of a crow, rose from his seat at her father's heavy oak desk, ushering Phoebe to a chair beside her aunt. His impassive face as he resumed his seat betrayed nothing of what was to come.

"'I, Abel Pardoe, being of sound mind . . .'"

Siveter's expressionless voice droned on through the bequests to servants, only changing when he came to her father's provision for Phoebe herself.

"'Next I come to my beloved daughter, Phoebe Mary Pardoe. By the time of my death you will have been Mrs Montrose Wheeler for many years and as such mistress of your own home and in need of nothing. Therefore I leave you what you have always had and enjoyed: my love.

"'Lastly, to my brother Samuel, and my sister Annie who has imprisoned him for the last forty years – to you, Annie Maria Pardoe, I bequeath the sum of one thousand pounds annually and the house you live in for your lifetime. To my brother Samuel Isaac Pardoe I bequeath this house and all its contents together with Hobs Hill Coalmine, Dangerfield Lane, the Crown coalmine, Moxley, and all lands, property, goods and monies pertaining to me. May God give you the courage to use them to buy the freedom I never had the courage to give you.'"

The numbness she had felt since her father's death shielded Phoebe from the full impact of what the lawyer had said and she sat there while her aunt ushered him out. Mrs Banks, their cook-housekeeper, offered to help her upstairs.

Now, opening her eyes, Phoebe stared at the moon-filled squares of the windows, their regimented line like the yellow eyes of demons about to strike, while in the shadowed belly of the room figures from her nightmare continued to move.

'You understand, Phoebe, Uncle Samuel needs continual quiet. To have a young girl about the place, especially one with the comings and goings of a fiancé, would be much too upsetting for him,' her aunt had said not two weeks later. 'Therefore I am asking you to make other arrangements.'

'But Uncle Samuel is already in continual quietness, is he not, Aunt?' Phoebe remembered her own answer and the fulminating look that crossed the older woman's face as she added, 'Is he not chronically deaf?'

'And are you not chronically rude?' her aunt had retorted waspishly, then drawing black gloves over thin stick-like fingers, drove home her winning blow. 'I want you out of this house by one week from today, and be sure you take nothing that was paid for by your father.'

'But Father paid for everything,' Phoebe had protested. 'My clothes . . . everything.'

Her aunt moved to the door, waiting while the maid opened it. 'Then you will have less to carry. But your uncle would not want you to suffer any hardship. Therefore you may take two dresses and two changes of underwear, and to be certain you take no more, I will send my own housekeeper to pack them.'

'Surely I may take my jewellery?'

'All paid for by my brother, therefore part of his estate and now part of Samuel's.'

'Not all.' Phoebe followed the spare grey-haired woman, whom for all their family connection she hardly knew, out into the late-autumn sunshine. 'I have several pieces left me by my mother.'

Annie Pardoe did not hesitate in climbing into her pony trap. 'Paid for, no doubt, by my brother.' Picking up the reins, she clucked the horse forward. 'Unless you have a deed of gift you will be wise to leave any such pieces where they are.'

Phoebe concentrated hard on the tiny moon-filled spaces, willing the nightmare memories to go away, but on they went, passing before her eyes like some awful dance. She had been writing to Montrose when the Wheelers' carriage had arrived from Oakeswell Hall, and she had felt so relieved. Montrose had obviously been informed of what had happened and was arranging for her to be moved to his parents' home until after their marriage. Grabbing her bonnet and smiling at her maid, Lucy Baines, Phoebe rushed out of the house.

'Miss Pardoe . . .'

The formality of the greeting from Montrose's mother did not surprise Phoebe who had always found the woman cold if not positively unfriendly; neither did the absence of her husband who would be at his place of business at this hour of the day.

'Miss Pardoe,' Violet Wheeler sat stiff-backed facing Phoebe, 'have you written to my son informing him of your situation?'

'No.' Phoebe shook her head, wondering how such a sharp-featured, cold-natured woman could ever have been given the name of so lovely a flower.

'I thought perhaps you may not have, therefore I myself informed Montrose of your position. Under the circumstances I must inform you there can be no question of a marriage between you. As an officer in the Guards Montrose must be seen to make a good marriage – he cannot afford to tie himself to a wife unable to bring with her a good social standing.'

Phoebe remembered the physical sickness that had come over her at these words; how she had stuffed a gloved hand into her mouth.

'I know this must come as a disappointment to you,' Violet Wheeler went on with no more compassion than if she had been wishing her young visitor a pleasant walk about the gardens, 'but both Montrose's father and myself agree that it is for the best.'

Of course it was for the best – the best for Montrose.

'And your son, Mrs Wheeler,' Phoebe had managed, swallowing the sickness filling her throat, 'does he also think that breaking off our marriage is for the best?'

'Montrose will take the advice of his father,' Violet Wheeler's sharp features tightened, her nostrils flaring with controlled anger, 'whilst you would be wise to take mine and say no more than that you feel unable to go through with the marriage so soon after your father's death.'

Phoebe turned her head sideways, staring into the darkness of a room she shared with nine other women. In the space of three weeks she was orphaned, homeless and jilted. Violet Wheeler had said her son must have a wife who could bring with her a good social standing. What she really meant was Montrose must have a wife with a good financial standing.

Three days after Aunt Annie's visit her housekeeper Maudie Tranter arrived to supervise the packing of two dresses and two sets of underwear in a large carpet bag.

'Miss Annie says I am to see that all wardrobes and cupboards are locked in my presence and that I am to take the keys back with me.' The woman looked apologetically at Phoebe. 'She also said I was to take your jewellery box . . . I am sorry, Miss Pardoe, but that was what she said and I have to do it or lose my position.'

'Please don't worry, Mrs Tranter,' Phoebe had tried to reassure the woman, 'no one is blaming you, of course you must do as my aunt says.'

'I've made an inventory of everything in that box,' said Abel Pardoe's own housekeeper who had watched the packing. 'That sees us all safeguarded, Mrs Tranter. Your mistress can't go saying as how anything has gone astray. Tell her this sealing tape was set around the box in your presence and this here is the inventory I spoke of with a copy already sent to Lawyer Siveter's chambers in the High Street for her to check by.'

Fanny Banks's quick fingers passed brown sealing tape three times around the box before handing it to Annie's housekeeper. 'Now, as you've seen to all you came for, you best be off back to that crow you call your employer. As for me, I'll be leavin' when Miss Phoebe do.'

With Fanny Banks treading on her brown skirts, Maudie Tranter dropped Phoebe a quick bob and disappeared from the room, her footsteps almost at a run on the polished wood of the corridor and stairs.

Phoebe herself had left the next day, bidding goodbye to a tearful Mrs Banks who was joining her sister in Chester and a defiant Lucy who vowed to 'go into the workhouse rather than work for that sour-faced prune, Annie Pardoe'.

Try as she might Phoebe had never been able to remember more than walking down the long tree-lined drive away from the large house that had been her home since birth. She knew only that somehow or other she had walked the three miles across open grassland to Hobs Hill coalmine. There Joseph Leach had half carried her into the tiny brick building he called 'the office'. Injured in an explosion underground years before, her father had kept him on ostensibly as tally keeper, though the times her father had taken Phoebe with him on his regular visits to the pithead it seemed Joseph oversaw just about everything. Prising the carpet bag from her fingers, he sat her on the one chair, listening as tears and words poured from her.

'Joe . . . Joe . . .'

Even now, in the quiet of a prison cell punctured only by the breathing of its occupants, the shout seemed to throb against her ears.

'Joe . . . there's bin a cave in!'

'Christ Almighty!' Joseph Leach turned for the door as it burst open.

'Joe.' A figure black from head to foot with coal dust,

the white circles around his eyes the only patch of colour, announced, 'There's bin a fall – roof gone.'

'Where?' Joe asked tersely, all thoughts of Phoebe gone from his mind.

'North tunnel.'

'Bugger it!' he rasped. 'I knew that bastard would go, I said it would. Who's down there?'

'Manny Evans's gang.' The begrimed figure made no acknowledgement of Phoebe's presence.

'Eight men,' Joseph said instantly, with no reference to anything other than his own sharp brain. 'Right, you send young Billy for the doctor then meet me at the mouth.'

After that the girl was forgotten as Joseph organised the rescue.

Though no sound from the pit head told the women of the town what had occurred, the sight of the doctor's trap following the path across the heath told its own story and soon they stood just beyond the green-painted wooden gates with her father's name painted tall and white across them – Phoebe could see them clearly from the small office, women with chequered shawls about their heads, each face chalky with fear.

'How many, Joseph?' Alfred Dingley jumped from the trap, a black Gladstone bag in his hand.

'Eight, sir. Emanuel Evans, Evan Gittins, Charlie Norton and 'is lad Tommy, Sam Deeley, David Walker, Ben Corns and Meshac Speke.' Joseph reeled off the names as he swept papers and ledgers from the table that almost filled the office, clearing a space for the doctor to work on any injured men.

'Where?'

'North tunnel about thirty yards in. We can get to about ten yards of 'em at a guess. I've got a gang in now clearin' rest, but the shorin's be weak. We got to watch rest of roof don't come in atop of 'em.'

'You are sure there are no more than eight?'

Joseph had pointed to a line of nails hammered into the

brick wall of the office, each bearing a round metal plate the size of a penny. 'Tokens be all in an' Davy's be all gone for North tunnel an' there be nobody else in that part o' the mine. I'll 'ave the tokens checked again though, if you wants, for the other seams?'

'No need.' Alfred Dingley glanced at the wall where the Davy lamps were hung as each man checked in when coming from underground.

Phoebe ran out into the yard after the two men as a shout of 'They'm through' rang out, watching them make for the mouth of the mine. Her offer of help went unanswered.

Slowly, the iron cage was winched again and again to the surface, the cries of the women reaching across the yard as they recognised their men, but each in his turn waited for the raising of the cage until the last survivor, Charlie Norton, stepped out, his fifteen-year-old son carried in his arms.

In the darkness, Phoebe threw an arm across her face, desperate to obliterate the screams of the lad's mother. They had been lucky, Joseph had said later, but what use was that to Sally Norton?

'You did very well.' Dr Dingley had smiled at Phoebe as the last of the men's cuts were washed and bandaged. 'Now you'd better let me take you home, my girl.'

But Phoebe had refused, saying she preferred to walk, not wanting to admit the truth of having no home and Joseph said nothing of what she had told him.

'You'd better cum along o' me,' he said, watching the doctor drive horse and trap through the gates, 'my Sarah'll know what to do.'

And she had, leastways until Annie Pardoe landed on her doorstep.

It hadn't taken long. A fresh ripple of anger swept over Phoebe and she flung her arm from her face as if fending off an enemy. News had a way of travelling fast and it was news in the town that Sarah Leach had taken in Abel Pardoe's daughter. Days from the cave-in at Hobs Hill mine her aunt had driven down to the Leachs' cottage and marched in. The whole thing was over before it began: the house was part of Samuel's legacy, as were most others in this area, her aunt said, and either Phoebe went or they did – and with them Joseph's job at the mine.

'Yer father was good to me, I can't turn me back on 'is wench.'

Joseph's protest at her leaving echoed in Phoebe's mind. He and his family were reluctant to see her go but as Sarah admitted, jobs were hard come by, especially for 'a bloke wi' a bad leg'.

Phoebe stared upward. The light against the windows was changing as her life had changed, but where the sky was brightening her life grew ever darker. Turning on to her side she closed her eyes, squeezing the lids tight, fighting away a memory she could not escape . . . *fifteen years' hard labour.*

Chapter Two

Phoebe breathed deeply, savouring the warm July air, not wanting to return to the stifling steam-filled prison laundry. Last night had been only one more in a long line of sleepless nights but Liza Spittle's visit to her bed had left her terrified, too afraid to sleep even after Tilly Wood had half throttled the woman. Phoebe pegged the last cloth to the line, her hand shaking. Liza wasn't the sort to give in easily, sooner or later she would try again.

'Thinkin' of doin' a runner, Pardoe?'

Sally Moreton stood in the doorway of the laundry, the long cane swishing alongside her skirts.

Phoebe picked up the empty basket.

'Wait!'

The order cracked across the yard. Phoebe stood still, watching the other woman march the length of the washing line, her cane lifting each of the cloths in turn.

'Wot 'appened last night?'

'Last night?' Phoebe hedged, knowing Sally Moreton would already have been told everything.

'Don't play the innocent with me, you bloody thief! I want to 'ear wot 'appened.' The cane whistled past, close to Phoebe's ear.

'I didn't know anything had happened.' She waited for the blow she knew the lie would bring. 'We all sat as usual, mending linen after clearing the dining hall, then at eight-thirty we dispersed to the dormitories and prepared for bed. Then at nine the light was put out and everyone went to sleep – at least that is what happened in our dormitory.'

'"At least that is what happened in our dormitory,"' Sally

Moreton mimicked, bringing the cane down again. 'Listen to me, you little snot! If nothin' 'appened 'ow come Liza Spittle can 'ardly shift 'er 'ead on 'er neck this mornin'? An' 'ow come when 'er talks 'er sounds like a glede under a door? Got a touch of this new influenza as 'er or is it somethin' else grabbed 'er by the throat? Somethin' like another woman?'

The cane tapped warningly against the drab grey skirts of the laundry superintendent. Phoebe knew that it would take very little to bring it lashing across her face.

'Lost yer tongue, 'ave yer?' Sally Moreton grinned, showing large uneven teeth, bases blackening with decay. 'You nearly lost a lot more last night. 'Ad a visit from Liza so I 'ear. Enjoy it, did you?'

Phoebe gripped the empty basket, holding it close against her as Sally Moreton stepped nearer.

'Play wi' these, did 'er?' Sally's free hand closed over Phoebe's breast and squeezed. ''Er likes tits does Liza, especially young tits.' She smiled again, bringing her face close to Phoebe's. 'The sort that is still firm. But it ain't just tits satisfies Liza, 'er likes more, 'er likes a bit of what's down 'ere . . .' The hand holding the cane knocked the basket aside, allowing the other to press between Phoebe's legs. 'I know what Liza likes. We 'as the same tastes if you see what I mean!'

Dropping the basket, Phoebe pushed the woman, causing her to take several steps backward. 'You disgust me!' she spat.

'So I disgust you, do I?' Sally Moreton brought the cane to rest against the palm of her left hand, eyeing the girl whose mouth was still swollen from yesterday's blow. It was going to be more than her mouth would be swollen this time! 'Did Liza disgust you an' all . . . could it be we ain't good enough for Miss 'Igh and Mighty Pardoe? Or is it Tilly Wood 'as staked a claim?'

'Tilly Wood isn't like that!' Phoebe flared. 'She hasn't got your filthy ways . . .' She stopped as the cane found its mark, the force of it splitting her lower lip as it threw her backward.

'So Sally Moreton 'as filthy ways, 'as 'er?' The cane whistled through the air, slicing across Phoebe's shoulder. ''Er ain't to yer liking.' The cane struck again. ''Er disgusts you, do 'er?' The cane flashed downward, cutting across Phoebe's cheek, then lifted high into the air again.

'Stop that!' Agnes Marsh caught the superintendent's arm, halting the blows raining on to Phoebe. 'You bloody fool, Sally. Ain't you got more sense than to beat the kid senseless this time o' the day?'

'I don't let nobody mouth off at me!'

'Nor you should,' Agnes allowed, 'but daytime ain't the time to teach her a lesson, you should know that.'

'No, it ain't, Agnes.' Sally Moreton lowered the cane, her eyes on the girl still shielding her head with her arms. 'But it won't always be daytime, will it? Then this one will really find out what it means to mouth off at Sally Moreton.'

'That's it, Sally.' Agnes Marsh, deputy superintendent of the prison laundry, released the woman's arm. 'Do what you like in the dark – that way there's nobody can point the finger. As fer 'er,' she jerked her head towards Phoebe, 'Governess 'as sent fer 'er, wants 'er upstairs.'

'What for?' Sally looked quickly at the woman beside her.

'Didn't say, just sent Mary Pegleg to say as 'er wanted to see Prisoner Pardoe in 'er office, now.'

'You 'eard 'er.' Sally reached out with the cane, poking Phoebe in the ribs. 'Get yerself up there . . . an' mind, I'll 'ear of every word what's said so you better be careful what you tells our new lady Governess about yer little . . . accident.' She touched the cane to Phoebe's bleeding mouth then stood aside. 'Get yerself to the bathroom and wash afore you go upstairs.'

Her eyes clouded with pain Phoebe picked up the fallen basket, carrying it into the steam-filled laundry and depositing it beside her washtub. All eyes followed her as she walked from the laundry; all eyes registered the bloody mouth and weals like scarlet ribbons criss-crossing her cheek, among them the eyes of Tilly Wood.

'Wot did 'er say?'

The evening meal of bread and potatoes finished and the dining hall cleared, the women prisoners sat at the long wooden tables, each with a piece of mending.

'She said I wasn't to be assigned to the laundry from now on,' Phoebe answered in a whisper.

'A sined? Wot does that mean?'

'It means 'er don't 'ave to scrub no more bloody jam rags, that's what it means.' Mary Pegleg, her duties as general dogsbody for the prison Governess finished for the day, sat with the others, the wooden stump attached to her left knee thrust out beneath the table. Tilly Wood looked up from her place opposite Phoebe but said nothing.

''Ave you bin sprung, Pardoe?' a thin whippet-like woman asked.

'No,' Phoebe shook her head, 'I am not being released.'

''Er's goin' into the sewin' room.' Mary Pegleg supplied the information with an air of importance. 'I 'eard through the door. I 'as to sit outside Governess's room case I'm wanted, an' I 'eard 'er say as 'ow Pardoe was to work in the sewin' room from now on.'

'By all the Saints in Heaven, I wish it were me!'

'Governess ain't that daft,' the whippet-faced woman grinned. 'Tek you in there an' Christ knows 'ow many would get clobbered.'

'It's not bloody fair! A bloke lathers the 'ide off of a woman an' 'e gets away wi' it. A woman 'its a man an' 'er finishes up doin' twelve months in 'ell, washin' other folks' dirty linen.'

'That's true an' all, Bridie Trow,' came another whisper, 'but you hit the man with a wooden stool, nearly knocking his brains out!'

18

'Holy Mother o'God, an' that's a dirty lie.' Bridie looked up from the sheet she was mending. 'Oi could never 'ave knocked out the man's brain for 'e 'ad none in 'is 'ead to start with.'

'Hey up, Steel Arse is comin'.'

The sudden whisper stilled the women's giggles and all heads bent to the sewing.

"Alf-past eight . . . pack up.' The ever-present cane swished as the superintendent of the laundry surveyed two hundred silent women. 'Put the sewin' in its proper basket then prepare for bed. Each dormitory will be inspected before lights out at nine.' She stood watching the women file silently from the hall, her eyes following the thin figure of Phoebe Pardoe.

'So 'ow come the sewin' room . . . an' why you?'

Hands and face washed, a rough calico nightgown swamping her stringy body, Tilly Wood sat on the end of Phoebe's bed, the other occupants of the room covertly listening.

Phoebe glanced at her hands, encased in the white cotton gloves which Hannah Price, the prison Governess, had given her to protect them while they healed. 'It seems Mrs Price was invited to a friend's house at the weekend. While she was there they visited the Goose Fair at Wednesbury and Mrs Price purchased a petticoat from one of the stalls. She asked who had made it because she would like to buy more but was told that would not be possible for the girl who was responsible for the petticoat had been sent to prison in Birmingham. Being told the name "Phoebe Mary Pardoe", the governess guessed it might be me. When I told her my home was in Wednesbury she asked to see some of the sewing I had done here in Handsworth, then she said I was to be assigned to the sewing room but my duties would not begin until my hands were healed.'

'An' yer face?' Tilly asked, looking at the weals still red

against the swollen flesh. 'What 'ad the Governess to say about that?'

'She asked what had happened. I told her it was an accident, the drying racks had slipped and caught me on the face.'

'Best way,' Tilly nodded. 'This is a new government prison, it ain't like the old 'uns with everybody packed in a single stinkin' underground cell, an' Hannah Price is first woman to run a prison as I know of. It will be a 'ard job keepin' it if I know anythin' about men – one breath about 'er bein' unable to control we women an' 'er'll be out. Besides . . .' she threw a meaningful look at Liza Spittle '. . . we can sort out our own problems.'

'Find yer own bed, Tilly Wood.' Sally Moreton strode into the long room, her cane slapping the foot of each bed as she passed. Reaching Phoebe's, she paused. 'Seems you 'ave more than one visitin' yer bed at night, Pardoe.' She touched the cane to Phoebe's breast. 'Already gettin' more than tits to play with, are they? P'raps we better move you from more than the laundry.' She smiled, showing her blackened teeth. 'Mebbe that little room next to mine? Be nice an' private there you would, nobody to come pawin' you in the dark.'

In her bed, Tilly's strong fingers tightened on the rough blanket.

'Now the lot of you, listen!' The cane cracked against the iron frame of each bed like a series of pistol shots as Sally Moreton proceeded to the door. 'There'll be no lovers' meetin's tonight, no moonlight walks from bed to bed . . . you 'ear that, Liza Spittle? Each of you stays put where you am now. Ignore Sally's warnin' an' you'll wish yerselves dead!'

Turning off the one gaslamp, she left.

'Goodnight to you an all, Mrs Moreton,' Bridie Trow called softly after the departing wardress.

'An' arsehole to yer warnin',' another voice added, just loud enough to be heard.

20

'Ar, an' you can stick yer cane up that!' Mary Pegleg laughed in the darkness.

'Sure, Mary, an' that's not the place old Steel Arse will be pushin' 'er cane in 'er lonely room,' Bridie Trow said crudely. 'It's not that 'ole she'll be a pokin' stick into, may the Divil an' all 'is demons escort her into Hell!'

Tilly Wood pulled the blanket up to her chin, remembering the weals on Phoebe's face, the broken mouth swollen to four times its size. The Devil could have Sally Moreton but it would be Tilly Wood gave her to him.

Phoebe stared at the windows high above her bed. Why had her aunt turned her out of her own home? Why after that had she ordered Joseph Leach to turn her out of his? Why did her aunt hate her so much? Why had Montrose not come to see her or even sent a note? The questions kept sleep from her.

'. . . *I find you guilty of wilful theft* . . .'

The words seemed to echo through the quiet room.

'*I want you for my wife, Phoebe.*' The figure of Montrose Wheeler rose in her mind, so tall and handsome, so dashing and attentive. '*I want to take you to London . . . to Paris . . . I want to show you off to the world . . . I love you, Phoebe, and I want you to be my wife.*'

But he hadn't loved her enough to write, he hadn't wanted her badly enough to come for her when the home she thought hers forever had gone instead to her aunt and uncle.

And her aunt had made sure she went from it quickly, just as she had made sure she had also gone from Joseph's home.

But Joseph had not left her entirely without help. He had taken her to see Elias Webb, a stumpy irascible man who owned property on the edge of the town.

'I wants no truck wi' the Pardoes,' he had shouted, his face red and angry when Joseph told the reason for their visit. 'It was Abel Pardoe ruined my business when he sold Monway Field to an iron merchant – pulled my mill down, 'e did, a mill I'd ground flour in all me life, ar, an' me father afore that, an' then she . . . Annie Pardoe . . . I wasn't good enough fer 'er . . . wanted no mill owner fer a 'usband did that one . . . bloody stuck up bitch! No matter who got 'urt so long as it wasn't Annie Pardoe.'

'Then why let 'er 'urt another, Elias,' Joseph had asked, 'why when you can stop it?'

"Ow can my lettin' Abel Pardoe's wench 'ave my 'ouse 'urt that bitch of a sister of his'n?" Elias had demanded.

"Cos your 'ouses are about the only ones left in Wednesbury as don' belong to Pardoe or Foster or Platt, or else to folk who am beholden to 'em. Annie Pardoe not only turned 'er own brother's wench out of 'er father's 'ome, 'er turned 'er out o' mine. Said if 'er didn't go, I 'ad to – an' lose me job at the pit an' all. An' if Annie Pardoe 'as seen wench off two places, what meks you think 'er will let Abel's daughter rest in any if 'er can do anythin' about it?'

Elias had looked at her then, Phoebe remembered, his eyes bright and calculating in his red face.

'Why let the sins of the parents fall upon the children, Elias? Especially the sins of Annie Pardoe.' Joseph drove home the last nail.

'That 'un!' Elias had almost spat the words. 'Annie Pardoe is still the same heartless . . . done!' He struck the table palm down. 'You can 'ave the 'ouse but it will cost you two 'undred an' fifty guineas . . . tek it or tek yerself off.'

Joseph had tried to get Elias to lower his price but Phoebe had agreed. To own her own house, however small, a house her aunt could not turn her out of, would be worth two hundred and fifty of the three hundred guineas her maternal grandmother had left her.

Wiggins Mill stood some way out of the town, close to its own pool. Set in a hollow, it was sheltered from the winds blowing off the open heath, the Birmingham Navigation Canal at its rear. With a scullery, kitchen, large living room and smaller parlour, three fair-sized bedrooms, together with the usual outhouses and a stable, it had become hers the following day.

And a week later Annie Pardoe had arrived.

'And this is where you intend to live?' she had asked, looking down her nose at the furniture which the remainder of Phoebe's guineas had bought from John Kilvert's pawn-broker's shop in Union Street. 'And what do you intend to live on?'

Refusing the offer of tea, her aunt wiped a gloved finger across the chair Phoebe indicated then refused that too.

'. . . or is there someone prepared to keep you – for a price?'

Staring at the squares of moonlight high on the shadowed walls Phoebe felt again the heat that had risen to her face and the cold steady rise of anger in her stomach. She had despised Annie Pardoe then: before that moment she had held no real feelings for the woman who was her father's sister, but at that moment the seed of hate was sown.

'Aunt,' her voice had been steady though she was taut with fury, 'this house is my home and how I choose to make my living is my business and no one else's. My father's will did not name either you or Uncle Samuel my guardian, therefore you have no jurisdiction over me. That being so, you will not interfere in my affairs.'

Her aunt's face had twisted with what Phoebe had hoped was derision but knew to be hate.

'What do you expect people will say . . . a young woman living alone outside the town?'

'That I'm what you already think me,' Phoebe had answered, 'a whore.'

Sally Moreton strode through the prison laundry, thin cane swishing beside the skirts of her grey uniform, her hair scraped back to form a knot at her neck, adding to the severity of her features.

'Call them clean?' She stopped at a basket of cloths, their sides ragged where they had been torn into strips.

Martha Ames looked at the cloths she had scrubbed at for over an hour. 'They look clean to me, Mrs Moreton.'

'Well, they don't look clean to me. Look at 'em!' Sally Moreton's black-booted foot caught the wicker basket, tipping it over to one side. Poking the contents with the cane, she strewed them across the flagged floor. 'Look at this . . .' She ground a boot into a wet cloth. 'An' this . . .' Her boot came down on another, leaving a dirty mark on each. 'An' wot about these?' Hitching her skirts, she trampled the freshly scrubbed cloths, spreading a pool of water across the floor.

Martha Ames stared silently at the cloths that had had her knuckles bleeding. She knew better than to argue.

'They'm bloody filthy!' Sally Moreton shouted, her tall man-like frame towering over Martha. 'Filthy, like all o' you scum!' She glared at the other women, watching silently. Only Tilly Wood's eyes refused to fall before her glare. 'We'll 'ave 'em done again,' she shouted, kicking the cloths across the floor, 'we'll 'ave the 'ole bloody lot done again. You!' She pointed to Bridie Trow. 'Get them boilers emptied. An' you,' she bawled at the ferret-faced Nellie Bladen, 'get fresh water in them tubs. An' you lot . . .' she glared around the steam-filled laundry, '. . . you all do the same. You are going to start all over again.'

'But, Mrs Moreton . . .' The pale consumptive face of Nellie Bladen blanched further as the superintendent swung back to her. 'That'll tek the rest of the mornin'. It'll be afternoon afore we can start washin' agen.'

'Are you arguin' wi' me?' The cane lifted, coming down hard across Nellie's thin shoulders.

'Steel Arse ain't took kindly to Phoebe Pardoe bein' teken out of 'ere,' a voice whispered behind Tilly Wood, 'looks like we am all goin' to be made to pay.'

'When I tell you what to do, you do it . . .' The cane rose again, coming down across Nellie's bent back. 'You don't talk about it, you *do* it!'

Tilly's hand tightened about the thick wooden stick she used to lift clothes from the boiling water in the huge copper.

'You 'ear me, scum? You do it.'

Nellie was already on the floor when Sally Moreton fell across her, unconscious from the blow Tilly Wood struck to the back of her head.

'That bastard has dealt 'er last blow.' Tilly looked at the figure of the wardress almost covering the thin woman half-conscious beneath her. 'Quick, you lot, 'elp me get Nellie out from under this swine.'

Bridie Trow grabbed the shoulder of the woman who seconds before had seemed set to beat Nellie Bladen to death, and heaved her aside, rolling her on to her back.

'Christ Almighty!' Martha Ames breathed. 'What've you done, Tilly? We'll all be done for when Sally Moreton comes to.'

'Holy Mother an' all the Saints.' Bridie Trow crossed herself. 'We'll all be swingin' on the end of a rope, so we will, when 'er tells Justice about this.'

''Er won't be tellin' Magistrates nor nobody else,' Tilly said, grabbing a cloth from a basket standing ready to be taken to the washing lines in the yard. 'Steel Arse 'as caned the last woman 'er'll ever cane an' spoke the last words 'er'll ever say.'

The cloth stretched between her hands, Tilly sank to her knees at Sally Moreton's head. 'Sit on 'er,' she said, looking up at the women grouped around. 'Bridie, Martha, sit on 'er – an' one of you watch the door.'

Then as the two women sat on the unconscious wardress, Tilly placed the folded cloth over the woman's face and held it tightly until any sign of breathing had stopped.

'That's you got yer comeuppance,' Tilly breathed, getting to her feet.

'An' may the Divil 'ave the dealin' of it,' Bridie added, crossing herself again.

'We'll all be meetin' 'im when Governess sees that.' Martha

touched a foot to the dead woman. 'We'll all be as dead as this one.'

'No, we won't.' Tilly looked at the woman on the floor. 'Find Mary Pegleg an' tell 'er to report to the Governess there has been an accident in the laundry . . . an' tek your time.'

''Ow do we mek this look like an accident?' Martha asked. 'The woman's dead.'

'Sure an' 'as no one ever died of an accident before?' Bridie answered as the woman watching the door set off on her message. 'Try holdin' yer gob for a second, Martha Ames, an' listen to Tilly.'

'Leave 'er be.' Tilly held out a hand to the women who stepped forward, about to lift the whimpering Nellie. 'Let 'er lie. Now listen to me. Sally Moreton was tellin' Nellie to tek the cloths outside for peggin' out when 'er started to gasp. 'Er clutched 'er chest, staggerin' about knockin' that basket over, then 'er cried out, a funny stranglin' cry in 'er throat, an' then tumbled 'ead first over Nellie there, nearly knockin' 'er unconscious. You two,' she pointed to Bridie and Martha, 'an' meself rolled Sally over an' called out 'er name, but gettin' no answer thought we best send for the Governess.'

'What d'you reckon will 'appen then?'

Tilly looked at Liza Spittle who until that moment had remained a silent observer. 'Do you reckon as the Governess will believe you?'

'I do.' Tilly looked at the woman who revolted her. 'An' I reckon summat else, Liza, I reckon you'd better keep yer mouth shut, 'cos what Tilly Wood does once 'er can do again – only next time it will be *you* lyin' there.'

'Won't the Governess be after sendin' for the doctor though, Tilly?' Bridie's look was as anxious as her question.

'I'm bankin' on 'er doin' just that,' Tilly answered. 'That Poor Relief doctor as looks after this place is more interested in the bottle than in patients. 'E's drunk no matter when 'e's sent for, be it day or night. It's my guess 'e'll tek one look at Sally Moreton, listen to what we tells 'im 'appened, an' say 'er died of an 'eart attack.'

'Amen to that,' Martha murmured.

'Holy Mother o'God, smile on the man an' grant he be as drunk as a fiddler's bitch!' And Bridie Trow crossed herself again.

Chapter Three

'Are you all right?' Bridie Trow had watched Phoebe from the start of the evening meal. 'You've not touched your taties other than chase 'em round the plate like a bobby after a babby.'

'Yes . . . I'm all right.'

'Like my arse you're all right!' Martha Ames popped the last of her own potatoes into her mouth, speaking as she chewed. 'I seen you comin' from the sewin' room an' you was cryin'.'

'Cryin'!' Tilly Wood stopped eating. 'What about . . . 'as anybody 'ad a go at you?'

'No.' Phoebe didn't look up, unable to keep more tears from filling her eyes.

'Then what am you cryin' for, Phoebe?' Mary Pegleg eased her wooden leg to a more comfortable position under the long scrubbed table top.

''Er's cryin' for to go 'ome,' Liza Spittle laughed, the beetroot mark on her face seeming to darken. 'Well, you'll cry a long time, Pardoe – about fifteen year I'd say.'

'Shut yer gob, Liza Spittle!' Bridie's eyes flashed.

'"As anybody said summat you didn't like, Phoebe? 'As anybody upset you, Phoebe?"' Liza Spittle minced, then laughed coarsely. 'You lot mek me sick the way you dance round 'er. 'Er ain't no different from the rest on we. 'Er was thievin' an' 'er was catched, now 'er's got to do time like we all 'ave so let 'er be . . . the more 'er cries the less 'er'll piddle.'

29

Tilly looked across the table, her thin face pinched with distaste. 'If you wants to chew yer next meal, Liza, then tek my advice and keep yer mouth closed.'

'Liza's right in a way, Tilly,' Mary Pegleg put in. 'Phoebe ain't no different. We all feel like 'avin' a cry at times, an' there be times when a good cry meks you feel better.'

'Give me half hour after lights out,' Liza smirked, 'then I'll mek 'er feel better. What Liza does is better for 'er than fartin' around wi' words. Ah bet you can remember 'ow it felt when that fiancy o' your'n touched you up, eh, Pardoe?'

Picking up her plate, Tilly tipped the remainder of her bread and potatoes on to Mary Pegleg's then swung the empty plate fast and hard, smashing it full into Liza Spittle's face.

'You was told to keep yer dirty mouth shut, Liza!' Tilly put the dented metal plate on the table as Sally Moreton's replacement began to move towards them. 'You should 'ave done just that, but then, they say there's no fool like an old fool.'

'What's going on here?'

Emily Pagett had been superintendent of the laundry for the month since Sally Moreton's death. She carried no cane but every prisoner in Handsworth gaol knew she was not to be played with.

'Phoebe . . . 'er's . . . 'er's a bit upset.' Nellie Bladen's consumptive face turned an even more sickly yellow.

'Why is that, Phoebe?'

Brushing at her cheeks with her fingers, Phoebe glanced up at the wardress. She had no occasion to see this woman other than at mealtimes, her place of labour being changed to the sewing room, but Tilly and the others had said she was not without sympathy.

'I . . . I was just remembering . . .'

''Er was saying that 'er father's bin dead twelve months today,' Tilly chipped in as Phoebe faltered. ''Er was very close to 'er father.'

'It happens to everybody, Pardoe.' Emily Pagett turned her

glance to Liza Spittle, trying to staunch the blood spurting crimson between her fingers. 'And what's happened to you, Spittle?'

'Sure an' 'tis the nose on 'er face, 'tis bleedin'.' Bridie Trow was angelic in her innocence. 'Sure an' it does that sometimes.'

'So her nose is bleeding. And what has happened to her tongue, why can't she use that? It's usually to be heard if she thinks none but inmates are around.'

'It'z juzt a doze bleed,' Liza snuffled through her fingers, 'it 'appenz zumtimes.'

'I see, just a nose bleed . . . not caused by anything specific like a snide remark or the promise of a midnight visit?' The wardress raised her voice so it carried over the clatter of forks. 'In the four weeks since my arrival in Handsworth I have come to know almost all of you women, and you have all come to know me and to know I will have no stepping out of line. Keep yourselves orderly, do your work well and there will be no trouble. That is *exactly* what I want and expect . . . no trouble.'

The clatter of forks resumed, no prisoner raising her head, each afraid that to catch the eye of the laundry superintendent might in some way constitute a challenge.

Her voice once more at a normal level Emily Pagett looked at Liza, blood smeared across her face, merging the beetroot mark into one red mask. 'Looks nasty, Spittle,' she said. 'Better get along to the washroom and get it cleaned up. You wouldn't want to get it knocked, now would you? That *would* be painful . . .' Then, her eyes still on the woman shuffling from the table, she added. 'And you, Tilly Wood, best try getting that plate back into shape. And next time, use your hand – there's less evidence that way.'

'How did you know?'

Phoebe slipped the rough calico nightgown over her head, fastening the flat cloth-covered buttons up to her throat.

31

'Took no guessin'.' Tilly fastened her hair in a plait, leaving it to lie across one shoulder. 'You've said one or two bits o' what 'appened afore you come 'ere, one o' em bein' as 'ow your father died sudden like.'

'God rest the puir man!' Bridie crossed herself.

'I never expected it.' Phoebe stared down at her hands, now lying in her lap. 'Father sometimes stayed away if his business took him to London or Southampton but he always told me first. I had no idea he had not come home that night until Mrs Banks announced his bed had not been slept in. Then when I heard about the accident . . .'

'Don't go over that.' Tilly fastened the buttons of her own nightgown. 'No use in rakin' spent coals.'

'Let 'er get it out if 'er wants to.' Martha Ames came to sit beside Phoebe on the low iron bed. 'Spit it out, wench, it'll feel better when you do.'

'It all happened so quickly,' Phoebe said quietly. 'Father dead, his will leaving me penniless, Montrose no longer wanting to marry me, and Aunt Annie turning me out of my own home . . .'

'By Patrick an' the Saints, ye puir girl! An' it's little wonder the Divil got his hooks into yous. So how did you manage, you never 'avin' to strike a blow yerself afore?' Bridie asked.

'I never would have managed without Joseph Leach and his family,' Phoebe answered. 'It was Joseph and his son Mathew who hired a horse and cart to transport the furniture from the shop to Wiggins Mill, and Sarah Leach and their daughter Miriam did most of the organising of the rooms. But it was providing food that gave me my worst moments. It was over an hour's walk from the house to the town and I would bring back only enough for one day. It was Sarah taught me to plan ahead, to buy in stones rather than in ounces, and it was she who got the carter to bring what I needed from the town and drop it at the crossroads on his way to and from Dudley. From the crossroads I had to carry it the half mile to the house. There were times I just wanted to give up . . .'

'I know that feelin'.' Nellie Bladen's sickly face looked death-like in the anaemic yellow light of the single gaslamp. 'But we keeps on goin' somehow.'

Phoebe smiled, recognising knowledge gained the hard way. 'Yes, Nellie, we keep going on. It didn't seem so bad once Miriam and Sarah finally taught me to cook . . . not so bad, that is, until I realised my very last pennies were gone.'

'Eeh, ma wench, 'ow did you manage?' Martha pressed a hand over Phoebe's, her eyes on the girl's face.

'I didn't know what to do,' Phoebe replied quietly, interrupted only by Liza Spittle's moans as the rough calico of her nightgown scraped her swollen nose. 'I only knew I wasn't going to take my trouble to Joseph and Sarah, they had done enough already and with my aunt only too ready to take their home . . . that was when Lucy Baines arrived. The carter had brought her to the crossroads then directed her to Wiggins Mill. I had not seen her since that last day at Brunswick House. She had found work at Sandwell Priory across the valley at West Bromwich. It was her first real day off, she said, and Sarah had told her how to find me.

'We talked a lot and laughed over some of the mistakes I had made while learning to fend for myself, then it came out about my last pennies being spent. She asked me about my jewellery, why didn't I sell it? I would get enough money to tide me over comfortably until I got work or was married.'

'But you said that fi-nancy o' your'n 'ad given you the push!' Mary Pegleg began, then stopped as Tilly's hand smacked against her backbone.

'Lucy seemed to think that was the least of my troubles.' Phoebe smiled again. 'I was better off without a "bloke with not enough oil in his lamp to light his way home", were her words, though what she meant exactly I don't know.'

'I do,' Tilly broke in for the first time since Phoebe had begun to speak. ''Er meant as 'ow your Montrose Wheeler 'adn't enough sense to hold on to a good thing when 'e'd got it, an' I fer one agrees wi' 'er. You be better off wi'out a bloke who only wants a woman for 'er money.'

'Tilly's right, Phoebe,' Mary Pegleg nodded. 'You be fortunate to 'ave found out what 'e was afore you married 'im. There be them among us as don't an' it's too late to do anythin' about it once you're wed. I know, that's 'ow I come to 'ave this.' She tapped her knuckles against the wooden stump below her left knee.

'So what did you do, Phoebe?' Martha asked, stealing Mary's moment of glory.

'I reminded Lucy of what my aunt had said. My mother's jewellery and mine must have been paid for by my father, and unless I had deeds of gift confirming they had been given to me, then they were part of the estate and as such belonged to Uncle Samuel.'

''Er sounds a proper old cow,' Nellie Bladen muttered. 'I wouldn't mind meetin' 'er one dark night. ''Er wouldn't bloody know 'er arse from 'er elbow when I'd finished wi' 'er.'

'An' the Lord give strength to ye,' Bridie Trow said fervently, 'an' the demons o' Hell be there to pick up the pieces.'

'And did you 'ave these deeds of gift?' It was Tilly who asked the question.

'No.' Phoebe shook her head. 'So when my aunt's housekeeper arrived to collect the keys to the house she was given both jewellery boxes, my mother's and my own.'

'So if your maid saw as 'ow the jewellery was took by your aunt's 'ousekeeper, 'ow come 'er asks you why you don't sell it?'

'I asked the same question,' Phoebe answered, 'then Lucy asked something else I found puzzling. What had I done with the dresses I had taken with me? I said I had not worn them since coming to Wiggins Mill, I had used only the underwear, the dresses were in a box in my bedroom. At that Lucy grabbed my hand and dragged me after her up the stairs. In the bedroom she flung open the box and threw the dresses across the bed. "Your bloody dried up fart of an auntie took your mother's jewellery but the old bag didn't get your'n," she said.' Phoebe halted. Less than a year ago she had never heard such words; now she could speak them without so much as a blush.

'But that 'ousekeeper of Annie's, 'er took both boxes, least tha's what you said.' Mary Pegleg sounded confused.

'So she did, Mary,' Phoebe answered, 'and I said the same to Lucy who laughed. She agreed Mrs Tranter had been given two boxes each containing pieces of jewellery – none of which, she said, was that given to me by my maternal grandmother. *That* she had removed from my box, replacing it with some of my mother's. She said Aunt Annie didn't know what jewellery my mother and I had so she would never know what or if any were missing.'

'Sure an' if that girl's brain is not the gift of the little people oi'll be after askin' what is?' Bridie Trow grinned. 'So tell me, what had she done wi' the trinkets an' all?'

'Sewn them in the hem of my dresses.' Phoebe looked at the women grouped around her. 'Mrs Banks and Lucy had taken my grandmother's jewellery out of my room as soon as Aunt Annie had left Brunswick House and together they had sewn it into the hem of two dresses, the two Lucy packed into a bag while Mrs Tranter watched.'

'Oi said it was the gift of the little people the girl had.' Bridie grinned again. 'Sure none but they have the guile to think of doin' the loike, sewin' baubles into a frock. Jesus, but Paddy O'Flaherty 'imself couldn't come up wi' better, an' him the smartest man in all Oirland.'

'So why 'adn't you sold the jewellery?' Tilly watched Phoebe's face, waiting for an answer.

'Because neither of them had told me what they had done. They both thought if I knew I would insist the jewellery go to my aunt, then Mrs Banks left for Chester, and with the worry of getting a new post and then not being allowed time off up until she came to see me that day, Lucy could do nothing but hope I'd found them.'

Seated on her own bed, Liza Spittle touched a finger to her broken mouth. 'If you found you 'ad jewellery to sell,' she said, trying hard to speak without moving lips swollen beyond recognition, ''ow come you was 'ad up fer thievin'? 'Ow come you am in 'ere doin' fifteen years?'

'You sew very nicely, Pardoe.' The prison Governess examined the stitches Phoebe had put into a church Psalter. 'Father Heywood will be pleased with these, I'm sure. Tell me . . . who taught you to sew like this?'

Hannah Price's office was at the front of the plain purpose-built prison and from where she was standing Phoebe could see out across the heath, out where people were living ordinary lives, where they could walk with soft meadow earth beneath their feet, where they could stand with the sun and wind on their faces, out where her own life had once been worth living.

'Mrs Banks, Ma'am.'

'Mrs Banks was your tutor?'

'No, Ma'am.' Reluctantly Phoebe turned from her view of the outside world. 'She was my father's housekeeper. I did have a tutor,' she explained, seeing the Governess's enquiring look. 'Mr Caleb Priest was my tutor until I reached the age of thirteen then my father thought my education needed a woman's hand. He engaged Miss Stephenson who did not think I would need the skill of needlework, but I enjoyed it. When she left I used to sit with Mrs Banks and Lucy. That was when I learned to sew.'

'I see.' Hannah Price returned the Psalter. 'Tell me, Pardoe, do you prefer to work out your sentence in the sewing room, or would you rather be in the laundry or the kitchens?'

Phoebe's hand tightened on the beautifully embroidered Psalter. To have to return to the laundry, even without the presence of Sally Moreton . . . a cold sickness rose in her stomach; fifteen years' hard labour, the Magistrate had said, and the woman watching her across the room had the power to return her to a labour that paralysed the soul.

'I . . . I prefer the sewing room, Ma'am.' Phoebe swallowed the sickness of despair. 'I . . . I hope my work is satisfactory?'

'It is.' Hannah Price nodded, the slant of sun through the window catching the chestnut brown hair she had coiled into a knot on the back of her head. 'And so is your behaviour. Your superintendent tells me you have given no trouble while you have been here and I have received no report of any disturbance in your dormitory.' Crossing to the table that served as a desk, she sat down, her hands clasped on its surface. 'In view of that, Pardoe, and of the excellence of your work, I am placing you in charge of the work of the prisoners in the sewing room. I hope you realise the trust I am placing in you?'

'I do, Ma'am.' It took Phoebe long seconds to find her voice, the sickness of fear subsiding into relief. 'And I will do my best to honour it.'

She had not been returned to the steamy hell hole of the prison laundry and to the hated task of washing menstrual cloths, a task Sally Moreton had taken particular joy in making totally hers. Phoebe looked at the Psalter she was embroidering. Fifteen years . . . how many Psalters would she sew in that time?

'Eeh, Joseph, I can't believe it!' Sarah Leach looked across at her husband. 'I can't believe Abel Pardoe 'as bin dead over a year.'

'You can believe it all right.' Joseph peeled off his moleskin trousers, dropping them beside shirt and waistcoat on the floor of the tiny scullery of the one up, one down that housed them, their twenty-year-old son and fifteen-year-old daughter. There was little enough room to move in the place but there would have been less had the rest of his seven children lived beyond babyhood.

'I 'elped to gerrim out an' our Mathew 'elped to carry 'im 'ome.' He slipped into the tin bath Sarah had prepared for him, the warm water easing his crippled left leg, that being the only thing that had prevented him helping to carry Abel Pardoe's body.

''Ow did it 'appen?'

Reaching for the Sunlight soap Sarah kept on a cracked saucer, Joseph lathered his face, blowing like a seal breaking the surface. 'Crownin' in,' he spluttered, 'along of Bilston Road, I told you.'

'I know you did, but I still can't believe it.'

Picking up her husband's clothes, she carried them into the small yard they shared with five other families and threw them across the rope Joseph had fastened for her between two slim tree trunks he had trimmed and hammered into the earth. Proceeding to beat them with a cane carpet beater, she coughed, catching some of the billowing coal dust in her throat. There were those in Wednesbury did this once a week, same as their men took a weekly bath, but in her house it was a nightly affair. Sarah gave the finishing whacks then gathered the clothes, carrying them back to the scullery. Wealthy they were not, but clean they would be.

'Did anybody see it 'appen?' She took up the conversation from where she had left it.

'Don't think so, not many comings and goings up that end during the week.' Joseph scooped handfuls of water, throwing it over his hair, revealing brown beneath the black. 'Folks is all at work 'ceptin' fer Sunday, an' most o' that is spent in Chapel.'

'What did Miss Phoebe 'ave to say?' Sarah had heard it all before but felt the need to go over it again.

'Not a lot, too shocked I reckon, though 'er did say as 'ow 'er father didn't go 'ome at all that night.'

'Oh!' Sarah placed trousers, jacket and waistcoat across a wooden stool. Then, 'Joseph . . . do you reckon 'e wuz theer all night . . . in that 'ole?'

'I doubt it, Joby Hackwood would 'ave found 'im. Them dogs o' his'n could find anythin' – sharp as a razor be them dogs an' Joby 'isself not far off. No, if Abel Pardoe 'ad met wi' that 'ole that night, Joby would 'ave found 'im.' His bath finished Joseph dressed. "Sides, 'e were facing wrong way.'

Carrying the tin bath out the back, Sarah emptied it into the communal drain that ran through the street of miners' houses then brought it back into the scullery against the arrival of her son.

'What do you mean, 'e were facin' the wrong way?' In the tiny living room she passed Joseph his clay pipe from the mantle then the precious tin with the last few strands of shag tobacco.

Joseph packed the tiny white bowl of the home-made pipe, pressing the tobacco firmly down with his thumb, testing the draw of it with loud sucking breaths before holding a taper to the fire. 'It were soft Johnnie as found 'em . . .'

'Wot! Minnie Pritchard's lad? I thought 'er kept 'im close, not let 'im roam about?'

'Lad 'as fits, Sarah,' Joseph held the lighted taper to the bowl, answering through short puffs, 'that . . . that don' . . . that don' mean as 'e's daft. Lad 'as a brain . . . it's folk around 'im as is daft . . . too daft to let lad be.' Knocking the taper against the bars of the grate blackleaded to a shine like silver, he extinguished the flame, dropping the taper back into a clay pot in the hearth. 'If that mother o' his'n let lad out to work . . .'

"Ow can 'er?' Sarah was quick to defend the woman. 'Lad 'as fits . . . 'e ain't responsible. 'E can't be trusted to act proper.'

'It's folk who believe that am the daft 'uns, Sarah.' Joseph leaned back into the chair set close to the fire, pulling heavily on the small pipe. 'Lad were responsible enough to come straight to pit an' tell me what 'e'd found. If that ain't actin' proper then I don' know wot is. Seems right responsible way of carryin' on to me, an' don' 'e always put isself down somewhere when 'e feels a turn comin' on?'

'I feel sorry for 'em both,' Sarah added coals to the fire, 'the lad an' 'is mother. What the good Lord was thinkin' on the day 'e was got . . .'

'Nobody knows the ways o' the Lord, Sarah, an' it's a wise 'ead that don' puzzle over 'em.'

'That be true enough.' Picking up her mending, Sarah carried it to the hard-backed settle beneath the small window. 'Any road up, it were lad found 'im, you say?'

Joseph tapped the white bowl against the palm of his hand, loosening the tobacco. 'Ar, leastways nobody else 'ad, not to my knowledge anyway.' He replaced the slender stem in his mouth, holding it between his teeth. 'Along about three o'clock he come runnin' into yard like a bat out of 'ell, babbling on about Bilston Road cavin' in and oss an' cart at bottom of 'ole.'

Sarah waited while Joseph tapped his pipe.

'I could see lad was upset,' a wisp of grey smoke curled from Joseph's lips, 'so I left office to Manny Whitehouse an' went wi' 'im.'

'What if gaffer 'ad come an' you not at the pit? You could 'ave lost yer job.'

'No fear o' that 'appening seein' it was 'im at bottom of that 'ole!'

You didn't know that at the time, tekin' off after soft Johnnie, Sarah thought, though was wise enough not to say it.

'Any road,' Joseph puffed, 'soon as I seen trap I knowed who it was 'ad gone in. I sent Johnnie 'ome an' went back to pit for men to raise Abel.'

'So, what about 'is facin' wrong way?' Sarah asked again as Joseph settled into silence.

'Well,' he removed the pipe from his mouth, his gaze on the glowing coals, 'if gaffer 'ad bin on his way from pit to the 'ouse, as Miss Phoebe thought, then oss would 'ave bin facin' t'other way, but it were facin' *toward* Bilston with its back end toward Brummagem.'

Sarah held the needle in mid-air, a puzzled frown drawing her brows together. 'What's wrong wi' that?'

'Think on it,' he answered. 'Abel Pardoe left 'ome that mornin' fer pit only 'e didn't come to pit that day. Miss Phoebe said 'e 'adn't come 'ome from pit in the afternoon nor 'ad 'e bin 'ome all night. Joby Hackwood is certain sure there was no 'ole in Bilston Road that night nor up to eleven o'clock next mornin' when he says 'e was runnin' 'is dogs along the edge o' cornfield . . .'

'Seein' 'ow many rabbits was runnin' likely,' Sarah said drily.

'Whatever 'e was doin', there was no 'ole in Bilston Road at that time or 'e would 'ave seen it, so Abel must 'ave run into it between eleven an' two. It would tek the hour between then an' three for young Johnnie Pritchard to sort out what to do then get isself over to the pit to get me.'

'I still don't see what you reckon is wrong?' Sarah stabbed the needle into her mending.

Joseph blew another stream of blue-grey smoke, the smell of shag tobacco mingling with the smell of coal. 'What's wrong is this. Oss 'ad its back end toward Brummagem,' he said, using the local term for Birmingham, 'that means Abel Pardoe was on 'is way back from there.'

'But 'ow can you be sure?' Sarah asked.

'I'm sure enough,' Joseph replied, his glance still deep in the heart of the fire. 'I 'appens to know Abel spent a deal of time there.'

'Doin' what . . . business?'

'Of a sort.' Joseph sucked on his pipe.

'What sort?' Sarah removed the thread from the needle, using the eye end to unpick an untidy stitch.

'Use yer 'ead, woman.' Joseph bit on the stem of the clay pipe. 'What sort of business does a man do at night? Not the sort 'e does in any office! It's my belief Abel Pardoe 'ad a kept woman – either that or he med regular visits to some knockin' shop.'

Sarah almost dropped the needle. 'Eeeh, Joseph! You mean Abel Pardoe . . .'

'That's just what I mean,' Joseph continued where Sarah's shocked voice left off. 'I mean Abel Pardoe had spent that night in Brummagem with a prostitute.'

'Thank the good Lord that never came out.' Sarah held the needle poised in mid-air. 'Phoebe Pardoe went through enough with that aunt of hers wi'out 'earin' such things about 'er father.'

'Seems nobody else figured it,' Joseph sucked once more on the slim white stem of his clay pipe, 'or, if they did then they'm keepin' quiet about it same as we 'ave.'

'That poor girl in prison these twelve months,' Sarah sighed, resuming her mending. 'I can't believe that neither, 'er would never steal anythin'.'

'Magistrate said 'er did.'

'Magistrate don't know everythin',' Sarah snapped, a catch in her voice. ''E don't know what a nice carin' wench young Phoebe was.'

'Magistrate don't need to know.' Joseph stared into the glowing heart of the grate. ''E knowed only what somebody wanted 'im to know an' in my opinion that somebody be Annie Pardoe. My guess is it be 'er as supplied that evidence, if what was said in that court could be called evidence, an' that were just enough to put Abel's daughter down the line for fifteen years.'

Chapter Four

''Er's sewin' what!' Martha Ames's face creased with a mixture of amusement and disbelief. 'Hey, Phoebe, you 'ear that? Mary Pegleg reckons you be sewin' salt cellars.'

'Psalters.' Phoebe joined the laughter of the women. Apart from a half-hour break for the midday meal she didn't see them until evening. 'I'm sewing Psalters . . .'

'That another of 'er new ideas?' Liza interrupted scathingly. 'Gets a good many of them does new Governess.'

'An' all of 'em to the good so far.' Martha looked at her fellow prisoner, the beetroot stain livid on her cheek. 'Though I reckon I could suggest one we'd all find to our liking.'

'Oh, ar, an' what's that, Martha Smart Arse?'

'That 'er 'as you put down.'

'What them Psalterers for then, Phoebe?' Nellie Bladen asked as the second flush of laughter died away.

'Jesus, Joseph and Mary!' Bridie exclaimed, making the regular sign on her chest. 'Sure an oi can't be after believin' what my own ears be tellin' me, Nellie Bladen.'

'So what am they tellin' you?' Nellie's ferret features tightened. 'One thing they ain't tellin' you for all the sign o' the cross you keep mekin' . . . they ain't tellin' you Bridie Trow is an angel nor ever likely to be!'

'That's where you be wrong altogether, so you be.' Bridie's native brogue thickened. 'If oi'm not after bein' an angel when oi'm dead it would be meanin' oi was to spend the rest of me after loif with the loikes of you – an' the good Lord will never be permittin' the loike of that.'

'And what is it the good Lord will not permit?'

The women's smiles faded as Agnes Marsh halted her patrol at their end of the long table.

Bridie, eyes still malignant, half turned on the bench seat. 'Nellie Bladen was after sayin' that oi'll be livin' wi' the loike of herself after oi be dead.'

'Well, you both have one consolation.' The wardress smiled spitefully. 'After you've finished in Handsworth you'll be used to each other . . . and to the place you'll both finish up in when you're dead. Now get this lot cleared and get ready for lights out or you might be wishing yourselves there now.'

'Sour-faced cow!' Nellie muttered, watching the wardress move down the room toward its one door. 'I know what 'er could do with.'

'An' p'raps you would like to tell 'er,' Liza Spittle dropped the apron she had been mending into the large basket set beside the table, 'to 'er face.'

'Why don't you when you am doin' it wi' 'er in the store room, you dirty bugger. Don't think we don't know what goes on in there.'

'It don't bother me what you think, none of you, I'll do what it teks to get by in this place.'

'An' that means mauling the tits off any woman who'll let you an' a few that's bin too frightened to refuse.' Martha Ames dropped her own mending into the basket then turned a disdainful glance on Liza. 'Yer nothing but a filthy swine, Liza Spittle, no wonder the Devil marked you one of his'n.'

'You still didn't tell me what a Psalterer was?' Nellie Bladen whispered to Phoebe as they left the dining hall.

'It is a book of Psalms.'

'A book! But you can't sew a book, Phoebe.'

'No, of course I can't.' She smiled, following Nellie out of the dining hall. 'What Mary should have said was that I am embroidering covers for Psalters.'

'Trust Mary Pegleg to get it wrong.' Nellie turned toward

the washroom. 'That woman couldn't get anythin' right, not if 'Ell fetched 'er.'

Soaping her hands and face with carbolic, Phoebe thought of the events of the morning. Hannah Price had sent for her, asking that she make two Psalter covers. She wanted them as a gift for the Vicar of St James's church in Wednesbury. Now Phoebe felt the same tug at her stomach she had felt when the Governess told her of her visit to a friend she had in the town. How long before *she* could visit friends? Phoebe buried her face in the rough cotton that served the prisoners as towels. She knew how long . . . fifteen years.

Phoebe stared at the familiar rectangles of moonlight, her brain refusing her the sanctuary of sleep. She had thought her troubles were ending when Lucy gave her the jewellery. If only she had known . . . her troubles were just beginning.

She had pawned a ruby ring first, choosing to take it to John Kilvert, the pawnbroker who had sold her the furniture, hoping to redeem it in a few weeks.

What a hope! Phoebe turned her face to the wall, finding no solace in the well of shadows.

The ring had been followed by a marcasite brooch and that by a cornelian bracelet. One by one the pieces had gone, John Kilvert giving her a fraction of their worth and that fraction swallowed by the purchase of food and the small amount of cotton she bought to make garments to sell, garments that brought her even less than her jewellery. Finally it was her grandmother's sapphire necklace. John Kilvert's eyes had glowed when she unwrapped it from her handkerchief and laid it on his counter. He had scrutinised it carefully then said, 'Two pounds ten, tek it or leave it.'

She had had to take it as the pawnbroker well knew. Two pounds ten shillings . . . careful as she had desperately tried to be, it had lasted less than six weeks.

Too proud to tell Sarah and Joseph of her circumstances, she had agreed to go with them to the Advent Fayre one

Saturday evening. 'The gentry will be there,' Sarah had said, 'mebbe they might buy some of your petticoats. Heaven knows they'm pretty enough.'

Only she had no material to sew petticoats and no money to buy more. But she would be expected to take something that could be sold to benefit the church. She hadn't thought about her two dresses until she went to bed. The next morning she had chosen the white one sprigged with tiny red flowers and carefully taken it to pieces, using the cloth to make two dresses for a child, trimming one with red ribbons and the other with pink.

Standing behind the stall allotted to her and Sarah Leach, Phoebe had seen Montrose's mother sweep into the market place and saw the doffed caps and bobbed curtsies of the townsfolk as the woman and her companions halted a few moments at each stall. Maybe they would pass her and Sarah by, maybe Violet Wheeler would not recognise her in the flickering light of candles set in jars, but even as she pressed into the shadows Phoebe knew it would not happen.

'Mama, look, how delightful.'

The two women and a girl Phoebe guessed to be around her own age paused at her stall, the cold November breeze fluttering the feathers of their bonnets.

'Look, Mama.' The girl touched a gloved hand to the dresses Phoebe had made. 'Don't you think they are pretty?'

'I do, my dear.' Lady Dartmouth smiled at her daughter then asked,'Who made these?'

'I did, Your Ladyship,' Phoebe answered, aware of the warning in Violet Wheeler's eyes.

'They are very pretty and well stitched.' Lady Dartmouth held one of the dresses closer to the lighted candles. 'Don't you agree, Mrs Wheeler?'

Montrose's mother made a pretence of examining the stitches. 'Yes,' she answered, already turning in the direction of the next stall, 'quite.'

'Mama,' the girl picked up the second dress, 'do you not think these would make the most admirable Christmas gifts for the children of the servants? You know how much you enjoy the giving of something useful.'

'They would indeed be admirable, my dear, always provided the children are not boys, eh, Mrs Wheeler?'

Forced to turn back Violet Wheeler managed an acid smile. 'As you say, Your Ladyship, useful only if they are not boys.'

'Tell me,' Lady Dartmouth returned her hand to the warmth of her fur muff, 'have you more of these?'

Phoebe shook her head. 'No, Your Ladyship.'

'Pity.' Lady Dartmouth made to move on but her daughter stayed.

'But you could make more.' The girl's cheeks glowed red in the cold of the November night. 'How many could you make before Christmas?'

'Two would be all I had cloth for.' Phoebe avoided the glare of Violet Wheeler. 'You see, Your Ladyship, I made those from a gown of my own and I have only one more.'

'You mean you made something as pretty as this out of an old gown?'

Not so old, Phoebe thought, that particular dress had been a gift from her father on her last birthday.

'Then there is no problem.' The girl turned to her mother. 'I have lots of dresses I do not wear any more. I may give them to be used may I not, Mama?'

'Of course, Sophie,' Lady Dartmouth nodded, 'that is a very good suggestion.' Then turning her glance on Phoebe added, 'My daughter and I will be returning to the Manor on Thursday of this week. You may call whenever my daughter wishes.'

'Oh, come the next afternoon.' The girl turned to Montrose's mother. 'I'm sure you too will find a few dresses for such a worthy cause, Mrs Wheeler. After all, the proceeds will go to the church, so when may she call upon you?'

Even in the darkness of the November evening Phoebe saw the colour drain from the woman's face. 'I . . . she . . . she may call Thursday afternoon of this week at three o'clock.'

'So,' Lady Dartmouth was clearly to be delayed no longer, 'bring the dresses to the Manor one day before Christmas Eve. I will send a list of how many and what sizes to the Vicar.' She turned to her daughter. 'And now, Sophie, I insist on returning to Oakeswell Hall, this night air is much too cold for either of us.'

'Looks like Violet Wheeler 'as designs, invitin' 'er Ladyship to Oakeswell.' Sarah Leach watched the departing trio.

'Designs,' Phoebe breathed, relieved when the carriage drove away, 'how do you mean?'

'Mean!' Sarah handed over a pot of her preserve, taking a threepenny piece and handing back a penny and a halfpenny to a woman with five children hanging on her skirts. 'A man wi' half an eye can see what I mean. Violet Wheeler 'as set 'er sights on that young un for 'er lad.'

'You can't mean . . .'

'I can an' I do,' Sarah said. 'That woman intends for 'er son to wed Lady Sophie, daughter of Sir William and Lady Amelia Dartmouth of Sandwell Priory.'

Phoebe remembered the feeling that coursed through her then; it wasn't pain, no, she couldn't call it pain, it was more like pity . . . pity for a young girl being prepared like a lamb for the slaughter.

She had gone to Oakeswell Hall at the appointed time to find a servant waiting for her at the gate, the dresses, two of them, draped across her arms. Phoebe Pardoe was not to be admitted even to the grounds of her former fiancé's home.

The visit to Sandwell Priory had been so different. Phoebe turned her eyes back to the greyish-yellow rectangles high up on the wall. She had looked down from the ridge of high ground on to the house nestling in the valley, its tall windows reflecting the pale watery November sunlight, windows that seemed to go on and on along the expanse of the huge building. Brunswick House was by no means small but it would fit a hundred times over into that house. She had stared until a flurry of snow blew across her face then set off down the path to the valley. A mile or so further on she had stepped aside, hearing the rumble of an approaching carriage.

'It is you, isn't it?' Lady Sophie leaned from the window, calling for the carriage to stop. 'You are the girl I spoke to at the Fayre, are you not? The girl who is to call today?'

'I am, Your Ladyship.' Phoebe bobbed a curtsy.

'Edward,' she went on to someone in the carriage, 'this is the girl I told you about, the one who makes such delightfully pretty dresses.'

The carriage door had opened then and a tall blond man of about twenty or so had jumped out.

'Forgive my sister,' he said, 'it is a failing of hers to keep people standing in the cold.' He smiled, a smile that lit deep blue eyes. 'Allow me to assist you into the carriage?'

'No.' Phoebe took a step backward. 'No, thank you, I . . . I'll walk.'

'Nonsense.' The man smiled again. 'I will not hear of such a thing, the day is far too cold. And besides,' he held out a hand, 'it is coming on to snow.'

'Of course you must ride with us.' Lady Sophie added her smile and voice to her brother's. 'There is plenty of room.'

Phoebe had made no more demur, accepting the man's hand as she climbed into the carriage.

'My sister told me of meeting you but she failed to tell me your name?'

Across the carriage the blue eyes had smiled deep into hers.

'My name is Phoebe . . . Phoebe Pardoe.'

'How do you do, Phoebe?' He said her name slowly as if wanting to hold it in his mouth, to keep it inside of him, a part of himself.

'My sister you have met already, allow me to present myself – Edward Dartmouth.'

He had introduced himself simply. Phoebe knew he was Edward Albert Richard Dartmouth whose family had owned the Priory for nearly five hundred years, but he had given himself no airs and graces.

At the Priory Sophie had heaped dresses into her arms, their colours mixing like some exotic rainbow, then laughed as Phoebe gradually disappeared beneath them.

She had not seen Lady Dartmouth, Sophie apologising for her absence, explaining that her mother's evening visit to the market had given her a chill. 'Poor Mama,' Sophie had laughed. 'She says the things she does for the church should guarantee her a healthy eternity, though she does wish it would do the same for her earthly existence.'

Four maids had eventually carried the dresses down the great staircase. Phoebe watched for a glimpse of Lucy as they passed but she was not among the servants who crossed the vast marble hall and down a wide fan of steps to the carriage Sophie insisted Phoebe should travel home in. Edward stood beside it.

'I could not forgive myself should I let you go home alone.' He had helped her into the carriage then, his eyes never leaving her face. Phoebe had not wanted him to accompany her, ashamed for him to see her dilapidated home and the tumbling outhouses, but once there he had kept her hand in his while the coachman carried the dresses indoors. 'You must allow me to call you Phoebe,' he had said softly. 'Please tell me I may?'

Phoebe closed her eyes but the face of Edward Dartmouth was printed on the lids. A handsome face, a face with more than admiration revealed in those deep blue eyes.

Lucy had been at Wiggins Mill one day when Edward paid a visit, one of many since Phoebe's going to Sandwell Priory.

'You wants to be careful, Miss.' Phoebe remembered Lucy's warning. 'Could be 'e's here after more than you should give 'im.'

'He's a friend, Lucy.'

'There's friends and friends.' Lucy's reply had been tempered with the same warning. 'The sons of gentry is no friend to the likes of us, Miss. Not unless they want a special sort of friendship. You take a tip from me an' tell 'im not to call 'ere no more.'

But Edward had not tried to take advantage of her. He had been so courteous and yet so full of life, insisting on her going out for walks along the canal bank, teaching her to skim stones across the water, piling logs on to the fire then sitting at her feet as she sewed. She had known he loved her, known even before he told her. In the darkness of the quiet dormitory, Phoebe remembered.

Samuel Pardoe put down his brush, turning from his latest landscape painting. 'It has been a year now since Abel died.' He spelled out the words on his fingers as he had been taught in childhood. 'It seems so very long, Annie.'

Annie Pardoe watched the brother she had lived with all of his fifty-two years. He had always been slight of build even as a child but of late had become markedly more frail, seeming to dwindle into himself, fading a little more each day.

'Twelve months is a long time,' she signed in return, 'but there it is. Abel is gone and we must learn to live with the fact.'

'But Phoebe is not gone,' Samuel's fingers moved quickly, 'yet we have not seen her since her father died. Why is that, Annie? Why does Phoebe not come to see us?'

'I told you, Samuel . . .' Annie walked to the window of the room that had been turned into a studio for her brother, avoiding the need to look into the face that was so like that of Abel, then after a moment turned to sign: 'Phoebe said she never wanted to see either of us again.'

'But I think perhaps if we went to see her . . .'

'No, Samuel!' Annie Pardoe signed rapidly then dropped one hand to her side as if the movement gave her pain. 'We will not go to see her. She made the decision to leave this house, hers was the choice and we must abide by it. If it be that she changes her mind then she will be welcome to return. Until that time we will have to wait and pray.'

Samuel applied another touch of paint to the canvas, his thin hand almost transparent, then signed again. 'I wonder why Abel left everything to us? It seems so very strange.'

'I see nothing strange in a man entrusting his business and property to someone old enough and wise enough to look after it.' Annie breathed deeply, holding her hand tight against the spot beneath her rib cage, then released it to sign, 'Phoebe was very young. Abel thought we would be the better guardian of what was his until she married.'

'The better guardian of what was his . . .' Samuel left off painting. 'Phoebe was his but he did not name either of us her guardian, did he, Annie?' His eyes reflected a sadness he could not voice.

'Our brother did not appoint anyone as guardian to his daughter,' Annie crossed to the door, 'simply because he thought to see her married long before he died. I have called to see our niece several times, Samuel, hoping to persuade her to come and live with us, but each time I have been met with hostility. It hurts us both to know that she has cut herself off from her family, those who have loved her from her birth, but we cannot force her to come home, my dear.'

'Annie,' Samuel signed as she opened the door, 'what happened to the idea of her marrying Gaskell Wheeler's son?'

She hesitated, the hand on her ribs pressing a little harder, then, 'I'm afraid she took the same headstrong, foolish action she took toward us,' she answered. 'She said she had been pressured into accepting Montrose Wheeler against her will, and now her father was no longer here to enforce the marriage, she would not do so. The Wheelers were understandably upset but agreed to say that following the unforeseen death of her father, Phoebe felt she could not marry so soon, therefore a postponement had taken place.'

'Is she alone?' Samuel's fingers fluttered like wounded butterflies.

Annie looked into the thin face and sad grey eyes of her brother and the pain beneath her hand worsened. It had not been his fault, he was not to blame for what fate had ordained for him or the life Abel Pardoe had ordained for her – he was not to blame yet she could not forgive him.

'No, she is not alone.' Her answer was sharpened by the pain. 'Abel's housekeeper went with her and so did her maid. They are all well cared for, I instructed Lawyer Siveter to pay an annual allowance. Phoebe might have turned her back on us, Samuel, but we will never turn ours upon her.'

Leaving the room before he could ask any more questions, Annie paused outside the door, her eyes closed, her hand pressed to the pain that refused to be ignored. Samuel had asked the same questions before and she had told the same lies.

Opening her eyes she walked to her bedroom, taking a small cardboard box from a drawer in the table that stood beside the heavy fourposter bed. Abel had slept in that bed, Abel and his pretty wife; so many nights, so much happiness. Taking the lid from the box, she put two of the white tablets it held into her mouth, swallowing them with water from the carafe on the table. Yes, Abel had shared this bed, this room with a wife while she . . . what had she had . . . what love had Annie Pardoe known, whose bed had she shared?

Putting the lid back on the box, she replaced it in the drawer, covering it with a layer of lace-edged handkerchiefs.

She had shared neither love nor bed with any man thanks to her brother. Abel could never be made to pay while he was living and death had carried him beyond her reach. No, Abel would not pay for a life he'd snatched away, a life he had destroyed so he could live his own. But Abel's daughter would . . .

Is she alone?

Samuel's question echoed in her mind, and in her mind she answered but this time with all the truth of vengeance. No, Phoebe was not alone. Some two hundred women shared her home, a home she would inhabit for the next fifteen years.

'Well, if it ain't the Governess's little pet.'

Liza Spittle's narrow eyes watched Phoebe coming along the corridor that led to the kitchens, a tray balanced in her hands. 'Ain't you goin' to stop an' 'ave a chat wi' Liza?'

'Move out the way, Liza,' Phoebe said as the other woman moved her large frame, blocking the narrow passage. 'You know prisoners must not hang around the corridors.'

'There's a lot of things not allowed in this bloody place,' Liza grinned, showing discoloured teeth, 'but the bastards 'ave to catch you at it first.'

'I have no wish to be caught,' Phoebe edged to one side in an attempt to pass, 'especially talking to you.'

'We don't 'ave to talk.' Liza stepped closer, the beetroot mark pulsing like some living thing on her cheek. 'You don't need to talk for what I want.'

'Liza, please move.' Phoebe was becoming alarmed. Why wasn't Liza in the laundry?

'Lucky me, bein' given the job of clearin' dinner plates,' she grinned as if answering Phoebe's unspoken question, 'otherwise we wouldn't 'ave this chance.'

'Chance?' Phoebe tried to control her trembling. She knew Liza Spittle had not given up in her twisted desire and for that reason took care never to be in her company without Bridie or Tilly.

Liza stepped forward again, wedging Phoebe against the wall. 'The chance for me to show you what you missed 'cos of that interferin' bitch Tilly Wood.' She leaned forward, pressing the tray into Phoebe's middle, her hand lifting the skirts of Phoebe's prison uniform, sliding high up over her thigh.

'Leave me alone!' Phoebe tried to use the tray in an effort to push the woman away from her, turning her face from the sour fumes of her breath. 'Please, for God's sake, don't!'

Liza laughed, a husky sound deep in her throat. 'They all says that first time.' Her voice was deep as a man's, her mouth touching the side of Phoebe's neck. 'But then it changes – it changes to, for God's sake, please do.'

'Stop!' Phoebe's cry cracked on a sob. 'Please, I . . . I'm not like that . . .'

'You will be.' Liza's tongue licked upward against Phoebe's ear, her hand moving toward the vee between her legs. 'You will be when Liza gets through.'

'No, please.' Phoebe's control had gone, the tears spilling down her cheeks. 'Please leave me alone. Please, for God's sake!'

'If you won't do it for God, then do it for me!'

Tilly Wood's voice rang out behind Liza as she was swung away, one arm twisted high up her back.

'I warned you,' Tilly snarled, her gaunt face twisted with contempt. 'I warned you afore, Tilly Wood tells not even the Lord 'imself twice . . .'

Grabbing the collar of Liza's grey calico frock, she spun her backward against the opposite wall.

'. . . but you don't tek a tellin', do you, Liza Spittle?'

Tilly struck out, the back of her hand slamming hard across Liza's face.

'. . . so yer goin' to 'ave to be shown that 'ands off means what it says.'

Across the narrow corridor Liza's small eyes glittered with a feral light as they flicked from Tilly to Phoebe then back to Tilly. 'I'm goin' to do fer you, Tilly Wood,' she breathed, wiping the blood from her mouth with the back of a hand. 'This time I'm goin' to kill you.'

She lunged forward, her large masculine frame threatening to obliterate Tilly who turned aside, thrusting a foot in her way. Liza stumbled but the force of her attack carried her forward, the sickening crunch of bone against brick covering Phoebe's sobs as she hit the wall beside her. Then Liza was falling, slipping sideways as she went down, her cracked skull sliding slowly over Phoebe's shoulder and breast, down along her skirt, trailing a long slow smear of red across grey.

'What did the Governess 'ave to say about it?' Martha Ames asked as the women prepared for the nine o'clock light out.

'I couldn't 'ear all that well,' Mary Pegleg answered. 'But 'er sent me to get Agnes Marsh an' that one looked none too 'appy when 'er went into the Governess's office, an' 'er looked a damn' sight less when 'er come out again.'

'But sure an' you must have heard somethin'?' Bridie said, slipping her nightgown over her head then folding the drab grey prison dress before placing it regulation fashion across the foot of her low iron bed.

Mary Pegleg unfastened the straps that held the wooden stump below her left knee, balancing it against the wall beside her bed. 'Well, I 'eard 'er tell Agnes as 'ow this was the first prison to 'ave a woman in charge an' that it would only tek summat like a brawl between the inmates to convince the Board that a woman wasn't fit for the job an' that 'er would be replaced wi' a man.'

'Sure an' that would be a black day for all,' Bridie said, buttoning her nightgown. 'Hannah Price has been fair in her dealin's with us women an' all. Could be we might have had a Governess the loike of Steel Arsed Sally Moreton, God rest her puir soul.'

'Did 'er say anythin' about Tilly?' Nellie Bladen looked across to Phoebe, sitting silent on her bed, her face pale and empty, then whispered, 'Is 'er still locked away on 'er own?'

Mary Pegleg rubbed a hand over the rounded nub of bone where her leg had been amputated. 'I 'eard summat about police, but I don't know if Governess said 'er was sendin' fer 'em or keepin' thing quiet from 'em.'

'Get the bobbies in 'ere an' it'll be more than Hannah Price will be teken out.' Martha Ames looked from one to the other of the women, their faces mirroring the tension that had held them all afternoon and evening. 'We'll all go, an' there's some of us in 'ere knows where to. 'Ell itself would be a better place.'

'Do you think Liza will die?' Nellie's normally yellow skin took on a deathly gleam under the sullen glow of the one gaslamp.

''Er looked near enough to it when we carried 'er to the infirmary,' Martha answered. 'Reckon 'er'll be lucky to last the night.'

'Holy Mother of God!' Bridie's hand lifted, making the sign of the cross several times in rapid succession.

'Did Agnes Marsh send fer the doctor, does anybody know?'

''Er couldn't.' Mary Pegleg eased her thin body into her bed, covering it with the one rough blanket before answering the question. ''Er 'ad to wait till Hannah Price got back from meeting with the Board an' that wasn't till after seven o'clock gone. 'Er said it was too late to get the doctor out then, that it would 'ave to wait till mornin'.'

'Too late my arse!' Martha spat. 'What 'er meant was the bloody doctor was too blind drunk by that time of the night even to stand up, let alone treat anybody.'

'Well, whatever 'er meant, 'er didn't send fer 'im,' Mary Pegleg stated flatly.

'Oi wonder what he will be makin' of it when he does come?' Bridie said.

'I don't know,' Martha shook her head, 'but this much I can say – drunk or sober there be no way 'e can call this a 'eart attack.'

'What will 'e call it . . . will it be murder?'

'Liza Spittle ain't dead,' Martha shot a glance at Phoebe but Nellie's words seemed to have passed over her head, 'so 'ow can 'e call what 'appened murder?'

Crossing to Phoebe's bed she pressed her back on the pillow, pulling the coarse blanket up to her chin before going back to her own place.

'But what if Liza do die?' Nellie persisted.

'If 'er does then any tears I shed won't be for 'er,' Martha said acridly. ''Er was nothin' but a filthy bitch sniffin' round women, 'er 'ad it comin' to 'er an' I fer one ain't sorry as 'er's copped it. The one I'm sorry fer is Tilly Wood.'

'What's goin' to 'appen to Tilly would you say, Martha?'

'Lord knows!' She looked at the other woman, death marked plain across her thin consumptive features. 'Depends on what the doctor and the Governess 'as ter say ter the Prison Board.'

Bridie crossed herself fervently. 'Then may the sweet Mother o'Jesus be puttin' the words into their mouths.'

Chapter Five

Phoebe lay awake in the hard narrow bed. She had not spoken since the affair in the corridor, she had not joined the discussions of the women, her mind empty, somehow detached, hearing nothing yet registering everything.

Tilly had offered no resistance when Agnes Marsh ordered two wardresses to take her away, only the eyes that had long forgotten laughter staying on Phoebe's face as they took her. What would they do to Tilly? She was already serving a life sentence for manslaughter . . . if Liza Spittle died Tilly would be accused of murder and it was certain she would hang. But she was no murderer; she had told Sally Moreton a lie about snapping her husband's neck to frighten her, it was the push down the stairs had broken it. No, Tilly Wood was not quite guilty of murder . . . yet.

Oh Lord! In the darkness, listening to the breathing of the sleeping women and the consumptive coughing of Nellie Bladen, Phoebe prayed, 'Oh Lord, don't let Liza die.'

High on the wall the windows showed a paler shade of darkness. Why was I sent to return that tray to the kitchen? Why was Liza Spittle clearing the dinner plates? Why was she in the corridor at that precise moment? Why was there no one else clearing the dining hall?

Questions vied for prominence in her brain. Lord, if only her father had not met with that terrible accident, if only her Aunt Annie had not acted as she had, if only she had never made those children's dresses, Lord if only . . . but how often had the Lord heard those words?

Above her the small rectangular windows lightened with infinite slowness, like lids lifting to reveal strange hypnotic eyes, and she turned her head away. But out of the shadows Lucy danced towards her, Lucy with eyes glowing and lips smiling.

'I'm getting wed.'

Phoebe heard the laughing happy voice rise from the depths of buried thoughts. 'Mathew an' me, we are goin' to be wed.'

Phoebe had joined in the girl's delight, returning the hug Lucy enfolded her in. They had talked a long time in the kitchen of the mill house, Lucy baking scones and mixing an amount of bread dough Phoebe thought must last a year at least, then she had asked about a wedding dress.

'I hadn't thought about it,' Lucy answered, setting the cloth-covered dough to rise besides the hearth. 'Well, not really thought about it, though I would like somethin' nice, somethin' new, I suppose, if the truth be told. But that's out of the question on what I get paid at the Priory.'

'And Mathew?' Phoebe had asked.

'Can't really ask him to sport me a dress from the money he makes, Miss Phoebe.' Lucy collected wooden mixing spoons, dropping them into the large brown earthenware bowl. 'Mathew had his wages docked same as the rest of 'em at the pit.'

'Docked?' Phoebe remembered the surprise she felt, but had it been surprise or disgust? 'Do you mean my aunt has reduced the wages of the men working at the mine?'

'Yes, Miss Phoebe, I do,' Lucy answered. 'Both of 'em, the Hobs Hill pit and the Crown mine at Moxley, and the folks who depend on it am feelin' the pinch real bad.'

'But why?' Phoebe asked. 'For what reason?'

'Annie Pardoe said as how price of coal had fallen an' men could take lower wages or take their hook.'

'She said that!'

'Well, not in them exact words.' Lucy carried the utensils

she had used in her baking to the long shallow sink in the scullery, returning for the kettle singing softly over the fire. 'But that was what 'er meant: the men could either accept a lower wage for a day's work or they could leave the pit altogether. And as you know, Miss Phoebe, that would leave them without a home as well as a job 'cos most houses in Wednesbury belong to Annie Pardoe, least at that end of the town they do.'

Phoebe might have asked what part her uncle had played in all of this but deep down she knew Samuel would know nothing of it.

'Mind you,' Lucy carried the kettle into the scullery, pouring hot water over a bowl and spoons then putting the kettle aside to be filled later at the pump in the yard, 'some of 'em couldn't be much worse off if they did leave. They 'ave little enough in their tins to feed a family *and* pay rent, and Annie Pardoe ain't one to let rent man call twice and get nothin', so some of the women an' kids am goin' more than hungry.'

'What of Joseph and Sarah?' Phoebe reached for a cloth to dry the dishes but it hung forgotten in her hands.

Lucy placed the freshly washed baking bowl on the wooden board Mathew had made to stand beside the sink. 'They are fairin' up to now though Joseph had his wage docked same as others, but they only manage 'cos Sarah can do most things herself.'

Sarah was a marvel, Phoebe thought, cook, housekeeper and gardener rolled into one, growing vegetables Joseph could no longer tend after the accident that had left him lame. But how long could she manage now money was short?

'So how will you and Mathew be fixed with him not earning as much?'

'It's going to be harder.' Lucy took the cloth from Phoebe and set about drying the bowls and spoons. 'There be no use in my denyin' that, but I'll have my position at the Priory and Mathew will 'ave his job at Hobs Hill. We can afford to rent a little house . . . just.'

'But you said yourself the wage at the pits had been reduced and what if you start a family? They won't keep you on at the Priory if you have children to care for. And if the situation at the pit gets any worse . . .'

'We've thought of that, Miss Phoebe, and we both know that if we wait for things to be perfect we will never be wed so we decided to go ahead. There will be hard times and worry for us whether we wed or not so we have little to lose except each other.'

Why had her aunt reduced the wages of the miners? Had the market price for coal really dropped or was there some other reason for her action? Phoebe picked up the bowls and spoons, carrying them back into the kitchen, replacing them on the rough wooden dresser set along one wall. Could it in some way have anything to do with her aunt's obvious dislike of Phoebe herself?

'So when will you and Mathew be married?' she asked as Lucy bustled into the kitchen, setting the freshly filled kettle over the glowing coals.

'Next month, the fifteenth,' Lucy's face radiated her joy, 'that's my birthday. Mathew said to have the wedding on that day then we would have two things to be happy for. Ooh, I am looking forward to it.'

Just as I was looking forward to my own wedding, Phoebe thought, watching the happiness light the other girl's eyes, only mine never took place.

'We want the ceremony to be at St Bart's.' Lucy lifted the bread dough on to the table, scoring it with a knife before placing it in the oven to bake. 'Just family and a few friends. We both hoped you would come, Miss? It won't be grand or anything.'

'I'm hardly grand myself, Lucy,' Phoebe smiled at the half apology, 'and I would like to come very much.'

'Would you?' Lucy placed the cooled scones on to a prettily flowered plate, embarrassment touching her cheeks with pink. 'I mean, could . . . ?'

'Would I . . . could I what?' Phoebe laughed.

'Well, Miss, me and Mathew thought . . . we hoped you might be my attendant.'

'Bridesmaid!' Phoebe grabbed the young girl, hugging her. 'Lucy, I would be absolutely delighted, and I think I have something upstairs you might be delighted with too.'

Holding on to Lucy's hand, Phoebe raced through the sitting room and up the stairs to a bedroom draped with the dresses Sophie had given her and which as yet she had not taken to pieces to make up into garments for children.

'What about one of these for a wedding dress?' she asked.

Lucy stood quite still, her eyes wide. 'You mean . . . you mean I could have one of these . . . to keep?'

'Of course to keep,' Phoebe laughed. 'Try them, I'm sure they will fit. You and Sophie are much the same size, and if need be we can soon make a few adjustments.'

'Which one?' Lucy stepped forward, touching first one and then another of the dresses. 'Which one can I try?'

'Try them all.' Phoebe snatched up a blue muslin gown trimmed with silk forget-me-nots, pressing it into Lucy's hands. 'And take whichever you wish.'

'Ooh, Miss Phoebe,' Lucy held the gown almost reverently, her eyes playing over the others, 'do you think I should?'

'No, I do not think you should!' Phoebe answered emphatically. 'I *know* you should. Now get out of that skirt and blouse and try every one of those dresses.'

Trying the blue gown, Lucy preened before a long cheval mirror that had come from Kilvert's pawn shop, then discarded it for one of pale creamy yellow, the skirt caught around the hem in half hoops of yellow tea roses.

'That looks lovely, Lucy,' Phoebe said, scooping up the girl's dark hair into a yellow silk ribbon, 'and we could make some silk rose-buds to dress your hair. The whole effect would be marvellous.'

'Oh, I do like it, Miss Phoebe,' Lucy breathed, touching a hand to the high waist, 'it's so pretty.'

'Then it's yours,' Phoebe smiled.

'But what if Miss Sophie should see me?' Lucy turned, her eyes filled with concern. 'Wouldn't 'er get mad seein' as how 'er give you these to make kids' frocks?'

Phoebe knelt, smoothing the creamy folds about Lucy's feet. 'I really don't expect the Dartmouths to turn up at Wednesbury Parish Church to witness the marriage of Mr Mathew Leach to Miss Lucy Baines, even though she'll be the prettiest bride in the country. And even if they should, I'm sure Miss Sophie would be delighted you chose to wear her gift on the most special day of your life.'

'Then if you be sure, Miss, I think I would like it to be this one. Only . . .'

'Only what?' Phoebe stood up.

'Only it do seem a shame not to try them others on, I'll not be gettin' another chance to wear such frocks!' Lucy grinned.

'And I will not be getting another chance to rescue the bread from burning.' Phoebe sniffed then dashed out of the bedroom. 'You carry on,' she called, hurrying downstairs to the kitchen, 'I'll be back in a minute.'

'Am the loaves all right, Miss?' Lucy asked when Phoebe returned a few minutes later.

'They look delicious. You are so good at cooking, Lucy.'

'Like you with sewing, Miss.' Lucy paraded a pale green sprigged dress. 'Those little frocks you've made for the kids look real pretty, I reckon Lady Dartmouth will be right pleased wi' them.'

'I hope I can get them all done in time for Christmas.' Phoebe helped to extricate Lucy from the swathes of pale green. 'There are more than I had expected.'

'Then you mustn't use your time making rose-buds or nothin' for my wedding frock,' Lucy mumbled from beneath layers of muslin.

'I shall make just as many rose-buds as it takes, Lucy Baines.' Phoebe took the dress, draping it across a chair.

'And anything else we think is necessary to make your day perfect.'

'P'raps I can 'elp, on my day off? I ain't much wi' a needle but I'm willing to try.'

'You already help enough, Lucy, I don't know how I would manage without your coming here. Sarah and Miriam tried hard to teach me to cook but I am still not very good, I'm afraid, so your help in that department is invaluable.'

'Mathew says my scones are as good as his mother's.' Lucy beamed.

'And Mathew is right.' Phoebe draped the green dress higher on the chair, leaving its folds free of the floor. 'Their only drawback being you want to go on eating them and that is not so good for a girl's shape.'

'Eeh, Miss, you need 'ave no worries in that direction.' Standing in white frilled bloomers and chemise, Lucy looked at her former employer. 'It might not be my place to say it but I reckon as you could be doin' wi' a bit more meat on your bones. You be gettin' to look right scrawny, beggin' your pardon.'

'Well, all that delicious bread of yours will soon remedy that.' Phoebe picked up the last of the dresses Sophie had given her and one which Lucy had so far refrained from touching. 'Now, Miss Lucy, I think you should try this on.'

Lucy looked at the gown, its folds streaming to the floor like a jade waterfall. 'Ooh, no, I couldn't, not that one . . . it's much too grand.'

'Nonsense.' Phoebe held it out. 'I agree it might not be as suitable to your colouring as the yellow but try it anyway. You will never know unless you try.'

'I . . . I don't think I should . . .' Lucy hesitated, a longing to feel the rich taffeta against her skin pulling her one way; a reluctance to dare try anything so grand and costly pulling her in the opposite direction.

'Oh, come on, Lucy.' Phoebe held out the dress, its fabric gleaming in the wintry sunlight, entering the tiny window sheltered by the eaves. 'Where is your sense of adventure?'

'Well, if you say so.' Lucy held up her arms for Phoebe to slip the gown over her head. 'Though I don't think it's goin' to suit me.'

'We will see.' Phoebe pulled the heavy fabric down over Lucy's shoulders then stopped as the girl cried out.

'It's somethin' in the frock,' she said, pushing the gown right down to the floor and stepping out of it. 'Somethin' cold and . . . and . . .'

'And what?' Phoebe put an arm around the frightened girl, leading her away from the dress folded in upon itself like a green island on the bare wooden floor.

'I don't know,' Lucy answered shakily, 'it . . . it felt cold and . . . and hard . . . across my chest.'

Phoebe stared at the mound of taffeta. She couldn't just leave it, she had to find out what it was lying coiled inside that dress.

'Stay here.' She pushed Lucy into the open doorway of the bedroom then, her own heart thumping, walked back to where the gown lay heaped.

'Eeh, don't touch it, Miss,' Lucy said, fear making her voice sound hollow, 'don't touch it!'

'Don't be silly, Lucy, it's probably nothing more than a dressmaker's pin that has been overlooked.' Sounding far more confident than she felt, Phoebe reached for the gown. Teeth gripped together she shook the material, then as nothing happened, lifted the dress, holding it at arm's length.

'Eeh, I could 'ave sworn there was somethin' in that frock,' Lucy said, courage returning sufficiently for her to step back inside the bedroom. 'I could swear I felt somethin'.'

'Well, let us look.' Phoebe laid the taffeta gown atop the pale green muslin draped over the room's one chair.

'I'll look.' Lucy came to stand beside her. 'I know whereabouts it was.'

Opening the bodice wide, she examined the inside of it. 'Oh my Good God!' she exclaimed, drawing back as though from the hand of death. 'Oh my Good God, will you look at that!'

'I want you to tell me exactly what happened.' The Governess of Handsworth Prison for Women looked at the thin figure of the girl standing in front of her desk. 'You were in the corridor at the time Liza Spittle was injured, were you not?'

'Yes, Ma'am,' Phoebe answered, her voice little more than a whisper.

'What were you doing there?'

Phoebe looked across the desk at the woman she knew held Tilly's life in her hands. 'I was returning a lunch tray to the kitchen, Liza blocked my way, she would not move when I asked her to let me pass . . . then . . . then she tried to force herself upon me.'

'She tried to do what?' The Governess's face blanched, her mouth pinched with disgust. 'Are you telling me Liza Spittle tried to behave like . . . like a man?'

'Yes, Ma'am,' Phoebe whispered, looking down at her feet. 'It happened once before and Tilly Wood helped me then.'

'As she did yesterday?' The Governess spoke as though she held a bad taste in her mouth. 'Tell me, Pardoe, where were the wardresses whilst all of this was going on?'

'Mrs Marsh accompanied me almost to the kitchens,' Phoebe lied, aware of Agnes Marsh standing just behind her, aware also that the woman had been asleep in her room instead of being on duty and knowing that to say so would bring vengeance not only upon herself but also on Tilly and the others. 'Then we heard the noise of a bucket being dropped on the stairs and she went to see what had happened.'

The Governess raised an enquiring glance to the wardress.

'It was one of the new intake, Ma'am,' Agnes Marsh took up the lie. 'She was scrubbing the top landing and knocked over the bucket, sending it down the stairs. I stayed to see to her mopping up before anybody could slip on the wet stairs, then I saw to her getting fresh water and soda to start

67

again, and when I got to go to the kitchen Liza Spittle was lying unconscious in the corridor.'

'I see.' The Governess returned to Phoebe. 'You say Tilly Wood helped you? How come she was in that part of the building and not in the laundry?'

'I checked on that, Ma'am,' Agnes Marsh put in swiftly. 'She'd been sent to fetch the cooking cloths and towels from the kitchens ready for the afternoon wash.'

'Allow Pardoe to answer my next question,' Hannah Price answered coldly. 'Tell me, what assistance did Wood give?'

Phoebe swallowed hard, her eyes still on her shoes. Please God, help me to answer without making things worse for Tilly, she thought. Don't let me put her in greater danger than she is in now.

'She pulled Liza away, then when Liza tried to attack her, stepped aside. Liza crashed her head into the wall. It all happened so quickly, Ma'am, then Mrs Marsh came and had Liza taken to the infirmary and Tilly was locked away. That is all I know.'

Hannah Price glanced at the blank sheet of paper lying on her desk. Was that all the girl knew, or was it all she was prepared to say she knew?

'Have you seen Spittle this morning, Mrs Marsh?' she asked without looking up.

'Yes, Ma'am,' Agnes answered. 'There is no change from last night. She is still unconscious.'

'In that case there is no sense in sending for the doctor.' The Governess picked up a pen, dipping the nib into a glass ink-well and beginning to write on the paper before her. 'I will send an interim report informing the Prison Board that one of the inmates is unwell, and this evening I will ask the doctor to call. Spittle should have recovered sufficiently well by that time to relate to him what occurred.'

Spittle should have recovered by that time, Agnes Marsh thought, beginning to usher Phoebe from the Governess's office, or was Hannah Price giving the doctor time to drink away his senses? Either way it suited them both. The last thing the Governess or Agnes Marsh wanted was a murder inside the prison, and if Liza didn't make it then that would be another bonus.

'Excuse me, Ma'am.' Phoebe ignored Agnes Marsh pushing her towards the door. 'May I please ask a question?'

Hannah Price paused in the writing of her report and looked up at the young girl whose eyes no longer studied her own shoes but were on her, steady and unblinking. Was she truly a thief? Had she really robbed the home of Sir William Dartmouth? In all honesty Hannah could not bring herself to believe so; this girl was very different from all the other prisoners in Handsworth, so well mannered and polite, so obviously well bred it would be hard for anyone to believe her a criminal, but the law had pronounced her such and the law must always be upheld.

'Yes, Pardoe, what is it?' She signed to the wardress to wait.

'It is Tilly Wood, Ma'am,' Phoebe said, showing no trace of her true feelings. 'What is to happen to her?'

The Governess balanced the pen back and forth between thumb and forefinger as though testing its weight, her lips pursed tightly together. Phoebe waited, each tick of the tiny carriage clock sounding like the boom of a cannon in the still room.

'Ah, yes, Wood.' The balancing of the pen stopped as if some decision had finally been reached. 'I do not think it necessary to mention the involvement of any other prisoner at this stage, so for the time being Prisoner Wood will return to the laundry.'

'Thank you, Ma'am.'

Hannah Price looked up at the quiet answer and knew it was more than a simple thank you. Much, much more.

Chapter Six

Phoebe pushed the needle tiredly into the cloth, her eyes aching from a sleepless night, a night that had followed the pattern of so many since her confinement to Handsworth Prison, for though her body rested her brain refused to sleep. But last night it had not been for herself she had worried but for Tilly: locked up in solitary isolation, a place Phoebe herself had only heard of, a place the mention of which reduced the rest of the women to hushed tones.

But Tilly was free of that for the moment at least. Phoebe pulled the gold wire thread through the cloth, seating it with the tip of a finger. And what of Liza . . . would the Governess send for the doctor this evening, and if so . . . ?

'May I see?'

Phoebe looked up as a voice broke into her thoughts. She placed her needlework in the prison Governess's outstretched hand.

'This is very fine.' Hannah Price examined the Psalter cover. 'You sew very well, and such an elegant choice of colour, I know Phi— Father Heywood will be pleased when he receives them. You should be able to place yourself in some dressmaking or millinery establishment upon your release.'

Phoebe took the piece back as the Governess moved on along the line of sewing women. She should be able to secure a position. It was so easily said but who would employ a convicted thief?

'I find you guilty of wilful theft . . . you will serve a term of fifteen years . . .'

She pushed the needle through the cloth. Fifteen years for a crime of which she was innocent.

'Oh my Good God, will you look at that!' Lucy's shocked words rose to the surface of her mind and Phoebe saw again the bodice of the jade taffeta gown spread wide, revealing the necklace caught up inside it.

''Ow do you reckon that got there?'

Lucy's words replaced the quiet hum of the sewing women's conversations.

'I don't know,' Phoebe had replied, 'but we must return it to the Priory.'

'How come it hasn't been missed?' Lucy looked up from the floor of the bedroom. 'And it can't 'ave been or I would 'ave heard about it. Word gets round fast in that house.'

'It must have become caught when Sophie removed the dress,' Phoebe said, seeing how the mounting had become hooked into the dress lining. 'She probably wouldn't feel it through her petticoats, but surely when her maid came to put the gown away she would inspect it first for any mark or stain?'

'Not that one, Miss.' Lucy watched her free the necklace. 'I know 'er and lazy isn't the word I'd be using to describe 'er. She would 'ave had 'er marching orders long since but Miss Sophie is too soft. Everybody downstairs says they don't know how 'er gets away with half of the things she gets up to, but get away with it she does.'

'Maybe, Lucy, but to overlook something as valuable as this must be more than careless.'

Lucy looked at the necklace, emeralds dripping like huge green tears through Phoebe's fingers.

'Aye, Miss,' she said thoughtfully. 'Like you says, more than careless.'

They had taken the necklace to the kitchen where they both sat looking at it spread on the table, its stones gleaming in the pale sunlight, the gold of its setting turned red by the glow of the fire.

'Eeh, it's so beautiful,' Lucy sighed. 'A girl would feel like a queen with that round 'er neck.'

Phoebe glanced up, her mouth curved in a smile. 'Much as I want you to look and feel like a queen on your wedding day, Lucy, I couldn't offer to let you wear this.'

'Would make no difference if you could,' Lucy drew back as if the necklace were a living thing, 'I wouldn't dare to. Why, I'd be scared to death!'

'And rob Mathew of his pretty bride? Then it is as well this does not belong to me.'

'What *will* you do with it, Miss Phoebe?'

'Return it to Sophie as I said.'

'I 'ave to return to the Priory, do you want me to take it for you?'

'No, Lucy,' Phoebe answered as the girl reached for the cloak she had hung on a nail set into the kitchen door, 'I would not want to put such a responsibility upon you. The dresses were given to me and I must be the one to return the necklace. Not to do so personally would be most impolite.'

'If you say so, Miss Phoebe.' Lucy tied the ribbon of her bonnet beneath her chin. 'But you be careful you say nothin' to anybody as to why you be visiting the Priory. There's folk about these parts as can't be trusted.'

Lucy had left Wiggins Mill then, and for the first time since making it her home Phoebe had felt truly afraid of being alone. The next day she had wrapped the necklace in a piece of white linen, pushing it deep into the pocket of her skirt, then wrapping her cloak tight about her had set off across the heath toward the Sandwell Valley.

She had reached the rise above the Lyng Fields, so called for their covering of tiny purple wild flowers, when Edward had caught up with her.

'Couldn't you have sent someone with word?' he said, dismounting from the huge bay horse and listening to her reason for visiting the Priory. 'I would have sent the carriage for you.'

'I have no one to send.' For some reason Phoebe did not mention Lucy and her connection with his home. 'Besides I have no wish to impose, your family has already been very kind to me.'

'Yes, but out here all alone,' Edward took her hand, concern loud in his voice, 'there's nothing out here for miles around . . . anything might happen.'

'And nothing.' Phoebe smiled. 'Really, I am quite safe.'

'I suppose I know that,' he touched her hand to his lips, 'but I would prefer you didn't walk the heath alone, Phoebe. I only wish I could accompany you but I have an appointment with my father at two and it is almost that now.'

'I would not want to be the reason for your being late for Sir William.' Phoebe withdrew her hand. 'Please go, I will be all right.'

'Well, at least let me take the blamed trinket for you. It's near enough an hour's walk from here to the Priory and I can send a carriage to take you home.'

'No, Edward,' Phoebe returned firmly. 'No carriage. I want to walk back to Wiggins Mill. The fresh air will do me good.'

'If it doesn't kill you from cold first, and it will be dark before you get there.' He glanced at the grey snow clouds gathering over the valley.

'Then hadn't you better take this so I can be on my way home?' Phoebe drew the linen bundle from her pocket, unwrapping the necklace and handing it to Edward. 'Please would you give my apology to your sister and explain I did not know this was caught inside one of the gowns she gave me until yesterday evening?'

'My sister would lose her head were someone not there to fasten it to her neck.'

Edward tossed the necklace up into the air and Phoebe watched the tiny flashes of green flame dance circles in the light as it descended into his palm.

'I still wish you would let me send a carriage out to you.'

He dropped the necklace into his pocket before swinging easily into the saddle.

'I shall be perfectly safe, Edward.' Phoebe stepped back from the horse, a sudden breeze catching the animal's nostrils and causing it to prance restlessly.

Edward reined the bay, speaking softly and touching the animal's neck. 'Sophie will certainly wish to thank you herself.' He looked down at Phoebe, the breeze fanning her sherry-gold hair about her cheeks. 'May I bring her to Wiggins Mill tomorrow?'

The horse neighed loudly, its hooves stamping restlessly at being held in check, and Phoebe raised a hand to wave, relieved at not having to answer.

One week later she had been arrested.

'Governess wants to see Phoebe.'

Mary Pegleg limped into the sewing room, delivering her message to Agnes Marsh.

'What for?' The wardress's voice was sharper than usual and as she looked at Phoebe her eyes held a touch of concern and a heavier touch of warning. Whatever the Governess wanted, Agnes Marsh had better come out of it white as snow if she were to keep the promotion of Superintendent to the sewing room and not be sent back to that hell hole of a laundry.

''Er didn't say.' Mary Pegleg leaned against the door jamb easing her weight from the wooden stump attached to her left knee. ''Er just said to tell you 'er wanted to see Phoebe right away.'

'You better get yerself to the office then, Pardoe.' Phoebe put her sewing on the end of the long trestle table, feeling the eyes of the other prisoners on her as she went towards the door.

'Pardoe!' Agnes Marsh came close, her mouth merely a slit as she breathed, 'Mind what you tell 'er. Things could be made pretty bad for you . . . there are worse places inside this prison than the laundry.'

Mary Pegleg limping alongside her and Agnes Marsh marching behind, Phoebe walked along the gloomy corridors that led to the Governess's office. How many more years would she spend locked away? Her fingers curled tightly as the memory of flashes of green fire darted across her brain. She had not stolen Sophie's necklace, they had found it caught up inside a dress, she and Lucy, but neither she nor the maid had been believed.

Edward and his sister had not called the next day or any day. She had seen no one until the day the constable arrived. She had to go with him to the Magistrates' Court, he said, and no, he could not tell her why, the Magistrate would tell her that.

They had walked the several miles to Wednesbury where she had been taken to the Green Dragon Inn at the entrance to the Shambles. It was in an upstairs room there that the Magistrate had heard evidence against her.

It was alleged that she had visited Sandwell Priory and taken away several dresses, the gift of Miss Sophie Dartmouth; in the process she had stolen an emerald necklace, the property of the said Miss Sophie.

That had been the point at which John Kilvert had been asked if she was the woman who had pawned several pieces of jewellery at his shop.

'She is, Your Honour.' The pawnbroker's shifty eyes had fastened on her and his high-pitched reedy voice carried around the room. 'Some very valible jewellery, and where could the likes of 'er get such from lessen 'er stole it?'

'We will decide that, Kilvert.'

But the Magistrate's voice had held no rebuke and the pawnbroker had smirked at Phoebe as she stood up from her seat.

'Are you now prepared to tell us what you have done with the necklace?'

She had not been asked if she had taken Sophie's necklace, she had been told she had, told she had stolen from a girl who had helped her.

76

'The necklace you speak of,' Phoebe tried to stay calm, to keep the mounting fear out of her voice, 'I . . . we found it hooked inside a gown given to me by Miss Sophie.'

'We?' The Magistrate had looked at her over heavy spectacles. 'Do I take it someone else was with you?'

'Yes,' Phoebe answered, the trembling in her stomach increasing as she realised Lucy was not present and neither was Edward. Did he know she was being accused of stealing the necklace she had given to him? Of course he must know, the complaint must have come from the Priory, so where was he? Why wasn't he here to tell them it was a mistake . . . to tell them she had been returning Sophie's property when he had overtaken her, that he himself took the necklace from her?

'Well, was someone else involved in this theft?' The Magistrate leaned across the table that served as a desk.

'There was no theft.' Phoebe stared at the other three people in the room: the constable sent to bring her here, John Kilvert her accuser, and a woman dressed in black, her face hidden behind a heavy veil. 'Please, you must believe me, I am telling the truth. We found the necklace caught up in the bodice of the gown and . . .'

'*We* found?' The Magistrate leaned back in his high wing chair. 'You had better say who it is besides yourself makes up this we.'

'It was Lucy, my mai— my friend. She was visiting me and we decided to try on the dresses before taking them apart. We found the necklace inside a green gown. We guessed it belonged to Miss Sophie, seeing she had given me the gowns, and Lucy asked if she could return it that day when she went back to the Priory.'

'And did she?'

'No, Sir.' Phoebe swallowed hard, seeing the look of satisfaction cross the hard features of the man facing her. 'I thought that as the gowns had been given to me, mine was the responsibility of returning the necklace.'

'Which you obviously did not or we would not be here today.'

'I did not return it to the Priory.' Phoebe felt a cold desperation take hold of her: they did not want to believe her, this man had already decided she was guilty. 'The . . . the day after finding the necklace, I went to return it. I had crossed the Lyng Fields and was about to go on when Edward Dartmouth overtook me. I told him the reason for my journey and he offered to take the necklace for me as the weather was worsening and it would take me several hours to get home.'

For several minutes the room remained silent except for the anxious fidgeting of the pawnbroker. Across the table the Magistrate fingered long white whiskers then, leaning forward, he glared at Phoebe.

'You are saying that you returned a valuable emerald necklace to Edward Dartmouth, that he did not return it to his sister, and that therefore he is in fact the thief?'

'No! No, I . . . I'm not . . . Edward wouldn't . . .'

'No more.' The Magistrate's palm came down hard on the table. 'I have heard enough. You stole a necklace and now try to place the blame upon the son of a respected family, a family who have held their seat in West Bromwich for hundreds of years. You accuse a man who is not present to answer for himself against your lies. Well, I will answer for him. Edward Dartmouth would never commit such treachery against his own. You are a liar and a thief, and it is only out of regard for the young man's father, Sir William Dartmouth, that I will exercise leniency and not inform him of what you have said here, for to do so would result in your incurring a far heavier penalty than the one I am about to pass.'

He then reached out a hand to the wooden gavel lying in front of him.

'Phoebe Pardoe, I find you guilty of wilful theft. I order you be taken to a place of imprisonment . . .'

A rustle of black skirts told of the woman's leaving the

room as the gavel struck hard against the table. Behind her black veil Annie Pardoe almost smiled. Her meeting with Sophie Dartmouth's personal maid had paid off. That girl's attempt to extract money in return for her silence regarding a missing emerald necklace had failed, but the charge of theft Annie had forced her to lay against Phoebe had not. The Magistrate's final words followed her through the door.

'. . . you will serve a term of fifteen years' hard labour.'

'Wait there, Pardoe.'

Agnes Marsh held out a hand as they reached the Governess's office. Mary Pegleg limped to the stool set against one wall where she was allowed to sit between running messages.

'Why has she asked to see me, Mary, do you know?'

'No idea.' Mary Pegleg answered the question in a whisper. 'I ain't bin 'ere the whole time though I knows there be someone in there with 'er 'cos I 'eard 'em talkin' when I come up from the kitchen. Sounded deep, the other voice, like a man's.'

'Is it the doctor?' Phoebe asked worriedly. 'Has the Governess sent for the doctor, is Liza worse?'

'I don't know,' Mary hissed. 'Was some shemozzle goin' on downstairs, summat about a visitor, but I didn't 'ave chance to find out who it was. Though like I said, it sounded like a man an' 'er in there seemed in a right tizzy, 'er voice all excited, what I could hear.'

'Maybe it is Father Heywood.' Phoebe's reply was almost a prayer. 'Perhaps he has called regarding the covers for the Psalters.'

'Let's 'ope it is.' Mary Pegleg shifted position on the stool, one hand rubbing her amputated leg where it sat in the cup of the wooden stump. 'At least let's pray to God it ain't the doctor. We don't want to see 'im 'ere while 'is brains is still in 'is skull.'

The door to the Governess's room opened and Agnes Marsh stepped out, her mouth tight with resentment.

'You're wanted inside, Pardoe,' she said, barely allowing her lips to free the words. 'And you, Pegleg, get your arse off that stool and get down to the kitchen. Tell them Her Highness is wanting a tray of tea sent up to her office – *now*.'

Waiting for an answer to her tap on the Governess's door, Phoebe remembered the Magistrate's words: 'Out of regard for the young man's father I will exercise leniency and not inform him of what you have said here, for to do so would result in your incurring a far heavier penalty.'

Chapter Seven

Inside the Governess's office, its desk lit by a larger window than elsewhere in the prison and set about with comfortable leather high wing armchairs, Phoebe bobbed a curtsy to the woman standing behind the desk.

'Pardoe, this is Sir William Dartmouth.'

'*A far heavier penalty*'. The words screamed in Phoebe's brain, the room whirling around her in a mad dance of chairs, desk and people. '*A far heavier penalty* . . .'

'Are you all right, Miss Pardoe?'

Phoebe felt hands to either side of her as her legs began to crumple.

'Sit here,' the distant voice commanded. Then, 'Have you sal volatile, Mrs Price?'

'Smelling salts, Sir William.' Somewhere above the void that threatened to swallow her, Phoebe heard the Governess answer, 'I have smelling salts,' then coughed as a small bottle was held beneath her nostrils.

'No, do not get up!' Sir William Dartmouth touched a hand to her shoulder then walked to the fireplace that held a fire both winter and summer. 'I have something I wish to say to you.'

He hesitated, waiting for Hannah Price to acknowledge the tap on the door. A woman in the drab grey dress that marked her as an inmate entered carrying a tray, depositing it on a small oval table set against one of the wing back chairs. She glanced at Phoebe before leaving.

He had been told. Phoebe's fingers curled, pressing her

nails hard into her palms. He had been told she had accused Edward of not returning the necklace to his sister. But she had made no such accusation. Why hadn't Edward told them he had the necklace, and why after so many months had his father decided to seek his own revenge?

'You will take some tea, Miss Pardoe?' he said as Hannah Price poured the steaming liquid into a china cup. 'My presence here has seemingly upset you.'

A china cup! She had not drunk from a china cup in over twelve months. Phoebe made no move to accept the tea the Governess held out to her. A tin mug was all she had to drink from now and would be all she would have for fifteen years – and how many more? How many more years had this man demanded be added to her sentence?

'You were accused of stealing a necklace from my daughter . . .'

Phoebe raised her gaze, her soul in her eyes. 'I did not steal it,' she said softly, 'I was returning it to the Priory.'

'So I understand.'

Hannah Price returned the cup to the tray, leaving her own untouched as she studied the girl who had already served a year in Handsworth gaol.

'I gave it to Ed— to your son. He said he would give it to Miss Sophie together with my apology. They were both to call at Wiggins Mill the next day, but they never came.'

'Miss Pardoe . . .' Sir William hesitated, looking into the fire for several moments then faced her again, squaring his shoulders as if preparing for an unpleasant task he would have preferred to leave to someone else.

Frightened of what she knew was about to come Phoebe stared at Edward's father, standing tall against the fireplace, tan knee-length coat accentuating his powerful physique, hair that had once been black crested with a dusting of grey above the temples, and eyes that in the dim light of the room might have been grey or even black.

'Miss Pardoe,' he said again, as if searching for words, 'I

was told of what passed between yourself and the Magistrate the day after you were sentenced, but yesterday I was told more . . .'

Phoebe's throat closed and her head began to pound. Yesterday he had been told more and today he would have retribution.

'Yesterday,' he went on, 'I spoke to Lucy Baines, or I should say I spoke to Mrs Mathew Leach. She told me you would not allow her to return my daughter's necklace but said that you yourself would do so.' Breaking off, he turned towards the Governess. 'We will not go on with this any longer. Mrs Price, you have the Magistrate's signed document?'

'Yes, Sir William.' She touched the folded sheet of white paper lying on her desk as he moved to take up his hat and gloves lying on a small table just inside the door of the room.

'Then I will say good day.' He inclined his head the merest fraction as Hannah Price dropped a curtsy. 'Miss Pardoe.' The same slight movement of the head and he was gone.

He had spoken to Lucy. The pounding of her head mounting to a sickening crescendo, Phoebe gripped the arms of the chair. Why had he not mentioned Edward? Why had he not spoken to his son?

'Sir William took the trouble to bring this himself.' Hannah Price picked up the sheet of paper, holding it unopened in her hand.

Phoebe stared at it, the world slowly dropping away from her. He had taken the trouble to bring it himself, to see the girl who had attempted to accuse his son of theft, attempted to blacken the character of his family, to see the girl whose life he was taking away. How many more years were written on that paper? How many more years to serve in hell?

'It seems a mistake has been made . . .'

Hannah Price's face swam before Phoebe's eyes.

'. . . the necklace you were accused of stealing has been

found. This,' she tapped the paper against her fingers, 'is an authorisation from the Magistrate. You are free to go.'

'Sir William Dartmouth himself?' Sarah Leach looked in disbelief at her son and his wife seated in her tiny living room. 'Billy-me-Lord in your 'ouse? Eeh, it's not to be believed.'

'What did 'e say?' Joseph tapped his pipe against the bars of the fire.

''E said as how his family had returned from Europe the day before and 'e had asked his son if he knew anything of Sophie's missing emerald necklace,' Lucy answered. 'It seemed at first as though he knew nothing of it then he remembered taking it from Phoebe and dropping it in the pocket of his riding habit.'

'So?' Sarah urged as her daughter-in-law paused for breath.

'So 'e says 'e sent a footman or some such to search the coat an' 'e comes back wi' the necklace in 'is hands,' Mathew took up the story.

'Oh, thank God . . . thank God!' Sarah wiped her eyes on her apron. 'Now she'll be free – Abel's daughter will be free to come 'ome.'

'Oh, aye, I reckon as Phoebe will be free to come 'ome,' Mathew went on, 'but what sort of freedom will it be? Nobody will want to know a gaolbird, innocent or not. I reckon as Phoebe Pardoe ain't gonna be a whole lot better off outside o' that prison than she were inside of it, 'specially if that aunt of 'ers can do anythin' about it.'

'What does that mean?' Joseph scraped the bowl of his clay pipe with a slender bladed knife then blew down the stem.

Mathew looked over to where his father sat beside the shiny blackleaded grate. 'I mean that in my opinion Annie Pardoe is somewheres to be found in this business. She 'olds something against Phoebe, the facts tell that themselves – turnin' her out of her father's house, tekin everythin' that was hers 'cept what Lucy saved for her – an' it's my guess it was her in that Magistrates' Court in the Green Dragon.'

"Ow can you tell that?'

'I can't really, Mother.' Mathew turned his glance to Sarah, scalding tea in a large brown earthenware teapot. 'But I got talkin' to the bobby as fetched Phoebe to the Magistrate . . . 'e gets into the Gladstone most evenings when 'e ain't on duty . . . an' 'e said the woman come in a carriage – a carriage wi' A.P. on the door.'

'A.P.' Sarah held up the teapot, the first cup half filled. 'Abel Pardoe.'

'Yes, Abel Pardoe,' Mathew said. 'The carriage was Abel Pardoe's an' the woman as rode in it were Annie Pardoe. An' 'er went to the Green Dragon to hear 'er own niece sentenced to fifteen years an' never lifted a finger to stop it!'

'God 'elp us,' Sarah murmured.

'Ar, an' 'e will 'ave to an' all if anybody 'ears you goin' on like that.' Joseph glared at his son. 'Keep yer opinions to yerself, my lad. Annie Pardoe 'as done thee badly as it is but 'er's capable of doin' a damn' sight more so be ruled by one older and wiser an' keep yer tongue between yer teeth.'

'Did 'Is Lordship say what was to be done about Phoebe?' Sarah resumed filling the cups, handing a larger mug to Joseph.

'He said he would see to everything himself,' Lucy accepted the cup from her, 'but he didn't say what it would be.'

'Billy-me-Lord be a fair man,' Joseph said, using the name by which the locals addressed Sir William. 'If 'e 'as said 'e will see to things then see to 'em 'e will. Reckon we will just 'ave to bide our time til' Abel's daughter be 'ome.'

'There's no telling when that will be,' Lucy said, swallowing her tea, 'but when she does come I want to have a fire going and something hot ready for the table. So drink up your tea, Mathew Leach, it's a long walk to Wiggins Mill.'

'Aye, the wench will be wantin' a bit o' comfort,' Joseph nodded as Lucy dropped a kiss on his head. 'If you can let we know when 'er is back, Mother an' me will walk over to the mill.'

'I'll do that, Father.' Mathew grabbed his cap from one of the several nails hammered into the door that opened on to the street, respectfully holding it until he was out of the house. 'Bye, Mother.' He folded Sarah in his arms, feeling the thinness that had come in the last few months, and in his soul cursed Annie Pardoe afresh. Her money grubbing was robbing his mother of her life as surely as Phoebe had been robbed of hers. 'We will be back to see you on Sunday.'

Reaching the corner where the road curved away out of sight of the house, he turned to wave to his mother and in his heart he made a wish: May Annie Pardoe not live to see Sunday!

The heavy door banged behind Phoebe. She was free! There would be no more days locked inside Handsworth Prison for Women, no more backbreaking hours in that laundry or sewing until she could barely see the needle, no more wardresses barking orders at her. Closing her eyes she breathed deeply, feeling the fresh air bite at her throat. She was free, free to go home, but Tilly Wood would never go home.

Phoebe had not been allowed to say goodbye to any of the women who had shared her existence for more than a year; even Mary Pegleg had not been sitting on her stool outside the Governess's office when she had come out. Given the clothes she had arrived at the prison in, she had changed, Agnes Marsh in attendance, then had been taken to the door of the prison, passing no other prisoner on the way.

'Excuse me, Miss . . .'

Phoebe opened her eyes to see the man who had come to stand at her side, wearing a high black hat and knee-length boots teamed with deep blue coat.

'Sir William asks if you would be good enough to ride home in the carriage?'

'*Sir William took the trouble to bring this himself.*' The

words echoed in her mind. But he had not come to lengthen her eternity, he had come to bring her freedom.

'Miss!'

'What . . . what did you say?'

The coachman looked at the girl in the shabby brown dress and cloak, her bonnet tied over lifeless hair snatched back from a drawn pallid face. This was not the usual kind to ride in the Dartmouth coach, but then again it was certain sure she wouldn't get far on foot. 'Sir William, Miss,' he said again, 'asks if you would kindly take the carriage home?'

Phoebe glanced about her, seeing for the first time the outside of the high prison building. She had not seen where they had brought her in that black-painted cart with its iron-grilled window, nor even known apart from hearing 'the women's gaol in Birmingham'. Now she saw a bare stretch of heath broken only by a group of scraggy trees some distance to the left and a path leading to the right, and realised she had no idea in which direction home lay.

'Yes . . . yes, thank you.'

Holding both hands to her skirt, feeling every sharp stone through the worn soles of her boots, she half stumbled to where the carriage stood waiting. Then the door closed and she was on her way home. Home! Leaning her head against the cushioned upholstery, she allowed the pent up tears of months to flood her cheeks.

'Allow me!'

Phoebe felt the soft cloth pressed into her ungloved hands and opened her eyes to see Sir William Dartmouth.

Across the narrow space that separated them he saw the sudden fear return to her eyes and felt disgusted at a system that treated a young girl in such a way as almost to destroy her; but it was a system he himself had long upheld.

'Forgive me for not giving you an explanation,' he said quietly, 'but I felt the sooner you were out of that place, the better.' He glanced at her hands, nervously twisting the white lawn handkerchief, then went on, 'I was informed of the outcome of your appearance before Gideon Speke, and of the term of imprisonment to which he had sentenced you, and I felt no regret. My family's friendship seemed to have been abused and my daughter's property stolen. But yesterday I found that nothing had been stolen and that I had been wrong. Because of my action you have been made to suffer great hardship. I can only offer my most sincere apology. I will, of course, make reparation in any way you wish.'

Reparation! Phoebe stared out of the window but the passing streets and imposing buildings of Birmingham went unseen. How could any reparation make up for what she had been through . . . for what she knew was yet to come?

'Your home is at Wednesbury, I believe,' he resumed, covering her silence. 'If you will tell me where I will have Aston take us there.'

'Brunswick House,' she answered, only half registering what he had said.

'Brunswick House!' He leaned forward slightly, a small frown creasing his brow. 'You live at Brunswick House?'

'No . . . I . . . I'm sorry.' Phoebe forced her mind to attend her words. 'I do not live at Brunswick House. My home is Wiggins Mill on the outskirts of the town.'

'Then why say Brunswick House?'

For a moment Phoebe thought she heard the note of accusation so many voices had held over the past months and her head rose defensively. 'Possibly, Sir William,' she said clearly, 'because I once did live there.'

'Brunswick House?' The frown deepened, his eyes narrowing in concentration. 'That was Abel Pardoe's house . . . his sister got it if I remember rightly. And you . . . your name is Pardoe . . .'

'Yes, Sir William.' Phoebe looked straight into his dark eyes. 'Phoebe Pardoe. I am Abel's daughter.'

'So she is to be set free?' Annie Pardoe looked at the man

seated in her drawing room, one hand tugging nervously at long white side whiskers.

'There was nothing I could do,' he answered. 'Sir William Dartmouth himself came to withdraw the charge, said the necklace had been found and demanded the girl be set free at once.'

'And you signed the document of release?'

'I had to, Annie.' Gideon Speke had been unnerved at Sir William's appearance in his office; he was a powerful man and not only in West Bromwich, there was no telling what he would do if he found out.

'Yes, I suppose you did.' Annie stood up, black skirts rustling. 'But hear me, Gideon Speke. You took my hundred pounds to put her away and if anything comes of her being found innocent 'tis you will bear the brunt. I will swear before God I paid you one hundred pounds to try buying her freedom, and that you pocketed that money while hearing no evidence in her defence. One word, Gideon . . . just one word and you will never sit on the Magistrates' bench again!'

So Abel's girl was free! Annie Pardoe closed the door on the departing Magistrate. She had been denied little more than one year of her life while she, Annie, had had no life at all. Slowly she walked through the house and out into the garden. She would not let it rest here. She had taken her niece's home and all she possessed save the paltry sum her maternal grandmother had left her, but all that would not pay for what her own brother had taken from her. Revenge tasted sweet and Annie craved its sweetness. There was more yet to be had and she would drink it to the very last drop.

Turning, she walked back into the house and up the stairs to her room. Putting on her cloak and settling a black bonnet on her head, she went to the room Samuel used as a studio.

'I have to go out for a while,' she signed on her fingers. 'I do not expect to be very long. Is there anything I can get for you while I am in the town?'

Samuel shook his head, his mouth unsmiling as he regarded his sister. Annie had always worn a look of bitterness but of late that look had changed; to what he could not rightly say but it was a look he liked even less.

'Has Tranter brought your hot drink?'

Samuel rested his brush on the palette. 'No,' he signed back, his fingers moving rapidly, 'I told her not to.'

Annie did not question his answer, knowing that in the years Maudie Tranter had spent with them she too had learned the sign language that enabled Samuel to speak.

'Then we will have one together when I return.' Annie Pardoe looked at the brother she had cared for for so many years. His features were thinned and gaunt compared to a year ago but they were still a carbon copy of the man who had been a brother to them both, still with the same keen eyes, 'Take care not to get cold, dear.' Her gloved fingers fluttered like the black wings of a crow. 'You know how unwell you have been of late.'

Samuel picked up his brush, watching his sister leave the room. The house always felt easier when she was not in it.

Annie drove the small trap, guiding the mare along the Holyhead Road that linked Wednesbury to its neighbouring towns. Passing the Monway Steel Mill of which Samuel, thanks to their brother, was part-owner, she turned off across the heath towards Hobs Hill mine, stopping at the huddle of small houses some half-mile away.

'I will say what I came to say.' She had marched straight into Joseph Leach's cottage, ownership relieving her of the necessity of waiting to be asked. 'My niece has besmirched her father's name, she has been imprisoned for theft, therefore she will be unwelcome in any house of standing.'

'But my Mathew's wife says Miss Phoebe is to be set free.' Sarah Leach stared at the woman who seemed to fill her small room with darkness. ''Er says as 'ow they 'ave found out Miss Phoebe never done it, 'er never stole no necklace.'

'Nevertheless,' Annie drew in a long breath, the effort flaring her nostrils, 'the slur remains, my brother's good name has been stained, and I will not have it perpetuated by accepting the girl's presence in any property I and my brother Samuel own. And this house forms part of that property. I tell you, Sarah Leach, you have Phoebe inside this house for one minute and you are out, bag and baggage. What's more, I will see to it that the cripple you call a husband will get no job in Wednesbury.'

'There be only one thief in Abel's family,' Sarah muttered, watching the trap pull away, 'an' that be you, Annie Pardoe. You 'ave teken everythin' that should 'ave bin his daughter's an' may the Good Lord pay you for it!'

Chapter Eight

Sir William Dartmouth watched the face of the girl he had just seen released from prison. Its pallor and thinness did not completely hide its fine-boned quality, or the unhappiness shading her green eyes detract from their lovely almond shape. He had known Abel Pardoe for many years, they had done business together on a regular basis, he buying much of the coal Abel's mines produced together with steel from his Monway works, but they had not mixed socially. Now he was looking at the daughter he had not realised the other man had, a daughter whom he guessed bore a quiet beauty beneath the mark of Handsworth Prison.

She had not spoken since telling him she had once lived at Brunswick House and though she had stared out of the window for the rest of their journey he guessed it was not the passing scenery that held her attention.

'Is this Wiggins Mill?' he asked as the carriage rumbled over a stony path worn by the carter's wagon. 'Miss Pardoe?' He leaned across, touching a hand to hers, still twisting the handkerchief, then withdrew as Phoebe jerked backward, the shadow in her eyes deepening. 'I asked, is this your home?'

'Yes.' Phoebe looked across to where the old house began to rise out of the hollow that sheltered it, the stilled windmill standing sentinel on the adjoining high ground. 'Yes, this is Wiggins Mill.'

The coach drew to a halt and almost immediately the coachman was opening the door.

'Miss Pardoe,' Sir William waited until she stepped down, 'you are no doubt in need of rest but perhaps you will do me the courtesy of calling at the Priory as soon as you feel able? There is a lot I still have not said and we must discuss how you may be compensated.'

Phoebe looked at her home. She was free, she did not have to bite back her words any longer and never again would man or woman order her life.

'Sir William,' she turned back to him, a cool gleam of assurance clearing the shadows from her eyes, 'I will call at the Priory but only to return your handkerchief. As for compensation, there is no need of any. A mistake has been made and a mistake has been rectified, we need say no more on the subject. Will the day after tomorrow be convenient for me to return your handkerchief?'

'I will send the carriage for you at eleven.' Then, as Phoebe made to reject the offer, he smiled. 'And *you* need say no more on *that* subject.'

'Miss Phoebe . . . oh, Miss Phoebe, you're home!' Lucy raced around the corner of the house as the carriage drove away. 'Oh, it's so good to see you.'

'And you, Lucy,' she breathed as her friend's hug threatened to stifle her.

'Welcome home, Miss Phoebe.' Mathew Leach smiled at the two women, laughing and crying at the same time.

'Mathew!' Phoebe broke free to hug the man she had known from childhood. 'But . . . but shouldn't you be at the pit?'

'Come in, Miss Phoebe.' Lucy's voice lost some of its joy. 'There's a fire in the grate an' tea on the hob an' I'm dyin' to butter you one of my scones.

'You see, Miss Phoebe,' she said when at last Phoebe stopped wandering through the rooms of her home and settled in the warm kitchen, 'when I was sacked from the Priory and Mathew was given the sack from the pit we had nowhere to go like an' . . . well, I thought the mill could do wi' being kept an eye on an' you wouldn't mind us being in one of the outhouses. We never used the 'ouse, Miss, honest we didn't. I just come in every day to dust and keep the rooms aired.'

'You mean, you were both removed from your employment?' Phoebe left the scone untouched. 'But why? For what reason?'

'Mathew was sacked for questioning the reason for your aunt reducing the wages at the pit an' meself? Well miss, Sophie's maid said I must 'ave put the necklace in one of the dresses sent to Wiggins Mill, that I knowed you as a friend and would be able to retrieve it when I visited you and then sell it. So the housekeeper up and sacks me. Matters of the servants is left to 'er when 'er Ladyship is away, Sir William is never bothered with little things like sacking a maid.'

'They don't 'ave to give a reason,' Mathew said sourly. 'Pit owner or gentry, meks no difference – when either of 'em wants you out it's a case of pick up yer tin and go.'

'But how have you managed with no wage between you?'

'Well, like I said, Miss,' Lucy took up the thread, 'we had nowhere to go. We thought yer aunt might turn nasty if we lived with Mathew's parents an' we couldn't live here without being wed so we just got Father Heywood to say the words over us then we come here. Oh, Miss, I hopes you don't mind?'

'Of course I don't mind, but Lucy . . . your lovely wedding? Didn't you get it after all?'

'No, Miss.' Lucy smiled at her husband. 'But I got the man and that's all that matters.'

'We'll be gone in the mornin', Miss.' Mathew turned towards the door. 'I'll go see to our bits an' pieces an' when Lucy is finished over 'ere 'er'll pack the beddin'.'

'She will do no such thing!' Phoebe answered vehemently. 'And neither will you. You will stay here and glad I'll be of your company. I . . . I wouldn't want to stay here alone . . .'

'We understand, Miss, and we thank you,' Lucy cut in, seeing the shadow return to Phoebe's eyes. 'Mathew and me we'll mek it up to you, really we will.'

'There is nothing to make up.' Phoebe smiled. 'We are friends, and wage or no wage will survive somehow. In fact, you two seem to have found a way already, judging by the food on this table.'

'That's Mathew, Miss,' Lucy beamed. 'You remember he was quite handy with hammer and saw? Well, he gets a few odd jobs from folk in the town, mending a chair or mekin' a stool, little things like but they buy flour and vegetables. And I do a bit of sewing like you used to only I don't get no dresses from the nobs.'

'Neither will I again, Lucy.' Phoebe sipped the hot tea she had poured. 'Those doors are closed forever, I'm afraid.'

'But you didn't never tek anything!' Lucy's glance was bright with anger. 'Them at the Priory knows you never and so does Magistrate.'

'I don't think that will make any difference.' Phoebe shook her head as the other girl offered more tea. 'The very fact that I have been in prison will be sufficient for the nobs, as you called them, to reject my company.'

'Then bloody nobs ain't worth associatin' wi'.'

'Mathew!' Lucy glared at her husband. 'Language.'

'Beg your pardon, Miss Phoebe,' Mathew pulled open the door that led on to the yard, 'but that's the way I feel,' he said, going outside.

'Please don't tek no notice of Mathew.' Lucy gathered the used cups on to a wooden tray. 'But the losin' of his job 'as made 'im bitter. I keep tellin' 'im it's no use his feelin' that way but I might as well bang my 'ead against a brick wall for all the good it does. ''E just won't take a tellin', says all moneyed folk am the same: all out for themselves an' sod the likes of folk who grind for 'em. There be times I think he'll never be the same as he was.'

Never be the same. The thought lingered as Phoebe followed the other girl into the scullery. She understood Mathew's feelings. Things might never be the same for any of them. She was free, but what freedom would Wednesbury allow a girl who had been in prison?

Phoebe came up the rise from Lyng Fields, feeling the softness of the earth beneath her feet, and stood on the crest of the high ground cradling Sandwell Valley, looking down on the ancient Priory. Cool air fanned her brow and she lifted her face to it, revelling in its touch. She had deliberately not waited for the carriage as Sir William had told her to, ignoring his instruction. Never again, she told herself, closing her eyes to the delicious taste of freedom, never again would any man or woman order her life.

A breeze lifting out of the valley caught her skirts, lifting them like unseen fingers, and she pressed a hand to them, delighting in the touch of the brown bombazine after so many months of wearing drab grey calico. But the women who had been her companions of those months were still wearing grey uniforms. Her mind flashed to Tilly. She would be dressed in grey calico the rest of her life. If only they had given her time to say goodbye to the woman who had befriended her . . . but she had been rushed from Handsworth Prison as though she carried the plague and now she would never be able to tell Tilly how glad she was to have known her and to have been her friend.

Opening her eyes, she looked down at the house nestling on the floor of the valley, its mullioned windows seeming to stare back at her. Sir William Dartmouth had waited outside that prison, waited until she emerged through its heavy door; he had brought her home in his carriage, but for what reason? Reparation for what his son had caused to happen to her? Maybe, but any such feeling would be momentary, passed and forgotten in a week. As Mathew had said yesterday, all moneyed folk were out for themselves, they and they alone were all that mattered to them, and the more money they had the less those without it counted for. Well, she had none but she would count for something. Lifting her skirt, she set off down into the valley. Somehow, some way, Phoebe Pardoe would count for something.

At the foot of the high ground the valley widened into a flat swathe, the grass-covered earth rolling away to green eternity. It had been green around Brunswick House, Phoebe remembered, the lawns edged with beds bright with flowers, a shaded arbour leading to her favourite rose garden, but there had been nothing like these vast acres spreading endlessly, the ancient house at their heart.

Passing at last beneath a great stone arch, she began to walk along the sweeping approach, itself lined with magnificent beeches, their arched branches almost meeting overhead as if in imitation of the stone.

'Hey!'

The shout coming from the hushed silence of the morning took her unawares and she stopped, both hands clutched to her brown cloak.

'Where do you think you be goin'?'

A man in late middle age, his shoulders hunched, stepped from behind a tree.

'Don't you know this 'ere be private property?'

He stepped towards her and Phoebe saw his earth-stained hands move toward the heavy buckle belt fastened about his breeches.

'Of course I know.' Phoebe lifted her chin, putting every ounce of her failing confidence into her voice. There was no one around; in fact there might only be herself and this man in the world, so empty was the spread of ground. 'This is Sandwell Priory and I am here by appointment.'

'Appointment, eh!'

The man's hands still hovered about the fastener of his belt and Phoebe felt her heart jerk. What did he intend to do? Whatever it was there was no one to see.

'Yes, by appointment.' Phoebe stood her ground as he came closer. 'I am here to see Sir William . . .'

'*You*, 'ere to see Billy-me-Lord?' The man sniffed derisively, eyeing her plain brown dress. 'You'll be tellin' me 'as 'ow you be a personal friend of 'is next.'

'Hardly.' Phoebe stared into the man's eyes, pale rheumy eyes that seemed to swim in a mist of water. 'Though I do wish to return this.'

Thrusting a hand into the pocket of her cloak, she pulled out the freshly laundered handkerchief, its crested initial worked in pale blue, and held it towards him.

'Oh!' He stared at the handkerchief, his manner changing as if the owner himself had suddenly appeared. 'It's . . . it's just that 'er Ladyship don't like town folk using the main drive, an' with you not bein' in a carriage like I thought as you . . .'

'That I was one of the town folk?' Phoebe returned the handkerchief to her pocket. 'You thought correctly, I am.'

'In that case . . .' the hands stopped hovering, dropping instead to the man's sides '. . . you should 'ave come by the back way, up against Ice Pool. That way there would be less chance of them up at the 'ouse seein' you. You best go back. There be a path around to the left of the arch will lead you to the stables. You can get to the servants' quarters that way.'

'Thank you.' Phoebe's mouth did not relax.

'I ain't seen you afore,' the man went on as she turned away. 'You be the new maid?'

'No.' Phoebe halted then swung around to face the lovely stone mansion. 'I am not the new maid and neither do I enter a house via the servants' quarters.'

Feeling those watery eyes on her back she marched up the arrow-straight drive, her mouth set in a straight line. Her home might be a hovel in comparison to that of Sir William Dartmouth but she was mistress of it and servant to no man, and that was the way her life would remain.

She had almost reached the steps that led from left and right, forming an arc up to the main entrance of the Priory, when a footman in dark blue livery appeared as if from nowhere.

'You shouldn't have come this way.'

His voice was hushed, almost reverential; no servant in her father's house had been expected to speak this way.

'So I have been told,' Phoebe answered loudly.

Closing the space between them, the man glanced at the house before grabbing her elbow. 'Then why did yer? You must 'ave been told 'er Ladyship don't like servants usin' the main drive. C'mon, out of it, there'll be trouble if 'er sees you 'ere.'

The hand on her elbow tightened and for a fleeting second Phoebe was back inside that corridor with Liza Spittle's hand pushing her back against the wall, the old sickness rising in her throat.

'What is going on here?'

The words were not loud but they acted upon the footman like a starting pistol. His hand fell away from Phoebe's elbow and he stepped back as Sir William Dartmouth rounded the corner of the house.

'I asked what is going on here?'

The sickness that memory had provoked faded as he approached. Glancing at the footman, Phoebe saw the pale line of anxiety now lining that man's lips. So it was the same here in West Bromwich as it was in Wednesbury! Positions once lost would be hard to replace, especially if a man were to be dismissed with no references.

'I have a stone in my shoe,' Phoebe lied, 'your footman was about to assist me.'

'I see.'

I know you do, thought Phoebe, catching the look of gratitude in the servant's eye as he was dismissed. First you think me a thief, now you see me as a liar.

'I will send for one of the maids.'

'Please don't bother.' Phoebe bent, and removing a shoe, shook it, displacing the imaginary stone. Then she slipped her foot back into it. 'A woman learns to do these things for herself in Handsworth Gaol.'

'Take him back to the stable.' Sir William turned to the groom who had followed him from the back of the house. The man began to lead away the magnificent black horse and its master turned back to Phoebe.

'That will keep them in conversation for a few days.' He smiled.

Phoebe glanced at the departing groom, remembering how the slightest deviation from the usual could set the women's prison humming for days. The slightest deviation! What Tilly had done to Liza Spittle was no slight deviation . . . what would happen now to Tilly . . . what would the Prison Board do to her?

'Shall we go inside?'

The question cut across those thoughts spinning in Phoebe's mind, bringing her attention back to the man half smiling at her.

'There is no need.' She fished in her pocket then held out the folded square of white lawn. 'I can return this to you here. It is all I came for.'

'But that is not the only reason I wished you to come.' He regarded her from deep grey eyes. 'You have not yet been given a full explanation of the facts of what happened on that day, nor have you received my family's apology.'

'I have received my freedom,' Phoebe answered, her own gaze clear and steady, 'that is enough. Nothing more is necessary or wanted, therefore I wish you good day, Sir William.'

'Maybe it is enough for you,' his voice was suddenly hard, cutting through the quietness covering the beautiful valley, 'but what of my son? All he can do is apologise, Miss Pardoe. Would you deprive him of what little solace that can give him?'

Edward! How many times had he filled her thoughts during those long nights, how many times had she seen in her mind that handsome face, those vividly blue eyes? Yet strangely she had not once thought of him since meeting his father.

'Will you not at least let the boy speak for himself?'

Only a brief nod indicating her agreement, Phoebe followed him into the Priory. Dismissing all offers of attention, Sir William led her through the spacious rooms, each exquisite in its furnishings, until he came to a door concealed in an alcove in a corridor lined with portraits.

'My wife will be in here,' he said, pushing open the door and waiting until Phoebe passed inside.

Much smaller than the rooms through which she had already walked, this held a more intimate feel, the home of laughing children and shared secrets. Phoebe glanced quickly at the photographs in silver frames dotted on tables, the deep chairs carelessly scattered with bright cushions, the spectacles beside the newspapers that marked this a family room.

'Amelia, my dear, Miss Pardoe is here.'

Lady Amelia Dartmouth laid aside the book she had been reading. 'Miss Pardoe, do forgive my not welcoming you but I was not informed . . . William, why did no one tell me of Miss Pardoe's arrival?'

'Never mind that for now,' he replied as his wife drew Phoebe to a chair, 'ring for Edward and Sophie.'

'You will take tea, my dear?'

Phoebe looked at the elegant woman, remembering her from the evening market, only then her bonnet had hidden the traces of gold that still shone among the carefully dressed fading hair and her cloak had covered the stately, tightly corseted figure.

'Thank you,' she murmured as Amelia Dartmouth issued softly spoken orders to the man who responded almost immediately to the pull of a bell cord.

'Phoebe!' Edward was first into the room, rushing to where she sat in a deep brocade chair. 'Oh, Phoebe, I'm so sorry.'

'Edward!' his father cautioned as a maid entered with a silver tray. 'We will wait for your sister.'

He had grown. Phoebe glanced over to where Edward stood beside his father. He was taller than she remembered but still lacked three or four inches beside the older man. He had the same blue eyes and golden hair of his mother but the stance of his father, the assurance that a life of wealth and position bestows.

'Phoebe . . . Phoebe, I'm so happy to see you!' Sophie burst into the room like a boisterous puppy, grabbing both of Phoebe's hands and pulling her out of the chair. 'Was it positively awful in that prison?'

'Sophie!' Lady Amelia's voice was sharp.

'Sorry, Mama,' she said, giving Phoebe's hands a squeeze before releasing them.

'Miss Pardoe,' Sir William said as Phoebe accepted the delicate porcelain cup Sophie handed her, 'my son has something to say to you.'

'Yes, Phoebe.' Edward's blue eyes clouded. 'That day I met you coming here to return a necklace you told me you had found caught up inside a dress that Sophie had given you, I said I would return it in your stead.' He looked at his mother and Phoebe thought that despite his height he seemed just like a little boy, seeking encouragement in making a confession.

'Go on, Edward.' His mother smiled, a world of understanding in her eyes.

'Well, after I left you, The Prince caught his foot in a root or something and came down heavily.'

'The Prince?' Phoebe questioned.

'The bay I was riding,' Edward replied, 'he was a son of Satan, my father's black, and sometimes he showed it. He did that day anyway . . .'

'He was restless, I remember.' Phoebe put the delicate cup and saucer aside, her tea untouched.

'He always reacted to a sudden breeze that way.' Edward glanced at his father, still standing before the Adam fireplace. 'As if he wanted to race the wind. Anyway he got the bit between his teeth and set off like a bat out of hell. We were half across the valley when he came down, and when I couldn't get him to his feet I went for help. By the time it was all sorted out I had completely forgotten about the necklace in my pocket.'

'The Prince was a particular favourite of Edward's.' Amelia Dartmouth stretched a hand toward the tall young man who was her son. 'His father gave him the foal when it was born, you could say they grew up together were it not to sound so sentimental.'

'Edward was devastated when they had to shoot The Prince,' Sophie put in. 'It was days before he could bring himself to speak to anyone.'

'By that time,' Lady Dartmouth took up the explanation, 'the chill I had caught that evening at the street market had worsened, and it was decided we should leave for Europe earlier than originally intended. So you see, Miss Pardoe, both Sophie and Edward were out of the country when you . . .' The explanation trailed off, his mother holding on to Edward's hand.

'What my wife was about to say was that she and our son and daughter were abroad when you were arrested and imprisoned, and I did not acquaint them with that information in my letters to them. Therefore the fault is mine . . .'

'William,' Amelia Dartmouth's brow creased in a small frown as she turned to her husband, 'my dear, you were not to know the necklace would be found.'

'As you say, Amelia,' he nodded, 'but that does not excuse my behaviour. When James Siveter informed me that a young woman had been found guilty of stealing the necklace, I did nothing to ascertain the truth of what had happened.'

'But what could you have done?' his wife asked. 'You must accept the law.'

'As we all must,' his already dark eyes seemed to darken further, 'but we need not accept that the law has been presented with the true facts. I should have set in motion my own investigation.' He turned to Phoebe. 'As it was I did not, and therein lies my guilt. I was too ready to believe the friendship of my family had been abused and for that I offer my profound apology, Miss Pardoe, and ask in what manner I may make reparation?'

Phoebe rose, her plain brown garments a stark contrast to the elegant testimony to wealth that lay all about her.

'Sir William,' she said quietly, 'I told you yesterday that a mistake had been made. It was a mistake for which I attribute no blame and require no reparation. I know that as soon as you were told the truth you lost no time in securing my release. I know also that neither your son nor daughter would have wished for such a thing as my imprisonment, but now the truth is out and the necklace retrieved there is no need for the subject to be raised again.'

She turned to the woman who still clutched her son's hand, as if thinking he might be marched away to some prison. 'Thank you for receiving me, Lady Dartmouth. Now I must return home.'

'May I come to see you tomorrow, Phoebe?' Sophie was on her feet. 'I do so enjoy talking to you.'

'Sophie,' Lady Dartmouth smiled for the first time, 'Miss Pardoe may wish to rest for a few days before being concerned with callers.'

'I should be happy for Sophie to call at Wiggins Mill whenever you feel she may, Lady Dartmouth.' Phoebe dropped a polite curtsy.

'Does that invitation hold for me too?' Edward released his hand from that of his mother.

'Again, only when your mother permits it.'

'Don't bother ringing for Compson.' Sir William stepped forward as his wife made to pull the bell that would ring for a servant. 'If Miss Pardoe will allow, I will see her out myself.

'I really cannot permit you to refuse to take some form of compensation for what we have done to you.'

They had passed once again through rooms Phoebe would have loved to linger in and stood now at the foot of the curving stone steps that fronted the great house.

'You can't force me to accept either.'

'As it seems I could not force you into waiting for my carriage to collect you this morning.' William Dartmouth looked down into a face too pale and too thin but one that nevertheless whispered of beauty and character, and he smiled. 'Perhaps you will permit it to take you home?'

'Thank you, Sir William, but I prefer to walk.'

'What!' He laughed then, low in his throat. 'And get another stone in your shoe?'

'I may even take them off and walk barefoot.' Suddenly Phoebe too was smiling. 'That would give your servants even more cause for conversation. Good day, Sir William.'

Sir William Dartmouth watched the slight brown-clad figure walk away and found himself admiring the courage and honesty of the girl, the resilience that had brought her through months of imprisonment yet blaming no one at the end of it. He remembered the astuteness and honesty of the man he had known in the world of business.

'Yes, Miss Phoebe Pardoe,' he murmured, watching her disappear along the drive, 'you are truly Abel's daughter.'

Chapter Nine

Phoebe put the last of the breakfast dishes back on the kitchen dresser then settled the kettle over the coals. She would make a broth later against Lucy and Mathew's return from town. They were both trying so hard to make a living, Mathew trudging the streets in search of odd jobs and Lucy baking every night then selling scones and pies in the market place by day, while she . . . Phoebe looked around the small kitchen, its red flagstones boasting a pegged rug against the door, dresser arrayed with an assortment of plates and cups, the table whose twice-daily scrub had the wood almost white . . . apart from keeping the house clean, what was she doing?

She turned back to the fire, staring into its red heart. She couldn't go on like this, she couldn't continue to live off Lucy and her husband. In prison she had dreamed of being home, of earning her own living, of being beholden to none save herself yet . . . 'Why?' she whispered to the flames. 'Why can't I do it, why can't I at least try?'

The coals settled, sending a small glowing ember sliding between the bars of the grate. Phoebe watched the trail of sparks it made as it fell against the fender, sparks that glittered and then faded into nothing, as her life had once glittered only to fade.

If only her father's death had not come so soon, if she had been married to Montrose, her life would have been so different. Different! Reaching the tongs from the companion set that stood beside the range, she picked up the fallen ember, replacing it on the fire. Yes, her life would have been different but her world would still be empty for how long would happiness have lasted once she'd found out that Montrose's real reason for marrying her was her father's money? And now it seemed Sophie had been earmarked to become Mrs Montrose Wheeler.

Replacing the tongs, she walked restlessly into the small living room with its meagre pawnshop furnishings. Mrs Montrose Wheeler! Phoebe touched a finger to the blue glass top of the oil lamp sitting in the centre of the round chenille-covered table and knew which she would rather have.

The skirts of her brown dress swishing, she ran up the stairs and into the bedroom she had once used as a workroom, the lethargy that had lain over her since leaving prison falling away like a discarded shawl. She knew how she could make a living. Opening a chest that stood against the window wall she took out the small dresses she had made for Lady Dartmouth, dresses that had never been given as the presents they were intended for. They were pretty. She lifted them one at a time, holding them against the light from the window. There were women in Wednesbury who either hadn't the skill to make their children's clothes or else were too busy working to keep them to have the time to try. Lucy said there were customers for her baking, maybe some of those customers would buy clothing. Draping the dresses across a table she used for cutting out her patterns, she counted them. There were eight ready for sale now and she still had some of the dresses Sophie had given her.

Turning to a larger chest standing on the opposite wall she raised the domed lid and stood stock still. The pale green gown stared up at her.

'. . . *I find you guilty of wilful theft* . . .' Phoebe's hand tightened on the mahogany lid as the room swam away from her.

'. . . *I sentence you to be taken to a place of imprisonment and there you will serve a term of fifteen years' hard labour . . .'*

Hard labour . . . imprisonment . . . fifteen years . . . wilful theft . . . I sentence . . . fifteen years. . . . The words twisted and turned in her mind, louder and louder until they screamed in her head; life draining out of her, Phoebe's fingers loosed the heavy lid and it fell with a bang, the noise of it chasing away the ghosts of the past. She stood for several seconds, her breathing rapid and short. She was free of the walls but not yet free of the prison. But she would be free, determinedly she lifted the lid of the chest and took out the green gown, totally free.

Laying the gown across the one chair the room still held she hesitated at a sound from downstairs. Sophie? Edward? It couldn't be Lucy or Mathew, they would not return before evening. She crossed to the window and looked out to where the Dartmouth carriage would be standing . . . only there was no carriage.

It could have driven up unheard but it could not have left the same way. Maybe she had imagined the sound? She stood listening until the crash of breaking china told her she had not imagined it.

Maybe it was Lucy, maybe she was unwell. 'Lucy!' she called, running from the room and downstairs to the kitchen. 'Lucy, are you all right?'

'It ain't Lucy . . .' a voice behind her halted her progress toward the scullery '. . . it's me!'

Phoebe turned toward the voice. A man stood inside the kitchen, blocking the doorway to the living room. He was about five feet ten and aged around thirty, and eyed her brazenly.

'Who are you? What do you want?' Phoebe asked, suddenly knowing a new fear as his eyes wandered over her.

'Who I be don't matter.' He spoke through lips that seemed too thick for his narrow face. 'What I want, though, that be a different matter.'

'I have no work to give you.'

He smiled, spreading the thick lips, showing teeth that were strong but in need of a rub with baking soda. 'It ain't work I'm after.'

'I . . . I don't live alone here.'

'Oh, I know you don't.' His eyes glittered, he knew her fear and was feeding on it. 'I know about Lucy and 'er 'usband, same as I know about you and your visit to Sandwell Priory last week. 'Ow much did 'e give you?'

'I don't understand.' Phoebe tried to move into the scullery but the man was at her side before she had taken two steps.

'Don't play me for a fool, Miss Bloody Fancy Pardoe,' he grated. 'You understands all right an' comin' on all innocent won't pull the wool. My eyes am wide open. I knows the Dartmouths won't be lettin' things go wi'out payin' you somethin' . . . now wheer is it?'

'I did go to the Priory last week.' The fear in her was stronger now and she knew he sensed it as an animal senses fear. What would he do when he found nothing here of value? 'But I went there only to return a handkerchief Sir William had lent to me, nothing more. I . . . I took nothing from them.'

'So Phoebe Pardoe got nothing?' He moved closer. 'Look, I warned you, don't play clever wi' me. I know you done twelve months an' more on account of Mr Bloody 'igh falutin' Edward Dartmouth an' that last week you went to the Priory to collect. You talked to the 'ole bloody lot of 'em . . . compensation is what you talked and compensation is money. You got money an' it's that money I've come for . . . now wheer is it?'

One hand flashed upward, grabbing her hair, snatching her head backward. 'You might as well tell me,' he brought his face close, the thick lips only inches away, ''cos I'll find out one way or another and one of them ways you're gonna find very painful.'

'I . . . told . . . you,' Phoebe fought to speak against the constriction of her neck being pulled backward, 'I was given

nothing . . . the Dartmouth family . . . they gave me . . . no
. . . no money.'

'Lyin' bitch!' He released her hair, the same hand smacking
viciously across her face, knocking her against the dresser,
sending plates hurtling to the floor. Grabbing a poker, he
thrust it deep into the glowing fire. 'If you ain't told me
wheer you 'ave the money 'id by the time that's 'ot, you'll
'ave a face nobody will bear the lookin' at.'

He wouldn't believe her, he was convinced she had been
given money by the Dartmouths and nothing she said would
alter that. Phoebe swallowed hard, her thoughts unnaturally
clear. If she could get out of the house she might be able to
make a run for it.

'All right,' she said, wiping a hand across her smarting eyes,
'Sir William did give me money but it's not here . . .'

'Then wheer is it?'

He grabbed at her again, cinching her arm, pulling her
forward. There was no smell of coal dust, Phoebe thought,
and no tiny burn holes in his trousers so he was not a miner
nor did he work in an iron foundry. That meant he wasn't
local for there was little for men to do otherwise around
Wednesbury. So how did he know about her being in prison
or about her visit to the Priory?

'I said, wheer is it?' He reached his free hand to the poker,
its steel tip indistinguishable from the crimson coals. 'But you
can take yer time, it's gonna be a pleasure gettin' you to say.'

'It's outside.' Phoebe prayed her words would convince
him. 'I thought it better not to bring it into the house. No
one would expect so much money to be left out there.'

'Wheer outside?' He drew the poker out of the fire.

'In the old mill.'

'That's better.'

He dropped the poker, letting it rattle down the bars of
the grate on to the stone hearth, dragging Phoebe with
him out of the house and across the yard to where the
windmill stood on a little rise.

'Wheer abouts did you put it?'

Phoebe winced as he jerked her arm. 'Up in the corn loft. There's a pile of empty sacks against the wall, I hid the money under them.'

'Yer best be tellin' the truth,' he threatened, almost frog marching her towards the door of the disused mill, 'yer'll regret it if you ain't.'

If only he would release her arm! Phoebe tried to form a plan: she could run back into the house and bolt the doors. But he did not release her. Kicking open the wooden door, he pushed her before him into the mill.

'The corn loft, you said?' He glanced upward then down to where a rickety ladder lay half buried in the dust of the floor. Holding her with one hand, he struggled to raise the ladder then rest it against the floor of the loft.

'You first.' He leered, his almost canine teeth taking on a yellower hue in the light streaming from the doorway.

Phoebe struggled up the ladder, her feet catching in her skirts, threatening to throw her off the narrow uneven struts.

'Stop there an' don't go movin' . . . if you know what's best for you.'

Pushing her as he followed from the topmost rung of the ladder, he kicked it aside, laughing as he made for the heap of sacks lying in a corner.

This would be her only chance. There would be no more tricking him when he found there was no money under those sacks. Moving slowly, holding her skirts so they wouldn't rustle, she got to her feet, inching towards the edge of the corn loft floor. He had kicked away the ladder but that wouldn't stop her.

'Go on . . . jump! Makes no odds.'

Despite her caution he had heard and was watching her, on his knees among the empty corn sacks.

'You'll break one leg at least, mebbe both, but you won't need legs for what I'm gonna do to you . . . after I've got yer money, that is. Go on, jump . . . you won't crawl far.'

He began to laugh again, a laugh that had her spine crawling. 'What I'm gonna do to you . . .' She had heard those words before; the image of Liza Spittle's birthmarked face floated before her eyes and the sour smell of her filled Phoebe's nostrils. Closing her eyes, she jumped.

Annie Pardoe slipped the key into her black bag and left her bedroom, going to her brother's studio.

'I am going into the town,' she signed, the movement of her hands setting her bag swinging from her arm. 'Doctor Dingley has prescribed a medicine for your headaches and I do not trust Isaac Jackson to send it before teatime. That man is not nearly the chemist his father was.'

Samuel put his brush on a table beside a palette smeared with paints and looked at his sister. He could hardly remember seeing her dressed in any colour other than black, as though she were in constant mourning; neither could he remember seeing her smile, he could only recall the bitterness that had eaten away at her over the years, a bitterness of her own making. Yes, Annie *was* in perpetual mourning, grieving for a life she thought duty had required her to forgo and nurturing bitterness against the brother she blamed for taking it.

'There is no need for you to go,' he signed, his long fingers moving in rapid succession, 'my headache is quite gone.'

'Yes, it is now,' Annie's fingers relayed words of care she had never truly felt, 'but what of the night-time, dear? You know how sometimes you cannot sleep for the pain in your head. I think it better I fetch your medicine myself.'

'If that is what you wish.' Samuel's fingers seemed to flow into each other, one sign blending into another with the practice of years. 'I will take a turn in the garden until you return.'

Going into the adjoining room that was her brother's bedroom, Annie took a lightweight coat from the panelled wardrobe. Returning to the studio, she held it out to Samuel.

'You must take care,' she signed as he took the coat and slipped it on, 'you know how quickly you take the influenza.'

Yes, he knew. Samuel followed her out of the studio, making his separate way into the garden. He also knew how much he wished the influenza would take him.

Annie drove her small trap along Walsall Road turning off when she reached Oakeswell End, directing the horse toward the chemist's shop that topped Dudley Street. She would collect the medicine Alfred Dingley had prescribed and then she would complete what she had intended all along.

Ignoring the sidelong glances of the women and the looks of dislike from men she had laid off from the pits on one pretext or another, and whom the iron foundries would not take on, she trotted the horse a roundabout route, avoiding where possible the more heavily frequented roads until she came to Bescot Fields. This part of Wednesbury was still mostly pasture with only a few farms holding out against the industrialisation that had engulfed the town like the black plague; here she had lived so many years before coming to Brunswick House, here at the end of a beaten track hidden by high hedges was the house Abel had given to her and Samuel. It had not been sold or let to tenants and neither would it be until her use for it was gone. Samuel took no interest in the property or businesses left to him by Abel and none in this house: his painting was his only interest, which suited her. She turned the horse off the track, driving round to the back of the house where the trap would be screened. Yes, it suited her very well.

Leaving the horse to crop at the overgrown flower border she took the key from her bag, letting herself into the house. She would not open the shutters. The years had taught her the geography of this house and she moved easily through its shadowed dimness. In her old bedroom she drew a box from the back of a narrow shelf obscured by a marble-topped washstand set in front of it.

A finger of daylight poked between the heavy velvet curtains. Annie carried the box over to it. She removed the lid and breathed deeply, a feeling of satisfaction coursing through her. It was still there. From the depths of the box she withdrew a small finely wrought glass bottle. By the finger of daylight she read the label: 'D'Amour'. Elias Webb had thought her his the day he gave her the bottle of French perfume. But the perfume and its giver had long gone from her life.

Discarding the box, she thrust the bottle into her bag and left the house, locking it securely before climbing into the trap and leaving her former prison to its silence.

Phoebe struck the packed earth with a jarring thud and lay still. Above her, his narrow face pulled into a grin, the man watched, then satisfied she was either unconscious or worse, turned back to searching the heap of sacks.

Hearing his movements above her, Phoebe knew he had not followed. Carefully, a prayer in every move, she pushed herself to her knees, then to her feet. By what miracle she had not broken her legs she didn't know and didn't stop to reason, her one thought was to make it back to the house and bolt herself in. Gathering her skirts in both hands she tiptoed toward the open door and was almost through it when she heard him shout.

Running the last few yards, she hurled herself out of the door, slamming it behind her, eyes skimming it in search of a bolt or securing bar. But there was no way of locking it; there had been no need for locks at Wiggins Mill.

'Hey! Come here, you bloody bitch . . .'

The shout was followed by a grunt. He was down from the corn loft, had jumped as she had.

'Think you could fool me, did you? You'll 'ave nuthin' to think with when I catch you!'

Phoebe heard the scuffle as he got to his feet. She was already halfway across the open ground separating the mill from the house when she heard the door slam open against the wall.

'You won't bloody get away . . .'

The shout followed her as she ran.

'You've got that money somewheers an' I'm gettin' it!'

The last came out in a gasp as he threw himself at Phoebe's back, his hands fastening in her skirts and dragging her to the ground.

'Would 'ave gone a lot better wi' you if you had just told me wheer the money is 'cos now I'm gonna knock the truth outa you . . .'

'I told you the truth.' Phoebe tried to move but his weight sprawled half across her was too much. Her face pressed against the earth, she went on, 'I was given no money at the Priory.' It would not be enough. Her brain began to work calmly; she had to be more convincing, tell him something his thieving mind would accept. 'They . . . they offered me a hundred pounds . . .'

She stopped as he rolled off her then snatched her over on to her back, a hand about her throat. ''Undred pounds!' His fingers tightened on her neck, lifting her head then banging it hard down on the ground. 'An' you told me you got nuthin', you bloody lyin' cow!'

'I . . . I didn't take it.' His fingers tightened about her throat and behind her eyes tiny fireworks began to explode. 'I . . . I told them . . . it . . . it wasn't enough.'

His fingers relaxed but stayed about her neck; above her his thick lips drew back. 'Not enough! You told 'im a 'undred pounds wasn't enough?'

'Y . . . Yes . . .' Phoebe coughed.

'You! You told the 'igh an' mighty Billy-me-Lord Dartmouth that a 'undred pounds wasn't enough?' He laughed. 'What a bloody cheek . . . I bet 'e 'ad near enough an' 'eart attack.'

'He . . . he wasn't pleased.'

'Pleased!' Her attacker laughed again, the sound rolling off the walls of the old windmill and away toward the canal. 'I bet 'e wasn't bloody pleased, 'is sort ain't used to bein' refused, not no way. So . . .' he stopped laughing '. . . if you didn't take 'is 'undred quid, what did you tek?'

Phoebe lifted her hands to the one still holding her by the neck and pushed. 'Nothing.'

The fingers tightened again, banging her head twice against the hard earth. 'You keep arsin' around wi' me an' you gets yer brains knocked out,' he hissed. 'I don't believe you didn't get summat, you was one of a sort once till that sister of yer father's took the lot from you . . . oh, I know all about that.' He grinned down at her, his yellow teeth parted. 'Same as I know you to be too smart to miss the chance of gettin' your 'ands on some of Billy's money, so don't tell me you got none.'

'I got a lot *more* than a hundred.'

The flicker of greed in his eyes told Phoebe this was what he wanted to hear, this would convince him, this he might just accept. Pushing against his wrist, she stared up at him.

Holding her stare for a full minute, he tried to gauge the truth of what she had just said then dropped his hand.

''Ow much more?'

'A lot.' She sat up, coughing as a stream of air gained free passage to her lungs. 'Only I don't get it until this afternoon.'

'Go on.' He watched her rub her throat, his eyes lowering to her breasts.

'They were all there, like you said,' Phoebe tried to ignore his look, 'Sir William and Lady Dartmouth and their son and daughter. They said they were sorry I had been inconvenienced . . .'

'Incon-bloody-venienced.' He laughed again, the noise of it rolling in waves from the mill to its outhouses before washing out over the low embankment that bordered the canal. 'That sounds just like 'im – somebody does twelve months in the shit an' 'e calls it a inconvenience!'

Taking her chance, Phoebe got to her feet, brushing spears of dried grass from her skirts. 'I told him much the same. I also told him that this particular inconvenience was going to cost him ten thousand pounds or I would go to the newspapers. I said I was sure they would relish reporting how so prominent a member of the gentry had allowed an innocent girl to take the blame for a crime his son had committed.'

'But the necklace was found!' His eyes glittered up at her.

'Was it?' Phoebe flicked a dried straw from her sleeve, trying to guess how long she could stall him. Maybe Sophie or Edward would call and maybe not, reason told her, they had called only two days before. 'Or was it a replica? After all, who would know? And who would really care? The public's interest would not be in the recovery of the necklace but in the suffering of a young girl, and that suffering would only increase in the telling.'

'An' 'e went for it?'

He stood up, his tongue skimming his thick lips, and Phoebe stepped backwards, making a breathing space between them.

'Not at first. He argued that I would never be believed, but I argued that the damage to his family's reputation would be already done and that he might never be quite believed again in anything he tried to do. I said the aristocracy is a cautious breed. It cares to take no chances with the unreliable in case its own unreliability is brought to light.'

'Clever.' He smiled his approval. 'I said you was one of 'is own sort, y'ave brains as well as looks.'

Deep inside Phoebe shuddered at the glance he played over her but forced herself to stay calm. 'Clever enough,' she said, avoiding his eyes, 'to turn a hundred pounds into ten thousand.'

'Christ Almighty,' he breathed, 'ten thousand quid . . . it's a bloody king's ransom!'

'But it's a king's ransom I earned,' Phoebe said, 'over twelve months in hell I earned that money, and I told them either they pay what I ask or I tell the whole story plus more . . . much more.'

'So 'e agreed?' His eyes slid again to her breasts. 'Billy-me-Lord is payin' you ten thousand quid.'

'This afternoon.' Phoebe turned towards the house. 'He had to go to the bank. He said that he never kept that much money in the house, so if you come back around four o'clock you can have half.'

'Why go?' He grabbed at her, pulling her hard against him. 'It will be more pleasurable to wait 'ere . . .'

He pressed his face to the side of her neck, pulling at her flesh with his thick lips, and this time Phoebe could not hold her shudder inside. Grasping his hands, she tried to force them away, a sob of terror escaping her as he turned her in his arms. 'I . . . I'll give it all to you if you go.'

'I intend 'avin' it all,' he grinned, thick lips shining wetly, 'an' the money besides.'

Hooking one foot behind her ankle he brought her down, her spine hitting the ground hard, driving the wind out of her.

Already unbuckling the belt holding up his trousers, he looked down at her. 'Relax,' he grinned again, 'you'll enjoy what I've got fer you.'

Their hold released, his trousers fell around his ankles, revealing the naked flesh beneath, then he was on top of her, one hand clawing at her breast while the other slid her skirts above her hips.

'*You'll enjoy what Liza's got fer you.*'

Once more Phoebe was against that prison wall, the stink of Liza Spittle in her nostrils, the vileness of her touch rising like gall in her throat.

'Stop!' She struggled to push him away, to rid herself of the threat of his body. 'Please stop!'

'It ain't stop you'll be sayin' in a minute,' he said thickly, his hands fumbling at her underwear, 'you'll be sayin' more . . . please, more.'

'No . . .' Phoebe screamed as his fingers touched against her bare skin. 'Liza, no . . . o . . . o!'

Chapter Ten

Maudie Tranter slipped out of the back entrance of Brunswick House, her cloak covering a wicker basket.

Annie Pardoe would be gone most of the afternoon and there was little likelihood of Samuel's needing anything, poor man. Maudie shook her head. He seemed to become more drawn into himself every day, eating hardly enough to keep a sparrow alive, and those headaches! She reached the lane that backed the house, turning left towards Hall End. Yes, Samuel Pardoe's headaches just seemed to get worse despite the medicines Alfred Dingley regularly prescribed.

'Come in, Maudie.' Sarah Leach left off scraping the potatoes she had freshly pulled from the vegetable patch, wiping her hands on a square of white huckaback. 'It's good to see you, the seein' ain't often enough.'

'An' likely to be less.' Maudie followed her through to the kitchen, letting the basket on to the table with a groan. 'It gets to be a longer walk out 'ere each time a body comes, or at least that's the way it feels.'

'Give us yer cloak.' Sarah took the heavy woollen cloak, her eye on the basket.

'Eeh, ma wench!' Maudie dropped heavily on to a hoop-backed chair, its cane seat welcoming to her thin frame. 'Why do you still go on livin' out 'ere? You would be better off nearer the town an' Joseph wouldn't 'ave near so far to trot to the pit.'

'Try tellin' 'im that.' Sarah smiled, lifting the kettle from its bracket above the fire and scalding the tea in her brown earthenware pot. "E says 'e is 'ere till they carries 'im up Church Hill an' settles 'im agen 'is mother and father.'

'P'raps 'e's got the right idea 'spite what I says.' Maudie watched the flow of dark brown liquid being poured into Sarah's china cups, kept for visitors. 'Wednesbury ain't the place it once was – all steel foundries wi' their smoke an' dirt messin' place up, an' now them newfangled toob works.'

'Toob works?' Sarah asked, adding milk to the tea before passing one of the cups to her visitor. 'What do toob works be?'

'They be factories as meks toobs – 'ollow stems of steel. All sizes they can mek – long an' fat, short an' thin, big or little.'

'What they be for then?' Sarah pointed to a small glass bowl filled with sugar. 'These toobs.'

'I'm buggered if I know!' Maudie spooned sugar into her tea. 'But I reckon 'er up at Brunswick 'Ouse does. Seems as 'er's dabblin' in a lot of things lately.'

'Is 'er buyin' these 'ere toobs then?' Sarah asked over her cup.

'Not buyin' 'em.' Maudie sipped her tea, savouring both it and the moment; she didn't see much of folk and when she did she enjoyed the glory of imparting news of the doings of Annie Pardoe. 'But I reckon 'er's puttin' money into the mekin' of 'em.'

'Well, 'er certainly ain't puttin' any into them pits o' their'n,' Sarah answered, placing home-cooked scones and a jar of her own damson jam on the table. 'Joseph says that Hobs Hill mine is near to cavin' in just about everywheer and that the Crown mine up at Moxley ain't much safer. What wi' all that an' their pay bein' docked, the men would pack in tomorrer if they could get set on anywheers else. Eeh, wench, what changes we've seen since Abel went!'

'There's been changes all right,' Maudie lifted a scone to the plate Sarah passed her, 'an' not all in them pits neither.' She sliced the scone, ladling it with thick dark jam. 'You knows 'ow long I've been wi' Annie Pardoe an' 'er brother, an' in all them years I ain't known 'er 'ave doin's wi' nobody other than tradesmen, but now . . . well, all I knows is summat is goin' on.'

"Ow do you mean?' Sarah helped herself to a scone.

'There's bin a caller to Brunswick 'Ouse several times over the last few weeks an' always when Samuel be sleepin' . . . 'e sleeps quite a bit, 'e does, these days.'

She paused but Sarah did not speak, not wanting to put her visitor off her stride. Maudie was easily diverted and any news of Annie Pardoe's doings was too good to miss.

Maudie drank the last of her tea and waited while the cup was refilled. Spooning sugar into it, she went on, 'It's always the same man: Clinton Harforth-Darby 'e says 'is name is, an' you should see Annie when 'e comes. All sweetness an' light 'er is, apologisin' for Samuel's absence sayin' as 'e regrets bein' unable to come down . . .' she stirred her tea vigorously as though the action would ease some of the contempt her words roused '. . . as if 'er would ever suffer the poor bugger to come downstairs. Keeps 'im up theer like a rooster in a pen, 'cept Samuel will never get to perform like no rooster.'

'Does 'e know what's going on?' Sarah chanced Maudie changing tack. 'I mean, the say-so in all business matters be wi' 'im surely? 'E must sign papers an' things, Annie can't do that.'

'That's what you think.' Maudie accepted a second scone. 'It's what a lot of folk think seein' as 'ow the lot was left to Samuel, but Maudie Tranter knows better . . .' Sinking her teeth into the light scone, her eyes fastened on Sarah's, relishing the interest she saw in them. 'I heard 'er tell this Harforth-Darby that 'er could sign in 'er brother's stead, that 'e 'ad given 'er power of a tur . . . I can't remember the exact word but it must be legal like 'cos Harforth-Darby passed her some papers an' I seen 'er sign meself.'

'You seen Annie Pardoe write 'er name on papers that man give 'er? Eeh, I wonder what they was for?"

Maudie touched a finger to each side of her lips checking for stray crumbs before sipping her tea. 'That I don't know,' she shook her head, 'but it was summat that set a smile on that man's face that stretched from ear to ear. An' there's another thing.' Maudie finished her tea, refusing a third cup with a shake of her head. 'Last time 'er went out, 'er bought a new frock . . .'

'Who, Annie Pardoe!' Sarah asked, disbelief plain in her voice.

Maudie nodded. 'Ar, an' not just a new frock but a new lavender-coloured frock.'

'God luv me, I don't believe it.' Sarah stared at the other woman. 'After all these years, Annie Pardoe in a frock that ain't black? I can't remember last time I seen 'er outa black.'

'Oh, 'er ain't wore it, it's hangin' in 'er wardrobe. 'Er don't know I've seen it – but then, there's one or two things as Annie Pardoe ain't knowin'.'

'P'raps they be goin' somewheer special?' Sarah swung the kettle on its bracket away from the fire as the hiss of steam became louder. ''Er an' Samuel, I mean.'

'Oh, ar,' Maudie smiled acidly, 'an' pigs might fly. That one never goes out nowheer, and garden is as far as 'e goes, an' I can't see as Annie 'as bought 'erself a new frock to saunter round the roses.'

'I never could understand that, Maudie,' Sarah said, sitting down again. 'From a babby 'e never went anywhere on 'is own, 'e was always wi' his mother, an' after 'er went 'e was only seen wi' Annie – an' that weren't often, poor sod. 'E was always kept close to their skirts an' yet from what I remembers of 'im 'e was a good-lookin' lad, same as Abel. Would 'ave been the mekin' of 'im to 'ave wed.'

'Ar, well,' Maudie sighed heavily, 'it be too late fer that now even if 'e 'ad the mind. That sister of his'n wouldn't 'arbour no other woman in the 'ouse an' I can't see Samuel goin' against 'er, not now.'

'Poor soul,' Sarah shook her head in unspoken sympathy,

'but whatever the reason 'e's been kept close all 'is life it couldn't a' been 'is brain or Abel would never 'ave left 'im everythin'.'

'It ain't 'is brain,' Maudie agreed, 'there be nuthin' wrong up top. 'E might not go out of that 'ouse but it ain't 'cos 'e's short of 'is marbles.' She tapped a finger to her forehead. ''E's just got no interest in nuthin' 'cept for 'is paintin'.'

'Seems to me 'e ain't never been allowed no interests. Eeh, that family am goin' to 'ave a lot to answer for, an' not only on account of Samuel neither. There's young Phoebe an' what they've done to 'er.'

'That were all Annie's doin', an' all,' Maudie replied. 'I tell you, Sarah, Abel Pardoe would turn in 'is grave if 'e knowed what 'ad 'appened to that girl of 'is'n.'

'There was no call to go turnin' the wench out of 'er own 'ome,' Sarah said, 'that were nuthin' short of vicious. Surely Samuel 'ad summat to say about that?'

''E might 'ave done,' Maudie rose reaching her cloak from the nail in the door, 'supposin' 'e knowed the truth of it but I 'ave me doubts about that. More likely 'is sister 'as filled 'im up wi' all sorts of lies.' She fastened the cloak about her throat. 'But like I said, Annie Pardoe don't know all. Might be as one day 'er will 'ave one or two surprises comin'.'

''Ow do you mean, Maudie?' Sarah waited for Annie's housekeeper to finish fastening her cloak.

'I ain't sayin'.' Maudie dropped a hand to the wicker basket still on a corner of the table; she wasn't one to give all her news in one sitting. If it were worth the telling it were worth the holding, for a while longer anyway. 'But mark my words, Annie Pardoe be in for a shock.'

'No . . . Liza, don't . . . no . . . o . . . o!'

Phoebe's screams ricocheted off the walls of the mill and its outhouses as she struggled to push the man away.

'You won't be sayin' no fer long,' he grunted, snatching at her drawers, the cotton of them tearing in his hand. 'You won't be sayin' anythin', you'll just be moanin' wi' pleasure when you gets this up you . . .'

'Somebody is goin' to get summat up 'em but I don't think it's goin' to be no woman!'

'What the bloody 'ell . . . ?'

'Is this yer 'usband, Missis?'

Her movements jerky, like a badly controlled puppet, Phoebe sat up, pushing her skirts down over her legs, grasping the torn bodice of her dress and holding it across her breasts, fear still bubbling in her throat. The man who had attacked her was jerked to his feet by the scruff of his neck.

'Am you married to 'im?'

'No!' Phoebe looked up at the figure dangling like a rag doll in the grip of a tall, broad-shouldered man.

'So you ain't 'er 'usband!' The tall man shook her attacker effortlessly. 'Then how come you be sprawled across 'er wi' your bare arse to the sun?'

'Let go, you interferin' bastard . . .'

Phoebe made to get to her feet as her attacker struggled to free himself, wanting only to get inside the mill house and lock herself away, but fell back as her legs refused to hold her.

'Oh, I'll let you go.' Placing two fingers in his mouth, the tall man gave a series of sharp whistles. 'When I've done wi' you.'

'You'll be sorry, you bloody canal rat.' The man who had come to rob Phoebe tried to kick backward but the trousers draped around his ankles prevented him. 'I've got mates . . .'

'An' do they all go around doin' what you intended doin' 'ere?' The tall man twisted the other around. 'You call attackin' a woman fun, I suppose? Well, I call punchin' the daylights out of scum like you fun – an' I'm goin' to 'ave me some fun right now!' One hand holding Phoebe's attacker by the throat, the other smacked into his yellow teeth with the force of a sledge hammer.

Her face turned away, Phoebe heard the cries as fists found their mark again and again.

'Bert . . . Bert, no more . . . you'm like to 'ave killed 'im!'

'I could bloody kill 'im lief as look at 'im.' Anger darkening his face, the tall man answered a woman in black skirts, a white cotton poke bonnet fastened over her brown hair, as she ran up to him. 'Makin' too free wi' what God give 'im.'

'Well, 'e won't make too free wi' it no more for a while.' The woman looked at the semi-conscious figure lying on his back, legs sprawled apart. 'Mind, the Lord weren't too lavish in first place wi' what he give this one.'

"E can still do more than enough harm wi' it all the same.' He dropped a hand to the handle of a knife tucked in his wide leather belt. 'I've a mind to cut the bugger off. That way 'e won't force it up no other woman as don't want it.'

'No, Bert!' The woman put a restraining hand over the one fondling the knife. 'I reckon 'e'll 'ave learned 'is lesson by the time 'e gets round to usin' that again. Best you do what you always do when you've knocked a man senseless an' I'll see to the wench.'

Turning away as the tall man caught the other by the collar, dragging him away, trousers about his ankles, the bare flesh of his buttocks scraping the rough ground, she moved to where Phoebe still sat, arms huddled across her chest.

'It's all right, ma wench,' she said softly, going down beside Phoebe and drawing her into her arms. 'It's all right, it's all over now.'

'Tilly . . .' Phoebe sobbed against the woman's shoulder. 'Oh, Tilly.'

'That's it,' the woman murmured soothingly, 'cry it up, wench, cry it up. You'll be better for gettin' it out.'

'We best get 'er inside.'

The man called Bert returned and stood looking at the two women huddled together on the ground.

'You be right.' The woman got to her feet, gently urging Phoebe to follow suit. 'A cup of sweet tea is what 'er's wantin'.' Then, seeing Phoebe flinch as the man made to help her up,

'It's all right, me luv, my Bert won't 'arm you, you'll be safe wi' us.'

''Er don't look as though 'er can make it on 'er own.' Bert stood still a moment then, reaching out, swept Phoebe up in his arms.

'Not in there, Bert,' the woman cautioned as he turned toward the house, its rear door still wide, 'we don't know what that bloke might 'ave taken out of there an' we don't want stickin' wi' the blame. We'll take 'er wi' us till 'er feels better. Might be somebody will be lookin' for 'er by then.'

'Try to drink some of that, ma wench, it'll do you good. You be in my 'ome.' Phoebe felt the cup held against her mouth.

'Tilly,' she cried, turning her face away, 'Tilly . . . it was Liza, oh God, it was Liza!'

'I ain't Tilly.' The woman placed the cup on top of a low cupboard built against a wall. 'An' it weren't no Liza as was 'avin' a go at you, it was a man.'

'Tilly . . . ?' Phoebe opened her eyes, looking for the first time at the woman who had helped her.

'No, ma wench, like I told you, I ain't Tilly an' it was no Liza sprawled across you, it were a man.' The woman smiled, her face kind beneath its bonnet. 'But you be all right, 'e's gone, an' after what my Bert give 'im I don't think 'e'll be back – not unless 'e be glutton for punishment.' Taking the heavy cup from the cupboard top she held it out to Phoebe. 'Try drinkin' this. It's only tea, but then our means don't stretch to alcohol.'

'Thank you.' Phoebe took the thick cup, swallowing the hot sweet liquid.

'Theer you go, Mam.'

Phoebe looked up as a lad of around nine years old squeezed into the narrow room, placing a prettily painted tin jug on the cupboard top.

'The water you wanted.'

'Eh!' The woman glanced at Phoebe. 'I 'ope as you don't

mind but I sent the lad for water from your yard. That was what brought Bert to your place earlier. 'E was supposed to be comin' to ask if we could 'ave a jug of water, this in canal be none too clean for drinkin'.'

Phoebe handed the cup back, her tea finished. 'What happened?'

'Me dad kicked the shit outa some bloke as was attackin' you,' the boy answered, eyes gleaming.

'An' you will get it belted out of you when I tells 'im what you've just said!' The woman aimed a swift blow to the side of the lad's head. 'What've I told you about that sort of language? You might live on a barge but you ain't no canal rat an' I ain't 'avin' you talk like one.'

'Sorry, Mam, sorry Miss.' The lad smiled, his face proud beneath a shock of brown hair. 'But me dad still kicked the s . . . stuffin' outa that bloke. Says 'e won't be maulin' no women for many a day.'

'Out!' The woman aimed a hand at the boy who ducked expertly. 'Get out and help yer father. Eeh!' She turned to Phoebe, 'Kids today. Their mouth be grown up afore their backsides be free of the napkin.'

'Was it your husband who . . . who pulled him off me?'

'Ar.' The woman nodded. ''E could tell from your screamin' that what that one was about 'ad none of your consentin' so 'e dragged 'im off you and give 'im a punchin' 'e won't forget in a 'urry.'

'Where is he now?'

'Who? The one as 'ad you pinned beneath 'is tackle?' The woman made a noise of contempt in her throat. 'Bert will 'ave chucked 'im where it'll go rusty if 'e don't get 'isself out, an' sharpish. 'E'll be in the cut, an' if 'e drowns I 'ope there's none to mourn 'im.' She poured more tea from a tall pot, pink roses and green leaves bright against its black enamelled body. 'I thought we should bring you 'ere to the barge, I didn't want nobody thinkin' we was in any place we shouldn't be, 'sides . . .' she placed the heavy platter cup on the cupboard top near to Phoebe '. . . if anythin' be missin' from your place, could be folk might think we took it.'

'He . . . he didn't take anything.' Phoebe picked up the cup, glad of something to do with her hands. 'He came for money, had the idea I had some hidden at the mill, and it was his intention to rob me of it.'

'An' did 'e?'

'No.' Phoebe shook her head. 'I didn't have any money at all, much less the amount he expected me to have.'

'You don't 'ave to say any more if you don't feel you want to,' the woman sipped her own tea, 'though usually it feels better to get it out like.'

'I was upstairs.' Phoebe stared into the tea. 'I heard him downstairs and thought it was Edward or Sophie. When I went to see he grabbed me and threatened to burn my face with a poker if I didn't give him the money.'

'But you 'adn't got any?'

'No.' Phoebe went on staring into her cup as if the events of the past few hours were being played out in its depths. 'But he wouldn't believe me. I thought if I could get him across to the mill I might be able to run away while he was searching it so I told him I had hidden the money in the old corn loft, but he forced me up there with him.'

'But you was outside when Bert come across you.'

'He kicked the ladder away,' Phoebe ignored the interruption, 'so I jumped. He didn't come straight down. I slipped out and made a run for the house.'

'An' that's when 'e catched you?'

'Yes.' It was little more than a whisper. 'I told him then that the money he thought I already had was to be brought to the mill that afternoon. I said if he would leave right away I would hand it all over to him when he returned.'

'An' 'e said 'e would 'ave the money an' a bit more besides,' the woman finished for her. 'The dirty swine! 'E deserves all my Bert give 'im an' more. The rope is too good for the likes of that one, but it ain't always the ones that am guilty as pays the price.'

'I find you guilty of wilful theft . . . you will serve a term of fifteen years . . .'

The Magistrate's words rang in Phoebe's ears. The woman was right: it was not always the guilty who paid the price.

Maudie Tranter let herself in at the rear entrance of Brunswick House and stood for a while in the kitchen, her ear registering the silence. The mistress wasn't back yet. Removing her cloak, she hung it in a cupboard in the scullery, sitting her bonnet on a shelf above.

She had timed her visit well as always, arriving back before Annie returned. Running her hands over her tight-drawn hair, she returned to the kitchen, a bitter smile touching the corners of her mouth as she replaced the wicker basket in its place beside the large pine dresser. Annie Pardoe had cut the wages of the miners to the bone; it was only fitting that some of the contents of her larder had gone to one of them.

Going out of the kitchen she crossed the hall, the slow tick of a longcase clock measuring her steps as she climbed the stairs. Halting outside Samuel's bedroom she listened for movement but, hearing nothing, moved along the corridor to the room used as a studio. Tapping the door out of respect for the man whose ears had been sealed in the womb, she went in. Samuel was not there. Maudie breathed more easily. He was still sleeping, so neither of them would know she had been out of the house.

She was halfway down the staircase when Annie let herself in at the front door. 'Mister Samuel must still be sleeping. I have just been to see if he wanted anything but he is not in his studio.'

'Has he woken at all while I have been out?'

'No, Ma'am,' Maudie answered. 'There 'asn't been a sound out of 'im the whole afternoon.'

'Bring his tray in about five minutes,' Annie turned towards the staircase, 'we will be in the sitting room.'

In her room she removed her cloak and bonnet, hanging them in a large wardrobe, letting her fingers caress the lavender silk of the gown the cloak would conceal. Soon she would wear no more black, soon she would wear the colours her lost youth had never known, soon now . . . very soon she would share a bed as Abel had shared his. Her body would know the touches his had known. Soon now . . . soon.

Opening her bag she took out the pretty glass bottle, holding it to where the light from the window caught the faintly golden contents, then crossing to a chest of drawers she placed the bottle in the bottom one, covering it with a layer of silk petticoats carefully wrapped in blue tissue paper.

Pushing to her feet, she gasped, clutching at a point below her left breast as a pain ripped through her. Her breathing rapid, she stumbled to the bed and sat for several minutes before taking the bottle of tablets from the drawer of the side table. Pouring a little water from the carafe that always stood beside her bed, she swallowed a couple of small white tablets. Two minutes later she made her way to her brother's bedroom, the medicine she had collected from the chemist in her hand.

In the kitchen Maudie laid a tray with tea and thinly cut sandwiches of salmon and cucumber. Samuel had taken salmon and cucumber for tea almost daily for the fifteen years she had served as housekeeper; in fact, everything remained the same in Annie Pardoe's household – or at least it had until Harforth-Darby had arrived on the scene. She scalded the tea, setting the white china pot on the tray. She didn't trust Harforth-Darby with his smarmy ways, he was buttering Annie Pardoe up sure as shooting, and just as sure she was in for a disappointment. Maudie set milk and sugar on the tray. If Annie thought she was going to get that one to the altar then she was shouting into an empty gulley, lavender frock or no lavender frock!

Carrying the tray to the sitting room, she set it beside Annie, her eyes taking in the tired sunken features and thin frame of the man who sat opposite.

'You be on your last legs, Samuel Pardoe,' she murmured, closing the door on brother and sister, 'an' it's my idea there be them as is ready to kick 'em out from under you.'

Waiting until the door closed, Annie poured tea, handing one of the cups to Samuel.

'It is just as well I went to collect your medicine,' she signed. 'I swear that Isaac Jackson took near enough an hour to prepare it. Seems tradesmen don't care how long they keep you waiting these days. I tell you, dear, things are no longer the same.'

Samuel smiled wearily. 'Things have not been the same since Abel died.'

Annie watched the rapid flickering of his fingers. 'What do you mean, not been the same?' Her own fingers formed the question.

'Let us not try to delude each other. You have always seen to my welfare, Annie, and I thank you for that though it has not been in the best of ways. It was our parents' thinking that turned my home into a prison. You have merely carried on where they left off. Oh, I know I could physically have forced my way out of this or our former home but what good would that have done? So in that way things have not changed.

'No, Annie, things changed when we heard Abel's will, when we came to Brunswick House. Feelings between you and me have never been what our brother thought them to be. You have always been bitter, blamed Abel for putting you in the position of nursemaid to me, blamed him for your never having married and saw his leaving me his fortune as a means of repayment for what he did. I can't blame you for those feelings, Annie, but since Abel died the bitterness in you has grown. I can never give you back the years you have spent with me but there are some things I can do . . .'

Annie sat stock still, her eyes on Samuel's dancing fingers, a feeling of alarm, fear almost, beginning to rise in her throat.

'. . . you see, I too feel that Abel acted wrongly, that your life was yours to do with as you wished and not as his money dictated. I know I should have told you this twenty years ago but I never found the way. That was my mistake and I'm sorry for it. I also think it was wrong of him to leave everything to us, literally denying his own daughter what was rightfully hers. That was Abel's mistake but it is one I can do something about . . .'

Samuel saw the apprehension on his sister's face deepen into something more at his mention of Abel's daughter and he felt a sudden deep pity. Annie had fed on her bitterness for years. What would she do when she heard all he had to say?

'It is my intention to return Brunswick House to Phoebe,' the movement of his fingers continued, 'together with the mines and partnerships in the Monway steel works and everything else her father willed to me, except a sum of money large enough to keep you comfortably for your lifetime and maybe recompense you somewhat for the years you have spent with me. You do, of course, have the house at Bescot. Whether or not you choose to live in it will be your decision.'

Annie stared at her brother, her brain numbed by what he had told her.

'As for myself,' he went on, 'I don't think Abel or Phoebe would object to my buying a small house somewhere. And not to worry,' the same weary smile touched his lips but the old sadness remained in his eyes, 'you and my parents can rest easily – I am not about to break my bonds. The shame I brought to the family will die a secret.'

The sharp sting of pain below her breast broke the numbness encircling her and Annie stood up, her glance sweeping the now empty room. Samuel was going to give everything back to their niece. She pressed a hand to the pain, will-power forcing the nausea out of her throat. But it was not only Samuel's to give, it was *hers*; she had spent half a lifetime earning that money, earning the power it brought, and Samuel would not take it from her.

"Ave you finished with the tray, Ma'am?' Maudie entered the room, one look at her employer telling her that the suspicion she had held for some time had proved correct, Annie Pardoe had been given a nasty shock. She smiled over the tray as Annie swept out.

'Ar, you've 'ad a shock, Annie Pardoe,' she whispered, carrying the tray to the kitchen, 'a big 'un. But there be more to come yet . . . much more.'

'Excuse me, Sir, but might you be Lucy's 'usband?'

'Who are you?' Edward Dartmouth looked at the tall well-built man coming toward him across the mill yard.

'My name is Bertram . . . Bertram Ingles.'

The reply was polite but there was none of the deference men usually adopted when addressing Edward.

'Might I ask what you are doing here?'

Edward looked at the man standing inches above himself, shirt sleeves rolled halfway between wrist and elbow, trousers held up by a broad leather belt blackened with wear, brass-studded clogs on his feet.

'I've come for water.' He lifted the black enamelled bucket painted around with a band of brightly coloured flowers. 'An' I asks you agen, Sir, be you Lucy's 'usband?'

'I am not Lucy's husband.' Edward's gaze circled the outbuildings. 'How do you know of her?' The gaze came back to the man now almost barring his way. 'And where is Miss Pardoe?'

'If Miss Pardoe be the young woman as lives 'ere then 'er is on my barge.'

'Your barge?' Edward said sharply. 'And how does she come to be there?'

'You've no need to come out fightin'.' Bert saw the flame kindle in the younger man's eyes. ''Er be wi' my Lizzie. I come for to ask permission to draw drinkin' water from the

135

pump there earlier on today an' I found a young woman wi' a bloke sprawled across 'er, 'is trousers round 'is ankles . . .'

'Phoebe!' Edward interrupted. 'Did he . . . ?'

'Rape 'er?' Bert shook his head. 'Though it weren't for the want of tryin', an' 'e would 'ave an' all 'ad I not come across 'im when I did.'

'This man,' Edward brought his riding crop across the palm of his left hand, anger drawing his mouth in to a tight line, 'where is he now?'

'Coolin' what's left of 'is ardour in the cut,' Bert said, a nod of his head indicating the canal, 'though I doubt there was much of that left after I'd finished lettin' daylight into 'is guts.'

'You didn't give him enough!' Edward's eyes glistened with rage. 'You should have killed the swine, and even *that* would have been too good for him.'

'I think I near enough did do for 'im.' Bert smiled grimly. 'Leastways 'e won't be botherin' no woman for a long time yet.'

'More likely never again if I can find him, and I will!' Edward slapped his palm with the crop. 'I'll find the man and finish what you started . . . in the meantime, take this for your trouble.'

Bert Ingles looked at the sovereigns Edward drew from his waistcoat pocket and his face hardened.

'Any trouble I took on young wench's behalf was a trouble I would tek for any woman,' he said angrily, 'an' if it were a trouble then it be one I don't need payment for. You put your money back in your pocket, lad, an' put this bit of advice wi' it: next time you offer payment to a barge man for preventin' a wench bein' raped, mek sure you steps away pretty sharpish or you be likely to find yourself in the cut wi' the light shinin' on *your* innards.'

Edward stared. What was it with these people? First Phoebe and now this man. Both had refused money though it was obvious neither had any: both had almost nothing to support them but both burned with the same fierce pride.

'My apologies, Mr Ingles.' He slipped the coins back into his pocket. 'I had no wish to offend.'

'None teken, lad.' Bert smiled. 'Now if you'll wait till this bucket be filled, I'll tek you to . . . what did you say wench was called?'

'Miss Pardoe,' Edward answered, a liking for the tall rough-mannered man already formed. 'Miss Phoebe Pardoe.'

Edward followed, stepping gingerly from the narrow towpath on to the moored barge, picking his way through an assortment of buckets and ropes clustered into the small space between the prow and the cabin, almost three-quarters of the barge housing a cargo of coal on top of which sat a young boy and an even younger girl, both watching his progress through solemn eyes.

'You pair stop on top,' Bert said to them as he led the way down four steep steps that gave on to the family's living quarters.

'Phoebe,' said Edward blinking against the gloom, 'are you all right?'

''Er's all right.' Lizzie glanced at her husband standing on the steps, the confined space not enough to hold them all. 'Though 'er's 'ad a bad fright.'

Head and shoulders stooped against the low roof, Edward squeezed down the cabin that seemed barely a yard wide. 'Let me take you home, Phoebe.'

'I don't think much of you doin' that,' Lizzie said firmly. 'That wench 'as 'ad a shakin' up an' the last thing 'er needs is to be left on 'er own, so lessen there be somebody wi' 'er in that place of 'er'n then I says 'er's best left 'ere.'

'I think perhaps that would be best.' Edward looked at the bargee's wife, a white poke bonnet still covering her head even though she was in what was her sitting room. 'It would not be proper if I stay alone with her and neither can she be left on her own whilst I fetch Lucy from the town.' He touched a hand to Phoebe's, resting in her lap.

'Don't fetch Lucy, Edward.' She looked up at him. 'I have

suffered no harm and don't want her worried. If it is all right with Mr and Mrs Ingles I would prefer to stay with them until Lucy and Mathew return. They are always home about seven.'

'That ain't no bother to me nor Bert.' Lizzie caught the nod from her husband.

'Thank you.' Edward squeezed Phoebe's fingers gently before turning towards the hatchway. 'You may have refused my money, Mr Ingles,' he said when they both stood once more on the towpath, 'but surely you will not refuse my thanks for your solicitousness.'

'I won't refuse.' Bert took the hand the younger man extended, shaking it warmly. 'An' though it don't be necessary, it be appreciated.'

'Surprised me, that 'as,' he said, half to himself, watching Edward stride away towards the mill, its redundant windmill standing sentinel on the low rise that hid the house from the canalside.

'What 'as, Dad?'

'That one,' Bert answered his son, eyes following the figure moving rapidly away. ''E don't come from no miner nor no foundryman neither, that one 'as a different breedin', yet I thought all moneyed folk was above thankin' the likes of we. But 'e ain't.'

'Dad,' the boy asked as his father stepped aboard the barge, 'what's titty us ness?'

'Eh?' Bert glanced sharply across the expanse of coal.

'Titty us ness,' the boy's eyes gleamed roguishly, 'that's what that bloke thanked you for ain't it?'

'They ears been flappin' agen?' Bert picked up a nut of coal, 'they need a set o' doors fastened to 'em.' He threw the coal laughing as his son rolled clear, 'Cheeky young bugger,' he muttered fondly.

Chapter Eleven

Phoebe looked up from the small dress she was sewing, waves of fear flooding through her at the sound from outside the house. Putting her work aside she tiptoed to the window that looked out towards the track leading to the town, breathing her relief when she saw the trap she knew to be Sophie's.

Running swiftly downstairs she opened the door, her smile of welcome fading when she saw her caller.

'Good afternoon, Miss Pardoe.' Sir William Dartmouth inclined his head with a slight, barely perceptible movement. 'I hope I am not inconveniencing you by calling?'

'No . . . not at all.' Phoebe could not entirely hide her surprise.

'Edward told me of the unfortunate incident that took place yesterday,' he said when she did not ask him into the house. 'I trust you were not injured . . . in any way?'

'No.' The tiny pause so significant in its meaning was not lost on Phoebe; he had been told not only of the assault upon herself but also the nature of that assault. 'I was not injured . . . in any way.'

'I am relieved to hear it,' he said, watching the colour rise to her cheeks. 'My wife and I were concerned to hear of what happened to you, as was Sophie. Both of them were anxious to call upon you but my wife is ill with influenza and Sophie is not happy to leave her mother at the moment. But given your permission they will call once Amelia is well again.'

'I shall be happy to see them.' Phoebe stepped aside,

clearing the doorway. 'Forgive me, Sir William, won't you come in?'

Stepping inside, he allowed her to take his gloves, and when she set them on a small mahogany stand, followed her to the tiny parlour.

'Will you take some tea?' Phoebe asked when he was seated. 'I am afraid I have nothing in the way of wine.'

Tea. William Dartmouth smiled inwardly. It was every Englishwoman's placebo. 'No, thank you,' he said. 'I will not detain you. I came only to assure myself and my womenfolk that you had taken no harm.'

'None, I assure you.'

'That is as well, for the fellow who attacked you will pay hard enough when he is caught, and he will be, you have my word on that.'

'I think he has probably paid enough already,' Phoebe said, 'judging by what I hear Bert Ingles did to him.'

'Ah, yes, Edward told me of him. A bit of a rough diamond if I'm not mistaken.'

'You're not!' Phoebe's eyes flashed green fire. 'But then, diamonds are valuable rough or cut, are they not? And the Ingleses will always be highly valued friends to me.'

He glanced around the small room with its tired, well-worn furniture. This child of Abel Pardoe's might have little in the way of worldly goods but courage and integrity she had in plenty.

'You are not here alone, Miss Pardoe?'

'Of course I am, this is my home, where else would I be?'

'But I understood a woman and her husband were here with you.'

'Lucy and Mathew,' Phoebe nodded, 'but they go into Wednesbury every day.'

'Leaving you in this place by yourself?'

'Sir William, I am not a child.'

'That much is obvious,' he replied tersely, 'and therefore

the greater the danger. This Lucy . . . she must stay home, you must not be alone here again.'

'Sir William,' Phoebe said coolly, 'Lucy is the mainstay of this house at the moment. Her earnings provide most of their living and all of mine. Mathew works hard but odd jobs pay little in Wednesbury, so you see it is impossible for Lucy to stay here all day. My explanation is more for Lucy's sake than for yours. I would not have you think she left me on my own from choice.

'There is one more thing I have to say and it is this: do not ever use the word "must" to me. I have earned the right to be my own mistress and no man or woman will ever dictate to me again.'

William Dartmouth glanced at the down-at-heel furniture. 'Accept the money I still offer and neither of you would need to work again.'

'Don't seek to still your conscience with money.' Anger made Phoebe's voice sharp. 'I asked for none and I shall take none.'

'That is your prerogative.' He smiled. 'As will be your answer to my next question, always supposing you choose to give one for of course I should not dream of saying you must.'

'You can ask.' Phoebe caught the hint of amusement behind his grey eyes and her own mouth relaxed into a smile.

'This Ingles fellow – he told Edward that when he came upon that man attacking you, you were screaming about someone called Liza, and a little later you thought you were talking to a Tilly. Neither is a suitable name for a man. Tell me, was anyone else involved? Did the one who assaulted you have an accomplice?'

Phoebe's smile faded. 'No,' she said, looking to her lap where her fingers had automatically twined together at the memory of Handsworth Women's Prison. 'At least, there was no one with him when he . . . when he came here.'

'So who are the women whose names you called?'

She didn't have to tell him, Phoebe thought, he had no claim upon her, no right to ask questions. She could tell him that and then ask him to leave.

'Liza Spittle was a prisoner in Handsworth,' she said, surprised by the decision she could not recall making. 'She . . . she had certain tendencies . . . she . . . she tried . . .'

'You mean, she tried to force herself on you much the same as a man?'

'Yes,' Phoebe said, not knowing why she wanted him to know what Liza had done and grateful when he spared her the strain of the telling. 'And Tilly helped me . . . twice. She warned Liza not to touch me in . . . in that way again, and when she did try a second time Tilly tripped her up and Liza hit her head against the wall. I think she was hurt quite badly . . . she . . . she may even have died, and if so the Governors might say it was murder and Tilly would hang. But it wasn't! Tilly couldn't . . .'

'Is Tilly an inmate of the prison also?'

Phoebe nodded. 'She always will be. She is serving a lifetime sentence for manslaughter. They . . . they said she killed her husband but . . .' She looked up, her eyes defiant behind their cloud of unhappiness. 'I don't think she did. Tilly is no murderess no matter what any judge may have said.'

He rose, collecting his gloves from the small stand where Phoebe had placed them and opening the door himself.

'You are a very stubborn young woman,' he said, smiling. 'You refuse my offer of compensation, then you tell me never to use the word "must" to you again, and now you say you do not believe the verdict of a court.'

'It would not be the first time a court had been wrong, would it, Sir William?'

Pulling on his gloves, William Dartmouth looked at the girl whom he knew would openly defy him on any matter she felt to be right. 'Yes,' he inclined his head in a gesture of farewell, 'a very stubborn young woman, but one I admire. Good afternoon, Miss Phoebe Pardoe.'

* * *

'Me mam says to ask can I fill this from your pump?'

Phoebe smiled at the lad, his grin cheeky, his toffeedrop eyes bright beneath tumbling brown hair.

'Of course,' she answered. 'And when you're done come into the kitchen. I've got a big fat scone that is just asking to be eaten.'

''As it got sultanas in it?'

'Yes, big ones . . . this size.' She made a circle with thumb and forefinger.

'Oooh, bostin'.' His eyes gleamed with anticipation. 'I like sultanas. Our Ruth don't, 'er picks 'em out when we 'ave cake. Me mam says 'er shouldn't, it's bad manners to pick, but I don't mind 'cos our Ruth, 'er gives 'em to me.'

'I might be able to find one without sultanas for Ruth.' Phoebe recognised the barge man's word for something good or pleasant.

'Eh, don't do that, Miss!' He grinned, putting down the large flower-painted jug then wiping his palms against the sides of his trousers. ''Er enjoys picking 'em out as much as 'er does the eatin' of the rest.'

'In that case, we will find her one with extra sultanas.'

'We am leavin' tomorrer,' he said, perched on a stool in the kitchen, pulling sultanas from a scone and squashing them between his teeth, savouring each one before swallowing it. 'We as to tek them coals to London.'

'London?' Phoebe watched him work his way around the edge of the scone, the plate she had offered it on forgotten on the table. 'That's a good way off.'

'Ar, it is,' he nodded, recovering a crumb from his knee and stuffing it in his mouth beside a sultana. 'You ever been there, Miss?'

'No, I haven't.'

'I don't know as you'd like it.' He surveyed her over the scone. 'It's quite a big place, an' dirty the parts I've seen of it, an' folks pushin' an' shovin' as if they don't 'ave a minute to live.'

'It can't be much dirtier than Wednesbury.'

'It is, Miss, you can tek it from me. Wednesbury is a picture compared to London. Oh, the buildin's 'ere am black wi' smoke an' soot but the streets, well, they ain't filled wi' everybody's rubbish like, am they? I mean, they don't drop their paper on the roads or throw the peelin's out the windows here, do they?'

'They don't do that in London, do they?'

One foot tapping a half-laced boot against the leg of the stool, he considered a partly concealed sultana. 'I don't know about the places the nobs live in,' he twisted the scone, considering the sultana from all angles, 'but the ones we dock in, the basins like, well, you finds all sorts o' stuff throwed down there. Me mam, 'er don't like London an' I don't think you would either.'

'In that case I shan't go.' Phoebe placed several scones in a dark blue paper bag that had once held sugar. 'But I do quite fancy the seaside.'

'Me an' all.' He gave way to temptation, pulling the sultana free. 'An' our Ruth. Me dad says we might pick up a load that 'as to go to a port one day . . . a port is like the seaside, ain't it, Miss?'

'Mmmm.' Phoebe twisted the top of the bag to make a fastening. 'I imagine so. A port has ships and ships sail on the sea, so a port must be the seaside.'

''Ave you been to the seaside?'

Settling the bag of scones on the table, Phoebe went into the scullery, fetching a jug of milk from a bowl half filled with water to keep it cool.

'Not since I was a very small girl.' She filled a glass with the frothy white milk, setting the linen cover back over the jug before returning it to the scullery.

'Didn't your parents 'ave the money to tek you more than once?'

'It wasn't the money,' Phoebe placed the glass of milk before him, 'my mother died while I was still quite young and my father was too busy with his business to take me to the seaside.'

'Never mind, Miss.' He looked across at her, his eyes round and brown as a well-used penny, a seriousness in them that outstripped his years. 'Like me mam says, we all 'ave our cross to bear, but when we get that load for a port you can come with we. Mam an' Dad won't mind.'

'Speaking of your mother, Mark Ingles, she is not going to be at all pleased if you keep her waiting much longer for that jug of water.'

'Bugger me! I'd forgot all about the water.' He jumped from the stool, shoving the desecrated scone into his mouth.

Phoebe followed him into the yard, handing him the bag of scones as he finished filling the jug.

'An' you'll forget me language, won't you, Miss?' He grinned up at her, crumbs edging his lips. 'Go on, Miss, be a pal, say you ain't 'eard me say what I said?'

'All right,' Phoebe laughed, 'I didn't hear you say what you said.'

'Ta, Miss.' He sauntered off across the yard, raising the bag of scones above his head. 'Tara for now.'

'Miss Phoebe,' Lucy said thoughtfully, 'whoever it was come 'ere to rob you, 'e knowed about you bein' up at the Priory, 'e even knowed as you seen all of the family together, so it seems to me 'e is either a footman or else somebody who works in the 'ouse told 'im about you bein' there.'

'I . . . I hadn't thought about it.' It was true she had not thought of how the man had known of her visit, or of the fact she had been in prison, but she had lived through the nightmare of his attack again and again through the long night, jangles of fear setting her nerves dancing at every sound, only the knowledge that Lucy and Mathew were staying in the house preventing her from screaming.

'Well, I 'ave.' Lucy went on talking as she tipped flour into a bowl. 'An' if I 'ave then Sir William is sure to 'ave an' all. 'E ain't no fool that one, 'e can put two an' two together an' come up with 'alf a dozen.'

'Do you think that was the real reason for his coming here today?'

'Don't know.' Lucy spooned a small amount of salt into the flour. ''E didn't ask any questions about 'ow anybody might know, did 'e? But that don't mean anythin'. 'E might not 'ave said as much but you can take it from me 'e 'ad thought of it.'

He might have thought about it but Phoebe wanted only to put the whole episode behind her. She wouldn't forget, she would never forget, but right now she wanted only to leave it, to talk of anything except that.

Phoebe reached for the tongs settling fresh coals on the fire, then rinsed her hands and set about greasing pie tins with a dab of lard on a scrap of cloth.

'He asked whether I had suffered any harm from being attacked.'

'What the 'ell did 'e think? It certainly ain't done you no good. Bloody soft question to ask!' Lucy exploded.

'He said Sophie and Lady Amelia were concerned and that they would call later.'

'Huh!' Reaching a small shallow basin from the dresser, Lucy pressed it into the pastry, making a series of circles. 'Why didn't they come with him?'

'Lady Amelia has the influenza.'

Taking the circles she had cut from the pastry, Lucy pressed them into the tins. 'It was their son's fault you was gaoled but even so their sort don't usually call on the likes o' we.'

'The likes of us are as good as any Dartmouths, Lucy,' Phoebe answered, pounding a pot of boiled potatoes with a wooden spoon. 'The only difference is they have money and we do not.'

'*You* could have.' Lucy scooped the remnants of the circles together, rolling them with quick deft movements, making a further mat of soft pastry. 'You was offered it an' I think you should take it. It's nothin' you don't deserve.'

Phoebe lifted the large pot of mutton from the fireplace where it had stewed gently from early morning. Draining the stock into a bowl, she added the meat to the mashed potato. 'Accepting money will not alter what happened. I prefer to earn my living.'

'Well, I think you'm daft.' Tasting the mixture of meat and potato, Lucy nodded and Phoebe began filling the pastry-lined tins.

Finishing the filling of a dozen pie tins, she draped a cloth over the unused mixture, setting the pan in the hearth. 'Lucy,' she asked, passing a smaller basin the other girl had pointed to, 'do you think my dresses would sell in the town?'

Lucy pressed the basin into the pastry, cutting out smaller circles. 'The bits an' pieces I've managed to make 'ave gone well enough an' they ain't near so good as your'n. Mind, I couldn't make much, what wi' the baking.'

Phoebe watched smaller circles of pastry being placed over each pie tin, Lucy fluting the edges between finger and thumb. 'But what you did make sold each time?'

'Ar.' Lucy nodded. 'Could 'ave sold more but like I says, it's 'avin' the time to sew.'

Dipping two fingers into an egg she had beaten, Phoebe traced the lid of each pie. 'What about your pies and my dresses?'

'What you mean, Miss?' Lucy was already busy with the next batch of pastry.

'Put them together.'

'Eh?' Lucy paused.

'Well, not together as such.' Phoebe began to load the oven with pies. 'What I meant was, if you bake and I sew we could pool the money we make.'

'No, Miss Phoebe,' Lucy began, cutting out larger circles, 'your little frocks is worth much more than mutton pies.'

Closing the oven, Phoebe straightened. 'Your mutton pies have fed me since I came home, Lucy.'

'Oh, ar!' Looking up she ran her eyes over the girl she had once worked for. 'Well, they ain't made you much fatter. Anyway you give Mathew an' me a place to stay . . . well, you did in a manner o' speakin' 'cept you wasn't 'ere to speak to, an' then when you come out you didn't make we go. Way I sees things, a mutton pie an' the odd scone don't count for much against that.'

'It counts for a great deal with me,' Phoebe said, oiling more pie tins with a knob of lard, 'so we are equal, neither of us owes the other anything.' Lifting the pan from the hearth, she spooned the remainder of the filling into the pastry-lined tins then carried the empty pot into the scullery to be washed later.

'Do you really think my clothes would sell?' She asked again, uncertainty edging her question. 'Money is not all that plentiful in Wednesbury, is it?'

'Not in all quarters it ain't.' Lucy finished fluting the edge of the last pie. 'But then everybody don't work for Annie Pardoe. Some o' the men 'er finished at the pits as got taken on at Hampstead mine. Seem to be doin' all right an' all judgin' by the number of pies them women o' their'n buy.'

'But everyone has to have food,' Phoebe said, moistening pastry lids with beaten egg.

'Ar, an' they 'ave to wear clothes an' all or they gets a slow walk to Wednesbury police station wi' a bobby on each arm.' Lucy stretched her aching back. 'Tell you what . . . why don't I take them little frocks you made for Lady Dartmouth an' see if they sell?'

'I had thought of trying, I was getting them out of the trunk when . . .' Despite the heat of the kitchen Phoebe's face paled. The fear of what had happened was still vivid. It haunted her nights and filled her days but she knew if she admitted as much her friend would stay home and that would mean very little money coming in, and Mathew and Lucy had things hard enough. Going to the oven, she took out the cooked pies, hoping the action would cover her hesitation, masking what she could not say.

Lucy rattled the cooking utensils, gathering them for washing. If that bastard hasn't drowned in the cut then I hope he's dropped down a mine shaft! she thought. Either way may he rot in hell for attacking a woman. 'I will just get this lot shifted an' we'll 'ave us a cup of tea,' she said, rubbing her hands in the bowl of warm water on the hob. 'Put the kettle back over the fire, Miss.'

Phoebe swung the iron bracket, bringing the kettle to rest over the hot coals, then picking up the basin of water, followed to where Lucy had carried bowls and dishes to the scullery.

'I'll empty this in the yard,' she said, going to the scullery door. 'Will I give Mathew a shout?'

'If you will, Miss.' Lucy set the dishes against the large brownstone sink. ''E'll be just about gaspin' for a cup of tea.'

'Lucy . . .' The three of them were sitting in the kitchen of the mill house, cosy with the glow of the fire and the smell of fresh-baked pies and scones. 'What did you mean when you said not everyone in Wednesbury works for Annie Pardoe?'

'What do you mean, what do I mean?' Lucy asked in the tongue-twisting Black Country style.

'It seemed strange your using my aunt's name. She can't have anything to do with the business, that is solely Uncle Samuel's responsibility.'

'P'raps yer father thought it would be,' Mathew looked up from the fire, 'but Annie soon put the mockers on that. It's 'er as 'as all the say in what is or what isn't to be done, an' who is to be finished an' who ain't.'

'Aunt Annie might say things,' Phoebe nursed her cup between her hands, 'but she can't do more than that, she cannot sign her name to anything. Only Uncle Samuel can do that.'

'Seems like 'er can,' Mathew replied. 'I called in me mam's afore I come 'ome an' 'er said Maudie Tranter 'ad visited earlier. Maudie told 'er that Annie be gettin' a gentleman visitor . . . quite reglar it seems . . . an' Maudie 'eard 'er tellin' 'im Samuel 'ad given 'er some sort of power . . . power of a turn summat or other, me mam couldn't rightly say, but whatever it be it means Annie Pardoe can sign any business paper in place o' her brother.'

'Power of Attorney,' Phoebe said, suddenly understanding the sacking of men and the reduction in wages. 'My aunt has Uncle Samuel's Power of Attorney.'

'What does that mean, Miss?' Lucy asked.

Phoebe let her head sink tiredly against the back of her chair. 'It means my aunt has control of everything my father left to Samuel.'

'An' that means 'alf of Wednesbury,' Mathew said. ''E might just as well 'ave left it to the Devil.'

A loud knock on the scullery door jangled Phoebe's frayed nerves and the jerk of her hands set the tea dancing madly in her cup.

'You be all right, Miss,' Mathew said calmly. 'Just stop you theer, I'll see who that be.'

'I would like a word wi' Miss Pardoe, would you ask 'er if 'er will see me?'

Phoebe breathed out long and slow, feeling the tension loosen from her stomach as she recognised the voice of Bert Ingles.

'Come in, Mr Ingles,' she said, going to the scullery. 'I hope you don't mind the kitchen? It's a bit cramped but it's warmer than the sitting room.'

'I'm used wi' being cramped, there's not much living space on a barge.' Bert Ingles nodded to Lucy and Mathew as Phoebe introduced them.

'What can I do for you?' Phoebe smiled.

'I come to bring you these.' He fished in the pocket of a jacket that should have had a decent burial long ago, pulling out two brass locks. 'Me an' Lizzie got to talkin' after we brought you back 'ere yesterday evenin' . . . well, like we said, you can bolt these doors from the inside but we couldn't see 'ow you would fasten 'em on the outside, not so as nobody could get in like, an' Lizzie said there was bound to come times when you 'ad to leave the place, so we thought if you put these on the doors you would at least be certain nobody had got in while you was away. You would 'ave no more nasty surprises waitin' for you, if you follow what I mean.'

'That is very kind of you, Mr Ingles, I am most grateful to you and to your wife. It will be a great relief to me knowing the doors of the house are securely fastened.'

'They will be with these.' He looked proudly at the locks he held, one in each hand. 'Nobody will get them open wi'out the keys. These am no ordinary locks, I made these meself.'

'You made 'em?' Mathew took one of the locks, turning it over in his hands. ''Ow could you do that on a barge?'

'I didn't make them on the barge.'

'Oh,' Mathew looked up, 'then where?'

Shaking his head at Phoebe's offer of a chair, Bert Ingles went on, a strong hint of pride lacing his explanation: 'Them locks be my own design. You can't buy them in no ironmonger's. I made them just before me father died. You see, Miss. . .' he looked at Phoebe '. . . me father was a lockmaker out at Willenhall, an' 'e taught me the locksmithing.'

'But the barge,' Phoebe said, 'I thought you worked the barge?'

'So I do, Miss,' he answered, 'but I ain't always done that. I worked wi' me father up to three years ago. It wasn't until 'e died though that I found 'e had run at such a loss I couldn't pay the brass founders an' everybody else that claimed 'e owed them wi'out selling up.' He shrugged. 'So that is what I did. There were nothing for it after that but to get a job, any job that would feed the wife and kids. That's how I come to be working the canal.'

'What be so different about this?' Mathew turned the lock he was holding, sending darts of gold flickering from the polished brass.

'I'll show you.' Fishing a key from his jacket, Bert took the lock, inserted the key in it. 'See?' He turned the key, the action shooting out a metal bar.

'Ar, it's locked,' Mathew said, a quizzical frown pulling his brows together. 'I don't see nothin' different in that.'

'But it's not locked, not altogether.' Bert Ingles smiled. 'You see, this is a doubler.'

'A whater?' Lucy asked.

'A doubler, Missis.' Bert passed her the lock. 'Least that's what I call it. You see, it's a double barrel lock.' He took the lock back, turning the key a second time, and another bar shot out. 'Now,' he handed the lock to Mathew, 'try openin' it.'

Mathew tried turning the key but it wouldn't budge. He tried again then looked at the man watching him. 'It's stuck,' he said. 'The key must be jammed or summat.'

'It's not the key nor the lock that be jammed.' Bert retrieved the lock. 'That's what you are meant to think. You see, anybody not knowing how it works would think the same, and thinking they had got the key stuck would leave off trying to get in.'

'Well, if a burglar couldn't get in, all supposin' 'e managed to get 'old of the key, 'ow do you expect we to do it?'

'Like this.' Bert laid the lock on the table so they could each follow what he did. 'You turned the key anti-clockwise to operate the bolt,' he said, glancing at Mathew, 'that would be the normal way to operate a lock, but I reversed the mechanism. On this the key has to be turned clockwise to lock it.'

'Clever.' Mathew pursed his lips admiringly. 'But what about the doubler bit?'

'This is where the key does get stuck,' Bert answered, 'least you would think it had 'cos you won't pull it out at this stage. You 'ave to turn the key once more, that releases a second bolt an' also the key; it's a double safeguard. Even if a burglar cottoned on to the fact the key had to be turned back way round from usual, its getting stuck would cause him a bit of a headache.'

'An' pickin' the lock an' then findin' it still didn't open, 'e would likely pack in tryin' altogether?' Mathew grinned. 'That's what I calls useful.'

'It is a very good way of locking doors,' Phoebe said. 'They will save me a deal of concern whenever I have to go anywhere. How much do I owe you, Mr Ingles?'

'You don't owe me anything.' He laid three more keys beside the locks on the table. 'Me and Lizzie be just glad we could be of help.'

'But I couldn't . . .'

'Ar you could,' Bert Ingles looked suddenly embarrassed, 'just show me where you keep your screwdrivers and such and I'll have them locks on the doors in no time.'

'I'll give you a hand.' Mathew picked up the locks. 'Tools am in the barn.'

'Eh! What do you reckon to that?' Lucy asked as the two men left the kitchen.

'I reckon you are going to have to pay for those locks, Mrs Leach.'

'Me!' Lucy gasped. 'I ain't got but ninepence in me purse.'

'Bert Ingles won't take money,' Phoebe handed her a clean cloth from the airer strung across the fireplace, 'but I don't think he would refuse four of your mutton pies.'

Chapter Twelve

'I said to sell them . . . both of them.'

Annie Pardoe sat in James Siveter's office in his chambers in Lower High Street, her voluminous black skirts entirely hiding the small chair beneath her.

'You will have no trouble, I have been asked to sell them on several occasions.'

'Miss Pardoe,' the solicitor cleared his throat, 'does your brother know of this intended sale?'

Annie's eyes narrowed and her mouth tightened. 'If you want to continue to be our solicitor, James Siveter, I advise you to do as I instruct. My brother gave me his full Power of Attorney and that means I can act as I see fit, and I see fit to sell the Hobs Hill coal mine and the Crown. It also means I can replace you in your capacity as Samuel's solicitor. Your sort are two a penny.'

James Siveter rolled his long-handled pen between his fingers, experiencing a strong desire to tell the woman sitting opposite his heavy desk to take her business with her to the nearest canal and jump in with it! But it was a desire he curbed; she was right when she said she could replace him, and while not exactly two a penny solicitors were not hard to come by. He could not afford to lose business, however wrong he felt it to be.

'I will bring the necessary papers to Brunswick House first thing tomorrow.'

'No!' Annie's tight mouth showed no sign of slackening. 'You will not come to Brunswick House. I will sign an agreement of sale while I am here. You can get the purchaser's signature today – we have already agreed the price. I shall call here again tomorrow at three and I expect the business to be concluded.'

Why the rush? James Siveter thought, filling out the necessary documents. And why was Annie Pardoe here instead of sending for him to come to Brunswick House as he had always done? Power of Attorney or not, she obviously didn't intend Samuel knowing of today's doings.

'I will get this to the purchaser as soon as . . .'

'You will take it to him now!' Annie snapped. 'I want this finished and done. Three o'clock tomorrow.'

Holding the door for her to pass, the solicitor watched as she swept into the street. So she was selling both coal mines, and quickly . . . too quickly even for Annie Pardoe. Yes, it was a safe bet Samuel knew nothing of it, just as he likely knew nothing of what she had sold already: the shares in the Monway steel foundry, the Moxley iron works, together with a string of smaller businesses and houses. And what was she doing with the money she'd had for them? He had drawn up no new contracts. Whatever she had done, he, James Siveter, had not been consulted. Closing the door, he returned to his desk. 'I wonder?' he mused, taking up the papers Annie had signed and putting them into a small valise. 'I wonder, Samuel, do you have any idea just how close you are to having nothing?'

Leaving the solicitor's office Annie had turned her trap left along the bottom end of Lower High Street, guiding the horse left again into Finchpath Lane. This way she could avoid the wheels of the trap becoming caught in the tramlines. There was also less likelihood of her being seen by going back to the house via the heath. She flicked the reins, urging the horse into a trot. What the folk of Wednesbury didn't see they couldn't talk about, and she wanted no talk of what she had been about today.

Samuel had spoken of reverting his legacy to Phoebe, of

giving back what his sister's sacrifices had earned. How easily, she thought bitterly, how *easily* her brothers disposed of her life, ordering hers to the comfort of their own. Abel had enjoyed that comfort, enjoyed the pleasures of his pretty wife, and now Samuel wanted the comfort of a conscience cleared of taking Phoebe's inheritance and his sister was to have no part in that decision. But she would not let it happen again; she had been given a second chance at living, a chance to have all Abel had had in every sense of the word, and this time she would not let it go. Tomorrow she would have the money from the sale of the mines and the next day she would give it to Clinton.

She clicked her tongue, encouraging the horse, seeing the figure of Clinton Harforth-Darby in her mind. In his mid-forties, he was a handsome man, tall, always well dressed, his dark hair just hinting at grey, with clear intense eyes and a manner only real breeding bestowed. Calling to see Violet Wheeler at Oakeswell Hall she had first been introduced to Gaskell's cousin, and the next afternoon he had come to Brunswick House.

The reins forgotten in her hands, she let her mind play over the events of the past weeks, events that had led her to the threshold of a new life. With the death of his wife a year ago Clinton had sold his sugar plantation in the West Indies to return to England. Interested in the manufacture of the new metal tubes, he had come to Wednesbury to discuss with Gaskell the possibility of starting up a business. That was when he and Annie had met. From that moment she had, for the first time in twenty years, been treated like a woman and not a servile catspaw. Clinton was not like her father had been, nor Abel, treating women as though they didn't have the capacity to understand anything beyond the kitchen. He had talked to her about going into the manufacture of tubes, how he saw the business expanding over the years; he had told her how Gaskell had wanted to be a partner in the venture but Clinton had refused him. He had more than enough money to finance any business, he said. He did not want a partner, what he wanted was *her*.

Annie's heart gave the same crazy bounce it had when Clinton had said those words two weeks ago. He wanted to marry her, to make her his wife. She, Annie Pardoe, would become Mrs Clinton Harforth-Darby, *she* would marry into the Wheeler family not Phoebe, and she would take the Pardoe money with her. Clinton had brushed it aside when she had told him that Samuel owned everything. It was of no consequence, he had said, he wanted her for his wife not the paltry amount her brother might have bequeathed. However, if it interested her, she could go on being the legal representative for Samuel. It was then he had given her the ring, placing it on the third finger of her left hand, a square-cut amethyst the size of her thumbnail.

It was kept in a drawer in her bedroom. Annie thought now of the lovely ring hidden beneath layers of petticoats, the same petticoats that covered the perfume bottle that had been Elias Webb's gift to her. Clinton would announce their engagement at the Wheelers' house during the party they were giving before their son's regiment left for India. Until then she would not wear it, and by then everything that had once been Abel's would be hers.

They had often talked of the new premises he would build for the making of metal tubes during Clinton's visits, her interest seeming to fire his own as she suggested sites in or near the town, pointing out their nearness to the canal that would be needed to transport the tubes. That was when Clinton had said she would have made an ideal partner for his business except she was to be his wife, refusing to entertain the idea she could be both; it had taken her some time to get him to agree, Clinton eventually suggesting she become a steel tube manufacturer in her own right; the premises, the machinery, the raw steel, everything in her name. Only that way would he be happy.

And now the coal mines, the mainstay of all that had

once constituted Abel's wealth and then Samuel's were gone. Tomorrow she would have the money that would start her in her own business and the beginning of a new life.

'I was pleased to hear Sophie's news.' Phoebe glanced at Edward walking beside her. 'She was so excited when she called on Thursday.'

'Her coming engagement to Montrose Wheeler, you mean?' He stopped, picking up a stone and skimming it into the canal. 'I wish I could feel as happy for her.'

'But you don't?' Phoebe knew she was stating the obvious.

'No.' He sent a second stone winging after the first. 'The Wheelers are simply intent on making a good match, just as they were with . . .' He stopped awkwardly. 'I . . . I beg your pardon, Phoebe.'

'Just as they were with Abel Pardoe's daughter?' She smiled. 'You don't need to apologise for telling the truth, Edward.'

'You knew!' He turned to her, surprise lifting his fair eyebrows. 'You knew they wanted you for your father's money rather than for . . . for . . .'

'For myself?' She gazed at the circles spreading on the surface where the stones had struck the water. 'No, not at the time. I only realised that when his mother told me she had written to tell him of my Uncle Samuel's inheriting everything that was my father's, and he did nothing . . . he never even wrote to me to tell me he no longer wished to marry me.'

'He left that to his mother also?'

She nodded. 'It was a shock then but at least I have been saved from a marriage that could have brought me no real love, and I am grateful for that.'

'But what will save Sophie?' He kicked a boot savagely into the spongy earth. 'Her dowry will not be signed away to an uncle, she will be handed over like so much coal or wheat, she and all she has will become the property of Montrose Wheeler – and it will be God help her after that.'

'Does your mother know how you feel about Sophie's marrying Montrose?'

'My mother thinks that it is a good match. I truly believe she is of the opinion that love grows only after marriage.'

'And Sophie . . .' Phoebe watched the circles spread into nothing. 'Have you said anything of your feelings to her?'

'No, how could I when she is so happy? I can't tell her, Phoebe, I can't be the one to hurt her.'

Far better the bubble be burst now, Phoebe thought, than let it carry her to the moon only to break there.

'What of your father?' she asked. 'Have you confided in him?'

Edward plucked a blade of grass, twisting it between his fingers. 'I have said nothing to him but I think he knows I feel such a marriage would be wrong, and that like myself he would rather Sophie widened her social circle, met other young men before making her choice. But like myself Father could never bring himself to hurt her.'

'So Sophie will marry regardless of how you and Sir William feel?'

'Maybe not.' He rolled the blade of grass between his fingers then flicked it out over the water. 'My father has no wish to see Sophie hurt and that is why he has set the date for her betrothal to Wheeler to take place when we return from Europe, which puts it several months into next year. At least that way he is giving her a little time to find out if her emotion is love or not. And who knows? She may meet someone she would rather marry than Gaskell Wheeler's son . . . anyway that is what I hope, and I think it is my father's hope too.'

And mine, thought Phoebe, no trace of jealousy colouring it. No girl should marry a man only to discover his passion was for her money. She had been saved from that. Pray God Sophie would be too.

Returning the wave of a small girl on a passing barge, Phoebe turned from the peaceful lure of the water. Sophie's visits once a fortnight were not so disruptive to her work but Edward had begun to call at Wiggins Mill weekly and sometimes more than that. She had to find a way of telling him she could not spend a couple of afternoons a week out walking with him. 'I really must return, Edward,' she began. 'I ought not to be here, it's not fair on Lucy and Mathew.'

'How do you mean, not fair?'

'Surely you must see it is not right for me to be out walking when both of them are at work? I should be working too. I have a living to make as they do.'

'There's no need for any of this,' he waved a hand in the direction of the mill, 'you should not have to work for your living.'

'Then how would I manage?' Phoebe's laugh held more irony than humour. 'People need money to live, Edward, and it does not grow on trees.'

'You would not need money,' he caught her hand, his blue eyes intense, 'not if you became my wife. I love you, Phoebe. I have since that moment I helped you into the carriage the day you came to the Priory to collect those dresses. Marry me . . . say you will be my wife?'

What would that hold for both of them? Phoebe looked into his face, so like his mother's, and knew the answer. Sir William Dartmouth's son and heir married to a woman who had been in prison . . . what gossip that would provide! What houses would receive them merely to see his gaolbird wife, only to ignore them politely from then on. She knew Edward would argue his love was strong enough to withstand the attitudes of others, but would it be? Yes, he loved her now, she had seen it in his eyes each time they met, but was it real or just the misguided infatuation of a young man attempting to right a wrong he had caused, and would a year from now see him regretting such a marriage?

Gently she released her hands. She could not take that risk. She had too much respect for his parents, Edward carried too old a family line, too ancient a name, to have anything threaten it. And marriage to her, a woman accused and convicted of theft, however wrongly, would do him no good in the eyes of society.

'I won't marry you, Edward,' she said softly. 'I will not marry anyone yet.' She smiled up at him. 'Perhaps in a year or so, providing you feel as you do now, you will ask me again.' She turned away, the cloud of disappointment on his face hurting her too. Trying hard to sound matter-of-fact, hoping that way to lighten any embarrassment her refusal of his offer might have caused him, she went on, 'In the meantime, whether we like it or not, I have work to do.'

'Phoebe,' he said as she would have walked on, 'is there anyone else?'

'No, Edward,' she replied, the truth of it shining from her eyes, 'there is no one else.'

'Eeh, what a to do in the town today!' Lucy dropped into a chair as Phoebe dished up the evening meal she had prepared. 'You know Charles West, the jeweller in the High Street . . . well, 'e was robbed the night afore.'

'Robbed!' Phoebe stopped filling Mathew's bowl with the soup she had simmered all day. 'Who did it?'

'Nobody knows,' Mathew answered. 'It 'appened durin' the night by what I 'eard.'

'Heavens!' Phoebe finished filling his bowl then ladled soup into her own. 'Was anyone hurt?'

Mathew took a chunk of crusty bread, dipping it into his soup. 'No,' he said between bites, 'nobody 'eard anythin', not a sound. Charlie West never knowed it 'ad 'appened till he went for 'is cash this mornin'.'

'But the money from the shop,' Phoebe looked up from her meal, 'surely he doesn't leave the takings in the shop overnight?'

'No, 'e don't,' Mathew helped himself to more bread, 'an' 'e don't put it in no bank neither. Seems whoever broke into 'is 'ouse last night knowed that, 'cos money was all was took.'

'Were the police called?' Phoebe asked.

Lucy nodded but it was Mathew answered. 'Ar, they was called but them bobbies don't seem to know whether they be comin' or whether they've been. It seems Charlie West wasn't the only one to get 'is pocket lightened last night. Hollingsworth the pork butcher, 'e was 'ad, an' so was Samuel Platt the iron founder up on King's Hill.'

'All on the same night? No wonder the police were at their wit's end. I don't remember anything like this ever happening in Wednesbury before.'

'I don't either.' Lucy spooned her soup. 'Me mam says nothin' like it *as* ever 'appened, least not as long as 'er's been alive.'

'Which is from the time of Adam, ain't it?'

'Watch it, Mathew Leach!' Lucy waved her spoon at her husband. 'You ain't so big 'er can't tan your arse.'

'Now *that* we would have to watch.' Phoebe joined in their laughter.

'Do you think it could be somebody local? The burglar, I means,' Lucy said finishing her soup.

'Won't know that till 'e be found.' Mathew cut a wedge of cheese from the block Phoebe placed on the table. 'An' Lord only knows if that'll ever 'appen. 'E could be miles away by now.'

Her sweet tooth preferring a sultana scone instead of cheese, Lucy spread it with the dark red damson jam Mathew's mother had sent from last summer's bottling. ''E could be,' she agreed, sinking her teeth into the scone, 'or 'e be down a disused mine shaft like that murderer we 'ad some years back. You know, 'e killed that woman Mary . . . Mary summat or other.'

'Mary Carter?' Mathew placed his cheese between two slices of bread, pressing the whole together with the heel of his hand. 'Bad business was that by what I've 'eard me mam an' dad say.'

'Any murder is a bad business.' Lucy popped the last of her scone into her mouth.

'Ar, that's right an' it ain't wrong, but that particular murder ended more'n one life, so it seemed, an' there was folks in Wednesbury was party to it 'appenin'. Me dad reckons there was no nicer bloke you would wish to meet than Joseph Bradly.'

'My father never spoke of a murder taking place in Wednesbury,' Phoebe said. 'At least, I never heard him speak of one. What happened?'

'Sit you down, Miss.' Lucy bustled up from the table. 'I'll get the teapot.'

Taking his cue, Mathew stayed silent but as the tea was poured Phoebe asked again.

'You don't want to be 'earin' about no murder, Miss Phoebe.' Lucy set the teapot firmly on the table. 'Anyway it all 'appened long ago.'

'Then my knowing can't hurt anyone,' Phoebe replied gently, realising Lucy wanted to protect her from anything she might find painful. 'Really, Mathew, I would like to know. There seems to be such a lot to this town I never knew of before.'

'If yer sure . . .' Mathew glanced at Lucy who lifted her shoulders resignedly. 'Joseph Bradly lived up along Church Hill, right against the old church. 'Is wife 'ad died while their daughter Anna was no more'n a babby an' Mary Carter used to go up to the 'ouse every day to do for 'em like. Well, 'er went missin' an' when 'er was found drownded in Millfields Pool folk said as 'ow Jos Bradly was one who done it; seems they kept on sayin' it till the poor bugger 'ad more'n 'e could stand.'

'What did he do?'

Mathew looked across the table at Phoebe then away to his mug of tea, his tongue stilled by sudden embarrassment.

'What did Joseph Bradly do, Mathew?'

''E . . . 'e got pie-eyed,' Mathew stared resolutely into the mug, 'too drunk to know what the 'ell 'e was about, then 'e . . . 'e went 'ome an' raped 'is own daughter.' The last came out in a rush. If he didn't say it quickly, he wouldn't say it at all.

'What a dreadful thing to happen!' Phoebe breathed.

'Ar,' Mathew nodded, ''er couldn't 'ave been more'n sixteen or seventeen accordin' to what was said. Left Wednesbury 'er did, left a babby . . . a lad, Aaron 'e was called . . . don't know what 'appened to 'er after that.'

'And her father, did he stay in Wednesbury?' Phoebe stirred milk into her own tea.

'Me mam said 'e couldn't do no other, not wi' a babby.'

''E could've put it into the workhouse,' Lucy joined the conversation.

'Me mam said that an' all.' Mathew leaned back, his meal finished. 'But me dad said 'e was too fine a bloke to leave a babby in the workhouse, no matter 'ow it was got.'

'Was anything ever proved?'

'Seems years after a bloke was brought up from a shaft 'e 'ad dropped into, and 'e said it was 'im killed Mary Carter.'

'So Joseph Bradly was cleared of suspicion of murder?'

'Cleared of suspicion by law but not by folk of Wednesbury,' Lucy said, collecting dishes into a pile. 'They 'ad got their claws into 'im an' wouldn't let go. Me mam said the same old tales kept flyin' around.'

'Did his daughter return?' Phoebe helped with clearing the table.

Lucy glanced at Mathew. 'Ar, 'er returned,' he said. 'At least Mam says 'er did, but only after 'er father 'ung 'isself.'

'Oh, how awful!' Phoebe looked from one to the other. 'What an awful thing to happen to a family.'

'Ar.' Mathew rose from the table, preparing to go to the workshop he had fashioned from one of the smaller outbuildings. 'First murder an' now these burglaries, there be some right crackpotical things goes on in Wednesbury.'

Burglaries! Phoebe helped carry the dishes to the scullery for washing. She had almost forgotten them. Thank God for the locks Bert Ingles had given her!

* * *

Samuel was sleeping. Annie had given him the draught Alfred Dingley had prescribed against wakeful nights, doubling the dose he had recommended. She wanted no interruptions. Everything had gone smoothly; her prices for both mines had been accepted, as she'd known they would be, and the cash for them paid without question. Siveter had wanted to ask questions, she knew, but had thought better of it; there wasn't much of Samuel's inheritance left for him to have the legal handling of, but words from her could still harm the lawyer's reputation and he would not risk that.

Reaching a box from beneath the fourposter bed Annie opened it, setting the contents in neat white piles on the counterpane. The last of everything of value apart from this house and the one at Bescot was gone, everything that had once been Abel's was sold and the money for it lay staring up at her. 'Everything!' Annie scooped the money together, the wads of notes thick in her hands. 'Everything you had, Abel.' She laughed low in her throat. 'Everything you ever owned is here in my hands, and tomorrow it will buy back my life.'

Leaving the money scattering the bed like a sudden snowstorm, she crossed the bedroom to the chest of drawers. Opening the bottom one, she took out the amethyst ring. Soon it would be on her finger for all to see, soon the whole town would know she was to be Clinton's wife. Carefully she replaced it, her fingers touching the perfume bottle, almost stroking it, before drawing one of the silk petticoats from its blue tissue paper.

Closing the drawer, she dropped the petticoat on the bed, watching several banknotes rise in the draught of air as it landed then settled back on the silk. That would be her life from now on, surrounded in money, covered in money . . . Abel's money.

Unbuttoning her black grosgrain town dress she stepped out of it. Throwing it across a chair, she slipped off her heavy cotton petticoat. She would not wear black for Clinton's coming . . . she would never wear black again.

Sliding the silk over her head, Annie let it down over her hips, her hands caressing the soft luxury of it. No, she wouldn't wear black again nor cotton either. Clinton would see her in nothing but silks and satins. Going to the wardrobe, she took out the lavender dress. She would wear it for his coming this afternoon.

The last of the tiny self-covered buttons fastened, she took a lavender fichu from her bag. She had bought it from Fosbrook's in Union Street before going to the solicitor's. Setting it on her head, she secured it with hairpins then stood looking at her reflection in the full-length cheval mirror. Stylish the dress might be but it did not give her back her youth, it could not remove the lines that bordered her mouth nor return the bloom to her skin.

Why was Clinton marrying her? She asked herself the question she knew others would ask. It wasn't for her looks. Annie touched a hand to her face. She had never been blessed with them; what there had been in the way of looks had been given to Abel and Samuel, not that they had done Samuel a lot of good. She turned away from the mirror. He had not fared much better with his life than she had with her own.

Annie gathered the banknotes, putting them neatly into the box and closing it. Looks and life, fate had denied her both, and Samuel had ideas of taking the latter away again, of returning everything to Phoebe. 'But you are too late,' she breathed, picking up the box. 'Just as it's too late for Abel's daughter.'

Chapter Thirteen

Phoebe put down her sewing, stretching her aching back, listening to the quietness of the old mill house. Handsworth Prison had been quiet, every voice hushed to whispers save those of the wardresses, but it had been a harsh jarring quiet that left the brain reeling from its unsung staccato melody. Here it was gentle, its touch lenient to the mind, settling courteously over mill and heath. Here the quiet soothed and healed.

It wanted over an hour before Mathew and Lucy returned from their day's work, the meal was simmering in the oven, she had time for a walk. Running downstairs, cheating herself of time to change her mind, she slipped out of the back door, securing the lock Bert had fitted before slipping the brass key into the pocket of her brown dress.

Refusing to let her eyes linger on the brooding pile of the corn barn she turned in the direction of the canal. It would be pleasant there with the barges passing on the way to the ports Mark Ingles dreamed of.

Coming up out of the hollow that sheltered the mill house she looked toward the ribbon of water. There was no passing barge, only a finger of smoke spiralling toward the sky, the air too lazy to spread it. Shading her eyes from the remains of the sun, she stared. It had been an extra warm day but by no means hot enough to set the heath ablaze, so how come the smoke?

''Ow do, Miss?'' The shout accompanied by a wave brought a smile to Phoebe's face and she walked on to where the

Ingleses sat grouped about a small fire above the towpath.

'I didn't know you were back.'

'Got back yesterday.' Bert took the shawl his wife handed to him, spreading it on the grass and gesturing Phoebe to sit down. 'Fetched a load of timber up from London way an' dropped it off at Moxley, shoring for the coalmine there.'

'But the barge,' Phoebe glanced to the empty waterway then back to Bert, 'where is it? You don't usually leave it while it's being reloaded.'

'Ain't no barge, Miss,' Lizzie said, staring at the fire trying its best to boil the kettle of water balanced over it, 'an' there ain't no load – least not for we there ain't.'

'No barge? I don't understand . . . what has happened to it?'

'Nothing 'as 'appened to the barge,' Bert poked the fire with a stick, 'barge is loaded an' off.'

'Mr Ingles,' Phoebe looked from one to the other, 'Lizzie, will you tell me what has happened, if not to the barge then to you . . . why are the four of you sitting here?'

'We come up yesterday . . . early on . . . wi' a load of timber for Moxley like Bert said,' Lizzie answered. 'We was expectin' to load coals for London like we usually does only the gaffer at the mine, 'e said there was no load for we an' that we was to get our things off the barge right away. There was already another bargee wantin' to take 'er off up to London.'

'But I thought the barge was yours . . . your home?'

'Our 'ome, yes,' Bert turned away, his face to the canal, 'but not our property. Now the owner 'as done a deal wi' new mine gaffer to put only 'is men on the barges.'

'New?' Phoebe looked at the man, his back still toward her. 'Do you mean Moxley mine has a new manager?'

'Not only a new manager.' Bert kicked out, sending a shower of grit from the path, spraying into the water. 'A new owner, an' that new owner 'as no place for Bert Ingles.'

The mine was sold! Phoebe sat back on her heels. Uncle Samuel had sold Moxley mine, and what of Hobs Hill? Was that also sold, was Joseph Leach too out of a job and a home?

'We would 'ave been further along but totin' our stuff as well as Bert's tools 'as slowed we more than we thought,' Lizzie said. "Sides the walkin' is a bit tough on the little 'un. The lad 'e can manage it but the babby . . . 'er just ain't used to it.'

'Further on to where?' Phoebe asked, watching the boy go to stand beside his father. 'Where will you go? Where will you live?'

Lizzie glanced at her husband, his shoulders slumped forward. 'It ain't too bad, sleepin' out is quite pleasant, an' anyway Bert will find work soon.'

She smiled but behind the expression Phoebe read a different story. Sleeping out? They had slept out last night, and would again for how many nights? And what about food? No job meant no money and that in turn no food. She looked at the tiny girl huddled against her mother's skirts. How in God's name could people behave in such a way as to throw a man and his family out of their home? What sort of man was it who had bought her father's mine?

'Mr Ingles,' she got to her feet, 'why not stay here for a few days, give yourself a chance to try for work in Wednesbury? There must be something there.'

'An' if there ain't?'

'Then you have gained a few nights' rest and lost nothing.' She picked up the shawl, shaking it free of dried grass and handing it to Lizzie.

'I could go wi' you, Dad, mebbe we could both find work.'

Bert dropped a hand to his son's shoulder but remained gazing into the green depths of the canal.

'Best we stop alongside o' the cut, Miss,' he said. 'That way I can keep in touch, ask if barges 'ave 'eard of work to be 'ad in other parts. News travels fast along the cut.'

'A couple o' days wouldn't make no odds, Bert,' Lizzie

said gently. 'You need not traipse into the town, you could come down 'ere 'an wait o' the barges passin', but the little un . . . 'er could do wi' a few nights restin' in one place.'

'The barn is dry and there are plenty of corn sacks in the loft,' Phoebe said. 'It isn't much, I know, but you would be more comfortable than sleeping beside the canal.'

'Thank you, Miss.' Bert's gratitude was plain to see. 'We be grateful for your kindness. A few days an' then we'll be off . . . the Ingleses will be a nuisance to none.'

'I'm all for 'elpin' folk but four more mouths to feed . . . eeh, Miss Phoebe, 'ow we goin' to manage that?'

'It will be difficult, I know, but the clothes I have made sold well . . . I have the money from those.'

'True,' Lucy heaped flour into a bowl, 'but it won't last long spread over four of 'em.'

'I couldn't let them go any further, Lucy, that little girl of theirs looks far from well.'

'I noticed.' She rubbed fat into the flour. 'It can't be 'ealthy on them barges, all cooped up like rabbits in a hutch, an' the damp . . . it's a wonder they ain't all sprouted fins.'

'So can we manage?'

'Reckon so,' Lucy answered, 'but not for long.'

Phoebe began the ritual of greasing pie tins. 'We won't have to for long.'

Lucy looked up from rolling pastry. 'It won't be no easier, Miss Phoebe, watchin' 'em go, I mean, whether they be 'ere a short span or a longer.'

Phoebe took each circle of pastry as Lucy pressed it out, positioning it in its tin. 'Maybe they won't need to go.'

'Look,' Lucy stopped cutting circles, her eyes on Phoebe filling pastry cases with meat and potato, 'I wouldn't bank on Bert Ingles findin' work in Wednesbury. Joseph told Mathew that there might be quite a few men lookin' for jobs, wi' Moxley mine changin' 'ands.'

'Who has bought it?' Phoebe put the heavy pan of meat and potato in the hearth, covering it with a cloth.

Lucy reached for the smaller dish with which to cut pastry lids. 'Joseph couldn't say. Told Mathew nobody 'ad wind of the buyer, not yet. Let's just 'ope that whoever it is keeps 'em workin' . . . like Joseph says, there might be a few others lookin' for work in Wednesbury so don't go ratin' Bert Ingles's chances too 'igh.'

Waiting while Lucy placed the lids on the pies, Phoebe dipped her fingers in milk, spreading each with a thin film of moisture. 'Maybe he won't need to go to the town for work.'

Lucy refilled the bowl with flour, a fine white cloud mushrooming up to settle along her brows and lashes. 'What do you mean?' she asked. 'What you thinkin'?'

Phoebe turned from stocking the oven, her cheeks red from the fire. 'Locks,' she said simply, 'I'm thinking of locks.'

'I ain't with you, Miss.'

'I have been thinking a lot about those burglaries in the town.' Phoebe came to stand beside the table.

'Me an' all. They worry me they do. Who knows where 'e might strike next? Makes you scared to go to bed nights.'

'Well, if they worry us here . . .' Phoebe glanced around the kitchen with its worn chairs and mongrel assortment of second hand pots and dishes '. . . imagine how worried some folk in the town must be.'

Lucy began to make her second batch of pastry. 'Ar, there be plenty like we. An' if *they* be frightened, 'ow must all the nobs be feelin'?'

'Exactly! How must they be feeling . . . mine owners, iron and steel founders, brewers, grocers, tavern keepers? Think of it, Lucy, the list is endless and Wednesbury has plenty of them as well as plenty like us. All these people have something to lose, and all of them, rich or not so rich, would pay to make their home secure, don't you agree?'

''Course I do, but I still ain't wi' you.'

'People will pay for security.' Phoebe covered the batch of pies waiting their turn in the oven. 'We can give them that security.'

'We!' Lucy exclaimed. ''Ow?'

'Wait.' Phoebe wiped her hands on the white huckaback cloth kept 'specially for the baking then went out through the scullery, running across the yard to the barn where Mathew was helping the Ingleses settle in.

'Mr Ingles.'

Lizzie Ingles looked up from covering a heap of straw with her shawl, her face clouding with disappointment as she saw Phoebe standing in the doorway,cheeks red and arms crossed over her breasts.

'It's all right, Miss.' She picked up the shawl and began to fold it, the children watching from a corner. 'We understand, you can't let we stop 'ere after all. Just give we a minute to get we things an' we'll be gone.'

'I did not come to ask you to leave, Lizzie, I said you could stay here and you can. I . . . I only wish it were more like a home.'

'It could be.' Lizzie looked around the barn, at the rusting implements and unused flour sacks. 'If only . . .'

'If you ain't askin' we to go then what was you wantin' to ask, Miss?'

Phoebe smiled at the children, each sitting on a broken quern, then looked to where Bert stood watching her. 'Mr Ingles . . . Lizzie, would you come to the house, please? And you too, Mathew, I have something I wish to discuss with the three of you.'

'You two mind what you be about,' Lizzie pushed to her feet as she spoke to her children, 'no messin' wi' anything an' no larkin' around. You can finish makin' up this bed for the pair o' you.'

In the kitchen Lucy had finished her evening baking, the bowls and basins already stacked against the scullery sink and the brown earthenware teapot filled and waiting.

'What be all this about, Miss?' Bert asked as Phoebe reached cups from the dresser.

'It's about your locks, Mr Ingles.'

'Locks?'

'Locks, the ones you made for me.'

'They ain't broke, am they?'

'No, they are not broken,' Phoebe said, 'they work very well. I was wondering if you could make more?'

'I could,' he looked puzzled, 'but for what reason? Beggin' your pardon, you 'ave the doors to the 'ouse secured an' them barns don't 'old nought save a few old tools. An' if it's Mathew's place you was thinkin' of I already 'as a lock made for 'im, made it on me last trip to London. We intended leavin' it on your doorstep afore we moved on from the cut.'

'Thanks, Bert, that's good o' you,' Mathew said. 'I knows missis was worried about 'er bits an' pieces, we bein' out all day.'

'I wasn't wanting locks for myself . . . well, not for my own use.' Phoebe passed round the tea. 'The point is, do you think you could make . . . say a dozen . . . of the same sort as you fixed to my doors?'

'A dozen!' Bert set his mug on the table. 'That's a few locks, Miss.'

'Could you make them?' She asked, emphasising her words.

'Reckon I could,' he mused, 'I 'ave me patterns an' me files. I brought them wi' me.'

'What else would you need?' Phoebe caught the look of enquiry that flashed from Mathew to Lucy and the shrug of the shoulders she returned.

Bert pursed his lips. 'Brass or steel . . . place to work . . . a fire . . . a anvil . . . then you could manage.'

'How long would it take to make them?'

'Depends.' Bert thought for several moments. 'A week, p'raps, depends on 'ow much time you 'ave to give to the work.'

'If you had nothing else to do,' Phoebe asked, 'could you make a dozen locks in one week?'

'Ar,' he nodded, 'supposin' I 'ad a week.'

'Mathew,' Phoebe turned her attention to Lucy's husband, 'where could we get the metal Mr Ingles would need?'

'Bagnall's,' Mathew answered, his tone revealing the puzzlement this conversation was causing him. 'Bagnall's in Dudley Street will 'ave what 'e needs. I could tek 'im in wi' me an' Lucy tomorrow . . .'

'That be easy to say,' Bert interrupted, 'but money be needed to buy metals an' I've got precious little o' that.'

'Don't worry about money, Mr Ingles . . .'

'That's all right for you to say, Miss,' Lizzie put in, the same cloud of anxiety that Phoebe had seen in the barn settling over her eyes, 'but we 'ave the kids to feed an' no prospect of work to fetch more money in. I don't want to sound ungrateful, God forbid, but what bit o' money we got can't go bein' spent on makin' locks.'

'I think you have every prospect of work, Lizzie,' Phoebe smiled, 'or at least your husband has.'

Standing behind his wife's chair, Bert dropped a hand to her shoulder. 'What do you mean, Miss, I 'ave the prospect o' work?'

Phoebe looked at each of the people grouped in her small kitchen. 'I have a proposition to make, a proposition that will involve all of us. I will provide the necessary materials for the making of a dozen double barrel locks and a place for Mr Ingles to work. Food and keep for himself and his family will be his wage for the time it takes. For your part, Mathew, if you are willing, I would like you to show the lock to as many shopkeepers and tradesmen as you can. Given the recent robberies I don't think they will take much persuading to buy one, and the fitting of them could provide you with extra work.' She paused then. 'So both of you, what do you say, will you give it a try?'

'I'm game.' Mathew grinned.

'And what about you, Mr Ingles?' Phoebe smiled at the man who looked as though he had been kissed with a pole axe. 'Are you game?'

'A week off the road . . . food for the kids?' Bert grinned. 'Game? I'll say I'm bloody game . . . thanks, Miss, thanks for everythin'. I . . . I'll make you the best bloody locks ever to come out of Willenhall!'

Phoebe held out a hand. 'Then we are in business, Mr Ingles, and if things go as I hope, we will discuss a more usual wage for your labour.' She smiled at Lizzie. 'All, of course, provided your wife agrees to your settling here?'

'Oh, I agree, Miss.' Lizzie laid a hand over the one resting on her shoulder. 'An' my Bert will make you the best locks you ever seen.'

'You said your proposition included all o' we?' Lucy spoke for the first time since the Ingleses had entered the kitchen. 'So where be my part in all o' this?'

'You have the most important part.' Phoebe threw an arm around her one-time maid. 'Even the strongest of men can't work without food. We need your cooking to pay Mr Ingles's wages. What I have to ask you, Mrs Leach, is this . . . are you up to it?'

Picking up a pie warm from the oven, Lucy passed it to Bert. 'Here,' she laughed, 'you tell me, Bert . . . am I up to it?'

'Didn't you hear anything . . . anything at all?'

Maudie Tranter looked at the woman she had worked twelve years for, twelve years and not one good word in all of them. Annie Pardoe was a woman twisted with jealousy and spite, a woman who deserved all she got and more. And more she would get, Maudie could feel it in her bones.

'No, Miss Pardoe,' she said, her feelings well hidden. 'I slept all through the night, never 'eard nothing.'

Annie glanced around the dishevelled room, the mantelpiece relieved of its silver candlesticks and silver framed miniatures of her mother and father, and the desk littered with papers snatched from their drawers, strewn like white confetti over the carpet.

'You am a light sleeper, Miss, didn't you 'ear nothin' neither?'

Annie looked sharply at her thin angular housekeeper, standing with hands clasped together over a white apron that reached to the hem of her black skirts, unsure whether the woman's voice held a note of sarcasm.

'No, I did not!' she snapped. 'Mr Samuel has slept badly for several nights and I have stayed up with him. Last night I took a draught in order to get some sleep myself.'

''Course, Mr Samuel wouldn't 'ear anything, not the way 'e is.'

'Precisely.' Annie glanced once more at the room, just this one, the one with the desk and little else of interest or value apart from the few bits of silver. No other room had been disturbed, so what was the thief looking for? Whatever it was he'd expected to find it in the desk and had almost torn it apart in the search. 'Whoever it was must have come in through there.' She pointed to a door still open on to the garden. 'The Leathern Bottle gives right on to this property. He was probably drinking in there all night. I knew we should have had that dividing wall heightened.' She crossed the room, slamming the door shut. 'Go at once and bring the constables.'

Much good they'll do, Maudie thought, returning to the scullery and reaching her cloak from the cupboard. Whoever had been rummaging in that desk I doubt the bobbies will find him. That lot ain't sharp enough to catch a cold!

In the room Abel had used as a study Annie gathered up the strewn papers. Bills of sale for property that had once been Abel's but none that pointed to what had become of the proceeds of those sales. There had not been time yet for her to receive the title deeds for her tube works but, thank God, she had already given the money to Clinton.

'Sergeant down the station says as constables be out,'

Maudie said an hour later. She would have liked to take the time to call on Sarah but commonsense had warned against it. Annie Pardoe could time a walk to the police station and back almost to the minute; she would know for certain if there had been any gossiping on the way.

'Out!' Annie glared at the impudence of the man. 'What did he mean, the constables were out?'

"E meant they wasn't in,' Maudie enjoyed replying.

This time Annie was sure of the sarcasm. 'As you will be out of a position if you try your lip on me, Maudie Tranter,' she said, anger barely held in check. 'Now, if you don't want to go from this house a sight quicker than you came into it, you will tell me exactly what that fool at the station told you.'

I know what I'd like to tell you, you bad-tempered old cow, and one day, with God's help or the Devil's, I will! Maudie's thoughts gave her little consolation and she answered sullenly. "E said as constables were out 'vestigatin' a break in up at Julia Hanson's place an' across at William Purchase, top end o' Chapel Street; said 'e would send 'em along 'ere when they reported back to the station, but 'e couldn't say 'ow long that was like to be.'

Julia Hanson and William Purchase, Annie mused as her housekeeper left the room, one a brewer, the other a grocer and general dealer, both likely to have money and like as not that money kept in the house. But what was the motive for breaking into Brunswick House? Unless . . . she touched a hand to the papers she had sorted ready to replace in relevant drawers of the desk. Unless someone knew of the cash she had got from James Siveter. She made her way to Samuel's room. And if they did, who but James Siveter could have told them?

'No, there has been no damage,' she signed in answer to her brother's question. 'Some papers scattered about the desk and the silver taken from the study. I have informed the constables. They will be here later.'

'Later?' Samuel's question flicked from his fingers.

'Two more houses were robbed last night,' Annie answered, 'Julia Hanson's and William Purchase's.'

'A brewer and a general dealer.' Samuel's fingers moved with the transient fluidity of a mayfly. 'Our burglar chooses his victims well, though why us?'

Annie shrugged. 'Who knows?' she replied her own fingers having none of the grace of movement her brother's held. 'Perhaps he thought to find money here. Thank heaven we keep little but petty cash, enough for small unforeseen events, no more.'

'This event was certainly unforeseen but nothing was taken that cannot be replaced – except, of course, for the miniatures of our parents and there is the possibility they will be returned.'

'We can always hope, but I do have my doubts.'

'No one was harmed, that is truly all that matters.'

All that mattered! Annie turned away, unable to disguise the contempt she knew must show in her face. How like Samuel to adopt that attitude . . . how typical of the weakness and ineffectuality he had shown all his life, the incapacity born of relying first upon their mother to attend to all then transferring that reliance to herself. And what of that reliance once she was married? And what of the condition that had kept Samuel confined to one house or the other for the greater part of his life? How would Clinton accept that? Would he accept it or would he . . . ?

'I must prepare for the constables' arrival,' she signed, quickly leaving the room before Samuel could answer. Clinton would not have to accept, Clinton would never know; no more would she be her brother's keeper.

Chapter Fourteen

'Ar, sold 'em both.' Sarah Leach looked at the young woman seated at her table. The years since her father's death had left their mark but it was the mark of confidence, of a sureness in herself; that prison had taught her a valuable lesson and not one any Magistrate would have expected: it had taught her that even in 1900 a woman had to fight and fight hard for any sort of life of her own. Many would have gone under given what this one had been dealt, but Abel Pardoe's daughter had learned how to fight.

'For what reason?' Phoebe's question caused the older woman to shake her head in a slow rhythm. 'Were the coal seams running out?'

'Joseph says they be gettin' thinner, but they 'ave a few years left in 'em yet.'

'Then why?'

'God knows, ma wench, an' 'e ain't tellin'.' Sarah stirred the tea she had poured. 'Who can tell what they at Brunswick 'Ouse might do next?'

'I can't understand Uncle Samuel's actions . . . to sell the coal mines!'

Sarah went on stirring, the spoon rattling against the cup. 'Who's to say it be yer uncle doin' the sellin'? Maudie Tranter said that aunt o' your'n 'ad the legal power to sign in 'er brother's stead, an' the Lord knows 'er would do it, tek 'er spite out on any 'er can. There's a few poor buggers lost their livin' 'cos of Annie Pardoe.'

Such as Bert Ingles, Phoebe thought, though he was one

of the lucky ones. The locks he made were selling as fast as he could produce them, there need be no more tramping the country in search of work for him and Lizzie had the comfort of a permanent place to make a home . . . but there were others not so fortunate.

'Sarah!' She pulled back from her thoughts, sudden agitation in her voice. 'Joseph . . . he hasn't . . .'

'Been given 'is tin?' Sarah intervened. 'No, ma wench, 'e still 'as 'is job at Hobs Hill. Seems to be just cut people as 'as been laid off . . . eh, what will them wimmin an' their babbies 'ave to live on? Meks my 'eart bleed to think on 'em.'

'Then you think my aunt is the one who has sold the mines?'

Twisting in her chair, Sarah swung the kettle from the fire, stilling its shrill hiss of steam. 'Think o' it,' she said, turning back to face Phoebe. 'Like you said you can't imagine yer uncle actin' in such a way as to put men an' their families on the streets, an' neither can I. It's true nobody 'as seen much o' him but 'e were a caring soul, never a bad word for nobody an' wouldn't 'arm a fly. But the other 'un, that Annie, 'er was a bad bugger from the start. No . . . if it was me 'ad to say who was the back of all this then it would be 'er as I'd name.'

Phoebe fingered her cup, looking at the tea she had not touched. 'Do you think Uncle Samuel knows what is happening?'

'If 'e don't then you ain't the one to tell 'im,' Sarah said sharply. 'That woman 'as 'armed you enough wi'out you givin' 'er the opportunity to do more. 'Er turned you out o' yer father's 'ouse, not carin' twopence where you went, an' naught but two frocks an' two pairs o' bloomers to go in.' She could have added that she had suspicions it was her aunt who had got her sent down for fifteen years, but bit this back. 'Mark my words an' keep well away from 'er, that woman is poison.'

What Sarah had said was true, her aunt had turned her out with virtually nothing, so perhaps it was true she was the one who'd sold off the mines. Phoebe stared at her tea, now cold in the cup. If only she could speak to Uncle Samuel, but she knew there was little chance of getting past his sister.

'So 'ow is it wi' you?' Sarah took the cup from Phoebe, going into the scullery and tipping the contents into the slop pail standing beneath the shallow ironstone sink.

'I am well, Sarah.' Phoebe watched a second cup of tea being poured.

'No after effects?'

Phoebe took the cup, adding sugar and milk. She knew what lay behind the question, knew it referred to the attack that had been made upon her, and knew also it was asked out of genuine feeling for her welfare and not morbid curiosity. 'No,' she answered, 'no after effects, though I am glad Mathew and Lucy are at Wiggins Mill with me.'

'And not only them, I 'ear.'

'You mean the Ingleses.' Phoebe sipped her tea, more from politeness than thirst. 'They were one of the families laid off. It seems the new owners had their own bargees. Mr Ingles and his wife and children were on the road when I came across them, I'm only thankful I could help them.'

'Turned out well for both of you so our Mathew tells me, but tek care, ma wench, don't get in so deep as you can't get out. 'Elpin' others is all well an' good so long as you don't get drownded in your own pity.'

'I'll try not to.' Phoebe smiled. 'And you and Joseph are always there to give me advice.'

'As long as you don't get too uppity to ask for it.'

'Joseph won't allow that.' Phoebe's smile widened. 'He never would allow Abel Pardoe's little girl to get above herself, and to him I am still a little girl.'

'Ar, Joseph always 'ad a soft spot for you.' Her tea finished, Sarah set her cup to one side. 'An' to 'im you always will be naught but a babby, but I knows an' you knows babbies 'ave a way o' growin', an' you be growin' to a beauty.'

'Has Joseph said yet who bought the mines?' Phoebe reached into the bag she had brought with her, her cheeks pink from the older woman's compliment.

'Nobody really knows, though Billy-me-Lord's agents 'ave been nosin' around for the last few days.'

'Sir William Dartmouth bought them!' Phoebe straightened up, her embarrassment forgotten.

'Like I says, nobody 'as spoke of 'im but I think as the facts says it theirselves. I reckon Billy-me-Lord be the new owner of the Crown and the Hobs Hill mines.'

Phoebe held the paper she had taken from her bag, her hand resting on the table, worry in her eyes as she looked at Sarah. 'I hope he doesn't make any more changes,' she said, 'people in the town need their jobs.'

'That be right an' don't be wrong,' Sarah agreed, taking two pots of damson jam from a cupboard. 'Pity that aunt o' your'n didn't 'ave the same feelin'.'

'What will happen . . . to men who might be finished, I mean?'

Sarah hesitated, a pot in each hand. 'Be my guess as young 'uns . . . they wi' no family to keep . . . will move on, the others'll like to stand the line.'

'Stand the line?'

'Ar,' Sarah nodded again, the movement slow and deliberate, 'men wantin' work gathers in the market place every mornin' an' stands in line 'opin' that any with work to be done will choose them. Some gets lucky and some goes wi'out . . .'

'The ones who are not chosen,' Phoebe's words dropped into the pause, 'what happens to them?'

Sarah sighed heavily. 'Work'ouse like as not, poor buggers.'

'Oh, no!' Phoebe's eyes widened. 'There must be something else.'

'Ain't nothin' else.' Sarah put the pots on the table. 'If you don't work you don't eat, not in this town. It's the work'ouse or starve, there be no such thing as charity in Wednesbury . . . things be too 'ard for them wi' next to nothin', an' them as 'ave plenty keep it to theirselves. That's the way of it, ma wench, an' you heed what I've told you an' don't go thinkin' you can tek on every man as gets 'is tin. That business o' your'n is doin' well enough but you ain't your father, you ain't Abel Pardoe.'

'No, I'm not Abel Pardoe,' Phoebe said quietly, 'but I am Abel's daughter.'

Phoebe walked toward Upper High Street, the pots of jam alongside the papers in her bag. She didn't get to visit Sarah as often as she would have liked and Joseph would be disappointed she had not waited to see him but as she had explained she was still not up to walking home alone, crossing the heath in darkness. This way she would finish her business and walk home with Mathew and Lucy.

She thought again of Sarah's pleased expression when she had shown her the poster now rolled up in her bag and told her how every shopkeeper she'd asked had agreed to display one in their premises. 'The Invincible', it proclaimed in two-inch type, 'Pardoe's Patent Locks'. They would be seen by all who used the shops, and for those who didn't she was on her way to the office of the *Express and Star*; an advertisement in the newspaper would reach every businessman in the town.

'Good day, Miss Pardoe.'

Phoebe turned at the sound of her name. She glanced first at the figure in tall hat and dark knee-length coat, then at the building he was vacating, and couldn't quite repress a shudder. The Magistrate had sentenced her to fifteen years from that building. 'Good afternoon, Sir William,' she returned.

'It was my intention to call upon you later in the day.' He replaced the hat held raised as he spoke.

'Perhaps I can save you the bother of the journey.' Phoebe wanted to move on, move away from that building and the memories it evoked.

'It is no bother, Miss Pardoe.' Grey eyes that could so easily be black regarded her evenly.

'Nevertheless it is some distance and an uncalled for journey if I can help you here.'

'I wished to tell you the man who attacked you has been gaoled. But we can't talk here . . .' He glanced at the women, their heads draped in shawls, who'd turned to look in their direction as Phoebe caught her breath sharply, a hand touching her throat. 'My carriage is to the rear.'

Gaol! Phoebe tried to breathe past the lump filling her throat. She would not wish a gaol sentence on any man, but for what he had tried to do to her . . .

'May I drive you home? I will give you the details on the way.'

'Home? No . . .' The spectres of that man's attack and of Handsworth Women's Prison fused together in her mind. 'I . . . I am not going home.'

'Then maybe we can talk inside.'

'No!' Phoebe's cry as he indicated the Green Dragon Hotel drew fresh inquisitive stares. 'I . . . I'm sorry, Sir William,' she said, 'I have no wish ever to enter that place again.'

He glanced first at the hotel and then at her, realisation dawning. The Magistrates' Court. Of course, she must have been sentenced from here. 'My apologies,' he said, 'I had not thought.'

'It is of no consequence.' Phoebe looked up, not all traces of fear gone from her face. 'If you have finished what you had to say . . .'

'I have not finished.' William Dartmouth interrupted what he knew to be a dismissal. 'If you will not allow us to speak somewhere else then it will be said here on the street. It seems one of my wife's maids overheard Sophie and her mother discussing our meeting that morning at the Priory. She presumed I had given you money and said as much to a man she was walking out with. He in turn thought to take it from you. That man is now in custody and will be spending a very substantial part of his life behind bars.'

'And the maid?' Phoebe asked. 'Is she to be dismissed her position as Lucy was?'

'Lucy?' He drew his brows together enquiringly.

'Mrs Leach, the girl you questioned at Wiggins Mill.'

'Why did she not come to me sooner with what she knew of what had happened to the necklace? Why say nothing until I questioned her?'

'Because she was warned not to.'

'Warned not to?' He frowned. 'Just what exactly does that mean?'

Phoebe looked straight at him. 'It means,' she said, her voice calm and clear, 'that Lucy was warned that to involve Ed— your son – in the affair would prove disastrous for her. She tried telling Lawyer Siveter what she knew but he said you would see to it she came to regret bringing the Dartmouth name under suspicion, then she was dismissed your wife's services.'

'She was in service at the Priory?' he asked, then before Phoebe answered, added, 'I was unaware of that, it had not occurred to me. Perhaps you will be good enough to tell Mrs Leach she will be reinstated immediately.'

No apology, Phoebe thought, no word of regret for what had happened to Lucy, just a calm proposal of her reinstatement.

'Does it not occur to you that she may have no wish to return to your employment?' she asked coldly.

Sir William Dartmouth looked at the young woman, her eyes cool and steady, and found the admiration he had first felt at their earlier meetings re-kindling in him. Not many men would speak to him as she did: his title and his money made no impression upon her and certainly did not intimidate her.

'That must be her prerogative – if you will forgive the use of the word "must".' The faintest hint of a smile appeared at the corners of his mouth. 'I wish you good day Miss Pardoe.'

'You said that?' Lucy asked later when Phoebe told her of her encounter. 'You said that to Billy-me-Lord?'

'I did,' Phoebe smiled broadly. 'Naughty of me, wasn't it?'

'Naughty or no, I bet it took the wind out o' 'is sails.'

'He did look somewhat surprised,' Phoebe said, still smiling.

'What did 'e 'ave to say to that?'

Waiting while Lucy served a customer to the last of her scones, giving her change from a sixpenny piece, Phoebe answered, 'He said that must be your prerogative.'

'My what?' Lucy shook her head as a woman, shawl drawn tight about her shoulders, enquired after a meat pie. 'What on earth does that mean?'

'It means that yours must be the choice. You can return to work at the Priory tomorrow if you wish, his wife will return you to the position you held there before.'

'Oh, ar.' Lucy sniffed scornfully. 'I'll be there bright an' early in me best cardi an' me boots blacked . . . like bloody 'ell I will! Go back to skivvyin' for the Dartmouths? I'd sooner go on the roads.'

'Were they unkind to you?' Phoebe watched the hurrying women pass from stall to stall, their purchases shoved into deep-bottomed baskets draped over one arm.

'The Dartmouths?' Lucy handed a broken scone she had placed to the side of her own stall to a small girl, her face pinched and thin, a ragged dress hanging from her bony shoulders, receiving a smile in payment. 'Not Miss Sophie or 'er mother, an' I never 'ardly seen Edward or the master. No, it was that lot below stairs. Talk about mean! They'd take the sugar out o' your tea an' then come back for the milk . . . no, I ain't goin' back there no more.'

''Ow much for this?'

A woman in skirts that had parted from their colour long ago and now hung like panels of rust from below her chequered shawl touched a finger to a child's white dress, its full skirts edged with a ribbon of cornflower blue, another of the same caught around the waist.

'Six an' eleven to you, luv.' Lucy smiled encouragingly. 'It's a lovely little frock an' all muslin.'

'It be pretty enough,' the woman ran a wistful eye over

the dress, 'an' my Ginny would look a picture in that come Sunday.' She looked at Lucy. ''Er's to be confirmed.'

Holding the dress closer to the woman, Lucy spread its skirts. 'Bein' confirmed, is 'er? Well, 'er couldn't 'ave a prettier frock for it than this.'

'That's right enough,' the woman fingered the dainty material, 'but 'er wouldn't get much wear out o' it after. It ain't the stuff to stand up to wear.'

'Muslin is stronger than it seems,' Lucy said, 'an' it's so easy to wash. You only needs to show this to the wash tub an' the dirt drops out o' it nor it needs no ironin' neither.'

'It *is* a special day.' The woman lingered. ''Er won't never get confirmed again, but near enough seven shillin' for a frock . . . that'd keep the kids for a week.'

'It might do,' Lucy withdrew the dress a fraction, 'but which would your little wench remember longest – a meal or the lovely frock 'er mother bought for 'er confirmation?'

'You'm right!' The woman drew a purse from the depths of her rusty skirts. 'I'll tek it, an' what me old man don't know 'e can't grieve over.'

Lucy wrapped the dress in a piece of brown paper, religiously saved from cloth Phoebe had bought from the draper and haberdasher in Upper High Street. ''Er'll do you proud in this,' she said, handing the woman a penny change.

'You know,' the woman wedged her package on top of those already in her basket, 'if I was the one made these frocks you wouldn't find me in Wednesbury for long.'

''Ow do you mean?' Lucy shot a sidelong glance at Phoebe.

'Well, they'm so pretty, ain't they? I tell you, if I 'ad the touch in me fingers to make such I would be in one o' they big fancy places like Brummagem or London. Folk there would pay twice as much for summat like this.' Returning the purse to her pocket, the woman turned away.

'You know, Miss Phoebe,' Lucy watched the customer, her old-fashioned black bonnet set on top of hair turned prematurely grey, disappear among the shoppers, 'I reckon there be some Wednesbury folk got more in their 'eads than coal dust.'

'But there is one at least with six shillings and elevenpence less in her purse,' Phoebe answered solemnly. 'Do you really think she should have spent so much on a dress? She said it would have kept the children for a week.'

'Don't you worry about that one,' Lucy said, after selling a woman a pink petticoat. 'If 'er couldn't 'ave afforded it 'er wouldn't 'ave bought it. 'Sides, 'er will sell it for four or five shillin' once 'er own kid be finished wi' it an' then when next one be too big for it, it will fetch a couple o' bob from somebody else, an' after they be done it'll still fetch a tanner or so from old Kilvert. There's always customers at the pawnshop either pledging bundles in or buying.'

'As I bought this.' Phoebe touched one hand to her jade green suit, the jacket trimmed with darker green frogging.

'You paid for it, didn't you?' Lucy said, a slightly indignant note in her voice. 'You didn't beg from nobody so you 'ave nothin' to feel 'shamed over. 'Sides it suits you, it really does. You look lovely, Miss.'

'Lovely enough to impress the printer?' Phoebe smiled.

'You'll knock 'is eyes out.' Lucy grinned. 'Just don't let 'im charge too much for that 'eaded notepaper an' order forms you be goin' to get 'im to print for you.'

'I won't.' Phoebe took the pots of jam from her bag. 'But could I leave these with you? I don't think Mr Simpson will be too impressed by my handing him two pots of damson jam with the designs for my bill headings.'

''E might take a bit off the price if you gives 'im a pot o' me mother-in-law's damson.' Lucy took the jam, setting it to the side of her stall. 'You never knows your luck.'

'I know I had better be off.' Phoebe closed her bag. 'I am putting off your customers.'

'Miss Phoebe,' Lucy said as she made to leave, 'mebbe you should wait for Mathew to come, let 'im go with you like? Might be best for a man to do the talkin'. After all, you ain't used to talkin' prices.'

'Then the sooner I get used to it, the better,' Phoebe said. 'I intend to be talking quite a lot of prices in the future and not all of them to a printer.'

Well, let's 'ope you stands up a bit stronger to that printer than you would to that woman just bought the frock, thought Lucy as Phoebe walked away. If I 'adn't been 'ere you would 'ave finished up givin' it to 'er. There's such a thing as bein' too soft . . .

'What did Simpson sting you for?' Mathew asked as the three of them walked home.

'A shilling a dozen.'

'A shilling a dozen!' Mathew was clearly disgusted. 'Why, that be pure bloody thievery. I'll go see 'im tomorrow an' tell 'im 'e can stick 'is bleedin' printin' wheer the monkey sticks its nuts. A shillin' a dozen! Who does 'e think 'e is coddin'?'

'He wasn't fooling me, Mathew.' Phoebe switched her bag from one arm to the other. Crammed now with butter and cheese, a pork hock wedged between the pots of jam, it weighed heavily.

'But a shillin' a dozen, Miss!' Lucy came in on Mathew's side. 'That does seem a bit steep.'

'I did not accept that price unconditionally.' Phoebe winced as her foot twisted against a stone. 'We came to an agreement.'

'An agreement?' Mathew sounded far from reassured. 'Like what?'

'Like fourpence a dozen when I order a gross or more.'

'Well, that's more like it.' Mathew hitched the hessian sack of potatoes higher on his shoulder. 'But will you ever be orderin' a gross?'

'I will be ordering many gross,' Phoebe answered, 'order forms, bill forms, receipts and notepaper, and the price will be the same for all of them.'

'Phew, steady on, Miss!' Mathew laughed. 'Lock business

191

be goin' well enough but I can't see it goin' on. After all, Wednesbury ain't all that big a town, it will only buy so many.'

'Mathew be right, Miss,' Lucy said. 'It don't pay to get carried away. Don't spend your money on fancy 'eaded paper you might never get to use.'

'Mathew *is* right,' Phoebe agreed, 'Wednesbury is not all that big a town. But then it is not the only town, and what we have sold in one town we can sell in another.'

'But 'ow?' Lucy made a detour, avoiding a puddle in the track. 'I mean, it takes folk to sell locks an' we . . . well, we all be busy doin' what we be doin'.'

'I have thought of that,' Phoebe said confidently. 'When the time comes I shall find somebody.'

'Always supposin' you find somebody to sell locks for you, Bert couldn't mek no more,' Mathew pressed home his point. ''E is workin' flat out now.'

'To say nothin' of 'avin' to buy in more metal,' Lucy supported her husband. 'An' that might be the 'orse you can't ride. Brass founders don't let stuff out on the strap, least not to likes of we they don't. You got to be big in business to get things first and pay later.'

What they were saying was perfectly reasonable. Phoebe trudged on in silence, but she had taken a gamble, made her play as her father would have said, and now she must follow it through.

Across the heath the windmill stood silent witness to one such as herself, Elias Webb, who had sold her Wiggins Mill, had made his play but for him the cards of fortune had not followed through. But hers would. Phoebe clenched her teeth, defying the laughter of the fates. One way or another she would win through, she had to if the Ingleses were not to be put back on the road.

''Ello, Miss, 'ello, Mrs Leach.' From the edge of the yard the Ingles children waved then raced to meet them, the boy leaving his sister in his wake.

'I will take that for you, Miss.' The boy took the bag from Phoebe, easing it on to his shoulder in imitation of Mathew before going to walk beside him, matching his step, in his own mind at least very much the man.

'I can carry summat as well as our Mark.' The girl looked up with serious eyes. 'I'm as strong as 'im.'

'No, you ain't.' Her brother sniffed scathingly. 'You be only a girl an' they ain't as strong as men, am they, Mr Leach?'

'They ain't that, lad.' Mathew grinned. 'But I reckon most of 'em be prettier an' our Ruthie be prettiest o' the lot.'

'But I am strong, me mother says my 'elp be in . . . in . . . invalible.'

'Well, I could certainly do wi' some 'elp,' Lucy said tactfully, 'this basket be fair breakin' my arm.' Lowering it to the ground, she took out a shank end of mutton wrapped in paper tied round with string, handing it to the child. 'If you could take that it would be a powerful 'elp.' She smiled at the small girl, the meat cradled like a doll in her arms. 'But you 'ave only to say if it gets to be too 'eavy. We 'ave two strong men 'ere can carry it.'

'I can carry it, Mrs Leach,' the child said proudly. 'I can do lots of things. I 'elped Mother make a 'ot pot today, peelin' 'tatoes an' carrots, an' 'er let me 'elp wi' jam roly poly.'

'That sounds like a real meal for a workin' man,' Mathew said. 'Jam roly poly, that's my favourite puddin', you'll 'ave to show Mrs Leach how it's done.'

'I will.' She looked up at Lucy, her little face wreathed in smiles. 'It's real easy.'

'I 'opes as you ain't fond o' too much jam in your roly poly,' the boy said, hitching the bag on his shoulder as Mathew hitched the potato sack.

'I like jam, the more the better,' Mathew answered.

'A pity that.'

'Why, don't you have any more jam?'

'Oh, ar, Miss,' the answer was jaunty, 'me mother 'as

another pot o' jam, but we don't get much on a roly poly. Least there won't be much on this'n.'

'Why not?' Phoebe asked as they crossed the yard to the house.

''Cos our Ruth keeps eatin' it!'

'So that's what meks 'er such a little sweet'eart.' Mathew lowered the sack of potatoes to the ground, sweeping the child into his arms and whirling round with her. 'Who wants jam when we 'ave our Ruthie?'

'It's time our Ruthie was in bed.' Lizzie Ingles came from the barn she had turned into a home, smiling at her daughter's delighted squeals. 'An' you too, my lad,' she said, looking at her son. 'I told the pair o' you more'n half an hour gone.' She turned to Phoebe. 'I never can get 'em to bed afore you all be back.'

'I wonder why?' Taking her bag from the boy, she drew out two fat round lollipops. 'It couldn't have something to do with these, could it?'

Shoving the joint of meat into Lucy's hands, the little girl jigged up and down, eyes shining at the promise of the sweet. 'I wants the red one.' She pulled at Phoebe's arm. 'It's my turn to 'ave the red one. Our Mark 'ad it last time.'

'Then if Mark had the red one last time it must be your turn to have it this time.' Phoebe handed her the sweet.

'I've got the red one!' The child jigged away, holding the lollipop in the air like some coveted trophy. 'I've got the red one!'

'You'll 'ave a red bottom, Ruth Ingles, if you don't say thank you,' Lizzie said sternly. 'You know better'n to take what somebody gives an' return no thanks. Whatever 'as 'appened to your manners, girl!'

The child stopped dancing. 'Beg pardon, Miss.' She came to Phoebe, her pretty mouth drooping. 'I'm mortal sorry.'

'That's all right, Ruth.' Phoebe caught the twitching of Lucy's mouth. 'I was always forgetting to say thank you when I was a little girl, and to tell you the truth I sometimes forget now.'

'Do you, Miss, do you honest?'

'Honest.' Licking a forefinger, Phoebe made the sign of the cross over her heart. 'Cross my heart and hope to die if what I have said is just a lie.'

'Ooh, you knows that an' all, you can't never say that if you 'ave told a lie.' The child's mouth lost its droop, turning upward in a smile. 'So you must be tellin' the truth, Miss, you do forget sometimes.'

We all do, Phoebe thought, bending to hug Lizzie's daughter, remembering playing the same scene so many times with her father. We all do.

'Now say goodnight.' Lizzie caught her daughter's hand as Phoebe released her.

'Goodnight.' The child lifted her face to each in turn, receiving a kiss on the cheek. 'Thank you, Mrs Leach, an' you, Mr Leach.'

'Why can't we make that Aunty Lucy and Uncle Mathew?' Lucy said, her face on a level with that of the child.

'I don't know if we could,' the answer came solemnly, 'it might not be 'lowed 'cos you ain't a real aunt, am you?'

'No,' Lucy said softly, 'but I love you as much as a real aunt, and Mr Leach loves you as much as a real uncle.'

'I'd like to,' the child said pensively, 'but I don't know if it's 'lowed.'

'Why don't we ask your mother?' Lucy looked up at the face of Lizzie Ingles.

'It's allowed.' The woman smiled, her eyes cloudy behind tears. 'It's allowed.'

Clasping her red lollipop in one hand, the other held by her mother, the girl walked away then stopped to look back at the three adults. 'I do love you all,' she said simply. 'I'm so glad we come to live 'ere.'

'I would like to call you Aunt and Uncle an' all if it's all right wi' you?'

Mathew looked at the face turned up towards his own, seeing the disappointments and knocks life had already dealt the young son of Bert Ingles, seeing apprehension of another. He held out his hand, shaking that of the boy offered to meet it. 'It's a sight more'n all right, Mark,' he answered huskily. 'That would mean more to me than a medal from the Queen.'

'I'm so glad we come to live 'ere.' The words echoed in her mind as later Phoebe prepared for bed. She was glad too. Having people about the place during the day gave her a feeling of security, and the knowledge they were close, combined with the locks on her doors, had given her confidence to sleep alone in the house, freeing Lucy and Mathew to go back to sleeping in their own home.

Yes, she was glad they had all come to live at Wiggins Mill. Picking up her nightgown from the bed, she held the soft cotton to her face, the memory of rough calico vivid in her mind. She was glad they were all here, Lucy and Mathew, the Ingleses with their children . . . if only she could have brought one more. If only she could have brought Tilly . . .

Chapter Fifteen

Annie Pardoe sat in the neat parlour of Brunswick House its
graceful bay window overlooking well-kept lawns. She paid
a man twice a week to see to the upkeep of the gardens
and made sure he earned his money. Annie Pardoe paid
no one to sit around. There had been little alteration since
Abel's time though she had seen to it that no laburnum or
yew grew there and had grubbed them out herself from the
garden of the house at Bescot years before. She caught her
breath, holding it till the twinge of pain below her left breast
subsided. Yes, she had grubbed them out – but not until she
had made good use of them.

'Papers, Miss.' Maudie Tranter entered the room, a newspaper neatly folded on a cloth-covered tray. Wait till you reads
that, she thought as Annie took the newspaper, you'll have
another shock. Making her way back to the kitchen Maudie
thought of what she had seen in the *Express and Star* and how
the woman in the parlour would react in the knowledge that
her housekeeper always read the newspaper before taking it
into her. Maudie enjoyed her thoughts.

In the parlour Annie spread the newspaper on the oval
mahogany table, fixing on to her nose the reading glasses
that hung on a silk string about her neck. She had made
a lifetime's habit of taking the papers, reading thoroughly
through them before allowing them to go to her brother.

'Hmmph!' she snorted, reading of certain elections to the
town council. 'Not an ounce of brain between the lot of
them.' Slowly she turned the pages, finding some reports

of interest to her, others not, but reading them all until her eye caught the advertisement.

Annie's fingers dropped to the corner of the page she had been about to turn, her eyes devouring the large caption: 'The Invincible'. The heading topped a representation of a lock under the sub-heading 'Pardoe's Patent Locks'. She read the advert through once and then again. Phoebe! She pressed a hand to her side but it did not still the pain biting beneath her breast. It could only be Phoebe!

Her thoughts flew to the man who had promised to make her his wife. What if he saw the advertisement? The name was the same, Pardoe, how long would it take him to wonder if it carried with it any relationship to her? He was no fool, he would put two and two together sharp enough, then how long before he found Pardoe's Patent Locks was run by her niece?

The pain jabbed viciously, bringing her teeth together, nostrils flaring with the effort of controlling it as she read the advert through again. If he should find out . . . if he discovered her niece had not quit Brunswick House of her own choice but had been virtually thrown out . . . And what of Samuel? What would his reaction be to seeing that piece in the newspaper? He had already made clear his intention of returning everything to Abel's daughter, what would he do when he found there was almost nothing to return? But it didn't matter what Samuel thought. Annie's eyes stayed glued to the advertisement. She had taken care her brother would never carry out his threat. No, it did not matter what Samuel knew, but Clinton . . . Clinton must never know. She would kill this lock business stone dead before it got started.

Leaving the newspaper on the table she walked upstairs to her bedroom. Slipping a smart grey day coat over her matching dress, she pinned a feathered bonnet over her hair. Clutching her bag, she went downstairs without calling in on her brother.

'I am going out,' she said as Maudie appeared from the kitchen, 'I don't know what time I shall be back.'

Maudie watched her mistress wriggle her fingers into grey chamois gloves. I was right, she thought, closing the door after the departing Annie, you've had a shock right enough and it won't be the last. And you taking to dressing up in fine colours won't ward them off. There be others waiting on you, Annie Pardoe, ones you won't walk away from.

Annie walked briskly along Spring Head, following it into the market place cutting across toward Great Western Street. She had not taken the horse and trap, they would be too conspicuous left standing outside the Great Western Railway Station, for today she meant to take the train to Birmingham.

'You can sit in the ladies' waitin' room, Mum, it's the next door along the platform. There be a nice fire burnin' in there.'

The man in the tiny ticket office touched a finger to the peak of his dark green cap as he handed Annie a ticket.

Putting it carefully into her bag, she nodded. It might be best to sit in the room set aside for women, there would not be many of them using the train, not when the steam tram was a cheaper way to travel. But today the train suited Annie. The fewer folk to see where she headed, the better pleased she felt.

Choosing a seat that gave a clear view of the door and of any who might choose to enter, Annie sat in the empty room. It was a bind having to go to Birmingham but it was safest. She would not be known there and there would be few in Wednesbury who knew that town in any detail. The advertisement she had read only an hour before lodged in her mind, till she felt her mouth tightening like a trap. The hundred pounds she had paid the Magistrate had been a total waste of money. What had it bought . . . a fifteen-year sentence that had been set aside after little more than one! What had that fool been about? He should have made the sentence one that couldn't so easily be revoked. It was a pity they had ceased transportation, that way Phoebe would have been out of the country, but now her niece was free and broadcasting her presence by way of advertisements, one at least published in the *Express and Star* and God only knew how many in other publications and places. Annie pressed her hands together in her lap. If you want a thing doing right, do it yourself. This time she would do it herself, and this time it would be done right.

The conductor's call of 'Snow Hill' told of having reached Birmingham and Annie alighted. Who was stupid enough to give a name like Snow Hill to this place? she wondered, taking in the soot-grimed archways of the railway station. Black Hill would have been more appropriate. Leaving the station, she followed the line of shops beside it; tailor, draper, grocer, milliner, each jostled the other, elbowing for room in the narrow streets, but she passed them by without a second look at the overcrowded windows. Pie shop, beer hall. Annie walked on, her eye scanning signs painted over shop fronts proclaiming the name of the proprietor and the wares he sold until she read: James Greaves, Hardware and Ironmongery.

Annie caught the train back to Wednesbury, six pot menders and six mousetraps in her bag. The purchase of these would raise no eyebrows in Brunswick House: pot menders were often used in her kitchen to close small holes worn in iron pots and pans and mousetraps were always set in the cellar. Mousetrap! She gazed through the window at the dingy houses set regimentally close alongside the railway line. The trap she was setting would catch more than a mouse . . .

'Has Mr Samuel been downstairs?' she asked when she reached the house.

'No, Ma'am,' Maudie answered. ''E took 'is lunch in 'is room though 'e didn't touch it none, an' when I popped in the studio about three o'clock 'e was asleep in 'is chair. 'E seems to 'ave slept more than ever these past few days.'

'That will be his medicine.' Annie took the pot menders and mousetraps from her bag, handing them to her housekeeper.

'The doctor increased the strength a little . . . you have been careful only to give him the prescribed dose?'

'Two teaspoonfuls, measured 'em out meself, Ma'am, an' 'e swallowed 'em right off, then 'e sat in 'is chair an' 'as been there all day far as I know.'

'And he ate nothing?'

'Nothin' at all,' Maudie shook her head, 'not even a bite. I carried 'is tray down same as I carried it up . . . nothin' 'ad been touched at all.'

'Perhaps a cucumber sandwich will tempt him?' Annie turned to the stairs. 'I will go in to him when I have removed my coat. Prepare a tray now.'

'Perhaps a cucumber sandwich will tempt him,' Maudie mimicked under her breath as Annie went up the stairs. 'As if she cares whether he eats anything or not. It's all bloody top show wi' that one an' underneath it all 'er couldn't care twopence whether the poor bugger lives or dies!'

In the kitchen Maudie put the hardware on the dresser and stood looking at it. Pot menders and mousetraps, nothing unusual in that – 'cept Annie Pardoe never bought anything without it had been asked for a dozen times and she, Maudie, hadn't asked for either. And why walk into the town, why hadn't she taken the horse and trap as always? And why jaunt off down into Wednesbury to get them herself when she could have had them sent up with provisions? Taking out a tray she spread it with a freshly laundered cloth and set it with china. Annie Pardoe was up to summat as sure as God made little apples, Maudie told herself, and like as not Samuel wouldn't come out of it too well.

In her room Annie spread the newspaper she had brought up from the parlour. She had spent a couple of hours with her brother before leaving him for the night. She turned a page. He had not eaten a cucumber sandwich earlier and neither had he taken any dinner, but she had expected that. She turned a second page. She had told Maudie Tranter she would go herself tomorrow and ask the doctor to call. But that would do nothing for Samuel. Her eyes scanned the columns of print, coming to rest on the advertisement for Pardoe's Patent Locks. No, nothing would help Samuel.

Going to the marble-topped washstand she slid open the narrow drawer that ran almost the full width of it, taking a sheet of paper from beneath the pile of towels. Returning to the table, she placed it beside the newspaper then took from her bag the bottle of ink and the cheap pen she had bought before taking the train back to Wednesbury. Reading the advert through one last time, Annie dipped the pen into the ink and began to write.

Phoebe heard the crunch of carriage wheels along the track and put aside the dress she had almost finished making. Going to the window, she watched it drive to the front of the house, her feelings mixed. She liked Edward, liked him very much, and was happy for him to call . . . but if only he would call less often. She had tried to tell him of her need to work, to explain the strong necessity for it, but he only said to marry him and be done with tiresome necessities.

She watched him climb from the carriage, the light glinting on his fair hair. She knew he loved her and that he would do his best to make marriage to him happy . . . so why couldn't she say yes? Why wouldn't she marry Edward Dartmouth? Turning from the window, Phoebe left the room. She didn't know why.

'Phoebe, I am so glad you are home. I told Edward we ought to send a card before we visited.'

'Sophie, how nice.' Phoebe's smile was a mixture of pleasure and relief. She had turned from the window before seeing Sophie and now the pleasure of her visit brought the added relief of not having to walk with Edward.

· 'Don't bother with tea,' Sophie said when Phoebe offered refreshments, 'just sit down and listen. You are invited to a farewell ball.'

'A ball?' Phoebe was surprised. 'Where?'

'At the Priory.' Sophie's face glowed with delight. 'Where else did you think!'

'That's just it,' Phoebe said, 'you gave me no time to think.'

'What is there to think of?' Sophie rushed on. 'Father is giving a ball and you are invited. There is nothing to be thought about.'

Phoebe looked from Sophie to Edward. 'You said a farewell ball?'

'My mother is to leave for Europe sooner than had been intended.' He smiled, misreading the reason for the question in her eyes. 'The influenza she suffered recently has not cleared as we would have hoped and her physician has recommended a warmer climate.'

'I am sorry to hear your mother is not yet fully recovered,' Phoebe returned her gaze to Sophie, 'please give her my regards.'

'Oh, Mother is not too ill,' Sophie burst out with the thoughtless disloyalty of youth, 'she simply has an over-fondness for Italy, and of course we have to go too which means I will not see Montrose for several more months. The whole thing would be totally unbearable were it not for the shopping en route. You really can buy the most exquisite lace in Paris. I intend to buy my whole trousseau there. Montrose . . .'

'My mother and sister cannot travel alone,' Edward put in as his sister paused for breath, 'I am to travel with them to our villa in Tuscany then I shall return.'

'Will that not be doubling a journey?' Phoebe asked, knowing he had interrupted Sophie because he hated to think of her with Montrose Wheeler and wanting to spare him as much as possible. 'To have to return to Italy again to escort your mother home will be very tiring.'

He smiled, the thought of her concern for him deepening the vivid blue of his eyes. 'I will not be returning there a second time,' he explained. 'My father will be joining Sophie and Mother after Christmas. He will bring them home.'

'With us leaving in two weeks there will be no Advent Ball at the Priory this year,' Sophie burbled on, 'hence the idea of a farewell ball. Mother has sent invitations to absolutely everybody and here is yours.' She took a cream vellum envelope from her bag, handing it to Phoebe. 'It will be absolutely wonderful and I hope to persuade Father to let Montrose announce . . .'

'It is kind of your parents to invite me,' Phoebe cut in but this time it was not to spare Edward, 'though I cannot accept.' She could not attend a ball at the Priory, she hadn't a suitable gown for one thing, and to ask her to one which Montrose would be attending . . . hadn't anyone told Sophie the man she wanted to marry had already been engaged to the daughter of Abel Pardoe, and had broken that engagement when he found out she had no money?

'But why?' Sophie demanded. 'Is it because of Montrose? You have no cause for worry there, Phoebe. He told me what happened himself. Told me you asked to be freed from your engagement to him – that after the shock of your father's death you felt you could not marry for some time, and later you found you no longer loved him and begged him not to hold you to your promise so of course he did not. But now he loves me and we are to be married. And you,' she squeezed Phoebe's hand, 'are not to worry over my feelings. You are to accept Mother's invitation and that is that!'

So Montrose had told Sophie! Phoebe glanced at Edward, reading the distaste in his face. It was not her recollection of events she had just heard but what effect would it have on Sophie should she ever find out the true story? And what effect would it have should she discover Montrose was marrying her purely and simply for her money; that for him love played no part in marriage.

'I'm so excited,' Sophie trilled on, 'I am to have a new gown, pink, Montrose says I look ravishing in pink . . .'

I wore a pink gown on our last evening together. Phoebe's thoughts suppressed Sophie's voice, drowning it in waves of memory. Montrose said I too looked ravishing in the colour. He held me in his arms while he vowed his love for me, while he told me he could not wait for our marriage, while he told me the same lies.

'. . . he is to get leave from his regiment . . .'

Wrenching her thoughts back to the present, Phoebe glanced across to where Edward sat.

'Sophie dear,' he rose, 'we really must not take any more of Phoebe's time.'

The girl jumped to her feet, colour rising to her cheeks. 'I'm sorry, Phoebe, I do prattle on. Mother is always telling me about it.'

'And so am I,' Edward laughed, 'to say nothing of Father's efforts in that direction, all of which are wasted.

'You will come, Phoebe?' He hung back as Sophie reached the carriage.

'It's not possible, Edward.'

'Why not?' The intensity of his question was echoed in the pressure of the hands he placed on her arms. 'Is it because of my forgetting that damned necklace?'

Releasing herself from his grip, Phoebe glanced at his sister but her back was still turned to them.

'You know it isn't, Edward.'

He looked at her, frustration and the need to know lending his eyes a desperation she had not seen before. 'Then why, Phoebe?' he asked hoarsely. 'Why?'

'Edward,' she smiled patiently as though dealing with a demanding child, 'for a single girl to attend a ball she requires a female chaperone or a male escort. It might have escaped your notice that I have neither of these, on top of which I own no gown suitable for a ball.'

'The escort part might have eluded me,' Edward admitted, his eyes clearing, 'but it had not escaped my father. He has expressed the wish that you give your permission for me to be your escort for the evening, and I sincerely hope you will agree. As for a gown, I . . .'

'No.' Phoebe cut short the offer she knew would follow. She would take none of the Dartmouths' money, not even enough to buy a gown to attend their ball; she wanted no reparation and she certainly did not want their charity. 'Thank you, Edward, but I prefer to provide my own gown.'

'Then you will come!'

'I think you had better be going.' Phoebe avoided answering what was more statement than question. 'Your sister is waiting.'

'A ball, and with Edward Dartmouth your escort!' Lucy held the cream card with its gold edging as though it were a priceless object. 'Eeh, Miss Phoebe, how lovely. What will you wear?'

'Nothing.' Phoebe took the card, putting it behind a jug that held pride of place on the dresser.

'Well, that'll give the women the vapours and the men a rare treat, though I 'adn't thought it of you, to go 'ob nobbin' in naught but that you were born in, Miss Phoebe.' Mathew stood in the doorway of the scullery.

'Trust a man to be there with 'is ears flappin'.' Lucy turned a reproving look as her husband grinned. 'What you be in 'ere after anyway, Mathew Leach?'

Phoebe smiled, joining in with his infectious grin. 'Yes, what do you be in 'ere after?' she asked, using the same lazy dialect, 'listenin' to wenches gossipin'.'

'Well, you be wi' one can do that all right.'

'Don't push your luck, me lad.' Lucy stretched a hand ominously towards an iron pot set on the hob.

'All right, all right.' Mathew raised both hands in a gesture of surrender. 'Bert says to tell you, Miss, as brass for locks be runnin' pretty low.'

'He knows he can get more whenever he needs it.'

'Ar, 'e do know,' Mathew answered, 'but 'e still reckons to tell you beforehand like, says that's the way it should be.'

'Tell him to get what he thinks necessary,' Phoebe said.

'I will come see him myself as soon as I finish helping Lucy with tomorrow's baking.'

'What did you mean when you said you would wear nothing to the Priory ball?' Lucy whisked about the kitchen gathering utensils.

'What I said.' Phoebe lifted the pot from the hob, placing it on a cloth she had set on a corner of the well-scrubbed table, then set about pounding the boiled potatoes with a wooden spoon. 'I will be wearing nothing to the Dartmouths' ball for the simple reason that I will not be going.'

'Eeh, Miss Phoebe, whyever not?' Lucy was already wrist-deep in flour.

'I can't Lucy.' Phoebe attacked the potatoes with a new savagery. 'I . . . I wouldn't feel right. Everyone there will know what my aunt did.'

Lucy banged lard indignantly into the flour, sending it surging upward in a cloud. 'Ar, they will, an' they'll know what an old bitch 'er is an' all.'

Phoebe ladled cubes of mutton into the mashed potato, folding them in with the spoon. 'They will also know about the business of the necklace.'

'That an' all.' Lucy rolled the pastry. 'An' they'll see that the Dartmouths 'old nothin' against you . . . not that there be anythin' for 'em to 'old . . . but you see what I mean. Billy-me-Lord can't be apologisin' any more clear, an' that's what 'e be doin'. In front of the 'ole bloomin' county 'e's apologisin', an' your refusin' to go to that ball be like chuckin' 'is apology right back in 'is face. It do an' all, Miss Phoebe.'

She had not thought of it in those terms. Phoebe watched Lucy working dexterously at her pie-making. This could well be Sir William and Lady Dartmouth's way of proclaiming the fact she had been wrongly accused of stealing their daughter's necklace and that despite her lack of fortune she was accepted in their home. For her to refuse would be seen as churlish, and worse, in her own eyes, would rank as rudeness. But to attend . . .

'I realise how my refusal may be received, Lucy, but it can't be helped. I haven't a dress anywhere near grand enough for such an occasion.'

'Is that all? Lord, it would take a bloody sight more than that to keep me from goin' to a grand do like that. Surely you ain't gonna let a frock keep you from it?'

'Not a frock, more the lack of one.'

'That be nothin' as can't be remedied,' Lucy said, watching Phoebe carry pies to the oven and load them in. 'You can buy a frock easy as winkin'.'

'You can if you have money, which I have not . . . well, not to spend on ball gowns anyway. They cost a small fortune.'

'Spendin' some on yourself won't 'urt for once.'

'Spending that much would. I need that money to buy metal if we are to go on producing locks. I will not throw it away on a gown I will never wear again.'

'I seen a lovely bolt o' satin in Underwood's window,' Lucy sounded almost matter-of-fact, 'the loveliest shade of pale yellow you ever did see – just like butter cream. Make a bostin' frock it would.'

'Make!' Phoebe stopped filling pies to stare at Lucy. 'I couldn't make a ball gown.'

'O' course you could.' Lucy loaded her bowl with a fresh helping of flour, adding salt and lard. 'You already makes frocks, don't you?'

'Little ones, yes.'

Lucy looked up from rubbing fat into flour. 'Well, then! this will be the same 'cept bigger.'

Phoebe half smiled. Lucy made it all sound so easy, make herself a gown . . . as if nothing were simpler. Supposing she did manage to make a gown, that would only be a part of what she would need. There were other things.

'A dress is not the whole of it, Lucy,' she said. 'Given that I had one, I would also require gloves and shoes . . . a bag . . . a fan. And jewellery, what of jewellery? I have absolutely nothing in that line at all. The last of Grandmother's pieces went before . . . before . . .'

'Before you were sent to prison,' Lucy finished for her. 'Jewellery be a bit o' a sticky 'un. Wonder if Bert could make anything?'

Phoebe set the second batch of pies aside, spreading the white huckaback cloth over them until there was room in the oven. 'Mr Ingles is not a jeweller.'

'I know 'e ain't.' Lucy paused from mixing dough. 'But 'e makes things out o' brass, don't 'e?'

'Brass is not gold. If it were we would be quite wealthy for there is several pounds of it in the workshop.'

'Pity it isn't,' Lucy floured the wooden pin and board then scooped the dough from the bowl a few quick light movements rolling it into a creamy mat, 'I wouldn't mind bein' wealthy . . . not too much, mind you,' she grinned cheekily, 'just enough to make the 'ole of Wednesbury sit up and take notice.'

'Oh, I understand,' Phoebe laughed, 'nothing too blatant . . . just the odd million would do.'

'I just thought as seein' Bert was so 'andy with the brass like 'e might be able to make summat as would pass for jewellery,' Lucy said when they both stopped laughing.

'And how would I explain my neck turning a delicate shade of green halfway through the evening?'

'Oh, ar!' Lucy grimaced wryly but her eyes were laughing still. 'I 'adn't thought o' that. Mind, that would put you one up over the nobs . . . you'd 'ave summat they 'adn't got.'

'How very true. But I think I prefer to do without a green neck. It doesn't seem me somehow.'

'No! Well, p'raps you be right.' Taking the last remnants of dough Lucy shaped it into the figure of a man, giving it sultana eyes and four sultana buttons.

'Ruth doesn't like sultanas,' Phoebe said as Lucy blobbed jam where a nose would be.

'I know, but Mark does!' Lucy sprinkled the figure with

a coating of sugar before placing it in the tin alongside the scones, then looked across the table to where Phoebe was watching. 'Seriously though, Miss, apart from the jewellery there ain't nuthin' you couldn't get if you wanted to go to that ball.'

'I will not spend a great deal of money on . . .'

'You wouldn't 'ave to,' Lucy said quickly. 'Gloves you can get from Underwood's, ones that reach up over the elbow for no more than ninepence. An' they 'as feathers an' buttons. Eh, Miss, wi' your sewin' I reckon as you could make a lovely frock for little or nuthin'.'

'Hardly nothing.' Phoebe covered the scones then began to take cooked pies from the oven. 'How much is the material going to cost? Think how many yards it will take . . . Lucy, the whole thing is out of the question.'

'I don't know how many yards it'll take nor 'ow much the cost would be!' Lucy banged bowls and dishes together impatiently. 'An' neither do you 'cos you ain't asked so 'ow can you say it be out of the question? An' afore you says anythin' about shoes an' the costin' o' them you could always try John Kilvert's place.'

Phoebe straightened up, her cheeks reddened by the heat of the oven. 'A pawn shop!' she exclaimed. 'A pawn shop is not going to have dance slippers.'

'There you goes again!' Lucy rattled spoons and knives into the large mixing bowl. 'You'm a right one for reachin' a answer afore askin' the question, Miss Phoebe. Who's to say what old Kilvert 'as got stored away in that pawn shop . . . it ain't always the ones looks down an' out is down an' out, there be others 'ad to visit 'im, others popped pledges as they couldn't redeem.'

'But dance slippers?' Phoebe shook her head. 'Really, Lucy, I can't see there being such as that in a pawn shop.'

'You said that when that old brown cloak o' your'n got to be too bad off lookin' to go into town in any more, but you found that good green suit in one. What I says is if you don't try you won't know. Time to say a thing can't be done after you 'ave tried an' not t'other way round.'

She could always ask, she didn't have to buy anything. Ninepence for gloves . . . say threepence for second hand slippers . . . twopence for a dozen buttons . . . trimmings . . .

Gathering the rest of the used dishes from the table, she followed Lucy into the scullery.

Maybe it could be done, but jewellery, what of that? Phoebe smiled inwardly. Perhaps the Queen may have pawned the Crown Jewels.

'Lucy,' she asked, 'you did say the satin you saw in Underwood's shop window was a *pale* yellow?'

'Yes, Miss.' Lucy looked up from scouring pots. 'A lovely colour it be, like butter fresh from the dairy. Set your colourin' off to a tee it would.'

Pale yellow. Phoebe picked up the drying cloth and began to wipe the dishes Lucy had stacked on the board beside the sink. At least it wasn't pink.

Annie Pardoe wrote quickly, her well-formed copperplate hand rapidly covering the sheet of paper. She had bought the ink and the pen in Birmingham, that way she did not have to use that which was on the desk in the study, and the paper together with its envelope was the last of a birthday gift she had received from Abel many moons ago. She had kept one sheet of paper and one envelope, hiding them away for so many years, hiding them away but never forgetting them, knowing only that one day they would serve to hit back at him. Abel had died before she had found a way to strike, but that would not rob her of the revenge she had longed for all these years. Abel might be beyond her reach but his flesh and blood were not.

Folding the sheet of anonymously white notepaper she slipped it into the same self-effacing envelope, sealing it before writing an address across it in the same sure style. Abel was in his grave but his daughter was not. Slipping the envelope into her bag, she replaced the top on the bottle of ink, wiped the pen nib on a scrap torn from a corner of the newspaper, then slipped both into her bag alongside the letter.

Tearing the advert from the newspaper she slipped it into the drawer of the washstand, burying it beneath the towels. Abel was beyond her vengeance but she would destroy his daughter.

Thrusting a long hat pin through her hat, fastening it securely to her head, Annie checked her bedroom with a long seeking stare. The newspaper was folded neatly against her bag, the scrap of ink-stained paper was in the pocket of her coat, there was no sign of a letter having been written. Taking up her bag and the newspaper she left the room, passing that of her brother without looking in.

'Mr Samuel is still sleeping,' she said as she entered the kitchen, the lie sliding easily from her tongue. 'I thought it best not to disturb him. Take him a breakfast tray at eleven o'clock. I am going to ask the doctor to call, I am not at all sure Mr Samuel's health is improving despite the medicines.' Going into the scullery she deposited the newspaper with others kept in a wooden soap box alongside the stove to be used for lighting the house fires, then carried on, leaving the house by the rear door.

'Don't think Mr Samuel's health is improving?' Maudie watched from the scullery window. 'O' course it ain't improvin' an' you don't care for all you pretend to. You don't fool me, Annie Pardoe, you don't fool Maudie Tranter not for one minute you don't. You tell me you be going to fetch the doctor but it be my guess you be about more than that. You be up to summat, that much I be certain sure of, up to summat as sure as God med little apples.'

Standing to the side of the window so her watching presence would not easily be seen from outside Maudie waited until Annie had left, driving her small trap around to the front of the house. And still Maudie waited. She wouldn't put it past that sly bitch to come back into the house from the front. For several minutes she stood listening then, assured her mistress had gone, crossed the scullery to the soap box. Picking up the top newspaper she checked the date printed on the front page and smiled mirthlessly. 'You 'ave to get up early o' a mornin' to catch me, Annie, ma wench,' she murmured, then scanned the date on several papers until she found the one delivered to the house the day before. Turning to the page number she had made a mental note of, she smiled again. The advertisement for Pardoe's Patent Locks was missing.

Annie drove the trap at a steady walking pace, she was in no hurry and had no desire to draw attention to herself. She spoke to no one and none spoke to her, her long practice of ignoring people producing in them an almost total disregard for her. Passing to the left of Oakeswell Hall she skirted the black and white Tudor house, following the track across open ground the locals called the Mounts and coming around towards Hill Top. At the foot of the swell of ground Annie reined in the horse and sat looking at the black-grey water. Millfield Pool had formed when several gin pits had flooded, their vertical shafts filling with water which merged at the surface to form a large pond. The flooding of those shafts had taken many men, drowning them in their sludgy surging tide before they could scramble free, and it had taken others since.

Taking pen and ink from her bag she climbed from the trap and walked to the rim of ground overlooking the pool. 'You robbed me, Abel,' she whispered to the still menace lying at her feet, 'you robbed me of my life. Now watch while I rob your daughter of hers.'

Throwing the small bottle she saw it wing outward then thump into the water. She sent the pen after it, standing watching the spreading circles mark their watery grave. Taking the scrap of paper from her pocket, she stared at it for several moments. 'Vengeance is mine, Abel,' she whispered, rolling the paper between her fingers and letting it drop into her palm. Slowly raising her arm, stretching it out towards the water in macabre benediction, she tipped her hand, letting the balled scrap roll off the tips of her fingers. 'Vengeance is mine!'

Chapter Sixteen

'I wrote me name for it, Miss, I 'opes as that be all right? I 'ad no way of knowin' 'ow long you would be like, an' the postman, well, 'e 'ad other letters 'e 'ad to be deliverin'.' Lizzie Ingles's features struggled between a worried frown and an uncertain smile. 'I thought as if I wrote me name to say as I 'ad taken it in place o' you it would be all right.'

'It is all right, Lizzie, thank you.' Phoebe smiled and the other woman's face brightened. 'I wonder who it can be from?' She turned the white envelope but apart from the address written in neat flowing copperplate it bore no identifying mark.

'Only one way to find that out, Miss,' Lizzie said. 'That be to open it an' read it, an' that be best done over a nice cup o' tea.'

'I agree with you there, Lizzie.' Phoebe picked up the brown paper-wrapped parcel she had set down at her feet as Lizzie had met her. 'It's a fair walk from the Tipton Road. I got a ride from the carter as far as there but even so I am ready for a sit down and a drink.'

'Would you like me to make it for you, Miss?'

'That's good of you, Lizzie, but you must have work enough without waiting on me.'

'Nothing as will take 'arm from waitin' a while.' Lizzie opened the door that led into the mill house through the scullery and waited for Phoebe to pass inside. 'Bert an' Mark be in the workshop an' the babby be playin' around the back there.'

'Then you have time to join me. I will enjoy a cup of tea the more for having your company.'

Phoebe placed the parcel on the table in the kitchen, the letter beside it, unbuttoning her coat and hanging it beside the old brown cloak she kept now for working about the yard. 'I will take it upstairs later,' she said, seeing Lizzie eye the coat she needed to keep looking its best.

'I'll run it up for you, Miss.' Lizzie released the coat from its nail, her boots rattling on the stairs as she whisked up to Phoebe's bedroom.

'You really shouldn't,' Phoebe said as the woman skipped back in to the kitchen. 'You will have me too idle to scratch myself.'

'You, idle!' Lizzie poured boiling water on the fresh tea leaves waiting in the pot. 'That'll be the day. I've yet to come across a wench as works 'arder'n you an' I've met a few in me time. You sews most o' the day, then you 'elps with the filin' down o' the locks in the workshop, then o' nights you 'elps Lucy wi' 'er cookin'. No, you ain't idle, Miss. Whatever thoughts you might be 'oldin' about yourself that 'un be wrong.'

'I bought the most beautiful material for a gown.' Phoebe began to untie the string securing the parcel, Lizzie's compliment painting her cheeks a ripe pink. 'It is every bit as lovely as Lucy said and not nearly as expensive as I would have thought.'

'Eh, that's real pretty!' Lizzie made to touch the delicate lemony-cream fabric then pulled her hand away. 'An' it be just the colour for you with your hair.'

'There were others.' Phoebe added milk and sugar to the tea Lizzie poured for her. 'Green, blue, a really deep scarlet and a soft sugary pink. They were all so nice I was spoiled for choice.'

Sweetening her own tea, Lizzie sat opposite Phoebe in the warm kitchen. This girl must have had silks and finery, all the comfort and luxury her father's money could buy, and yet it hadn't spoilt her. There was nothing bay-windowed about her, and nothing vicious either. Even the months spent in that rat hole of a gaol hadn't altered her nature. Lizzie drank her tea. That son of Dartmouth's came visiting too regular for it to be a way of apologising for what he had done. His sort might say it once if you were lucky but not a couple of times a week. There was more to his coming than that. He was looking to make this wench his wife and if he got to do it he could count himself fortunate. This one would be no high-faluting, sit-on-her-arse lady of the manor. This one would care for the folk who worked for her.

'I got these to go with it.' Phoebe delved into the basket she had carried, taking out an assortment of buttons and lace. 'I thought feathers might be a little too much, what do you think?'

'I think you made just the right choice.' Lizzie admired the lace and touched a finger to the pretty pearl buttons. 'You'll be pretty as a picture, Miss, an' no coddin'.'

'But a ball gown,' Phoebe said, holding the elbow-length gloves she had bought against the material, then looking worriedly at Lizzie. 'I hope I haven't taken on more than I can handle. A ball gown . . . it's so different from a child's dress.'

'A bit fancier, Miss, I'll give you that,' said Lizzie, gathering the teacups, 'an' a bit on the bigger side, but that be all an' that ain't different, not really.'

'You make it sound so easy,' Phoebe called after her into the scullery, 'I almost believe it myself.'

Lizzie returned from the scullery drying her hands on her rough apron. 'You believe it, Miss, 'cos it be the truth. Lizzie Ingles wouldn't lead you up the garden path, 'er tells you the way 'er sees things an' no lies. Now you best be gettin' that there cloth up to your workroom afore summat be findin' itself spilt on it.'

'Did the metal come?'

'Ar, Miss, brass founders delivered it about an hour after

the three of you left this mornin'.' Lizzie watched as Phoebe gathered her purchases into one parcel. 'Bert says as there be enough for a couple o' dozen doublers an' p'raps a bit left over as'll make a few close shackle padlocks, an' 'e says as it be good quality metal an' all.'

Thank heaven for that, Phoebe thought, remembering how she had declared to the brass founder that any dross delivered to her would be returned unpaid for and her business taken elsewhere. She had trembled inside, seeing the scorn in his eyes as he had listened to a woman trying to play at business, but the scorn had faded as she had declared the price she was prepared to pay for brass or steel, changing to veiled admiration as she stated she would pay not a penny more.

'Don't forget your letter, Miss.' Lizzie nodded to the envelope that had become hidden beneath layers of brown paper. 'I'll be off now.'

'Thank you, Lizzie,' Phoebe said as the other woman left through the scullery. 'I will just take these upstairs and then I will see what it is.'

'. . . *one gross of Invincible locks to be delivered by the close of business on the last day of the month* . . .'

Phoebe stared at the words written neatly across the sheet of notepaper, its heading boldly proclaiming James Greaves, Hardware and Ironmongery. An order for one gross of locks, the first in answer to her advertisement. She read the remainder of the letter: '. . . *should you find yourself unable to comply with my requirements please notify me by return post.*'

The end of the month. Phoebe made a swift mental calculation. That left twenty-one days all told, including Sundays. It could not be done. She sank heavily to a chair, the letter in her hand. Her very first order and it could not be met. The start she had prayed for and it was over before it had begun. Folding the letter, she returned it to its envelope.

'It is as I have told you before, your brother's constitution has been weak from childhood.' Alfred Dingley pulled on his chamois leather gloves. 'I can prescribe medicine to help him sleep or to relieve pain should he have any, but there is no real cure for what truly ails him. You know it, Miss Pardoe, and I know it, and sadly so does he.'

Picking up the black Gladstone bag that was his constant companion, the doctor pressed a hand to his patient's shoulder before leaving the bedroom. 'He is getting weaker,' he said as he reached the front door. 'You can try him with beef tea or with some chicken broth but nothing too heavy.'

'My brother eats so little,' Annie said with mock solicitude, 'I worry so for him.'

'Worrying heals no wounds.' The doctor raised his tall black hat the merest fraction. 'And seeing you fret will only add to his suffering. My advice is to treat him the way you have always done – give him no intimation of how things really stand with him, though it is my guess he needs none.'

'How do you mean?' Annie asked, her hands shaking just enough.

Placing his valise on the seat, the doctor climbed into the carriage. 'I mean your brother is probably already acquainted with the fact that he has just a few years left on this earth.' Taking up the reins, he raised his hat again. 'Good day, Miss Pardoe. I will call one week from today.'

A few years? Annie returned to the house. Alfred Dingley was wrong. Her brother Samuel did not have a few years left on this earth, he had less than a few days.

She had taken so much care. The seeds of yew and laburnum painstakingly collected from the garden of the Bescot house. Several seasons' worth gathered and stored before the shrubs had been rooted out and burned, leaving nothing that could be traced. Dried and ground to an ultra-fine powder and added to water, the seeds had produced a liquid that held death in its pale golden heart, death that had slept within a perfume bottle waiting the time to strike. That time had come on the day of the burglary.

Annie stood before her cheval mirror admiring the sheen

of her pearl grey dress. Samuel had said how nice it was to see her in a colour other than black. How much more becoming soft shades were to her, how particularly well the grey suited her. It had suited well that day. She touched her fingers to the pocket in her skirt, concealed by the folds of taffeta. She had taken the bottle from the drawer and put it in her pocket. Samuel had been so taken up with examining the other rooms in order to ascertain whether anything other than the few silver ornaments had been taken he did not see her add the liquid from the bottle to the glass of sherry she had poured for him. Clinton had arrived just at that moment. He had heard of the burgling of her home, he said, and had to call to satisfy himself no one had been harmed.

It had not mattered to her then. She had almost smiled as she had poured a second glass of the pale golden sherry for Clinton. It had not mattered that he had met Samuel, theirs would be only a short acquaintance. Placing the glasses on a small silver serving tray she had been interrupted by the arrival of the constables and had left the two men to their drinks while she showed the policemen to the study.

Clinton had been taking his leave when she returned and she had walked with him into the tree-shrouded drive. She would have the deeds to her industrial properties the next day, he had told her, then kissed her cheek before leaving.

Turning from the mirror she crossed the room to the chest of drawers. Sinking on to her knees she pulled open the bottom drawer, taking the box with its amethyst ring from beneath the tissue-wrapped petticoats. Slipping the ring on to the third finger of her left hand she twisted and turned her wrist, admiring the dancing spurts of purple flame shoot from the heart of the stone. Soon she would wear it beyond this room, soon it would shine where all could see.

She felt no regret for what she had done to Samuel, for bringing early the death that Alfred Dingley foretold. Any regret she might have felt was gone, eaten away by her wasted years; nor did she feel any guilt. That must be Abel's for the shackles forged by his money.

Returning the ring to its box, Annie slipped it back beneath the petticoats and stood up. She would be Clinton's wife and Samuel would be gone from her life. Soon she would be free from all she had despised for so long, free from all that had held her prisoner while her youth slipped away, a freedom that had no place in it for Samuel and none for Abel's daughter.

Abel's daughter! Annie turned away from the chest of drawers, catching her reflection in the mirror as she did so. She had once been as Abel's child, young, pretty enough, full of happiness, eager for life and the promise it held. But the promise had been broken, life had not been given to her, it had been snatched away, snatched by a brother intent on his own happiness to the detriment of her own; a brother who could not himself be made to pay for what he had done to her but whose daughter would pay.

Annie smoothed her grey dress but her eyes were on the reflection of her face, on the tired skin, on the lines about her mouth, on the creases across her brow, on the look of age. The gall of bitterness rose within her. 'The sins of the parents shall be visited upon the children,' she whispered. 'She will pay, Abel . . . to the very last penny.'

'It's just impossible.' Lucy read the letter then passed it to Mathew. 'Six or seven locks a day . . . it can't be done.'

'I know.' They were in the kitchen of Phoebe's house, the evening meal having been cleared, the table holding only the letter Mathew had placed at its centre. 'The first reply to my advertisement and I can't fulfil the order.'

''Ave you talked of this wi' Bert?'

'What is the use?' Phoebe glanced at the tall young man, shirt sleeves rolled above the elbow, a broad belt about his waist. His sleeked back hair was still wet from a wash at the outdoor pump.

'Maybe none,' Mathew answered, 'but you should talk to 'im all the same.'

'Like Miss Phoebe says,' Lucy turned to her husband, 'it ain't no use talkin'. Talkin' don't make no locks.'

'It don't cost nothin' neither.' Mathew's retort was sharp. 'You think I should have shown the Ingleses that letter?'

'I don't think as 'ow it would 'ave 'urt none even if it didn't do no good. Seems only right to me some'ow that Bert be told.'

'I don't see as tellin' Bert will make no difference no'ow,' Lucy said stubbornly. 'It might only make 'im feel bad 'cos 'e can't do what that order asks.'

'Lucy has a point, Mathew.' Phoebe picked up the letter, folding it into its envelope. 'Bert works so hard, I would not want him to feel that losing this order was due to him.'

'Nor you should.' Mathew's lower lip came forward as it always did when he felt his argument was the right one. 'But it seems the bloke 'as the right to know 'is locks not just be sellin' well but could be sellin' a damn' sight better.'

'An' that be supposed to make 'im feel good, is it?'

'It would bloody well mek *me* feel good!' Mathew frowned at his wife. 'A bloke slaves 'is guts out, it shouldn't be too much for 'im to know the job 'e be doin' is a good 'un.'

'You are right, of course, Mathew.' Phoebe stood up, the letter in her hand. 'Bert should see the order. I will take it to him now.'

'I realise it cannot be done but we thought you should see the order, it shows how well your work is being received.' Phoebe waited while Bert Ingles read through the letter.

'It can't given the way we be now,' he handed back the letter, 'but that don't mean to say as it couldn't be done at all.'

''Ow be that then?' Mathew asked, his broad shoulders almost blocking the doorway of the small workshop. 'I don't follow.'

'It be logical,' Bert answered. 'One bloke on 'is own can't be doin' everythin', but give 'im a little 'elp . . .'

''Elp?' Lucy squeezed in against Mathew. ''Ow can we 'elp? We be knowin' nothin' of lockmakin'.'

'Mathew do.' Bert smiled. ''E's picked it up real well, an' Lizzie does most of the filin' down, an' Miss Phoebe there 'elps out wi' that, an' the lad works the bellows an' fetches coals up from the cut.'

'Coals!' Phoebe asked, perplexed.

'Ah, Miss, coals.' Bert turned to her. 'You needs coal to fire the forge an' we gets it from the barges that pass along the cut.'

'You mean the bargees give you coal?'

'Not gives,' Bert grinned, 'they comes 'ere for fresh water an' leaves a few buckets o' coal the side o' the cut afore they goes. It's fair trade.'

'But . . . but don't they get into trouble? It . . . it's like stealing.'

'No, it ain't, Miss.' Lizzie smiled. 'The coal bosses, they knows as cut men can't carry everythin' they needs for trips to London or the coast an' they makes allowances like. They knows a bit o' coal 'as to be swapped for water an' such.'

And may the Lord shut His ears to your lies, Lizzie Ingles, she thought, glancing away. Any hint of a bargee exchanging coal for any reason would have the coal bosses slamming him into gaol, but then, what the eye don't see, the heart don't grieve over.

'So if we all be already doin' what we can to 'elp, 'ow come you says the fillin' o' that order could be done?' Mathew asked.

'I reckons as 'ow it could be given another bloke or two, a few more hours workin' a day, an' a bit o' proper machinery to work wi'.'

'But we don't 'ave another bloke!' Lucy stated the obvious.

'Then there be the metal, Miss,' Lizzie added. 'You 'ave to

'ave money for metal. Bert sometimes gets carried away. 'E don't always see obstacles till 'e cuts 'is nose on 'em.'

'I see this order could be the start.' Bert looked at Phoebe. 'This could lead to others. Get this done an' I reckon you will be lookin' at the beginnin' of a business that could grow into summat big.'

'Buying brass and steel is one thing,' Phoebe was touched by the note of hope in Bert's voice, knowing how his dreams had ended with his father's death, 'but buying machinery is another.'

'You wouldn't 'ave to.'

'Then how?'

'I think as Bert be thinkin' of 'is own,' Lizzie put in. 'The rest of 'is tools still be in a out'ouse back of 'is father's place. They were never sold . . . nobody 'ad use for 'em seemed.'

'Until now.' Phoebe's mouth set in a determined line. 'We are going to use them. What has happened once will happen again and next time we will not have to refuse an order.'

'What you thinkin' of?' Lucy asked, recognising the determined expression.

'I am thinking we should discuss this further but not here in the workshop. Come across to the house, all of you. And with your permission, Lizzie and Bert, I would like Mark to come too. He helps in the workshop, he should be part of any decision that is made.'

'So,' Phoebe looked at the circle of people grouped about her kitchen, 'we need metal, we need men, and we need equipment. Where do we find them and how much will it cost?'

'The equipment be no bother,' Bert said. 'There be several bench vices, an anvil, 'ammers, tongs, chisels, files, the lot in my old place. They only needs bringin' 'ere, and findin' space to work be no 'eadache.'

'Then we must find a way of bringing them here.'

'Reckon a couple of Lucy's best mutton pies would see to that.' Bert grinned as he had in the workshop, the excitement of regaining his own equipment showing in his eyes.

'I see,' Lucy laughed, 'it's bribery now, is it?'

'Summat like that.' Lizzie looked up from her chair by the fire, her daughter on her knee. 'Bert be good at that.'

'See, Miss,' he went on, 'the 'ole lot, bench an' all, could be brought 'ere by barge.'

'But you don't work the barges anymore, Bert, so how does that help us?'

'No, I don't work the barges any more,' he answered, 'but I knows many who does an' there be one alongside towpath who be goin' up to Wolverhampton tomorrow. That will take him through Willenhall and right past my old place, an' 'e will be back 'ere the same afternoon. 'E would cart the lot for nuthin' more'n a couple of pies.'

'Could the man do that? Alone, I mean. Some of the things you need must be quite heavy?'

''E would need another man. I thought as I might 'ave to go wi' 'im.'

'Would there be anythin' I wouldn't recognise?' Mathew caught the flavour of the discussion. 'If you give me a good description, could I find the things you want?'

Bert thought for a moment before nodding. 'Reckon you could, ain't nothin' special.'

'Then why don't I go?' Mathew looked at Phoebe, her hands resting on the table, still holding the letter with its order for one gross of locks. 'That way Bert could carry on with the locks 'e is workin' on.'

'But what of your own work?' Phoebe asked.

'Ain't much of it at the moment,' Mathew answered wryly. 'Don't seem to be anybody wantin' odd jobs done right now an' what locks I'd be sellin' round the town could be countin' towards the gross we be needin'.'

'We are still left with the matter of employing another man,' Phoebe said.

'I've 'ad me brain on that one an' all,' Bert said again, 'if it's all right to say?'

'You've 'ad nuthin' but good ideas so far Bert so let's be 'earing what else you 'ave to say.'

Bert smiled at Mathew's words but his eyes were on Phoebe.

'Mathew has said what we all feel.' She smiled encouragement. 'Without you there would be no lockmaking business. You have solved all the problems so far, I am sure you will be helpful again.'

'Well, Miss, way I look at it is this. Mathew there 'as a good 'and for the locks, 'e 'as picked the job up a treat, 'sides which 'e as the strength needed for usin' 'ammer an' anvil. Now 'e 'as said as 'ow odd jobs 'ave dropped off so why not give 'im the job of workin' along o' me?'

'I had never thought of that,' Phoebe said, 'but how would Mathew feel about it? And what of Lucy?'

'I wants Mathew to be 'appy in what 'e is doin',' Lucy said as her husband's eyes turned to her. 'Whatever 'e chooses I know 'e does it for the best.'

Reaching for her hand Mathew folded it in his own, his smile broad. 'I'd like to work wi' Bert, Miss. Tattin' for jobs be no way to mek a livin'. Seems this lock business is goin' to tek off an' bein' in on it would give a man a reglar job like.'

'So we have our new hand,' Phoebe tapped her fingers against the envelope, 'now what we must do is work out the finances.'

Almost an hour later Phoebe pushed across the table a sheet of paper covered with figures and leaned wearily against the back of her chair.

'If only I had not bought that material to make a gown we might just have managed. I'm so sorry, Bert.'

'Ain't your fault.' Lizzie handed her daughter across to Mark who placed a protective arm about his sister's thin shoulders. 'You wasn't to know about no order comin' in.' Taking the pot from the dresser, she set about making tea.

'Of course it ain't no fault of your'n.' Lucy turned to help Lizzie with the tea. 'It was your money, you 'ad a right to spend it any road you wanted.'

'What say we goes through it once more?' Bert intervened.

Her calculations were correct, Phoebe knew. To go over them a thousand times more would only bring the same result: she just did not have sufficient money to buy the metal and pay the extra wages and no amount of checking the figures would alter that. But she leaned over them again, not having the heart to say no as she saw the dream dying in Bert's eyes.

'Let's all have a cup of tea an' p'raps things will look better.' Lizzie handed out the steaming cups while Phoebe buttered a scone each for the children.

''Scuse me, Miss.' Mark pulled a sultana from the edge of his scone, eyeing it with the look of a connoisseur, 'but you said as since I was workin' along o' me father I should be paid a reglar wage.'

'So I did, Mark.' Phoebe saw the astonished face of the boy's mother and the tightening of Bert's hand on his broad leather belt.

'Well, Miss,' Mark kept his eyes on the sultana, avoiding the warning glare that was in his father's eyes, 'I don't want it.'

'You don't want it?' Phoebe glanced quickly at the angry face of his father then back to the boy. 'But, Mark, we all agreed that a shilling a week was a fair wage.'

'It's a bostin' wage, Miss, only you can keep it toward payin' for metals. But when you gets paid for them locks, I will tek a shillin' a week.' His toffeedrop eyes gleaming with the air of a satisfied businessman clinching a deal, he popped the sultana into his mouth.

His anger forgotten, Bert touched a proud hand to his son's shoulder. 'He be right, what you reckon to pay 'im do be a good wage. Reckon lad 'as shown the way we was lookin' for,' he said. 'You can 'old my wage over till job be done an' locks paid for an' all.'

'I could not do that.' Phoebe looked up, astonished at Bert's words. 'Thank you, both of you, but you cannot work for nothing.'

''T'wouldn't be for nuthin',' Bert answered solemnly. 'Look at it my way. As things be Lizzie an' me 'as a roof for the children an' food for their bellies. Anythin' over an' above that be a luxury, an' luxuries can be gone wi'out. I know Lizzie will agree to what I says an' it be this. We will do as we did the first week we come 'ere. We 'ave enough to live on for the next three weeks so Mark an' me will tek no wage. You can make it up once locks be paid for.'

'Lucy an' me be of the same mind,' Mathew came in quickly, preventing Phoebe's refusal. 'We can manage same as Bert an' Lizzie.'

'I don't know what to say.' Phoebe's eyes glistened.

'Ain't nuthin' to be said, 'cept get these cups outa the way an' let's go over them figures again.' Bert came to stand at her shoulder. 'This time we're goin' to make 'em work.'

'We are still short,' Phoebe announced later as Lizzie carried her sleeping daughter out of the kitchen, Mark at her heels. 'I don't see there is anything more we can do.'

'I do 'ave one more suggestion.' Bert ran a hand through his hair. 'You 'ave down there the wage for another workman along o' Mathew. That be countin' for 'alf a crown a week. Now Mark, 'e knows lockmakin' inside out. Long nights on a barge leave a lad wi' little to do. 'E 'as a good brain, an' what's better 'e listens to what 'e be told. 'E can do all I do 'cept for the anvil an' that be a bit too 'eavy for 'im as yet.'

'So what are you saying?'

'I'm sayin' this. You got to pay 'alf a crown a week for summat my lad can do, and on top o' that you will need a couple weeks to show a new bloke the ropes an' a damn' sight more'n a couple weeks afore 'e can be left to work on 'is own, where the lad can do that now.'

Phoebe pressed a hand to her back, more tired than she wished to show. 'I don't understand, Bert.'

'I think I do,' Mathew said. 'You will be payin' a man's wage for a job 'e won't be able to do for weeks, the same job as Mark can do now, so why not let 'im work on the locks an' get another bloke to work the bellows an' bring up the coal, right, Bert?'

'Almost.' He grinned. 'My way you will be gettin' job done quicker an' for less money.'

'But if Mark is doing what a man would do he must be paid the same wage.'

'That ain't the way of things, Miss.' Bert straightened from where he had been stooped over the figures. 'Lad won't be doin' quite all a man would 'ave to, like I say 'e ain't up to 'ammerin' on a anvil, not yet. An' anyway, young 'uns gets paid less on account of the trainin' they be given. I 'preciates your thinkin' but I would rather 'e learned the usual ways of the world.'

'Bert be right in what 'e says,' Mathew nodded. 'This be one o' the facts you 'as to learn if you be goin' to run a business.'

'I expect so.' Phoebe smiled. 'And I understand we have no time to train a man in the skills of lockmaker, but we will still have to employ one to do what Mark was doing so where is the saving in that?'

'I said Mathew was almost right.' Bert pointed to the column of figures. ''Alf a crown for a bloke against ninepence for a lad, so why set a bloke on doin' a lad's work? Pumpin' bellows be a lad's work so why not get a lad to do it? It will cut nearly two-thirds off what you will pay in wages.'

Phoebe ran a swift eye over the figures, her tiredness evaporating as the import of what Bert was saying struck home. Mentally deducting the wages of Mathew, Bert and Mark, together with the revised wage of a youth, she felt a tremor of exhilaration. She could do it!

'Supposing you can make that many locks in a day, then we can accept our first order.' Rising from her chair, she held out a hand to each of the two men. 'Thank you,' she said simply, 'thank you both very much.'

'An' I'll thank you both to leave,' Lucy bustled into the scullery in search of baking tins, 'otherwise there'll be no mutton pies for that there bargee an' that'll put the cobblebosh on the lot of it.'

Taking his flat cap from his trousers pocket, Bert held it in his hand. 'I'll go down to towpath now an' 'ave a word wi' 'im, but 'e will bring my stuff right enough, no need to lose sleep over that. Night, Miss. Night, Lucy.'

'Goodnight, Bert,' Phoebe answered as he moved toward the scullery door. 'And, Bert, you have a good son in Mark.'

'Aye, Miss,' Bert fitted the cap to his head, 'Lizzie an' me, we knows that.'

Chapter Seventeen

'I instructed my own barrister to look into the affair of your time in prison.' Sir William Dartmouth looked at the young woman standing before him, hands folded across the front of a print dress, hair that was neither gold nor brown caught back in a knot that tried in vain to add years to her face. 'The result, I regret to say, showed a lamentable lack of justice. I have here a warrant signed by a magistrate – not, I might say, the one who consigned you to prison in the first place. What I ask is, will you return to Handsworth Prison for Women with me or would you prefer the constables to escort you there?'

Instructed my own barrister, I have a warrant, will you return, would you prefer the constables . . .

The words whirled together, dancing a crazy fandango, whisking in and out of her understanding. Phoebe clenched her hands together, hoping the bite of nails into flesh would stop the screams rising to her throat. He had not forgotten though he had been told of her innocence of the theft of his daughter's necklace, he wanted vengeance, never mind if the victim be free from blame. He had pretended friendship, even to the length of asking that his son be her escort to a farewell ball, and all the time he had been searching for a way to send her back to hell.

'You . . . you say you have a warrant?'

'Here.' He tapped the folded sheet against a gloved hand. 'Do you wish to read it?'

'No . . .' Phoebe breathed long and deep, fighting the nausea that was laying claim to her stomach. 'There will be no need, Sir William.' She could read it, Phoebe thought, fetching her coat, but she could not alter it. This time the Magistrate would not be wrong. This man would have his revenge and would make certain there could be no way he would be cheated of it.

Thanking the coachman for the hand he held out to help her up, Phoebe climbed into the carriage, her gaze on her home until it fell away below the rise of the ground.

How long had he been planning this? Phoebe watched the passing landscape but saw only the devils of fear dancing in her brain. Was it in his mind when she met him outside of the Magistrate's rooms in Wednesbury . . . was he thinking of it when he sent Edward and Sophie to invite her to the ball? And Edward, was he party to his father's action? Had he known of it even when he had asked her to marry him?

She closed her eyes, leaning her head against the padded upholstery of the carriage. No one save Sir William Dartmouth would know where she had gone or what had happened. Lizzie had watched from where she had been hanging washing on a clothes line Bert had set up beside the old windmill to catch the best of the breezes, but it had been too far for her to see any distress which might have shown. How long would Lucy and Mathew wait before making enquiries as to her whereabouts? Tomorrow? The next day? No, not that long, they knew she would not stay away from Wiggins Mill that length of time unless she had told them beforehand. And what if they went to the Priory? Would he see them, or would he have them dismissed without a word?

'Miss Pardoe, Miss Pardoe, we have arrived.'

This was not happening, it was a bad dream that would vanish when she opened her eyes, but it didn't and as she stepped from the carriage to be faced by that blank wall with its solid oak door Phoebe came face to face with the nightmare she had thought was over.

The door opened in answer to a knock from Sir William's malacca cane and they were inside. Inside the jaws of Hell.

Phoebe followed the grim-faced wardress in her grey soulless uniform, their footsteps sounding sharp in the carbolic-laden air of the narrow bare brick corridors. *I sentence you to fifteen years* . . . The words seemed to echo from the brickwork. How many years would it be this time? How much of her life would be spent paying for a crime she did not commit?

'Begging your pardon . . .'

The wardress had led them to a small, sparsely furnished waiting room Phoebe had heard of but had not seen and now stood looking at her, a faint shadow of near-forgotten concern on her long, drawn features.

'. . . but are you feeling unwell, Miss?'

Sensing Sir William move toward her, Phoebe stepped away.

'We do 'ave a infirmary 'ere, Sir,' the wardress looked at Sir William, 'if the lady would like to rest? She do look pale.'

'Thank you, but I am quite all right.'

Phoebe forced the words past a throat tight with fear. Resting in the infirmary would delay her return to the dormitory and the laundry only for as long as it took the man who had brought her here to leave. It had to happen, she had to return to the torture of long days and nights locked in this Godforsaken place, so why delay the inevitable? Let her sentence begin.

'Then I will tell the Governess you are 'ere.' The wardress bobbed the tiniest of curtsies. ''scuse me.'

'Miss Pardoe,' catching her arm as the wardress left the waiting room Sir William pressed her to a chair, 'are you quite certain you are not feeling unwell? You were very quiet during our drive here and now . . . as the wardress said, you are looking very pale.'

Looking very pale? Phoebe wanted to laugh but stared at him instead, rage at his treatment of her suddenly destroying the fear that had been suffocating her.

Pushing his hand from her arm she stood up, her features calm and icy as if carved from some glacial peak. 'I am looking very pale, how unwarranted of me!' Every word clipped into the quiet room like ice cubes falling into a glass. 'Please forgive my thoughtlessness. How ungracious of me to look so when you were kind enough to escort me here personally . . . how ignorant to repay that kindness by looking pale! So tell me, Sir William, how do you expect a woman to look when she is being returned to the grave?'

'Returned to the . . . I don't understand?'

'Of course you don't understand!' Phoebe spat, anger and fear overcoming her reserve. 'How could you understand? You to whom a girl dare not come with the truth for fear of tainting the name of Dartmouth. You who have been protected from reality all your life, whom the people raise their hat to, the powerful Billy-me-Lord, how could *you* understand what it is to be imprisoned? The degradation, the total lack of privacy, the utter soul-destroying mindlessness of it, the complete waste of a life . . . how would you know the torment of being accused of something you did not do, of having your life ripped away, of being condemned to a living hell, to be released only to be returned? To have the torment begin all over again!'

'Miss Pardoe . . .' He made to touch her then his hand fell to his side. He stayed where he was, watching the shades of passion flit across her face. 'I am sorry my bringing you here has caused you distress . . .'

'Sorry!' Phoebe glared contemptuously. 'You are *sorry* to have caused me distress? What did you expect returning me to prison would cause?'

'I did not think . . .'

'You did not think!' Phoebe cut across him, her tone lacerating. 'Do not insult me with lies, Sir William. You could have thought of little else all the time you were planning your revenge.'

'Revenge? I . . .'

'Yes, revenge.' She refused to let him speak, anger still uppermost. 'You pretended friendship towards me, you and your family, when all you really wanted was to have me

234

re-committed to this prison. Why, Sir William? Why when you know I am innocent, when you have the necklace back? Why . . . is it to show the great Sir William Dartmouth is not to be played with?'

'Miss Pardoe, listen . . .'

'To what? More lies?'

'Call what I have to say lies if you will, but you shall listen. I brought you here . . .'

'Good day, Sir William.'

He stopped in mid-sentence, turning to see Hannah Price standing in the doorway.

'Miss Pardoe, my dear, how are you?'

Habit bent Phoebe's knee to a slight curtsy as she faced the Governess of Handsworth Prison for Women, fear surging up through the anger.

'I am well, Ma'am,' she murmured.

'But you look so pale.' She glanced at the man standing tight-lipped beside the young woman who had spent over a year locked behind the walls of this prison, a young woman she had come to like, whose loyalty and courage she had grown to respect. 'Sir William, perhaps the infirmary . . .'

'No, Mrs Price, thank you but we will get our business over. I want no further delay.'

'As you wish.' The governess nodded to the wardress who had remained at the door and she stood aside, allowing a third figure to enter the room.

'You wanted to see me, Ma'am?'

Everything stilled in Phoebe: her mind, her heart, the very blood in her veins.

'Yes, come in. Would you wait outside, Mrs Marsh?'

'Yes, Ma'am.'

Phoebe refused to let the exchange register, waiting only for the voice that had stilled her world to speak again.

'I think you know one of our visitors?' Hannah Price said.

In the stillness of her soul, Phoebe waited.

'Phoebe?'

The voice was uncertain but Phoebe was not. She knew that voice, recognised it from the long months of her captivity. 'Tilly!' She whirled to face the gaunt-faced woman, her hair tied in the compulsory plaits, the regulation grey skirts hanging loose about her thin body. 'Tilly! Oh, Tilly!'

'Sir William.' Phoebe stood at the front entrance to Wiggins Mill, her cheeks pink with embarrassment of what she knew she had to say. He had remained silent during the drive back to the mill, watching her hold a sobbing Tilly in her arms, then had waited until she had been settled with tea in a china cup, the kindly Lizzie in attendance. 'Sir William . . .' Phoebe began again.

'You do not have to say anything.' He placed a hand on her elbow, leaving it there as he added, 'It was thoughtless of me to act as I did. There is no need for apology.'

'There is every need,' Phoebe said, her eyes still holding traces of the tears of relief and happiness she had shed. 'It was wrong of me to speak to you as I did.'

'I think harsh words a mild punishment given the circumstances.' His grey eyes grew warm. 'Were I in your shoes nothing short of a horsewhipping would satisfy my feelings, I do not consider you at fault in any way.'

'That is kind of you, Sir William.' The colour deepened in Phoebe's cheeks, 'but I was at fault. I should have asked your reasons for taking me back to that place before I railed at you.'

'What did you think my reasons were?'

'Revenge.' Embarrassed as she was, Phoebe forced herself to meet his gaze. 'I thought you planned to have me returned to gaol, to have me serve the sentence originally passed upon me or perhaps an even longer one.'

'You thought the warrant I had was an order returning you to prison?'

'Yes.'

'But you had not been brought before a Magistrate, there

had been no new charge laid against you, how could you have thought you were being returned to serve that sentence?'

'Fear makes you suspect many things you would not normally think. I was afraid – afraid of being locked into Hell.'

'Miss Pardoe,' his eyes darkened and the fingers holding her arm tightened, 'I would never have you afraid because of me. Believe me when I say I was thinking only of the pleasure my actions would afford you. Causing you fear or concern never entered my mind. You told me of the circumstances of your friend's trial, of how you suspected there had been a miscarriage of justice. I thought it would in some way make amends for the suffering my family caused you if I could get a review of Mrs Wood's trial. I put the whole of what I knew before my own barrister who set in motion a further investigation of the so-called murder of the husband. It appears that other occupants of the lodging house where they lived had witnessed the argument. They had seen the man strike his wife and her attempt to defend herself. They had seen him fall backward down the stairs, causing his death.'

'Why didn't they say so at Tilly's trial? Why didn't they tell the Magistrate that?'

'It appears the constables did not report there being witnesses to the fall.' He did not remove his hand nor did his eyes leave hers. 'Or at least that is what the prosecution claimed. My barrister pressed for a complete review of the trial on the grounds of suppression of evidence, with the result that Mrs Wood was given a Queen's Pardon. Had I thought to tell you of all this before we went to Handsworth Prison you would not have been subjected to so much worry. I am deeply sorry and apologise most profoundly.'

'You are sorry and I am sorry.' Phoebe broke into a smile. 'We are a sorry pair, you and I, Sir William.'

'Yes.' His fingers tightened fractionally and the grey of his eyes turned to smoke. 'A sorry pair,' he finished softly.

'Sir William,' she said as he withdrew his hand from her

arm and turned towards his waiting carriage, 'I will not forget what you have done, for Tilly and for me.'

I will not forget either, Miss Phoebe Pardoe, he thought, climbing into the carriage. I will not forget what you have done to me.

'Annie dear, tomorrow I would like to see James Siveter.' Samuel's fingers moved without hesitation. 'I told you I wish to return most of what Abel bequeathed me to Phoebe.'

Annie's mind moved like quicksilver. He could not know that Phoebe still lived here in Wednesbury. She scrutinised the newspapers closely before passing them to him, removing those advertisements that referred to Pardoe's Patent Locks, and there was no one who could communicate with him other than herself. She alone had learned to speak with her hands; even Abel had not troubled himself to do so, relying on her to relay what he wished to say to Samuel.

'I want the papers drawn up tomorrow.'

She caught the quick movements, her thoughts outstripping them. Let Samuel say all he wished it would achieve nothing. There would be no tomorrow. She had thought the poison she had concocted from the yew and laburnum seed would have acted more rapidly than this; she had tried it often in those early years, feeding it to mice then cats then a dog, and in every instance it had brought death in less than two days. But for Samuel it had not worked. He had shown no more than his usual signs of illness. Was that due to Alfred Dingley's potions? She doubted it. The medicines he prescribed were no more than coloured sugar water prescribed as a salve to his own conscience for the fees he charged.

'I will go to his office in the morning,' she signed. 'I will tell him what you want and ask him to bring the papers here to you when they are ready.' That way she could delay long enough, she thought. A day would be all she needed.

'No.' The shake of Samuel's head signalled his refusal while his fingers flashed the rest of his words. 'I do not wish Mr Siveter to call at the house. I intend to visit him in his office myself tomorrow.'

You may intend to visit him, Annie thought, but I intend you do not.

'Will you be kind enough to drive me there in the trap, Annie dear?'

'Of course.' She smiled, her hands moving nimbly. 'If you are feeling as well tomorrow as you are today then certainly we will visit Mr Siveter.'

If he was well. Annie resisted the temptation to laugh. He would not be!

Samuel looked about him, the colours of late summer glowing the borders to the lawns. He loved the garden in all its phases but perhaps this was his favourite time.

'Brunswick House is such a kind house,' he motioned, 'it is almost a shame to leave it.'

A shame for you, Annie's thoughts raced, but not for me. I shall not be sorry to see the last of this place, to see the last of Wednesbury. I shall have a home of my own at last, a home with Clinton.

'Like you say, Samuel,' her fingers answered, 'it will be a shame to leave, but if it will give you peace of mind then of course that is what we must do.'

'Thank you, dear,' he smiled his weary smile, 'you always were so understanding, I will ensure you are well provided for.'

'Nonsense,' she returned, 'whatever makes you happy is all I want. But tell me, dear, how do we go about finding Phoebe? We do not know where she went, she may not even live in Wednesbury any more.'

'I know,' Samuel answered, 'but I am sure Mr Siveter will have methods of enquiry. We may leave it to him to find her.'

'Then we will tell him to begin tomorrow.' Annie touched a hand to the pain below her breast. It troubled her more often as the days passed, forcing her to take the white tablets several times each day, waking her in the night with fresh demands.

'It's time for Mr Samuel's medicine, Ma'am.' Maudie Tranter set a tray on the wicker table set between the garden chairs. 'Will I measure it?'

'Yes,' Annie nodded, 'but carefully. Two dessert spoons, no more, we must not exceed the amount the doctor advised.'

Bloody hypocrite, Maudie thought, carefully filling the dessert spoon she had placed on the tray then pouring the liquid into a glass before repeating the process. 'Er wouldn't care if 'e swallowed the lot, bottle an' all. But the Lord missed nothing and he wouldn't be missin' Annie Pardoe's doings. There was evil in that one, an old evil that had festered from her mother's passing, an evil that wouldn't be quenched this side of the grave.

'Will I pour the tea, Ma'am?' she asked as Samuel took the glass, swallowing its contents.

'No.' Annie reached for the dainty flower-patterned milk jug. 'I will do it myself.'

Samuel would take his tea then would go to his room and rest, probably sleep for several hours. That would give her time. Annie took her own cup, sipping her tea as the seed of her plan germinated in her mind, temporarily banishing the pain from her side.

'I want you to go into town.'

'Yes Ma'am.' Maudie had answered the bell summoning her to the study.

'Mrs Gaskell Wheeler told me of a herbal tea she was sure would be of benefit to Mr Samuel,' Annie went on. 'I have written the name of it on this paper. Take it to the herbalist in Meeting Street and wait until it is made up, I want my brother to have it today.' She handed the paper to her housekeeper together with a florin. 'There will be change from that,' she said as Maudie turned to leave. 'That herbal tea will cost no more than sixpence.'

'I'll get 'im to mek a bill out,' Maudie said, and banged the door behind her.

Samuel had been sleeping half an hour, Annie looked at the fob watch she wore pinned to her dress, and Maudie had been gone five minutes. Opening the doors that led directly into the garden she walked its length, turning at the tall privet hedge that screened the brick boundary wall and making her way to the low bothy building housing garden tools.

It was not one of the days the gardener-handyman was employed at Brunswick House. What she was about to do would be observed by no one. Going into the building she searched quickly along the shelves. It was there, the cardboard carton the gardener had bought, a carton containing rat poison. He had shown it to her, labouring the importance of keeping it out of reach, stressing the potency of its contents.

Taking her handkerchief from her pocket, she tipped a little of the powder into it, wrapping it carefully in the folds of the small white square of cloth before pushing it deep inside her pocket. Then, after replacing the carton on the shelf, she left.

From his bedroom window Samuel watched his sister return along the garden and knew where she had been. The colour of the dress she wore had changed. She no longer wore black, but that was the only thing about his sister that was different. Inside the same bitterness that had plagued her youth plagued her still.

Entering the house through the scullery, Annie glanced at her fob watch, checking the time once more. Maudie Tranter would be another hour at least. She had time yet.

'What did you think when you knew there was to be a re-investigation?'

They sat together in the warm kitchen. The fire had settled low in the grate and one oil lamp spilled a pool of yellow light courted by shadows.

'I didn't know.' Tilly's eyes strayed for the hundredth time around the kitchen, not yet believing it would not disappear like some dream-built world at the chime of a clock.

'But you must have been given some hint? The Governess or the wardresses, surely they said something?'

'If they knowed they said nothin' to me.' Tilly returned her gaze to the glowing coals. 'You knows what it's like in that place. If anythin' good was goin' to 'appen then that lot would be as close-mouthed as a Jew in a presbytery. They'd keep it to theirselves on purpose, drag out the agony a bit longer.'

'I can believe that of the likes of Agnes Marsh but I had thought better of Hannah Price,' Phoebe answered. 'I always got the impression she acted fairly.'

'Ah, me wench, we all thought that, an' 'er was fair an' all. 'Er was a decent woman an' a good prison governess. You kept yer nose clean and you 'ad no worry from 'er.'

'Do you think she knew?'

'Can't say.' Tilly looked again to the rough wooden dresser, studying the motley assortment of cups and dishes. 'Maybe yes, then again maybe no. There was some comin' an' goin' about a week ago, 'er was off out somewhere two or three times, but we put it down to meetings wi' Prison Board.'

'Mary Pegleg heard nothing?'

'You can bet yer life 'er didn't.' Tilly stretched a hand to the lamp Phoebe had set in the middle of the kitchen table, running a finger over the gleaming brass body. 'Mary Pegleg gets to know summat an' 'er's like a cat wi' a maggot up its arse – 'er can't get it out quick enough.'

Phoebe bent over the spent fire, adding fresh coals, the move hiding her smile at her friend's rough language. Tilly had been in gaol a long time and the ways of others had touched her. It would take time for them to fade.

'If those meetings with the Prison Board concerned your release and Hannah Price said nothing of it to you, then she must have been told not to. I can't imagine there being any other reason for her to keep it from you,' Phoebe said, sitting down again.

'Like as not yer right,' Tilly nodded, 'an' come to think on it p'raps it were the sensible thing to do. I think if 'er 'ad told me there was a chance I'd be gettin' outta that place, then told me later that I weren't, I'd of got meself out another way.'

Phoebe looked perplexed. 'Another way? But surely there was no other way.'

'Oh, ar, there was, me wench.' Tilly looked up from the fire, her laughterless eyes haunted by the spectre of hopes long dead. 'A way I'd thought on many a time. A sharp knife across the throat gets you out of anywheer.'

'Oh, Tilly!' Leaning forward, Phoebe pressed the other woman's calloused hands. 'It's all over now.'

'For me it is.' Suddenly Tilly sounded far away. 'I'll never go back theer again, I'll put meself in me box first.'

Phoebe rose, kneeling before Tilly to put her arms about her. 'You won't ever go back, Tilly, I promise, I promise.'

Holding each other, the two women stared into the flickering flames of the rebuilt fire, each seeing their yesterdays in its heart.

'Phoebe,' Tilly asked after several minutes, ''ow come that man knowed about me an' what I'd done?'

'Sir William?' Releasing her, Phoebe stood up. 'I am afraid I told him after . . .' She broke off, the horror of the attack on her flooding back.

'After what?'

'Nothing.' Phoebe made a business of taking cups from the dresser and setting them on the table. 'Nothing.'

'Yer 'ands be shakin' an' yer face be the colour of a corpse. That don't be tellin' me it was nothin'.'

Locating a brown-coloured tin labelled 'Bournville', Phoebe spooned cocoa into the cups, spilling as much of the powder over the sides as went into them.

'A man came to the house,' she said, knowing Tilly would repeat her question until it was answered. 'I . . . I was upstairs. He thought I had been given money by Sir William and that I had it hidden somewhere.'

"Ad you?' Tilly watched the cocoa powder sprinkle like brown snow over the cups. It was her bet the girl had told nobody the full story of what had happened, and no matter what it had been it was better told and in the open; fastening it up inside herself would only see the fear grow.

'No.' Phoebe loosed the spoon into one of the cups, the clatter loud in the stillness of the kitchen.

'But 'e didn't believe you?' Tilly led her on, knowing each answer would relieve the pain.

'No, he didn't believe me. I thought if I could get him out of the house I might somehow escape him so I told him the money was in the old corn barn. He made me go there with him and while he was searching among the sacks I managed to run out into the yard, but he . . . he . . .'

Tilly rose from her chair. This was the part that was buried deepest, the core of the pain etched across that young face. Taking the tin from Phoebe's trembling hands, she stood it on the table then drew her into her arms. 'Get it up, ma wench,' she said softly, 'let it all come out, Tilly's got you.'

Slowly, between long shuddering sobs, the full story of the attack came out. Tilly listened without intervention. The dam was broken, let the water flow.

'I thought it was Liza,' Phoebe sobbed against her shoulder, 'I thought it was Liza!'

'Ssshh.' Tilly stroked her hair. 'Liza won't 'urt you no more, an' neither will anybody else so long as I be livin'.' She stood with Phoebe in her arms, holding her as she would a child until the sobbing had stopped.

'Now I think we're both ready for that cocoa,' she said, pushing Phoebe into a chair. 'An' I thinks I'll be meking it, you spills too much.'

'I never thought Sir William would do anything to help you,' Phoebe said, sipping the hot frothy liquid.

'An' why should 'e?' Tilly held her own cup cradled between both hands, savouring the heat on her fingers. ''E don't know me from Adam, so why put 'isself to all that bother?'

'He said he did it to try to make up for what his family had caused to happen to me.'

'Well, whatever 'is reason, I thank the Lord for it. 'E got me from Handsworth Prison when I never thought to see the outside of it never again.' She looked across at Phoebe, sudden concern in her eyes. 'Eh, wench, I've just thought! I never even said thank you. 'E's gonna think I'm a right 'un.'

'You didn't say anything as I remember,' Phoebe smiled at last, 'but I am sure Sir William will understand.'

'Do yer think as I might see 'im agen?' Tilly asked. 'Might 'e call 'ere agen sometime?'

Phoebe dropped her eyes to her cup, surprised at the answer rising silently within her. I hope so, Tilly, I hope so.

'P'raps it might be better to write 'im a note, just in case like,' Tilly went on. 'Would you 'elp me, Phoebe?'

'Of course.' She looked up. 'We will do it tomorrow and Lucy will post it for you in Wednesbury. The post office is just a stone's throw through the Shambles.'

'Is there work in Wednesbury?' Tilly asked. 'For a woman like me?'

'A woman like you!' Phoebe said sharply. 'What does that mean?'

'It means, will anybody employ a woman they know 'as been along the line.'

'If you are referring to a certain Tilly Wood,' Phoebe adopted her most cautionary tone, 'I advise you speak of her with respect. She happens to be one of my greatest friends and one who stands in no need of employment for she is to live, and work I might add, here with me at Wiggins Mill.'

'Oh, Phoebe, me wench!' Tilly choked. 'Phoebe!'

Carrying the cups to the scullery Phoebe washed them then returned them to the dresser, giving Tilly time to regain her composure, then she asked, 'Tilly, what happened to Liza?'

'Huh!' She snorted. 'A bad 'un that if ever I met one. It seemed for a long time as 'er wouldn't get over 'ittin' 'er face agen that wall, but 'er did. 'Appen there be no stoppin' the Devil's own, an' Liza Spittle was that all right. 'Er 'adn't been outta that infirmary no more than a fortnight when we 'ad a new inmate, pretty little thing wi' 'air the colour of corn fresh scythed an' eyes blue as a kingfisher's wing. Well, I don't need to tell it but Liza took a shine to 'er an' you won't believe this but so did Emily Pagett. You know, wardress as took Sally Moreton's place.'

'I remember.' Phoebe took a chair on the opposite side of the fire, resting her feet on the hearth.

'Well,' Tilly smiled sardonically, 'that pretty little thing looked like a angel but 'er weren't none. 'Er played them two women one agen another, lettin' both touch 'er up then tellin' each in turn the other 'ad forced 'erself on 'er. It would 'ave been summat for the rest o' we to laugh at if we 'ad any laughter left in we. Any road up, outcome was Liza 'ad the blue devils an' went for Emily Pagett wi' a knife.'

'Did she kill her?'

'No, me wench,' Tilly shook her head, 'though 'er nearly did. Knife just missed 'er lung so Mary Pegleg 'eard the doctor tell the Governess. Anyway, they took Pagett off to some 'ospital in Brummagem an' that be the last we seen of 'er.'

'And Liza?' Phoebe stared at the fire, seeing in its redness the birthmark that spread across the woman's face.

'Prison Board dished out thirty strokes of the cat.' Tilly's voice was devoid of emotion. 'No more than 'er deserved.'

'But is she all right?' Phoebe had to ask. 'She did get over it?'

Tilly was silent for a moment before answering the girl Liza Spittle had tried so many times to assault. 'Might 'ave been,' she said quietly, ''cept 'er 'ung 'erself wi' laces out of 'er own stays.'

Chapter Eighteen

Letting the fob watch drop back into place over her left breast, Annie listened. The house was silent, no movement from overhead. She breathed slowly. Samuel must still be sleeping.

Going into the pantry she brought out the one small chocolate-covered cake delivered to the house fresh each day. Samuel had never liked the taste of medicine, any medicine, complaining of the bitterness after every dose and the cake was a treat that took the taste away.

Annie placed it on a plate. Shaped like a cup, its thick chocolate sides daintily fluted, it was filled with a generous depth of fresh cream and topped with a thick chocolate lid embedded in which was a walnut. Working quickly, Annie removed the lid, scooping out the cream on to a saucer. Taking the powder from her pocket, she tipped it into the cream, mixing the two together. Would Samuel detect the taste? What if he left it uneaten after the first bite? Annie thought for a moment, then going back to the pantry brought out a box of finely powdered sugar. Adding a large spoonful to the cream, she folded it in then carefully returned it to its chocolate case, replacing the lid.

It was done! Putting cake and sugar back in the pantry, Annie cleared all traces of her activity from the kitchen then carried the plate to the scullery, washing both it and her hands and rinsing them in several bowls of water before drying them. Replacing the plate on the dresser in the kitchen, she returned to her chair in the garden, dropping her handkerchief in the stove as she passed through the scullery. Tomorrow she would not be talking to James Siveter, tomorrow she would be talking to Thomas Webb, Wednesbury's undertaker.

'The 'erbal tea, Ma'am.'

Annie opened her eyes, blinking rapidly, pretending to chase sleep from them. But she had not been sleeping though she had been dreaming – dreaming of her life with Clinton.

'The 'erbal tea.' Maudie held out a bottle in which a sludgy brown mixture reached almost to the cork. 'The 'erbalist said to give a small wineglass o' this twice a day.'

'Was that all he said?' Annie hitched herself straighter in the chair.

'No.' Maudie still held the bottle at arm's length.

'Then what else did he say?'

''E said we was fortunate to be 'avin' such fine weather though like as not we'd be payin' for it come winter.'

Snatching the bottle, Annie glared at her housekeeper. The woman deliberately tried to anger her. Was she hoping to be dismissed? Hope or not she would be in very few weeks from now. Rising from the chair, Annie stalked into the house, a smirking Maudie at her heels. 'I will leave this here.' She put the bottle of herbal mixture on the table Maudie kept well scrubbed.

'Will I be tekin' a draught up to Mr Samuel?'

'No.' Annie looked at the bottle then at Maudie, busy fastening the straps of her long white apron. 'No, you can bring a glass with the afternoon tray.'

'The bill for that be there on the dresser an' the change from the florin alongside o' it. You best count it.'

'Didn't you count it when the herbalist gave it to you?'

'Oh, I counted it,' Maudie looked bland, 'but then I ain't the one was worried over it.'

Sweeping to the dresser Annie snatched up the bill, reading the words 'One eight-ounce bottle of herbal mixture, sevenpence'. Scanning the change, one shilling, a threepenny bit and two pennies, she scooped them into her hand. 'Mrs

Gaskell Wheeler was confident this mixture would help Samuel.' She moved across the kitchen toward the door linking it to the rest of the house. 'And Mrs Gaskell Wheeler is most knowledgeable in the use of herbal remedies.'

Mrs Gaskell Wheeler this, Mrs Gaskell Wheeler that! Maudie grabbed the tea tray from beside the dresser, her thoughts acid. Annie Pardoe was possessed by that woman. Would kiss her arse if asked to.

'I think Mr Samuel would quite like his afternoon tea in the garden,' Annie went on. 'It is still so pleasant out there we should take advantage of the warm spell while we can. It is not often we get the chance with a climate such as ours. I will see if my brother is awake yet.'

She had thought of everything but as she moved up the stairs Annie went over it all again in her mind. The herbal tea had been Violet Wheeler's idea and Maudie Tranter had collected it. She, Annie, had left it unopened in the kitchen and would leave it to Maudie to administer it as she would leave it to her to give Samuel the cake. Should anyone question the cause of his death there would be no finger pointed at her and there would be no trace of poison having been added to either the herbal tea or the medicine Alfred Dingley prescribed.

And the cake? Who could prove poison had been added to that? Annie paused at the head of the stairs, pressing a hand to the pain that shot upward through her breast. The cake would be eaten. Samuel was too fond of sweet things to leave any of it uneaten. What if anyone asked the reason for there being just one cake? Annie pressed harder, clenching her teeth against the fire clawing at her side. Maudie Tranter would answer that. She could tell them Annie Pardoe never ate cake or sweet desserts. And the doctor? He would not look too closely, he had been expecting Samuel's death for too long. Pulling in a deep breath, she walked along the corridor to Samuel's bedroom. Yes, she had thought of everything, just as she had with that letter.

* * *

'They all be so pretty,' Tilly fingered the dainty dresses and lace-edged petticoats Phoebe had ready for market, 'an' they sells well, you say?'

'They have up to now.' Phoebe held a strip of ribbon against a length of delphinium-sprigged cotton cloth, matching the colours. 'Lucy says we could sell more.'

'Then sell more is what you must do!'

'It is not that easy.' Phoebe changed the ribbon for one of darker blue. 'I can't sew any more than I do already. I was hoping to buy one of Mr Singer's new sewing machines – I read about them in a newspaper Lucy had wrapped around some fish.'

'Bet that made a change from the smell o' brass filin's.'

Phoebe glanced across at Tilly, noticing the smile about her mouth, a smile that came more easily as each day passed.

'Then why ain't you?'

'Why haven't I what?' Phoebe went back to her first choice of ribbon.

'Why ain't you bought one o' Mr Singer's newfangled machines?'

'Money.' Phoebe spread the flower-strewn cloth on her workroom table and began laying paper pattern cut outs over it. 'I haven't got enough money. My clothing sells well but buying metal for locks swallows it as fast as I get it. I use every penny either on that or cloth or food.'

'An' what does this be for?' Tilly touched the delicate cream-yellow satin still lying in its paper wrapping.

'It was to have been for a ball gown.' Phoebe glanced at the gleaming satin then returned to her cutting.

'Was to 'ave been?' Tilly questioned. 'Why "was to 'ave been"? Why ain't it still goin' to be?'

'Because I will not have the time to make it,' Phoebe said, her lips pursed as she cut around a tricky piece of pattern.

Tilly waited until the manoeuvre was finished then asked,

'But won't the woman it be for be put out wi' your not mekin' 'er gown after gettin' that cloth an' all?'

'I don't think so.' Phoebe gathered the paper pattern pieces together, laying them aside. 'You see the woman was me.'

'You was mekin' yourself a ball gown?'

Phoebe gathered the pieces of cloth she had cut out. 'I had intended to do so but sometimes plans have to be set aside.'

'That means you ain't no longer goin' to mek it.' Tilly covered the cloth with its paper wrapping. 'Why?'

Sitting at her work table Phoebe began to pin the pieces of cloth together, matching sides to sides. 'Because it would be wrong of me to spend time sewing something that was not intended for sale, something that was bringing no money to Wiggins Mill when everyone else was working so hard.'

'But it must 'ave been special for you to 'ave spent money buying that cloth in the first place.'

'I have been invited to the Priory,' Phoebe explained. 'Sir William is giving a farewell ball in place of the more usual Advent Ball, the reason being Lady Amelia is leaving for the continent earlier than she would normally do. Her Ladyship took the influenza some weeks gone and is not yet over the effects.'

'An' you 'ad accepted the invite?'

'Not exactly.'

'Cockeyed way o' carryin' on, ain't it?'

'What is?' Phoebe asked, her mouth half full of pins.

'Buyin' stuff to mek yourself a fancy frock an' you not accepted the party invite exactly.' Tilly retrieved a pin from the floor, dropping it into the tobacco tin Phoebe kept them in. 'Strikes me you 'ad every intention of goin' to that ball. P'raps it could still be done if I 'elped you with the sewin' of it.'

'I did not know you sewed?' The words pushed past the pins still locked between Phoebe's teeth.

'There be a lot you don't know about Tilly Wood, me wench.'

Phoebe removed the pins from her mouth, putting them in

the tobacco tin that had once belonged to Mathew. 'This much I do know, you already work hard enough. You have taken on the running of the house and preparing the meals . . .'

'Lizzie does a fair share o' all that,' Tilly said quickly.

'And you do a fair share of the filing down of the locks.' Phoebe smiled gently. 'I wanted you to rest, Tilly, I didn't want you working just as hard as . . .'

'As hard as I had to inside.' She took up the words Phoebe couldn't say. 'Phoebe, wench, what I does 'ere at Wiggins Mill be paradise compared to Handsworth Gaol. I thank God every minute I breathes for what 'e done for me, an' 'elpin out wi' a bit o' sewin' ain't too great a burden. I'd like to see you go to that there ball.'

'Very well,' sorting a needle Phoebe broke off a length of blue thread, 'we will do a little each evening.' She looked up from threading the needle, her eyes smiling. 'Unless, of course, a fairy godmother should exist somewhere and decides to bring me a gown already made.'

'Oh, they exist all right.' Tilly picked up the tin of pins, staring into it. 'An' not all o' em be old neither. You be my fairy godmother, Phoebe. What you did for me be nuthin' short o' magic.'

'It was not I who got you released from prison, Tilly,' Phoebe reminded her softly. 'It was Sir William Dartmouth. He is the one who worked the magic.'

'Ar, wench, 'e is, an' grateful I be to 'im.' She replaced the tin on the table close by Phoebe's hand. 'Only some'ow I can't see 'im wi' wings an' wavin' of a wand.'

'Bert says the new lad Mathew got to work the bellows is doing very well,' Phoebe said when they had both stopped laughing.

''E is. Lad works like a little Trojan, nuthin' ain't too much trouble for 'im.'

'Do you think carrying coals might be too heavy?'

'No, wench, I don't. The lad be strong enough, Bert wouldn't set 'im no task 'e thought too much.'

'No, he would not.' Phoebe examined her line of stitching. 'Bert is a kind man.'

'They'm a nice family an' willin' workers the lot o' 'em.'

'Including Ruth. I have seen the way she gets under your feet, you can't do anything without her being there.'

'Ar, you be right.' Tilly smiled. 'But I don't mind that, 'er be a pleasant little thing, an' Lizzie 'as seen to it 'er knows 'er manners, never forgets a please or a thank you. An' talkin' of folk gettin' under other folks' feet, I better be off an' leave you to get on wi' what you be about.'

'How are the locks coming along?' Phoebe called after her.

'Nearly 'alf done,' the answer came back. 'Bert says you will 'ave 'em all on time.'

'How can you be certain?'

The evening meal finished, Lucy and Mathew sat for a few minutes before starting their evening's work.

'I can't, but it do seem strange me not seein' 'im once since 'e started.'

Mathew lit his pipe, sucking the stem much as his father did. 'P'raps 'e's found some other way.'

'Such as what?'

'Such as followin' the cut.'

'Could be as you're right but it wouldn't make a lot o' sense,' Lucy said. 'Cut would take 'im right out o' 'is way – 'e lives other end o' Wednesbury. Least that be what 'e told you, wasn't it?'

'Ar.' Mathew tapped his pipe against the heel of his hand. 'Then why would 'e be followin' the cut 'ome?'

'Who knows why kids do 'alf the things they does?'

'They does some daft 'uns, I'll give you that,' Lucy began to clear the table, 'but to go a mile or more outta your way 'ome after a day's work don't strike me as no kid's lark.'

'So what do you reckon?' Mathew blew down the stem of

his white clay pipe. 'You've got some bee in your bloomers, wench.'

'You watch the way you be talkin', Mathew Leach, I ain't no fish wife to be listenin' to your vulgarities.' Lucy flicked out with the cloth she had taken to the dishes but she was smiling.

'You ain't seen 'im, not once?' Mathew resumed, sucking his pipe.

'Not once,' Lucy affirmed. 'An' I thinks that be more'n strange. You know what I really thinks? I thinks 'e ain't goin' 'ome at all.'

Several puffs of blue-grey smoke curled into the room, suspended like a delicate veil above Mathew's head. 'Then where do 'e be goin'?'

Carrying the enamel bowl with its washing up water into the yard, Lucy emptied it into the drain running along its width then stared at the old windmill, secretive and brooding against the fading light. ''E be goin' there,' she whispered. 'It's my guess 'e be goin' there.'

Back in the outhouse they had made into a comfortable home Mathew finished his pipe, knocking the burned ash of the tobacco out against the bars of the fire. ''Ave you said anythin' to the others?'

Lucy fitted the cups and plates on to the rack Mathew had made and set on the wall, then folded the cloth she had dried them on and hung it across the length of string set across the grate. 'I thought as I would talk to you first.'

'You am sure?' Mathew put his pipe alongside the tin of shag tobacco on a cupboard that had come with a job lot of furniture from a tat man who had delivered it all for a shilling.

'Sure as I be talkin' to you.' Lucy reached for the white apron she wore only when baking, fastening the straps around her waist.

'Then we best tell the others.'

Phoebe listened, concern deepening on her face as Mathew spoke of Lucy's suspicions.

'He could not have crossed the heath without you seeing him?'

'I swear 'e couldn't, Miss Phoebe. A body can see for miles across there, it bein' mostly flat ground, an' I ain't seen 'im nowhere on it, not when I've been goin' in to Wednesbury on a mornin' nor when I've been comin' back at night. I be tellin' all o' you, that lad ain't passed me an' I says that shows 'e ain't goin' 'ome nights.'

'But his parents would have enquired before now surely?' Phoebe said. 'They must know where he is employed.'

'Maybe not,' Bert said. 'Maybe the lad 'as got no parents.'

'Was nobody wi' 'im that day I picked 'im out o' the line,' Mathew put in. 'Leastways nobody spoke to 'im when we set off.'

'If 'e don't 'ave no parents it could follow 'e don't 'ave no 'ome.' Lizzie looked at Phoebe. 'That would explain Lucy not seein' 'im on the way to an' from the town, wouldn't it?'

'It would.' Phoebe nodded. 'But if he is not going home at night, where is he going?'

Lucy's glance strayed to the rise of high ground, to the silent windmill painted black against the sky. 'I thinks 'e be goin' nowhere,' she said, 'not for the 'ole night anyway.'

'Then where is he spending his nights?' Phoebe asked, worry plain in her voice. 'I hope he is not sleeping on the heath.'

'I don't think 'e is,' Lucy glanced again at the windmill standing tall into the glow of the setting sun, 'I think 'e be sleepin' in there.'

'The windmill?' Bert followed the line of Lucy's eyes and her reasoning. 'Could well be. I could think of worse places a lad might get 'isself 'oled up in. You women wait indoors, Mathew an' me will go look.'

'You have been sleeping in the old windmill since the first day Mathew brought you here?' Phoebe said ten minutes later when the bellows boy stood in her kitchen, Mathew and Bert to either side of him.

'Yes, Miss,' the boy answered, chin on chest.

'But why? Is the walk from Wednesbury to here and back too much for you?'

'T'ain't too much!' The boy's chin came up defiantly. 'Ain't nuthin', that tiddly walk. I could walk six time further'n that wi'out feelin' tired.'

Bert placed a hand on the boy's shoulder, feeling the bones through his ragged coat. 'Tell 'er, lad.'

'Ain't nuthin' to tell.'

'If there ain't another reason you be sleepin' in that mill then Miss Phoebe be right in thinkin' the walk be too much for you, an' that bein' the case 'er might give you your coppers, lad, an' that means you'll be out o' a job.'

The boy looked quickly to Phoebe, the subtle warning Bert had given bringing fear to his eyes.

'You wouldn't, would you, Miss? You wouldn't go givin' me the sack?'

Phoebe looked at him. The sleeves of his threadbare coat were short of his wrists by several inches, his trousers halfway up his legs with more holes in them than sultanas in one of Lucy's scones, and her heart twisted with pity. What was it drove him to sneak back to sleep in the mill?

'I would have to if I thought it too far for you to walk, Josh.'

''T'ain't, Miss. Honest 't'ain't.' He looked down to where his toes peeped through boots that lacked the laces to fasten them. 'It's . . . it's . . . I ain't got no 'ome.' The reservoir of pride breached, the words tumbled from him. 'Me dad 'e buggered off years ago, left me mother to fend for 'erself an' me. We managed not too bad while she could tek in washin', then when 'er got sick we couldn't pay the landlord an' 'e chucked we out. It was the work'ouse or the road an' me mother wouldn't tek the work'ouse, least not till 'er could 'ardly walk no more. 'Er died the day after 'er went in. So you see, Miss, I ain't got other than the 'eath to sleep an' that windmill be a shelter from the wind.' He looked up at Phoebe. 'I didn't think as you would mind, Miss, I meant no 'arm, really I didn't.'

'And you did none.' Phoebe resisted the urge to take him in her arms, knowing that his fierce pride would resent any offer of childish comfort. 'But I wish you had told me.'

'You would 'ave chucked me out if I 'ad.'

'Miss Phoebe wouldn't 'ave chucked you out,' Mathew said.

'Mebbe 'er wouldn't,' the boy remained stubborn, 'but it was a chance I wasn't tekin'. Long as nobody seen me go in I 'ad a place to sleep.' He twisted free from Bert's hand. 'Who told you I was in there anyway?'

'Nobody told we,' Bert answered. 'Well, p'raps that's not strictly true. It were Mrs Leach not seein' 'ide nor 'air of you not comin' to work in the mornin's nor goin' back of an evenin'. Seemed strange to 'er that did, set 'er to wonderin' just 'ow you did get to Wiggins Mill.'

'I couldn't 'ave missed sight o' you, Josh,' Lucy said apologetically. 'The 'eath be mostly flat 'tween 'ere an' Wednesbury. You could spot a grass'opper a mile off.'

'I knows you didn't mean to drop me in it,' the boy tried to smile as he looked from her to Phoebe, 'an' I'm sorry to 'ave been the cause o' trouble, Miss. I won't go in the mill any more, you can be 'sured o' that. Just let me keep me job an' I'll bugger off every night cleaner than me father did.'

'You won't go nowhere every night, same as you won't be usin' that foul language no more.' Lizzie pushed further into the kitchen. ''E can't be sleepin' on that 'eath, Miss Phoebe, so unless you 'ave any objections 'e could bed down the side o' our Mark. There be room a-plenty in the corn loft, an' 'im an' Mark, they gets on well together.'

'Bert?' Phoebe looked at the man standing beside the young boy.

'That be all right by me, Miss Phoebe. Lad can stay wi'

Lizzie an' me long as 'e as a job at Wiggins Mill. An' if I knows Lizzie, 'er will look after 'im.'

'What do you say, Josh?' Phoebe asked.

A smile splitting his face, the boy looked at Lizzie. 'Bostin',' he breathed. 'I say that be bostin'.'

'I thought we would have afternoon tea in the garden, it is still quite warm enough,' Annie signed, finding her brother in his studio. 'And you do so enjoy the garden.' She stopped speaking, her mouth half open with surprise as she caught sight of the canvas on the easel. It was a finished portrait of Phoebe, only the paint that formed the signature still gleaming wetly. The face looked serenely back at her, a calmness beyond its years radiating from it. It was also the image of Abel's pretty wife, she realised.

'I . . . I did not know you had painted this.' Annie caught her brother's eyes on her and struggled to regain her composure. 'It is very good, especially considering you have seen so very little of Abel's daughter.'

Samuel's long narrow fingers moved rapidly. 'I worked from this more than from memory.' Going to a drawer set in a long bench-top table on the opposite side of the room, he drew out a photograph, handing it to Annie. 'It was in among some of Abel's papers. I found it when I went through them.'

Among Abel's papers? Annie stared at the photograph. She'd thought she had weeded everything out but obviously she had missed this and Samuel had said nothing of it, as he had said nothing of the portrait he'd now finished. What else had he said nothing of? What other secrets lay hidden from her? None that mattered, surely. She had held his Power of Attorney long enough to take everything from him save this house, and now it was too late for him to make good his intention of naming Phoebe his heir. She handed back the photograph. Their niece would get none of the wealth that had once been her father's.

'It is a very good likeness,' Samuel signed. 'We must hang it opposite the one of her father, they will look very well together. Perhaps James Siveter will find her and persuade her to come home. It would be nice to have her here with us, don't you agree, Annie?'

'Of course, dear,' Annie's fingers carried the lie. 'Nothing would give me more happiness than to have Phoebe return to us. We must pray that God will make it so.' She watched Samuel clean his brushes, immersing each in a jar of turpentine then wiping the bristles on a soft cloth. He could pray as much as he liked but he would find God as deaf as himself. She looked at the lovely painted face, her fingers curling into her palms. The portrait could hang with that of Abel but his daughter would never again live here.

She would sell this house, she thought as Samuel poured water from a tall flower-twined jug into a matching basin and washed his hands. She would sell it and give the money to Clinton to invest in more tube works. After all, there would be no need to keep this place on when she became his wife.

Clinton's wife. The thought stayed with Annie as they walked downstairs to the garden. How long would it be before they could marry? Not for several months that was certain, a suitable period of mourning for her brother must elapse before they could be wed, the proprieties must be observed. But Clinton would not mind the waiting, not when he saw her grief for Samuel's passing.

'Will you be wantin' tea now?' Maudie followed them into the garden.

'You have not mashed it yet, have you?' Annie asked sharply. 'I have no taste for stewed tea.'

You've no taste for anythin', if you asks me! Maudie sucked in her cheeks, looking at Annie's lavender dress with ill-concealed disdain.

'Tea ain't been mashed, not yet,' she replied. 'I knows 'ow you likes yer tea, an' so I should after all the years I've spent mekin' it.'

That won't go on for much longer, Annie thought. Once I am married you can count yourself dismissed. Aloud she said waspishly, 'Not long enough to do it graciously but I suppose we must make do. You may bring the tray now.'

Sour-faced old cow! Maudie returned to the kitchen. But then, that one had never had a good word for the doings of anybody other than herself – not that she had ever done good in her life.

'You have forgotten the herbal tea.' Annie looked at the tray her housekeeper set down on the wicker table.

'I ain't forgot nothin',' Maudie replied. 'I set it on a sep'rate tray. Seein' as 'ow Mr Samuel don't care for medicines I thought it might suit better for it to be on another tray altogether.'

'I see.' Annie began pouring milk into the cups. 'Then bring it out. It will do Mr Samuel no good left sitting in a bottle.'

'Yes, Ma'am.' Maudie turned away. If that mixture were only poison, she would gladly pour the lot down Annie Pardoe's throat!

'It is just a herbal tea, dear,' Annie's fingers signed rapidly to her brother. 'Mrs Gaskell Wheeler recommended it, she is convinced it will help you build up your strength, and I am sure Mrs Tranter has something that will relieve the taste should it prove unpalatable.' She looked at Maudie, carefully measuring the mixture into a cup, adding a little of the hot water from the tea tray. 'Have you something sweet?' she asked.

Maudie nodded a smile to Samuel, knowing he could not hear but wanting him to understand. 'Yes, Ma'am,' she said. 'I took a chocolate cake from the baker this mornin'. It be Mr Samuel's favourite sort.'

'Bring it for him then,' Annie said, 'he will take the herbal tea much easier with a chocolate cake to follow.'

Pouring the tea, she watched Maudie set the cake at Samuel's elbow then hand him the herbal mixture. Swallowing it in two long gulps, he handed the cup back to her.

'There now, that didn't be so bad, did it?' Maudie crooned to his silent ears. 'Now eat up your cake an' you'll soon forget the swallowin' o' that stuff.'

Annie picked up her own cup as Samuel took the cake, sinking his teeth into the chocolate-covered mound. Eat his cake and Samuel would soon be forgetting everything!

Chewing the last vestige of chocolate, Samuel touched his mouth with his napkin, eyes straying to the privet hedge that shielded the end of the garden. Annie had walked the length of it and when she had walked back she had held a hand close against her skirts.

It had gone as she'd known it would. Annie stood beside the four-poster bed that had been her brother's marriage bed. Samuel had eaten the cake. The ground yew and laburnum seeds had not worked, why she could not guess, but the poison she had mixed in the cream of that cake would. This time there would be no mistake. Come the morning Samuel would be dead and she would be free to enjoy her life as Mrs Clinton Harforth-Darby.

The pain that had gnawed at her all day spiralled up from her side and into her breast, the rawness of it stealing the breath from her lungs. Sinking on to the bed, she groped for the bottle of small white tablets, taking two into her mouth even as she poured a glass of water from the carafe on her night table. Waiting for the pain to pass, she checked the fob watch pinned to the shoulder of her dress. It wanted a quarter of an hour to nine o'clock. Samuel always retired at eight-thirty, he would already be in his bed.

Annie forced herself to stand. She must say goodnight to him as she always did. Tomorrow he would be beyond remembering whether she had or not but that sharp-nosed Maudie Tranter would remember the least thing that was different, and though you may not see Maudie Tranter, you could be certain the woman missed nothing.

Tapping on Samuel's bedroom door as her mother had

insisted everyone must though no sound passed his barrier of silence, Annie pushed open the door.

'Goodnight, dear,' she signed.

Samuel's hands rose like white wounded birds. 'Goodnight, Annie,' he signed, a slowness in his fingers. 'You always did what you thought best. Thank you, dear.'

What did he mean? Annie asked herself, leaning down to kiss his brow. Then in the soft glow of the oil lamp she caught the look in his eyes. He knew! Samuel knew what she had done. He was thanking her for giving him death!

Chapter Nineteen

Dead!

Phoebe walked across the heath toward Wednesbury, her mind still trying to reject the news Lucy had brought with her the night before. Her Uncle Samuel was dead.

She had not seen him since the reading of her father's will. In all that time he had not tried to contact her, not even when she was in prison. True she had never seen a great deal of Uncle Samuel, even as a child, but for him to ignore her very existence seemed somehow unnatural.

Reaching the town, she walked along Lower High Street, taking the turning that would lead her past Oakeswell Hall. She glanced at the black and white half-timbered building as she passed its curtain wall. Would Sophie live there when she married Montrose? The thought brought a twinge of pain, but it was pain for Sophie not for herself.

At the gate of Brunswick House she paused. This had once been her home, a place of happiness and love. Now it held neither. She had always been so glad to return here yet now she wanted only to turn and run. But she had to go in. Uncle Samuel was her father's brother and she must show her respects.

At the door she tugged the bell pull, her eyes avoiding the mourning wreath set at its centre. Her aunt hated her, that much had been made plain, but she was not here for the sake of her aunt.

'Eh, Miss Phoebe!' Maudie Tranter looked at the girl standing on the doorstep. 'What be you doin' 'ere?'

'Lucy told me my Uncle Samuel has passed away.'

'Ar, Miss, 'e 'as. In the night it was . . .'

'Who is it, Mrs Tranter?'

Inside Phoebe shivered at the sound of her aunt's voice but she stepped determinedly into the hall. 'It is me, Aunt.'

Annie Pardoe's hand flew to her side. She had not expected this, had had no intention of informing Abel's daughter of his brother's death. 'What are you doing here?' she rasped. 'You are not wanted in this house.'

'You made that clear enough more than two years ago,' Phoebe replied.

'That will be all, Tranter.' Annie glared at the listening Maudie, waiting until the door leading off to the kitchen had closed behind her. 'If I made it so clear,' she said, turning back to Phoebe, 'then how come you are here now?'

'I was given the news my Uncle Samuel was dead. I have come to Brunswick House to pay my respects, and that is the only thing I am here for.'

'Respects!' Annie let her gaze travel slowly over her niece. 'What respect does it show to come dressed in green? You have not even the respect to adopt mourning.'

'I apologise for the colour of my clothing,' Phoebe's chin came up, 'but this is all I have. You did not allow me an extensive wardrobe, did you, Aunt?'

'I want you to leave.' Annie placed a hand on the door handle.

'And I want to leave, Aunt, very much, I find you a most unpleasant person to be with, but I will not leave until I have done that for which I came.' Phoebe walked to the foot of the stairs. 'Is Uncle Samuel in his room?'

'No,' Annie looked towards the door of the parlour, 'he is in there.'

Phoebe stood for a moment, unmoving. Uncle Samuel had not wished her to visit him in life. Would he wish the same in death? Was her presence in this house an intrusion he would have resented? Somewhere deep in her heart she felt that to be untrue. He had been so kind to her on the few occasions they had met. Taking a long breath, she walked into the parlour.

Nothing had changed. The chiffonier held the same Staffordshire china figurines, the same high-backed sofa stood against the wall, only the mahogany table below the central ceiling gasolier was different. It stood where it always had but its heavy Brussels lace cloth was gone and in its place was draped the black velvet that had lain beneath her father's coffin and now lay beneath Samuel's.

Phoebe stared at the features that seemed to be cut from marble, her heart full of tears that would not reach her eyes. Though his eyes were closed and no smile lingered at his mouth the strange haunted look that had constantly drawn his face was no longer there. Her uncle seemed to have found a peace in death he had never known in life.

'Aunt,' she said softly, 'why do you hate me so much?'

Stood on the opposite side of the coffin Annie felt the breath catch in her throat but the rising gall of bitterness was too much for her to swallow.

'Your father stole my life!' she screamed. 'He took it, him and his fancy wife, and gave me this in return.' She struck the side of the walnut casket with her hand. 'I have had no life of my own now for nearly twenty years, I have known a living death all that time and it was your father's gift to me. He made me responsible for Samuel – Samuel who could not be cared for by any other than his own family, who could not be taken into your father's house for fear of causing distress to his pretty wife. Oh, yes, *she* must be shielded from his affliction.'

Phoebe looked from the face of her dead uncle to that of her aunt, twisted with bitterness. 'Affliction?'

'Yes, affliction!' Annie spat. 'That which kept him from leading a normal life, which kept him from taking a wife, which used up my life in keeping his secret.'

'But surely Uncle Samuel's deafness was not a good enough cause to turn him into a recluse.'

Annie's eyes burned as she answered, 'No, it was not a good enough cause. But it was not only deafness my brother suffered from – it was this!' Reaching into the casket she lifted the long white robe that covered her brother's body, snatching it open to the waist.

Phoebe gasped then turned away, her senses stunned.

'That was what made my brother a recluse!' Annie cried viciously. 'That was the shame that must be kept hidden from the world. That was what kept him from taking a wife for what woman would marry a man who was no man, who was neither male nor female, but had the genitals of both!'

'How strange we meet in the same place, Miss Pardoe. Miss Pardoe!' Sir William Dartmouth caught the arm of the young woman whose eyes set in a chalk-white face seemed to look straight through him. 'Are you feeling unwell?'

'Uncle Samuel,' Phoebe mumbled. 'Uncle Samuel, he . . . Lucy will . . . I must . . .'

Supporting her with his arm as she sagged against him, he helped her into the George Hotel. 'A doctor, quickly,' he ordered the attentive manager. 'Then a brandy. Move, man!'

'Nothing physically wrong,' Alfred Dingley said an hour later. 'She is suffering from some sort of shock, though . . . I have given her a sedative that will help but she needs rest and will get that better at home than she will here.' He nodded towards the door of the upstairs sitting room Phoebe had been taken to. 'I will have a carriage sent round to take her. Was there anyone with her, do you know?'

'She was alone when I met her in the street,' Sir William answered, 'so I presume no one was accompanying her, and as for a carriage there will be no need. I will see Miss Pardoe gets home. Send your account to the Priory.' He stood aside for the doctor to leave. 'Good day, Doctor.'

Tapping first at the door he went into the room where Phoebe sat, the wife of the hotel manager hovering at her elbow.

'Are you feeling better, Miss Pardoe?' he asked.

She looked up, the shock still showing in her eyes. 'Yes,' she said. 'Thank you, Sir William. I am sorry to have been so much trouble.'

'You were no trouble.'

'That is kind of you to say.' Phoebe stood up, her legs still not quite her own. 'But I have delayed you. I thank you again for helping me. I can manage on my own now.'

'Were you alone?'

'Yes.' Phoebe smiled at the woman handing her her bag.

'You said something about an Uncle Samuel and Lucy, were they not with you?'

Phoebe breathed deeply, her fingers curling tightly about the bag. 'My uncle is dead, Sir William. I have just come from paying my respects and I was going to speak to Lucy.'

'Lucy?' He frowned slightly. 'Is that the Lucy you told me was once in the employ of my wife?'

Phoebe nodded.

'Mrs Leach, so where is she now?' he asked.

'She will be in the market place.'

Sir William looked at the woman still hovering close to Phoebe. 'Send to the market place. See if Mrs Leach is there.'

'I know 'er, Sir,' the woman bobbed a curtsy, 'I'll fetch 'er.'

'There is no need,' Phoebe protested, 'I can go there myself.'

'Go to Mrs Leach,' Sir William spoke to the woman, ignoring Phoebe's protest, 'ask her to be good enough to come here, and tell your husband to have my carriage brought to the door.'

'Yes, Sir.' The woman bobbed again then disappeared through the door.

'I am sorry to hear of your uncle's death,' he continued to Phoebe, 'please accept my condolences. If I can be of assistance, do not hesitate to contact me.'

Phoebe walked from the room and down the stairs to the lobby. 'My aunt will be handling everything,' she said. 'She has cared for my uncle for many years.'

'Miss Phoebe, are you all right? What happened?' Lucy rushed in from the street.

'Lucy!' Phoebe caught her hands, holding them tightly. 'Lucy, I am so glad you are here.'

'Miss Pardoe has suffered something of a shock,' Sir William answered Lucy's enquiring glance. 'The doctor says she will be all right but she is in need of rest. Will you see her home?'

'O' course.' Lucy put an arm about Phoebe. 'You take a seat, Miss, while I finds the carter. 'E'll be 'avin' a drink in the Turks 'Ead round about this time. 'E'll give us both a ride as far as the Tipton Road.'

'Do not trouble yourself with the carter, Mrs Leach,' Sir William said as Lucy made to get a chair. 'My carriage is just outside. My driver will take you home and return for me here.'

'I'll collect your things from the market, Mrs Leach. They will keep 'ere till you collect them.' The manager's wife hovered nearby, eager to be seen offering assistance.

'Ta, Mrs Jinks.' Lucy led the way out of the lobby. 'I'll pick 'em up tomorrer.'

'Sir William, there is no need for me to take your carriage,' Phoebe hesitated at the door, 'a ride with the carter will do as well.'

He smiled suddenly, a light dancing behind his grey eyes. 'Miss Pardoe, you once told me that I should never use the word "must" to you again, but I will if I have to. Now spare me the retribution that would bring by accepting my carriage.'

Phoebe smiled. 'I would not have retribution fall upon you, Sir William, so I will accept. And thank you.'

Inside the carriage Phoebe leaned back, her eyes closed against the horror of what had taken place at Brunswick House, a house that had once held so much love and laughter and now held so much unhappiness.

Poor Uncle Samuel. She flinched as the picture of his thin disfigured body flashed before her closed eyelids. To have spent a lifetime with such a deformity would be terrible enough for any man to suffer, but knowing his sister's resentment, thinking that he was responsible, albeit indirectly, for her solitary life, as he must have done, could only have added to that suffering; and Aunt Annie, so consumed with her bitterness, so twisted with hate for her own family, had she ever made any attempt to hide her true feelings or had she shown them to Samuel as she had shown them to Phoebe?

Behind her closed lids a pale finely drawn face smiled back at her, a gentle kindly face, but one whose blue eyes held the shadow of pain.

'Are you all right, Miss Phoebe?' Lucy asked, feeling the shudder that passed through her.

Phoebe saw again the figure of her aunt standing over the casket which held that malformed body, her face distorted with the hate she held for her brother's child. All right? Phoebe turned her face, pressing it into Lucy's shoulder. Would she ever be all right again?

Five days to the end of the month. Phoebe looked at the calendar. She had crossed off each day as it ended, making a note of the number of finished locks. Now less than thirty were needed to make the gross. They had all worked so hard; even Ruth had helped put the finished locks in the wooden soap box Josh had got from the carter.

Brushing her hair, Phoebe remembered the grin on the boy's face as he had related his deal with the man. She had sent Josh with twopence to pay for the box. He had offered the carter one penny.

'A penny!' Zach Coates had laughed. 'It cost me more than that to cart it out 'ere.'

'It'll cost you twice as much if you 'as to cart it back,' Josh retorted. 'You might as well let me 'ave it.'

'Not fer a bloody penny I ain't. I might as well use it fer firewood, at least it'll keep me warm.'

'Why not swap it for this?' Josh had opened the sack he had carried with him across the heath, displaying the lumps of coal. 'It'll burn a lot longer than the few sticks that old box'll mek an' give off a lot more 'eat.'

'An' where 'ave you pinched that from?' Zach had demanded.

'Never you mind,' Josh told him. 'If I tell you you'll only get a 'eadache worryin' about it an' you'll 'ave to pay tuppence for a bottle of Aspro to cure it. So you see, you'll still be outta pocket.'

'You be a right bloody smart arse, don't you!' Zach grumbled, handing the soapbox down to Josh.

'Ar, an' you'll be a right 'ot 'un if you stands too near that coal,' Josh returned, handing over the sack. ''Eat that gives off is more than the fires o' Hell you've 'eard talk about.'

Tying a ribbon to the plait in her hair Phoebe could not resist a smile. Josh had bounced into the workshop, placing the box on the floor, his grin wide as the heath as he handed back the two pennies.

He was a nice boy. Phoebe climbed into bed, the smile still warm on her lips. Things were going so well, maybe he could stay on after the locks were finished.

Climbing into bed, she turned off the oil lamp that stood beside it on a table and lay back, staring at the moonlight filling her window. It was the same moonlight as filled the windows of Handsworth Prison only the spectres it held were different. In gaol the moonlight had brought memories of her life outside. Now it often brought memories of her life locked away behind those walls. How many women were lying behind them now, their freedom snatched away, and how many were staring at the moonlight?

She would never forget. Every moment spent in that place was etched deep in her soul, every word and every blow. No, she would not forget, nor would she forget Sir William. He had brought the release she thanked God for each night, but more than that he had shown her kindness at every opportunity. But why? For what reason? If he had been indebted to her because of her imprisonment he had more than made up for it. Or could it be her friendship with his son, did he know of Edward's feelings toward her? Phoebe looked away from the light of the window but the tall figure of Sir William Dartmouth remained lit in her mind. No, that was not the reason behind his kindness to her. A man with an ancestry graced by the best families in the county for so many generations would not allow his son to break with tradition. Whatever reason lay behind his friendship she was sure her possible marriage to Edward played no part in it.

Edward . . . Phoebe closed her eyes. Was he blind to his illustrious name? Could he honestly not see his parents could never accept her as his wife, a woman who had been in prison, or was he just too stubborn to accept it? He had asked her to marry him again when he and Sophie had called, bringing their mother's regrets that Phoebe would not be attending the ball and also her condolences for Uncle Samuel's death.

Phoebe turned restlessly, her eyes returning to the moonlit window. She had refused as gently as she could, trying not to hurt Edward, and now he was gone, left for Europe with his mother and sister. Painful as she knew it would be to him, she had felt bound to tell him she did not love him, her feelings were not those of a girl desiring to be his wife. He had smiled then, masking the hurt, and Phoebe had seen the strength of his father in him. Edward Dartmouth had been hurt but that hurt would never be allowed to affect his friendship toward her. Phoebe closed her eyes again but it was not Edward who stayed with her as she drifted into sleep. It was not his mouth that smiled or his eyes that watched her. The face that bent toward her was that of Sir William Dartmouth.

'That is the last of them, Tranter.'

Annie Pardoe folded the sheet of paper, slipping it into the envelope she had just finished addressing. There had been more messages of sympathy for the death of her brother than she would have expected and she had let a suitable time elapse before answering them. Let people believe her too grief-stricken to write replies before the two weeks that had gone by. Gathering the envelopes together, she handed them to Maudie.

'People will understand why it has taken so long before I answered their messages,' she said, wiping the pen nib clean of ink before moving from the desk. 'They will realise how much pain it causes me.'

Pain my arse! Maudie thought caustically. The only pain Samuel caused you was the pain of wanting him out of the way, and that pain worsened with the arrival of that Harforth-Darby!

'Take them to the post office now.' Annie took half a crown from a small black lacquered box, handing it to her housekeeper. 'That will be more than enough to pay for stamps.'

'Yes, Ma'am.' Maudie did not bob a curtsy. 'An' there'll be change an' all, I know that wi'out yer tellin'.'

Annie bit back the anger that rose in her as Maudie walked from the study. Maudie Tranter knew a lot of things and in a very few weeks she would know one more. She would know she was out of a job.

Following her from the study, Annie walked up the stairs. Maudie had seen her leave the study, she would think the last of the letters written as she had been told, but there was one more yet to do. Watching from the window of her room she saw Maudie leave the house by the rear door, crossing the yard and taking the path that led through the grounds to a door set in the garden wall. Looking at her fob watch, Annie remained at the window. She would give Maudie five minutes before writing that last letter.

The minutes gone she took the sheet of writing paper from where she had slipped it into the packet of her skirts. It was not exactly the same as the one that had lain so long in the drawer of her washstand but it was white and that was near enough. Going to the wardrobe she took her bag from the shelf, taking out a fresh bottle of ink and a new pen. She had thrown the others into Millfield Pool not thinking of the letter she must write now but her visits to Alfred Dingley's consulting room had afforded the opportunity to purchase more. Stress, the doctor had called the pain in her side, stress due to the passing of her brother but it would cease with time. She'd known it had to come, he had told her, slipping tablets into a small brown glass bottle. They had all known, even her brother himself. Annie levered the cork from the bottle of ink. Yes, Samuel had known. The look in his eyes as she kissed him goodnight had told her so.

Reaching once more into her bag, she took out the bill she had been given when she went back to that shop near Birmingham railroad station. It had been clever of her to pretend to have forgotten to buy pot menders when she bought those mousetraps. It had given her two receipts.

Fetching the small nail scissors she kept in a drawer of her dresser, she carefully cut the heading from the receipt. Quickly pouring a small amount of water from the carafe on her night table she placed it beside the ink then, drawing her handkerchief from her pocket, tipped into the water the spoonful of plain flour she had taken from the pantry while Maudie Tranter had been on her half day off. Using the long handle of the pen she mixed the flour and water to a paste then, with the tip of one finger, smoothed a little of it on to the back of the heading she had cut from James Greaves's receipt, attaching that to the top of the sheet of white paper. That done, she carefully washed pen and glass in the bowl on the washstand, wiping them on the towel folded beside it. Opening the window, she emptied the water she had used on to the flower border below. Maudie Tranter would find no trace when she came to clean.

Annie sat at the table and began to write. Tomorrow she would post this letter herself and the ink and pen would follow the others to the bottom of Millfield Pool.

The letter finished and sealed, all trace of its having been written hidden away, Annie returned her bag to the wardrobe, caressing the silk of the pearl grey gown and the rustling lavender taffeta. She must wear black for appearance's sake but once the period of mourning was over she would never wear it again. She would wear only gowns of coloured silk, the colours Clinton liked. Soon she would be with him. But how soon would that be? Annie tried to push away the thoughts that held sway in the shadows of her mind but they would not be denied.

Three weeks and more, it had been all of that since she had given him the money which the sale of the last of Abel's bequest had brought. Three weeks and she had heard nothing from him. He had told her she would have deeds of ownership to land on which to build her tube works in a couple of days, but those days had grown into weeks and she had seen nothing of him or the papers. But he would come, he would! She closed the door of the wardrobe, gritting her teeth as a spasm of pain bit upward to her breast. Clinton would come.

'Change from the post office.' Maudie entered the sitting room where Annie now sat, a newspaper spread across the table.

'Leave it there.' A nod of her head indicated the opposite side of the table but Annie did not look up.

'Do there be any mention of the Wheelers' trouble in the paper, Ma'am?' Maudie asked.

'Trouble!' Annie looked up sharply. 'What trouble? What are you talking about?'

'I 'eard it when I was comin' from the post office.' Maudie stood with hands folded in front of her. 'Two women was sayin' as 'ow Oakeswell 'All be in mournin', said as they 'ad it from one o' the maids.'

'In mourning?'

'That be what them women said, I 'eard for meself.'

'But for whom?' Annie asked, not quite believing what her housekeeper had said. 'Is it Gaskell?'

'Don't know, Ma'am,' Maudie replied. 'They said as nobody knowed.'

'How ridiculous! There couldn't be a death in the house without its being known who had died.'

'No, Ma'am, but there could be one as 'adn't took place in the 'ouse. That way could be the maid wouldn't know who it was 'ad died.'

'Well, it is no member of the family,' Annie glanced at the newspaper, 'otherwise there would have been an entry in the Obituaries column and there is none. Most probably it is a remote aunt of Mrs Wheeler's. She did sometimes talk of one living in southern France.'

'Likely that be who it is then.' Maudie turned to leave then paused as Annie spoke again.

'Nevertheless it is only polite to call and offer my sympathy, I shall go to Oakeswell Hall now.'

Fastening her cloak, Annie thought rapidly. She would go to the post office first and post the letter she had written. Then she would make her way to Oakeswell Hall, passing Millfield Pool where she would dispose of pen and bottle of ink.

From childhood she had been used to harnessing pony to trap and needed no help with either. Twenty minutes from hearing the news Maudie had brought, Annie was driving across the open ground that skirted Millfield Pool.

'I heard it being talked of in the town,' she said when she was shown into Violet Wheeler's sitting room, 'and felt

I must call and offer my condolence were it true for I saw no announcement in the newspaper.'

Violet Wheeler sat down, her black skirts flowing over the edges of her chair. 'Gaskell made none.'

'Then your husband is still with us, thank the Lord.'

Ordering tea from the housemaid who answered her ring, Violet looked at her visitor. 'Gaskell? But of course he is still with us.'

Uncomfortable beneath the other woman's gaze, Annie apologised. 'Forgive me, but with there being no announcement . . .'

'Of course,' Violet cut in, 'but as you say, Gaskell is still with us, thank the Lord.' Waiting as the maid reappeared with the tea tray, then with a bobbed curtsy left again, she went on, 'My husband is recently returned from London.'

'It is not Montrose, I hope?' Annie said. 'Not your son?'

Violet poured the tea with the grace of long practice. 'If you mean you are hoping it is not my son's death we are mourning, Miss Pardoe, then your hopes are fulfilled. My husband was in London on a business trip, not concerning our son.'

So it was Violet Wheeler's aunt who had died. Annie took the cup held out to her. 'It relieves me to hear your son is well.'

'Yes, Montrose is quite well though he is disappointed that given the circumstances we will not now be holding a farewell reception for him before his regiment leaves for India.'

Replacing her cup on the tray, Annie stood up. 'I will not intrude upon you any longer, Mrs Wheeler. I came only to offer my sympathy in your loss.'

'Before you go there is something here we believe was intended for your brother.' Crossing to an elegant mahogany sideboard she took a large envelope from a drawer, handing it to Annie. 'Gaskell saw his name on this but it bore no address so he brought it back with him from London.'

'Oh!' Annie turned the envelope in her hand but it bore no mark other than the name 'Pardoe' scrawled shakily across it.

'It was among Clinton's effects.'

Effects! Annie's hand tightened convulsively on the envelope. Why was Gaskell Wheeler dealing with Clinton's effects? Why was Clinton in London when he had told her he would be in Wednesbury? The answer was staring her in the face. Clinton had gone and her money had gone with him!

'Thank your husband for me.' Annie's lips struggled with the words.

'Gaskell's cousin was so ill before he left Oakeswell Hall . . .' Violet Wheeler's words followed Annie to the door.

'Ill?'

'Yes, it all came upon him so suddenly,' Violet answered the query in Annie's voice, 'stomach cramps and symptoms so akin to fever he thought it a return of the malady that struck him when he lived in the Caribbean. He went to London to consult his doctor there and we heard no more until a mutual friend wrote to tell Gaskell that his cousin was dead. Who would have thought it?' She fluttered a handkerchief to her eyes. 'A man as vital as Clinton, dead in a couple of days.'

Clinton was dead! Annie stood in her own bedroom with no memory of the drive back to Brunswick House. He had died after so short and so unexpected an illness. Clinton was dead! Taking the scissors she had used earlier that afternoon, she opened the wardrobe door. Clinton was dead and with him her dreams. Stabbing the scissors into the cloth, she slashed the grey and the lavender gowns. Clinton was dead, she would have no need of colours. The gowns in shreds about the floor, Annie slumped to the bed. *Such a short illness, so sudden, dead in a couple of days* . . . Violet Wheeler's words reverberated in her brain, circling round and round. What was it that had caused the death of a man who had appeared the picture of health when he had last called on her?

When he had last called on her. . . . Annie stared at the remnants of the pearl grey gown. She had been wearing that when he had been shown into the sitting room, when she had handed sherry to him and to Samuel. She had given Samuel the glass she always used for him, the glass with a small air bubble in the stem, one that she could not confuse with her own. She had handed it to him as Maudie had announced the arrival of the constables. But she hadn't! Fear closed her throat as memory returned. She had not handed Samuel his sherry. The tray had been taken from her by Clinton.

So sudden. . . . The words seemed to scream in her mind. Stomach cramp followed by fever, the same symptoms the powdered seeds of yew and laburnum produced. She had not handed Samuel his sherry, Clinton had after she had left the room. That explained why her brother had not fallen ill as she had expected. He had not drunk the poison, Clinton had. She had killed Clinton!

Pain surged into her breast but Annie ignored it. She had killed Samuel for nothing, she had sold his inheritance for nothing, she would never be Mrs Clinton Harforth-Darby. And the money she had handed over to him, what had happened to that? Was it in some account that would most likely pass to Gaskell Wheeler? And the envelope Violet Wheeler had handed her, what lay in there? Reaching for it where she had dropped it on the bed, she looked at the name sprawled across it. Was it some lies as to her money or did it contain the barefaced truth? He had played her for a fool and now thank you, Annie Pardoe. Thank you and goodbye.

Breaking open the seal she drew out a letter, the writing spidery. '*Annie, my dear,*' she read, '*I wanted to bring you these myself but I am afraid I feel too ill. I will post them to you from London. You will be in my thoughts until I return. Yours, Clinton.*'

Taking the rest of the contents from the envelope, Annie looked at the stylised wording . . . *land and buildings appertaining thereto the property of Annie Mary Pardoe* . . .

Slowly she began to laugh, a low empty laugh that echoed round the room, laughing as her soul died.

Chapter Twenty

'They be a fine job, Miss, you'll 'ave no trouble wi' them.'

'Thank you, Bert, you have worked so hard.' Phoebe looked at the wooden soap box filled almost to the top with shining brass locks.

'I couldn't 'ave done it by meself, everybody 'as worked 'ard and that includes yourself.'

'Four days, Bert,' she reminded him, 'four days to delivery. Do you think we will do it?'

'We be good as done now,' he smiled. 'Mathew an' me we be on the last batch. Tomorrow will see the lot finished.'

'I must admit I had doubts when we started. It seemed impossible for you to have made so many in the time we were given.'

'Would 'ave been if Mathew 'adn't stepped in, an' them two lads 'ave worked like Trojans. I tell you, without that pair there would 'ave been no order to deliver in four days' time.'

'I wish I were the Queen."

'The Queen?' Mathew glanced up from the lock he was freeing from a vice attached to the work bench. 'Whatever do you want to be 'er for?'

Phoebe's eyes danced. 'Because then I could give you all a medal. You certainly deserve one.'

Josh looked up from pumping the bellows, his face red from his efforts. 'Medals be no good, you just 'ave to keep on cleanin' 'em. 'Sides, like me mother used to say, you can't eat medals.'

'In that case, Josh, I will make yours a fish supper.'

'That be more like it.' He looked across to where Mark was working alongside Mathew. 'What you say, Mark?'

'I say mek that two suppers, an' mek me eat both.'

'Them pair, eatin' be all they think on,' Bert joked. 'I swear neither of 'em 'as a bottom to their belly.'

'Hard work makes men hungry, which reminds me – Tilly and Lizzie said to tell you the meal was ready and waiting on the table.'

'I would rather 'ear news like that than that the Queen was to visit.' Josh laid the brass-studded bellows aside, running his palms along the sides of his trousers.

'Well, I might not be Queen, Josh White, but rubbing your hands on your trousers will not do for me nor will it do for Lizzie. You know her rule: no hands washed, no dinner given.'

Josh looked at his hands then at Phoebe, his grin cheeky. 'I might 'ave known there'd be a price to pay! Mind you, I wouldn't mind 'avin' a bath for one o' Mrs Ingles's dinners, only don't tell 'er I said so.'

''Ave you thought on what you be goin' to do wi' them locks when they be finished?' Mathew asked as they ate their dinner.

'Do with them?' Phoebe asked, a certain amount of surprise in her voice. 'I am going to deliver them to Mr Greaves, of course.'

Mathew chewed on some cheese. 'I know that be your intention but 'ow?'

'I've been wonderin' the same, Miss.' Bert looked up from his plate of cheese and pickles. 'Carryin' two or three o' them locks be one thing. Carryin' a gross on 'em be summat else.'

'Carryin' 'em be summat you ain't never goin' to do. You needs transport.' Mathew cut a slice of onion, sliding it into his mouth from the blade of his knife.

Across the long trestle table that the men had set up at one end of the corn barn, and where Lizzie and Tilly had laid the midday meal, Phoebe looked at them both, her brows drawing together in a worried frown. She had been so busy, so preoccupied with her sewing and with helping in the workshop, she had totally forgotten the need to arrange transport of the locks to Birmingham.

Mathew continued to eat. 'So what be you goin' to do?'

'I don't know,' Phoebe admitted. 'That part of it never seemed to enter my head.'

'We could 'ire a 'andcart?' Mathew suggested.

Bert nodded. 'We could, but it be a long push to Brummagem. It be all o' ten mile.'

'What about Zach Coates?' Mathew took a pull from the mug of beer he had brewed himself. 'If we could carry 'em between we up to the Tipton Road, 'e could put 'em on 'is cart down into Wednesbury and then on a train from there.'

Phoebe's frown turned to a look of dismay. 'That would mean paying carriage charges and a return fare for one of us to go with them.' She spread her hands on the table, defeat in the gesture. 'I just do not have the money.'

'Would it tek more'n four shillin', Miss?' Josh asked through a mouthful of food.

'I would not have thought so, Josh,' Phoebe answered, 'but I do not have four shillings.'

'I 'ave,' he swallowed noisily. 'Least I 'as three an' another 'un this comin' Friday'll mek four, so if as you says four shillin' be enough to pay to get them locks to Brummagem, then they'm as good as there already.'

'Those three shillings,' Phoebe looked at the tousle-headed boy regarding her with eyes like molten bronze, 'are they the same three shillings you have been paid as wages since you came to Wiggins Mill?'

'Ar.' He took another bite.

'And the fourth shilling is the one you will be paid for the work you have done this week?'

He nodded, the food in his mouth leaving no room for his tongue to manoeuvre.

'Thank you, Josh,' Phoebe said, her eyes grateful though her mouth would not smile. 'But I cannot take it. You will need that money to keep you until you find other employment.'

The boy's grin faded at her mention of finding work elsewhere but his eyes lost none of their brightness. 'I managed afore I come 'ere,' he said, allowing the food in his mouth to slide past his throat, 'an' I can manage when I be gone so you tek them shillin's an' get them locks to Brummagem. Could be when the bloke as 'as ordered 'em sees what 'e be gettin', 'e will up an' order another gross on the spot.'

Phoebe shook her head. 'No, Josh.'

'Why!' the boy demanded. 'That money be mine. I've earned it so I can do what I likes wi' it, an' I wants you to 'ave it.'

Pushing herself up with her spread hands, Phoebe rose from the table. 'You are right, Josh, that money is yours. You earned it and you are going to keep it, I . . .'

''Ang on, 'ang on!' he cut in on her refusal. 'I've been 'ere near a month as meks no odds an' in that time I ain't paid no board nor lodgin', I've 'ad three good meals a day an' supper besides, an' on top o' it all I've 'ad a bed. Now then.' Putting aside his knife, he held up his left hand, fingers curled into his palm. 'Three meals a day would cost tuppence a go an' they wouldn't be 'alf the tucker I've 'ad from Mrs Ingles neither, so wi'out supper I would 'ave been set back a tanner a day.' Two at a time he raised the fingers of his left hand, counting slowly before raising one finger of his right. Satisfied with his numbers he went on: 'A penny to 'ang the line in Joe Baker's lodgin' 'ouse would mek it seven.' He raised another finger. 'Sevenpence a day that would be, an' nowhere near the comfort I've 'ad 'ere so I reckons I owes you that money, Miss, an' a damn' sight more aside it.'

'If you owe anyone, Josh, it is Mrs Ingles. She is the one who has given you food and found a bed for you to sleep in.'

''E don't owe me nothin'.' Lizzie smiled at the boy. ''E 'as earned more'n a meal or two, the 'elp 'e gives me around the place, an' as for a bed, 'tain't nothin' outta me way lettin' 'im lie in the loft along o' me own so 'is money be 'is own to do whatever 'e likes wi' it.'

'There you am!' Josh grinned triumphantly. 'Now will you tek it?'

Phoebe shook her head. 'No, Josh, I will not.'

'What about the cut?' Mark had remained silent until now. 'You could get them locks straight into Brummagem if you sent 'em along the cut.'

''Course,' Bert nodded, 'I never give a thought to the cut.'

'What! An' you workin' the narrow boats this three year?' Lizzie smiled across at her husband. 'Some bargee you be, Bert Ingles. Back at the locks for a few weeks an' you forget the cut exists.'

'I 'ad forgot it an' that be no lie,' Bert said sheepishly, 'but Mark be right. Get that box o' locks on a boat an' you could bring 'em right into Gas Street Basin. An 'andcart from there an' you as 'em delivered.'

'It sounds easy, Bert,' Phoebe said, the worry in her tone not diminished, 'but will there be a barge going to Birmingham in the next day or two?'

'Sure to be.' The words were Lizzie's. 'Barges be up an' down to Brummagem as often as a barman serves beer on a Friday night.'

'Might be one comin' now.' Josh jumped up. 'Shall I go an' see?'

'Ar, lad,' Bert nodded, 'an' if one passes as ain't due for Brummagem ask if 'e knows when one is. An', lad,' Bert pointed a finger at him, 'no dawdlin'. There be work still to do.'

'Can I come?' Ruth scrambled up from the table. 'Take me wi' you, Josh, I want to come.'

''Old on to 'er,' Lizzie said as Josh looked at her for permission. ''Er can be off like a ferret down a rabbit 'ole if you leave go of 'er.'

''Er'll be all right wi' me, Mrs Ingles.' Josh caught the girl's hand. 'We'll be back quicker'n a navvy sups a pint.'

'There be a boat along o' the towpath.' Josh was back at the bellows in under five minutes. 'Bloke says if it be on for 'im to fetch water from the pump, 'e'll cart your locks up to Brummagem.'

'Can you carry on if I goes for a word wi' 'im?' Bert asked from the yard.

'Ar,' Mathew nodded. 'Mark 'ere can put me right should be I needs it.

'Settled?' he asked when Bert returned to the workshop later.

Sitting in his place at the workbench Bert took up a lock, removing it from the pattern mould. ''E goes up to Brum' wi' an empty boat, 'as a load to pick up from Gas Street in the mornin'. 'E 'as agreed to lay up 'ere for the night to give we the time to finish the last o' the order.'

'That be a bit o' good news for Phoebe.' Mathew put the lock he had finished on the pile set aside for filing down. ''Er was worried, you could tell that.'

'Well, the worry be groundless now,' Bert answered, 'but somebody 'as to go wi' them locks an' I don't think as Phoebe be the one. There be no other woman on that barge an' while I ain't sayin' as it be the bloke would touch 'er, I am sayin' as 'ow it wouldn't look right.'

'So what you reckon?'

'What I reckon is one o' we men should go wi' 'em.'

'It be the sensible thing,' Mathew agreed, 'an' that one should rightly be you, Bert. You can talk locks better'n me and you knows what they be worth. A bloke won't find it so easy diddlin' you as 'e would me.'

'Mmm.' Bert reached for a screwdriver. 'I'll go tell 'er when I've finished this, but we'll 'ave to bide by 'er decision.'

'It would have been the answer to our problem,' Phoebe said when Bert told her the reason for his being in her kitchen, 'but it will no longer be necessary. The locks are not going to Birmingham.'

'Not goin' to Brummagem?' Bert looked surprised. 'Then where do they be goin', Miss?'

'They won't be going anywhere, Bert. Perhaps you had better read this.' She handed him a white envelope. 'It came just a few minutes ago.'

Drawing a folded paper from the envelope, Bert read the neat copperplate hand. 'But why?' he asked. 'There be no reason given an' the month's end be three days clear away.'

'I do not know why.' Phoebe took the letter from Bert, her eyes scanning the heading James Greaves, Hardware and Ironmongery. He had given no reason in his letter, merely stating the gross of locks ordered on the second day of the month would no longer be required.

'I don't believe it!' Bert pushed a hand through his hair. 'I just don't bloody well believe it! Three days from finishin' an' the bloke 'as the gall to say 'e no longer wants 'em, an' not even a reason.'

'I am afraid we have to believe it.' Phoebe folded the letter, returning it to its envelope. 'But we do not have to accept it without a reason.'

'What you be goin' to do?'

'I am going to Birmingham, Bert.' Phoebe's chin came up. 'I am going to see Mr James Greaves.'

Phoebe sat on the slatted wooden seat of the steam tram, her bag with the one lock in it held close in her lap. The journey would take longer by tram but the fare by train was more than she had. The tram moved along Holloway Bank, complaining at the rise in the ground.

'Nice day, ain't it?'

A large woman in an even larger flowered hat nodded at Phoebe.

'Very nice,' she replied, her thoughts not with her words.

'It'll get nicer an' all if it don't get no worse.' The

woman's head bobbed, setting the flowers on her oversized hat wobbling dangerously.

'My rheumatiz says it be a-goin' ter rain.' A second woman joined the conversation.

'Oh, ar!' The flowers wobbled again. 'My old man says as 'ow 'e's goin' to get up off 'is idle arse tomorrer an' find isself a job – only tomorrer never comes, an' when it does 'e ain't in, so don't you go believin' all you 'ears.'

'You 'ave one o' them sort an' all, does you, wench!' The second woman laughed wheezily. 'I thought as I was the only woman wi' a bloke too idle to blow the froth off 'is beer.'

The large woman's assortment of chins wobbled in rhythm with the flowers on her hat. 'You knows what thought thought.' She laughed. ''E thought 'e weren't dead till they buried 'im!'

'Boundary,' the conductor of the tram called loudly. 'Boundary, all change.'

'Change?' Phoebe had been to Birmingham several times but always in her father's carriage. Now the conductor's call confused her.

'You 'as to get off 'ere, luv.' The large woman eased herself out of her seat. 'It's the boundary, did you want to go further?'

'I want to go to Birmingham.' Phoebe got out of her seat as the conductor called again.

The woman began to move along the narrow aisle separating the wooden bench-like seats, her ample hips brushing both sides. 'Wednesbury tram only runs as far as West Bromwich,' she said as Phoebe followed. 'To go on to Brummagem you 'ave to change at the boundary.' Alighting heavily, the woman eased her basket more firmly on to her arm then pointed. 'Just go a bit further down the road an' you'll see the tram for Brummagem. It be navy blue an' cream where this one be red, you can't miss it.'

Murmuring her thanks, Phoebe followed the way that had

been pointed. It took several more enquiries before she found the shop front announcing James Greaves, Hardware and Ironmongery. Taking a deep breath, she pushed open the door.

'Mr Greaves,' Phoebe took the letter from her bag, placing it address uppermost on the smooth polished wood of the counter that ran the length of the small dark shop, 'can you please explain to me why you have cancelled your order for one gross of Invincible locks just days before that order was due to be delivered to you?'

'I beg your pardon!' The man's smile faded to be replaced by a bemused look.

'I have no doubt you do,' Phoebe replied tartly, 'but begging my pardon is not enough. I require an explanation.'

'Are you sure you have come to the right shop?' He sounded almost apologetic. 'I have ordered no locks.'

'Yes!' Phoebe glared, her mouth tight with anger. A reason with or without an apology she would accept, but not bare-faced denial. 'You are Mr James Greaves, are you not?'

'I am, Miss,' the shopkeeper answered politely.

'And this, if I am not mistaken, is a Hardware and Ironmongery store?'

'It is.' He nodded, following Phoebe's cursory glance at the various articles of hardware hanging from every available space.

'Then this must be yours. Please read it and tell me if I am wrong.'

Taking the letter from the envelope, he fitted a pair of wire-framed spectacles to his nose, looking first over them to Phoebe's angry face then through them to read the words written on the paper. 'I am afraid you are wrong,' he said, after reading it through, 'I did not send this letter and neither have I sent any order for locks.'

'But it has your name and business address.' Phoebe took the letter, tapping a finger against the heading.

'I do not deny that,' he answered levelly, 'but I deny having written that letter. If you would care to look at this ledger you will see the handwriting is not the same as is on that letter.'

He could have disguised his writing. Phoebe glanced at the ledger. But why should he go to so much trouble? What did he have to gain from ordering a gross of locks then cancelling that order days before delivery?

'Then who?' Phoebe's hand fell limply on to the counter.

'I don't know who,' the man answered gently, seeing misery slowly spread across Phoebe's face, 'but it must be somebody who holds a grudge against you.'

Drawing in a deep breath, Phoebe folded the letter returning it to her bag. 'I apologise for having accused you of such an action, Mr Greaves,' she said, 'I should not have spoken as I did.'

'I understand, Miss. You pay it no more mind. These locks you spoke of, what be they like?'

'I have one here.' She took the lock from her bag, laying it on the counter where its polished brass gleamed against the dark wood.

'That ain't no botched up job.' James Greaves took the lock in his hands, examining it closely. 'This be a good bit o' work. Man as made this knows his job.' He looked up at Phoebe. 'Bet they teks a bit o' time making and all. And you have a gross, you say?'

He examined the lock again as Phoebe nodded. 'A man can be proud of making something like this,' he said. 'He's a craftsman and no mistake. Look here, Miss . . .?'

'Pardoe,' she supplied.

'Miss Pardoe,' he handed back the lock, 'I will be willing to take some locks off your hands.'

Phoebe sat on the steam tram, finding the journey home no less a strain than the outward one had been. James Greaves would take some of the locks but to whom could she sell the remainder? She looked through the window towards a sky that was already darkening. But it is not as dark as my horizons, she thought miserably. How do I tell

Mathew and Bert and Mark, and Josh there is no money to pay what I owe them?

'So there you have it.' Phoebe looked at Bert and the others grouped in her kitchen, their faces solemn. 'It appears that James Greaves did not send us an order for one gross of locks and neither did he send the letter that cancelled that order.'

'Then who the 'ell did?' Mathew had listened silently to all Phoebe had said and now his temper broke. 'Some stupid bugger wi' a twisted mind, an' if I finds out who it be 'e'll 'ave a bloody twisted neck to go wi' it . . .'

'You said as this Greaves bloke showed you a ledger of 'is 'andwritin'?' Bert said, interrupting Mathew's explosion, his own voice still level and calm. ''Ow good a proof do you take that to be?'

Phoebe looked up with eyes shadowed with disappointment and worry. 'Well, the ledger did go back several years and all the entries were in the same hand, quite different to this.' She touched the envelope lying on the table in front of her. 'I can't believe a man would go to so much trouble as to disguise his own handwriting to play a practical joke on someone he does not know, on someone he never even met before today.'

'There be no tellin' what folk'll do if they 'ave a mind,' Mathew cut in, his anger still hot.

'True,' Bert agreed soothingly, 'but what would the bloke be gainin' by doin' such? There was nothin' in it for 'im.'

'P'raps 'e thought 'avin' been turned down once 'e could get them locks cheap,' Tilly ventured her opinion. 'Mebbe 'e thought you would be only too glad to get shut of 'em.'

'There is no telling,' Phoebe answered wearily. 'The fact is I am left with a gross of locks for which I have no sale, and whether the ordering of them was a practical joke or not will not pay wages.'

'The ironmonger did offer to buy some of 'em and at the

price you first said. 'E made no attempt to cut you down, you told me?'

'None.'

'Well, to me that seems to say 'e wasn't tryin' to buy more on the cheap,' Bert thumbed the buckle of his broad belt. 'But like Tilly says, you never know 'ow a man's thoughts be turnin'.'

'Mine be turnin' to murder,' Mathew growled. 'Whoever it be 'as done this, pray God I never comes across 'im 'cos I won't be responsible for what I does to 'im – but it'll be a long time afore 'e walks again.'

'It's done now an' what's done can't be undone.' Lizzie took her daughter's hand. 'Best for all of you to get some rest. The problem will still be wi' us in the mornin', it can be talked on again then. Might be as you will see a way out when you be feelin' calmer.'

'Lizzie be right, Miss.' Bert followed his wife through the scullery to the yard. 'P'raps summat will make itself plain come mornin'.'

'I hope so, Bert, goodnight.' Phoebe stood as the Ingleses and Josh followed by Lucy and Mathew crossed the mill yard to their respective dwellings. They had all worked so hard, and for what! She looked up at the night sky, its inky void strewn with stars heavy with light. It could not all be for nothing, there had to be a reason. Why would someone want her to throw her last penny into a venture, only to see it sink? It didn't make sense. But then sending her to prison for a crime she had not committed had not made sense. She drew in a deep breath of the night air, carrying the sweet smell of the heath to her nostrils. She had been imprisoned but not defeated, and the failure to sell her locks would not defeat her either. Bert and Mathew had put their trust in her and it was up to her to ensure that trust was not in vain.

'But what can you do, wench?' Tilly asked later as she handed Phoebe a cup of steaming cocoa. 'It's all right you sayin' it's up to you to mek things good, but what do you reckon to do? You 'ave no money to pay the men an' none to buy more metals wi'. Not that you needs 'em with so many locks unsold.'

'I don't know what I can do,' Phoebe's hands shook as she put the cup on the table, 'I only know I have to do something. Mathew and Bert need their money to support their families and somehow I have to find that money.'

'Somehow, somehow!' Tilly fussed about the grate, banking down the fire for the night, the kettle already filled with water for the morning sitting on the hob above the oven. 'You can go on sayin' somehow till the cows come 'ome but it still won't put money in yer purse.'

'There has to be a way.' Phoebe closed her eyes, a thin film of tears glistening along the edge of her dark lashes.

'You could let James Greaves 'ave the dozen locks 'e said 'e would tek. That would be little, I know, but a little be better'n none at all.'

'And if I can't sell the rest, what then?' Phoebe spoke more to herself than Tilly. 'The Ingleses can't stay where there is no job to support them. They will have to move on, and that means being on the road for God knows how long, on the road with Ruth and Mark. And then there is Josh, what will he do? Go back to the streets of Wednesbury, standing in line for a job that breaks his back for a penny, sleeping under a hedge because that penny is not enough to buy him food and a bed. I can't let that happen, Tilly, I can't.'

'Mebbe you won't 'ave to, wench.' She rested a hand on Phoebe's slumped shoulders. 'The good Lord only lets we tek as much as we can bear then 'e teks the rest. 'E as give you a burden an' it be 'eavy for you, but 'e won't let it break your back. 'E'll lift it, you'll see. P'raps 'e won't tek it away altogether but 'e'll lift it enough for you to mek your way.'

'I don't mind for myself, Tilly,' Phoebe looked up, 'you and I have known worse, but I feel I have let the others down.'

'You've let nobody down, my wench!' Tilly said fiercely. 'You found 'em food an' a place to live when nobody else would 'ave 'em, an' they won't go blamin' you for what's 'appened. If it be as the Ingleses 'ave to move on then that will be 'cos the Lord is wantin' it that way.'

'No, Tilly,' Phoebe pressed the hand resting on her shoulder, 'the Lord has no desire to see children suffering on the streets or men dragging their families from town to town in search of work. While we have food in the house we will share it, and with God's help we will stay together.'

'Amen to that,' Tilly answered fervently. 'Amen to that!'

In the moonlit shadows of her bedroom Phoebe slipped her nightgown over her head. They would go back to selling Bert's work one or two a day as before, but the profit from that would not be enough to keep his family and pay Mathew for toting them around Wednesbury. That in turn would mean extra work for Lucy, trying to cover the shortfall with her baking, and the strain of the past month was already showing in her face. She could not go on like this much longer. And then there was Josh. The Ingleses could not go on feeding him when they had next to nothing to keep themselves with.

Going over to the window she stared out over the silent night: over the windmill, its folded sails thrust out like a cross stark against the dark sky, over the corn loft into which she had been forced by the man who had come to rob her, and to the spot in the yard where he had almost raped her. 'Why?' she whispered softly. 'Why is all this happening to me?' But out of the quiet shadows there came no answer.

'Can I see you for a minute, Miss Phoebe?' Bert stood cap in hand at the doorway to the scullery.

Leaving the breakfast dishes she was drying as Tilly washed them, Phoebe laid the huckaback cloth aside. 'Of course, Bert. Come in, please.'

Nodding a greeting to Tilly, he followed Phoebe to the kitchen but as she made to go through to the parlour he held back. 'It will do 'ere, Miss.'

Phoebe's heart skipped a beat. She had lain awake the

greater part of the night trying to find a solution to their difficulties but none had come. If her burden was to be lifted it seemed the time was not yet, and if Bert had come to tell her that he and Lizzie must move on she had nothing to offer that would hold them to Wiggins Mill.

'It's like this,' he twisted his cap between his fingers, 'Mathew an' me, we been talkin', an' we thinks as 'ow p'raps them locks would be better taken down to Liverpool.'

'Liverpool!' Phoebe exclaimed.

'Ar.' Bert looked at her, his eyes candid. 'Mathew an' me, we says we got nothin' now so if we get nothin' there then we lost nothin'. We thinks it should be given a try, but we 'ad to ask what you thought. 'Ow you felt about it.'

'Liverpool.' Phoebe sat down, her hands together on the table. The night had brought her no idea of what to do with the locks but the same could not be said of Bert.

'Ar, Liverpool, Miss.' He reinforced the theme, his voice enthusiastic. 'You see, Liverpool be the docks from where ships sail to America. Mathew an' me reckon if we can get them locks over there, they will sell.'

'How do you reckon that?'

Bert shuffled from one foot to another, his hand nervously throttling his cap. 'Well, Miss, from what I 'ear tell, you can sell spectacles to a blind man in that country.'

Trying but failing to hide the smile his words brought to her mouth, Phoebe asked from whom he had such information.

'Word gets round the docks,' he told her. 'Sailors comin' in from America an' the West Indies talks of 'ow the country be growin' that fast an' 'ow they be 'ungry for all sorts o' goods. They tells the cut men you can find a market over there for anythin', an' if they be buyin' goods fast as we can ship 'em over seems reasonable they 'ave to be stored for a time in warehouses. An' warehouses need locks – good locks as can't be broken.'

'And you and Mathew think our locks will sell over there?'

Bert smiled. 'Like Mathew says, they might not be the first locks to 'it America but they'll be the best.'

'But it will take weeks, Bert, maybe months, and you have already gone a month without wages. You can't go for several more. It is different for Mathew, he can go back to oddjobbing in the town and they have the money Lucy makes selling pies, but you and Lizzie will have nothing and I have not enough money to buy more metals for you to carry on while you are waiting – not unless we let Mr Greaves buy the one dozen locks he offered to take.'

'We've thought of that, me an' Lizzie, an' we both say the same. Leave the gross of locks intact an' send 'em off to America. We will find a way to manage till we gets word back.'

'But if they should not sell as you think, Bert,' Phoebe added a cautionary note, 'Lizzie and the children . . .'

'Lizzie an' Mark knows the score,' Bert said quickly. 'They also knows that should it fail to come off we will be back on the road, but if we never takes a chance then we'll never 'ave the answer, one way nor t'other, so the final word rests wi' you, Miss.'

'Has Mathew discussed this with Lucy?'

'They spoke of it this mornin' as he walked 'er to the crossroads.'

'And Lucy was in agreement?'

'Sees 'er was,' Bert nodded, 'but t'would be better all round to talk the matter over wi' all concerned brought together. That way everybody gets to 'ear all the fors and all the agens, and gets to say their piece fair like.'

'Agreed. But in the meantime have you thought of the cost involved in transporting the locks to America? It is going to be a great deal more than getting them to Birmingham and I did not have sufficient money to do that.'

'I 'ave thought of it.' Bert stopped mangling the cap he had taken to wearing to keep the dust of the workshop out of his hair. 'An' if you agrees then I think as we 'ave the answer. You see, while you was off to Brummagem to see James Greaves I went down to the cut side an' a mate of mine was takin' a load o' coal up to London. From there 'e 'as to pick up a load that'll take 'im to Liverpool. 'E will call 'ere day after tomorrow an' if I asks 'im 'e will take them locks wi' 'im. Won't cost no more'n a couple o' pies.'

'A couple of pies might get them to Liverpool, Bert, but it will take more than that to get them across the Atlantic. How do you propose we do that?'

'This way.' Bert stuffed the cap in his trousers pocket. 'The bargee as will be passin' 'ere in a day or two 'as a brother-in-law who is first mate on a cargo steamer that makes a regular run to America. 'E takes aboard various items to sell over there.'

'What sort of items?' Phoebe asked.

'Anythin' the bargee picks up along 'is route.' Bert grinned. 'Anythin' they think will sell, which seems to be most things. An' this brother-in-law sells them for a cut of the profit.'

'Is he allowed to take things aboard the ship to be sold for his own profit?'

'Put it this way,' Bert smiled, ''e is allowed to take aboard anythin' that nobody else knows about.'

Phoebe looked at him, uncertainty in her eyes. 'There is something that does not seem quite honest about it, Bert. He is taking things on board to sell for himself and not for whoever is paying for the ship to carry cargo, and that can't be right.'

'Crew be allowed to take their own box aboard,' Bert explained. 'Don't nobody ask if it be 'olding clothes or anythin' else. One box be all they be allowed, it be up to them what they 'ave in it, so if this first mate wants to fill it wi' things 'e wants to sell that be 'is concern so long as 'e don't overdo it. It be a recognised thing, Miss Phoebe, that be 'ow seamen makes up for the low wage they be paid, same as do cut men.'

'This brother-in-law of your friend,' Phoebe asked, 'is he

to be trusted? I do not wish to call his honesty into question but . . .'

''E won't do the dirty, Miss Phoebe.' Bert's grin faded. ''E knows the cut men, an' 'e knows to cross one o' them is to wake up one mornin' wi' a knife in your ribs. No, if 'e sells 'em you'll get your money, an' if 'e don't sell 'em you gets the locks back, 'e makes nothin' an' we makes nothin'. That way benefits nobody so you can rest your mind easy: if them locks will sell at all in America then 'e will sell 'em. You tell 'im 'ow much you wants for 'em, that way 'e won't bring you less, then you pays 'im for 'is part.'

Phoebe sat silent, thinking over what Bert had said. She had little to lose either way. 'Very well.' She met Bert's quizzical stare. 'We will discuss it together this evening and if everyone is agreed, we will send the whole lot to America.'

Chapter Twenty-One

It had been a month. Phoebe picked up the bucket of water she had filled from the pump in the yard. A month since the locks had gone off to Liverpool, a month in which the small workshop had been silent.

She carried the bucket into the scullery, emptying it into the copper to heat for washing the household linen, feeling the empty pull of her stomach. The food stocks had diminished quicker than she had expected due to her giving more than a share to the Ingleses and she would take from Lucy only the small amount her needlework paid for. How much longer could it go on? she thought, slicing thin slivers of Sunlight soap from a thick bar and dropping them into the copper. A few shillings a week to feed herself, Tilly, the Ingleses and Josh.

Josh! She stirred the soap slivers into the water with a wooden stick. She had not yet found the courage to send him back to the town yet she knew she was merely putting off the moment, that it had to come. 'But not yet,' she whispered staring into the soap clouded water, 'not yet.'

'What be not yet?' Tilly came into the scullery, her arms filled with sheets.

'I was thinking we cannot keep Josh much longer.' Phoebe felt almost relieved as she said the words she had admitted to no one but herself. 'Lizzie is finding it hard to feed her own even with our help.'

'I've known that for some time, my wench.' Tilly took the wooden stick, using it to push the soiled linen into the wooden tub that stood beside the copper, pressing the sheets beneath the soapy water. 'An' I knows you won't be able to 'elp much longer. There be almost nothin' left in the 'ouse.'

'Has Bert gone looking for work?'

'Ar 'e 'as.' Tilly took the wooden maid to the clothes in the tub, banging it up and down on the linen. ''Im an' the two lads, same as they does every day, but it be a waste o' time. There be no work, not even in the foundries seems like.'

Phoebe watched the other woman pound away at the washing, her thin body bent by the weight of the heavy wooden wash tool that pressed the dirt from the linen. 'Do you think he will wait much longer before taking to the road?'

'Who can say what a man like that'll do?' Tilly brushed a wet hand across her brow. 'All I know is you can see it's gettin' 'arder day by day for 'im, comin' 'ome wi' nothin'.'

'But Lizzie and the children, he wouldn't take them on the road again, would he?'

Using the wooden stick she had taken from Phoebe as a rod Tilly fished the pounded sheet from the wooden tub, lifting it across to the brownstone sink, sloshing clean water over it and rinsing away the soiled soapy suds before carrying the sheet across to the copper to be boiled. 'Could be Lizzie would refuse to stay behind,' she said, recovering from the effort of carrying the water-soaked fabric. 'A woman like Lizzie Ingles ain't easy separated from 'er man.'

Nor from her children, Phoebe thought, lifting another sheet into the wooden tub. Lizzie would not leave her children at Wiggins Mill while she and Bert went to look for work.

'When you goin' to tell 'em?' Tilly took the maid to the sheet in the tub, pounding it with a steady rhythm.

'Yer goin' to 'ave to,' she said as Phoebe turned away. 'You 'ave to tell 'em that sewin' night an' day you still ain't got the means to support 'em more'n another couple of weeks at the outside, an' you try to do more'n you be doin' already an' you'll work yerself into the ground an' that'll be a lot o' good to nobody.'

Tilly was right. Phoebe made her way slowly to her sewing room. She would tell them tonight. To tell Bert and Lizzie she could help them no longer would be painful but what would she say to Josh? How do you tell a young boy he must leave the home and people he loves? That would not be painful, that would be heart-breaking.

Pausing before the brown paper that held the creamy yellow satin, Phoebe ran a finger over the cloth. She was to have worn that to the Dartmouths' ball where she would have been Edward's partner. Edward who loved her and wanted to marry her. Her life would be so different had she said yes, had she loved him as he did her. But she did not love Edward, she did not love any man. Closing the brown paper back over the satin, she walked to her chair, taking up the petticoat she was making, but the stitches were blurred by the face in her mind. The face of Edward's father.

Her thoughts going again and again over the problem of keeping the Ingleses and Josh, Phoebe sewed until the light from the window was too dim to see the tiny stitches clearly. The whole day and only one petticoat to show for the hours of work. She smoothed the narrow pin tuck pleating that wound around the skirt above the flounces of cotton lace. If only she could afford one of Mr Singer's sewing machines! Laying the petticoat aside, she stood up, stretching the aching muscles of her back. If only she could buy just enough metal for Bert to make one or two locks it would help, but money would stretch just so far and buying brass or steel out of what little she earned was that much too far.

Maybe I don't need money. Phoebe stood stock still, the words singing in her brain. Maybe she did not need to pay for metal when it was ordered. Maybe she could pay at the end of the month like her father's customers always had. She could but ask. Tomorrow, she would ask tomorrow.

She had walked across the heath from Wiggins Mill and now stood in the ledger room of Thomas Bagnall's iron foundry, conscious of the dust on the skirt of her green coat.

'This way, Miss.'

Phoebe followed a small man, his shoulders permanently stooped from bending all day over ledgers.

'In 'ere, Miss.'

The man stood aside, holding a door open for Phoebe to pass into an inner office.

'Miss Pardoe.' Heavy-jowled, his hairline way back from the front of his head, Thomas Bagnall pushed himself to his feet as the door closed behind her. 'I 'aven't seen you in a long time. Sit down, my dear, sit down.'

'Thank you.' Phoebe perched nervously on the chair he indicated, aware of the glance that took her in from boots to hair.

'So, my dear, you're well, I 'ope?'

'Quite well, Mr Bagnall,' Phoebe said, unable to furnish the words with a smile. There was something in Thomas Bagnall she did not like and the sooner their business was finished and she could leave the greater would be her relief.

'Then what is it Thomas Bagnall can do for you?' He smiled, the heavy folds of flesh on his face shuttering his small eyes. 'Nothing 'olds more pleasure for me than serving a pretty woman.'

'I want to order some metal.' Phoebe tried not to wonder how his eyes would re-emerge from the enfolding flesh.

'That's easy done,' Thomas Bagnall's eyes stayed buried by his broadening smile, 'you only 'ave to say what it is you want.'

'Twenty-four pounds of brass and half that of steel.'

'That don't be much.' The folds of flesh gave a little ground, allowing his eyes to show.

'No, Mr Bagnall, it is a smaller order than my previous one but it will suffice for now.'

Dropping a thick-fingered hand on to a bell set on his desk he bawled the requirements to the same stoop-shouldered man who came in answer.

'We will 'ave that out to you tomorrow, Miss Pardoe,' he said when the clerk had left for the second time, 'if you will pay Simms on your way out?'

'I wish to speak to you about that.' Phoebe fingered her bag, her nerve threatening to run out on her. 'I – I wish to settle my accounts monthly in the future.'

'Monthly!' He smoothed the whiskers that ran the length of his flabby cheeks, at the same time coming from behind his desk to stand beside her chair. 'Now that be a different arrangement . . .'

Phoebe eased her knees away from the figure standing so close his legs touched hers. 'I am aware of that, Mr Bagnall, and though I have always paid in advance when purchasing metal from you, I believe it is not unusual to pay a month after delivery.'

'It's not unusual,' his small eyes glittered, 'not unusual at all between men. But you don't be a man.'

'I do not see that it makes any difference, I can pay as well as any man.'

'Except you ain't got any money.' Thomas Bagnall's smile registered triumph as he saw Phoebe wince. 'If you had the money you wouldn't be asking to pay at the end of a month, now would you, Miss Pardoe? And that being so we need to talk terms.'

'Terms?' She hitched herself further from him, sitting almost sideways in an effort to avoid the touch of his legs. 'Do you mean a charge for interest?'

'Some might see it that way.' The small eyes hovered about her breasts and his podgy hands pulled at his side whiskers as if tearing away her clothes. 'I see it as a way of saying thank you for a favour.'

'Do you charge a man interest for the privilege of settling his account after a month?' she demanded.

'How I conduct my business is my business.' He smiled, sending waves of flesh coursing toward his eyes. 'And if you want my metal without paying cash on the nail, you must meet my terms.'

'Which are?'

He touched a finger to her face, stroking it across her cheek and along the side of her throat. 'A little of your company, a private dinner somewhere secluded. Not much to pay for a month's credit.'

Not much to pay? Phoebe felt her stomach reach for her throat. A little of her company? Thomas Bagnall would want more than that.

'I find your terms too much!' Phoebe pushed to her feet, moving quickly to the door and snatching it open.

'P'raps you do but when you find nobody'll give credit to a woman then come back to Thomas Bagnall. You'll find his terms easier to fulfil when you've no money in your pocket and no food in your stomach.'

Phoebe walked back across the heath. She had not gone to visit Sarah or to see Lucy at her stall in the market place, knowing the contempt and disgust she was feeling would show in her face. But why had she avoided both of her friends? She sat on a half-buried stone, her feet aching from the long walk to the town and halfway back again. Why did she not want either of them to know what had gone on in Thomas Bagnall's office? Turning her face to the sky she closed her eyes. She had not gone to visit them for fear of their finding out what she only now admitted. She could not let the Ingleses take their children out on the road nor could she allow Josh to sink back into the poverty and misery of living in the streets. She had to go back to Thomas Bagnall, she had to agree to his terms.

* * *

'You have no need to take me.' Phoebe smiled at the stoop-backed clerk who looked up as she entered the ledger room. 'I know where Mr Bagnall's office is.' Knowing his eyes were following her, she went along the corridor that led to the comfortably furnished room she had been in less than an hour before. Pushing open the door without knocking, she stepped inside.

'Well, now!' Thomas Bagnall's self-satisfied smile obliterated his eyes. 'You've come to your senses, I see. I thought you would so I didn't cancel your order for steel and brass.'

He moved around the desk to stand close, his body brushing hers, bringing a fresh surge of revulsion to Phoebe's throat. If she were to help Josh and the others she had to do it now for she would never have the courage to do it later. Her voice little more than a whisper, her legs trembling with weariness from her long walk but mostly from fear of what she was about to agree to, she said, 'Dinner with you one evening, that was what you proposed as payment for extending me credit, was it not?'

He lifted a hand, stroking his knuckles across her breast. 'One evening for brass,' he said thickly, 'an' one for steel.'

'But you said one evening!' Phoebe pushed his hand away, her cheeks flaming.

'So I did,' he agreed, his tiny fat-shrouded eyes sweeping the length of her before settling on her face, 'and I'm still saying one. One evening for brass, one evening for steel. Those be my terms. You may take 'em or leave 'em.'

She had no choice. Trembling she turned to the doorway, stumbling through it in her eagerness to get away from a man who revolted her, yet a man to whom she must submit. 'Mr Bagnall,' she said, her voice low and shaky, 'I agree to your terms.'

'And what terms might those be?' Sir William Dartmouth caught Phoebe's arms as in her haste to be gone from the office she cannoned into him. Steadying her, he released her, asking again, 'What terms?'

'Miss Pardoe an' me had business together.' Thomas Bagnall's eyes receded behind their barrier of fat as he glanced warningly at Phoebe.

'How interesting!' William Dartmouth looked from one to the other, his glance pausing on Phoebe's flushed face. 'I am always interested in business and in the terms that conclude it. Perhaps, Miss Pardoe, you will tell me of yours?'

'It was nothing of consequence.' Thomas Bagnall stepped back from the doorway, leaving it clear for the other man to enter the office, but he did not move.

'What do you call "nothing of consequence" Thomas?' Sir William asked the question of the iron founder but his eyes were on Phoebe.

'Twenty-four pounds of brass and half that of steel, a piddlin' little order!' Bagnall snapped, annoyed at being questioned.

'Little indeed,' Sir William nodded, 'though it could have been more politely described in the presence of a lady, don't you think Thomas?'

What little could be seen of his eyes glittering venomously, the iron founder looked at Phoebe. 'I beg your pardon, Miss Pardoe,' he ground, 'a slip of the tongue.' Then to Sir William, 'Miss Pardoe was just leaving.'

'So I see.' William Dartmouth remained blocking Phoebe's way in the narrow brown-painted corridor that smelled strongly of the foundry. 'And hurriedly. Is that because you have other business, Miss Pardoe, or is it due to the terms you have just agreed with Thomas Bagnall?'

'I . . . I asked Mr Bagnall to allow me to settle my account at the end of the month from the date of purchase.' Phoebe straightened the quaver from her voice though her cheeks still flamed.

'That is the usual practice.'

'Not for me, Sir William.' Phoebe raised her head, a mixture of pride and despair in her green eyes. 'I have always paid the full amount at the time of placing an order but today it is not possible for me to do that therefore I asked for the month of credit I knew it was usual to extend to customers.'

'And the terms?' he asked, the temperature of his voice dangerously low.

'There were no terms. She asked for a month. I . . . I gave her a month, that's all we agreed.' Thomas Bagnall glared at Phoebe. 'There were no other terms.'

'And there will be none!' Sir William glanced past Phoebe to the other man, a world of meaning in his cold grey eyes. 'Miss Pardoe's order will be delivered in the morning and paid for one calendar month following that day and there will be no extra charge any sort whatsoever. The same terms will apply to any and all future orders she may wish to place.' He turned to Phoebe. 'Do you find those terms acceptable?'

'Most acceptable,' she nodded, 'thank you.'

Inclining his head so slightly his eyes did not leave her face, he answered quietly, 'Then your business here is settled. Good day, Miss Pardoe.'

The brass and steel would be delivered tomorrow! Bert would have the means of earning a living again! Phoebe walked home across the heath, her tiredness forgotten. She had a month in which to get the money to pay for the metals and thanks to Sir William she would not have to dine with Thomas Bagnall or suffer the attentions she knew would have followed. It was more than fortunate Sir William had arrived when he did, it was heavensent. She breathed a long deep breath of air flavoured with the scent of ling and wild flowers. It had been many months since her release from Handsworth prison but she still felt the same wonder and relief at being free to walk across the heath, just to stand and listen to the hymn of a skylark rising to the sky or the chorus of crickets in the grass. William Dartmouth had brought her that freedom just as he had brought another different kind of freedom today. 'Thank you,' she murmured using her inner eyes to look at the tall dark-haired man whose grey eyes seemed to smile back at her. 'Thank you.'

'When did he go?' Phoebe asked Tilly, her voice throbbing with concern.

'About a hour after yerself,' she answered. ''E come swannin' into the kitchen an' said 'e was off somewheres else to find work 'cos there was none to be 'ad in Wednesbury. It wasn't till later I found that in the parlour.'

Phoebe glanced at the coins lying on the table, a tiny pool of silver glistening in the last of the daylight.

'Did he say where he was going?'

'I've told you what 'e said, word for word,' Tilly answered patiently, ''ad 'e said more I would 'ave told you more.'

'I know, Tilly, and I am sorry to keep on questioning you, it's just that I am so concerned.'

'We all be that, my wench, but I don't see as worryin' yerself sick will do any good – you already be worn out wi' walkin' to that town an' back. Sit yerself down an' wait for Mathew gettin' in. Could be 'e was told more'n me.'

But Phoebe could not sit down. The meeting with Thomas Bagnall had unnerved her, and now this.

'Has Lizzie said anything?' She looked at Tilly peeling potatoes in an enamel bowl, black chip marks leaving a pattern of dots around its white edge.

'Nuthin' 'er can say.' Tilly hacked a hole in a potato, digging out the brown rottenness attacking its heart. ''E be gone an' that be all there be to it. Talkin' will mek no odds to that.'

Phoebe had talked yesterday of not being able to keep them all together at Wiggins Mill; now she had found a way, only she had found it too late. If only he had waited just one more day.

'That be Lucy and Mathew 'ome.' Tilly dropped a half-peeled potato into the bowl, rubbing her hands on her apron. 'Could be they seen 'im somewheres.' Following Phoebe into the yard she heard Lizzie already asking the question and Mathew's answer.

'I seen 'im this mornin' afore Lucy an' me went into Wednesbury an' I ain't seen 'im since.'

'Neither 'ave I.' Lucy shook her head.

'It ain't 'ardly dark yet.' Mathew glanced at the golden-red rim of the horizon. ''E'll be back soon, you be worryin' over nuthin'. It ain't as if 'e ain't never been out in the dark on 'is own afore.'

'Mathew's right,' Lucy agreed, ''e 'as most like gone into the town an' met up wi' somebody 'e knows. Give 'im an hour or so an' 'e'll be back.'

'I 'ope you be tellin' true, Lucy,' Lizzie said tearfully. 'I 'ope you all be tellin' true.'

'Tell you what,' Mathew scooped Ruth into his arms as she came squealing with delight into the yard, 'let me give my best girl a cuddle and then I'll go look for 'im.'

'Who you goin' to look for, Uncle Mathew?'

Kissing the little girl's cheek he set her down beside her mother. 'I'm goin' to look for the prince who will marry my little princess, but not till you be older.'

'Can I come? Can I, Uncle Mathew?'

Mathew smiled at the child, her tumbling red-gold hair caught with a strip of cornflower blue ribbon Lucy had bought for her. 'We can't 'ave a princess walkin' the 'eath an' gettin' 'er royal feet dusty.'

'You could carry me,' she answered, her eyes wide and serious.

'I might be able to, Ruthie,' Mathew hid his smile, 'but I be gettin' very old. Could be as I couldn't carry you back.'

Catching his hand the girl smiled up at him, craning her head back on her neck. 'Don't worry, Uncle Mathew, I will carry you back.'

'Come along, miss.' Lizzie caught her daughter by her free hand. 'You can carry yerself to the wash bowl and wash yer 'ands an' face ready for bed. Say goodnight to everybody.'

'You will let me know if you find 'im?' Lizzie asked when the goodnights had been said.

'Don't worry,' Lucy smiled sympathetically, 'I'll come right over.'

'I think I'll go wi' Lizzie,' Tilly said quietly. ''Er 'as took this 'arder than I would 'ave thought. I'll stop with 'er till Mark be 'ome then I'll be back to finish them 'taters.'

'I will finish them.' Phoebe looked towards Lizzie leading her daughter to the corn barn that had become their home. 'Stay with Lizzie as long as she needs you.'

'Who would 'ave guessed Lizzie would 'ave been 'it that 'ard?' Mathew lifted his cap, running a hand through his hair.

'When you grow to love somebody it be 'ard when they ups an' leaves wi' 'ardly a word,' Lucy answered. 'Beats me why 'e did it. 'E ain't goin' to find no better 'ome than 'e's got 'ere.'

'He did it because he thought we could not keep him at Wiggins Mill any longer,' Phoebe said. 'He was no fool, he knew how long it had been since any money other than the few shillings my sewing brings had come into the house. He knew I could not support them all for much longer so he left.'

'Poor soul!' Lucy sighed. 'An' now 'e is Lord knows where, but at least 'e as *some* money in 'is pocket an' 'e is well used to mekin' it stretch as far as it'll go so at least 'e will eat for a week or two.'

'But he does not have any money.' Phoebe turned towards the house. 'He left what he had in the parlour.'

'What, all of it?' Lucy asked as Mathew set off to search the heath.

'All of it,' Phoebe nodded. 'All four shillings.'

'Poor soul!' Lucy said again. 'Poor little Josh!'

'If only he had waited, we will have brass and steel tomorrow enough for Bert to start again.'

'Eh, Miss Phoebe! How did you manage that?'

'It's a long story, Lucy.'

Catching her arm, Lucy hustled her towards the house. 'Then let's 'ave a cup o'tea wi' the tellin'. I'm that parched I couldn't spit a tanner.'

'Eh, the dirty old bugger!' Lucy exclaimed when Phoebe finished relating the happenings of the afternoon. 'I wonder 'ow the 'oity toity Rachel Bagnall would take to knowin' 'er old man be no better than a lecher!'

'I hope she never has to know.' Phoebe poured tea for both of them, handing a cup to Lucy.

'Prob'ly wouldn't worry 'er none.' Lucy blew indelicately into her cup to cool the steaming liquid. 'From what folk tell 'er ain't no better than 'er should be.' She looked up suddenly, shock slackening her mouth. 'Eeh, Miss Phoebe, you wouldn't 'a gone, would you? Wi' old Bagnall I mean!'

'I think that at the time I was prepared to do anything, Lucy,' Phoebe admitted.

'You would 'ave been called on to do more than eat a dinner wi' that dirty sod!' Lucy's shock retreated before an onslaught of indignation. 'Thank God Billy-me-Lord turned up when 'e did. Which reminds me,' she put her cup on the table, 'there was talk in the market today about the Dartmouths.'

'Sir William?'

''Im an' all,' Lucy said quickly, 'but mostly 'is family, about them comin' 'ome to England.'

Edward was coming home. The thought was pleasant but it brought no rush of excitement. It had been the truth when she had told him she was not in love with him but he had said that would change while he was in Europe, that when he returned he would ask her again to become his wife. But her feelings for him had not changed. Edward Dartmouth was a kind attentive man who would make a wonderful husband but she could never marry him.

'When are they expected?' Phoebe asked.

Across the table Lucy's eyes were bright. 'They ain't!' she said bluntly.

Phoebe's brows drew together with a hint of puzzlement. 'But you said they were coming home?'

'They *was*,' Lucy emphasised the last word, 'but it seems there was a almighty storm at sea somewheres an' the ship they was on was sunk. 'Pears there was quite a few of the passengers didn't find a place in them lifeboats an' was drowned.'

'No!' Phoebe's face blanched. 'No, not Sophie, she was to be married . . . she . . . she can't be drowned!'

'That seems to be what 'er father said,' Lucy continued. ''Cordin' to what be told in the market the ship was sunk some time ago but 'e wouldn't 'ave it that 'is family was drowned. 'E kept on waitin' for word that would tell they was still alive.'

'But it did not come?'

'Seems not.' Lucy picked up her cup, sipping the tea. 'Seems he 'eard to the contrary. 'E must 'ave for word to be goin' around.'

'I never thought when I saw him in Thomas Bagnall's foundry today, it didn't seem to register.'

'What didn't?' Lucy looked up from her tea.

Phoebe frowned as though trying to recall some inner picture. 'He, Sir William, he wore dark grey. The collar of his coat was faced with black velvet and he had a narrow ribbon of grosgrain about the sleeve. He was in mourning and I never noticed.'

'Don't blame yerself, Miss,' Lucy said soothingly, 'after what you 'ad just been through wi' old Bagnall, 't'ain't surprisin' you never noticed.'

'But *he* noticed.' Phoebe condemned her own oversight. 'He noticed my discomfort even in his own sorrow and I . . . he must think I am so heartless!'

Rising from her chair Lucy went to stand beside the girl she had once served as a maid, the girl whom life had moulded into a woman. "E won't think nothin' like that,' she said, bending to place her arms about Phoebe. "E could see you was upset an' 'e won't tek no insult from you not offerin' 'im sympathy. Billy-me-Lord be too fine a man to 'old a grudge, 'specially from summat 'e knows full well to be not meant.'

'I hope you are right, Lucy.' Phoebe turned to her friend, hiding her tears against her waist. 'He was so kind to me, I never wanted to hurt him.'

'You ain't 'urt 'im, Miss Phoebe.' Lucy stroked a hand across sherry-coloured hair, her voice gentle. 'You ain't 'urt 'im, an' when you be feelin' more like yerself you can write to tell 'im of yer sympathy wi' 'is loss, but for now go an' wash yer face while I finishes peelin' these 'taters. You will feel better for it.'

'Ain't no sign o'the lad,' Mathew was saying when Phoebe returned to the kitchen. 'Bert an' Mark went over towards Tipton way an' I went towards the Lyng but it be blacker than the devil's tongue out there an' wi' no moon I couldn't see no more'n a spit in front o' me an' same wi' Bert an' Mark. Ain't no more we can do tonight.'

'But he might be sleeping out in the open,' Phoebe protested.

"E might an' I can't say as 'e ain't,' Mathew answered, 'but it be no use our lookin' any more. 'Sides if it be as 'e left the parish like 'e told Tilly 'e was goin' to do 'e could be anywhere by this time. We can't tell whether 'e 'eaded for Brummagem or took Walsall way, an' in any case, even if we does find 'im we can't force 'im to come back to Wiggins Mill, not if 'e don't want to.'

'But he was happy here and the work with Bert interested him.'

'Ar, the work interested 'im,' Mathew looked from Phoebe to Lucy, 'but who knows 'ow long a lad's interest be 'eld by anythin'? They changes their minds quicker'n a kingfisher flaps its wings. One minute they be fascinated by one thing an' the next minute they wants no more to be doin' wi' it.'

'I don't think Josh was like that,' Phoebe said quietly. 'I think he left because he saw it as the only way to help the situation. He thought one less mouth to feed was one less to worry over. Why else would he have left every penny he had earned in my parlour?'

'You be right, Miss Phoebe.' Lucy added salt to the potatoes she had placed in a pan set over the coal fire. 'But so is Mathew. If the lad 'as med up 'is mind to go then there be nothin' we can do about it. We just 'ave to accept it.'

'Lizzie has taken it so hard you would almost think it was Mark had left.'

'Lizzie be a good soul,' Mathew said, ''er treated that lad like 'er treated 'er own. 'Tain't surprisin' 'er be tekin' it 'ard.'

'And Bert?'

''E were the same, treated Josh as 'e treated Mark.'

'One as worries me be Ruth,' Lucy said. 'That little 'un thought the sun shone out of 'is eyes, 'er followed 'im every chance 'er got. 'Ow do you explain to a child as young as that the one 'er took to be God 'as up an' left?'

'Lord!' Mathew breathed. 'Nobody thought about Ruthie.'

Phoebe stared at the window. The night sky had lightened into dawn and still she had not slept, her mind living and re-living the times spent with Sophie and Edward. Edward had loved Phoebe, and he had died knowing her love for him was not returned. And Sophie . . . she was so full of marriage plans, so happy at the thought of becoming Montrose's wife, and now she was lying somewhere on the sea bed. Son, daughter and wife, all taken in one swoop. Phoebe closed her eyes against the picture her mind formed yet again, a picture of people helpless against waves that engulfed then swallowed them. His whole family lost together, what must Sir William Dartmouth be feeling?

'Ruth . . . Ruth, where am you?'

Phoebe's eyes snapped open as Bert's voice rang across the yard.

'Ruth . . . Ruth, my girl, ah'll tan yer arse for yer if you don't come 'ere this minute!'

This time it was Lizzie's voice that rang on the dawn stillness. Flinging aside the covers Phoebe jumped from the bed, crossing quickly to the window that overlooked the yard. Bert and Lizzie, still in their nightclothes, were looking around the outhouses. Raising the sash, Phoebe called to ask what was wrong.

'It be Ruth.' Lizzie looked up at the window, her face a mask of concern. ''Er be gone from 'er bed.'

'Have you searched the barn thoroughly?' Phoebe realised the futility of her question only after asking it.

'We looked just about everywhere,' Lizzie said, her voice near to breaking, 'me and Bert been lookin' an hour or more.'

'I'll be down in a moment!'

'What be the matter?' Tilly came into Phoebe's room as she withdrew her head, leaving the sash open.

'Ruth.' Phoebe reached for her dress and petticoats. 'She is not in her bed and Lizzie and Bert cannot find her in any of the out buildings.

'Lord, not summat else!' Tilly threw up her hands in despair. 'If it ain't one thing it's another. When is it all goin' to end? I'll get me dress an' then I'll be down. That poor woman . . .'

Phoebe threw off her nightgown, scrambled into her day clothes. Unmindful of her unwashed face or her uncombed hair she thrust her feet into her shoes and ran downstairs to the yard.

'How long has she been gone?' she asked, reaching Lizzie's side.

'I don't know for true,' Lizzie answered, her face crumpling. 'I put 'er into 'er bed last night like always an' when I woke this mornin' 'er were not in it no longer.'

'Try not to worry.' Phoebe held the crying woman, realising the unreasonableness of her request but hoping it at least sounded confident. 'We will have her home in no time. She has probably gone over to the windmill to pick you some flowers. I noticed some very pretty ones around there the other day.'

'Or 'er might 'ave gone across by the cut.' Lizzie's body shook. "Er might 'ave 'eard we talkin' after 'er 'ad been put to 'er bed. We said about Josh 'avin' left, an' Bert was sayin' 'ow 'e might never come back.' She stepped out of Phoebe's arms. 'You know 'ow 'er 'ad taken to the lad,' she said, her eyes darkening with fear. 'Summat tells me 'er 'as gone lookin' for 'im an' 'er'll 'ave little fear o' the cut. 'Er'll 'ave no understandin' o' the danger of it.'

'But she may not have gone to the canal.' Phoebe tried to sound reassuring. 'Why should she have?'

'I know 'er 'as.' Lizzie spoke more to herself than to Phoebe. "Er 'eard Bert say the lad could well 'op a barge somewhere an' barges means the cut an' that be where my babby 'as gone! My Ruth be somewhere in the . . .'

'Don't talk like that!' Tilly snapped, coming into the yard in time to hear Lizzie's fear. 'That babby o' your'n be up to 'er arse in flowers over by that windmill an' 'er father will 'ave 'er back 'ere afore you 'ave time to blink, so stop yer snivellin' an' go mek 'er some breakfast to come back to!'

'Tilly is right,' Phoebe said as Mathew and Lucy joined them. 'Ruth will be back before you know it. Leave it to the men. You come with Tilly and me, a cup of tea will help.'

'Will it?' Lizzie sagged against Tilly. 'Will it 'elp that?'

Phoebe turned, following the line of Lizzie's stare. 'Oh no!' she whispered. 'Please God, no.'

'Ruthie!' Bert's agonised shout rent the quiet sky as he caught sight of his daughter, her white nightgown clinging to her small body, her red-gold hair a bright splash against a dark jacket. 'Ruthie!' he shouted again, running towards the boy who carried her in his arms . . .

• • •

'I were a few yards, along the cut,' Josh explained as Lizzie held her daughter, dry and in a fresh nightgown, tight in her arms. 'I know I'd said as I was leavin' Wednesbury altogether but when it come to it I couldn't, I just wanted to be near all of you, especially Mrs Ingles.'

'But why go in the first place, Josh?' Phoebe looked to where he sat, his fingers curled about the girl's hand.

'I knowed you was short o' money, Miss, an' 'ad been for some time. It sort of makes sense, don't it? One less body in the 'ouse meks one less mouth to feed so I went, but I come back when it was dark. I found a place to sleep the other side o' the lock. I would 'ave liked to have slept in the old windmill but I wouldn't 'cos I 'ad promised Miss Phoebe I wouldn't never sleep in that place again an' there were nowheres else so I kipped along o' the cut.'

'Thank the good God 'e put you there, lad.' Bert took the child from his wife, carrying her into the loft to her bed.

'But if you was sleepin',' Mark asked, ''ow come you knowed our Ruth was in the cut?'

'I was sleepin',' a puzzled look crept over Josh's face, 'an' I was dreamin'. I was dreamin' o' me mother only it were not me mother. Well, the face were not me mother's, it were Mrs Ingles's, but 'er were wearin' a lovely white frock an' 'er face were all shinin' like a light were on it an' 'er called me name.' He paused as if living the dream again. ''Er called me name two or three times an' then 'er told me to get up an' bring Ruth 'ome. I said as Ruth already be 'ome but 'er just smiled an' said it again. "Josh, get up and bring Ruth 'ome."'

He looked at the group of people watching him. 'I 'eard 'er say it plain as day an' then I woke up. I looked all around but I couldn't see nobody an' I was just goin' to lie down again when the water up along the canal by the lock went all bright wi' the sun an' I seen summat white floatin' in it. Well, I run like buggery to see what it might be an' . . . an' it were Ruth. I went in 'ead first an' brought 'er out but I couldn't bring 'er to wakin' so I carried 'er back 'ere to 'er 'ome like I was bid.'

'You did well, lad.' Tilly pushed a dish of thick porridge to each of the two boys.

'You did that.' Lizzie caught her husband's hand as he came down from the loft. 'An' don't you ever go leavin' we again, Josh, or I'll 'ave Bert 'ere belt the 'ide off you. This place or any other the Ingleses might find theirselves in be your 'ome an' we be your family.'

Josh looked up, a spoonful of porridge hovering at his lips, his eyes filled with something near to longing. 'Mrs Ingles,' he asked, 'could . . . could I call you Mother?'

'It was a strange dream Josh had,' Phoebe said as she walked with Tilly across the yard toward the mill house, 'strange but very fortunate.'

'It were fortunate all right an' a dream it might 'ave been.'

'Might?' Phoebe stopped walking and looked at the woman beside her. 'Now just what does that mean, Tilly Wood?'

'Mek on it what you will,' she answered, 'but to me that were no dream young Josh 'ad.'

'What else could it have been?'

'I ain't sayin',' Tilly's mouth set in a straight line, 'but the lad said as the sun shone on the water just about where that little wench was floatin', didn't 'e?'

'Yes,' Phoebe answered, puzzled by Tilly's attitude.

'Well, it 'pears to 'ave escaped everybody's notice but there ain't no sun, leastways none as can be seen through clouds that be thicker than a grorty puddin'.' She glanced skyward. 'There's been no break in them from first light. I knows 'cos I ain't been to bed. I sat watching against that lad comin' 'ome.'

Chapter Twenty-Two

'But this is more than I expected.' Phoebe looked at the banknotes on her kitchen table then to the man shuffling from one foot to another, clearly uncomfortable at being inside the house. 'It is more than I asked.'

'Ar,' he nodded, 'I knows that but my brother-in-law says they Americans were willin' to pay more for such good locks so 'e sold 'em for more. That bill 'e sent along wi' 'em be from man as bought 'em an' tells the price 'e paid. You will see when you check that it all be there.'

'I am sure of it,' Phoebe smiled, 'but why has your brother-in-law not taken his percentage?'

'You trusted 'im, Miss. Now 'e be trustin' you. If it be as you be satisfied wi' the deal 'e struck then you will be sendin' 'im what 'e earned, that be the way 'e looks at it.'

'I am more than satisfied and I think Bert and Mathew are too.'

'It be a right good deal so far as I sees it.' Mathew grinned delightedly. 'Bert was right to suggest it.'

'There be a market for many more, so I was instructed to tell you, an' they can cross over same way as before.'

'Take some time,' Bert said thoughtfully. 'We couldn't go on workin' flat out like we did to make that gross, not all the time we couldn't.'

'Well,' the man shuffled again, his clogs loud on the red scrubbed flags of the kitchen floor, 'I be away up to London termorrer and back this way along o' a week. I will call, if you allows, for water an' you can be givin' me yer answer

319

then. An' if you don't mind, Miss, would you keep me brother-in-law's cut till I be comin' back 'cos it don't be doin' to 'ave money wi' you on the barges?'

'It'll be 'ere when you wants to pick it up,' Bert said, following the man from the kitchen, 'an' there'll be some for you an' all for the 'elp you 'ave been.'

"Elp where you can,' the bargee refastened the muffler wrapped about his neck, 'that's what me mother learned all 'er kids, an' if you can't be a 'elp then don't be a 'indrance.'

"Er couldn't 'ave learned you better,' Bert said, shaking the other man's hand. 'Safe journey to London an' I'll see you a week from now.'

'That went better'n I'd guessed,' he said as he re-entered the kitchen. 'Seems you 'ave a solid market if you wants to follow it up, Miss Phoebe.'

'We *have* to follow it up, Bert.' Phoebe glanced at the bill signed 'Hiram B. Rosmeyer'. 'It would be foolish not to. The only thing we have to decide is how many locks we can make in a month. As you have said, you can't work at the pace you were before so how many would you expect to make?'

'That depends,' he mused. 'As we be now I would say between a dozen or dozen an' a 'alf a week.'

'Half a gross a month,' Phoebe calculated quickly, 'two months before we could ship another worthwhile batch.'

'The market could be gone in that time,' Mathew said, 'could be somebody else will get a notion to do the same thing an' if they be quicker at it than we . . .' He shrugged his shoulders.

'I don't see we can do anything about that, Mathew.' Phoebe looked rueful. 'You all do your best and no one can do better than that.'

'Might be a way o' speedin' up the makin' . . .' Bert touched a hand to his chin. 'Mathew an' me 'ave both spoke o' the way young Josh picks things up. 'E be a quick learner an' already knows near as much of locksmithin' as do Mark. Now if we could tek 'im off the bellows an' set 'im to work on the benches along o' we three then you could turn that dozen an' 'alf into two dozen or more a week.'

'But who would work the bellows? You need those to keep the forge burning, don't you?'

Bert nodded. 'We need the bellows, that be right enough, but they don't need to be sat over full time. What I was thinkin', if Mathew be agreeable, was for each o' the four on we to tek the bellows to the forge when we uses it an' the two lads to tek a turn when Mathew an' me be too busy. An' as for the coal, I was of a mind to suggest that Mathew an' me hauls a load up from the cut each night.'

'Easy done,' Mathew grinned, 'I could knock up a cart on a couple of wheels to mek it less of a task.'

'I think though, Miss, in all fairness Josh should 'ave the same wage as Mark, learn the way o' the world ain't paved wi' gold like fairy tales would 'ave 'em believe.'

'Whatever you say, Bert.' Phoebe smiled her thanks. 'Pardoe's Patent Locks are in the export business.'

She had smiled confidently at Bert and Mathew but counting the banknotes later that evening Phoebe felt that confidence seeping away. Deducting the wages owed to the men and to Mark, and the money she would pay Bagnall tomorrow, plus setting aside even a minimum for food and household expenses, left the sum much depleted. Then she would need to order a further supply of metal if the workshop was to be kept in full production and that she would pay for in advance – she would take no more chances with the odious Thomas Bagnall. Phoebe counted in her mind. She was playing near the edge but she had done that before. Folding one of the white five-pound notes she shoved it deep into her bag. Perhaps it might be enough for what she wanted.

Leaving the iron foundry Phoebe smiled to herself. Thomas Bagnall had been surprised to find her settling one account two days before it was due to be paid and paying for a further, larger supply in advance.

With the five pounds in her bag she walked along Dudley Street, turning left against St James's Church, following Holyhead Road toward the Lodge Holes coal mine.

Joseph had given her the idea when she had visited on Sunday. He had mentioned that the old pit ponies were to be brought out of the mine and sold. Phoebe shuddered to think of these animals, most probably condemned to the glue works after years toiling underground, but that was the way it had always been.

Joseph had somehow seemed more than usually lame, needing Mathew's arm to walk around Sarah's tiny vegetable plot, and Phoebe knew they were worried for his job. If the new mine owner sacked him then they would have to leave their home.

Holding her skirts free of the dusty ground Phoebe left the road, striking left across open ground that gave on to the mine.

But Joseph had not been sacked as yet, and if she could only keep a supply of locks going to America, then maybe in a couple of years she could help Joseph and Sarah to find a new home.

'Please let things work out this time,' she breathed to the morning. 'Please don't let this order be a hoax.'

It was going to be hard work turning out the number of locks Bert had specified every week and she really ought to be at the mill helping all she could or at least busy on her needlework, Phoebe thought, feeling guilty at being away from the house. But for a few hours things were going to have to take their chances.

Reaching the large wooden gates that closed off the pit yard from nothing but open land, Phoebe saw her father's name, not painted out as yet. Nothing moved fast in Wednesbury. Loosing the skirts of her green coat, she took a deep breath and stepped hesitantly across the yard trodden black with coal dust. Today she would not be dealing with Joseph Leach, as she would have a few years before, now she would be doing business with a new yard foreman. Joseph had been dismissed when the mine had changed hands.

'Can I 'elp you, Miss?'

Phoebe smiled at the man who answered her knock on the door of the office. Of medium height but powerful across the shoulders, his splendid moustache wiggled as he spoke.

Phoebe swallowed the smile the dancing moustache threatened to bring to her lips. 'I have reason to believe you are bringing several ponies out of the pit today?'

'Ar, Miss, so we am.'

'Then I would like to purchase one of those ponies.'

'Purchase!' The moustache jigged. 'What do you mean, Miss?'

'May I step inside?' She glanced about the yard, seeing the heads of several men turn in her direction. Maybe Joseph would be in the office.

'Well, it be all dusty in 'ere like, it ain't clean for a lady.' The man hesitated, clearly unused to his working domain being encroached on by a woman.

'We won't let that worry us.' Phoebe stepped inside, glancing about the shed she remembered so well: at the heavy ledgers on a bench to one side, the row of nails hammered into one wall, each with a numbered tag that indicated a man underground, and the table where the dead Norton boy had been laid by his father. Pushing the image away she looked at the man who stood as if trying to bar her entry into a holy sanctum.

'As I said, I wish to purchase one of the ponies that are to be brought up from the pit.'

'You can't, Miss,' he said. 'Them ponies ain't to be sold.'

'What do you mean, they are not for sale!' Phoebe demanded.

'What I says, Miss.' The moustache danced indignantly at her question. 'Them ponies ain't to be sold, not to you anyway.'

'Not to me, but they are to be sold?' Phoebe pressed.

'Mebbe,' the man conceded grudgingly.

'Then why not to me? Why can I not buy one of them?'

''Cos you can't, that's all I know.' He touched a hand to his top lip as if to prevent the moustache leaping from his face. 'The ponies ain't to be sold.'

'You mean perhaps they have been sold already?'

'Maybe they 'ave, then maybe they ain't.' He held on to the moustache that seemed to want to lead a life of its own. 'All I know is what I'm told, an' I was told them ponies was not to be sold.'

'But they have always been sold,' Phoebe defended her case.

'They might 'ave bin, but that were before. This be now an' things am different. Seems new bloke don't want them ponies sent to no glue works.'

A tiny frown formed over Phoebe's eyes. 'Then what does he intend doing with them?'

'Look, Miss,' the man began to sound exasperated, 'I already told you I only knows what I'm told an' I ain't bin told that.'

'Then if you do not know perhaps you will direct me to someone who does?'

'You best talk to the manager,' he said stiffly, 'if anybody be told diff'rent it'll be 'im.'

Phoebe was taken aback. The pit ponies had always been sold off at the end of their working life to any who saw fit to buy them. It had nearly always been the glue works but others had never been barred from buying. 'Then please show me to the manager. Perhaps, as you say, I had best speak to him.'

'Can't do that.' The man grinned, triumphant in his small victory. ''E ain't 'ere.'

'Then where is he?' Phoebe felt a strong desire to slap both moustache and its owner.

'Could be anywheres in the pit, might be one place might be t'other, ain't no tellin'.'

'It is clear you did not win a Sunday school prize for honesty nor one for helpfulness,' Phoebe snapped.

'Maybe not, Miss Pardoe, but *I* did so perhaps you would do better to talk to me?'

Phoebe turned at the sound of a voice that echoed almost nightly in her mind, a faint hint of pink staining her cheeks.

'Might I ask what you are doing here?'

'Sir William,' the blush on her cheeks deepened at the unexpected encounter. 'I – I was told some of the pit ponies would be finished today.'

He waited, eyes taking in the bloom of her face.

'Oh!' His well-defined eyebrows lifted quizzically. 'Were you also told the ponies were to be sold to the glue works?'

'No.' She looked away awkwardly. What was he doing at the mine? Why did she suddenly feel like an erring child?

'But you presumed they were?'

Phoebe lifted her head, re-engaging his eyes defiantly. Wanting to buy a pony to save it from the glue works was no crime. 'Is that not what always happens to ponies taken from the pits?'

'Not all pits, Miss Pardoe.' He glanced at the yard foreman watching them covertly and the man turned back to his ledgers. Sir William led her out. 'Certainly not those belonging to me.'

'You bought my father's mines?' Phoebe asked, surprised.

'I did,' he nodded, 'and that means no more ponies from here or the Crown at Moxley will go to the glue works. Once their working life is over they will be returned to pasture at Sandwell Priory.'

'Then if they are to be put to pasture, why can I not buy one?'

Almost at the gates that closed off the pit head from the open heathland, he halted. 'Why do you want a pit pony?' he asked bluntly. 'When these animals have served so long underground they are virtually worked out. They will not be useful for heavy work.'

'I do not want a pony for heavy work.'

'Then what do you want it for?'

She did not have to tell him, of course, chances were he would not sell her a pony if she *did* tell him, but then she had nothing to hide.

'I wanted it for Ruth.'

'Ruth?' His brows rose again.

'She is the Ingleses' daughter – they live at Wiggins Mill,' Phoebe explained. 'There was an accident and she fell into the canal and though she seemed to suffer no serious injury she has not been the same child since. She used to be so full of life, always playing about the mill, but now she seems so withdrawn. I thought a pony of her own, one she would have the caring of, would give her something of interest.'

'How old is Ruth?'

'She is just a child, no more than eight years old.'

'Would she be able to handle a pony?'

'I am sure of it,' Phoebe answered. 'Her family worked the barges along the canal so she is well used to horses – that was why I thought a pit pony used to being handled by young children would suit her.'

He smiled, his eyes taking on a new warmth. 'Then perhaps we should discuss the possibility of furnishing Ruth with a pony, but here is not the most suitable of places.' He looked at the film of black dust covering her shoes and edging the hem of her coat. 'Might I suggest we go to the Priory?'

'The Priory is at least an hour and a half's walk and I have little time to spare, as I'm sure is the case with yourself, Sir William.'

'You are sure of so many things,' he said. 'Sure my ponies are to be sold off to make glue and sure I do not have time to discuss the provision of one for Ruth.'

'I beg your pardon,' Phoebe coloured afresh at his mild rebuke, 'but I have so little time and a walk to the Priory will take a great deal of it.'

'Not so much if you will accept a ride in my carriage.' He

smiled again. 'It would also relieve me of walking there as I must if you refuse.'

'But could we not just agree a sale here?' she protested.

'I think the pit ponies deserve the peace of the pasture,' he answered, 'even though Ruth would cherish one of them.'

'Then there is no cause for me to accompany you to the Priory.'

'There is every need if you wish the child to have a pony. Please,' he said, seeing the query on her face, 'there is a pony there that will answer your needs perfectly if only you will take enough of your precious time to look at it.'

It would take more of her time than she had accounted for. Phoebe thought of the others working at the mill. She really ought not to be away so long but Ruth seemed so dejected, so apart from them. If two or three more hours would serve to restore the child's interest in life then it would not be too much to pay.

'She's beautiful,' said Phoebe later, stroking the sand-coloured pony nuzzling her hand. 'What's her name?'

'Pippin,' Sir William answered quietly. 'Sophie gave her that name when the mare foaled. She said the newcomer was the colour of the pippins in an apple she fed to the mother.'

'I was so very sorry to hear of what happened to your family.' Phoebe saw the sadness shadow his face. Then in an effort to chase away a little of the shadows, she asked, 'Was this Sophie's horse?'

'The mother was Sophie's so I suppose the foal was too.'

'Then I cannot possibly take her from you.'

'Why not?' He signalled a groom who came and led the horse back to its stable. 'Sophie would have wanted the child to have it, and I want her to have it. I also want her to have this.' Leading the way to a long stone building set with graceful arched windows, he swung open a pair of heavy doors showing a line of broughams and carriages at the end of which stood a small blue-painted governess cart. 'This was my daughter's when she was a child,' he said, going over to it. 'Now I wish it to be Ruth's.'

'But I can't!' Phoebe thought of the five-pound note at the bottom of her bag. It could not possibly be enough to purchase horse and cart.

'Would the child not like it?' he asked, turning to her.

'I'm sure she would.' Phoebe glanced again at the cart, its blue-painted side edged with a pattern of daisies. 'But . . .'

'Once more you are sure,' he said gently, 'so why the "but"?'

'Ruth would love the horse and the cart would be her delight,' Phoebe decided only the truth would conclude this discussion, 'but five pounds is all I have and I know that to be insufficient to pay for them.'

'I am not selling you the horse or the cart, they are a gift.'

'No!' Phoebe's mouth set in a straight line. 'What I cannot pay for I will not take, whatever the need. Thank you for your kindness but I must refuse.'

Touching a hand to the pretty cart he seemed to see into the past, to the child who had once ridden in it so happily. 'If you will not accept a gift from me, accept it from Sophie,' he said softly.

Seeing the droop of his shoulders and hearing the pain in his voice, Phoebe's heart twisted with pity. If only she could take him in her arms and hold him until the pain had gone but she could not. Offering a gift on Sophie's behalf then having it refused would add to the hurt he was feeling. But such a gift . . . Phoebe hesitated, torn between her wish to spare him any more hurt and her decision to accept no man's charity.

Almost as if he sensed her thoughts he turned suddenly, a half sad, half amused smile at the edges of his mouth. 'I will make a bargain with you, Miss Phoebe Pardoe. You are, I take it, familiar with the handling of a horse?'

'I both rode and drove my own governess cart until . . .' She paused. 'Until a few years ago.'

'Then you take this.' He touched the prettily painted cart. 'Tell the child's parents I wish to make a gift of it to their daughter. With your permission I will drive over to Wiggins Mill tomorrow and if they do not wish to accept it I will have it taken away and no more will be said on the subject. Agreed?'

'Agreed.' Phoebe smiled, a part of her already looking forward to tomorrow.

'I ought not to have said I would do it,' she said that same evening.

'Then why did you?'

Why had she? She pondered Lucy's question. Was it because she wished to repay a kindness? Part of her owned to that but the greater part denied it. She had agreed to William Dartmouth's request, not to humour him but out of a desire she could not acknowledge.

'Why did you agree to be 'is 'ostess at the staff Advent Ball?' Lucy asked, her hands deep in flour.

'I suppose it was because he might otherwise have cancelled it,' Phoebe answered, 'and that would have been disappointing to his workers. It is the one really big celebration in their working year.'

'Why 'ave to cancel?' Adding water to the bowl, Lucy began to knead her pastry.

'Sir William explained he has no female relatives, no one he could call upon to fill the role of hostess for the evening.'

'An' so you said as you would do it?' Tipping pastry on to a board, Lucy began to roll it out. 'Was it 'cause 'e gave that 'orse an' cart to the Ingleses?' She looked up, her eyes asking a question she did not speak.

'It seemed churlish to refuse when he had been so kind.'

Phoebe avoided Lucy's eyes, knowing her own would betray the secret she had only fully recognised in the long reach of a sleepless night, a truth that had hit her like a bolt from the blue. She did not feel only pity for William

Dartmouth – she felt love. She had felt it for a long time, she realised, hugging the truth, trying to drive it from her mind as the hours passed. She could not love Edward because she had always loved his father!

'I reckon the ball'll do you good,' Tilly joined in. 'A chance to meet folk and mix a while wi' others will bring you no 'arm.'

'Perhaps not.' Phoebe spooned filling into pastry cases. 'But have you two thought about my gown? Brown grosgrain is hardly suitable for an Advent Ball.'

'Seems like that there satin'll 'ave a use after all.' Tilly carried pies to the oven, packing them inside in neat rows. 'And before you starts on about tekin' time from yer other sewin', I will tek that on till yer frock be done.'

'I don't have much choice, do I?' She smiled at Tilly.

'Not lessen you wants an argy bargy,' her friend replied, 'an' Tilly Wood don't lose no argument – 'er be determined to win.'

'An' you can forget 'elpin' in the workshop.' Lucy lined a fresh batch of pie tins with pastry cases. 'Me an' Lizzie can see to the filin' down.'

'Did I ever tell the two of you?'

'Tell we what?' Lucy asked.

'Tell you how dear you both are to me,' Phoebe said softly.

Annie Pardoe pressed a hand to the pain eating away below her breast. It was constant now, sometimes vicious, sometimes bearable, but always with her. Taking the bottle with its white tablets from the drawer of her bedside table, she eased the cork from its neck then angrily banged the bottle down on the polished mahogany surface. The pills did no good, they did not ease the pain, nor did the laudanum that fool Dingley had prescribed.

Her steps slow and heavy, she crossed the room, drawing a large brown envelope from the chest of drawers and carrying it held to her chest as she returned to sit on the huge bed. Her breathing regulated by spasms of pain, she stared at the sprawled writing before her. Her name in Clinton's writing, his hand shaking as a result of the poison she had given him. But it was not meant for you, my love! Her heart screamed. It was not for you. But he had taken it and had died and with him had died all her hopes, all her reasons for living. But Clinton would not be forgotten. Pressing the button mounted on the panelling beside the bed, she waited until Maudie Tranter entered the room.

'I . . . I have some letters . . . to write,' she said, pain interlacing the words so they came out haltingly. 'Bring . . . bring me pen and ink from . . . from the study. I . . . I will write them here.'

'Yes, ma'am.' Maudie glanced at the pill bottle, its cork still removed. 'Will you be wantin' paper an' envelopes?'

'Yes.' Annie paused, a sudden jab of pain forcing her eyes shut. 'Yes, bring paper and envelopes.'

It's a doctor you be needin', Maudie thought as she went to get the things Annie had asked for. And if you don't be callin' on one soon it won't be a letter you'll be writin' – it'll be yer will.

Drawing the documents from the brown envelope, Annie stared at the titles to properties Samuel's legacy had paid for, properties she was to have built a new life upon, a life shared with Clinton. But now he was gone and without him her life no longer held meaning.

'Will you be wantin' a tray in the garden, ma'am?' Maudie set the writing materials on the table that had been moved near the grate in which a fire was laid but as yet unlit. 'Or will I fetch a pot o' tea up to you 'ere?'

Annie glanced at the fob watch pinned to the left shoulder of her black dress. 'I will have tea here in . . . in about . . . an hour,' she said, pain snatching at the words.

'Very good, ma'am.' Maudie left the room. There don't be many hours left to you, Annie Pardoe, she thought, making her way to the kitchen. With or without the potions of old Dingley, you be walking the last stretch and how far that be only God in Heaven be knowing, and he won't tell.

Alone once more, Annie glanced at each of the documents Clinton had intended to post to her. She had doubted him, had judged him guilty of theft. But you will have it all, my love, she thought. You will have it all, every penny, as you would have had when I became your wife. I would have given it to you then as I give it to you now.

Crossing to the table she sat down, her black skirts rustling in the quiet room. Dipping the pen into the ink, she began to write.

Slicing cucumber sandwiches, Maudie placed the wafer thin triangles on a china plate, arranging a few sprigs of watercress across them before covering them with a food net. It had been an hour since she had taken the writing materials to Annie's bedroom and though she knew her mistress would probably not touch the sandwiches or even drink the tea she would take it up to her nonetheless. Annie had eaten less and less every day since hearing of that man's death. Maudie filled the tiny flowered jug with fresh milk, setting a dainty bowl of sugar beside it on the tray.

I guessed you would not be getting him to no altar, Annie Pardoe, she thought, scalding tea from a kettle bubbling softly over the kitchen fire. But I never thought he would avoid it by turning up his toes.

Taking the tray upstairs, she tapped at Annie's door with the toe of her boot, waiting for the call that would give her permission to enter and tapping more loudly when it did not come. Balancing the tray awkwardly on one arm when her second tap went unacknowledged, she turned the door knob and pushed open the door.

Annie sat on the bed, her voluminous black skirts spread over the cover like a storm cloud.

'I brought your tray.' Maudie crossed to the table set before the fireplace but seeing that the letters Annie had written were still open upon it, she took the tray to the washstand, setting it down beside the jug and bowl.

'Will I clear the table or will you take yer tea on yer bed?' she asked, shoving bowl and jug a little further along the marble top of the washstand. 'Do you want to tek yer tea at the table?' She turned, repeating her question when Annie did not answer.

'I'll pour you out a cup.' Pouring a little milk into the fragile china cup, Maudie filled it with tea then carried it across to where Annie sat on the bed, a large sheet of paper in her hands.

'Drink this up while it be 'ot.' Maudie held the cup towards Annie. 'C'mon, tek it.' She offered the cup again. 'It be fresh brewed, the way you like it.'

Annie carried on staring at the paper in her hand and Maudie tutted with irritation. Maybe she didn't fancy the tea now she had it but it was only good manners to answer a body. But then, when had good manners ever bothered Annie Pardoe? Never, unless that Clinton be about, and then it was all please and thank you. Clinton Harforth-Darby! Maudie put the cup beside the open bottle of tablets on the bedside table. What kind of a name had that been to go to bed on?

'Don't leave yer tea standin' there,' she said, the irritation she was feeling colouring her tone. 'It'll get stewed an' you knows you don't like stewed tea.'

Pausing as she turned to leave, Maudie looked at the woman seated on the bed. She hadn't spoken but that in itself was no surprise. Annie Pardoe often ignored her. But she hadn't moved either, not even to shield the paper she was holding from the possibility of being seen by another. That boded no good. But her eyes be open, Maudie told herself, 'er be readin' that paper so 'er be all right!

'Yer tea be to the side o' you,' she said again. 'Leave what you be doin' an' drink it afore it gets cold.'

Returning the few steps to the bedside table, she took up the cup with one hand, the other touching Annie lightly on the shoulder – only to draw away again quickly. Annie Pardoe was holding a sheet of paper and her eyes were open but she was stone dead.

'Oh my Lord!' Maudie breathed. 'Oh my dear Lord!'

Her hands shaking, she set the cup back on the table beside the still full bottle of tablets. Whatever had killed Annie Pardoe, it was not an overdose of them. She looked to where the body had fallen backward at her touch, the head lying a little sideways on the pillow, the open eyes seeming to watch her.

'I thought you was on the last stretch,' she murmured into the stillness, 'but I little thought you was *that* near thy end. May the Lord rest you, Annie Pardoe.'

Bending to lift the dead woman's legs on to the bed, Maudie noticed the hand that still held the paper had dropped palm down across her breast, showing a large amethyst ring on the third finger.

'That be yer weddin' finger!' she said as if Annie could hear. 'That must be a engageyment ring but I never seen you wi' it afore.'

She bent to look closer at the ring. 'Did 'e give you that?' she asked the silence. 'Or did you buy it yerself to mek it look like 'e was goin' to marry you?' Ignoring the open eyes, she eased the paper from the already cold fingers, reading the letter Clinton had written. *In his thoughts till he returned* . . . Carefully she replaced the single sheet of paper. Then he was going to marry her, seemed like. But if he was, it was unlike Annie to have let the fact go untold.

Glancing around the room, her eyes lit on the letters Annie had written that afternoon. Picking them up she read the neat copperplate hand. *'The Last Will and Testament* . . .' Maudie continued to read to the last word.

'You bitter, twisted old bugger!' she gasped, her hands falling to her sides. 'May the Lord see fit to forgive you for I never could.' She lifted the letters, looking unbelievingly at the second one. She could understand the feeling behind the first, if a woman wanted to leave her all to a man then that was her prerogative, but to write a letter like this to a girl who had done her no harm! Still unsure of what her eyes had told her, Maudie read again the letter addressed to Phoebe.

I want you to know whose was the hand behind the one that signed you to prison. I paid the Magistrate £100 to have you put behind those bars. It was I told Lawyer Siveter to advise Lucy Baines not to take what she knew of that necklace to the Dartmouths, and it was I paid John Kilvert to testify that you had pawned jewellery once before in his shop– jewellery he knew to have been stolen from another town altogether. But you were released, released from your prison though there was no release for me from the prison that held me. Abel's child was free but Abel's sister remained in the prison he had paid for.

Then there was the order for one gross of Pardoe's Patent Locks. How did you feel when you received that? I cut the heading from James Greaves's bill and pasted it to my own letter, and I did the same to the one you received cancelling that order.

And why? I will tell you why. Your father took my life. To me fell the task of living with Samuel, of ensuring no one would ever discover the twist of fate that held him and me prisoner in the same house, that none would ever learn of the affliction the medical world held out no cure for. Your father took my life so he might live his to the full. I could not make him pay so I exacted that payment from you, and though you might still live after I do not you will not have a penny of that which was first your father's and then Samuel's, for everything of that is for my husband that was to have been.

Signed, Annie Pardoe.

"Ow could 'er do all that to 'er own flesh an' blood?' Maudie said when she had finished reading. "Ow could 'er do such bad things to a young wench who 'ad never done 'er no 'arm?'

Glancing at the first letter that was Annie's will she scanned the words again: '. . . *all land, property and jewellery belonging to me shall be sold, the realisation such land, property and jewellery shall produce is to be used for the erection of a monument to be dedicated to Clinton Harforth-Darby and is to bear the inscription, "Dear to the heart and to the memory of his betrothed, Annie Mary Pardoe . . ."*'

Maudie dropped the letters back on to the table. How could there be a spite so strong as to strike at a wench from the grave, as Annie Pardoe was here striking at her own niece? She had turned her from her father's house and even now was denying her the last of what should rightly be hers.

Maudie looked again at the figure on the bed and the papers spread about her. Going to the bed, she picked them up, quickly scanning words she did not understand but guessed to be legal proof of ownership of the properties they named. And all this was to be sold to build a monument to a dead man and feed the pride of a dead woman!

'An' Phoebe be to get nothin',' she said aloud. 'P'raps that be what you 'oped, Annie Pardoe, an' for all I know you may be 'opin' for it still but you reckoned wi'out Maudie Tranter. An' if you wants to stop me now you 'ave got to get up from that bed to do it!'

Seating herself at the table, Maudie began to copy the wording of the will until she reached the words 'shall be sold'. Careful to spell each word correctly, she changed the text to read 'shall become the property of my niece, Phoebe Mary Pardoe', then she signed Annie's name.

Taking both of Annie's letters, she pushed them into her pocket. They would burn on the kitchen fire. 'If what I be doin' be wrong, Lord, then you must punish me for I'll not change it,' she murmured. Then, slowly and methodically, she searched the room for any other paper Annie might have written and that could be compared with the Will now on the table.

Satisfied the room held no other documents she went to the rooms Samuel had used and searched them, finding nothing. She would collect the tray then search each of the downstairs rooms. Only then would she go for the doctor. Once more in Annie's bedroom she looked again at the dead figure, feeling no pity for the woman who could plot so much wickedness against her own kin. Reaching for the cup, she changed her mind. It would look more natural for it to be there; she would tell them she had left the tray earlier and on going back for it had found Annie lying on the bed and the letter she had said she wished to write on the table.

'You 'ave 'urt that wench enough, Annie Pardoe,' she murmured, leaving the room to go downstairs. 'You'll not 'urt Abel's daughter no more.'

It had been a month since Phoebe had agreed to William Dartmouth's request for her to stand as hostess for the annual party he gave for the household staff. The creamy satin falling in soft folds about her feet, Phoebe wondered if she had done right to consent to attend this evening at Sandwell Priory. Sir William had called at Wiggins Mill several times since the day he had shown her the little cart and the horse, each time saying he wished to enquire after Ruth's well-being, and with each of those visits she'd had to try harder not to read more into his grey eyes than friendship. That she loved him she could not deny, but to imagine that love returned was foolish as well as hopeless. Sir William Dartmouth might take another wife but he would not look for one at Wiggins Mill.

'You look beautiful, Miss Phoebe,' Lucy said, adding the last tiny yellow silk rose-bud to Phoebe's hair.

'Do you think he will expect jewels?' She looked at her reflection in the cheval mirror. The gown held her body in a close sheath, the satin drawn to the back in heavy swathes and the front of the skirt relieved by a trail of yellow roses

Lucy had spent hours making. The décolleté neckline was ornamented with one yellow rose, showing the swell of her breasts.

'That man 'as more sense than to go lookin' for jools other than the ones that be shinin' in yer eyes,' Tilly said, taking the gloves Phoebe had bought so many months before from the drawer and handing them to her. "E don't need no finery − 'e can see what a woman be wi'out artificial 'elp.'

'Tilly's right,' Lucy added, 'you don't be needin' no jewels. They couldn't mek you look any more beautiful than you do now.'

'I hope you are right.' Phoebe took up her gloves and after checking one last time in the mirror, followed the two women downstairs.

'Afore you go, Miss,' Lizzie came hesitantly to the door of Phoebe's front parlour, 'the lads an' Ruth 'ave somethin' for you. Would you mind if they come in?'

'Of course I would not mind.'

'Eh, Miss, you look bostin'!' Josh was first through the door, his eyes round with admiration as he looked at her. 'Don't 'er, Mark?'

'Good enough to eat,' he grinned. 'I might even be tempted to tek you out meself, Miss.'

'Cheeky young sod!' Lizzie cuffed her son but could not help smiling.

'I think you looks like a princess!' Shy at being in the front parlour, Ruth pressed against her mother's side.

'Go on, Ruthie,' Josh urged the child, his hand gently taking hers, 'give Miss Phoebe what we got for 'er.'

The little girl looked up at her mother and at her nod allowed Josh to pull her forward. 'We buyed this for you, Miss,' she said, shyly holding up a fan of the palest lemon lace, each of its struts tipped with a tiny yellow crystal. Then as Phoebe bent to take it she piped, 'It be a new one, it ain't from the pawn shop.'

'Oh, you sweetheart!' Phoebe felt a rush of tears as she took the child in her arms. 'That is exactly what I needed.'

'We thought you might like a fan,' Mark's cheeky lopsided grin stretched across his mouth like a wedge of melon. 'You can 'ide yer yawns be'ind it if you gets bored.'

'I don't think I will be bored, Mark,' Phoebe said, giving Ruth one last hug before turning to him. 'Though I might need it to hide my embarrassment at having no jewellery.'

'No need for you to feel embarrassed,' Josh said gallantly. 'There ain't not one thing you could do would better the way you look.'

'Josh be right, Miss.' Mark wasn't to be outdone in the field of compliments. 'Ain't nothin' would mek you look prettier'n you look now. Ya looks real beautiful an' that be no lie.'

'When experts such as them two agree you look beautiful then you can be sure it's beautiful you look,' Lucy said.

'You could marry a prince,' Ruth said solemnly, 'you be beautiful enough to be a princess.'

'If I do,' Phoebe smiled, 'it will all be because of my lovely fan.' She flicked it open, holding it below her eyes. 'Any prince would be glad to marry a princess with a golden fan.'

But she did not want to marry a prince, Phoebe thought as she rode in the carriage sent to collect her. The man she loved held a title, albeit not a royal one, but he did not want her for his wife.

'Good evening, Miss Pardoe,' William Dartmouth greeted the young woman alighting from his carriage. 'Ruth is well, I hope?' He escorted her into the great hall of his ancient house.

'As well as she was when you called three days ago.' Phoebe smiled up at him, glancing quickly away as she met the look in his eyes, a look she so wanted to be saying what she knew he never would.

'And the boys?'

'Cheeky as ever.' Phoebe held out the fan. 'They bought me this.'

'Rogues, the pair of 'em.' He smiled. 'But rogues with good taste.'

'Mark said he might be tempted to take me out himself.'

'Did he!' Sir William laughed, the sound drawing the glances of his staff lined up to be presented to Phoebe. 'The young hound! There'll be many a man takes a horsewhip to that one before he settles, though I say again I admire his taste.' He glanced at Phoebe, seeing the colour steal the paleness from her cheeks. 'You look very beautiful, Miss Pardoe.'

'I think we should look to your guests.' She turned towards the line of waiting men and women.

'Our guests,' he murmured at her elbow. 'For one night at least allow them to be that.'

Later William watched the young woman dancing a waltz with his estate manager. For something like four hours she had mixed easily with the people of the estate, men and women alike, a smile and a word for each, her simple manner making her readily acceptable to them. Watching her now, the light from the chandeliers glistening on the bronze silk of her hair piled high on her head, tiny buds of yellow satin nestling in its coils, her slim body outlined by the lines of her gown, he felt a pang of jealousy that the arms holding her and the eyes looking down on her smiling face were not his. Impatient with his own thoughts, he turned to his steward.

'It is all going very well,' he said. 'Give my thanks to everyone in the morning and tell them I was very pleased at the effort they have all made.'

'I will, sir.' The steward smiled, pleased at these words of thanks.

'And now I think we should announce supper.' William watched the man make his way to the end of the great hall, to where the musicians were seated in a large alcove, not sure whether announcing supper or wanting Phoebe out of the arms of his estate manager was the real reason behind his having the music stopped. Watching the man escort her back to him, William carefully lowered his gaze, hiding the answer that throbbed in his heart.

'A glass of wine, Miss Pardoe?' he asked as the estate manager took his leave of them.

'I would find a glass of lemonade more acceptable,' Phoebe answered, a little breathless from the constant round of dancing.

'Lemonade it shall be.' He led her to the supper table. 'May I help you to a plate of something?'

Phoebe shook her head. 'Like the princess in the story, I am too happy to eat.'

'Unlike the princess in the story,' he said softly, 'don't disappear when the clock strikes midnight.'

'How does Pippin be gettin' along, Miss?' The groom who had led the horse from its stable to show to her smiled as Phoebe came up to the supper table.

'Being spoiled terribly.' Phoebe's own smile broke out spontaneously. 'She is loved by all of us but especially so by Ruth.'

'The master told us of Pippin's new mistress and with his permission we would like to send her an Advent gift.' He looked at Sir William and when he nodded permission the groom handed Phoebe a package. 'It be from all the 'ouse, an' we 'oped you would take it for we an' give it to the little girl.'

'May I peep?'

'Ar, Miss.'

The groom nodded and Phoebe peeled away a layer of brown paper, exclaiming with delight at sight of blue leather reins. 'How lovely! Ruth will be enchanted. Thank you all so much, it is so kind of you.' She smiled at the assembled staff, all of whom had their eyes turned to her and all of whom shared her delight.

Arranging for the gift to be placed in the carriage against her return, William Dartmouth accepted the glass of lemonade handed him by one of the housemaids, dressed now in a pretty print frock. 'You are a victim of your own popularity,' he said as Phoebe was kept continually busy answering the polite addresses of his staff, 'you have made too favourable an impression and I fear you will have to pay the penalty.'

'Talking to people as friendly as these is no penalty.'

'But you would like a quiet interlude before the evening resumes?'

She nodded. 'It would be nice. I have not been called upon to be hostess to a party before and it is tiring.'

'Exhausting would be my word for it. Let's go to the drawing room, it will be quiet there.'

He led the way to a room furnished with sofas and chairs upholstered in a deep cream brocade, the curtains over high arched windows echoing the same colour and the huge square of carpet patterned in cream and soft peach.

'I admit I prefer a glass of something other than lemonade.' Crossing to a large figured cabinet he drew out decanter and glass, filling the latter. Raising it to his lips, he looked at the young woman sitting on the sofa, her hair turned to glistening amber by the soft light, her lovely face smiling at him – and turned quickly away, staring into the fireplace.

'Miss Pardoe,' he said, the thickness in his throat not quite under control, 'I believe my son asked you to become his wife?'

Phoebe's smile faded. 'Edward did me that honour.'

'But you refused?'

'Yes.'

'Not once but several times, is that not so?'

Phoebe stared into her glass, the happiness of the evening draining away. Was this why he had asked her to come to Sandwell Priory? Was this why they were now alone in this room, so he could bombard her with questions? Glancing at a side table, she looked at the silver-framed photographs of his family, at Edward's face staring solemnly back at her. 'It is so,' she answered quietly.

He remained staring into the empty fireplace. 'Might I ask the reason or would that be considered too rude?'

Putting the lemonade aside, Phoebe took a long trembling breath. He had brought her to his home in order to question her and she would answer his questions, all of them, and then she would return to Wiggins Mill. 'No, I do not consider there to be any rudeness in your question. The reason for my refusals was simple: I did not love Edward in the way a woman should love the man she agrees to marry, and I would marry no man I did not love.'

'I see.' He waited for several moments, the silence marked by the ticking of a graceful clock on the mantel, above his head. Then: 'Was there someone else?'

Phoebe watched him, her emotions crying out to comfort him, knowing the pain these questions must be causing him, understanding his wish to know as much as possible of the son he had lost. 'When your son asked me to marry him there was no one else,' she said gently.

'And now?' He swivelled to face her, his question hard and sharp.

Phoebe hesitated, taken aback by the knife edge of his tone. 'I . . . there . . . no, I am not being called upon by anyone.' In the hushed light of the room Phoebe saw the play of emotion on his face, saw his fingers about the glass whiten with tension.

'I ask your pardon,' he said. 'I had no right to ask such a question.'

'No, you did not.' Phoebe looked at his face, still handsome behind the pain. 'But had I not wished to answer then I would not have done so.'

'Miss Pardoe . . . Phoebe.' He wrestled with the words, wanting to say them yet stubbornly denying them freedom. 'I, I . . .'

Phoebe remained silent. Whatever it was William Dartmouth had to say to her, he must say it alone.

'Miss Pardoe, had my family lived I would never have said to you what I must say now. Had Edward survived I would not have spoken, whether you had married him or not. You have told me there is no gentleman calling upon you, that you have promised marriage to no one.'

His fingers closed tighter, threatening to crush the glass in his hand, and a film of perspiration glistened on his forehead.

'That being so, allow me the honour of asking you to become my wife?'

Phoebe felt the rush of blood leaving her face, the fan falling from fingers suddenly without strength. Why did he want to marry her? Did he still feel Edward was somehow obligated to her, an obligation he must make good by making her his wife? That alone could be the reason, she decided.

'Sir William.' She spoke evenly though her heart was breaking. This was the thing she had dreamed of for so long; she loved this man deeply but he saw marriage to her only as a means of reparation. 'Edward was under no obligation to me, you have no debt to repay.'

'For God's sake!' He flung the glass from his hand, shattering it against the stone of the hearth. 'I love you. God help me, I love you!' He turned back to the fireplace, one hand on the mantel, his head bent, the anger in his voice replaced by a mixture of longing and recrimination.

'I have loved you since I brought you from that prison, may Heaven forgive me. It was wrong of me but I had no power to prevent it. I loved you even as Edward loved you, the thought of you married to my son or to any man haunted my days. I know it is useless to speak of it, I am afraid I allowed my emotions to override my judgement. It is unforgivable of me to have spoken to you as I have. I realise you would not dream of marrying me . . .'

'But I have dreamed of it,' Phoebe interrupted, her own voice soft with an answering surge of love. 'I have dreamed of it for many months and I dream of it still.'

'Phoebe!' He turned from the fireplace, his face lit with hope. 'You said you would never marry a man you did not love.'

She smiled across at him, her eyes tender with love. 'Nor would I, but I love you. I think I always have.'

'Phoebe!' He crossed the room with one bound, snatching her roughly into his arms. 'My love – oh, my love.'

He loved her, *he loved her*, and he wanted her for his wife. Phoebe leaned against him as he kissed her. But how would a wife who had been in prison be accepted among his circle? Would marriage to her slowly destroy his life? And children, what if they had children? What would they think of having a mother once accused of theft?

Pulling away from his arms Phoebe put her fears into words, asking each of the questions her soul told her she must.

He smiled at her, his grey eyes a deeper shade with the love he no longer feared to show. 'I want you for my wife because I love you. I love you so much I cannot conceive of life without you. I love your honesty and integrity, your loyalty and tenderness of conscience, your dignity and your constancy. I want more for my children than the emptiness of a society that prizes none of those qualities.

'The world is changing, Phoebe, and we must change with it. It might take some time for people to forget the past but give them that time and they will see for themselves that trueness of spirit that would never allow you to commit any crime.'

He drew her into his arms again, looking down into her radiant face. 'You told me once that I should never use the word "must" to you again, but I am going to do so one more time. Your father is unable to answer my request so you *must* do that yourself. Phoebe Pardoe, I ask for your hand in marriage. Will you marry me?'

Turning her face up to him, her eyes soft with love, Phoebe smiled. 'My father cannot answer you, William,' she murmured, 'but the answer would be the same. That answer is yes, you may marry Abel's daughter.'

For the Sake of her Child

For my parents. With my very deep love and gratitude for a truly wonderful childhood.

Prologue

'Shit!' George Walker swore vehemently, feeling the sharp stone bite into the ball of his right foot. ''Ang on,' he called to Ben Corns who, hands in pockets and head down against the cold April morning, was picking his way along the narrow path that was a short cut from the drab back-to-back houses of Lea Brook to Brinson's steel foundry. 'Summat in me shoe.' George hopped on one foot while rearranging the layer of cardboard he had cut and fitted to the inside of his shoes the night before, to cover holes that stretched from side to side.

'Summat in thee shoe?' Ben sniffed, too cold to take his hand from his jacket pocket to wipe away the drip festooning the end of his nose. 'Well, whatever it is, it ain't no sole. Thee wants to tek them to old Harris an' get 'im to put a bottom on 'em.'

'Oh, ar?' George shoved his bare foot back into the shoe only prayer was holding together, wiggling it around, trying to slide the cardboard insole to a more comfortable position. 'An' what do I pay 'im with? John Harris is a good cobbler but he ain't no saint. You can't pay, then he don't mend. Like I says, he don't do nothin' for love.'

Ben sniffed harder, his top lip curling back towards his nose in an effort to dislodge the enlarging drip.

'So 'is missis tells my Kate. He only meks the effort on a Saturday night, an' 'er 'as to buy 'im an extra quart of Old Best afore he can rise to that – and at best it's over in two minutes. 'Er reckons as 'er don't know why 'er bothers, 'er

1

would get more pleasure from drinking the quart o' Best 'erself!'

Their laughter rang out in the sharp cold dawn, sending a cloud of startled crows shooting into the air.

George stared after them for a moment, watching the effortless way they lifted clear of the dismal smoke-blackened buildings.

Wednesbury ... He glanced behind him at the untidy strangle of decaying houses that was his end of the dirty little Midlands town. Christ, no wonder they called it the Black Country!

'George ... hey, George!'

Ben Corns's call broke into George's thoughts, something in the tone telling him to hurry up.

'What's up?' He hobbled along, his right foot held awkwardly sideways; the cardboard was precious thin, every stone threatening to pierce it through. This damp would see it off soon enough and that meant sparks from pouring steel under feet as good as bare.

'What's up?' he asked again, catching up with Ben who was staring down at the grey-black water of Millfield Pool.

Millfield Pool had once been a shaft of the Bluefly Coalmine; it had flooded following an underground explosion that had taken nine men with it, among them George's own father. There were folk in the Brook said Millfield Pool was haunted, that the calls and cries of the trapped men could still be heard on summer nights, but that was claptrap – old women's talk. George didn't cotton to such daftness. Nevertheless his eyes found a way of drifting away from the slatey mouth of the dead mine.

'Down theer. Look, George.' Ben pointed towards a mantle of green weed that circled the pool. 'Look theer in them weeds.'

George didn't want to look. He didn't believe in no tales of hauntings – bloody silly old women with nowt better to do than talk such daftness! – yet still he didn't want to look into the waters that had swallowed his father; waters that had added a thousandfold to the misery of an already poverty-stricken existence. In his earliest years he'd had to finish school at dinnertime to spend the rest of the day, and much of the night, running and fetching for anyone who would pay a penny; then at nine years old start working dawn to the early hours, doing anything that would add a few coppers to his mother's earnings from skivvying up at The Lodge. He could likely have earned more if he'd gone to the mine but his mother would have none of it. It had taken one, she told him, it wouldn't have another. So it had gone on until they could manage no longer and he had taken work at Brinson's.

'George . . . oh, bloody 'ell!'

Ben grabbed his arm, causing him to bring his right sole down hard on the ground. He winced, not knowing if it were caused by the sudden jab of pain through his foot or from the sight of black cloth being spread by the breeze ruffling the calm surface of the water.

'Oh, Christ, it's 'er . . . it's Mary Carter!'

Ben's work-grimed fingernails pressed through the thin cloth of George's jacket, the drip on the end of his nose jiggling as he looked up at his friend who was a clear six inches taller than himself.

'Don't you talk so muttonheaded.' George shook off the hand with its mute demand and looked again at that patch of black. 'I'll tell thee summat, Ben Corns, you've got Mary Carter on the brain. Didn't Beth Haywood say as how the wench buggered off wi' a bloke from around 'Ampton way?'

The drip jiggled precariously with the shaking of Ben's head. 'Mary Carter wouldn't buggar off wi' nobody. I'm tellin' thee, George, somebody 'as done for 'er.'

'Done for 'er?' George echoed the words scathingly. 'More like somebody's done *to* 'er. Probably copped for a babby and took off rather than face the music, not that you can blame 'er for that, knowing the Lea Brook . . .'

''Er weren't 'avin' no babby.' Ben grabbed his elbow. ''Er wouldn't look at a man after 'er Jed was took an' you know it. I'm tellin' yer, George that's 'er down theer an' if you'm so sure it ain't then you won't be agen goin' an' 'avin' a look.'

A push to George's elbow added to the challenge, but George hung back, reluctant to accept, for fear of going near the water that terrified him.

'That ain't anythin' other than some old rags.' He shook his friend's hand from his elbow. 'Kids likely throwed 'em in.'

Ben sniffed loudly but unsuccessfully.

'Well, if they'm just old rags you won't mind goin' an' provin' it.'

The challenge was unmistakable: refuse it and George would be the laughing stock of the foundry for weeks to come; accept it and he risked worsening the nightmares he still suffered from, of men drowning in Millfield Pool.

'If we am late we'll get quartered,' George countered, hoping the reminder they would lose pay if they were a minute late arriving at Brinson's would deter Ben from challenging him further. But his ploy fell on deaf ears. Ben was determined to see if his supposition was right.

'Go on,' he urged, 'whatever it is down theer, it can't eat yer.'

Unwilling to lose face before the men at the foundry . . . because hear of it they would, Ben was too fond of a good story to let the pleasure of telling it go by . . . George slithered down the shallow bank that gave on to the edge of the pool, feeling the scree of coal chippings shredding the cardboard from his soles.

'Can yer reach it?' Ben asked, as close to George's rear as a dog after a bitch in heat.

Gritting his teeth, George stretched out a hand and grabbed the slime-covered cloth.

'It's 'eavy,' he muttered, heaving at the sodden mass, 'you'll 'ave to give me a hand.'

4

Together they freed the floating cloth from its anchor of weed.

'Oh, Christ!' Ben breathed as a wreath of brown hair appeared on the grey water. 'Oh, Christ . . .'

Detaching itself from his nose, the pearly dewdrop fell on to the swollen, blotched face of Mary Carter.

Anna Bradly sat on one of the two wooden chairs that, together with a scrubbed wooden table, almost filled the tiny kitchen. Her feet, bare below the cotton of her blue print dress, rested on the drab hearth.

How long had it been? Leaning her head sideways, she let it rest against the rough brick of the wall. Light from the oil lamp on the mantelpiece caught the movement of her rich auburn hair. How long since Mary Carter had been pulled drowned from Millfield Pool . . . how long since the accusations had started?

Mary Carter had come twice a week to this house since Anna's mother had died in childbirth ten years ago. Mondays were given over to washing. The fire already lit beneath the brick-lined copper before she arrived, she would hang her shawl on the nail behind the kitchen door and go straight into the poky wash-house. Anna had been allowed to watch as she ladled heavy buckets of steaming water into the round wooden washtub and sometimes Mary let her help cut thin slices of yellow scrubbing soap and drop them like dusty curls in among the wash.

Thursday Mary baked.

Anna breathed deeply, remembering the smell of freshly baked bread and sugar-topped cinnamon cake. This had been her favourite day. A half-burned coal settled further into its glowing bed, sending flakes of grey ash falling into the hearth.

Anna looked back across the years since her mother's death. Standing on a chair beside a table white from years of scrubbing, she would pour the liquid yeast and sugar mixture into the huge earthenware bowl of fluffy white flour after Mary had said the devil had been raised.

'Does yeast and sugar really raise the devil?'

She remembered the smile on Mary's face as she answered, but even more clearly remembered the answer she had never understood.

'There's more than yeast and sugar can raise that one.'

Only now could she see just how true that was.

The coals settled again and Anna stared into the depths of the fire, hypnotised. Oh, the devil had been raised all right! Only not in a cup of yeast and sugar water.

It had been on a Friday morning. Two men crossing the fields to work had seen the floating mass of clothes caught in the reeds; they had pulled the body on to the narrow path skirting the water-filled mine shaft . . . the body of Mary Carter.

'Death from misadventure' had been the Coroner's report but people hereabouts had called it murder, a murder they accused Anna's father of committing. That had been three years ago and not one of them had set foot in this house since.

At thirteen Anna had taken on the running of it, watching the taunts and jibes turn her father from a quiet man to a morose, withdrawn shadow.

He had murdered Mary Carter, they said, because she'd refused his advances. She would have nothing to do with his filthy suggestions so he had forced himself on her, then, knocking her senseless, thrown her into Millfield Pool.

Anna closed her eyes. Her father was innocent, that much she knew. Mary Carter had always arrived at the house after he had left for work and had long gone home before he returned. How could he have murdered her?

The hollow echo of the old tin bucket rattling across the cobbled yard woke Anna. The low fire now gave little light, and for a moment she could not make out the shape looming in the doorway as the door was thrown back on its hinges.

'Where are you, you bloody bitch?'

The harsh shout rang in the silence. Her father was drunk again. This had become the pattern of his life: trying to sink his pain at the bottom of a pint tankard.

'Where are you . . . you lying, stinking bitch?'

Stumbling forward, he half-fell across the table, sending the cups she had set out for tomorrow's breakfast crashing to the floor. Anna stood up, reaching for the oil lamp, turning the wick a little higher. She would help him to bed as she had done so many times; once there he would sleep off the beer.

'There you are, Mary Carter!'

He had pushed himself upright. Eyes glazed with alcohol and hatred stared at Anna. Her hand fell away from the lamp; he had called her by that name before, always when the accusations had been flying thick and his drinking heavy.

'No . . . it's me, Father . . . Anna.' She didn't move, watching the swaying of his head as he continued to stare at her.

'Do you know what you've done to me, Mary Carter?' The question was thick and slurred. 'Do you know what I've gone through because of you? The lies and insults I've suffered. Do you, you cow, *do* you?'

'Father.' Anna spoke softly, carefully. She had never seen him this bad before. 'Father, it's me, Anna . . . Mary has gone home.'

'Do you know what they are saying down there, those bastards!' He banged a heavy fist on the table, setting the knives dancing a crazy jig. 'I'll tell you what they're saying: they are saying I screwed you, forced you when you said no, then knocked you senseless and threw you into the pool.'

Swaying, he moved around the table, dim light filtering through the open door, turning him into frightening solidity. His hands hung at his sides, his head lolled tipsily forward on his neck. 'But that's not true, Mary Carter, and you know it. Screwed you? – Pah! – Christ knows I never laid a finger on you.'

Across the short distance Anna could smell the beery fumes

exhaled with each breath. Something must have happened, someone in The Collier must have baited him more than usual for him to have drunk himself into such a state. Nervously she stepped forward, bare feet soundless on the flagged floor.

'C'mon, Father, I'll help you upstairs.'

His eyes continued to stare. Locked on her face, they did not see her, but what they did see contorted his expression to a twisted mask of bitterness. He moved slowly, head thrust forward, feet shuffling on the stone floor and Anna wanted to cry out but was afraid. If she remained calm he would recognise her and that terrible look would be gone from his face.

'No, by God, I never laid a finger on you. Was that why you did it? Was that why you told your cronies that every time you came to this house I made you lie with me? Was that pretence to cover the fact that I never did?'

He came closer. The dull yellow pool of light cast by the oil lamp flickered over his face, touching the long smear of blood on his left cheek, paling before the glitter of his almost transparent blue eyes.

'And why didn't I, did you tell them that, Mary Carter? Did you tell them Jos Bradly takes no whore?'

Anna clutched her hands tightly, pressing them against her sides as her father took another swaying step towards her. She had thought to help him to bed but now instinct told her to get to her own room. He would shout and swear for a few hours, smash a few dishes, but she could clear up in the morning. Right now she was safer out of his sight, for in his drink-fuddled mind he was seeing not her but Mary Carter.

'For months I've taken the brickbats,' he began again, but this time he didn't shout. His words were little more than a whisper, almost as if he were talking to himself. 'For months they've pointed the finger at me, accusing me of that which I never thought to do. Well, now I've changed my mind. I've taken the insults so I might just as well take the pleasure.'

For the first time in her life Anna was afraid of her father.

He would never harm her in his normal state. But tonight he was not normal, he was in drink. And there was worse than that wrong with him; the long months of mental torment since Mary's death, months of being a social outcast, treated like a leper by those who had called themselves his friends, had at last broken him.

Heart thumping, she stepped sideways. The light from the lamp, what little there was of it, was shining into his eyes. If she moved slowly, chances were he would not notice.

But she was wrong. One hand shot out, grasping the hair tied at the back of her neck and at the same time wrenching her forward, her scream muffled by the rough material of his jacket.

'You can go, Mary.' Above her head the words came out in a quiet sing-song voice. 'You can go, but this time it will be the truth you'll tell those bastards.'

Pulling back her head, Anna's anguished cries did not register on his fevered mind. Wiping his free hand across his face, mixing blood and sweat together, Joseph Bradly swore with the soft vehemence of one who has waited long for vengeance. Then, grasping the neckline of the cotton dress, he ripped it violently downward, tearing the cheap thin material to the hem.

For a moment he stared at the creamy skin above Anna's bodice then that garment too was torn away, his hand leaving a smear of blood across her breast.

'This is what you've talked of so often to your dirty-minded women friends, you filthy, bloody bitch! That you were crucifying a man didn't matter to you, did it? Well, now you're going to pay.'

'Father . . . please, Father, it's me, Anna. Father, please . . .'

Anna's screams died as a blow to the side of her head sent her spinning to the floor and the blackness of nightmare began. A nightmare that would stay with her for the rest of her life.

His weight pinning her to the floor, he dragged away her underclothes, freeing his own body as he did so. Then, with

9

one knee forcing her legs apart, he drove deeply into her. Each thrust was like a red hot knife but Anna was already beyond pain. Her mind closed to what was happening to her body, she did not cry out. Eyes closed too, she waited while her father vented his rage and passion.

At last it was over and with a low grunt he rolled away from her.

Anna lay still, his sweat drying cold on her bare skin. Above her the yellow flame flickered a warning of the lamp's need for oil but she did not move. How long she lay there she could never later remember but at last, limbs as numbed as her mind, she pushed herself to her feet.

Her dress lay half under the snoring man stretched on the floor and there she left it. Pulling the remnants of her underwear about her, she walked slowly upstairs.

Moonlight silvered the tiny room that had been hers from birth, but Anna saw none of its magic. In a trance-like state she filled the bowl on the wash stand from its matching jug, unaware of the icy sting as she plunged her hands into the water, lifting palmsful to her face. For long seconds she threw the water over a face almost as cold, then stripping off her torn garments, reached for the thick greyish bar of soap. Again and again she scrubbed herself, covering every inch of her body, ignoring the sting of carbolic where the violence of his entry had lacerated her. She scrubbed her breasts, washing away the smear of blood; scrubbed her stomach where the flesh felt sticky; and still she scrubbed, trying to wash away the smell of his breath from her nostrils, the touch of his sweat-soaked flesh, the memory of what he had done to her.

Silver light turned a cold grey before Anna finally slipped a clean white calico nightdress over her frozen body. Her hair, still wet from the merciless scrubbing, dripped spots of icy water on to the front. In the small mirror hanging from a nail on her bedroom wall she watched them spread and join, forming a smear, the way the blood from her father's hand had smeared her breast. It was only then, hands blue with cold covering her face, that she sank into a heap on the bare wooden boards and cried: the desperate, hopeless crying of a soul doomed to everlasting torment.

The same grey light paling to opalescent pearl fingered past the undrawn curtains of the tired kitchen. The last embers of the fire had long settled and the lamp gave no more light. Groaning from the stiffness of his cold limbs, Joseph Bradly stood up. Shaking the last clouds of alcohol from his brain and remembering. That whore Mary Carter had got what she deserved. From now on the insinuations of the townspeople would carry some truth at last. Satisfaction in the grim set of his mouth, he reached for the poker, stabbing ash from the grate with hard jerky movements. Now she would have something to talk about, the bloody bitch. It was this last thought that halted his assault on the cold cinders. Mary Carter was dead! He had seen her bloated corpse laid on the path by Millfield Pool. He couldn't have been with her last night, it could not have been her, but he had . . .

Turning from the grate, he saw in the faint blush of morning the heap of torn blue cotton where he had lain. He reached for it, the iron poker dropping loudly to the stone hearth. He knew this dress. He had seen delight spread across the face of the child he had bought it for. Lifting the cloth to his face, he could smell the faint scent, as if the pattern of cornflowers gave off a living perfume . . . and then he knew. Last night he had not wreaked vengeance on Mary Carter. Last night he had raped his own daughter.

Chapter One

The long climb up Church Hill seemed neverending. Glancing at the black, smoke-grimed walls of the ancient Parish Church that crowned it, Anna thought it still seemed as far away as when she began the trudge up Ethelfleda Terrace.

Back aching with the effort of freeing every step from mud that threatened to suck her down, swollen mound of a stomach making her lean awkwardly back, she willed herself on.

Pulling her foot from the squelching earth, she gripped the basket she was carrying, forcing the bamboo handle painfully into the flesh of her palm. But the pain went unnoticed, hidden beneath the breath-snatching agony that suddenly lanced through her.

Clutching at the nearest gate, Anna leaned heavily against it, her breath coming in short frightened gasps.

It had started, she thought through the pain. The long hopeless months of waiting were about to end. The child that had been set inside her with so much pain and bitterness was about to enter the world, about to begin a life that would be led the same way, could only continue in the malice and hatred that had been her lot since the finding of Mary Carter's body.

One hand gripping the grey splintered wood of the garden gate, Anna gasped, waiting for the pain that flared through her to diminish. Drawing in a long ragged breath, she lifted her head, glancing along the path of beaten earth that led to the door of the house. But though the curtain at the window twitched, no one emerged to help her.

She was Jos Bradly's daughter, his whore. No decent woman in Wednesbury would be seen helping her.

Sweat bathing her face, Anna pushed herself upright. She had to climb the hill. She must get home or give birth like some animal in the hedge.

Stopping every few yards, panting against the recurring stabs of pain, she dragged on to the house that once had held so much happiness for her, the house where her mother had loved and cherished her for the first seven years of her life.

Pushing open the door that gave on to the kitchen, she stumbled inside, grabbing the edge of the table that almost filled the little room, fighting the red hot spasms that threatened to cut her in two.

'Mother . . .' she moaned softly into the emptiness. 'Mother, help me . . . help me.'

But her mother could not help her. Her mother had died ten years before, died in the agony Anna was suffering now, the boy she had carried dying with her.

Letting the basket fall to the table, Anna breathed hard. She must fight the pain. She was alone and would be until past her usual bedtime. Only then did her father return to the house that had become his prison and her penitentiary.

Trying to keep her breathing calm and even, she took an enamel basin from the shabby wooden dresser. She was placing the eggs she had bought into it when fresh searing pain ripped through her, jarring every nerve with searing, brutal agony. The eggs jerked in her hands, splashing the front of her with oozing stickiness.

Anna gazed at her dress, the terror she had known once before returning with stark clarity.

Her stomach had been covered in the same slimy mess when he had finally lifted himself off her.

'No! No, mother, no!'

The cry was dragged from her as she rubbed at her dress in a vain attempt to wipe it clean.

*   *   *

It was too early to go back.

Jos Bradly walked out of the yard of the steel foundry in silence; no friendly wave acknowledged his going, no voice called a goodnight.

Shoving his hands deep into his pockets, he walked quickly in the direction of Church Hill. This was the wrong way, he told himself, he had never gone home before ten since . . .

He closed his eyes, momentarily trying to shut out the scene that never left him.

He never went back to the house until he knew she would be in bed, until she would not have to look at the man who had raped her. And he would not see, at least in the flesh, the hurt and fear in his daughter's eyes.

But tonight, try as he might to tell himself he must not return, his steps carried him home.

He could see from the gate that the door to the kitchen was wide open. Suddenly sick with new fear, Jos ran up the narrow path.

She was there, a crumpled heap on the kitchen floor, her red-gold hair covering her face – a face he did not need to see to know it was crumpled with pain.

'Anna! Anna, my little wench!'

Blood draining from his face, he stepped towards her then turned back to the open door.

Clear of the house he began to run, streaking away down the hill as if Gabriel's Hounds were already snapping at his heels.

'Will yer come, Polly?'

He fell into the tiny house that was one of a ribbon of tumbledown dwellings edging Trouse Lane.

'Say yer'll come? There's none other I can ask. I don't want none o' they touchin' 'er.'

Polly Shipton twisted round on her stool, her withered left leg dragging on the bare flagstones. She had wondered where he would turn when the girl's time came. Well, now she knew.

15

She looked up at the face she had known since childhood, a face smeared by tears mixed with the dirt of the steel foundry.

Was it true what they said of him? Had he murdered one woman and then raped a young girl, and that girl his own daughter?

Polly sighed. She didn't have the answers and was never likely to have them.

'Please, Polly . . . yer must come.' At his sides, Jos's hands balled into fists. 'Anna, my little wench, 'er was on the floor. I . . . I couldn't . . . I don't know how!'

Shoving herself from the stool with her sound right leg, Polly reached for the heavy woollen shawl hanging on a nail in the scullery door. She pulled it close as she followed Joseph Bradly past the mocking eyes of the quickly gathered women – women who took care to keep their opinions in their mouths until he had passed.

Hobbling painfully, Polly kept her own head high. From this day on she would be as much an outcast in the town as the man she was following. No matter. Whatever else he might be, he was now a man sharing his daughter's agony, and the fact that she would be ostracised and ignored for helping either of them was of no consequence compared to a young girl's pain.

'It be all right, Anna.'

Pushing past Jos into the kitchen, she bent over the girl huddled on the stone floor.

'It'll be all right, me wench. Polly Shipton 'as come to be with you, Polly will take care of you. Come on now, there's a good wench, let's 'ave you upstairs.'

Hair plastered to her cheeks with sweat, Anna lifted her head and Polly saw the look of terror in her eyes as Jos Bradly bent to take his daughter in his arms.

'No . . . o . . . o!'

The scream filled the tiny kitchen and Polly Shipton knew she need go no further to find the father of the child struggling to enter the world.

* * *

16

Standing beside the wooden crib, Anna stared at the son she had borne a month ago, hearing in her mind the taunts and sneers that met her whenever she ventured out of the house.

She tucked the blanket closer around the sleeping child.

It had grown into something of a sport; women gathering in twos and threes as she approached, calling after her from the safety of their married respectability.

'That father o' 'er's . . .'

Words emerged from the shadows of her mind like silent wraiths.

'. . . 'e be bloody jailbait. 'Ow come the bobbies ain't fetched 'im afore now?'

They passed their taunts from one to the other, each woman raising her voice, ensuring Anna could hear.

'Ar, why ain't they? 'E killed Mary Carter, we all knows that, an' 'e be the one who 'as fathered that babby. That by blow belongs to Jos Bradly as sure as there be a God in 'eaven.'

'You didn't hear them, did you, sweetheart?'

Anna stroked a finger across her son's downy head.

'You didn't hear what they said or realise what they think, and you never will my precious . . . you never will.'

But those women had been partly right. Anna sat on her bed, one hand resting on the crib that her father had made for her own birth.

The child now sleeping in it was Jos Bradly's, in that they had been correct, but the rest of their accusations bore no truth. There was no God in heaven. She looked at the sleeping child, her heart filling with pain at what she knew was in store for him as he grew.

No, there was no God in heaven. Had there been she would not have been raped.

Rising from the bed, she lifted the child from the crib, a wild surge of love and sorrow sweeping through her as the tiny body touched her own.

17

'They have judged him too,' she murmured, her mouth against the tiny head, 'my father and yours. They have all judged him and, right or wrong, he will pay their price. All the years of his life will not wash away the sin of which he is guilty, even though he would have suffered death before committing it had he been sober.'

In her arms the tiny face crumpled, one arm freeing itself from the swaddling blanket, and Anna rocked gently back and forth, her lips touching her son's face, soothing away his complaining cry.

'Shhh,' she whispered, folding one finger into his clutching palm. 'Shhh, no one will hurt you. No one in this town will ever call lies and filth after you.'

But as she lifted the tiny hand to her mouth, Anna knew they would.

Anna placed the wicker laundry basket in a small hollow to shield it from the wind, checking the blanket that covered the child inside.

'You will be warm there,' she murmured, 'but Polly will be cross if she learns I brought you with me. You see, neither of us ought to be out of the house. We can't go into a shop or into anyone else's house until I have been churched.' Not that anyone in Wednesbury would have me inside their gate, much less their house, she thought. She gazed across the heath towards Ocker Bank. But if she were not churched, her son would be even more of an outcast for who would so much as glance at a child whose mother had not asked God to forgive the sin of conceiving it, whether in wedlock or out of it? But why? Anna thought. Why be forced to beg forgiveness for a sin which she had played no part in committing?

No, she had no desire to go to the Parish Church, no desire to pass the women who would be standing with shawls draped over their heads, tongues wagging, as they watched her walk alone. But she knew she would do it, for the sake of her son.

If only her mother had not died. If only . . . Anna looked into the distance where the glow of furnace fires turned the sky scarlet. There were not enough 'if onlys', not enough to give her back her life.

Beside her the baby snuffled and Anna bent to check that his face was free of the knitted blanket. Of all the people in Wednesbury, Polly alone had stood by her; Polly Shipton who had taught her so much yet had refused to tell of the herbs that would cause the child to leave her body before its time was due.

'You will come to know Polly Shipton.' Anna smiled at the sleeping child. 'She will teach you about flowers and herbs as she taught me. Look.'

Snapping a dandelion at the base of its stalk, she held the golden head over the basket.

'These can be made into soup or a drink.'

Suddenly Anna was six years old again, her tiny hands clutching Polly's skirts as they walked across the heath just beyond the town.

'Not just the flower, me wench, take the root an' all.'

Anna's mouth curved in a smile as she remembered.

'What will we make?' she had asked, running from one golden cushion of flowers to another, eager to grab them all at once. Polly had halted in her task of gathering the gleaming crop.

'Well, if you take them from the earth properly we can make several things. But you go snatchin' the 'eads off 'em an' we won't be makin' a lot of anythin' for they dandelions will be no use.'

She had hesitated then in her own task of gathering the delicate white flowers of the elder and had sat beside Anna, spreading her dark skirts on the green of the heath, and taught her to make chains from the white and purple clover. Anna draped them proudly about her neck to show her father.

She had chattered all the way back to Polly's house, dancing

19

into the kitchen and watching excitedly as she gathered an assortment of pots and pans.

'You wash them flowers.'

Polly had stood her on an old wooden chair at the scullery sink.

'And mind you scrub all the soil off the roots.'

Anna twisted the flower she held in her hands, reliving the gentler days of the past.

Polly had kept an eye on the washing while herself drying the plants on a piece of cloth then together they laid them in the oven to roast before grinding the dried roots to make herbal tea.

'Now then.'

Polly had taken the cloud of white flowers from her basket, spreading them across the kitchen table.

'We be goin' to make these into creams and lotions that will keep that pretty skin of yours soft an' fresh, spite o' the muck that spews from them factory chimneys.'

'Like this?'

Anna had taken a sprig of white flowers, trying to make it stay on her face without holding it.

'No, not like that.'

Polly laughed, scooping up several handfuls of flower heads and dropping them into a pan of water bubbling over the fire.

'We 'ave to boil them first.'

'Like taties in a broth?'

Anna held out a tiny hand filled with fragrant snowy blossom.

'Yes, me little wench.'

Polly took the offering, dropping it beside her own in the pan.

'Just like taties in a broth.'

Now Anna sank to the ground beside her sleeping son, a wealth of loving memories in her head.

'She also taught me how to make wine from berries,' she

whispered, touching the tiny hand that had pushed from beneath the covers. 'But you watch out, young man. It makes your nose tingle. And besides, not all plants are so kind as elder flowers.'

'It won't 'urt after a minute or so.'

Anna heard the words across the years and saw again the crippled woman bend over her as she cried at the pain of a nettle sting.

'Let Polly show you 'ow to chase away that nasty old sting.'

Followed by a tearful Anna, she had gone into her tiny garden, selecting a broad leaf from a plant growing at the base of a tree heavy with apples and rubbing it over the white blisters erupting along Anna's fingers, spreading the soothing juice over the skin.

'There you be, me little love, it'll be better now.'

Then she had picked an apple from the tree, giving it to Anna before taking her indoors where she had nursed her on her knee while the apple was slowly eaten.

'Polly taught me so much,' Anna whispered, stroking a finger across the soft cheek of her child. 'She taught me what was good and what was bad. And what will you be taught, my darling? What will the bastard son of Jos Bradly be taught?'

'You must go, me wench.' Polly Shipton looked at the pale face of the young girl dressed in a plain brown dress, red-gold hair braided and tied with a ribbon. 'You must be brave for the sake of the child.'

For the sake of her child. Anna took the shawl the older woman held out to her. Everything she had lived through, the taunts and jibes she had endured, had been for the sake of the child, but how much more could she stand?

'I would come with you but you know the child mustn't leave the house until you've bin churched an' I can't leave him 'ere in the house alone.'

No, the baby could not be allowed outside his place of birth until she sought the atonement of God, the God whom her

21

Sunday school teachers had taught protected and loved. But where had his protection been the night she had been raped? And where his love?

Anna walked slowly from the house that stood in the lee of the smoke-blackened church, thankful that the distance at least was small. Behind her women stood beside their garden gates, their eyes as well as their criticisms on her. Passing beneath the lych gate, Anna turned from the path leading to the church door, following the worn turf to the spot where her mother lay buried. 'Sacred to the memory of Leah Ruth, beloved wife of Joseph Bradly', she read, tears blurring her vision.

'He didn't mean it, Mother,' she whispered, 'he didn't mean it.'

'Have you a covering for your head?'

The robed figure of a priest she did not recognise stood beside the pew where Anna knelt in the empty church.

She felt for the shawl, only to realise it was gone.

'You should have your head covered when you enter the house of God.' The priest did not bother to disguise the irritation in his voice. His rest between the end of Sunday school classes and the beginning of evening service was being disturbed by the churching of a girl who did not deserve the holy mercy.

Anna remained silent. Father James did not demand she cover her head before entering the church, but then this was not Father James.

'Oh, well!' The priest sighed audibly. 'We will carry on. Only next time be sure and cover your head.'

The service would be short, Polly had assured her, but to Anna, listening to words she had never heard before and giving the responses urged on her by the priest, it seemed to go on for ever.

And then it was over and the priest was gone, leaving her alone in the church. To the right of the altar steps stood a life-size replica of Christ, one hand reaching out; to the left,

22

a figure of the Virgin cradling her infant son. Anna gazed at it and wept.

Back in the house Polly Shipton held out a cup of tea to the young girl whose hands trembled like leaves in the wind. One ordeal was over but there was a lifetime of others ahead, one of them being the christening of the child that lay sleeping in a laundry basket beneath the window of the tiny living room. Who beside herself would stand godparent to a bastard? Two godfathers and one godmother were the church's requirements for a boy child. Polly sipped the strong hot tea she had poured for herself. Where in Wednesbury could there be found two men to stand godfather to the offspring of a rapist and his daughter?

She sipped again, feeling the liquid hot against her throat. The answer was plain – nowhere.

Anna tucked the baby inside her shawl, then passed the knotted corners over her head.

'We are going to buy you some milk,' she crooned softly to the tiny face peeping up from the folds. 'Yes, some milk. You'll like that, won't you?'

Picking up her basket, she slipped the handle over one arm, cradling her son to her with the other. Once out of the house she held him close against her, shielding him from the breeze and from the hostile stares of the women who drew their skirts closer to their legs as she passed, as if proximity to a sinner would somehow contaminate them.

She had not been right into the town since the birth of the child, Polly bringing the few things they needed on her daily visits. Cripple Polly. Anna held her son tight. What would have happened had that woman not stood by her?

Reaching the bottom of Church Hill, Anna crossed over Trouse Lane, turning into Meeting Street. This way she could avoid the High Bullen with its shopping women.

She was on her way home, milk and butter tucked into her basket, when she passed a group of them chatting outside

Tedd's wet fish shop. Anna felt her heart jump as they stared, then closed around her as she drew level.

'Well, if it ain't Jos Bradly's whore.' A dark-haired woman with a front tooth missing grabbed the shawl that held the baby. 'An' this must be the bastard he's fathered.'

Instinctively Anna stepped back but a second woman stood firm against her.

'Maybe it is, maybe it ain't,' the second woman said. 'Depends on 'ow many men 'er's had beside 'er own father.'

'Well, let's 'ave a look then.' The gap-toothed woman grabbed at the shawl, pulling it from the sleeping baby.

'Let's see what sort of kid a father and 'is daughter mek.'

'Don't touch him!' Anna flared, snatching the shawl from the woman's grasp. 'Don't you dare put your dirty hands on him.'

'Ooh, you hear that, Liza?' The third member of the trio wiped a hand across her nose. 'You've got dirty hands.'

'You should be careful who you call dirty!' The gap in her teeth looming wide, the woman snatched at Anna's hair, dragging her head back painfully. 'A bloody whore like you!' The woman's eyes gleamed with a captor's delight over her helpless prey. 'We don't like your sort, an' we ain't 'avin' you here.'

The woman pitched her forward, throwing her against a wall. Dazed by the force of the impact, Anna stumbled away, clumps of mud and stones finding their mark as she went.

'Don't go comin' down 'ere,' the woman who had grabbed her head shouted after her. 'You bring your spawn this way again an' you'll be sorry. Get out of Wednesbury, you bloody whore, and tek your by blow with you . . .'

Somehow she managed to reach home, though Anna never remembered how.

'Lad is all right,' Polly said when she called later. 'He's teken no harm and you will be all right as well in an hour or so.' But she stayed the whole day nevertheless, seeing to the baby and preparing a hot meal.

'Little 'un is sleepin'.' Polly eventually reached for her coat, hanging from a peg at the back of the sitting-room door. 'An' you should be too. Get yourself a few hours afore 'e wakes for next feed. Jos's meal is ready in the oven, you 'ave nothing to do.'

Anna watched her friend limp away down the hill, then climbed the stairs to her room. Her father would make no call on her. Coming home as late as possible, he would take his meal to his bedroom and be gone at first light next morning. He could go on like that while the months of summer held but what would he do when the ground was frozen hard? Anna stared listlessly at the whitewashed wall. Her father could not be out of house and home for the rest of his life, but neither could he decently be in it or suspicion of them would fester, father and daughter, the evil minds of some seeing them living as man and wife.

'But it's not true,' Anna cried softly. 'My father is not like that, he would never harm me, it's just not true.' Neither was it true that he had killed Mary Carter, she thought hopelessly, but they believed he had and would go on believing it, the same as they would go on believing she was her own father's whore.

'It doesn't stop.'

Eyes brimming with unshed tears, Anna looked at Polly Shipton who sat beside the kitchen table, her crippled leg in its high laced boot jutting out beneath her black skirts.

'I don't think it will ever stop. Every time I take him out of the house there are filthy insults and people throwing stones.'

'It be bad for you, me wench, but it be new to folk yet. Give them a year or two and they'll get used to seein' you with the child. Give them time and they will forget how he was got, find summat new for their tongues to wag on.'

But Polly knew they would not forget and neither would they ever allow Anna to forget. She was a branded woman and one who would never know peace or real friendship in the town again. Strange, she thought, watching her cross to the child sleeping in its basket beneath the window. The working-class people of Wednesbury would endure poverty, they would pull together in hardship, but immorality among their own they would not countenance. Their eyes became closed to the real rights or wrongs of a case and, victim or not, there would be no place in this town anymore for Anna Bradly.

'No, they will not forget, Mother Polly.' Unconsciously Anna used her childhood name for the woman. 'No matter what else may happen they will not forget, and as long as I am here they will not let him forget. But I can't let my child pay for what happened. He and I should not have to bear the brunt of what my father has done.'

Polly sat quietly. The girl had not finished; there was more yet to be said.

'I cannot stay here.' Anna kept her eyes on her baby. 'If he is to have any life at all, I must go.'

'Go?' Polly asked sharply. 'But where? You 'ave no kin as I be knowin' of.'

'No, I have no kin other than my father,' she answered dully.

'Then where would you go, wench? You can't just pick the lad up and leave. You must 'ave shelter for 'im.'

'I have thought of that.' Anna reached into the basket, one finger fondling the baby's cheek. 'I have thought of it night after night, of his life and my father's. What will they be worth with me here? They both have little on which to build a future, but with me gone, at least they stand a chance.'

'Leave the child behind?' Polly looked at the girl she had helped to rear, the girl she had loved as her own, and saw the anguish in her face. 'Is that what you really want?'

'No,' Anna cried. 'I want *him*, I want my *son*, but I cannot condemn him to a lifetime of taunts, I love him too much for that. I love him too much to keep him.'

'Have you said anything of this to Jos?'

Bending over the child as it stirred in its sleep, Anna murmured softly, soothing it before answering.

'No, I have said nothing to my father. If I tell him what I feel, I know he will be the one to leave. But it would be hard for him to start again. Trying to find work would be difficult enough, but to leave behind all that he had with my mother . . . no, I cannot do that to him.'

'But you will be leaving all you have,' Polly said gently. 'All that you love in the world. Will you be able to do it, Anna wench?'

'Oh, help me, Mother Polly!'

Anna ran to the cripple woman, sinking to her knees and burying her face in her lap, choking on her sobs.

'Help me . . . take my son and care for him . . . love him for me, Mother Polly . . . love him for me.'

'Ar, I'll tek 'im for you, me little wench, an' I'll love 'im for you too.' Polly stroked the red-gold head pressed against her knee. 'I'll love 'im as I love you.'

Mother Polly would take her son, she would care for him and raise him as she had raised the motherless child of Jos Bradly. She would find the first tooth, hear the first words; she would feel the tiny arms about her neck, she would soothe and comfort . . .

'But he's mine . . . mine!'

Almost blinded by tears, Anna pulled open a drawer in the chest set against her bedroom wall, taking out her few belongings and placing them one by one in the shabby carpet bag standing open on the bed. Then she paused as a gleam of pink showed in the sallow light of the oil lamp.

Holding it in her fingers, she looked at the shiny strip of ribbon, one diamond-shaped piece of paper glued to its centre.

Peter! Her mind flashed back across the years. She had been eight years old and Peter a grown-up thirteen, already earning his living. They had spent their childhood together, he indulging her childish games, always there, always protecting; even helping with the Sunday School outing because she had cried until he said yes.

Anna walked slowly to the crib, holding out the shiny ribbon as if the sleeping child could see it.

'You would have liked Peter,' she murmured, half to herself and half to the child. 'And you would have liked the Sunday School outings: riding on long low carts all done up with flowers and ribbons, the horses with ribbons in their manes and tails, the sugar buns and lemonade. You would have climbed the trees and most likely fallen into the stream . . .'

Peter had fallen into the stream. Anna left off speaking, the rest of her memories for herself alone. Peter, his brown hair shining in the sun, trousers rolled to his knees, laughing at her as he tried to catch one of the tiny fish. She had demanded a tiddler to take home in a jar, and he, unable as always to refuse her, had waded into the water. That was when she had seen the pretty orange butterfly and wandered off after it. When he could not see her and she had not answered his call, Peter had panicked and in scrambling too quickly from the stream, slipped and fallen back into the water.

He had found her downstream and persuaded her a dead butterfly would be of no use. She had tried her usual childish ploy of tears but he had not given way.

'Let the poor little thing be.'

Anna felt the tears in her throat as she remembered the tender way he had dried her eyes.

'I will give you something that can't die.'

He had taken her by the hand, matching his longer stride to her short one, leading her to where he had left his coat on the river bank. And from the pocket he had taken a pink ribbon with one diamond-shaped piece of paper at its centre.

'One day, Anna,' he had said, 'you will have a whole string of diamonds.'

Now crossing to the window of her cramped bedroom, she looked out through her tears, over the darkened town to where the steeple of the church rose like a pointing black finger.

Those had been his words as he tied the ribbon about her neck, but Peter had died from meningitis and she had died inside the night her father raped her. There would be no more diamonds in her life.

Anna pulled the slip of ribbon through her fingers as memories of yesterday ran through her mind. Then she turned back to her son. Tenderly lifting the tiny head, she slipped the ribbon about his neck. The people of Wednesbury had claimed one innocent victim, they would not have two.

Lifting the child from the crib, Anna held its tiny body close to hers. Peter had always protected her just as she must now protect her son. She would do that the only way she knew how. He must not suffer because of her. To keep him safe she had to leave him, give him into the care of Mother Polly even though it meant breaking her own heart.

Kissing the tiny face snuffling after her breast, Anna felt as if the world were shattering around her. This would be the last time she would hold him, the last time she would tell him of her love for him, for when morning came she would have to leave this house, leave everything in the world she loved. She would do it for the sake of her child.

Chapter Two

A thin drizzle of cold rain dripped from a weeping sky as Anna stepped out of the train. She had wanted to stay in the closed security of the third-class compartment but the little money she had saved so carefully from the weekly allowance her father left on the kitchen table every Friday morning would only buy her so many miles, and a courteous conductor punching a neat round hole in her ticket had said those miles were up.

The carpet bag no weight in her hand, she shivered against a wind which drove freezing spots of water against her thin body, using its superior strength in an effort to force her out of the strange town she had just entered.

Coseley. She read the name on a board fastened against the grimy brickwork of the little platform. However far the two shillings and six pence she had paid for her train ticket had carried her, it wasn't far enough to escape the smoke and dirt of factory chimneys.

Anna lifted her eyes, half-closing them against wind-blown flurries of rain, and squinted up at chimneys rising dark and menacing in a drowned sky. She had changed one industrial town for another, but at least in this one nobody would know her.

The sudden scream of a steam whistle startled her and her fingers clutched convulsively around the handles of her bag, before her shoulders slumped in relief. It was only the hooter of one of the factories, signalling the end of a shift.

Suddenly the empty street was filled with people. Women and young girls seemed to pour from every side alley, their wooden clogs clattering on the shining wet cobblestones.

'Excuse me!' Anna reached out, touching the arm of a woman hurrying past.

'Aye?' she demanded.

'Could you tell me, please . . . is there someone around here who . . . who takes paying guests?'

'Paying guests!' The woman shook off Anna's hand impatiently, her face frowning in the circle of her black woollen shawl. 'Not as I knows of.'

'But there must be.' Panic coloured Anna's reply. She was in a strange town and already it was getting dark; she had to find a room somewhere.

'Must be?' Again the woman echoed Anna's words before her own. 'Then yer must find it for yerself, I have my man's meal to get. If I stand 'ere talkin' to yer much longer the men's shift will be finishin' and 'im comin' home to an empty table.'

She pulled the shawl tighter with an indignant tug, holding each corner in hands pushed beneath heavy breasts, and turned on her way, long black skirts swinging around urgent feet.

Anna stood and watched her disappear down the long street. In the distance the lamplighter came slowly towards her, lighting each street lamp in turn; behind her the clanging bell of a laden trolley bus sang its strident song. And then, as suddenly as it had filled, the street was empty.

A trickle of rain slid over the brim of Anna's cheap straw hat, slithering down her neck, soaking into the high collar of her blouse.

From a distance a train sounding its readiness to depart seemed to taunt her, to say it could carry her home.

'You won't.' Anna's defiant whisper banished the temptation. 'Nothing will take me back there, I'd rather die first.'

'Are yer lost?'

Anna twisted sharply, startled by the question. On the

pavement stood a girl of about her own age, pulling a thick shawl protectively over her mousy hair.

'I've been watching you from in there.' The mousy head gave a small backward toss.

'There', Anna saw, was a small, ill-lit shop, its tiny window filled with an Aladdin's Cave assortment. Huge pink hams, plate-sized pies, sausages and black puddings, jostled for space against brightly coloured packets and boxes.

'I was just gettin' some barley for me mam, she's settin' tomorrow's dinner on the fire.' The girl's face broke into a rueful grin. 'Forget 'er 'ead, me mam would, if it wasn't tied on. She's bin in Bella Castleton's twice today an' still forgot the barley.'

'It's easy to forget,' Anna replied, wishing the words held some truth for her. Forgetting was a luxury and this life held no promise of luxury for Anna Bradly.

'It is for me mam, and so it ought to be – she's practised all 'er life.' The girl's laughter pealed out, ringing off a long row of identical small houses joined in homage at the foot of majestic mills. Houses where lamps were fast being lit in the windows. The sight hurt and Anna felt frightened and alone. Soon curtains would be drawn, Coseley would close its eyes, and she would still be on the street.

'Where did you want to get to?' The rain didn't seem to bother the girl. 'I 'aven't seen you round these parts afore, 'ave I . . . you got relations in Coseley?'

So many questions and Anna did not want to answer any of them, but reticence would not find her shelter.

'No, I'm a stranger here. I was hoping to find a place to stay. A . . . a guest house.'

The wind bit through the thin cloth of her old green coat and she pulled the lapels together across her throat.

'Do you know where I can find one?'

'Eee, wench, there's nowt like that in Coseley, we don't get visitors as such 'ere. You should 'ave gone into Birmingham.

Like as not you would find plenty o' them guest 'ouses there. Birmingham's a big town.'

'Thank you.' The reply trembled on lips white with cold. Anna hitched the carpet bag more comfortably in her frozen fingers. She had better go back to the railway station. At least there would be a fire in the waiting room. Perhaps they might let her sit in there until morning.

'You'll not get a train to Birmingham tonight, wench.' The girl still stood before her, raindrops like crystal freckles on her pert young face. 'But if it's nowt grand you're after, you could always try Maggie Fellen.'

'Maggie Fellen?' Anna tried to keep the hope out of her voice. 'Can you tell me how to find her?'

'I'll do better than that, I'll take you to her. She lives just against our house. C'mon, let's get in out of this rain or we'll both be growin' flippers!'

The sound of Anna's worn shoes was lost beneath the clatter of wooden clogs as the girl guided her along a street of grey, effacing sameness, turning left along a narrow alley to emerge into another street that could have been the first one for the long rows of tiny houses were an exact match, their doors leading straight off the narrow footpath, windows half-shrouded in lace curtains.

''Ere we are, number seventy-six, that's our 'ouse, and Maggie Fellen is seventy-eight. The number of 'er 'ouse, I mean, not Maggie.' The happy laughter broke out again and in a pool of waxy yellow light from a street lamp the girl's eyes twinkled roguishly. 'She'd 'ave my guts for fiddle strings if she 'eard me say she was seventy-eight. She's a mite particular is Maggie Fellen, and not just about her age either.'

Pushing open a door which Anna noted had been left off the latch, the girl stood aside.

'I'll 'ave to give me mam the barley before I go round next door. She'll be wonderin' what kept me as it is.' One eye closed in a wink. 'I can always tell 'er Bella Castleton kept me natterin', and that's not a hundred miles from the truth.

But come in with me, me mam likes meetin' folks. She can natter almost as good as Bella Castleton. If ever they 'ave a competition for who can talk longest and say least, I reckon they two would 'ave a rare battle.' She waved Anna across the whitewashed step. 'Go on, wench, get you in afore the rain soaks the mat.'

Leading the way along a short, narrow passage, the girl called over her shoulder, 'Me mam will be in 'ere.'

After the harsh grey streets, the kitchen of number seventy-six seemed to shout with colour. Anna blinked against the yellowness of the gas mantle, aided in its fight against the shadows by a brass oil lamp crowned with a fluted white opalescent glass shade. On one wall a wooden dresser displayed a proud collection of blue and white willow pattern china, while another was taken up by the fireplace. Baking ovens polished to the brilliance of jet, bowels filled with crimson coals, glowed a welcome.

Putting the blue paper bag of barley down on a table white from constant scrubbing, the girl pulled Anna forward.

'Mam, I'm tekin' 'er round to Maggie . . . Mrs Fellen's. She's lookin' for a room. I found 'er in front of Castleton's shop.'

'I bet 'er found you afore you was lost, wench, knowin' my girl.' The woman's plump face creased into a wide smile. 'But come yer in, now yer 'ere . . . eee, but you be sodden through.'

Shooing a sleepy marmalade cat from a chair next to the fire, the girl's mother drew Anna to it.

'Sit yerself down, wench, and tek off them wet shoes. You'll be tekin' that influenza if we don't get you out o' them wet things, and soon.'

Already filling a brown earthenware teapot from a huge iron kettle steaming quietly to itself, she called, 'Get a fresh cup, Essie, then go and ask Maggie Fellen to step round. If she can't find wench a room then we'll have to squeeze her in with us somehow, for she can't be out there no more tonight.'

Stirring sugar into the cup she filled with fresh-brewed tea, the woman offered it to Anna, brown eyes studying her pale tired face. The girl had gone through torment and not long ago, judging by the look in those eyes. It wouldn't take much more to break her.

'Our Essie is a good wench but a little empty-headed at times.' She smiled as Anna took the mug, sipping the hot liquid immediately. 'She fair rushed off without sayin' your name.'

'It's Anna . . . Anna Bradly, Mrs . . .' She broke off awkwardly. She had followed this woman's daughter into their home and not thought of asking their name.

'I'm afraid I'm empty-headed too sometimes. You see, I didn't ask her name either.'

'It's lost no brass, wench.'

Reaching into a drawer of the dresser, the woman pulled out a length of clean white huckaback, passing it to Anna to use to wipe the droplets of rain from her face.

'That one is Hester, my first. And I'm Mary, Mary Cresswell.'

'How do you do, Mrs Cresswell?' Anna answered politely, but her face had long since lost the ability to smile. 'Hester did find me standing outside the shop. I had just got off the train and was looking for a room. I had thought to find a guest house somewhere in the town.'

'Not this one, Anna.' The name was already comfortable on Mary Cresswell's lips; there was something she liked about the thin, frightened-looking girl lost in the depths of her old chair.

'Coseley is hardly grand enough for that sort o' thing, nobody stops by here longer than they 'ave to.'

She was interrupted by Hester pushing aside the floor-length red chenille curtain that hung across the door to keep out draughts. She was followed by a woman who looked to be in her late thirties. Rich brown hair drawn into a flat knot at the back of her head gave a sharp, almost severe look to her well-shaped features. The obligatory shawl covered her shoulder. Beneath it a snow-white apron reached almost to the hem of the skirts that touched her clogs.

'You asked me to come, Mary.'

The words were for her neighbour but the woman's steady grey eyes remained on Anna. Already she had taken in the soggy straw bonnet, well-worn green coat and carpet bag.

'Aye, Maggie.' Mary Cresswell reached for another cup while her daughter took off her wet shawl and shook it before hanging it behind the scullery door.

'This 'ere is Anna Bradly and she's lookin' fer a place to stay.'

'Oh, aye!' Maggie Fellen took the mug held out to her. 'And what's that to me?'

'Well, I knew you 'ad a room that's empty since . . .' Hester coloured violently and looked to her mother for help.

'Hester told her there might be a chance of your lettin' her come to you. It was a kindness on my girl's part to a wench not knowin' her whereabouts.'

'A kindness to a stranger is one thing,' Maggie Fellen returned in clipped tones, 'bringin' me a lodger is something else again. I have no mind for tekin' in lodgers, especially one I've never clapped eyes on afore.'

'I know that as surely as yourself even if it seems my wench did not. But since you're 'ere, sit yourself and drink your tea. There's no brass charged for sittin'.'

The pale grey eyes stayed on Anna's face as Maggie Fellen drew up a straight-backed wooden chair and sat beside the table, one hand curved about her mug. Anna dropped her own glance to the steam beginning to rise as her coat dried in the fire's heat.

'Will you be in Coseley long, Miss Bradly?'

The woman did not call her 'Anna' as Hester's mother had done. But the tea and the fire had warmed away some of her desperation and Anna looked at her levelly.

'I can't say yes or no to that yet, Mrs Fellen. It depends upon whether or not I can find work here.'

'Where did you work afore?'

It took Anna by surprise. She had not thought to be questioned about her background. Sipping her tea, she gained a little time, then, meeting the grey gaze with complete candour, answered, 'I kept house for my father. I have done for three years, ever since I was thirteen. My mother died when I was six and my father did not marry again.'

'And what about your father now? Who will look to him now you 'ave up and left him?'

Anna could feel the tears gathering in her throat but banished them determinedly from her eyes. Her voice quiet and steady, she spoke the one lie she had worked out in the train.

'My father is dead, Mrs Fellen.'

'Eee, you poor wench!' Mary Cresswell leaned forward, patting Anna's knee with a podgy hand. 'No wonder your little face looks as if it's been drawn through a needle's eye. You be such a skinny one, all eyes.'

'It's not easy to bear losin' a loved one.' Maggie's grey eyes dropped and for a moment only the fire spoke, crackling out its own questions, spitting back its own replies.

'So, the tape being cut, you be off and running?' Maggie Fellen commented, then took a long sip of tea.

Behind her mother's chair Hester fidgeted, uncertain what to make of the exchange.

'Not running, Mrs Fellen.' Anna was suddenly dignified beyond her years. 'There was nothing left for me in Wednesbury, nothing to hold me except the unhappiness of losing my family. I had to start on my own, find a way of earning my living. It . . . it seemed a good idea to find fresh ground on which to do it.'

'Well, y'ave got spunk, wench, I'll give you that.' Mary Cresswell heaved her over-proportioned frame out of the chair she had settled in and picked up the bag of barley, emptying it into an iron saucepan, then stirring the contents with a long-handled spoon.

'A fresh start canna do you great harm and I don't see anything against you mekin' one in Coseley. As for work, our Hester can tek yer on up to Rewcastle's Mill when you've a mind. They'll set you on up there all right.'

Leaning sideways, Anna placed her empty mug on the table.

'Thank you, Mrs Cresswell. You and Hester have both been very kind.'

'Kind nothing!' The large woman blustered, giving the stewpot an unnecessary stir. 'Isn't that what the good Lord placed us on this earth for? My mother taught her brood to do people a good turn whenever the chance was given, and if you couldn't do them a good turn, then you shouldn't do them a bad one. It's a rule that's always stood me in good stead. Help others and the Lord will help you.'

Leaving the spoon in the pot, she turned, hands resting on ample hips, mouth a straight line.

'So what say you, Maggie Fellen? Do you find the wench a place, 'cos if not I do. And that bein' so, she'd best be off in scullery and get them wet things off.'

'She can 'ave the room.' Maggie Fellen rose, pulling the shawl across her breasts. 'But if she proves to be carryin' then either you or the Lord better find her a place, Mary Cresswell, for I'll have none of that in my house.'

'Carryin'!' Hester's mother laughed. 'She don't look strong enough to be carryin' 'erself, let alone a babe. Look at 'er, she's as thin as a stick.'

'Aye.' At the door, Maggie held the chenille curtain aside. 'And you should know better than to let that fool you, Mary Cresswell. When a body is expecting, they're thin afore they get fat.'

'You need have no fears, Mrs Fellen.' Anna's cheeks were scarlet. 'I am not expecting, but if you feel that I will be a nuisance then I would rather not come with you. If Mrs Cresswell could just let me stay here tonight, I will find some other place tomorrow.'

The grey eyes flicked back to Anna standing in front of the fire, the old carpet bag in her hand, and for the briefest second they held admiration.

Here's a girl I can trust, Maggie Fellen thought, and suddenly she did. A smile lifting her thin mouth, she held out a hand.

'Come on, wench, let's get you home and Hester can come and help you settle if she's a mind.'

Chapter Three

Anna climbed into the train carriage. The long buttoned skirt of her green coat refused to stretch and she had to lift the hem, displaying a little of her shapely calf above black sidebutton boots.

Catching the ticket collector's appreciative grin, she blushed, settling quickly into a window seat and fumbling in her bag for the fare. The carriage filled slowly, mostly with women with children at their skirts, heavy baskets unwieldy on their arms, but eventually it was full and lurched forward, rattling alarmingly over the noisy points.

It would take almost an hour to run from Birmingham to Coseley, stopping at every tiny village along the way, but Anna didn't mind. She had come to enjoy this monthly excursion to the large steel town.

'Did yer have a good day, Mrs Dalby? Where did yer pigeons come in last race, Bert, or has yer missis put them in a pie yet?'

The conductor, a short red-faced man, had a word for each passenger as he made his way slowly along the narrow aisle. As he clipped her return ticket, he smiled at Anna. He had seen her several times; come to live over at Coseley so he'd been told, and she looked a right bonny wench. Pity she never smiled.

'You likin' Birmingham, me wench?' he asked as she slipped her ticket into the bag resting on her knees.

Anna glanced back at him, green eyes clear beneath her straw hat.

'I do,' she nodded, 'but I prefer Coseley. People there are not in such a rush.'

'I know what you mean, wench.' He pushed back his boater with its navy blue band, scratching a finger along his receding hairline. 'I find meself wonderin' what them there folk do with all the time they saves, rushin' from pillar to post all day.'

'It's certain we'll never see you rushin',' a woman in another compartment called good-naturedly. 'I reckon we shall all see the Second Coming 'fore ever we see you break into a sweat.'

Pulling the boater back into place, the conductor moved on, a grin splitting his florid face.

'Now then, you just behave. You don't want for me to tell your man the high jinks you gets up to in Birmingham.'

A storm of laughter greeted his remark and Anna turned her eyes to the window. Trees dressed in the green of late-summer; fields, having given their bounty, waiting for the plough. Between the towns the countryside had a quiet beauty she never tired of looking at.

The fields around Wednesbury would be green, their skirts of grass looking even more beautiful swirling around buildings dark with the soot of foundries and the dirt of coal mines. Would her son be out among that greenery, up on the heath where she had carried him in a laundry basket? Polly Shipton could not carry him and her father would be working and there was no one else. I had to go, she sobbed inwardly, I had to leave, it was the only way to protect you. But I love you, my darling . . . I love you so much.

The train grumbled to a halt and a woman on the seat beside her gathered her several hessian shopping bags, calling a cheery goodnight as she stepped down. People here were so friendly.

Anna watched the hedges dance away as the train pulled itself onward. People had been friendly enough in Wednesbury until . . . She closed her eyes, feeling the familiar surge of pain, that remembering her home and son always brought. Then, lifting her lids, she swallowed hard. That was·in the past; her home was here now with Maggie.

It didn't seem like six months since Maggie Fellen had taken her in, giving her the room that had been her son's until he had left his job at Rewcastle's to try his hand in America.

Maggie herself never talked of him, as she never asked questions of Anna. From the start she had respected her privacy, asking no more than she had that night in Mary Cresswell's kitchen, and now the liking they had for each other was more than just respect; Anna knew she loved fierce, outspoken Maggie, and though her landlady might never say it, she had a strong feeling her love was returned. Perhaps in time Anna might be able to bring herself to tell her what had happened to drive her away from home. But not now, not yet, it was still too raw.

How greatly her life had changed. Anna's body rocked with the motion of the train. A home with Maggie, a job at Rewcastle's, and two pounds a week – a fortune. She felt like a queen every Friday when she drew her wages from the office and watched the clerk enter the amount in the huge ledger, and later smiled at Maggie's grateful, 'Eee, wench, that's too much,' as she slipped one of those pounds into the painted tea caddy on the mantelshelf.

The other pound was her own and she had known from the first what she intended doing with it. The second pay day she had asked about a bank, saying she felt she ought to save some of her money. But there was no bank in Coseley, so if she couldn't keep her brass under the bed like other folk, Maggie told her, then she would have to traipse all the way into Birmingham.

But it hadn't been a bank so much as a Post Office that Anna wanted and that had not taken long to find. Her letter was already written. Slipping a ten-shilling note into the envelope she had sealed it, placed a stamp on one corner and dropped it into the post-box.

She had addressed it to 'Polly Shipton, care of Siverter's

shop'. The letter had conveyed little more than her thanks for the woman's help. The money, Anna wrote, was to help with the child, for she knew Polly would have the rearing of him. Adding that she would send two pounds every month, she had signed the letter simply 'Anna'. She made no mention of her father, nor did she give an address.

She had not dared to look back at her baby because on doing so she could never have left him, but neither could she stay with him, living with the finger of scorn always pointing at her and thus at him. It was better this way. He would grow up never knowing her but she would carry him in her heart until they buried her.

'Coseley . . . this is where you get off, wench.'

A touch on her shoulder brought Anna out of her reverie.

'Thank you. I was day dreaming.'

Clutching her bag, she scrambled up from the slatted wooden seat and called her own shy goodnights to the few people left on the train. Holding her skirt, she watched her feet, pretending not to see the hand the conductor held out to help her down from the high step. He swung himself back aboard.

'Be seein' you, take care now.'

The train trundled away, trailing a cloud of grit-filled smoke behind it. Anna watched for several moments then turned to cross the street. Maggie would have the tea brewed and the Saturday night meal of sausages and mash would be ready and waiting.

'Oh!' Anna gasped as her foot twisted on an uneven cobblestone, almost throwing her off balance.

'Steady, girl.'

The street lamps had not yet been lit and the greyness of dusk had masked the figure that stepped towards her. Tall and hatless, a man reached for her.

'No . . . oo!' Anna's scream ripped through the silence. Even now the thought of a man's hand touching her set a flood of panic welling up in her. Intent on escape from the shadowy form, she began to run but tripped, falling to her knees.

'I told thee to go steady.'

The voice was quiet and this time its owner made no move towards her, offered no hand as she scrambled to her feet.

'Is tha hurt?'

Anna brushed a hand across her coat in embarrassment. Fancy falling down like that, and screaming too. It was a wonder every house in Coseley hadn't thrown wide its doors.

'No, I'm all right, thank you.'

'Then hadn't tha better do that on path? If carter comes round corner, tha'll be right in way and he might not be too wide awake, especially if he's called in Black Bull as he usually does.'

'Yes . . . I . . . yes.'

Still not lifting her eyes to the man beside her, Anna stepped forward then lurched again as her right foot came down unexpectedly flat on the cobbled surface. The heel of her right boot had torn completely away.

'Damn!' she swore, not quite beneath her breath.

'Twisted your ankle?'

'No.' Anna turned, searching the road behind her. 'It's my heel, it's come off.'

'Must have been as you got off that train. You stepped down a mite sharp.'

'I'll go back and look. It must be in the grass somewhere.'

This man had seen her react as the conductor had offered her his hand. Did that mean he had been watching her . . . waiting for her, perhaps? Anna's heart missed a beat. Had he watched her before, got to know she took a monthly ride to Birmingham and was here now waiting for her to come back?

'You stand on path, I'll go find tha heel.'

Anna watched him bend then straighten up, holding up a hand in triumph before rejoining her. She had been given a chance to run, either to the nearest house or into Bella Castleton's shop, and she had done neither.

Without knowing why she had waited for the tall angular man to find her broken heel, waited for him to come back across the road and stand beside her.

'Thank you.' She looked up into a finely drawn, clean-shaven face. Despite the shadows she could see it was not the face of a young man.

Hair she guessed to be dark drooped softly over a wide forehead and somehow Anna felt pleased it was not plastered with the brilliantine that seemed so much in favour with the men at Rewcastle's. Beneath thick brows a pair of eyes whose colour she did not even try to guess regarded her solemnly.

'If tha lets me have that boot, I could have this back on in no time.' He tossed the offending heel in the air, catching it as he spoke.

'That's all right, thank you. No doubt Maggie will know a cobbler somewhere. You . . . you've gone to enough trouble on my account as it is, Mr . . .'

She had not meant to ask his name and was glad the gloom of late-evening hid the sudden flush that flooded her cheeks.

'No trouble, lass, and the name is Edward, Edward Royce. And yours is Anna Bradly, tha's the lass as lives with Maggie Fellen.'

'How did you know?'

He smiled. The accusation in her tone seemed to amuse him.

'In a small place like Coseley a man gets to know many things, Miss Bradly. Besides it's not often we get a lass coming to settle here. Why, half of the ones we have already would give their eye teeth to be shot of the place.'

'Maybe.' Anna held out a hand, aware as she hadn't been before of her lack of gloves. 'I must be going, Mr Royce. Thank you again for finding my heel.'

Circling once more in the air, the heel came down again

in the wide palm of Edward Royce's hand, his fingers closing firmly over it.

'I live just at the back of Maggie Fellen's place, in Slater Street. We could walk along together. Unless, of course, you object?'

She did object, and yet perversely she didn't. After that first offer of a steadying hand he had made no move to touch her, keeping a distance of several feet between them as they talked yet.

'I . . . I have no objection, Mr Royce.'

Anna gave way to the part of her which said she was in no danger from this man.

Keeping pace with her awkward up-and-down step, Edward Royce walked beside her. He could smell the faint aroma of violets from her, so different from the chemical smells of the steel works or the cheap scrubbing soap that was the perfume of most of the women of Coseley, and wondered as he had a hundred times about the circumstances that had brought this girl here.

'I haven't seen you at Rewcastle's.' Aware of the silence between them, Anna tried to break it.

'An' tha won't if I can help it.' He caught the upward tilt of her head. 'Oh, I've nothing against Rewcastle's, their mills find work for most of the folk in Coseley, but not for me. I prefer things the way they are, I like to be my own man.'

'Nice evening.' Across the street the lamplighter lifted his long pole to the street lamp, turning on the gas and watching until the flickering mantle glowed a steady yellow.

'It is that.' Edward Royce lifted a hand in acknowledgement, the same wide smile coming readily to his face. 'Tell tha wife I'm askin' after her.'

'I will, lad, goodnight to yer.' Pole across his shoulder, the lamplighter moved on into the night. Anna watched him go. In this small community everyone seemed to know everyone else so it was little surprise the man walking beside her had known her name and with whom she lodged. They had reached number seventy-eight Roker Street and Anna asked again for her heel. She would not invite him in; it wasn't right to ask a stranger into Maggie's house.

'Why don't you go in and take off that boot? Tell Maggie Edward Royce is offering to mend it for thee.'

He lifted the heel, holding it between thumb and finger.

'If she raises an objection then I'll give thee this back and say no more . . . go on.' He pushed open the door that was as ever on the latch, catching the scent of violets once again as Anna whisked inside.

Chapter Four

'Well, what did he say?' Hester Cresswell wrapped a metal soup ladle, pushed it into a tea chest then stared across the packing benches at Anna.

'Go on, Anna, tell!'

'I've already told you half a dozen times.' Her green eyes smiled though her mouth did not yet remember how. 'It'll be no different if I tell it another half dozen.'

'I know, but Rachel wants to hear you tell it.'

'Eee, Hester Cresswell, I do not! You be tellin' lies.' Rachel Orme's huge brown eyes swivelled towards Anna. 'I was just interested, that's all, Anna. It's none o' my business if Edward Royce waits for you at the bottom of the road.'

'Waits for me?' Anna stopped, the ladle she was about to wrap held in her hand. 'What do you mean, Rachel?'

The girl's lower lip trembled slightly and she bent to the job of nailing a lid to a filled tea chest.

'Everyone knows, all Rewcastle's is talkin' of it. Every Saturday night Edward Royce waits for the Birmingham train. And for what? Nobody else goin' there ... the only one from Coseley goes into Birmingham is you, and it was you he spoke to and walked home on Saturday, Anna Bradly, you can't deny that.'

No, she couldn't. Anna wrapped the ladle, her fingers moving automatically.

The man had walked with her as far as Maggie's door, but as for waiting for her at the street's end ... he couldn't have.

'Eee, Anna, you ain't cross, are yer?' the girl twittered nervously as Anna dropped the wrapped ladle into the half-full tea chest and reached for another. Hester Cresswell let her mouth run away with her sometimes.

'What's to be cross about, Rachel? It's no secret after all.'

Anna's fingers resumed their customary swiftness and she was glad of a valid reason for not meeting the other girl's stare.

'The heel broke off my shoe when I came out of the station and Mr Royce very kindly found it for me, that's all.'

'Oh no it isn't!' Hester joined in. 'Tell it all, Anna Bradly, about how he walked you home.'

'You make it sound like one of those tuppenny romances Bella Castleton has in her shop.' Anna kept her eyes on her work.

'Ar . . . lovely,' Rachel sighed, a ladle forgotten in her hand. 'Lovely.'

'Well, it was nothing like that, and I hope you haven't been giving the rest of the girls the wrong idea, Hester.'

'Me! I haven't given anybody the wrong idea. Besides, you should know by this time they don't need any coaching. They can all have ideas quite nicely for themselves.'

'Well, they've certainly grabbed the stick by the wrong end this time if they think Mr Royce was waiting for me. I . . . I've never seen him before so why should he wait for me?'

'Well, he's seen *you* afore!' A little way along the line of women and girls engaged at the packing benches, the voice of Ella Barnes chipped in.

'Our Davy often goes down to Royce's workshop after tea, says he likes to talk to somebody that doesn't work for Rewcastle's. Makes a bit of a change for him. Well, any road, he was down there the other night, and accordin' to 'im Edward Royce could talk of nowt save you, Anna.'

Aware of a row of interested faces she stooped to pull a fresh sheaf of wrapping paper from a shelf that ran beneath the long benches. Edward Royce had talked of her? But why? For what reason?

'In that case, he and your Davy must be very short of topics for conversation!' She dropped the paper heavily on to the bench, slitting the string binding with a sharp flick of her knife.

'They wasna short last Monday by sounds of it,' Ella retorted quickly. Then seeing the colour sweep into the other girl's cheeks, added maliciously, 'Our Davy says if he didn't know Edward Royce better, he could swear as 'ow that man was sweet on you, Anna Bradly.'

'We can all understand your Davy sayin' that – he's puddled, poor sod, like the rest o' the Barneses.' Hester flew to Anna's defence, tiny golden flecks of anger sparkling in her hazel eyes. 'If all you've got to say is the drivel that brother o' yours spouts, then you'd best keep your mouth closed.'

'You mind your tongue, Essie Cresswell, or there's them that'll mind it for yer!' Ella Barnes's freckles seemed to join into a brown mass. 'Always 'ad too bloody much of a bob on yourself, you 'ave, though God only knows why. Y'ave never 'ad no more than one pair o' bloomers to your name, an' them none too clean neither!'

'That'll cost three-halfpence.' Eli Curran, foreman of the packing shops, declared as a ladle flew from Hester's hand, barely missing Ella Barnes. 'You should wait till shift finishes and break one another's heads outside. That way it's none o' my business and won't cost you yer hard-earned brass.'

'Serves you right, Essie Cresswell.'

'And you better put a sock in it an' all!' Eli turned a sharp look on Ella. The Barneses were trouble and well known for it, but he was having no ructions in his department.

'If I report you to the office, you'll be docked tuppence for stirring. You knows old man Rewcastle will have no arguments between 'is workers.'

'Then go on an' tell 'im, Eli Curran. We all know 'ow much you enjoys that,' the girl spat viciously.

'The same as you know I need give 'im no reason for sacking anybody.'

A buzz of speculation sped from mouth to mouth and the girl's face paled, anger draining away with the same speed it had risen.

'Now I suggest the lot of you get stuck in. This order is for dispatch tonight and if it doesn't go out the gaffer'll not wait for me to give anybody the sack – he'll do it 'imself. And like as not, he won't stop at one.'

'Phew!' Rachel released a long breath as Eli walked away. 'I reckon you got off light there, Ella. I really expected Eli to tell you to draw your pay.'

'So did I.' Ella Barnes wiped a hand across her face, leaving a grimy smear across one cheek. 'Either it's my lucky day or 'is missis spread 'er legs last night.'

'If you want it to go on being your lucky day, you'll shut your mouth now or I'll shut it for you!' Along the bench one of the older women looked at Ella Barnes, hands not needing the help of eyes to do the work of packing kitchen implements. 'Yer has a nasty tongue, Ella Barnes, and if I hear any more on it I'll gi' you what yer mother or father should o' given yer long since.'

A sullen look settled over Ella's face but she knew better than to argue with any of the older women. Like her mother their tempers were unreliable and their vengeance could be swift.

'Well, it's no surprise if Edward Royce is setting his cap at you, Anna,' a woman lifted a sallow smile. Her own youth stolen by perpetual pregnancy, she recognised the shyness of the young girl who had come to settle in Coseley.

'You make a fair picture. I saw hair just that colour in a painting once when my dad took me with 'im to old man Rewcastle's house. I peeked round the door 'fore my dad caught me and clipped my ear. Ooh, it was lovely that painting, but no more than yourself, Anna wench. Yer skin looks as clear and fragile as me mam's best china cup, and that 'air . . . 'ow do you manage to keep it looking so shiny in a place like the mill?'

'I've been wondering that an' all.' Rachel's candid brown stare fixed on Anna. 'Is it something you buy in Birmingham?'

'No,' she replied hastily, not wanting the conversation steered towards her trips to town and glad also of the chance of escaping the subject of Edward Royce. 'I just use my own cream for my face and make a rinse up for my hair. It takes all the hard soap scum out of it once I've washed it.'

'You makes yer own?' The older woman's enquiring eyes looked too large for her pinched face. 'I reckon I'd like to try some of it.' A sudden smile brightened her tired face and she patted her already swollen stomach. 'But I don't need to gi' my man any encouragement.'

'Where did yer learn to make them things?' asked Ella Barnes, forgetting her sullenness.

'At home.' The words were out before Anna really thought of what she was saying and the twist of pain that followed them brought a tiny furrow to her forehead. It still hurt to think of home.

'Did yer mam teach yer then?'

'No,' Anna answered, methodically wrapping each kitchen implement in a sheet of paper before placing it in the tea chest that stood half-full beside her. 'Mother Shipton taught me. She was a woman who lived alone.'

Curtains of memory opening, Anna gazed across the chasm separating her from the years of her childhood. She had been so happy then, with a mother who adored her, a father who doted on them both, and Polly Shipton, the woman the other children were so afraid of, the woman they said was a witch.

But Anna, despite her tender years, had recognised the loneliness of a woman who had lost the love of her life and tried to fill the gap by making herbal medicines for an ungrateful town. She had spent many long summer afternoons out in the fields and on the hills, helping gather herbs and plants then carrying the wicker basket back to the cottage, watching and learning as Polly brewed her lotions and tonics. She had been so safe in her own tiny world . . . a world that had been shattered the night her father had raped her.

'Did she tell you of anything that can shift freckles?'

'I don't know if they can be shifted, Ella, but she used to make a face wash that some of the girls in Wednesbury swore by. They said it certainly seemed to fade their freckles.'

Anna caught the girl's hopeful look; that covering of dark brown freckles was responsible for much of Ella Barnes's sour outlook. Feeling a surge of pity for the girl, she offered, 'I will make you some up, if you like, but mind, I can't promise it will work.'

'Oh, would you, Anna?' Ella Barnes looked almost happy. 'Eee, I'd be that grateful.'

The hooter blared its message. The female shift had ended. The women reached for their shawls hanging from nails driven into the walls either side of the packing benches, clogs beating a tattoo as they hurried their several ways. In an hour the men's shift would finish and a hot meal would be expected on the table.

Anna and Hester followed, the soles of Anna's boots almost soundless on the rough cobbles of the mill yard. She was glad the conversation stayed on face creams and hair rinses until they reached number seventy-eight.

'And what did you say?'

The meal of ham and salad and crusty bread finished, Maggie Fellen reached for the empty plates, carrying them into the scullery to be washed in hot water drawn from the huge black kettle.

'I told them it was nonsense, they were reading too many of those tuppenny romances they buy from Bella Castleton.'

Anna refilled the kettle from the single brass tap, carrying it back to the kitchen and setting it on the gleaming black range where the heat from the fire would have it ready boiled for supper.

'Then you be a fool,' Maggie told her bluntly as she returned to the scullery, picking up a rough huckaback cotton towel and beginning to dry the crockery. 'Why else do you think Edward Royce waited for the Birmingham train, and why else do you think he mended that boot and brought it back 'imself?'

'I don't think he was purposely waiting for the train.' Anna carried the dried plates and pots to the kitchen, giving each its own position on a wooden dresser such as every house in Roker Street seemed to possess. 'And as for my boot, he was just being helpful.'

'Oh, aye! He was being helpful, all right.' Maggie followed her, drying her hands on her long white apron. 'Only question is, who was he helping? You or 'imself?'

'Now what is that supposed to mean?' Picking up a plate only to replace it in its former position, Anna avoided that penetrating grey stare. The subject of Edward Royce, and the reason for his actions of late, embarrassed her.

'How on earth can his cobbling my boot be of any help to him? You told me he would take no payment for doing it.'

'True he would accept no brass for his efforts but that doesn't mean he has no intention of being rewarded for them.'

Picking up the cushion cover she was crocheting, Maggie settled beside the fire that burned winter and summer, her fingers moving deftly.

'And if you hadn't run upstairs swift as a scalded cat the minute yer 'eard 'is voice the followin' afternoon, when he brought yer boot to the door, yer would know that for yerself.'

Turning to the window Anna straightened a curtain, her nerves suddenly taut. Beyond the sky was a vast canvas of purple, blue and red. The sun was dying, its passing marked in breath-taking splendour.

Behind her, fingers idle for a moment, Maggie Fellen watched the girl she had taken into her home. Red-gold hair touched by the colour of the evening sky gleamed like some precious setting for the pearl of her skin. Pale green blouse and dark skirt following the curves of her body, the girl had a waist a man could span with his hands and no help from whalebone either.

'He's set his cap at you, wench.' Maggie bent to her crocheting, her own hair burnished by the light that slid past Anna. 'And you could do worse than take Edward Royce for a husband.'

'Maggie!' Exasperated, Anna swung round. 'I have no intention of marrying anybody. I'm happy the way I am, living here with you. I don't want to be married, and even if I did, that man would not be Edward Royce.'

'Maybe, maybe.' Maggie's fingers worked the cream cotton about the crochet needle. 'But what a woman fancies she wants isna always what she gets. And like I say, you could do worse.'

They were interrupted by Hester coming in the back way through the scullery.

'Mrs Fellen, me mam says to tell you she is 'avin' Kate over to do the cups and would you and Anna like to come round?'

'I thought Kate said she was finished with the cups?'

The crochet hook rested in Maggie's lap.

'Oh, aye, that's what she said. But like me mam says, when brass is short, yer'll do most things to feed kids.'

'Ar, your mam's right there, Essie.' Folding her needlework and putting it away in a raffia basket, Maggie walked to the door that closed off the narrow stairs from the kitchen. 'Thank 'er for me, will you, wench, an' say as 'ow I'll be round in a minute. I must tidy meself up a bit first.'

Anna waited for the door closing behind Maggie.

'What on earth is doing the cups . . . 'and who is Kate?'

'Kate O'Keefe,' Hester whispered back. 'She's Irish, lives over the other side of Coseley. Has about six kids an' none of them working. Times were bad in Ireland, they reckon, that's why they came here for her man to get a job in steel mills, but from look of the kids it don't seem they are much better off. Poor little buggers! Their arses hangin' out of their trousers an' a half-starved look on them most o' the time.'

'But what are the cups?' Anna heard the sound of Maggie coming downstairs and rushed to ask the question of Hester.

'Kate reads the tea leaves, she can tell your fortune from your cup.' Hester's explanation ended abruptly. It didn't do to be talking about other people's private lives when Maggie Fellen was around.

Reaching for her shawl, the older woman glanced coolly at Anna.

'Well, now you knows who Kate O'Keefe is, you might as well meet her for yourself. An' bring your brass. Kate 'as a good 'eart but also six mouths to feed besides her man.'

Mary Cresswell's kitchen was in its usual state of cheery chaos. Fire chased the shadows of early-evening, playing them over the blue and white willow pattern china that was Mary's pride and joy. Beside the hearth the black kettle sang its favourite song.

Billy, a year younger than Hester, had followed his usual pattern, going out as soon as he had finished his meal. Knowing that pattern, Anna's heart gave an unwanted twist. He would be with Edward Royce, she knew, in the tiny workshop Edward had told her had been left to him by his father, a master cutler, a true craftsman who had seen to it his son followed in his steps.

Traces of the five-year-old twins were everywhere; a picture book half hidden by a yellow jumper, shoes on the hearth, lined like a miniature guard of honour. Anna would have liked to cuddle them, loving their mischief, but tonight their mother had them out of the way, tucked up in bed. William Cresswell, Mary's husband, was out the back, flying his pigeons.

'Take off your shawl, Maggie. Kate will be here shortly. Anna, sit yourself down, wench. I'll just brew the tea.' Mary Cresswell turned to the dresser. Tonight was to be something of a social evening, calling for the use of her beloved wedding china. Setting the pretty cups and saucers on the snowy cloth, Hester gave Anna a covert look, eyes sparkling with merriment. She found the whole business a bit of a joke and her glance said so but her mouth remained sensibly closed. One wrong word and she would be out through the scullery door, her mother's clog following.

As if on cue Kate O'Keefe arrived as the hissing water bubbled into the painted teapot, sending out the fragrant essence of scalded tea.

'Is it bein' in ye are, Mary Cresswell?'

'Aye, Kate. Come you in, wench.'

'Sure and a foine evenin' it's bein'.' The full figure of Kate O'Keefe pushed aside the chenille curtain placed against the draught and stood poised in the doorway like an avenging angel.

Anna stared at the two perfectly round spots painted on her cheeks, at the black hair pulled into a knot on the nape of her neck. Eyes sharp and dark as a raven's wing swept the room beneath brows so straight they might have been drawn with a pencil and ruler.

'Evening, Kate. The little ones and your man are all well?'

'They are, Maggie Fellen, an' thanks be to Jesus.'

Pulling a chair to the table, the twinkle gone from her eyes, Hester offered, 'Would you like to sit here, Mrs O'Keefe . . . can I hang up your shawl?'

Giving the shawl to Hester, the woman beamed, heavy black skirts rustling as she lowered herself on to the chair.

'It's a deal of growin' ye've done, Essie Cresswell, since last oi came here. Who knows . . . perhaps the cup will be tellin' how long ye still have beneath your mother's roof?'

'Oh, Mrs O'Keefe, I haven't a lad yet.'

'Maybe not but nothing can be hidden from the cup. Itself will be tellin' me how far off the one is, an' all yer blushin' will alter it not a jot, Essie Cresswell.'

Mary's indulgent smile was turned to her daughter whose

looks were hers of years before. Cup or no cup, it wouldn't be long before some lad took her off to be his wife.

'Will you be startin' now, Kate?' Mary nursed the teapot in her large hands.

'Aye, that oi will, Mary Cresswell, as soon as one o' ye has the good sense to be introducin' me to this colleen.'

Across the table the dark eyes lanced into Anna as if already scanning her very soul and she felt a shiver run through her as she looked at the woman, perched like some huge bird of prey on the edge of her chair.

'You knows well who wench is,' Maggie answered, her voice a mite sharp. 'You visits too many houses in Coseley not to know, but I'll tell you all the same. She's Anna Bradly. She came from . . .'

'Sure an' there's no need of ye tellin' me anything more,' Kate O'Keefe cut in quickly. 'The cups will be doing that, and tellin' where she'll be goin' to, Maggie Fellen.'

'Going to?' There was more than a little fear in Maggie's tight reply. She hadn't realised how much Anna had come to mean in her life; the thought of her leaving brought cold fear.

'A body can swirl the tea and move the leaves,' Kate O'Keefe's soft Irish brogue filled the tiny kitchen, 'but they will find their own resting place, Maggie Fellen. They will say what they have to say and nothing can be changing that.'

Silence settled while Mary filled her precious cups with tea, holding the room in enchanted silence until the contents were drunk.

'Who'll be after bein' the first?' Kate pushed aside her own cup. 'Will it be yerself, Mary Cresswell?'

'There be not much of a fortune left for me, I be thinkin'.' Mary's loud laughter burst out. 'What bit is left can hang fire a while longer. Read the others first, Kate.'

'Then oi'll be taking Essie's cup. Pass it here, girl.'

Hands red and rough from constant work fastened about the dainty cup and Kate turned it slowly, peering into it.

'There be a lad for thee, Essie, but he be a ways off. Ye'll walk out of God's house with a foine man and work together well. The leaves say ye have a good life spread afore ye with all the comfort ye could ever want, but it's not near. Ye must be patient, Essie Cresswell, but rest assured that which the leaves promise will be given.'

'Is it a lad I knows?' Gold flecks shone like sequins in Hester's excited eyes.

'No, ye'll not be knowin' him, nor is he in Coseley. He waits on ye a long ways from this house.'

Kate replaced the cup in its saucer.

'Now what of ye, Maggie Fellen? Have ye any wish to be knowin' the future?'

Maggie smiled, a tight smile that found no echo in her slate-coloured eyes.

'Like Mary, most of my life is done, Kate, and there can be no change around the corner for me. But it can do no harm to hear you say as much.'

William Cresswell's soft encouraging calls to his pigeons wafted in through the half-open scullery door as the women watched Kate perform her ritual, turning Maggie's cup slowly between her rough hands.

'Ye have lost two men,' the soft brogue began at last, 'each to their own God. One who followed after wealth ye will see again in this life but once only. The other waits for ye beyond the veil . . .'

Despite lengthening shadows Anna saw Maggie's lips blanch and the hands resting in her lap curl about each other.

'. . . but ye be wrong in thinking life holds no change.' Kate hesitated, drawing in a long breath. 'Ye thought the Good Lord was after denyin' ye the daughter of yer heart but the girl ye desired for so long is yet to come . . .'

'Me havin' another child . . . now I know the cup is wrong.' Maggie laughed bitterly. 'My man has been gone many years and I've no thought to tekin' another.'

'The child will come,' Kate went on resolutely, ignoring the interruption. 'Though not of yer body, it will be the daughter of yer soul. Yours will be the carin' of it and ye will live to see the growin' of it.'

'Andrew?' Maggie asked softly, hope chasing disbelief from her voice.

'No, the child will not come from that direction but from one who will become as close to ye, an' it is not so far off. Within a twelve month ye will know. Ye are not to end yer days here in Coseley. The leaves tell of a foine house and a comfort ye never dreamed of, but some of yer heart will be here where much of yer days were spent in sorrow and where some still wait on ye. There will be hard times afore there be soft, Maggie Fellen, but better times are planned for ye.'

Putting the cup upright on its saucer, Kate turned a beady glance to the silent figure of Anna.

'An' what of ye, Anna Bradly?'

The voice had not risen yet Anna recognised the challenge. Kate O'Keefe's eyes passed behind her own, looking into the secret corners of her mind, probing, seeking, and Anna could not free herself from those black needle points.

'Oh, go on, Anna,' Hester urged, insensitive to the other girl's reticence. 'It canna do yer any harm.'

'Anna will not be tekin' a reading if she's no mind for it,' Maggie said quickly, recognising that something more than shyness held Anna back.

'But it's only a bit o' fun, Mrs Fellen, nobody teks any notice really.'

'So ye think it's a bit o' fun, do ye, Essie Cresswell?' Kate's bird-like glance swivelled to Hester. 'Then think on this: a month afore ye see yer twentieth year ye will take yer leave of Rewcastle's Mill. Ye will be mistress in yer own place and answerable to one only, and that one will be female. When this happens, come ye round to Kate O'Keefe's and tell her that no notice need be teken of what she sees in the cups.'

Beyond the door William Cresswell called coaxingly, tempting his pigeons from the sky, shooing them gently into their white-painted loft.

In the warm kitchen the fire whispered softly and in its glow Kate's black hair took on a darker shade. Her eyes, already brilliant, glowed like burning coals.

'Well?' She returned to Anna. 'Is yourself wantin' to hear what the cup has to tell or is it leavin' now Kate O'Keefe will be doin'?'

'What do I have to do?' Anna asked the question while every fibre spoke against it. Kate O'Keefe held some strange power; her black eyes seemed capable of passing through the barrier of flesh and travelling into the mind itself.

Kate's mouth curved in a tiny movement of triumph.

'Swirl the dregs in yer cup three times, slowly to the left. Turn it upside down into the saucer, then using yer right hand, pass it to me.'

Doing as Kate instructed, Anna handed it to her.

'You has no need, me wench.' Maggie saw the shaking of the small hand. 'Life will bring only what it holds, whether you hears the cup or whether you don't.'

'I . . . I do want to hear, Maggie.' It was half true. 'I would like to know what Kate can see for me.'

'You know your own way!' Maggie leaned back in her chair. She had said her piece and was done.

'Tap the bottom of the cup three toimes with yer marriage finger. That way ye chase tears that have no need of shedding.'

Kate waited solemnly until it was done then waited a while longer as Mary held a taper of paper to the fire, lifting it to the iron bracket fastened to the wall behind the table. The gas mantle began to glow and Mary turned up the light, filling the room with an eerie yellowish tinge. The taper thrown into the fire, Kate lifted Anna's cup and began to turn it.

'Holy Mother of God!' she swore, lifting her eyes to the girl facing her across the table.

She knows! The thought ran through Anna. Oh God, she knows, I can see it in her eyes!

'Yer've had yer troubles, mavourneen,' Kate's brogue thickened, 'an' they're not after bein' over yet. There be tears in yer cup . . .'

Tipping the cup sideways she watched the minute dribbles of milky tea hang against the rim then shook her crow-like head as most slipped obstinately back inside. She straightened it, peering once more into its depths.

'. . . an' it's refusin' to be dried, so they are. It's spillin' many more yer'll be, girl, for ye are not to be havin' an easy life, Anna Bradly, though there will be those to argue different. Toil and tears are the price ye'll pay . . . toil and tears.'

'But there must be something else, Mrs O'Keefe?'

'Shh!' Mary's sharp hiss silenced her daughter. Kate's eyes remained on the cup she was slowly twisting in her hands.

'Yer stay here will be short.' Kate's voice was hypnotic. She seemed almost to be in a trance, eyes glued to the mass of dark brown leaves. 'Ye're thinking never to wed but ye will. The man who will put the ring on yer finger is close by, but the man who will encircle yer heart is not in this land. There will be children . . .'

Kate paused and Anna's heart leaped again.

Instinctively she felt this woman knew of the son she had borne and of his fathering. She badly wanted to break the spell that seemed to bind her, to run out of Mary's kitchen and lock herself in her own little room in Maggie's house. But she couldn't, she could only brace herself as Kate lifted that piercing glance to her face.

'. . . one who is to grow with ye and one who will not.'

She had said *will* not *is*, thought Anna, clenching her teeth until they hurt. She knows one is born already . . . one who can never grow with me.

Kate's eyes softened, recognising the fear in the girl who was little more than a child herself. There was none would learn from Kate O'Keefe that she had already borne a child, one conceived from rape.

'There will be a parting that ye'll take hard, and deceit that will be as a smack in the gob.' Kate dropped her glance to the cup as relief shone in Anna's green gaze. They understood each other, a rough old Irish woman and a girl who had already been scarred by life. 'But from that parting ye will become yer own woman. The lives of many will be bound to yer own. Ye will have the carrying of them for it's yer back their fortunes will ride upon. Ye will work all the days of yer life, Anna Bradly, but that life will prove to be a great one, bejesus. Aye, a great one to be sure.'

Chapter Five

The train wheels clicked over the points with monotonous regularity but Anna didn't hear. She had posted two pounds to Polly as usual then wandered aimlessly around Birmingham until it was time to get the train home, and all the time one thought had whirled in her brain. Would he be there . . . would Edward Royce be at the end of the street tonight? The nearer the train carried her to Coseley, the more the thought pounded, refusing every effort of her will to dismiss it.

With a brief nod of goodnight to the passengers in her compartment, Anna stepped hesitantly on to the platform. The evening breeze carried back a steamy grey cloud of smoke as the engine pulled away down the track. She couldn't leave the station in case he was there, but at the same time, she told herself sharply, she couldn't stay here, jumping at every shadow like a startled deer.

Anna gripped her bag, her boots making little sound on the wooden platform as she made her way towards the street. If Edward Royce *was* there, and if he *did* speak to her, she would tell him flatly his attentions were uncalled for and unwelcome.

In the event she did neither. Emerging from the entrance to the tiny station, Anna felt colour surge to her cheeks and her tongue cling helplessly to the roof of her mouth.

'Good evening, Miss Bradly.' Edward Royce caught the scent of violets. 'I was waiting until tha came.'

The moon passing behind a cloud left the long street in

darkness before them. Roker Street suddenly seemed at the ends of the earth.

'Billy Cresswell said you would be away to Birmingham today but if he hadna I would still have bin here, just as I am every Saturday.'

He doesn't wear clogs as all the others do. Anna found herself consciously listening to the softer tap of leather. Nor does he cover his head with a flat cap.

'If tha are annoyed by my cheek, Miss Bradly, then I'll tell tha goodnight here. It's not my intention to cause tha any worry.'

Anna looked up then, catching the set of his jaw by the light of the re-emerging moon, seeing his mouth, straight and tense.

'I . . . I'm not worried, Mr Royce, but I am confused. Why should you wait for me?'

'I've asked myself that question many times. Why should I wait for thee when I would wait for no other lass in Coseley?'

They turned into the alley that led to Roker Street, its narrowness forcing them to walk closer beside each other, and Anna felt the brush of his arm against her own.

'I only know I must come.' They passed from the alley and Edward took a sideways step, widening the space between them. 'P'raps it's the thought of tha walking alone.'

'I don't think you should worry about me, Mr Royce.'

Anna stopped in front of number seventy-eight, painfully aware that no curtains hid her from the prying eyes of Roker Street. 'But it was kind of you and I thank you.' Her hand was already on the door.

'Miss Bradly, can I . . . do you think . . .?' He sounded suddenly awkward, like a schoolboy searching for the proper words. 'Would tha object to my calling on you tomorrow?'

Anna was stunned. This was the last thing she had expected and the last thing she wanted.

'I . . . I'm sorry, Mr Royce,' she stammered, pushing open

the door and swiftly stepping inside the house. 'I . . . I'm afraid my Sundays are always spent with Maggie.'

Anna carried the plates to the scullery, washed and dried them then returned them to the kitchen, placing them back on the dresser. Thoughts of Edward Royce's confession that he had purposely waited for her claimed her concentration so she didn't hear Maggie say she had a headache and was going to lie down.

'What?' Anna was still vague as Maggie opened the door leading on to the stairs.

'Eee! I don't know where yer've bin all morning, wench, but I do know as it's not here.' Maggie lifted her heavy black skirts from around her feet. 'I said, I'm not coming with yer today.'

'But we always go to the moor together on Sundays.' Anna turned from the dresser, the memory of her last words to Edward Royce rushing back to her.

'Aye, I knows that, but you'll have to manage on your own this afternoon. I have a head as thick as a mill chimney.' Maggie set a foot on the bare wood of the stairs that over the years she had scrubbed almost white. 'You can call me when you gets back.'

'I'm sorry.' Anna crossed to the foot of the staircase, guilty that her mind had been elsewhere. 'I didn't realise you were feeling bad, I'll stay here with you.'

'What good do you expect that will do? I be no babby as needs to be fussed on.' Maggie continued on up the stairs, her clogs loud against the wood. 'Besides, I thought you needed them herbs an' things for to mek creams for them wenches up at the mill?'

'I do.'

'Well, you'll not get them sitting here the rest of the day.'

Anna's eyes watched her straight back.

'They will have to wait . . . I would rather stay here with you.'

At the head of the stairs Maggie stopped, turning a questioning look at the girl below.

'Did you promise?'

'Yes,' Anna answered reluctantly, remembering Ella Barnes's freckles. 'But . . .'

'No buts, wench, a promise is a promise. If you're not going to keep it then you shouldn't mek it in the first place.' Maggie turned away into her own room. 'Wake me when you gets home.'

It was the first time Anna had come to the moors alone. On every side green space rolled before her to join the blue of the horizon. At each step insects hummed, flying up from the sun-warmed grass, settling again to their labour as she passed. Anna breathed deeply, loving the fresh clean air, the feel of the sun on her face. It was a different, lovely world. The words of a hymn her father and mother had often sung with her touched her memory and as she knelt to pick rosebay willow herb, butterfly orchid and delicately perfumed sweet briar, she sang softly: 'All things bright and beautiful . . .'

'I could help with that if tha let me?'

She had heard no one approach, the soft springy turf muffling the sound of footsteps. Taken by surprise, she gasped then twisted about to squint at the tall figure outlined against the sky.

'I . . . I've finished.' Scrambling to her feet, Anna brushed grass from her skirt with one hand, clinging to her canework basket with the other.

'Tha hasn't picked many.' Edward Royce passed a glance over the basket. 'Judging by the way the women at Rewcastle's are tekin' to those creams and lotions tha makes, I doubt that will be enough.'

'So you've heard about that too!' Anna's voice was tart. 'It appears you hear a good deal about me, Mr Royce.'

'Aye, I do.'

'Billy Cresswell, I suppose?'

'True enough he tells me of tha doings.'

'Billy Cresswell talks too much.'

'The lad thinks tha's something special.' Without asking, Edward took the basket, turning away towards a clump of newly awakening evening primrose, picking some with careful, precise movements. 'An' he's not alone in that.'

'Mr Royce . . .'

His words had unsettled Anna. Unsure of the feelings stirring inside her, she was nervous.

'Mr Royce . . .'

'Look, Anna lass . . .' Squatting on his haunches, Edward Royce turned his head towards her.

His hair had fallen across his brow. Anna saw how the sunlight burnished it. It was almost the colour of her mother's wooden chest, the same rich mahogany.

'It's true I like thee more than somewhat but tha need have no fear I'll push myself on thee. I'm no sprig of a lad that thinks every lass should fall flat on her face just because he looks at her.'

The same light caught his eyes, deepening them to the blueness of hyacinths, bringing a fresh batch of tiny lines to their corners as he screwed them up against the glare.

'I waited for thee purposely last night but my seeing tha here this afternoon is accidental. I come here sometimes when I need to think a thing out . . . I must say, I was surprised to see thee on this part of moor.'

'I don't usually come this far but today . . .'

'And where's Maggie?' he interrupted. 'I thought that tha always came up on to moor together?'

Narrowed against the sun, his eyes seemed to accuse her and his hands rested idly against his knees, waiting for her answer. They were strong hands, the fingers long with white half moons showing at the base of nails that were surprisingly clean. His wrists and forearms below the rolled sleeves of a striped cambric shirt were covered with short fine hairs that glistened in the sun.

'She . . . she wasn't feeling too well.' Suddenly conscious she was staring, Anna pulled her glance away to the line of houses in the distance. 'I really should be getting back to her.'

'Then it's as well I did come across thee.' He turned back to the business of collecting plants. 'Two pairs of hands can do most jobs quicker than one.'

He was right, of course and if she didn't fill the basket it would mean her having to come to the moor again one evening after work.

'Thank you, Mr Royce.' With a shy whisper, Anna bent to pull the fragrant plants.

'Phew!' Half an hour later Edward Royce flopped to the ground, rolling on to his back, eyelids closed. 'It's warm work, is that. I need five minutes before I tackle the walk back.'

Anna stared at him. He stretched a good six feet. He had said very little as they had worked and not once had he attempted to touch her. It would do no harm to sit just for a few minutes.

The basket between them, she sat down. Pulling up her knees, skirts tucked around her ankles, she gazed out over a forest of mill stacks rising above terraces of tiny two-up, two-down houses.

So like Wednesbury. There too factory chimneys dominated a skyline regularly turned to blood red as furnaces were opened to receive offerings of pig iron or to spew out molten steel. And there, as in Coseley, there was no way out, no employment other than the foundries and mills. That was what her son would grow up to, that was his future. And what of hers? It could only be the same hard work and little besides, despite what Kate O'Keefe had read in her tea cup. A bee hummed loudly, investigating the contents of the basket; beyond, in the distance, a lark rose from the grass, filling the sky with song. Somewhere there was a beautiful world but its doors were closed against the likes of Anna Bradly.

'Coseley is a small place, Anna . . .'

He had not asked to use her Christian name but neither

was sitting on the moors alone with him conventional. What the women of Wednesbury would have had to say about such 'carryings on' didn't bear thinking of.

'. . . but I would tek it against the big cities any day.' His eyes were still closed against the sky.

'Billy Cresswell told Maggie you had been to London.'

'It's true, I took my cutlery design and entered it in an international trade fair. When it took first place in its class I wrote to the King asking his permission to call it "King's Choice".'

'You wrote to the King?' Anna was more astounded than impressed.

Edward drew up one knee, resting his other foot across it. The buttons of his shirt opened just below the throat, showing the same covering of short glistening hairs. Anna quickly diverted her glance as his head turned and his blue eyes looked up at her.

'I wrote to Buckingham Palace. Whether the King will get to see my letter or whether it will be read by one of those aides he has is anybody's guess. They might even have thrown it away.'

'Oh, they wouldn't do that.'

Anna meant to look at his face but somehow her eyes were drawn to the line of hairs below his throat. Blushing, confused by her own feelings, she turned her attention to the basket, re-arranging the collection of plants.

'Mebbe not.' He sat up, his gaze on their small world of Coseley.

'I have the workshop my father bought when he moved here from Sheffield. It was he taught me the making of cutlery; he was a fine cutler and made sure I learned his skills. He would brook no shoddy workmanship. He also left me the house I was born in. That might be counted little enough by some folk but it's enough for me. I am my own master and as long as I can, I will keep it that way. I want no bending and scraping to ironmasters like

71

Rewcastle. Seems to be better to be your own man, for either way brings the likes of me no riches.' He wondered how to continue.

He had been aware of this slight girl with the head of red-gold hair since shortly after Maggie Fellen had taken her in and had long realised that he wanted Anna Bradly for his wife.

'What I'm tryin' to say, Anna, is this. Has tha any objection to my callin' on thee?'

You could do worse than tek Edward Royce for a husband. Maggie's words echoed in her mind. If she were walking out with Edward it would put an end to the way the lads at the mill looked at her, the whistles as she passed and the sniggers when they thought she was out of hearing. Yes, she could do worse than accept Edward, but would he still want her once he knew her past?

'Edward.' She hesitated. Maggie had listened to her story and at the end had shaken her head and said Anna had been in the way of the devil's temper that night, that Maggie Fellen would not be the one to continue his evil by throwing her out so long as she kept a decent life under her roof. But would Edward see things in the same light? Would he respect her privacy if he no longer wanted her for his wife? Somehow she felt he would.

'Edward.' She began again. 'There is something I have to tell you. It concerns my life before coming to Coseley . . .'

About to reply that there was no need to tell him anything, Edward turned to her. Seeing the look on her face, he remained silent. Whatever it was, she had the need to tell it.

'. . . my mother died from childbirth while I was very young. A friend, Mother Polly, took care of me while my father was at work and a woman from the town, Mary Carter, came to the house twice a week, to do the washing and the baking. Then, one day, Mary disappeared and when her body was found floating in Millpool my father was accused of her rape and murder. The official verdict was death by misadventure but that made no difference to the people of Wednesbury – they accused and taunted him for months, until one night he came home drunk. He . . . he mistook me for Mary and said he might as well do what he was accused of doing. He didn't mean to hurt me, he thought I *was* Mary, I know he did, but he . . . he raped me.'

Pausing, Anna gazed out across the heath, into the distance that held her child.

'I have a son, Edward,' she finished softly. 'I have a bastard son.'

He had not taken his eyes from her as she talked. He had seen the emotion in her face, sensed the effort the telling of her rape had taken. She need have told him nothing yet instead had told him all. She could have lied to him but deep within him he knew she had spoken the truth, the whole truth.

'Who has the lad now?' he asked.

'Mother Polly said she would care for him as she had for me,' Anna answered. 'I could not let a child suffer for something he had no part in, and I could not bring him with me with having no place to live and no one who would look after him while I work. But I love him, Edward, I send what money I can to feed and clothe him, and one day, God willing, I intend to have him with me.'

Turning her head, Anna looked him squarely in the eyes. 'I have told you what happened, Edward, and it is the truth. If you no longer wish to call on me then I understand.'

Standing up, he held out a hand and when she took it pulled her gently to her feet.

'Tha's told me lass,' he said gently, 'and I appreciate the telling, though it makes no difference to the feelings I hold for you. What happened was none of your doing, that is what I believe, and will always believe. Marry me, Anna, and we will make a home for the boy, together.'

* * *

The wedding, a year after that day on the moor, was a quiet gathering at the chapel, Maggie Fellen and the Cresswells the only witnesses as Anna joined her life to that of Edward Royce. He'd known that day on the moor that she had not loved him and he had not asked her for anything, even when she had felt the tension holding him like a coiled spring.

Laying a sparkling white cloth across the table, Anna smiled tenderly. She had not loved Edward then, but she did now, with a quiet peaceful love.

I'll not push myself on thee, Anna. On their wedding night they stood in a shaft of moonlight streaming through the open curtains of the small front bedroom in his Slater Street house. 'Tha need have no fear on that score. Ah love thee, lass, an' ah want thee, ah'll not deny, but ah'll lay no hand on thee unless tha wants it. Tha is my wife an' ah thank God every day. An' if that's to be the all of it, then ah can make best of it.'

Her hair had been loose of its pins and he had run his fingers through the dark fiery silk, holding her against him. She had felt the shudder run through him, the quickening of him pressing against the thin cotton of her nightdress, then he had left her, going to lie in the bed they had shared without further closeness for three months. Fear had kept her from loving Edward, fear that the pain her father had caused her would happen all over again, the same terror and revulsion. But that had been a dreadful mistake she knew, her father had been driven mad by lies and taunts. He had tried to drown that madness in drink which had only added to his insanity until he had raped his own daughter without knowing. But like her father Edward was kind and gentle, loving her with an undemanding love, and like her father he would not knowingly hurt her. She was the one hurting Edward, she was causing him pain, pain he did not deserve nor would force her to assuage.

'Edward!' She had called his name in the soft creamy moonlight and heard the quiet, almost sobbing release of breath as she whispered, 'Help me, Edward.'

Now Anna smiled into the fire, her memory sending pictures through her mind. She was to bear his child.

Behind her the latch opened noisily and she twisted towards the sound.

'Tha shouldn't have waited up, lass, tha needs to rest more with little 'un coming.' Leaving his shoes at the scullery door, Edward dropped heavily into a chair beside the glowing range, fatigue scoring lines across his face.

'I get quite enough rest.' Anna tried to keep her own tiredness from showing. There had been too many nights with Edward working into the small hours, but if he could manage, so could she.

'Has anyone stayed up at the new place with you?' Ladling soup into a bowl that had been warming against the fire, she placed it on the table, pushing a plate of bread close beside it.

'A couple of the men, but I sent them home about eleven. Ah can't expect a proper day's work out of a man who's worked half the night afore it!'

'Yet that is what you yourself are doing.' The worry of weeks echoed in Anna's reply. 'You push yourself day and night, Edward, and don't pretend . . . it's wearing you out. Why must it always be you who has to be there? Why can't this partner, whoever it is, take a turn?'

'He's seeing to the sales end, Anna.' More weary than he would ever admit, Edward changed his seat for a chair at the table but the soup remained untouched. Reaching for Anna, he pulled her close, his arms around her thickening waist, head resting on the child in her womb, breathing in the scent of violets.

'King's Choice is mine, the same as this child is mine, and I want the best for both of them, Anna. Don't you see, love, I have to succeed for both of you?'

A rush of tenderness softening her voice, Anna touched a hand to the head lying against her stomach. Edward didn't understand even yet that she loved him whole-heartedly, he

75

had no need to prove himself to her; perhaps it was her fault. She didn't lie in his arms smouldering with passion, but she loved him and he was enough for her.

'You have already succeeded for me, Edward,' she whispered into his mahogany hair. 'And our child will have the finest man in Coseley as a father, it will need no more.'

'I love thee, lass.' Edward did not look up. 'I love thee.' He buried his face closer to the gentle rise that was his unborn child, waiting for a reply he knew would not come.

Anna had married him and kept his house, she answered his physical needs, but not once had she said she loved him.

'Ah'm not wanting to eat.' Stifling the emotion pulling at him, he stood up, one hand grasping Anna's. 'Ah'm away to bed and for once tha can leave the crocks, they'll wash in mornin' . . . and this time, Mrs Royce, tha's not goin' to pretend neither. Ah can see tiredness in tha face.'

'I will bank the fire and come straight up.' Anna smiled into a face weary from more than hard work, and her heart twisted. She was failing him, she knew that, and yet . . .

'No tha won't.' Releasing her, Edward moved towards the scullery where the bucket of coal chippings was always kept. 'Tha's goin' to bed, ah'll see to fire.'

He did not follow at once. Anna had washed her hands and face in the water kept in a jug on the dresser at the foot of the brass bedstead and was already plaiting her hair when she heard his tread on the wooden stair. She wished he wouldn't work so many hours.

'There's water in the jug.' She tied the end of her long plait with a length of white ribbon.

'Ah had a swill in the scullery.' The icy water he had hoped would wash away desire had achieved nothing. His back turned towards her, he slipped off his shirt and trousers.

'Will it take much longer to get the new workshop set up?' Anna glanced at the sinewy back and the surge of warmth she had felt downstairs welled up in her. Suddenly she wanted to take him in her arms, to soothe away the weariness of body and heart.

'A few days, ah reckon. There's one big machine has to be delivered yet. Get that in and we should be all set.'

'Edward.' Turning off the oil lamp, Anna pulled back the curtains, looking down at the sleeping, moon-bathed street. 'It's not too late,' she said quietly. 'You can still withdraw from this partnership and wait until you can launch King's Choice yourself. You have always preferred to be your own boss and don't have to change for me.'

'But ah do, Anna.' He was behind her, his fingers playing with the long plait of her hair. 'Ah want to change the world for you, to give you the best that money can buy . . .'

'You have given me more than any money can buy, Edward.' She turned, seeing the line of his shoulders in the light from the window, catching the dark gleam of his eyes sweeping her face, and the heat from his body burned through her nightgown as she pressed against him, lifting her arms to his neck.

'I have you, and soon I shall have our child. I love you, Edward,' she whispered, shy as a new bride. 'I love you.'

'Anna!' He was hoarse with longing and uncertainty. 'Anna . . . oh, Anna, my love . . . my love.' His arms strong about her, he held her close in the moonlight, afraid that to move would be to lose what God had just given him.

It was Anna who broke away but only long enough to climb into bed and as Edward joined her she slid back into the circle of his arms, happy that tonight he would taste the fullness of her love.

'All things bright and beautiful . . .'

Singing the words of the hymn her mother had taught her so long ago, Anna tidied her already spotless kitchen. Satisfied all was as she liked it, she turned her attention to the gently bubbling saucepan against the fire. It was too early to add potatoes yet, Edward would not be home until late and she did not want them boiled away to nothing in the water.

'All things bright and beautiful, the Lord God made them all . . .'

Lifting the heavy pan, she put it on the hob that gleamed like black silver. Edward said she shouldn't work so hard, scrubbing and polishing, but she loved this tiny house as much as she guessed his mother must have done.

The girls would be here soon. Anna glanced at the clock ticking quietly on the mantelpiece above the fire. She looked forward to the visits of the wenches from the mill, enjoying their gossip and listening to their latest love stories. Anna smiled to herself as she reached down her precious china cups from the dresser. They had been a wedding present from Maggie and she still felt like a little girl playing house every time she took them from their hooks. Laying them ready on their delicate saucers, she took out the fruit cake she had baked that morning; she liked to have something to offer and the girls were always hungry.

'Are yer in, Anna?' Ella Barnes pushed aside the chenille door curtain.

'Of course, come in.' The same happy smile teasing her mouth, Anna welcomed her guests.

Tea made and poured, she handed Ella a small carton, watching her pleased grin.

'Eee, ta ever so, Anna.' Ella took the pill box filled now with a paste of grated horseradish and milk. 'It's workin' just fine. My freckles 'ave almost disappeared.'

They were not so thickly brown, Anna admitted to herself as the girl eagerly opened the box, sniffing at the contents, but that could be the result of her not worrying so much about them rather than the paste.

'Anna,' Rachel Orme's brown eyes gleamed excitedly, 'would yer do my face with cosmetics? You know, like them there rich women in tuppenny novels.'

'It won't be tuppenny novels your mother will be blaming

if I send you home with your face made up,' Anna said, smiling.

'You knows the sort o' women daubs themselves in paint and powder,' Ella mimicked Rachel's mother, 'the sort that's no better than they should be.'

'Oh, go on, Anna,' Rachel pleaded as the giggling died away. 'I've always wanted to see how I might look done up like wenches in Birmingham Music Hall.'

'You might see how they look done up in Birmingham 'ospital if your mother cops you.' Ella Barnes wagged a warning finger.

'But her won't, not if I washes it off afore I goes. Please, Anna, you never knows. I might look like one o' them film stars. Eee, think of it, "The Desert Sheik", starring Miss Rachel Orme.'

'It would tek more than Anna's cosmetics to turn thee into a film star,' Ella Barnes said, laughing. 'That would need a Fairy Godmother!'

'Well, at least I don't need no pastes to get rid of freckles,' Rachel shot, hurt by Ella's remark.

'No, you doesn't, but you could do wi' a load o' concrete to fill in holes where you had the chicken pox.'

'Now that's enough!' Anna had seen exchanges of this sort lead to tears before. 'I think it might be fun to try, Rachel, so long as you scrub it off before you go home.'

Delighted, she settled into a chair in Anna's bright kitchen, tucking the towel Anna handed to her round her neck, protecting the high cotton of her pink blouse.

'When is the babby due, Anna?'

Wiping Rachel's face with a scrap of white cloth dipped in rosewater before spreading a thick layer of ground oatmeal mixed with milk over her cheeks and brow, Anna smiled happily. 'Another month.'

'Is Edward pleased?'

'Of course he is pleased.' Hester came in through the scullery, a feathering of rain sparkling like tiny crystals on her mousy hair. 'Have you had that sort of daft question all night, Anna?'

'I didn't mean to be daft.' Ella's mouth drooped. 'I just asked, that's all.'

'Then tek a poker an' stir your brains a bit! Get rid of all the dust afore you asks the next time.'

Putting a paper-wrapped parcel on the table, Hester took off her shawl, hanging it on the wooden peg behind the door.

'Me mam has sent a matinee coat an' says to tell you there'll be some baby gowns along tomorrow. Her got them from the pawn shop, an unredeemed pledge, but 'er's got them in boiler just to mek sure as they're clean.'

'I'll never be able to thank your mother, Hester, but I am pleased. Every little helps just now with Edward starting his new line.'

Leaving Rachel until the oatmeal dried, Anna turned to Ella.

'Do you want to try?'

'Eee, Mrs Royce, I was 'oping you'd ask.'

'Maggie says to mek sure you're not standing on your feet too long.' Hester cast a stern glance at the girls in Anna's kitchen.

She enjoyed the company of the girls but they had turned it into a weekly visit and she now eight months gone; she should be resting with her feet up instead of running a beauty parlour.

'Maggie worries too much.' Massaging a thin film of cream scented with a hint of wild honeysuckle over Ella's upturned face, Anna glanced at her friend. 'And for that matter, so do you, Hester Cresswell.'

'Well, it needs somebody to. You seem to think you can keep going day and night.'

'I'll come to no harm.' Cutting two slices from a cucumber, Anna placed one over each of Ella's eyes. 'Is Maggie with your mother, Hester?'

'She was when I left. Seems they're havin' some kind of

competition, the way me mam's knitting needles and Maggie Fellen's crochet hooks are flyin'. I tell yer, Anna, that babby of yours will 'ave to wear these woollies till it's twenty-one to get through what that pair are mekin'.'

Behind them Rachel choked back a laugh. 'Don't go on like that, Hester Cresswell. If you meks me laugh it'll crack all of Anna's plaster work.'

'That's about ready to come off.' Pouring water from the hissing kettle into a large pottery bowl, Anna cooled it with a jug filled from the scullery tap.

Watching Rachel cleanse away the dried oatmeal, Hester asked, 'Edward is sure he's doin' the right thing, Anna?'

'He would rather have been on his own,' a tiny frown pulled the arch of Anna's eyebrows, 'but since the palace agreed to the name King's Choice and ordered a complete suite of cutlery, everybody seems to want it. Edward couldn't fill all the orders working alone so this seemed the only answer.'

Removing the cucumber slices from Ella's eyes, Anna wiped the lids with a rosewater-dipped cloth, patting them dry with a fingertip movement.

'A partnership was the sensible solution really,' she defended Edward's action. 'We hadn't the money for machinery and there was no way he could make that amount of cutlery by hand. A sixty-forty split was fair, he reckoned.'

'I don't know about the money side of things,' Hester took the bowl of water, emptying it into the scullery sink, 'but it seems to me your husband is doin' all the work. How many times has he bin home before eleven at night since this thing started?'

Anna stretched her back, feeling the baby kick inside her. Hester was right. Edward was gone all day and well into the night but he wanted to make sure everything was set up the way he wanted it; it was like Edward not to leave things to other people. 'We will have a better life soon,' he had told her last night, holding her in his arms. 'We are on a winner, Anna, and this is just the beginning. Soon you can have a nice house somewhere. P'raps we might even join the toffs in Woodgreen.' He had slept then, worn out from working since first light.

'What time be you expectin' him tonight?' Hester came back, drying her hands, her eyes speckled gold from the softly flaring gas light.

Bending over Ella, touching beneath the lower side of her lashes with a soft black drawing pencil, Anna didn't answer at once. Studying the girl's face, she smudged the lines she had pencilled, smoothing the starkness to a charcoal shadow that emphasised the almond shape of the girl's eyeline.

'I'm not sure. Edward is helping the men get a new machine bedded in. He doesn't know how long it will take.'

'While his partner is getting another trollop bedded in – and we all know how long *that* will take.'

'Eee, Hester Cresswell!' Ella Barnes looked up from the box of cream she had cradled all night. 'You better not let your mam hear you talk like that.'

'Well, it's true.' Hester turned on the girl from Rewcastle's Mill. 'An' everybody knows it. That one is willing to let anybody do the work just so long as it don't tek him from his pleasure.'

'Edward wouldn't be happy if he hadn't seen the job done for himself, Hester,' Anna said, smiling. 'Now make us all a cup of tea.'

'There you are, Ella.' A few moments later she handed the girl a mirror. 'It could be Miss Ella Barnes currently appearing in The Desert Sheik.'

Looking at her reflection, Ella's brown eyes widened with pleasure.

'Eee, Anna, I can't tell meself. Ooh, you be clever in cosmetics! You'll 'ave to teach me 'ow to do this for meself . . . Eee, what would me mam say!'

They were laughing when the beige-bordered chenille door curtain was pushed aside and Eli Curran stepped in from the street.

'It . . . it were a machine, me wench. It slipped.'

Hester's arm about her, Anna watched the men carry a door into her bright warm kitchen, a door on which they had laid the body of her husband.

'It were an accident.'

Eli pulled off his cap and stood twisting it in his hands.

''E were settin' up a press – you, know for stampin' out the metal for them knives an' things – when it slipped an' the lot come tumblin' over on top of 'im.'

Behind her the mill girls clung together holding on to each other, their frightened exclamations punctuating the dreadful hush that had settled, robbing the tiny room of its warmth.

'Where shall we put 'im, missis?'

One of the men helping to carry the door looked at Anna but his question was lost on her. Why was Edward lying down? Why didn't he smile?

'Over here.'

It was Hester who answered. Crossing quickly to the sideboard beneath the room's one window, she scooped up the wooden candlesticks and pottery bowl, dropping them on to the table among the cosmetic creams and lotions.

'We be mortal sorry.' Eli looked more at Hester than at Anna. 'There weren't nothin' we could do, the thing was over an' 'im under it afore you could wink.' He glanced towards the four men standing awkwardly shuffling their feet now their burden was laid down. 'If . . . if we be needed, then you know where to find we.'

'You have grease on your face, Edward.'

Anna crossed to the sideboard, a tiny smile lifting the edges of her mouth, and touched a finger to the smear of greasy dirt crossing his brow and cheek.

'You will have to wash that off before supper.'

'Come away, Anna.' Hester put an arm around her, turning her away as the men left the house. 'Edward won't be wantin' anythin' tonight.'

'Eh, Hester, is . . . is Edward Royce truly dead?'

The girl's words seemed to pierce Anna's mind, chasing away the numbing stillness.

Edward was dead!

Around her the room swirled in a crazy dance and in her womb the unborn child lurched.

Edward Royce was dead!

'You pair!' Hester spoke sharply to the girls as she held on to Anna. 'Stop actin' like bloody mawkins. This ain't the first dead body y'ave seen, an' God knows it ain't likely to be the last! Now go fetch Maggie Fellen an' me mam, tell 'em what's happened. I'll stop with Anna.'

'I did not love him as I should have done.'

Anna sat beside the cold grate that would remain fireless while her husband's body lay in the room.

Sitting beside her, Maggie held back a reply. Anna had said nothing since she and Hester's mother had come running. 'Edward Royce be dead,' was all the two girls had gabbled before racing off. She had said nothing they had washed the body and dressed it in its Sunday best, just stood silent and unmoving, staring at Edward's face.

'I did not love him enough. He deserved more.'

'You gave 'im all you could, wench,' Maggie said gently. It would be best to talk, to try to draw out the grief locked inside, better if Anna would cry it out.

'Did I, Maggie?'

Anna's eyes turned to the door where her husband's body still lay. It had been placed on chairs brought in by neighbours.

'Did I give him all I could?'

'O' course you did, Anna. You looked to 'im as well as you could an' 'e knowed that.'

'Looking after him was not enough.' Anna's voice was barely audible. 'It was not enough, Maggie, I should have loved him more.'

The weight of the child in her womb making her progress slow and unwieldy, she pushed herself to her feet and crossed to where her husband lay, only the bronze pennies holding his eyes closed saying he was not sleeping.

'It was not enough, Edward.' She looked down at his quiet face. 'You deserved so much more.'

In the hushed stillness she slipped to her knees, taking one hand in hers, holding her cheek against its marble coldness.

'I could not show you for so long,' she whispered, 'I could not tell you what lay in my heart, the *real* love that had grown and filled it. I could not tell you how I felt in those early weeks and now it is too late – too late to tell you it was fear that held me away from you, fear of what had happened before. But I loved you, Edward, I loved you. Oh, Edward, I'm sorry . . . I'm sorry!'

In the shadows Maggie Fellen watched, her own heart moved to breaking, but she made no attempt to bring Anna away. Let her pour it all out. Let the tears of sorrow be her comfort, for it was all the solace life might offer her.

Chapter Six

Anna didn't cry. Nor did the tears fall the day the plain deal box holding his body was lowered into the ground or that same night when pain carried his child into the world.

Hester Margaret was her daughter's given name, but from the moment Maggie had laid the tiny bundle in her arms and she had seen the golden fuzz of hair, soft as a summer morning, Anna had called her Misty.

'You have a half-brother, Misty.' She stroked a finger across the tiny head, feeling the child pull hard on her nipple. 'He has the same colour hair as you but his eyes are blue. I don't know his name and he will never know yours, but you have a half-brother, my little sweetheart, though the two of you will never meet.'

'Be you in, Mrs Royce?'

Anna glanced towards the door, kept on the latch like all the rest in this part of Coseley. Taking the child from her breast, she called, 'Come in.'

She recognised the man who shuffled self-consciously into her neat little kitchen. He was a clerk in Rewcastle's offices.

'Mr Rewcastle sent me, Mrs Royce.'

'It used to be Anna. What happened to change that, Joby?' Putting the baby in a drawer that served for a cot and covering her with a blanket, Anna turned towards the slight frame of Joby Timmins. 'So Mr Rewcastle sent you. What for?'

'He told me to ask you if you would come up to the Mill? I . . . I don't know what for.'

Maybe not, Anna thought, watching his glance fall before her own, but I bet you have a good idea.

'Did he say when, Joby?'

'Aye, Mrs . . . Anna, this afternoon, if you can manage?'

'I'll manage. Tell Mr Rewcastle I will be there at three.' She crossed to the door, holding it open for him. 'Is your family well, Joby? Last I heard your John was cutting his teeth with bronchitis.'

'Aye, but he seems all right now, poor little bugger. There was a time I thought we'd lost him.' Joby Timmins smiled, transforming a face worn by work and worry. 'Thanks for askin', Anna wench. And, Anna . . .' he leaned slightly closer '. . . look out for Rewcastle, he's a sly sod. I don't know what he wants to see yer for . . . well, not all of it any road. Just be careful, eh?'

She had left the baby with Maggie and sharp on three crossed the cobbled yard of the mill. Inside the offices, their walls covered with drab brown paint, Anna looked around with distaste. The workhouse couldn't be much drabber. She was about to sound the small brass bell on a table beside the entrance when Joby Timmins entered from an inner door.

'Mr Rewcastle is waiting for you, Mrs Royce.'

This time Anna did not question his formality. Here he would be expected to address her as any other visitor to the mill. He led her through a long room where several clerks burrowed industriously among mounds of paper though Anna knew their eyes followed her as she passed.

The office Joby showed her into smelled strongly of lavender wax polish and for the first time in her life Anna walked on a rug that had not been pegged from clippings of old clothes.

'Sit down, Anna.'

There was no formality here, she noted, sitting on the edge of the chair Jacob Rewcastle pointed to. Or was it a lack of respect? The great mill owner and an ex-employee? He smiled at her across the huge mahogany desk and Joby Timmins's warning echoed in her mind. 'Look out for Rewcastle, he's a sly sod.'

'I think you know how sorry I am about your husband . . . dreadful accident . . . dreadful.' His smile faded. 'But the business of life must go on. That's the reason I asked you to call and see me, Anna. Business.'

'I don't understand, Mr Rewcastle, what business do you have with me?'

'Not you directly.' He lifted a sheaf of papers, shuffling them together. 'My business was with your late husband. He borrowed a great deal of money from me to buy new machinery and premises, and now,' the heavy shoulders were raised in a shrug, 'now I must call in his loan, Anna.'

'But Edward said he had a sixty-forty arrangement. He was to take forty per cent of the profit from King's Choice in exchange for the money he needed right away to set it up.'

'I'm sorry, Anna. He must have wanted you to believe in him, I suppose.' The papers were shuffled again. 'The truth is your husband borrowed heavily from me, but I'm a fair man and seein' as how things stand with you, I've decided to let you keep the workshop.'

Across the desk small eyes peered at her, from within enveloping fleshy folds. Anna shivered inside. Jacob Rewcastle had no intention of being fair with her.

'After all,' he went on, dropping the papers he was holding on to the desk, 'it'll be little use to me once I get the new line into full swing . . . and you should get a good price for it.'

'The workshop?' Things were moving too quickly for her. Edward in debt to this man? But he wouldn't borrow money, not without telling her, and had spoken only of a partnership.

'Didn't he tell you? The workshop was part of the collateral he put up against the money I lent him.'

'And the house?' Anna's voice was strangled.

'That, too, since you ask.' Pushing himself heavily out of the brown leather chair ringed around with brass studs, Jacob

Rewcastle moved to Anna's side. She was a good-looking wench, with that thick bright hair and clear skin. Put her in a few decent clothes and a man could take her places.

'But you could do better than that hovel.' He brought a podgy hand down firmly on her shoulder.

So that was it, that was the real reason Jacob Rewcastle had asked to see her in the privacy of his own office. He thought he was on to a good thing: a woman who would share his bed and be only too glad to keep her mouth shut. Shoving his hand from her shoulder, Anna was on her feet, her eyes glinting like green ice.

'That hovel, as you put it, was my home. And shared with Edward, infinitely preferable to any you might offer.' She saw the dull flush spread across his heavy jowls but went on scathingly, 'if the house and workshop were pledged by Edward then take them . . . I will produce King's Choice somewhere else.'

'I don't think so.'

The shiver inside Anna turned to a feeling of cold dread. As much as this man had told her, the worst was still to come.

'King's Choice is no longer yours to produce.'

Jacob savoured the telling. This would show this young upstart her bread would be buttered thicker by his hand. He moved behind the desk, leaning back in his chair.

'The design was patented, and the patent is in my name. Edward Royce was no businessman.'

'You bastard!' Anna spat as she realised what he was implying. 'Edward would never do that. He worked too many hours on that design. You've stolen it . . . you're a thief, Jacob Rewcastle, nothing more than a common bloody thief!'

'Take care, Anna,' he warned softly, little eyes travelling over the black cloth coat rubbed bare along the line of buttons, the black gabardine skirt shiny from so many pressings, shoes he guessed had no bottoms to them. 'You're hardly in a financial position to pay off a libel suit. You'd better be sensible. I could see you quite comfortable, you and that daughter of yours.

There was never any contract signed, your husband only put his name to the loan paper, so it would be in your best interest in the long run to do as I suggest. Come on, Anna, you know I'm right.'

'The name is Mrs Royce!' Behind the filmy black widow's veil draped about her cheap hat, Anna's eyes glared. 'And don't bother to go any further. You have everything Edward ever had in his life except his wife, and her you will never possess!'

'Don't be bloody stupid, woman.' Piggy eyes darted to the office window beyond which Joby Timmins was bent over a ledger. 'You're going to find it hard.'

'That's the one thing I can be sure of right now.' Anna walked to the door, twisting the brass knob before she turned to look back. 'But there is also something *you* can be sure of. No matter how hard I find it, Jacob Rewcastle, you will find it doubly hard. I intend to take back all that was Edward's and more besides. My advice to you is: pray. Pray very hard that I stop at that!'

'Is something wrong, Father? I could hear voices all down the passage.'

Pressure from the other side caused Anna to release the door handle and step away. The man who came in gave her a sharp glance; she had seen him several times at the mill, the women pointing him out as Philip Rewcastle.

'I just made this woman an offer only to have it thrown back in my face.' Jacob glanced past them to Joby Timmins. His head was bent over the books but it was a certain bloody bet his ears were cocked. 'I don't like that, Philip, I don't like that at all.'

In his mid-twenties now, Philip Rewcastle knew all about his father's offers, especially those made to women, and despite her widow's weeds this one appeared young and not bad-looking.

'Perhaps the lady didn't like it either, Father.' Philip smiled full at Anna. 'Why don't we see if we can make things more acceptable, Mrs . . .?'

'Royce . . . Anna Royce.'

'What was my father's offer, Mrs Royce?'

Across the desk Jacob Rewcastle lost much of his colour and those small eyes seemed to retract further, almost invisible amidst the puffy flesh.

Anna's fingers tightened about the strap of her shabby bag. This was her first chance of revenge: to tell his son of the offer to become his father's kept woman. Beneath her veil Anna looked at Jacob Rewcastle's only child. He wasn't as tall as Edward had been, in fact he was little taller than herself. A pale grey topcoat emphasised his slender build, a hint of auburn gleamed in hair worn long enough to touch his collar and his side whiskers were worn fashionably level with his ear lobes. There was no moustache framing the attractive, almost feminine fullness of his mouth. Physically at least Philip Rewcastle was the complete opposite of his father.

'Your father offered to let me keep my husband's workshop.' Anna relaxed her fingers, allowing the moment to slide away. This was not the revenge she wanted. 'But it was part of a business arrangement they had made together and as such belongs to your father. It was . . . kind of him to offer its return but I don't want it.'

'This workshop, Father, where is it?'

'Slater Street. You know, runs along bottom of main mill.'

'Oh, yes. And this workshop, Mrs Royce . . .' Philip's eyes returned to Anna. 'Isn't it joined to the house?' At her nod he added, 'Which means that too was part of the arrangement.'

'I've said all I'm going to.' Jacob had recovered his composure but his voice betrayed fury. 'I offered and she said no . . . that's all there is to it. The house and everything beside it was pledged against a loan that cannot be paid. The property will be sold so I can recoup some of my losses. I'm not a bloody Philanthropic Society.'

'All Coseley knows that, Mr Rewcastle. To be frank, all Coseley knows exactly what you are.'

Anna turned to the door, not missing the admiration in Philip's face as he opened it for her. 'Good afternoon,' she murmured.

'Mrs Royce!' Philip Rewcastle dismissed Joby with a shake of his head, walking with her along the drab corridor. 'I'm sorry about all this, I'm sure I can get my father to change his mind.'

'Oh, but I don't want him to!' Anna blinked, finding the daylight harsh after the gloom of the building. 'You see, I wouldn't stay in a house of his even if he paid me.'

'Which constituted his offer exactly or I don't know my father.'

'I must go.' Not by the flicker of an eyelid did Anna confirm the truth of what he said. 'My daughter will need feeding soon.'

'But where will you live? You must let me help you.'

'No!' She jerked her head upward. 'I will arrange for my things to be moved as soon as possible. There is nothing apart from clothing that I want from the house. I trust your father would not deny me that?'

'Mrs Royce.' Anna glanced at the hand touching her sleeve then up at his face.

That was what had been at the back of her mind since he had first stepped into his father's office. Philip Rewcastle had pale smooth skin, she noticed. Smooth and clear as a woman's.

'The house . . . is there a key? We will need to send someone round to make an inventory of the property.'

The word meant nothing to Anna but it didn't matter anymore what happened to it or to Edward's workshop. The only thing that hurt was the knowledge, despite her passionate threat of a few minutes before, that she would never be in a position to take revenge on Jacob Rewcastle.

'You called him right, me wench, Jacob Rewcastle is a bastard and more.' Maggie filled the pot for yet another cup of tea.

It was the only solace she could offer this girl who even

now refused herself the comfort of tears; she had strength, there was no denying that, but strength alone couldn't put food into her child's mouth.

'Well, I can't see Edward handing over King's Choice as easily as that.' Hester cradled her goddaughter. 'It might well be as old Rewcastle said, Edward was no businessman. But he was no fool neither.'

'Aye, wench,' Maggie's spoon rattled noisily against her cup as she stirred her tea, 'there's bin sharp practice somewheres and you can wager your man knew nowt of it.'

Hester placed the sleeping baby in the blanket-lined drawer standing on the floor beside the fireplace and stood looking at the tiny puckered face.

'Edward might have left a paper of some sort. Yer should at least look, Anna. It's not just you that Rewcastle is robbing.'

''Appen Essie could be right. Least ways we might have a little peace if you goes on up there and searches.'

Anna hadn't been back to the house she had shared with Edward since the afternoon of her visit to Jacob Rewcastle's offices, and she didn't want to go now. It had not been an all-consuming love she had had for Edward but they had been happy enough; he always so keen to please her, she secure in the knowledge he would always care for her. But now he was gone and she was back where she had been two years before, living in Maggie Fellen's house, only this time there were two children, two tiny lives who had their beginnings in her and whom she must find a way of keeping.

'There was the box.'

She had barely murmured it but Hester turned sharp hazel eyes on her.

'What box?'

'A wooden one, about that size.' Anna indicated with her hands. 'Different coloured woods made a pattern of flowers on the lid. Edward said his mother had had it as long as he could remember . . . but there are no papers in it, I'm sure.'

'Oh!' Light fading from her eyes Hester Cresswell dropped to a chair, her fingers drumming against the sparkling white cloth Maggie always used. 'But couldn't there have been another . . . say in Edward's workshop?'

'I didn't go in there all that often,' Anna admitted, 'but I wouldn't think so.'

'There's no good in thinking.' Hester stood up, pushing the chair back. 'You've got to look. C'mon, I'll go with you.'

'But you have to go back to work . . . we . . . we'll go tonight.'

'Oh no we won't! You ain't backin' out again, Anna Royce. I owe it to Misty to see you does all you can to get her father's rights. As for going to work, if I thought Jacob Rewcastle would go bankrupt 'cos of me not turning up for shift, I'd never go again.'

'Go on, Anna, leave little 'un. She'll be safe enough wi' me.'

Maggie began to collect the cups. Anna watched her place them on the cheap wooden tray. Maggie liked things nice. Her scrubbed table always wore a fresh clean cloth; her bits and pieces of furniture shone. Suddenly the tears she had denied so long welled into Anna's throat. God, she prayed silently, make it possible, no matter how hard. Let me find the way to pay Maggie Fellen for her kindness to me.

'Eee, Anna, that teks some believing.' Together the two girls walked along Roker Street, turning into the alley that linked it with Slater Street. Hester's clogs rattled loud against the blue-grey cobblestones. 'You sure it was Philip Rewcastle?'

'Of course I am, you've pointed him out to me often enough. Besides, he called Jacob "Father".'

'Aye, and no one would do that lessen they had to!' Hester giggled, wrinkling her nose. 'Poor little bugger. But yer sure he said he'd help?'

'He said I must let him help me,' Anna stated flatly, having already gone over the scene in the office more times than was necessary for Hester to get the picture. 'In fact, he seemed quite kind.'

'I've no doubt, but don't you be fooled by him, Anna. There's summat about that one I can't quite figure.'

'Like what?' She felt a stone bite through the worn sole of her shoe.

Edward had refused to allow her to wear clogs, her feet were too dainty to be subjected to those monstrosities, he'd said, but that was a nicety that would have to go.

'Like the men he goes around with.'

'What's wrong with them?' They turned into Slater Street. The house and workshop were right at the end, separated from the line of terraced houses by a wide area of derelict land.

'It would be more to the point if yer asked what's right wi' 'em.'

Anna, who had only seen Philip Rewcastle briefly at the mill before as he had walked through her own department, found herself wondering where else Hester had seen him.

'He was strange when he were a lad.' Hester linked an arm through Anna's. 'Accordin' to me mam, old Jacob wanted him to learn steel trade from bottom up, on shop floor so to speak, but it wasn't steel trade he wanted to learn. Oh, he was interested all right but only in the men he worked with.'

'Well, wasn't that a good sign, being interested in the men who would one day be his employees?'

'Oh, aye?'

Hester cocked her head sideways, a half-disbelieving look in the glance she directed at Anna. She wasn't that gullible surely? True Anna had none of the coarseness some of the girls at Rewcastle's had, their bawdy jokes usually passing over her head, but Philip Rewcastle . . .

'The business he was interested in had nowt to do wi' steel,' she finished, watching for Anna's reaction.

'Me mam wouldn't say much when us kids were around,' Hester went on when there was none, 'but after a while he went away to some posh school, I believe, and now he's back – and a couple of right queer characters he's brought with 'im.'

'Queer!' Anna's eyes were on the house.

'Aye, bloody queer. One of 'em fancied his chances last week. Came into the packing sheds, they did, Philip Rewcastle and one of his posh friends. Big bloke, and underneath his fancy clobber like to have a few muscles.' Hester caught the corner of her shawl the breeze had freed and held it across her breasts.

'Well, they was strollin' down the shed when this one stops behind me and touches my hair with his fingers. "What about this one, Phil, old chap?" he says, all bay-windowed. "Surely you must have fancied a romp in the hay with this one?"'

'And what did Philip say?' Even now Anna wasn't quite listening.

'"Oh, don't be so bloody stupid, Robert,"' Hester mimicked wickedly. '"You know I have no interest in that sort of thing."' Hester's laughter rang out scornfully.

They had reached the waste land and Anna felt herself shrink inside. She ought not to have come, there was nothing for her here.

'Philip Rewcastle went to walk on then,' Hester was not oblivious to the emotion tearing at Anna and kept fighting it the only way she knew, 'but this friend of his wasn't having any. He puts his fingers under my chin and asks, "What about you, my little pearl? What would you say to an offer like that?"'

'What *did* you say?'

'I told him to stick it up his arse!'

It was just the right thing to say. Anna's laughter joined Hester's, dispersing the ghosts of yesterday.

'Let's go in the back, through the workshop.' Anna pushed open the gate in the surrounding wall, leading the way up the path.

* * *

'I told you there would be nothing here.' They had spent an hour searching the wooden shelves and cupboards, finding nothing but the tools that had been Edward's father's.

'I think we should go.'

'Not yet, Anna, we have the house to search first.'

'But maybe Jacob Rewcastle has had everything taken out?'

Anna thought of the few articles of furniture she had kept so carefully polished. They too had been Edward's parents' and she felt sick that Jacob Rewcastle should have the selling of them.

'And maybe he hasn't.' Pulling her by the hand, Hester walked determinedly across the pocket handkerchief of yard that separated the workshop from the house, then through the scullery into the kitchen.

It was the same as she had left it. Nothing had been moved, nothing taken away.

'There's nothing in here,' Anna whispered in the silence, 'or I would have seen it when I fetched Misty's things.'

'It'll tek no hurt from looking again.' Hester's quick fingers pulled open drawers and, finding nothing, pushed them closed.

'C'mon, Anna, yer no help standing there like a statue.'

As Anna predicted, they found no papers either there or in the tiny front parlour that had been her pride and joy.

'Where's the box you spoke of?' Hester straightened the red chenille table-cloth with an automatic movement.

'Upstairs in our bedroom.' Anna felt the fear return. That was the room she'd shared with Edward. The door they had carried his crushed body home on had been laid on the bed they had slept in together. She couldn't go up there, she couldn't look at it again.

'I know, love,' Hester's eyes were oceans of pity, 'but think of Misty. If you can't do it for yourself, do it for her.'

Steadying herself against the table, Anna drew a long breath. Hester was right, of course, she had to try everywhere, if only for her daughter. She had one foot on the stairs when she heard it, a long pulsing moan.

'Christ! What does you reckon that was?'

'I don't know.' Her own fear matched Hester's. 'Probably nothing, these old houses creak a lot.'

'They might creak but I've never heard one moan afore!'

Overhead there was a bump and the scrape of wood against wood.

'It must be the men from Rewcastle's.' Relief surged through Anna. 'Philip said they would need to make an inventory.'

'I don't know what one of them might be.' Hester's young face hardened. She had heard the same sounds before from her parents' bedroom when they thought she and their Billy were asleep, the same breathy moans. There was somebody up there all right, but whatever they were doing in Anna's bedroom, they were not taking any inventory!

'Stay back of me,' she ordered, stepping out of her clogs.

Anna never could think of it in later years without a feeling of pity. To be found like that, and by two young women!

They made no sound on the stairs and the bedroom door was open. Hester pushed it wider still. Two naked bodies writhed together on the double bed. Smooth creamy arms twined about muscular shoulders, long fingers fastening into dark hair; two smooth legs spread creamy columns each side of those covered with short dark hairs and a bare bottom tautened with each grunting push.

'Oh, please!' It was half a sob as the hard jerking body ground into the one pinioned beneath it. 'Please, more . . . more.'

'I'll give yer more, yer dirty sod.' Hester stepped forward, the clog she held in her right hand slapping against bare buttocks.

The muscled body with its covering of fine dark hairs rolled sideways off the one beneath, and Anna stared. Swathes of sweat-soaked hair lay across smooth cheeks like streaks of dried blood; where the widespread legs joined, a tight-curled mass of the same colour formed a halo around a penis robbed now of strength or vigour. But it was the eyes that held her, amber eyes drowning in agony, the eyes of Philip Rewcastle.

'Well, well!' The muscular man propped himself lazily on one elbow, his throbbing penis jerking with newfound life he made no effort to hide. 'So you changed your mind, little pearl . . . and you have brought a friend. How thoughtful. Don't you think so, Phil?'

'Shut up, Robert!' Philip Rewcastle reached for a shirt lying on top of the tumbled heap of clothing on the floor beside the bed, draping it across himself as he sat up.

'Not shy, are we?' Robert splayed his legs slowly and deliberately. 'Don't hide it. Show the little ladies what they can have if they behave.'

Closing the fingers of his right hand about the throbbing tube he lifted it clear of his stomach holding it up like a baton. 'C'mon girls, which of you wants the first ride?'

'I told you once before what you could do with that.'

Anna listened remotely, as though in another world. A furious Hester wasn't shocked at what she saw; it was as if it was no more than she'd expected.

'Then what about your friend?' He continued to flaunt himself before them. 'I wouldn't mind the odd hour with you, girlie, and from the look of you you could do with a nice little present . . . besides this one, I mean.'

Anna felt sick. They were on her bed, hers and Edward's, defiling it with their unspeakable activities – and now he was asking her to join in.

'That's enough, Robert!' Philip found the courage to look at her. 'I'm sorry, Mrs Royce. To say this is unfortunate would be ludicrous. Instead I will only ask why you are here?'

'The box,' Anna stammered. 'I . . . we came for my box.'

'Where is your box?'

He was very gentle, almost as if he was the one to have

caught her in some dreadful act and was trying to reassure her there would be no punishment.

'In . . . in the drawer of the chest.'

'Then could I ask you to get it and then be good enough to leave? I would get it for you, but for me to move would cause you more embarrassment and you've had enough of that already.'

As if in the grip of some horrible nightmare, Anna walked across the room, pulled open the top drawer of the chest in the alcove below the only window, and took out the small wooden box. Walking back to where Hester still stood in the doorway, she averted her eyes from the men, one still sprawled blatantly across the bed.

'You really don't know what you're missing,' Robert said mockingly.

'Maybe she don't,' Hester bristled, gold specks flashing in her angry glare, 'but I do, mister. A dose of the clap, that's what she's missing!'

'Why, you bloody little snot! I'll break your dirty little neck for that!'

He jumped up but Philip Rewcastle was as quick, nakedness forgotten as he held the other man back, his tawny eyes fixed on Hester.

'You will go now,' he said tonelessly, 'and if you know what's good for you, you will say nothing of what you saw here this afternoon.'

'There weren't a lot to see.' Hester stared hard at her employer's son, scorning his nakedness. 'An' if you be threatenin' me, Philip Rewcastle, you needs bigger assets than that to do it with.'

Outside the sun warmed Anna, freeing her from the icy grip of shock.

Philip Rewcastle and the man he'd called Robert had been making love. She shivered, fingers trembling around the pretty inlaid box. It was unnatural, obscene. How could anybody bring themselves to do such a thing?

'Eee, never mind, love.' Hester put an arm through Anna's. 'A lot of strange things 'appen in life, and it's my guess we both have a lot more to see afore we are done. I did try to tell you about Philip Rewcastle. I guessed when you were tellin' me an' Maggie what 'appened t'other day in 'is old man's office that he 'ad more things in mind than 'elpin' you. 'Elpin' hisself more like!

'Can't you see, Anna? He only asked about a key to the 'ouse so he could hold on to it. That way he could 'ave a little love nest for 'im an' that Robert to go to, all locked in safe and sound. Only he forgot the way in through scullery. If that's all the sense them posh schools 'is father sent him to 'ave taught 'im, then I reckon old Rewcastle should get his money back.'

'But even in . . . in there he tried to be kind.' Anna shuddered, seeing again the streaks of sweat-soaked auburn hair across his pale skin; seeing again that smear of blood across her own breast.

'Aye,' Hester pulled her away, guiding her steps towards the alley, 'that's another of his little tricks, I reckon. Get 'imself into folks' good books. That way they either won't see 'is slimy ways or else will turn a blind eye to them. Either way Philip Rewcastle comes out on top.'

Hester grinned suddenly, the cheeky grin of a naughty schoolgirl that lit up her plain little face and deepened her hazel eyes to molten gold.

'But he didn't come out on top of 'is mate Robert, it was the other way round wi' that one. Mind you, Anna, when I told 'im to stick it up his arse, I didn't think he'd take me serious!'

Her tinkling laughter echoed off the sombre line of terraced houses, but Anna did not join in. Whatever Hester thought of Philip Rewcastle, she could feel only pity for him. How strange to feel pity for a man who had everything: money, education, a good background.

But Anna knew with awful certainty that, like herself, Philip Rewcastle had nothing.

Chapter Seven

Anna opened her faded purse, already knowing the paucity of its contents before she did so. It had been three months since Edward was killed and apart from the few pence the girls from the mill gave her for her face creams and hair rinses, there had been no money since.

She tipped the few copper coins into her hand. Scarcely enough to pay Maggie for her board and keep.

'Will you watch Misty for me, Maggie? I'm just going out, I won't be long.'

Reaching behind the door for her black coat, Anna left the house, still pushing her arms into its sleeves. The bell rang over the door of the dark little shop and the dank musty smell of decay swept into her nostrils as Anna stepped inside.

Sam Castleton shuffled forward, puffing from the effort. Suffering from a collapsed lung, the intense heat and sheer physical effort involved in working in the steel mills made his former employment impossible for him so he had opened a pawn shop at the rear of the general grocery stone run by his wife.

'Aye?' Sam asked, the sun behind the figure in the doorway turning it into a silhouette he could not recognise.

'It's me, Mr Castleton.' Closing the door, Anna walked across the dusty floor, pulling her wedding ring free from her finger. 'How much can you let me have against this?'

'Eee, Anna, I didna know it was you.' He picked up the ring, looking inside it for the hallmark. 'Still no work, wench?'

'Not yet, Mr Castleton. Rewcastle's don't want anybody, it seems, and apart from them there's little else in Coseley.'

'Aye, aye.' Sam nodded sympathetically.

This girl had had things hard, and according to talk in Bella's shop, word was old Rewcastle didn't want her given work anywhere, and there were not many in these parts would go against that old swine.

'It's a good ring . . . twenty-two carat. I could let you have three pounds.' It was over generous even for twenty-two carat for the ring wasn't heavy, but what the hell? If she never redeemed the pledge he was out of pocket. 'That do for you, me wench?'

'Yes . . . thank you, Mr Castleton.' Pushing the white ticket and three pound notes into her purse, Anna turned away. 'Say hello to Bella for me.'

'Aye, I will that.' Sam watched the pathetic figure in the black coat and skirt bought from his collection of unredeemed clothing and shook his head.

Coseley could hold only trouble for Anna Royce, old man Rewcastle would see to that.

Back in Maggie Fellen's kitchen, two young girls giggled nervously.

'This wench at work knows some of the wenches in packing sheds at Rewcastle's,' the shorter of them volunteered as Anna took off her coat. 'She said you would sell the two of us some if we came. Eee, Mrs Royce, I 'opes you don't think it a cheek, our comin' to the 'ouse like?'

'No cheek.' Maggie stirred the fire beneath the kettle then reached for the cups on the dresser, her starched petticoats rustling. 'Shy wenches get nowt. If you wants anything, ask for it, I always say.'

'Aye, Mrs Fellen, me mam says that an' all.' The tall and lanky girl smiled, showing good teeth. 'But Chrissy an' me felt a bit awful like, coming to the house.'

'Nobody need feel awful about coming to Maggie Fellen's.'

Cups rattled busily on saucers. 'If I don't want 'em in then I tells 'em to leave.'

'Was it me you came to see?' The three pounds in her purse making her feel a little happier, Anna smiled at the giggling girls, clutching each other's hands in a state of delicious excitement. Had she ever felt as these two did now?

'Aye, Mrs Royce.' The girl called Chrissy spoke up. 'We . . . we'd like to buy some of that there face cream you 'as. Everybody says 'ow lovely it is . . . does wonders for the skin, so they say.'

'I don't think either of you girls needs face cream. You both have lovely complexions.'

'Oh!'

Anna saw disappointment chase laughter from two pairs of eyes. She had told them the truth and ruined their day by doing so.

'However,' she added, salvaging their happiness, 'you need to take care of it if you want to keep it.'

From Maggie's front room she fetched two small white pots, handing one to each girl.

'After you have washed your face, smooth in just a little of this.'

'Eee, it smells just grand.' Chrissy removed the lid, pressing her pert nose to the contents of the pot. 'Ta, Mrs Royce.'

'Yes, ta, Mrs Royce.' Chrissy's friend smiled her delight. ''Ow much do we owe you?'

'Oh, er . . . just leave something for the baby.' Anna hated taking money for anything she made.

'Mrs Royce!' About to cross Maggie's newly whitened front step, the lanky girl looked back at Anna. 'Benjie Freeth 'as just 'ad a big order come in. I heard me dad tellin' our mam last night. 'Appen he might be able to use somebody . . . that's if yer wants a job?'

'I was told you might have a vacancy, Mr Freeth?'

Anna had followed the two girls out of Maggie's kitchen,

hurrying to the little brick workshop standing in the shadow of the huge steel-rolling mills.

Benjamin Freeth, the circular cap that marked his Jewish faith fitting the crown of his head like a saucer, lifted his shoulders.

'So people know already! Time was when a man could have a minute to breathe in Coseley, but now . . .' He shrugged his shoulders again.

'If I was told wrongly, I apologise for disturbing you.' Anna shifted uncomfortably, feeling the rough floor against the soles of her feet. On the way home she would call in Bella Castleton's shop for a cardboard box and cut another couple of insoles for her boots. They were going to have to fight the good fight for a while yet.

'So I'm disturbed already.' A perpetually harassed face creased into a semblance of a smile. 'But to be disturbed by such a pretty face should count among a man's blessings.'

Miraculously finding a chair from beneath a welter of wood shavings, he brushed it clean with a thin hand, indicating Anna to sit down.

'Mine is not a large place, it pleased the good Lord that Benjamin Freeth didn't make it big, but thanks to Him at least I eat every day.'

Tucking his thumbs through the shoulder straps of the coarse carpenter's apron that reached almost to his boots, he watched Anna trying desperately to keep disappointment from showing in her face. He knew from her speech she was not from Coseley and from her clothing that she wasn't finding it easy.

'I couldn't pay a large wage and I could only take you for four days a week.'

Even then he would be stretching his resources, but if the good Lord hadn't stretched out His hand and sent His servant Moses to bring the children of Israel out of bondage there would be no Benjamin Freeth, Cabinet Maker, to give a job to anybody.

'Four days a week would suit me very well, Mr Freeth. Thank you. Thank you very much indeed.'

'I have a job, my darling.' Anna bent over the small truckle bed beside her own where Misty lay sleeping, one arm thrust free from the covers.

He had slept in that same way, Anna remembered, her heart jerking. Almost from birth he had fought to free his arms from the blanket she wrapped him in.

Climbing into bed, she watched the play of moonlight across her bedroom window, seeming to feel again the tug on her nipple, the tiny down-covered head nuzzling her breast. Did her son still refuse to have his arms placed beneath the bed covers? Was his hair still the colour of ripe corn, his eyes as blue as she remembered?

'Oh, my love,' she whispered, turning her face into the pillow, the pain in her heart crushing the breath from her body, 'my little love, I want you so much . . .'

'It doesn't pay as much as Rewcastle's,' Anna explained, cutting the cardboard box Bella Castleton had given her into shape and fitting the new soles inside her boots, 'but then, I will only be working four days. Mr Freeth said he always goes into Birmingham on a Friday. Something about there being no synagogue in Coseley and Saturday being the Jewish Sabbath he's not allowed to work. Seeing there is nobody other than him to supervise the place, I can't work those days either. But it's better than nothing, Maggie, if . . .'

'If what?' Maggie Fellen had listened quietly.

'It . . . it's a lot to ask, Maggie. Are you sure you can manage? Babies can be hard work.'

'Aye,' Maggie's grey stare remained level, 'and are you saying Maggie Fellen is past it?'

'You know I'm not.' Anna flung both arms round the older woman's neck, resting her head against the rich brown hair.

'But I love you, Maggie. You and Misty are my life and I don't want to risk your overdoing things.'

Her arms tightening, Anna pressed her face deeper into Maggie's brown hair. 'I couldn't go on without you,' she whispered. But I have to go on without my son, she added silently.

'*The girl you desired for so long is yet to come . . .*' Kate O'Keefe's prophetic words circled Maggie's mind '. . . *yours will be the caring of it.*' She would have the caring of Anna's child; would to God it had been under different circumstances.

'Thirty shillings a week isn't going to provide any luxuries but it will keep us, Maggie, and we should be thankful.'

'I could manage on less than a pound a week, Anna, I've always told you so.'

'I paid you a pound when there was just me.' Anna moved to the corner by the fireplace looking down at the face of her sleeping daughter. 'I won't pay you less now there's two of us.'

'The child teks no keepin'. You 'as 'er on the breast.'

'And you do just about everything else for her, and will do even more now I've got a job.'

'You could always send a bit less for the other 'un.'

'No, Maggie.' Anna bent to hook a finger into the curling fist of the baby. 'He can never know what I feel for him. I left a part of myself behind when I left my son. He'll never know my touch or my face but I'll not deny him money to keep him fed. Whatever happens, Maggie, I must send that. I . . . can't give him anything else.'

'I understand, love. Don't worry. While Maggie Fellen lives, neither you nor yer little 'uns will go short. Anna . . .' Maggie looked at her closely. 'Do you remember that night Kate O'Keefe read the tea cups in Mary Cresswell's kitchen?'

'Yes.'

'Well, she wasna quite right in what she said. She said I would 'ave the daughter denied my 'eart and mine would be the carin' of it, but she didna say I would 'ave *two* daughters. Misty is the daughter of my heart and I love her as my own, but even that is not the sort of love I bear 'er mother. That one is the daughter of my soul.'

Anna didn't move. Sunk on her haunches, her finger held in the tiny fist of her baby, she at last allowed the tears to flow.

'I don't know what time they will come, Anna.' Benjamin Freeth picked up the beautiful inlaid mahogany box, blowing any last speck of dust from its ivory velvet lining. A lot hung on whether the box met with the approval of the people he was expecting. Anna knew it was to be part of a presentation but to whom and just what it was to hold remained a mystery to her.

'Relax, Mr Freeth, they can only love this. It's the most beautiful one you've made, I'm sure.'

'Yes, Anna, it is the most beautiful. But then, it is to be given to the most important in the land so it is right it should be so.'

'You know,' Anna looked up from the table where she had been polishing the lovely casket, 'Maggie Fellen has a saying: "When a man has done his best, he can look anyone in the eye with pride."'

'Anna,' Benjamin smiled the slow smile that seemed to take an hour to stretch across his fine drawn face, 'that Maggie Fellen, she must be one smart woman.'

'Hello . . . Mr Freeth?'

Benjamin went to greet the new arrival.

'You cut it pretty damn' fine,' he shouted, 'them from London could be here already.'

Anna turned to watch, hoping he would greet his London visitors less irately, then felt a sudden chill touch her. The man handing a large box to Benjamin Freeth worked at Rewcastle's Mill.

'Stop yer fussin'. I couldn't get 'ere afore I was sent, could I?' The man pushed the box hard against Benjamin's chest.

'Seein' they 'aven't arrived yet, yer still 'as time to get that lot tarted up.'

Mumbling under his breath, Benjamin carried the box to the tiny room where Anna worked.

'This is what we've waited for, Anna, it should have been delivered already but . . .' He lifted his shoulders in protest. 'But who is Benjamin Freeth that folks should hurry? Check them, Anna, I don't want the tiniest speck or blemish. Benjamin Freeth, Cabinet Maker, does not supply boxes to hold goods of inferior quality. The best, Anna, that is what this must be. The best.'

'I'll be very careful,' she said, conscious of the old man's pride in his work. 'I'll go over every one.'

He shuffled out, leaving her to untie the string. Inside brown paper several tissue-wrapped articles nestled together. Peeling back the soft white paper, Anna stared at the beautiful hand-made knife . . . she had just unwrapped the first of King's Choice.

Anna laid the rest out before her, the complete range of flatware exactly as Edward had designed them; elegant handles flaring slightly at the bottom housed an intricate crest then flowed in classic lines to the bowls of spoons, the prongs of forks. Each piece was a masterpiece. Some craftsman had turned Edward's dream into golden reality, one he would never see. Edward Royce had poured his very life into the making of King's Choice and now he was dead.

'I took the liberty of bringing Lord Kenmore, Benjamin, seeing as how you might find it inconvenient to leave your workshop.'

Anna pressed the last spoon into place with a vicious movement.

Jacob Rewcastle! She should have known he wouldn't be far away; that was why King's Choice had been brought here instead of the lovely presentation box Benjamin had made being taken to Rewcastle's Mill. Jacob would want no hint that he was involved. It must seem that the project was still in the hands of the small producers it was meant to help. That way royal approval would be retained and King's Choice would be sold all over the world.

'But I never expected . . . you should have warned me, Mr Rewcastle. The place is not fit.' Benjamin's guttural accent thickened with anxiety.

A voice Anna did not recognise intervened brusquely.

'Nonsense. It was His Majesty's wish that we see where all the pieces were made . . . that includes the box.

'Now I would like to see the article to be presented, if I may?'

The cultured voice came nearer and Anna closed the lid of the casket, giving it one last quick wipe.

'Your clothes . . . they will be soiled,' Benjamin protested. 'I will bring it out here, there is more room.'

'Clothes are of no consequence.' In his elegant dark alpaca coat worn knee-length over pin stripe trousers, a silk waistcoat covering his brilliantly white shirt, Lord Kenmore strode into the tiny room at the end of Benjamin Freeth's factory. 'Is this the gift?'

Lifting the silver-topped malacca cane he carried in one gloved hand, he tapped the mahogany inlaid lid Anna had just wiped.

'It is, Your Lordship.' Jacob Rewcastle could not fit into the tiny room.

'Mmm.' Lord Kenmore ignored Anna, squeezed tight into corner. 'His Majesty will be pleased. My dear . . .'

He held out one hand stepping backward into piles of Benjamin's carelessly strewn templates, and handed a woman into the constricted space.

'If you will permit, Lady Strathlyn, I will leave you to make your decision. I wish to speak to Mr Rewcastle and Mr Freeth.'

'Of course, I will join you presently.'

Anna had seen fine dresses displayed in the windows of the shops in Birmingham and covers of magazines showing elegant models, but her mouth opened in admiration of the woman Lord Kenmore handed into the tiny workroom.

She wore a lavender silk twill three-quarter-length coat frogged down the front and with slightly padded sleeves corded in amethyst. The straight skirt worn beneath was of the same colour. On her dark head she wore a small lavender grosgrain hat, amethyst feather trimming shading at the tips to mauve. And even in the Birmingham shops Anna had never seen the like of these shoes! Pointed toes, cut low across the foot, small square heel . . . they were the exact colour of the hat, and covered in lavender lacework patterns picked out with tiny brilliants of amethyst and mauve.

'This is King's Choice?' she asked, touching the box with a lavender-gloved hand.

'Yes . . . yes, it is, ma'am.' Anna bobbed a nervous curtsy. Was that the proper way to address a lady as obviously grand as this one?

'Her Majesty asked if I would try holding them. Some cutlery causes her discomfort.' The woman touched a finger of one hand to the palm of the other. 'Her Majesty has a very small hand.' Then, when Anna did not move, added, 'Would you be kind enough to show it to me?'

Awestruck by the grandeur of the woman, Anna moved awkwardly, bumping against the table. Wisps of wood shavings curled into the air, floating on to the lovely coat, but the woman paid no heed.

'These are exquisite!' she breathed.

The rose blush of Britannia gold glistened against ivory velvet. Edward would have been so proud. Anna lifted a knife from its retaining slot, holding it towards Benjamin's distinguished visitor.

'Perfect.' Lady Strathlyn curled one gloved hand around it, holding it as though about to cut. 'A perfect fit. Her Majesty will find no discomfort in using these, I am sure.'

'Will Your Ladyship try the rest?' Anna took back the knife, laying it among its golden family.

'There is no need. The man who is responsible for the creation of King's Choice is a master of his craft. Their precision and balance, the way they fit into the hand, makes me feel their design was more than just a labour of the brain. Something of the heart is there also.'

'A great deal of his heart.'

'Oh!' Lady Strathlyn heard Anna's murmur. 'You know the designer?'

'He . . . he was my husband.'

'Was?' Cool blue eyes looked straight at Anna.

'Edward died, ma'am.' Anna touched a finger to the box holding the cutlery that was to be a royal gift. 'Before King's Choice was produced.'

'I see. So now you work for Mr Freeth?'

'Yes, Ma'am.'

'Mmm.' Lady Strathlyn glanced at the unpainted walls, the heaps of templates and layers of wood dust covering everything. 'I wonder . . . how do you keep your skin looking so clear and manage to have a real shine in your hair in all this dirt? I find it difficult enough in the palace or my own home. But here . . .' She patted her immaculate coiffure. 'Tell me what magic you use.'

Anna blushed at the compliment.

'I . . . I just use herbal preparations, Your Ladyship. Creams and rinses I make myself.'

They were interrupted by the return of Lord Kenmore and with a slight nod of her dark head Lady Strathlyn left Anna, who did not quite believe what had happened.

'What the devil . . .?' Jacob Rewcastle, coming to collect the box of cutlery, stopped at the sight of Anna. 'What the bloody hell are you doing here?'

'I work here, Mr Rewcastle.' Anna's voice kept an even tone though her heart lurched violently. Any meeting with Coseley's mill owner could only mean trouble for her.

'Do you now!' The piggy eyes became almost invisible. 'And just how long have you been working here?'

'Three weeks.'

'You'll not work another three, that I'll guarantee.' Snatching up the mahogany casket, he stared at her narrowly. 'In fact, Anna Royce, you'll work nowhere the hand of Jacob Rewcastle can reach.'

It was less than three as he had predicted. One week after collecting the presentation box from the workshop of Benjamin Freeth, Jacob Rewcastle bought him out.

'Like my Naomi says, Anna,' Benjamin told her, tears running down his thin cheeks, 'the business . . . we have no child to leave it to and we are both old already. "So sell it, Benjie," she tells me. "Sell it and stay home with your Naomi."' He lifted his shoulders in his predictable shrug. 'And that Jacob Rewcastle . . . sheeesh! A man can do without the trouble he can cause. I'm sorry, Anna, but what else could I do? If I refused to sell he would get a cabinet maker somewhere else and I would still be out of business. But with no money to show for it.'

'Don't worry, Mr Freeth.' Anna fastened her worn black coat and shoved a long hairpin through the black hat, fastening it to her piled up hair. 'I'll find work.'

The trouble was, she thought, walking home with her last thirty shillings, where was she going to find it?

The potatoes peeled and set in a pan against the fire, Anna stirred a spoonful of plain flour into half a cup of cold water. Taking the huckaback cloth from the side of the fireplace, she lifted out the tin tray. Maggie had made faggots this morning. Now Anna poured the flour and water mixture into the pan, stirring it into the juices of herbs and meat. Returning the tray to the oven, she carried the utensils to the scullery for washing.

The meal would be ready when Maggie returned from next door. She liked a chat with Mary Cresswell and Anna had insisted she go this afternoon, just for an hour or so. It would be a change for her not to have to be responsible for Misty. It had not been easy dashing home to breast feed the baby at noon and again at four o'clock, then dashing back to Freeth's, but Benjamin had been very good to her, never complaining if she were a few minutes late. Anna sighed, drying the little pot jug she had mixed the flour and water in. It hadn't been easy, but managing without the meagre wages he'd paid was going to be a sight harder.

A knock sounded through the silent house. Startled, Anna hurried back to the kitchen. Nobody ever knocked in Roker Street. The knock sounded again and Anna held aside the long chenille curtain, pulling the door open at the same time.

'Good afternoon . . . Mrs Royce?'

'Yes?' Anna answered a woman tastefully dressed in brown gabardine edged with a piping of cream braid matching her well-polished brown shoes. This was a woman she hadn't seen before.

'Oh, good!' She seemed relieved. 'My daily woman said you lived here. You . . . you are the lady that makes face creams, aren't you?'

'Please, won't you come in?' Anna remembered her manners.

'Thank you.' The woman stepped into the kitchen, her glance flicking around the neat room.

'It's my daughter's sixteenth birthday in a few days, Mrs Royce, and I would like to give her a little extra present. I know girls of that age like to experiment with cosmetics so I prefer her to have something safe and I have heard such good things of yours. Would you sell me some? A little cleanser perhaps. I . . . I don't know very much about that sort of thing.'

'It's a bit difficult, Mrs . . .'

'Paget. Lorna Paget. We live on the other side of Coseley, Wood Green Road.'

'Will you sit down, Mrs Paget?' Anna offered her a chair. 'As I said, it is difficult for me to sell you creams when I don't know your daughter's skin type. Is it dry or perhaps a little oily?'

'Does it make a difference, Mrs Royce?'

'I'm afraid it does.' Anna looked at the well-scrubbed face of her visitor.

The woman had probably never used more than the odd dab of rosewater in her life but was forward-looking enough to realise the same would not do for her daughter.

Over a cup of tea Anna carefully gleaned the information she needed, and when she offered to deliver the appropriate creams, Lorna Paget smiled gratefully.

'That would be very kind, Mrs Royce. Shall we say Thursday afternoon?'

Wood Green Road was a quiet tree-lined place. Houses here were built in twos but sometimes one house would stand alone in its own well-tended gardens. There were no long rows of terraces, their front doors standing next to the footpath; no perpetual grey blanket of smoke hanging above them; and no sentinel mills standing black and threatening on the skyline.

It must be wonderful to live in a place like this. Anna studied the houses hungrily. Here a child could play while filling its lungs with clean air, instead of the fumes of the steel mills the kids of Roker Street grew up with.

Number twenty-four was a neat, green-painted semi-detached, with white lace curtains closed decorously across the bay window. Turning into the neat flower-bordered drive, Anna felt sharp gravel bite through the thin layers of cardboard she had put in her boots and wondered if she ought to go round the back. That was the usual entrance for tradesmen.

But having already reached the front door she decided against it. The less crunching about on this gravel, the less her feet would suffer. Before she could change her mind she rang the brass bell.

A young lass in ankle-length black skirt, white long-sleeved blouse buttoned high up her throat, a small lace cap on her bright hair matching the starched apron, showed Anna into Mrs Paget's front parlour.

'This is most kind of you, Mrs Royce.'

Anna had wrapped her parcel in a sheet of brown paper Bella Castleton had given her, careful to place the black printed words 'Morton's Finest Quality Sewing Threads' on the inside. Now she waited while Mrs Paget unwrapped it.

'Oh, Mrs Royce, this is so beautiful . . . you must have spent so much time on it.'

She had. Anna smiled ruefully, remembering Maggie's disapproving sniff when she had decided the pretty inlaid box that had been Edward's mother's would hold the creams and rinses she had made for this woman's daughter. But Anna knew Edward would have taken the same pleasure she had in using the box to make a young girl happy.

Mrs Paget lifted the tiny glass jars from their separate compartments, removing the stoppers and sniffing the contents, reading the labels Joby Timmins had written in flowing copperplate script before easing them gently back into the boxes and closing the lids.

'Mrs Royce,' she said, brown eyes tear bright, 'I don't think this is the usual way you package your preparations. It is my belief that this . . .' she rested her hand on the pretty wooden box, '. . . was something that meant a lot to you, and I know the reason behind your giving it away. You wanted to please a young girl you have never even met, to make her birthday more pleasurable by giving her something she can keep and treasure. I won't forget this, Mrs Royce.'

'Five pounds, Maggie! Mrs Paget paid me five pounds!' Anna had run almost the whole way back to Roker Street and now she sat at Maggie's table staring at the white five-pound note. 'That's almost as much as I got in wages for a month at Rewcastle's or at Benjie Freeth's.'

'Aye, wench,'er paid you well. And you can add this to it.'

Maggie reached beneath her white apron, pulling a handful of coins from the pocket of her black skirt.

'While you was away I've 'ad no less than five wenches 'ere, all after buyin' your creams.'

Counting the coins, Anna was amazed to find they totalled almost fifteen shillings. Together with the five pounds Mrs Paget had paid her, she and Maggie would be able to manage for at least four, maybe even five weeks if she were careful, and she could still send money for her son.

'Your mother is very rich, Misty.' Anna dropped a kiss on the head of her sleepy daughter. 'Five pounds fifteen shillings, and it's all ours.'

'Anna . . . I've bin meaning to talk to you for some time now.' Maggie filled the pot from the steaming kettle on the polished hob. 'Sit you down and we'll have a cup of tea.'

'Is anything wrong?' Happiness drained from Anna. 'You're not ill, Maggie?'

'Eee, 'course not! Can't a body 'ave a conversation unless it be from their death bed? I've got summat to say an' I reckon now's as good a time as any to say it.'

She poured the hot brown liquid into china cups. She never could abide those thick pottery mugs big enough to hold half a pint. A woman felt more like a woman drinking her tea from a dainty cup. Anna took hers, adding milk and sugar, stirring too long.

'It's this way, me wench.' Maggie Fellen's grey stare was candid. 'Old man Rewcastle 'as a down on you and intends that nobody in Coseley will give you a job. So the way I look at it is this – it's time you worked for yourself.'

'But how, Maggie . . . doing what?' Perplexed, Anna's brows drew together.

'Wait.' Going across to the fireplace, Maggie lifted down a cocoa tin from the shelf above.

Anna dropped the money the girls paid for her creams into this tin, always a little too embarrassed to count it.

'How long has it been since you looked in there?'

Anna glanced at the chocolate-coloured tin. 'I haven't . . . I mean, I don't . . .'

'Exactly!' Maggie took a triumphant sip of tea, an unreadable expression lurking in the depths of her steady gaze. 'Well, you'd better look now.'

Slightly bemused by the turn her homecoming had taken, Anna eased off the lid, emptying the contents of the tin on to the white cloth. Sorting the coins, she stacked them, silver and copper. Pennies, halfpennies, threepenny bits, sixpences, shillings and florins, sprouted up from the cloth like brown and silver stalks.

'Good God!' Anna leaned back against the chair. 'I had no idea there was so much. It comes to almost eight pounds. I couldn't possibly have made all that.'

'Well, there's no way I could 'ave made it an' it don't grow on trees despite what fairy tales tell you. Anyway that's not the finish of it, y'ave made more than that.'

This time Maggie went upstairs, returning with an oblong cigar box.

'I got this from the carter,' she said, placing it at Anna's elbow. 'He asked if I'd took up smokin'.'

'The carter . . . but why?'

''Cos if I'd asked Bella Castleton for one 'er'd 'a wanted to know the top and bottom of what I wanted it for.'

'And what did you want it for?'

'To keep your brass in. It were gettin' over much for that piddlin' little tin o' your'n.'

Maggie tipped up the box and Anna gasped as gas light gleamed on gold sovereigns, silver crowns, half crowns and florins, all tumbling together in a glittering miser's hoard of coins.

'Maggie,' she croaked at last, 'where in God's name did this come from?'

'It's your'n, girl, all on it. I thought you had no idea 'ow much them creams of your'n was bringing so I took it out of that tin a little at a time and put it under my bed against a rainy day.'

'But all that, Maggie?' Anna whispered, afraid to touch the glistening heap. 'I couldn't have made that much.'

'Look, Anna.' Maggie sat down, facing her across the table that half-filled her tiny kitchen. 'You don't be knowin' what a winner you be on. Whoever taught you 'ow to make lotions and the like gave you a rare gift. Use it wisely, Anna, and you could kiss Roker Street goodbye.'

The gas jet spluttered and the yellow light dimmed then flared steadily, tinting Maggie Fellen's rich brown hair bronze.

'Look, wench, I told you at the start, there's no way you will be given work in Coseley or close by. Old Rewcastle has shit on you but by God 'e'll not wipe his arse on you an' all. Tek the money, wench, and set up for yourself. Keep your head low an' you'll be all right.'

'But, Maggie, this money . . . I know it's quite a sum but is it enough? And will my creams continue to sell? I think the girls at the mill only bought them because they felt sorry for me.'

'Don't be so bloody daft!' Maggie exploded. 'Brass is too bloody 'ard come by an' folk about 'ere gi' nowt away. If they buy owt it's because they want it. And think on this . . . if women 'ereabouts buy a thing it better be good or they tek it back and wrap it round throat of the bugger that sold it. An' I 'aven't heard you choking yet.'

Pushing the heap of coins towards Anna, Maggie smiled. It had hit the girl right between the eyes and she needed a minute to take it all in.

'Try it, wench,' she said minutes later when Anna's eyes showed understanding. 'Tek your money and get the things you need. My front room will serve as a shop if you sets up a few shelves. That way you won't need to splash out on hiring premises. And,' Maggie smiled widely, 'that way, if you falls then your arse won't get bruised so badly.'

'Mrs Fellen!' Reaching across the table, Anna took Maggie's rough hands into her own. 'I have heard more swear words from you tonight than I ever thought you knew.'

'Aye,' Maggie twinkled, 'an' you be like to hear more if you don't heed what I've said.'

'I'll heed you, Maggie.' Anna's face softened into tears. 'And you heed me. I love you, Maggie Fellen . . . I love you very much.'

Chapter Eight

Brushing her wealth of red-gold hair high on her head, Anna skewered it with pins then settled her black hat firmly with a long pearl-topped hat pin.

The deep green suit Edward had purchased for their wedding had been sold in order to buy the black skirt and coat she'd needed for his burying; the skirt and coat that had just received yet another pressing. She must look her best for what she was about to do.

It was six months since Maggie had shown her the money her cosmetics had made. Turning the front room into a shop had cost them nothing. William Cresswell had been coaxed into leaving his beloved pigeons and with his son's help a row of shelves had appeared in no time. Anna had resisted Hester's advice to paint them shocking pink, settling instead for a delicate shade of beige. Plenty of pretty lace, ruched and tied, turned the shelves into inner window displays, holding a select few of the products for sale. Replacing the chenille door curtain with a piece of bright yellow cotton Bella Castleton found for her, Anna had trimmed it with a froth of lace tied with a huge satin bow. Mary and Maggie had insisted they too were going to help and did so by washing the floor free from paint splashes and serving far too many cups of tea.

Anna fastened her coat. Maggie was minding the shop so there was no hurry. Outside the wind whipped about her legs, cutting through the thin coat, and she was glad she had used some of the recent profits to buy a new pair of button boots.

At least her feet would stay dry. The train seemed to take forever to get to Birmingham but once there Anna wasted no time. After posting off the monthly two pounds for her son, she strode along the main street until she came to the little shop, sandwiched between Monsieur Pierre, A-la-Mode Gowns and Beatrice, High Class Milliner. She heaved a sigh of relief. The premises were still to rent. Reading the notice in the window, Anna asked directions, finally reaching the address in Rooth Street.

Abraham Fine listened to her proposal to rent his shop for six months, bright eyes taking in her shabby appearance.

'You say you come from Coseley, Mrs Royce?' he asked when she finished.

Anna's happiness faded. Did Jacob Rewcastle's influence stretch as far as Birmingham?

'Forgive me if I seem impertinent,' he went on in his slightly guttural voice, 'but is it Anna . . . Anna Royce?'

'Yes, Mr Fine, I am Anna Royce.' If he was going to refuse to let her hire his premises then he might as well get it over with. Anna's eyes held his rheumy blue ones. She had survived worse disappointments.

'Then you know my good friend Benjie Freeth?' He smiled. 'A friend of Benjie Freeth's is a friend of Abraham Fine's. The shop is yours, Anna . . . do we sign a paper?'

She hardly heard the babble of voices in the third-class compartment on the way home. She had taken the first step.

In the six months of using Maggie's front room she had made enough profit to put what was left after living expenses into acquiring a second shop. Anna looked at her reflection in the window of the railway carriage. The shabby hat with its veil lifted off her face. The sparkling white cotton blouse fastened high about her neck . . . a blouse that was almost threadbare. But she was Anna Royce, a woman going places. She twisted her wedding ring, redeemed from the pawn shop, remembering her threat to Jacob Rewcastle. Her mouth set in a hard, determined line. Maybe he was not beyond her reach after all.

'But you went to Birmingham last week, you can't want to go again?' Maggie Fellen shook her head. 'An' I certainly won't go gallivantin' off on no train.'

Anna had been to Birmingham only the week before and Abraham Fine had done all he'd promised. Following her little sketch faithfully, the men he'd hired had made the shop ready in two days and she had placed her pots and jars in the lace-trimmed alcoves. Now everything was ready for her big surprise.

'Please, Maggie, just for me. I want to buy myself some new clothes and I'd like you to be there. Please come, Maggie . . . please?'

'I never could refuse you anythin', Anna, an' I'm still as daft. But what about Misty?'

'Mary Cresswell will keep an eye on her, she said as much.'

'You've got things nicely sorted out, ain't you, wench?'

I hope so, Anna breathed silently. I certainly hope so.

'I didn't know you was comin', Essie.' Maggie, feet feeling less than her own in the shoes kept against weddings and funerals, walked between the two younger women, her dark grey gabardine coat and long skirt smelling of mothballs.

'Aye, Mrs Fellen. Anna said I should see the shops in Birmingham and I agreed. Me mam says it's a waste of good brass train ridin' to Birmingham – but eee, I be that excited! It feels like Sunday school outing when we were kids.'

Sunday school outing! Anna glanced away. She and Peter had laughed so much on their last Sunday school trip when he had given her a necklace of pink ribbon with a paper diamond and she had worn it, as proud as the Queen of England. But what good were paper diamonds?

'My feet be killing me. Y'ave traipsed me all over the place and still you ain't bought anything,' Maggie complained.

They had stared in windows and walked in and out of shops most of the afternoon, Anna holding tight to her secret, wanting the moment to last.

'What about a nice cup of tea?' she relented, seeing the crease between Maggie's brows. 'I know a place where they make it just the way you like it.' She pushed a hand beneath the older woman's arm. 'And no one will see if you push those shoes off while you drink it.'

'Eee, Anna!' Hester's head swivelled with each shop they passed. 'I never thought there were places like this. Some of them are big enough to swallow half Roker Street.'

Anna laughed. She had thought the same on her first visit.

'There's one more I want you to see, Hester. It's not a big shop but I think you will like it.'

'Not until I've 'ad my cup of tea and five minutes sit down,' Maggie admonished vehemently. 'Your feet be younger than mine. You two could go on all day but I need a rest or you'll be carryin' me back to that train.'

'You can have your tea, Maggie.' Anna halted, pointing across the street to the elegant lettering painted in gold above a lace-draped window: Anna Royce. 'You can have it in there,' she said.

'Well?' Anna had made the tea in the tiny room at the back of the shop while her companions inspected every corner of it. 'What do you think?'

'Think!' Hester did another round of the prettily flounced shelves then perched on one of the spindly velvet-covered chairs. 'It's lovely, Anna, really lovely. Did you design all this yourself?'

'Yes, I sketched it out the day I hired the place from Mr Fine but it was he who got everything done for me. I just arranged the jars and pots.'

'Eee, Anna, who'd 'a thought it? Anna Royce with 'er own shop.'

'It would never have happened without Maggie.' Anna put an arm around the spare shoulders. 'She showed me the way.'

'You just needed a push, me wench.' Maggie bent over her tea.

'Stand behind the counter, Hester, I want to see what it would be like to be a customer.'

Anna stepped outside and when she re-entered Hester stood smiling behind the gleaming mahogany counter.

'Good afternoon, madam.' She inclined her mousy head just a touch. 'Welcome to Anna Royce.'

'Perfect!' Anna clapped her hands, happiness gleaming in the depths of her green eyes. 'I knew you would be. Hester, I would like you to run this shop for me. I'm asking you to leave Rewcastle's Mill and work for me here in Birmingham. It will mean a train ride night and morning but . . . but this is only the beginning, Hester. I intend to make a go of this cosmetics business. I intend Anna Royce to go a long way and I'd like you to come with me. You will have full control here and answer to none but me in anything you do. Will you do it, Hester?'

'I'll start on Monday . . . an' Rewcastle's can sing for a week's notice!'

Jacob Rewcastle. He must not find out why Hester was leaving the mill. If he did, she could say goodbye to her dream.

'Don't tell them you are coming to work for me, will you, Hester? You know how Mr Rewcastle would enjoy closing me down before I started.'

'I'll think of something, Anna.' Hester came out from behind the counter. 'Eee, fancy! Me, manageress of a real shop. It makes a right fine birthday present.'

'Of course!' Anna said, remembering. 'It's your birthday soon, isn't it?'

'Aye, I'll be twenty next month . . . eee, Anna!' Hester clamped a hand to her mouth. 'Does you remember?'

'I do!' Maggie Fellen regarded them both with steady grey

eyes. 'Kate O'Keefe said that a month afore you saw your twentieth year you would leave mill. You would be mistress in your own place and answerable to one woman only.

'Do you still think Kate's reading of the cups is just a bit of fun, Hester Cresswell?'

Chapter Nine

Anna loosed the button at the throat of her white cotton blouse, feeling the cool air touch her breasts beneath the thin covering. Her worn black skirt was heavy about her ankles and for one mad moment she wanted to tear it off, to fling it away together with her petticoats, and run, feeling the wind on her body.

The moor was a vast ocean of green with tiny wavelets of wild flowers cresting the grass that bent and swayed, first silver, then green, in the ebb and flow of the gentle breeze. How she would love to bring her son to the moor, to see him run with his sister over the soft grass, to watch him pick flowers for Misty as Peter had picked them for her. How she would love . . .

But Anna knew she could not claim the son she had given into the care of his father, she could not hold him in her arms. But she would always hold him in her heart, in her very soul.

As the pain of remembering pulled at her, Anna stared across the wide moor to where Coseley lay, a dark smudge against the landscape. Coseley and Wednesbury, both so alike, both bringing happiness and pain to Anna Royce.

She no longer came often to the moor, the thoughts such visits conjured being harder to bear each time. A herbalist now supplied the oils and essences of the plants she'd once picked, but when she could Anna still liked to gather some for herself; besides the isolation gave her time to be alone, time to think. Her basket was almost full but, reluctant to leave the peace of the moor, Anna walked to the spot where Edward had found her the wild honeysuckle. She smelled the delicate fragrance, touching her face to the scarlet and yellow blooms. It was one of her favourite perfumes, as it seemed to be with the many customers she was getting from the wealthier side of Coseley. Lorna Paget had preached the worth of her cosmetics with the zeal of a disciple and every day brought Anna fresh business.

She still felt dazed at the speed with which it was happening. Opening the shop in Birmingham in October, it had become popular in time for Christmas and she and Hester had both been run off their feet, keeping up with the demand there and in Coseley.

Hester. Anna smiled. The girl was changing. The 'thee' and 'tha' of her speech was fading, but there were no airs and graces. Hester didn't need any. The quiet dignity of her own nature was enough; now her mousy hair gleamed like brown honey and her plain little face had taken on a confidence that gave her a new radiance.

Breaking off a few of the fragrant blossoms and putting them into her basket, Anna turned toward Devil's Finger, the small waterfall that fell a hundred feet into a spray-filled chasm. Misty was at Sunday school with the Cresswell twins; an independent three year old, she loved being with the 'big' children. Anna relaxed. She could afford another hour here in the splendour of the moors before making her way home.

The sound of water falling over stones muffled approaching hoofbeats and Anna swung round, startled to hear a voice suddenly declare: 'Well, well, if it isn't Mrs Royce.' The darkly handsome friend of Philip Rewcastle looked mockingly down from a black horse, its flanks silvered with sweat. 'Aren't you afraid, out here all by yourself?'

'Not in the least.' Summer sun ringed his black head with a circle of blue, the devil's halo. It fitted him to perfection. 'So long as that is the way it is . . . but seeing I can no longer enjoy that luxury, I will say good afternoon.'

'Not afraid of me, are you, Mrs Royce?'

Anna glanced up at the handsome features. Some said the devil was handsome. This man was both, the devil and handsome.

The horse side-stepped nervously at the sound of his crop striking brown leather riding boots. He stared down at Anna, a mixture of disdain and lust in his brilliant eyes.

'Then perhaps you should be, Mrs Royce.'

Blood raced through Anna's veins. This was a man best avoided. He had been dangerous enough with Hester and Philip present, but out here, alone . . . Anna's free hand moved nervously to her throat, fingering the open button, and his hungry look followed, lingering over her breasts.

'Is that the invitation I think it is, Mrs Royce?' He bent forward, using the riding crop to pull at her unbuttoned neckline. 'I thought the last time we met you were more than ready to play.'

Angrily, she swiped away the gleaming cane with its snaking leather strip.

'You disgust me!' she spat. Then she was running as fast as she could through grass that suddenly seemed intent on grabbing her feet, holding her back.

At first only laughter followed her retreat then the drum of hoofbeats told her he was chasing her. Guiding his mount around and in front, he forced her to stop.

'I won't hear of your leaving, Mrs Royce.' An ugly smile twisted his mouth. 'You and I have some unfinished business. Where better to complete it than here?'

'I've got no business with you!' Anna replied, fear mounting inside her. 'You will please let me pass.'

'Will I?'

He was gloating, tormenting, feeding like some evil being on the fear he saw in her eyes. The gleaming cane snaked out, ripping her hair free from its pins, spreading it like a red-gold shawl about her shoulders.

'Lovely!' he breathed. 'Like fire. Do you live up to the

reputation that goes with hair that colour, Mrs Royce? Do you make love with the burning heat and passion of fire?'

There was no room now in that fierce gaze for disdain; it had been overridden, destroyed by the surging tide of lust. It sent a shiver of loathing and fear along Anna's spine. The fact that she was alone and defenceless was nothing to a man like him. In fact, he preferred it that way. If there were none to see him attack, there would be none to answer to.

There was nothing to be gained from talking. Dodging beneath the animal's chest, Anna streaked away, her hair a red banner floating behind her. She had only run a short way and already the breath was painful in her throat when hoofbeats throbbed behind her. Turning her head, she threw a backward glance across her shoulder. Through the hair whipped across her eyes she saw the horse approaching at a gallop, white flecks of foam flying from its mouth like flakes of snow on the breeze. Then her senses reeled, blue and green swirled into a kaleidoscope of colour as earth and sky rotated in turns about her tumbling figure; the horse had been spurred straight at her, its massive black shoulder catching her and sending her sprawling into the grass.

He was dismounted and rolling her beneath him before her senses had steadied. He ripped away the cotton blouse and chemise, his mouth closing over her nipple as his hand threw up the length of her skirts and pushed between her thighs.

'No!' Half-conscious, Anna tore at the head fastened to her breast but his teeth closed cruelly over the tender flesh and she screamed with pain.

Then, as quickly as his weight had rolled on to her, he heaved it away and Anna saw a riding crop strike, finding his face again and again.

Fighting against the brute strength of him, Anna had been unaware of the approach of a second rider. Now as she pushed her skirts down over her legs and pulled the remnants of her torn blouse across her breasts, she looked up into the tortured face of Philip Rewcastle.

'You lying swine, you filthy lying swine!'

The crop rose and fell.

'You told me you wouldn't do this again. You said you were finished with women.'

'Wait!' Flinging up his hands, protecting his face from the cut of the flailing whip, Robert backed away. 'You don't understand, Philip . . . listen to me, please.'

'I understand you, all right, you lying swine.'

But the whip fell still.

Anna had scrambled to her feet and without knowing it moved closer to Philip's chestnut mare, seeking the protection of her rider.

'No . . . you don't understand, Philip.' Robert's voice became soft and pleading, his dark eyes entreating. 'I was passing when I saw Mrs Royce. I stopped to give her the time of day and she asked if I would pull up some plant or other that was too strong for her.'

Scarlet trails of blood trickled across his forehead and through the thick black of his eyebrows, smearing into his dark eyes, but their gaze never flickered from Philip Rewcastle, even when Anna gasped at the outrageous lie.

'What else could I do than assist the lady, Philip? Then, when I was kneeling down, she lifted her skirts, spread her legs and pulled me on top of her.'

'Then shoved her tit in your mouth, I suppose!' Philip laughed, a harsh, haunted sound. 'Really, Robert, what kind of fool do you take me for?'

All the time he spoke Robert had been stealthily moving backwards and Philip let him go, widening the space between them.

'No fool, Philip. I know it must sound ludicrous but it's the truth. The woman wanted me to . . .'

The last was spoken on a note of hysteria as Philip looked down at Anna. For a moment his terrible expression softened, giving way to a gleam of pity.

'There is no need to ask what happened, Anna,' he said

131

quietly. 'Your eyes speak for you. The blame lies with Robert Daines. But he will never touch another woman, I swear it!'

'Philip.' Anna lifted a hand to the man who smiled a strangely contented smile, then felt it thrown aside as he pressed his spurs to the flanks of his mare.

With a strangled cry, Robert Daines turned and ran.

But Philip followed relentlessly, closing the gap between himself and the lover who had betrayed him. As Anna watched, the dark figure came to the edge of Devil's Finger and turned desperately, seeking another way. But it was already too late. Drawing level, Philip tugged viciously on the reins, snatching the mare's head back over its neck so that she reared.

The whinny of protest was followed by a longer, terrified human one. Front hooves lashing forward as she rose on her hind legs, the mare caught Robert Daines full in the chest, sending him flying, arms spread-eagled, out over the chasm then down, following the Devil's Finger into blackness. There was a momentary pause then the glint of sun on polished wood as Philip's crop whistled down on to the mare's flanks again and she reared once more.

Anna pushed her fist against her mouth, stopping her own screams, watching the animal fight against the slippery shale sliding away beneath her, taking horse and rider on a last journey into death.

They brought the bodies up from the chasm, the men of Coseley, and a specially convened Coroner's Court returned a verdict of 'Accidental death'. A week after the nightmare scene the body of Philip Rewcastle was laid to rest and that of Robert Daines returned for burial on his southern estate, and not once in all that time did Maggie question Anna's return from the moor, her blouse almost torn away, hair cascading loose about her scratched neck.

The whole town seemed unnaturally quiet following the funeral of the only son of Jacob Rewcastle, though his mill continued to belch out its black smoke and men drew molten steel from the fires of its belly.

In the front room she had turned into a shop, Anna moved restlessly, unable to rid herself of the horror of that afternoon. Outside the sound of a vehicle drawn by a trotting horse caught her attention. It was mid-afternoon; tradesmen had already made their rounds, even the 'Auntie Sally' man who could never be tied to any approximate hour to deliver the black syrupy disinfectant from which he drew his nickname.

Moving to the window, Anna caught her breath; a smart carriage drawn by a grey horse had stopped outside Maggie's door and Jacob Rewcastle was stepping out.

'You will come in?' Maggie pulled the door open before his knock sounded on it.

'It's Anna Royce I want to see.'

'I'm here, Mr Rewcastle, what can I do for you?' Anna emerged from the front room, her face blanching at sight of the basket he placed on the table. She had left it behind on the moor. Caught up in the drama being played out before her, she had forgotten it and later been too terrified to go looking for it.

'You *can* do summat for me.' Jacob brushed aside the offer of a chair. 'You can tell me the truth of what happened last Sunday up at Devil's Finger. And don't deny you were there. That . . .' he pointed to the basket though he didn't look at it. '. . . was found close by and I'm told it's yours. That's the truth, isn't it?'

'The basket is mine, Mr Rewcastle.' Anna's knees began to tremble. Why hadn't he been to see her before this? Why hadn't the basket been used to bring her before the Coroner's Court? Why had Jacob Rewcastle waited until now to face her with it?

'Then you were on the moor last Sunday?'

Wincing at the accusation behind the question, Anna nodded.

'And did you see my son?'

Across the table the puffy red face challenged her but beneath the bravado Anna could read the man's fear, a fear that silently answered her questions. She had not been brought to court because he was afraid she had seen what had happened, and afraid she had understood what lay behind it.

Strangely, Anna felt almost sorry for the man who had cheated her of everything she and Edward once had. He would never accept a denial that she had been present when his son had fallen to his death; it would eat away at him like canker in an apple. Fate had given her another chance to strike at him through Philip, but again Anna refused to do so.

'Yes, Mr Rewcastle,' she answered simply, 'I saw your son.'

'Did . . . did you see him fall? What happened?'

Turning away, Anna walked to the black-leaded grate, a fire burning there even though it was June.

To tell the truth about the tortured love that had driven Philip Rewcastle to commit murder would not bring back the dead or wipe away the memory of what Robert Daines had tried to do to her. It would have been easy for Philip to accept the lie the other man offered, to close his eyes to her innocence, but he hadn't. Philip Rewcastle had acted towards her as a gentleman, just as he had when she and Hester had come upon them in the bedroom of Edward's house, and as he had in his father's office. She would not repay that kindness by revealing he was hopelessly in love with a man.

'The dark-haired man . . .'

'Sir Robert Daines?'

'Yes. Your son called him Robert.' Turning to face him, Anna heard her daughter's laughter float in from the tiny back yard shared with the Cresswells and suddenly all concern over what she was about to say faded. Yes, she would lie, to preserve any respect Jacob Rewcastle still felt for his son.

'I was on the moor,' she said levelly, 'near Moses Table, when Robert Daines came up behind me. He rode me down with his horse and while I was on the ground, tried to force himself upon me. It was entirely the actions of your son that prevented him from raping me. Philip dragged him away, telling him what a fool he was, and while he was helping me to my feet, Robert Daines became very angry. He shouted that Philip was a fool, I was nothing but a mill wench and no one would bother if they both took me.

'When Philip pushed him away from me a second time, Robert Daines struck him in the mouth. Philip fell and lay still for a while . . . I think he caught his head on a stone. Robert Daines thought he was dead. Shouting that he would kill me too if I said anything of what had occurred, he began to run in the direction of Devil's Finger.'

Anna kept her glance on Jacob's eyes. 'A few seconds later Philip got to his feet. He shouted something about Robert not knowing the waterfall was there, then jumped on his horse and rode after him. I don't really know what happened next except one moment your son was reaching for his friend, then they both went over the edge.'

'So that's it! I guessed as much.' His face darkening, Jacob Rewcastle bent forward, placing both hands palm down on Maggie's white table-cloth, hatred spewing out with his words. 'My son died for nowt but a whore. Gave his life to save a woman who most likely spreads her legs willingly.'

'Jacob Rewcastle!' Maggie had not moved until this moment. Now she stepped forward, her face sharp with anger. 'This is my house. You 'as what you came for, though God knows yer tormented mind must twist what y'ave 'eard to suit yerself. But there's nowt about Jacob Rewcastle that frightens me so you best leave afore my clog finds your arse.'

Jacob straightened but his livid stare remained locked on Anna's pale face.

'I'll leave, Maggie Fellen,' he hissed, 'I'll leave, but when I have there'll be others to follow. You thought I didn't know about your little enterprise in Birmingham, didn't you? The shop run by Hester Cresswell . . . the one you're renting from Abraham Fine. Well, I do! And I tell you this and all: you've paid your last rent. There'll be no Anna Royce in Birmingham this time next week, and if you have any brains at all you'll see there's no place for you in Coseley or anywhere else I can find you.

'You took my son but by God you'll be sorry. You'll be sorry you ever heard the name Philip Rewcastle!'

'That was only part truth you spoke, wench, but I reckon as the Good Lord won't pay much mind to the rest.' Maggie turned from the window where she had stood watching Jacob Rewcastle drive away.

'Cryin' will get you nowhere. All you gets from that is the 'eadache. Wash your face an' tidy your hair. You can't be goin' out looking like a half-wrung mop.'

Anna sniffed, dabbing a handkerchief to her eyes. 'I . . . I'm not going anywhere.'

'That's all you knows. You be goin' to see Abraham Fine afore Jacob Rewcastle does.'

'But what good will that do? Rewcastle has money and there's little people can do against that.'

'How does you know?' For the first time Anna could remember Maggie snapped at her. 'Not every man in the world worships brass, an' it's my guess Abraham Fine is one of them or why should he 'ave let you 'ave 'is shop for rent he did? Common sense should tell you with a position like that it could fetch twice as much.'

Anna hadn't realised Maggie had quite such a business eye. As she looked at her now, slate-grey eyes cold as the steel that rolled from Jacob's mill, she might have been looking at a stranger.

Anna smiled faintly. 'It might be as well to give Mr Fine a little advance warning of Jacob's intentions.'

She hadn't known what to expect in going to see Abraham Fine but he and his wife Leah listened attentively as Anna told them of the threat to her livelihood.

'Jacob Rewcastle won't be satisfied until I've left this part of the country altogether, Mr Fine and I wouldn't want you to clash with him on my account so I will pay you three months rent to cover any loss while you look for someone else to take over the property.'

'We have heard from our good friend Benjamin the truth of this Jacob Rewcastle, and more of what he has done to you than you have just told.' Leah Fine shook her neat grey head, setting long gold earrings jangling. 'Perhaps now it is time for him to find out the whole world need not dance to his tune, eh, Abraham?'

'What my Leah is saying, Anna, is that we will not sell over your head, not to Jacob Rewcastle nor to anybody else. The shop is yours for as long as you wish.'

'But Jacob Rewcastle would give you a good price, more or less anything you ask, just to get me out . . . and be assured, Mr Fine, he won't give up without a struggle.'

'So who is afraid of a struggle?' Abraham's watery blue eyes strayed to his wife's gentle face. 'For nearly two thousand years our people have struggled . . . it's nothing new.'

'But the Lord has stayed with us, Abraham,' Leah added.

The tinkle of fine china as she poured coffee from a swan-necked pot then stirred in sugar and cream for Abraham sounded loud in the pretty chintz-upholstered sitting room. Anna accepted the cup offered to her, not knowing if she would like the strongly smelling drink. They had only ever had tea at home and Maggie never had anything else except a tin of cocoa in the house.

'Anna.' The skin on his hands almost transparent, the veins showing clearly, Abraham reached forward, putting his flower-sprigged cup and saucer on a mahogany table.

'I said we would not sell the shop over your head . . .' he paused, fixing that pale stare on her '. . . but what if I sold it to you?'

'Me!' Anna swallowed. 'But even if I had enough to buy it,

Jacob Rewcastle could always offer more, and he'd never let you sell to anyone else.'

'A man can sell what is his own to whomever he chooses.'

'Try telling him that!'

'Anna, we have talked of selling the shop for some time now and Leah thinks as I do. Our son Reuben does not want those premises. He already has a fine office for his solicitor's business.' He reached with his thin hand for his wife's, folding it about her fingers. 'It is our wish that you should have the shop.'

Her own hands shaking, Anna put down her cup beside Abraham's. It would be wonderful . . . her own shop . . . she might have the asking price, she was showing a handsome profit both in Birmingham and Coseley.

'Well, what do you say? My Abraham, he wants you to have it. Says you will love it as much as he did.' Leah lifted plump shoulders in the gesture Benjamin Freeth always used. 'Sheesh! Who should love a shop . . .'

I would, thought Anna, I know exactly how Abraham feels; to have given so much of your life to something then have it taken away by someone who wants it only for spite and revenge; to work as Edward had worked only to lose it all; and the losing would be hard for Abraham, even to someone he liked.

'If I can pay the price you ask, nothing would please me more than to take your shop and care for it, Mr Fine, but once Jacob Rewcastle finds out who has offered for it, you will get no peace until you promise to sell to him.'

'By that time it will be too late.' Abraham looked at the elegant long-case clock ticking in the corner of the room, then drawing his pocket watch from his waistcoat, checked it and replaced it in the slit pocket. 'Reuben will be home in a few minutes, Anna. Let's see what he suggests.'

Reuben Fine was tall and dark, almost as dark as Robert Daines though there the similarity ended. His eyes were those of his mother, brown and piercingly observant, but the rest of his features spoke of Abraham. Thick, straight brows topped a slightly hooked nose and his wide mouth smiled easily.

'But nothing could be simpler to remedy, Mrs Royce.' He too listened carefully to her fears. 'It would be sensible for you and my father to sign a legal document of sale . . . I know my father would be happy just to have a verbal agreement but in this instance it would be in the best interests of both of you to go by the book.'

Back at Roker Street Anna went up to the room she shared with Misty. Looking down at the tousle of golden hair and pinkly flushed face of her sleeping daughter, she knew she had been right to take the risk of buying the shop from Abraham Fine.

She had to fight Jacob Rewcastle on his own terms . . . this child, and for all she knew the boy back in Wednesbury, depended on her and she would fight any man for their sake.

Sitting on her bed, she spread out the legal document on the faded blue bedspread.

'We don't rent it anymore,' she whispered towards the old truckle bed Misty slept in. 'It's ours. For better or worse, darling, it's ours and I swear I will make a go of it. Oh, Misty! It feels so marvellous.' Anna held the paper to her breast. 'It . . . it's as if someone had suddenly given me a diamond.'

A diamond! Anna slowly lowered the document, staring unseeingly at the flowing script. '*One day you'll have a whole string of diamonds* . . .' The words danced in her mind, Peter's words. He hadn't meant a tiny scrap of paper glued to a pink string. This was what he had meant. She touched the crisp edge of the document, letting her finger trace the signature: Anna Royce. This was her diamond, her first paper diamond, and one day she *would* have a string of them.

Chapter Ten

Despite his threats, Jacob Rewcastle had not driven her from Coseley or closed her shop in Birmingham. He might be able to influence the men of his circle but the women were beyond his jurisdiction; they liked Anna Royce Beauty Products and they intended to have them. Anna closed her account book and leaned against the hard back of the wooden chair at Maggie's table. Takings were up every week; so much so that in Birmingham Hester was taking on a new girl.

''Ave you thought on what I said yesterday?' Maggie came in from the scullery, her questioning glance directed at the closed book.

'Yes, Maggie, and I can see the sense of it but . . .'

'But what? 'As you not got enough?'

'Money? Oh, yes, it's not that.' Anna rose, carrying the account book over to the dresser and putting it into a drawer. 'It's just that I feel nervous whenever I think of taking on something new.'

'What's new about it? You put the creams an' lotions into a fancy box for Lorna Paget, didn't you? So do it again. I'm sick to my back teeth of 'avin' to tell all those women from yon side that you don't 'ave any. For God's sake, girl, they're beggin' to spend their money an' if you don't be quick, somebody else will up an' tek it off them.'

She was right. Anna watched her black-skirted figure bustle out. Maggie had been right about her starting her own business and she was right in her advice to extend it to suit the more exclusive end of the market.

'Sleepin' money is idle money,' Maggie had said, 'make yours work for you.'

Anna pushed open the door of Wigmore Banking Company, her boots tapping on the tiled floor as she walked to the counter. Reuben Fine had suggested she come here. She was to meet him later at the shop. He always suggested they meet there if she needed his advice any time and Anna had a sneaking suspicion why. Hester Cresswell had turned into an attractive young woman.

'Can I help you?'

From his superior position behind the counter, the teller looked down his thin nose at her. 'Was you wanting something?'

His eyes were darting all over her, from the black hat pinned securely to the piled up red-gold mass of her hair to the shabby coat and shiny skirt.

'Yes, please.' Anna tried to smile but couldn't. There was enough vinegar in the man's face to pickle a barrel of onions. 'I wish to see the manager.'

At the end of the sharp thin nose nostrils widened like sluice gates opening while a thin smile hovered round his lips.

'I'm sure I can see to any business Madam might have.'

It was a definite snub, undisguised emphasis on the word 'Madam'; his open contempt for her clothes said it all. Anna squared her shoulders. Eyes cool as green ice played meaningfully on his own frayed cuffs and paper collar, the dark coat pressed as many times as her own. If she were going to do what she had come here to do, then she would do it properly. And the time to start was now.

'*You* might be sure of that, Mr Burrows.' Her quick gaze had caught the name plaque displayed on the counter. 'I am not. I do not deal with subordinates. I will discuss my business only with your superior.'

She had intended her voice to carry. Now titters of amusement spread among the other men working to either side of
the reddening, spluttering Mr T. Burrows.

'I do not have all day.' Trembling inside, Anna maintained
a calm front. 'You will tell the manager that Anna Royce
is here.'

She had added no 'please', had not said she would be
obliged if he would see her. She had issued an order and
was surprised at its effect.

John Harris leaned forward, resting his hands on the walnut
desk. He had heard of this woman sitting opposite him; one
got to hear many things in his line of business and it was
his opinion Jacob Rewcastle had robbed her. Business was
business, John Harris was the first to admit, but robbery was
also robbery and that was what had taken place over King's
Choice.

'I will be happy for you to bank with Wigmore's, Mrs Royce.'
He rang the small bell on his desk.

'Have this deposited to Mrs Anna Royce and bring her book
in here,' he said to the man who answered his ring.

Anna kept her mouth steady, fighting a smile as Mr Burrows
kept his glance away from her face. He was taking no more
chances with her sharp tongue.

'Er . . . forgive my forwardness, Mrs Royce.' John Harris
waited until the door closed behind the departing Burrows.
'But the money you have just placed on deposit, would it not
be better to make it work for you . . . investments . . . stock
perhaps?'

Anna did smile then, amused that he should choose the
same words as Maggie.

'Thank you, but I wish that money to remain untouched.
However, I would welcome your advice on another matter,
Mr Harris. I . . . I feel I can trust you to guide me in the right
direction.'

She lowered her long lashes. There was a time for putting

men in their place and a time for flattery. Lifting her glance, she saw his pleased reaction. Anna Royce was learning fast.

Quickly she outlined her business. 'And now I feel there is an opening for a more lavishly packaged product, one aimed at the more affluent who are looking for an unusual gift.'

John Harris was listening intently. 'So what do you suggest? Will it make another selling line or should I forget it?' Anna asked.

Touching the tips of his fingers to his lips, the bank manager remained silent. His own wife had purchased this woman's products and now bought no other. Handled properly, it could prove a profitable venture and maybe bring additional business the bank's way. There was a discreet tap on the door and Burrows re-entered the office, placing a slim black book on the desk then withdrawing like a shadow.

'It is a laudable idea, Mrs Royce.' John Harris opened the small book, checking what was entered in it before handing it to her across the neat desk. 'But for the bank to back you financially . . .'

'I'm sorry.' Anna watched the movement of hands so different from Edward's. His had never been so white yet there'd been a strength to them, a steadiness and calm which she badly missed.

'I must not have explained myself clearly. I don't want to borrow money from the bank, I do not intend to incur any debt. I want to feel my way slowly, Mr Harris, paying as I go, and this is what I will use to make my start. What I want you to tell me is whether it is enough to begin with?'

For the second time since entering his office, Anna lifted her old carpet bag from where it rested on the floor beside her chair. Placing it across her knees, she opened it, taking out several small thick linen bags. Not all of the words 'fine milled flour' had come off when she had washed them in Maggie's scullery sink but they were clean enough, leaving no trace of their original contents as she placed them on the shining desk.

'There's three hundred pounds there, Mr Harris, but if you think that insufficient, I will wait until I can add more.'

Anna heard his sibilant intake of breath.

'I would say you have ample funds to make a beginning, Mrs Royce. Do you wish to place this in a business account with us?'

Anna nodded, watching the pleased smile spread across his features as he rang the gleaming brass bell once more. An acid-faced Burrows carried her money away.

Anna fastened her carpet bag. She was pleased with the way things had turned out, just as Reuben had predicted she would be. He was a smart man, was Reuben Fine. But then, didn't Hester tell her so almost every evening?

'Mr Burrows,' John Harris showed her out of his office, pausing as they passed the chief teller, 'any time Mrs Royce is in the bank she is to be shown into my office immediately. Please let the rest of the staff know that also.'

Anna walked proudly from the building. What John Harris had just done clearly signalled his support of her, a helpful gesture towards a woman fighting in a man's world. Head thrown back, she strode on determinedly to her meeting with Reuben. Now she had two debts to pay, one to a mill owner and one to a bank manager. She would pay both.

Maggie was right as usual, Anna realised as she slipped on the moss green day suit and studied its effect in the fitting-room mirror. It deepened the emerald of her eyes and complemented the burnished gold of her hair. She had lost weight but that was not surprising, seeing she hardly ever had a moment to sit down, and she wasn't displeased. Her waist was tiny and her breasts high. She didn't need the restrictive whalebone corsets to give her that hour-glass silhouette that was so modish. She ran a hand over the stiff grosgrain. Edward would have loved to see her dressed like this . . .

'But, my dear, of course I took them. I couldn't possibly have disappointed him by refusing, now could I?'

Two shrill voices trilled loudly, their empty falseness jerking Anna from her memories. She would buy the green suit. Taking it off, she draped it across a tiny gilt chair.

'They are lovely – but they're not real, are they?'

'Of course they're real. Rubies are my favourite. I would never settle for less than the best. Fortunately he had drunk himself into a stupor before I had to earn them . . .'

Laughter trilled again, loud and unpleasant. Anna slipped on her brown skirt, fastening the small self-covered buttons. She had no wish to eavesdrop. Reaching for her jacket, she slipped her arms into it, shrugging it on to her shoulders, nimble fingers slotting the buttons through buttonholes.

'Stupid old man!' The woman's voice came clearly through the thin wall separating the dressing cubicles. 'Thinks he can get himself a son and heir and it will be with me. Hah! He doesn't know how wrong he is.'

'Is your friend not married then?'

'Yes, but she won't give him what he wants – probably too old to have any more children anyway.'

Drawing aside the curtain, Anna pushed the green suit into the hands of the assistant waiting discreetly.

'Thank you, I will take this . . . will you please bring it round?'

'Of course, Mrs Royce.' The woman smiled. 'Will you be in the shop or will I leave it with Miss Cresswell?'

'I'll be in the shop.'

'More children!' the thin voice piped as Anna began to cross the carpeted floor of Monsieur Pierre, A-la-Mode Gowns. 'He does already have children then?'

'Should I have the peach or the mauve do you think?'

Anna stepped through the doors and stood outside breathing in fresh air. She wasn't a fool, she knew there were women like that, but suddenly she would have liked nothing more than to shake the breath from the selfish bodies of the two she had just been forced to listen to. Perhaps it was a case of six and two threes. The man, whoever he was, was cheating on his wife and so perhaps deserved to be cheated in his turn. Nevertheless it made her feel a little sick.

'Did you buy anything?' Hester looked over her shoulder from the shelf she was dressing when Anna came into the shop.

'Yes. The assistant will be popping round with it in a few minutes, she has customers at the moment. Do you mind taking it for me? I . . . I have one or two things to see to.'

Hester nodded and Anna slipped quickly into the neat back room before her friend could question the faint flush of anger tingeing her cheeks. The tinkle of the shop doorbell followed but Anna remained where she was. It was probably Reuben, he usually called at this time.

'But I thought I had told you . . .'

Anna's spine tingled. It was the same voice she had heard moments before.

'. . . he only had one son. In his late-twenties he was, I believe, but he was killed. An accident, they said. His horse lost its footing and went over the side of a waterfall or something . . .'

Anna's head reeled and she clutched at the table for support. She was talking about Philip . . . the woman out there in the shop was talking about Philip Rewcastle; and the man who had bought her rubies, the man who hoped for a son, was Jacob Rewcastle.

'*He only had one son.*' The words rang through the dark hours of the night. '*He thinks he can get himself a son.*' They went on ringing in her mind as Anna walked to the station and bought her ticket, and they were still there a little over an hour later when she walked from the small station at Burslem. She felt guilty about leaving Misty and the front-room shop to Maggie yet again.

A freckle-faced boy grinned when she asked if he could give him directions to the pottery. He couldn't be much older than Misty, certainly no more than eight, but already his arms hung well below his sleeves and there was a marked gap between trousers and boots that only will-power held together.

'Aye, I can, missus. Which one does tha want?'

The cheeky grin was infectious and Anna smiled broadly.

'I don't know,' she admitted 'suppose you tell me?'

Wiping the back of his hand under his nostrils then running it down the side of a trouser leg, the lad chuckled.

'Well, tha could tek tha pick of any of 'alf a dozen but nearest one is Seth Gladwin's place. Though whether or not 'e's theer . . .'

Shoulders too wide for the jacket lifted non-committally.

'Why shouldn't he be there?'

''E might be off looking for somebody to buy rest of 'is stock. Seth 'as bin tryin' for weeks now and me dad says it'll be a miracle if 'e finds someone, but if tha wants I'll tek thee theer.'

At Anna's nod the boy turned along the steep cobbled street, his thin legs moving rapidly.

'Ar,' he volunteered, 'Seth is all but finished. Closin' its doors is Gladwin's like a good few others round 'ere.'

A pair of high doors led to Gladwin's Potteries. Anna slipped a threepenny bit into the grubby hand of her chatty companion and walked across the cobbled yard. To her left a huge bottle-shaped brick edifice rose to the sky. The rest of the court was boxed in on three sides by ramshackle buildings, one of which boasted a rickety wooden staircase leading to an upper storey. Anna glanced around, almost wishing she had accepted Reuben's offer to come with her. In her old carpet bag the walnut box Benjamin Freeth had made at his home to her instructions weighed suddenly heavy. The world of Burslem was strange to her.

'Can I help thee?'

Anna turned to the shadowed doorway of one of the side buildings and for one wild sickening moment she wanted to scream. The white potter's apron daubed with red clay reminded her of a smear of blood across her breast, the tawny streaks of hair across Philip Rewcastle's face . . .

'I . . . I wanted to see Mr Gladwin.' Her trembling fingers almost lost their grip on the carpet bag and it took several long breaths to fight away shadows of her yesterdays.

'I'm Seth Gladwin. Tha better come up to the office, tha looks about ready to drop.'

Anna followed him up the shaky staircase and into a tiny office whose organised chaos reminded her of Benjamin's workroom. Offering her the only chair, Seth Gladwin walked over to the high arched window where he stood looking at her.

'What was it you wanted?' he asked when they were both settled. 'As tha can see, there's little left.'

'I . . . I was told you were closing. I didn't know that before I set out.' Anna tried to keep her eyes from the smeared calico apron. 'I might have saved myself a journey.'

'Aye, Gladwin's Pottery is finished.' The whiskered face turned from her, looking down into the deserted yard. 'I'm glad me father isn't alive to see it. This pottery was his pride, his life and mine until . . .'

Anna waited but the man, whom she judged to be in his sixties, said no more, eyes fixed on the emptiness of the yard below as he too walked the corridors of memory.

'There's no more call, tha sees,' he said at last. 'Everybody wants this fancy foreign stuff. Hah! Ah wouldn't gi' tuppence for the best on it.'

Anna glanced at the few pieces in one corner of the room: thick workmanlike jugs and bowls, all in the same uninteresting white glaze. She could understand the change in preference. She too liked even workaday objects to be pretty.

'Is that the only type of pottery that can be made here?' she asked, ignorant of the whole process.

'No.' Seth Gladwin moved to a cupboard covered in a layer of red dust and took a cup from the shelf inside.

'I made this when ah was nobbut a lad and me dad fired it in that very kiln.' He nodded to where the bottle-shaped brick building was visible through the grimy window. 'Aye, ah liked to get a lump of clay and see what my fingers could mek of it.' He gave the cup to Anna. 'But me dad said as 'ow we would mek nowt out of stuff like that. Break too easy, he said, folk wouldn't want pieces as would break easy.'

Anna held the fragile cup in her hands. Delicate as a baby's breath and almost as transparent. She held it up, marvelling at the thinness of it, seeing how the light from the window filtered through. It was beautiful, even without the slim, question mark handle and fine glaze.

'You say you made this?'

'Aye, ah did.' Age had not dimmed his pride in his achievement. 'When ah were a lad ah did a few other bits and bobs . . . they're in cupboard if tha's interested?'

Anna was . . . very interested. Going to the cupboard, she took out pretty fluted jugs and elegant vases, fine as a summer breeze. How Maggie or Mary Cresswell would treasure one of these!

'They are lovely, Mr Gladwin.' She held a fragile tea-pot. 'I wonder you didn't make more of these instead of heavier ware?'

'No call for 'em. Good strong crocks was what me old dad always said. Gi' folk good strong crocks and tha won't go far wrong . . . only it seems folk no longer want 'em.'

Anna returned the lovely painted teapot to its shelf.

'So now you are closing down, what will you do with the stock you have left?'

'Truth is, ah think ah've sold all ah'm gonna shift. The rest will 'ave to be written off, same as kiln and buildings.'

'But you can get a sale for them, surely?'

'Not round 'ere.' Seth took a whisper-fine cup from the dusty cupboard. 'Reckon this is all ah'll tek from 'ere. Kiln will never be fired again . . . business is finished.'

He placed the cup on the table, turning to stare once more through the arched window.

'There's no selling any of it.'

Anna picked up the carpet bag she had left beside her chair, taking out the walnut box.

'Mr Gladwin,' she said quietly, 'would you be able to make me some small pots to fit this?'

Seth Gladwin turned.

'So that's what tha come 'ere for, Mrs . . .' For the first time since her arrival, he asked her name.

'Anna Royce.'

'Well, Mrs Royce, truth on it is tha's too late. Today will just about see me off. Ah've already finished the last of workers I 'ad.' He fingered the beautifully grained walnut. 'Bloke who made this is a craftsman, ah reckon, knows what 'e's about.'

'The pots I want for inside would have to be fine, like those in the cupboard. Can it be done?'

'It could, but tha needs china clay for that.'

'Can it be got?'

'Oh, aye.' Seth's glance met hers. 'Has to be brought up from Cornwall, though, does china clay.'

There was no breathless heat of excitement inside her nor the damp fear of doubt, just quiet conviction. Going back to the cupboard, Anna picked up a graceful jug.

'Mr Gladwin,' she asked calmly, 'given a buyer for Gladwin's Pottery, how much would you expect to sell it for?'

Fingernails lined with clay pulled at long side whiskers and heavy brows drew together quizzically as Seth Gladwin surveyed the woman who had walked unceremoniously into his works. Still young and with looks that would turn many a head, she was dressed clean and neat without a deal of money spent on it. Her speech was quiet, nowt lah-di-dah, and he had made easy conversation with her. Strange that . . . he wasn't given to talking overmuch to anyone, much less a stranger and that one female.

'I should have counted myself lucky to come out of it with a 'undred pounds,' he answered at last, held by her candid green stare. 'But as it is . . .' He shrugged, holding out the box to Anna.

Taking it, and putting it on the dust-covered bench that served for a table, she held his stare.

'I will pay you one hundred and fifty.'

'A hundred and fifty! Tha must be daft. 'Aven't ah told thee there be no call for pots anymore?' He could have said: 'Put the money down and works is your'n, lock, stock and barrel,' and didn't really understand why he hadn't.

'I would not be producing the sort of pottery you have been making, Mr Gladwin. My line of business calls for something entirely different, that was my reason for bringing the box. I want specialist ware: small jars with lids, hand painted if possible, to fit inside such boxes. Those jars would have to be as fine as this.' She touched the lovely scrolled jug. 'So what do you say . . . will you sell Gladwin's Pottery to me?'

It still took seconds to sink in, to recognise the genuine offer she was making.

'Aye, ah will that,' he spluttered at last. 'If tha wants it, it's thine.'

'I do want it, but there is a condition to the sale.'

'Oh, aye?'

Anna's gaze never flickered. She heard his disappointment, the feeling of 'I knew it was too good to be true', and smiled inwardly. There was a proviso to be met if she were to buy his building but somehow she could not see it causing him much grief.

'Yes, Mr Gladwin, I will pay you one hundred and fifty pounds for Gladwin's Pottery provided you stay on as manager. You will take sole responsibility at a wage of . . . shall we say . . . four pounds ten a week?'

Slowly delight spread over the work-lined face, smoothing away creases and lighting his eyes with an inner fire.

'Ah don't know how tha came to be here, Mrs Royce, but ah thank the good Lord for all 'is blessings.'

'Amen to that!' Anna replied with feeling. 'Now could we settle on how long it will take for you to get production going?'

Seth took the box again, lips pursed under their line of grey whiskers.

'That one is a big kiln, Mrs Royce, and expensive to fire. Tha could fit thousands of the jars the size tha's askin' for into one corner of it.' He glanced up. 'What I'm really sayin' is the cost teken overall will be pretty 'igh if tha only part-fills it.'

'I think, given your help, Mr Gladwin, we can overcome that particular problem,' she returned. 'I want the rest of the space taken up with the type of pottery you have there.' She indicated the delicate pieces she had handled. 'Can you find me the men and women to make them?'

Seth tugged his long grey side whiskers.

'There's bin no bone china med in these part for many a day but the old 'uns still 'ave the skills and the young 'uns the will. Aye, ah reckon we can gi' thee most anythin' tha asks.'

'Does that include painting the designs?'

'Aye, that an' all.'

His tired eyes were suddenly alive again and hope lifted his drooping shoulders. It was little short of a miracle for him and for folk in this part of Burslem. Seth thought of the men and women without work, without money to feed their families; if this woman did take on the pottery there would be many blessing her name.

'You can contact John Harris of Wigmore Banking Co., Birmingham, if you have any queries, Mr Gladwin.' Anna realised he would probably have his doubts about her. 'I will have my solicitor draw up a bill of sale at once.' She turned to go. 'I will leave the box with you, I presume you will need its measurements. As for the rest . . . if I sketch roughly what I have in mind, will you be able to make cups and things from that?' She smiled. 'I'm afraid I'm a total novice when it comes to pottery.'

If she had asked would he fly if she strapped two palings

to his arms, he would have said yes, but all he could do was nod. Tears were too close for him to speak. Walking with her to the gate, Seth fidgeted with the corner of his apron, too shy to offer his hand.

'I'm very glad I came here today.' Anna held out her own hand. 'I think together we will make it work but there is something that would help.' Seth took the tips of Anna's slim white fingers in an effort not to cover them with dried clay but she pushed her hand firmly into his. 'I might not know much about making crockery but I know that a name people have come to depend on can only help us both. Will you agree to my keeping the name Gladwin's Pottery?'

Words still would not come but Anna didn't need them; the answer was in the old man's eyes. If it were within his power, the venture they were about to embark on would succeed.

'Tha's finished then?' The tousled head of the boy who had brought her from the station popped round one tall door, split in a cheeky grin. 'Somebody has to show thee back to station.'

And another threepenny bit wouldn't come amiss, thought Anna, matching his grin.

'If you had told me you intended buying the business, I could have drawn up the contract and come with you . . . I did offer.' Reuben looked at Anna across the table in the back room of the Birmingham shop.

'Don't think I wasn't grateful . . . I just thought it would be taking you away from your work for nothing. Believe me, Reuben, when I went to Burslem yesterday I had no thought of buying anything other than cosmetic jars for my gift boxes.'

'That will be the truth, Reuben.' Hester's neatly dressed hair glinted in the light from the window. 'Anna didn't even know where to find a pottery until we asked the teacher up at the school, so how could she know one was for sale?'

He pushed forward the sheet of paper for Anna to read.

'Well, I think she made a very good deal. You are a clever girl, Anna Royce.'

'Thank you, sir.' Anna dimpled. 'But I would like you to come with me and ask Seth to sign this . . . I want to be perfectly sure it is what he wants too, Reuben.'

'I'll be there, Anna. But right now, may I borrow your assistant for a few minutes?'

What happens if he proposes? Anna thought, seeing the radiance in her friend's eyes as she followed Reuben. His real goal in coming here was Hester. They were in love, deeply in love, but a Jewish-Anglican marriage? What would Abraham Fine have to say about that? Not to mention Mary Cresswell.

She had washed the delicate pieces that Seth had insisted he wanted her to have and now studied one of the delicately moulded jugs. Placed discreetly in a draped niche, or set with one or two pretty jars, it would be displayed to perfection; a ruse secretly intended to catch the eye of her customers. Anna smiled to discover a deviousness that was new to her. She was becoming a true businesswoman with an eye to the main chance.

At the tinkle of the bell Anna turned to the door, her quick glance taking in the customer's blonde hair swept up beneath a classy blue hat, blue panne velvet coat trimmed with tiny blue bows and braid.

'Good afternoon, welcome to Anna Royce.'

She used Hester's words though for some reason she could not imitate her smile. Putting the jug quickly on the shelf she had chosen for it, she placed a small upholstered chair close to one of the tables Hester had suggested might be more acceptable to ladies than hovering at a counter, then waited until the woman was seated. Anna watched the hard face; paint and powder, going some way to disguise the effects of age, did nothing to soften the line of her mouth or the steely light of her blue eyes. Anna repressed a sudden shiver. She had taken a dislike to the woman on sight, but why . . . for what possible reason?

'May I show Madam something?' She had to say something, couldn't stand there staring like an idiot.

'Yes!' It was imperious, a command, and Anna's hackles

155

rose. 'That jug you were holding just now, I would like to see it.'

Her mouth set hard, Anna handed over the lovely porcelain piece. That voice had told her why she felt so much dislike for the woman in blue. It was the same woman who had come to the shop last week; the one she had overheard in Monsieur Pierre's, speaking so disparagingly of Jacob Rewcastle.

'This is very beautiful.' The woman twisted the jug in gloved hands. 'So very delicate, obviously Italian . . . they are so good at this type of thing. I often think it would be nice if our own country could produce such fine china but . . .' She shrugged, lifting soot-coated lashes. 'We just don't seem to have the skills.'

Anna clenched her teeth, no longer even trying to smile.

'Do you have this in pink?' The woman held out the jug. 'The continentals have such a wonderful eye for colour, you really can't get the like of it here.'

'Not yet, Madam,' Anna heard herself reply graciously while her every urge was to throw the woman out of the door. 'But we do hope to have some very shortly.'

'Ah! Such a distance to transport fragile china, I do understand. Where is it you import from? Milano . . . Roma . . . or Venezia? Oh! That divine Venetian glass . . . do you sell that too?'

'No!' Anna's insides clenched. She had never heard anyone talking of foreign places yet recognised the falseness of this woman.

I'll bet you've never been fifty miles out of Birmingham, she thought acidly.

'Pity. It's such marvellous glass.' Placing the jug on the small round table, the woman admired its graceful lines again. 'Do you have any more pieces like this?'

Grudgingly Anna brought out the rest of the porcelain Seth had given her and listened to the woman's admiration. She might be a gold digger, taking Jacob Rewcastle for all she could get, but she genuinely appreciated the beauty of Seth's work. As she listened Anna knew she had been right; she would be able to sell every piece of fine porcelain the pottery could produce.

Chapter Eleven

Had it really been that long? Anna looked at the two documents she had spread side by side on her bed. Was it really two years since she had bought Seth Gladwin's place, two years since adding the second paper diamond to her string? So much had happened since she came to Coseley: her marriage to Edward, then his death before the birth of her daughter – then had come the loss of King's Choice and the terrible death of Philip Rewcastle.

'*Toil and tears.*' Anna remembered the reading of the tea leaves. 'There's been a lot of that, Kate,' she whispered, 'a lot of toil and too many tears.' But both of the businesses had done extremely well. And now this.

She picked up the cream envelope, looking again at the crest on the flap, knowing the words of the letter by heart. 'Her Grace would be pleased if you would call on the afternoon of 19 May . . .'

'Granma Maggie says are you ready, Mother? Auntie Mary has sent the boys round to say Hester would like you to go next door.'

Anna smiled into the cornflower blue eyes of her daughter. At eight years old, she was chubby and golden-haired as a cherub, and the thought occurred to Anna just as it always did: were those other eyes still that strange transparent blue, was his hair still blond?

'I'm coming, sweetheart,' she said, shoving the papers together and pushing them into their box. Taking Misty's hand, she walked awkwardly behind her down the narrow stairs, her free hand closing around another imaginary hand and her heart aching for the smile and the touch of her son.

Hester was married. Anna thought nothing could ever be so beautiful as that exchange of vows beneath a canopy. Memories of her own wedding flooded her mind. Edward in stiff wing collar and Sunday suit, and herself feeling like a lady in the green outfit he had bought for her and which she had later sold to Sam Castleton to buy her widow's black. But it wouldn't be like that for Hester, she thought, fiercely protective of her friend's happiness. Nothing was going to spoil life for her.

'She's done you proud, Mary.'

'Aye, Maggie.' Mary Cresswell wiped her eyes.

'Her's a grand wench, an' that bloody pretty as well!' William Cresswell put in proudly. 'An' it's your turn next, Anna girl . . . it's time you were wed. It's bloody wicked, lettin' a wench as pretty as you go to waste.'

'You hold your swearin', William Cresswell.' Behind the frown Mary's eyes twinkled. Her William was a quiet man but a sensible one and what he had just said needed saying.

'Well, I'm right, it's not good for a woman to live life alone.'

'But I'm not alone. I have Misty and Maggie and a whole family of Cresswells to keep me company.'

'You knows what I meant and I still says you be wastin' your life,' he defended himself.

'I'll marry you, Anna.' Fourteen-year-old Bobby Cresswell turned a cheerful eye on the gathering. Almost as tall as his father, a shock of hazel hair fell in an unruly mop over his brandy ball eyes, the only thing that distinguished him from his twin brother for George had eyes almost as blue as Misty. 'I quite fancy the older woman.'

'You'll not fancy my toe up your arse, but that's what you'll get if you don't shift!' Mary fetched her son a swift slap on the ear. Wedding reception or no wedding reception, she was having no lip.

"Is bloody ears are far too big. I keep saying it's time William clouted 'em for 'im but I might as well talk to meself for all the notice that one teks. It's a good job 'e's startin' work tomorrer, that'll tek some of the lard out of 'im.'

Anna smiled at Bobby's infectious grin.

'Make a good job of working with Benjamin Freeth, and who knows? I might take you up on your offer, Bobby Cresswell.'

She had set Benjamin up in a small workshop where he made the wooden presentation caskets that held Anna's small jars of cosmetics. These had been a winner right from the moment they were introduced and now he needed assistance. Bobby was quick to learn and the old man had taken him on as an apprentice, along with his brother. Anna sighed inwardly. Two more lives tied up with her own.

A week after Hester's wedding Anna caught the London train. Reuben had agreed Hester should remain in charge of the shop. They were a modern young couple, he said, he didn't expect her to stay home all day just because she was now a married woman. Mary had said nothing to this. After all, women in her walk of life only stopped going to the mill long enough to give birth. A week later they were standing at the benches again. It was enough for her that her daughter was happy. Misty and the front-room shop were left to the care of Maggie.

Anna again felt guilty at leaving her daughter, even though it was only for a couple of days. Soon now she would take a few days off from the business and spend them just with Misty.

Leaning her fiery head against the seat, Anna closed her eyes, the words of the letter in her bag matching the rhythm of the train's wheels passing over the points. 'Her Ladyship would be pleased . . . Her Ladyship would be pleased . . . The letter had said 19 May. That was tomorrow. First she must find a hotel.

Stepping from the train at Euston Station, the noise and bustle of the crowds was overpowering and Anna hesitated.

'Do you 'ave to stand there right in other folks' way?'

An old woman with a covered straw basket on her arm bumped past, muttering angrily. Steam belched loudly from a massive green and gold engine and Anna started nervously at the shrill whistle of the guard; a cloud of black particles, floating in the grey breath of a departing iron monster, wreathed about her face, closing off the breath from her lungs and making her cough. Tears stinging behind smarting eyelids, she hitched the new valise she had bought for the journey more firmly in her hand, missing the comforting worn handle of her old carpet bag.

Outside, the street held a dark promise of rain. A breeze intent on mischief tugged at a strand of her red-gold hair, freeing it from the restriction of hat and pins then chasing it across her face. Yet even here there was little relief from people pressing and pushing from every side. It seemed to Anna that the whole world lived in this one street in London, and that the whole world was intent on pushing her out of the way. Buildings so tall and grand they terrified her rose all around, grey and suffocating as the walls of a tomb; nifty hand carts filled with fruit and vegetables were darting like coloured butterflies almost beneath the iron-bound wheels of carriages and cabs, and all the time the cries of street traders added to the din.

'Watch yer back!'

A barrow loaded with oranges was pushed close to her and Anna moved a step forward then retreated with a startled cry. A black lacquered carriage, its driver resplendent in black top hat and coat trimmed with red braid, whisked past just inches from her toes, throwing mud on to the skirt of the green suit she had bought at Monsieur Pierre's.

'Will you be wantin' a 'ansom, miss?'

A dirty-faced character, the front of his coat adorned with greasy marks, sidled from the crowd to stand too close to her.

'A . . . a what?' The strident yell of a costermonger exploded, confusing Anna with its suddenness.

'A 'ansom. You knows . . . a 'orse and carriage.'

'Oh . . . yes. I suppose so.'

Two dirty fingers were inserted in the character's mouth and he gave a loud whistle. Down the street a driver laid his whip to the flanks of a tired horse.

'Where you wanting to get to?'

Fumes of gin gusting from him, the sleazy man questioned Anna as the carriage halted beside them.

'I . . . I don't really know.' Confusion still dulled her mind, making it difficult to think. 'I was hoping to find a quiet hotel.'

'You ain't bin to London afore then?'

'No.' Anna hitched her valise closer in aching fingers.

'That explains why you was lookin' a bit lorst like.' His calculating gaze moved to the black valise as his grimy hand reached for the cab door.

Involuntarily Anna shrank away. The man's hand was filthy, dirt ingrained in the skin. Even the men at the mill never seemed this dirty, not after ten hours of forging and rolling molten steel, and they certainly didn't smell like he did. The gin was bad enough but each time he moved, the sour smell of ancient sweat rolled from his body in sickening waves.

'You leave it to me, miss.' He smiled, showing blackened teeth. 'I knows a quiet place . . .'

'I'm sure you do!' A black malacca cane dropped on to the hand that touched Anna's sleeve. 'Too quiet . . . Muswell Hill graveyard being the prime favourite, I have no doubt.' The cane tapped lightly several times on the grimy hand before the man who had joined them spoke again. 'On your way, you rogue, before I send for a constable. The lady can do without your kind of help.'

The black tip of the slender cane remained resting for a few seconds on the knuckles of the other man's hand, then it was lifted. Muttering about 'bloody interfering sops', the fellow sloped away into the station.

'Forgive my intrusion,' the voice at her elbow began

again, 'but I could not allow a lady to be accosted by such a rogue.'

'He was trying to help.' Anna brushed a hand over the mud on her skirt, succeeding in transferring most of it to her pale grey glove. She knew the stranger was watching and suddenly felt like an awkward girl.

'That was obvious, but it was himself he was intent on helping – to your purse, the moment he got the chance.' Opening the carriage door, he took the valise and put it inside. 'Will you allow me to give the driver the address to which you wish to be driven?'

Again Anna felt foolish. She had no place to go, having thought to ask after a suitable hotel once she arrived in London. She had not dreamed it would be like this, so crowded and impersonal, and after the last few moments felt even more inadequate.

'Perhaps I might suggest The Conway? It is a small genteel residence most suited to a lady travelling alone. It stands in Leicester Road, not far from here.' He smiled for the first time. 'Handy for any business you might have in this, our fair city.'

Taking her silence for acceptance, he handed her into the musty-smelling cab.

'I would take you there myself but I have the misfortune to be meeting someone . . . an old friend. In the circumstances I will take the liberty of offering my card now instead of calling at your address and leaving it there.' The smile flashed again. 'My poor dear mama would have a touch of *mal-de-mer* were she to hear of it.'

Reaching into an elegant silver case he withdrew a card, handing it to her before closing the door. Stepping one pace back, he gave a half bow. 'If I can be of any assistance during your stay, a sixpenny runner will find me at that address.'

He called to the cabby then, giving the name of the hotel, and Anna heard the whip crack and felt herself jolt forward as the horse heaved against the traces.

He had been tall, the sand-coloured velour of his coat complementing, almost caressing, the upright line of his body. His voice and manner were authoritative; hair free from pomade curled almost boyishly over his forehead; side whiskers traced his cheeks down to the line of his jaw. But it was his eyes Anna remembered most. Changing from grey to twinkling blue as he had spoken of his dear mama, then back to grey as he became serious once more. He had been charming, her knight in sandy armour, but who had he been and why bother to help her?

Anna looked at the card she still held between her fingers. 'Charles Lazenby', it read simply in bold black print, and Anna was too stunned to read the address.

'Her Ladyship will see you now.'

Smiling nervously, Anna followed the portly figure along acres of carpeted corridor.

Dressed in a black cutaway suit over a brilliant white shirt, he not only resembled a penguin in appearance but waddled like one too. Knowing she would fall flat on her face if she didn't stop gawking at her splendid surroundings, she forced her eyes to remain on the butler before her.

'Mrs Royce, Your Grace.'

His announcement over, the penguin closed the gilt-embellished door, leaving Anna alone on a blue carpet so vast it reminded her of the sea the day she had taken Misty to Rhyl.

'Do come in, Mrs Royce.' A woman rose from a small writing table beneath a sun-filled window, its light reflecting on the lavender silk of her dress, touching the immaculate coiffure of slightly greying hair. 'It was good of you to come . . .' Stopping mid-sentence, she lifted a pair of gold-rimmed lorgnettes, studying her visitor more closely. 'But I've seen you somewhere before. Yes . . . yes, of course, King's Choice!' She dropped the eyeglasses, letting them hang by a slim gold chain. 'You were the girl who worked at . . . at wherever it was.'

'Benjamin Freeth's, Your Ladyship,' Anna supplied with the suggestion of a curtsy.

'Ah, yes!' Lady Victoria Strathlyn waved a thin white hand. 'But you were such a frightened-looking little thing. My dear, how you have changed.'

Anna blushed, fighting the urge to look down at her skirt. She had rinsed off the mud as soon as she had got to her hotel room but a faint stain remained on the material.

'Sit down, Mrs Royce.' Giving a sharp tug to an embroidered pull hanging beside the stone fireplace, Lady Strathlyn settled into a high-backed chair. 'You must be wondering why I took the liberty of asking you to come all this way?'

Anna had been wondering. In fact the question had not left her mind since the letter had arrived, but she could wait. She was used to it by now.

A maid in a white lace-trimmed cap and apron entered with a tray, and as she laid it on a table beside her mistress, Anna gave a surprised gasp.

'Is something wrong, Mrs Royce?' Lady Strathlyn was watching her closely.

'No . . . no, it was just the surprise of seeing my china.'

'*Your* china?'

A tiny smile curving her mouth, Anna lifted her eyes confidently to the woman serving her tea. She had known the lovely porcelain produced in her pottery was worthy of the finest houses in England and now the proof was here in front of her.

'I always tend to think of it in those terms, Your Ladyship. I suppose because it is an Anna Royce design.'

'You mean, you are responsible for this?' Victoria Strathlyn looked from the tray to Anna. 'But I thought you worked for Mr . . . for that cabinet maker?'

Easing off her gloves, Anna accepted her tea, loving the touch of the paper thin porcelain cup and saucer.

'I did, but that was a long time ago. Now I manufacture my

own beauty preparations and am responsible for Gladwin's Pottery.'

'I must congratulate you on both, Mrs Royce. Each is exceptional in its way, and that brings me to why I asked you to call at Beldon House.'

Returning her own cup to the tray, Lady Strathlyn looked up. The woman sitting opposite her was no longer a half-starved, harried young girl. She handled herself well; she was polite in her speech and manner, but not unduly deferential. Whatever had happened to Anna Royce had changed not only her circumstances, it had changed the woman herself.

'Some weeks ago my son bought one of your beauty boxes for his sister. She showed it to the Princess ... they have been friends from childhood ... and in turn the Princess asked that one be made for her. As you will appreciate, Mrs Royce, Her Majesty could not journey to Birmingham where I believe my son purchased his sister's gift, nor would propriety allow that the Palace contact you directly. But like all mothers, Her Majesty desires to give her daughter the present she has asked for. Therefore it fell to me, as Lady-in-Waiting to Her Majesty, to write to you.'

Anna's mind began to spin. The Queen! The Queen had asked for her cosmetics. The Queen wanted to give her daughter an Anna Royce beauty box.

'Would you be prepared to supply one?'

'What? I ... I'm sorry.' Anna pulled her thoughts together. 'Forgive me, Lady Strathlyn, but ...'

'I know, my dear, it is not every day the Queen asks for one's products. You do realise, I presume, that my letter could not enlarge upon the true reason for your coming to London. Her Majesty does not approve of her ... shall we say ... private matters, being widely known.'

'I understand perfectly, Lady Strathlyn.' Anna put down her cup with fingers that shook.

*   *   *

'Excuse me, madam.' One of the hotel maids entered Anna's room when she called: 'Come in.' 'A gentleman asked me to deliver this, he's waiting downstairs.'

Anna took the familiar card and smiled at the request scrawled across the back of it: 'Have dinner with me and make my miserable life happy.'

'Would you ask the gentleman to wait? Please tell him I will be down in a few minutes.'

She had no intention of making his miserable life happy by dining with him, but she did want to thank him for his kindness yesterday. The maid curtsied and withdrew, leaving Anna to tidy her hair. She had taken a bath since returning to the hotel, hoping the warm water would help soothe her mind, but try as she would the wonder of the afternoon would not be dismissed and she still felt half-dazed. Pushing a last pin into the heavy swathes of her hair, Anna looked at herself in the cheval mirror.

'You have met a Lady-in-Waiting to the Queen,' she whispered. 'What will Maggie have to say about that?'

Charles Lazenby smiled as Anna joined him, his teeth white against his tanned skin. Why hadn't she noticed he was tanned when he spoke to her yesterday?

'Good evening, thank you for agreeing to come downstairs.' The voice was the same: musical, soft, yet not without strength, and the grey-blue eyes held open appreciation as they settled on her.

A faint blush painting her cheeks, Anna answered.

'I must thank you, Mr Lazenby, for helping me yesterday.'

'You find the hotel to your liking?'

'I do,' Anna nodded, her gaze shifting around the foyer. 'I could not have chosen better, Mr Lazenby.'

'Then if you are pleased, perhaps you will reward my efforts.'

'Perhaps!' Anna was amazed at her own answer, amazed how at ease she felt with this tall elegant man, amazed at the way she allowed herself to be drawn towards a sofa in a secluded alcove.

'My reward, should you grant it, Mrs . . .?'

'Royce . . . Anna Royce.'

'My reward, should you grant it, Anna, is that you call me Charles.'

'I don't think that is too much to ask after the help you gave me yesterday.'

His smile widened. 'Kind as well as beautiful, Anna, your bounty is double.'

Why did she not object to an almost total stranger addressing her by her Christian name? Anna thought as Charles Lazenby smiled again, his eyes changing from grey to twinkling blue. Surely it was not the most acceptable procedure but suddenly social etiquette no longer seemed so very important.

'And the answer to my question?'

'What question?' She frowned.

'My dear Anna, have you forgotten already? I asked if you would dine with me this evening?'

She had forgotten and his reminder brought her up sharp. He was little more than a stranger. She had spoken to him yesterday for the first time in her life, and that had come out of the blue. There had been no formal introduction, no one to vouch for him; it would be sheer madness to trust herself to him; better by far to thank him again and return to her room.

'No, no thank you.' She was terrified enough of the Conway: she had never stayed in a hotel in her life and worried that each move she made would be a wrong one. The thought of eating in a public dining room scared her even more.

'Please, don't say no, Anna.'

Perhaps she did owe him something in return for his assistance yesterday, and maybe, in the future, her business might require she dine in a public dining room. A start would have to be made sometime, it might just as well be now.

Putting on a brave face, Anna smiled.

'Very well Mr Lazenby, I won't say no.'

Seated at a secluded table, Anna stared at the array of cutlery and glasses set before her. What on earth were they all for? Nothing but a knife and fork was used in Roker Street, and only a spoon if the meal were broth; it had been the same in Wednesbury.

In deferential silence a waiter placed a small dish before her.

Did she use a fork or a spoon? Anna's hand hovered in her lap. Edward had shown her a setting of King's Choice but she had only appreciated its beauty, without asking what each implement was used for.

'How was your day, Anna?'

Charles picked up the fork furthest from his plate. Breathing an inward sigh of relief, Anna followed suit.

At last the meal was finished and she relaxed with her favourite cup of tea though Charles had expressed a preference for brandy. Around them other diners stole surreptitious glances at the tanned features of her handsome escort.

'I still can't believe what happened. It's too much like Bella Castleton's tuppenny novels.'

'Whose tuppenny novels?'

'Oh, they're not Bella's, not really,' Anna laughed. 'She doesn't write them, just sells them in her shop in Coseley . . . that's where I live. The girls at the mill love to read them. Filled with such soft notions as the rich young lord marrying the poor working girl, they are. Totally removed from reality. Perhaps that is their chief attraction.'

'And that idea holds no attraction for you, Anna?' There was an undercurrent in his question, a strange intensity that held them silent for a moment.

'I believe in facing reality,' she said, meeting his penetrating stare. 'It doesn't happen that way in real life. Girls like those in Coseley don't marry lords, rich or poor. Work is all they know or will likely ever know.'

'But you, Anna, given the opportunity, would you marry a rich lord?'

'Rich or poor, lord or mill worker, it would make no difference if I loved him.' Anna lifted her head, the movement stealing light from the chandelier then returning it in a thousand tiny red-gold sparks. 'But I don't believe in fairy tales . . . at least not that sort.'

She had thought her straightforward answer would dissuade him from his close scrutiny but it remained just as intense and his eyes had the look Edward's had often held when they had walked together on the moors above the village.

'What happened today was like a fairy tale. I still can hardly believe it.'

'Tell me about it and perhaps my cavalier actions can be practised once more.' Lifting his brandy glass, he eyed her closely. 'Though I shan't be able to say I don't believe in fairies, for you, Anna, have the golden beauty of Titania herself.'

'Who?' she asked quizzically.

'Titania . . . Queen of the Fairies.'

'Oh! Well, it wasn't the Queen of the Fairies I went to see this afternoon,' Anna replied. It poured from her then, the whole business of going to Beldon House, and Charles avidly watched the movement of her lovely face and the emerald fire in her eyes. She was every bit as beautiful as on the day he had seen her cross a street in Birmingham where he had followed her into a shop, only to find as he walked in that she was no longer visible.

'Oh, heavens!' Anna pressed a hand against her lips.

'Heaven is not my domain, Anna, but I will move it and earth too to take that crestfallen look from your face. Whatever it is that is worrying you can be overcome, you know . . . you have only to tell me what it is?'

'Me and my big mouth. Maggie says it's as big as a Parish oven and one day it will get me into trouble, and she's right.'

'You have a delectable mouth, Anna.' Charles replaced

the brandy glass on the table, topping up its contents from a cut-glass decanter. 'I'm sure it could give offence to no one.'

'You don't understand,' she said through her fingers, 'I promised Lady Strathlyn I wouldn't tell anyone that the Queen has asked for my beauty box – and in less than four hours I've revealed it all.'

'Have you told anyone other than myself?'

'No . . . just you, but it is still unforgivable, I made a promise and I've broken it. If the Palace or Lady Strathlyn were to find out . . .'

'They will never hear it from me, Anna.'

There was no reproach in his voice, just sadness. He had shown her kindness and she was repaying it with mistrust.

'Oh, I didn't mean it to sound that way!' Impulsively she put a hand on his.' Of course I don't think you would repeat what I've said. It's myself I can't trust . . . me and my big mouth . . . how long before I blurt the whole thing out again? And next time it might be to someone not so understanding as you.'

Closing strong fingers over the hand on his own, Charles Lazenby looked at the woman seated opposite, knowing he wanted her. Taking a moment to quell the strong desire her touch had stirred in him, he smiled reassuringly.

'It was the excitement that loosened your tongue, Anna. Given a few days it will fade. You will not feel the same need to share it with anyone. Believe me, you will not betray the confidence of Her Majesty.'

'I do hope you're right.' Anna was still not convinced. 'Maggie will give me a right tongue lathering when I get home, and it will be no more than I deserve.'

'You are returning home tomorrow?' he forced himself to answer naturally.

'Yes, the eleven o' clock train.'

'But you have seen nothing of London. That is a pity, Anna, for though you might have difficulty in accepting it

170

after that fracas at the station yesterday, it does have some beautiful sights.'

Withdrawing her hand from his, Anna played absently with her white damask knapkin. She had never used one before, and as with the cutlery only knew what to do with it from watching Charles. He was from an entirely different background to herself; everything about him, clothes, speech, manner, made that glaringly obvious. He was part of the world Jacob Rewcastle had tried to buy Philip into by sending him away to college. He might even be of the aristocracy, the wealthy titled gentry that had bred Sir Robert Daines, but there the similarity ended. There was no spiteful cruelty in this man, of that she felt certain, no unnatural trait that wanted only to see others cower before him.

'I would like to show you some of the city, Anna,' Charles began earnestly. 'Its theatres and art galleries, buildings and parks. The Albert Hall, Saint Paul's Cathedral . . . there are so many things I know you would enjoy.'

'I would enjoy seeing them, Charles.' She twisted the napkin, it helped keep her eyes from that handsome face. 'And Misty would love hearing about them, but there just isn't time.'

'Misty?'

'My daughter.' Anna did look up then, a tender smile playing about her lips. 'She's almost nine and interested in everything. In fact, Maggie says she's such a fidget, wanting to know the top and bottom of everything there's no keeping up with her.'

'Then why doesn't she give her some of those books to read?'

'Books!' Anna looked perplexed. 'What books?'

'Bella Castleton's tuppenny novels.'

Anna laughed aloud, drawing several enquiring faces her way.

'Maggie would never have that. Maggie Fellen took me in when I moved to Coseley. We live in the same house and she looks after Misty most of the time. Too much of the time, if truth be told.' The smile left Anna's eyes. 'I leave too much to Maggie, I know I do, nearly all my time is given to the business. It's not fair on her, and I've tried telling her so and getting her to agree to some help but she won't hear of it. Keep yourself busy and there will be no time for the devil to put his oar in, is Maggie's philosophy.'

'She sounds a sensible woman.'

'She is.'

'Then why not do as she says? Why sit here all evening when you could be busy seeing some of London? And think how fascinated Misty will be when you tell her all you have seen.'

It was a temptation. Misty and Maggie both would be enthralled to hear of what she had seen, but Anna hesitated. It wasn't right to go gallivanting about the place with a man who was almost a stranger . . . and especially not at night.

'I could hire a chaperone.' Charles smiled, understanding her dilemma. Edwardian England had not changed so much. It still imposed tight conventions upon women; its fierce public morality always ready to shred a tarnished reputation.

'But today has been a strain, it has tired you. Maybe a carriage ride through Regent's Park in the morning before you take your train?' He rose to his feet, tall and elegant in a deep blue evening coat reaching almost to his knees. He raised her hand gallantly to his lips. 'You will ride with me tomorrow, Anna?'

His mouth whispered the question but his eyes asked more. Deep dark tunnels, they drew her inexorably where she had no wish to go. There was no sense in prolonging things, nothing to be gained from agreeing to ride with him tomorrow. But on the other hand, Anna told herself flatly, there wasn't much to be lost either. When she got on that train tomorrow Charles Lazenby would melt from her life like mist in a summer sun.

At her nod of agreement he touched his mouth to the back of her hand and walked from the hotel, the elusive violet scent of her perfume filling his nostrils, his mind already wrestling with the problem of how to keep Anna Royce in his life.

Chapter Twelve

Anna had been back from London a week when Charles came to Birmingham.

'He left this, Anna.' Hester, wide-eyed with curiosity, handed Anna a familiar card. 'And he said he would call every day until he saw you. He's already been here twice but I thought I'd better not say where you lived.'

Anna took the card.

'You did right, Hester. Maggie's making enough fuss over moving house, she's no desire to live over against Woodgreen. "Yon side's too lah-di-dah," she says, so heaven knows what she would do if Charles Lazenby landed on her doorstep!'

'He was quite a looker.'

Anna laughed outright.

'You don't have to ask, Hester Fine, I've known you too long. What you mean is, who is he and how did we meet?'

Hester's hazel eyes twinkled.

'Kettle's on, come and tell me the whole story.'

'And now he's in Birmingham and intent on finding you, Anna?' Hester had listened wide-eyed. 'Eee . . . it really is like Bella Castleton's tuppenny romances. Just think . . . Lady Lazenby.'

'Now don't go getting ideas, Hester.' Anna tried to sound calm but as the bell tinkled and her friend disappeared into the shop, Anna's heart was racing.

Eight o' clock, Charles had said, earlier that morning when

leaving his card with Hester and even that was too long to wait before seeing her again. In the back room of the shop Anna slipped into the turquoise taffeta gown she had bought that afternoon from Monsieur Pierre's. It had been wildly expensive but for this one occasion she forgot the cost. She looked at herself in the mirror. Her stomach was flat and her breasts high, even after carrying two children . . . two. The eyes looking back from the mirror changed from green to transparent blue; her son would be almost thirteen now. Was he strong . . . would he be tall . . . did he know about her?

'I'll leave the door on the latch. Eee, Anna, you look gorgeous!'

Hester stood admiring her in the doorway.

'You're going to make the loveliest Lady Lazenby they've ever had.' She darted across the room, taking Anna in a close hug. 'Have a lovely evening,' she said, 'you deserve it.'

There was little time before Charles arrived and Anna, unable to keep still, began to rearrange a lace-draped alcove, placing a tall-necked, cloud-pink porcelain vase at its centre. 'The Italians have such an eye for colour.' She laughed at her own mimicry.

'I agree, but even the most gifted of them could not capture the beauty standing before me.'

Startled, Anna whirled round, colour tingeing her cheeks.

'Charles! I . . . I didn't hear you come in.'

'I had not meant to startle you but will not apologise for having done so.' He moved forward, smiling down at her. 'No man should apologise for being the cause of such wide eyes . . . such beautiful eyes.'

'I was day-dreaming,' Anna replied, a flurry of nerves filling her stomach.

'I think I too am day-dreaming.' His low, seductive voice wreathed about her like black smoke. 'That can be the only explanation for what I am seeing, a dream too beautiful to be true.' He watched the colour deepen in her cheeks, the brilliance of her eyes against the translucence of her skin.

What he had thought in London was true: Anna Royce was the most beautiful woman he had ever seen.

'I thought The Royal Hotel for dinner, if you have no objection?'

He stepped aside at the negative shake of her head, making no attempt to touch her as they went outside to the waiting hansom. He could wait.

'The key.' Anna turned back to the door. 'I mustn't forget to lock up. Hester would have a fit.'

Handing her into the hansom, he caught the elusive fragrance of violets, a fragrance that had haunted him ever since meeting this woman, as she had haunted his mind.

Anna's nerves were stretched taut. She trusted Charles Lazenby, it was her own disturbed emotions that made her nervous.

Their table was in a secluded alcove, some distance from the four-piece orchestra, and Anna, conscious of eyes following them as they crossed the beautifully appointed room, was glad of the privacy it afforded.

All around waiters moved on silent feet, black tailcoats worn over white shirts, and not one of them resembled a penguin.

'What are you hiding behind that Mona Lisa smile?' In the soft light her hair was a vivid crown, all the more alluring for not being adorned with a silly assortment of the feathers so beloved of society women.

'A what smile?' Anna asked, blushing again at what she saw in his look.

'Mona Lisa. It is a painting by Da Vinci, famous for the smile on the face of its subject. It has haunted men for centuries, driven them mad wondering what lies behind it. The same way that your smile is driving me mad now, Anna.'

'Well, I won't let you go mad wondering.' She met his eyes as she told him what had amused her. Listening, he smiled inwardly. He had always thought of Groves as a penguin waddling importantly through Beldon. Strange Anna should see him in just that way.

'What did you think of Beldon House?' Charles asked as their glasses were replenished.

'Whew!' Anna raised her eyes towards the ceiling. 'It defies description. I can only say it was absolutely breathtaking – all those pictures of people in strange clothes, and the furniture . . . I never thought such things existed.'

'And the people?' He watched the animated play of her delicate oval face, the fluttering descriptive movements of her slender hands.

'I only saw Lady Strathlyn.' Tentatively she sipped the wine he'd poured into her glass. 'I suppose there might be a husband somewhere but I know there's a daughter and a son because her Ladyship mentioned them. She was very nice. I expected . . . I don't really know what I expected.'

Creamy shoulders lifted in a shrug, closing the enticing valley between her breasts which peeped tantalisingly over the décolletage of her turquoise gown.

'Will you allow me to escort you home?' he asked, forcing his eyes away from the tormenting sight.

Surprised by the suddenness of his question, Anna glanced at his unfinished brandy. Had she said something to displease him? Had he for some reason become embarrassed at being seen with her? Not wanting to add to any possible unease, she rose.

Taking the short silk-lined cape from the back of her chair, Charles placed it around her shoulders, one finger touching the long curve of her neck beneath the sweep of her hair. Outside the night was a mixture of warm moonlight and darkest velvet sky. Anna couldn't resist staring up at it. It was a sky made for more than just a journey home. This was a night for walking on the heath, for making love in the shadows of Moses Table.

'Allow me, Anna.'

Charles touched a hand to her elbow and she was glad the darkness of the hansom hid the blushes painted by her thoughts. At her side in the shadowed closeness his arm touched against her, then as she would have moved, went about her, drawing her against the hardness of him, his other arm sliding around her back, the palm of his hand between her shoulder blades, its strength preventing her from pulling away – always supposing she had wanted to.

'Anna,' he breathed against her ear, 'my beautiful Anna.' His lips trailed her cheek, pressing a feathering of kisses to her parted mouth. 'My beautiful, beautiful Anna.'

Her eyes closed, everything spinning together in the dark as his mouth closed over hers.

'You're so lovely, Anna.' He broke away. 'I can't tell you how lovely. You are like an exquisite flower, so soft and fragrant.' His voice sounded faraway, drifting in her mind like an echo; a voice within a voice, carrying her on a spiral away from her own common sense.

'Anna.' He still held her close, his mouth against the perfumed silk of her hair. 'I want you to come to London with me. I want you to be with me always. I've wanted you since I first saw you cross a street here in Birmingham. I followed you into a shop, only to feel like a child that had lost some precious toy when I found you were not there.'

'You saw me in Birmingham?' A pulse beat in her brow, resting against his temple. From the recesses of Anna's mind came Lady Strathlyn's words: 'My son purchased it for his sister . . . Birmingham, or so I believe.'

'Lady Strathlyn's son bought an Anna Royce beauty box.' She drew away from him. 'He bought it for his sister.'

'I must confess . . . it was I.'

'But, but your name . . .'

'Is different to my mother's? She took her name and title from a second marriage.'

Pulling free, Anna sought his eyes in the gloom.

'Why didn't you tell me that night in London when we had dinner together? You let me go on about Beldon House and never said a word . . . why?'

He tried to take her back in his arms but Anna resisted, a little of her pleasure gone.

'You were like an excited child, Anna.' He took her hand in his, pressing the palm against his mouth. 'To tell you I knew the house would have robbed you of that excitement, and robbed me of seeing the pleasure in your lovely face as you talked. Why should I do that when the fact of where I live is unimportant?'

'Then why didn't I see you there?'

He released her hand. Light from a street lamp caught her eyes, endowing them with sudden brilliance. How could he tell her he had deliberately stayed away? That his mother was too shrewd a woman not to guess at the feelings he harboured for her visitor?

'Didn't I tell you I was meeting someone? The day you visited Beldon, I was with a very old friend who was returning from Europe.'

The carriage rolled smoothly on, the clatter of the horses' hooves loud on the cobbled road, the encouraging commands of the driver urging them on. Everything seemed the same as it had a few minutes before but somewhere there had been a change.

'Does that answer your question, my sweet interrogator?'

His hand still cupped her chin. Anna pulled away. She didn't know whether it answered her or not. Charles had no need to lie to her yet something inside warned her that he had.

'So, will you come with me to London, Anna . . . please?'

'And what would Lady Strathlyn say to that?'

'She wouldn't have to know,' he returned quickly.

Anna felt the last of her enjoyment drain from the night and her body tensed, waiting for what had yet to come.

'We would gradually introduce the idea of our being together.'

If he had any sense of the impropriety of his proposal, he didn't show it.

'I see!' Anna gathered the silk folds of her cape, holding

them almost protectively across her breasts. 'And will you be living at Beldon House too while this . . . acclimatisation . . . is going on?'

'Beldon House?'

She felt him turn, felt those cool eyes regarding her in the dimness, but made no effort to meet them.

'Of course! That is where I would be living if I came to London with you, isn't it?'

'No, Anna!' He was so casual. 'I had thought of something a little more private, somewhere we could more easily be alone. I could find you a nice little house in the suburbs, away from the bustle of London.'

And from Beldon House. Anna swallowed, tasting bitterness. That was what had really brought him to Birmingham. He wanted a new toy, one that would warm his bed. Well, he certainly fooled you, my girl, she thought with a grim smile. You thought he was helping you up there in London when all he was doing was softening you up, and now he's moved in for the kill. Suddenly she wanted to laugh, loudly and hysterically. Charles Lazenby was no different from Jacob Rewcastle except that when it came to the business of wanting a mistress, the older man didn't beat about the bush.

The carriage stopped in the quiet street in front of Hester and Reuben's house and Anna jumped down without waiting for help, not wanting him to touch her. On the footpath she turned to look back at the man leaning out of the window, his handsome face clearly visible in the moonlight.

'Anna . . .'

'That's a high wall you are sitting on,' she interrupted, 'it separates your world from mine. You should make up your mind which side you want to be on . . . it could be a long painful fall.' Forcing a smile to her lips, she went on, 'It was a pleasurable evening but as for your invitation, thank you, no. I will not be accompanying you to London.'

Climbing the stairs to Hester's spare room, Anna willed her jolted nerves to settle.

'Mark it down to experience,' she whispered, stepping out of the turquoise gown. 'You won't make the same mistake twice.'

'We just can't manage, Anna. Orders is floodin' in wi' each day, an' though I've taken on new 'ands, we can't keep up.'

'So what do you suggest, Seth?'

'I 'adn't wanted to bother thee, I knows tha's busy, but it seemed to me as tha should be told. It's a regular avilanche we bin gettin'. Orders for everything from a vase to a full bankitin' suite.'

Anna smiled at the old man's pronunciation but his meaning was clear enough. John Harris at Wigmore Bank had already told her of the rapid upward surge in her profits and advised her to invest them. She would do that, of course, but after her own fashion.

'So what do we do?' she asked again.

Seth pulled his side whiskers and pushed his lower lip before answering.

'If tha wants to fill these orders . . . and tha'd be a fool not to . . . then only way ah sees it is to get another place. This'n just ain't big enough.'

'Any suggestions?' Anna watched another tug of his whiskers, another pensive twist of the mouth.

'There's several seein' as nobbut us seems to be working. Theer's Boucher's down the road aways. Jeremiah 'ad two kilns a firing theer at one time. An' then theer's Myton's, they 'ad two an' all, mostly piss pots they med.'

Anna glanced away, a smile threatening.

Seth's choice of language was just his way; he meant no offence and she would take none.

She asked instead, 'Which would be best for our use, Seth?'

'Six an' two threes, Anna. They would both do. Both back on to cut, as this place does. Tha could still get pots away by barge.'

'Pots' was hardly an adequate description of the beautiful fragile porcelain but the old man would not thank her for another; they had been 'pots' whatever he or his father had produced, and 'pots' they would always be to him.

Anna went to the window overlooking the cobbled yard. It was no longer desolate and empty as it had been that first day. Now men and women hurried busily between drying sheds and packing houses, and the faces that glanced up smiled as they caught sight of her.

'Two kilns, Seth,' she said quietly. 'That would make them expensive.'

'Ah reckon not.' Behind her, he could see the set of her head, the determined grasp of her small hand on a window bar. 'They 'as two kilns right enough, whereas this place as just the one, but they've stood empty a lot longer'n Gladwin's an' all. Way ah sees it is this.' He pulled his whiskers, particles of dried clay flaking from his hands. 'Thee mek tha offer for whichever one tha chooses an' leave it at that. Neither Jeremiah Boucher nor Joseph Myton is like to refuse. They'n 'ad them dead potteries on their 'ands too long.'

Anna tapped a finger against the dusty glass. Could she work both places? Would the craze for her dainty tea services and elegant dinner suites last, or was she riding the crest of a wave that would ebb, leaving them empty again? Her finger ceased its movement. What she had done once could be done again. If and when fragile porcelain lost its hold on the market then it would be up to her to find something to take its place.

'What about the running of another place, Seth. You can't be in both. Can you find a man you can trust?'

'I reckon so, I knows all folk hereabouts and they'd give their hearts for a chance of a job. They'll serve thee well, Anna, as do the ones 'ere at Gladwin's.'

'But without you to teach them, Seth, will they be able to produce the type of ware I've come to expect?'

Seth tucked his thumbs beneath the string that held the clay-covered apron to his waist.

'There are some older ones who can teach the young 'uns, same as we did here. And besides,' his head thrust forward authoritatively, 'they'll have Seth Gladwin to answer to should they not come up to scratch.'

'Get them then, Seth, as many as you think we will need to run both Boucher and Myton, and leave the rest to me . . .'

'Tha's thinkin' o' gettin' both? That be four kilns extra to this 'un. I know tha has some kind o' magic in thee, lass, but . . . but does think tha can fill 'em all?'

'It's no magic on my part, Seth. Your skill has brought all this about, and I think it will keep us going for a long time yet.'

Turning from the window, Anna picked up the bag she had left on the dust-covered table, making a mental note to get the office cleared and into working efficiency.

'Can you find a sign writer?'

'A sign writer?' Seth repeated, his bushy brows drawing together in concentration. 'Theer's bin no call for such in these parts for long enough but I reckon I knows one. But what does want sign writer for?'

'Read this, Seth.' Handing him the letter, Anna watched him read and then read again, his old hands shaking. At last he looked up, tears channelling the lines of his face.

'If only my old dad could 'ave seen this.'

'The whole of Burslem is going to see it, Seth,' Anna said proudly. 'We are going to have a sign painted the width of those doors out there: "Gladwin's Pottery. By Appointment to His Majesty the King. Suppliers of Fine Porcelain."'

'But 'ow did tha manage this, lass?' He still held the letter in trembling fingers, looking first at it and then at the young woman who was breathing new life into his own.

'Remember the blue and gold banqueting suite you made nigh on a year ago? It was accepted by the Palace, and that,' she nodded towards the letter, 'is the outcome. We've only just started, Seth. Whatever the King has, all the big nobs want the same. You think we are flooded with orders now but just you wait . . . before very long Anna Royce china will be in every fine house in the country.'

She slipped the letter back inside her bag. This was the third of her paper diamonds, but precious as it was, it was not the one she desired most. That was King's Choice. And sooner or later, Edward, she vowed inwardly, I'm going to get it.

'Mary Cresswell is a well-meanin' soul and 'as bin as good a neighbour as a woman could hanker for, but I don't think as how 'er's right for shop.'

'I thought the same, I must admit, Maggie.' Anna looked up from checking her accounts. 'I will have to get a younger woman . . . question is, who?'

The front room that was part of Maggie's old house had been left mostly to Mary's care since they had moved to Woodgreen. Busier than ever, Anna found less and less time to go there.

'An' 'ave you thought of one in Birmingham? Young married wenches 'ave a way of gettin' pregnant.' Maggie watched Anna's pale face, her eyes enormous inside dark circles. Anna worked too hard, driving herself all the time, and for what? A revenge that would kill her in the getting.

'What if Hester starts a child? I can't see Reuben bein' so happy with her workin' when that happens, an' don't tell me you can manage yourself, y'ave enough on your 'ands.'

The same thought had plagued Anna for months now. How would she manage without Hester? True Ellen Passmore, the girl Hester had taken on, was confident and efficient, but had she got Hester's touch . . : could she make every woman who came into the shop feel cosseted, that Anna Royce existed solely to please her? These were all questions that needed answering.

'I will talk to Hester and sort things out but right now I must finish looking over these accounts. I'm seeing John Harris at the bank tomorrow and I want all the facts at my fingertips.' Keeping the accounts herself was time-consuming but there was only one other she would trust to do them in her place. Tomorrow she would go to see Joby Timmins.

'Something is pushin' you, Anna wench.' Maggie refused to be dismissed. 'I don't know what. All I do know is it wasn't pushin' you a few months since an' it's nowt to do wi' Jacob Rewcastle neither. You tek it steady, lass. The devil still rides though the back be sore, Anna. There's no chuckin' 'im off when y'ave 'ad enough.'

Maggie was right, of course. Anna, her head still bent, closed her eyes wearily then opened them again as the handsome face of Charles Lazenby imprinted itself upon the lids. Something *was* pushing her, burning as strong as the desire to regain King's Choice, and tomorrow she would take the first step towards dousing the flames.

Unlike a tuppenny novel heroine she wouldn't have a title but, by God, she would have everything else. She was only a mill girl, only good enough to be a rich man's mistress, was she? Well, watch me, Charles, she vowed silently. Just watch what a Black Country girl can do.

John Harris ushered her into his office with a glance at the long-faced Burrows. He had been hoping Anna would call at the bank; her profits were on a meteoric rise. It would be to her benefit to consider using some of the money for further investment.

'That's sound advice, Mr Harris.' Anna listened to his recommendation that she should buy stocks. 'But I have an idea of my own.'

John Harris smiled.

'You usually have, Mrs Royce, and so far they have all been sound. However, the way you are piling up capital, I felt I ought to offer my advice.'

'That is always welcome, Mr Harris,' Anna flashed him a smile, 'but I have decided on what I want to do . . . only to be frank I don't quite know how to go about it.'

John Harris pressed his hands together, tapping his fingers

against his lips and watching Anna with shrewd, assessing eyes. The shiny black skirt and worn coat were gone, replaced by a grey gabardine suit. Button boots he guessed had seen more cardboard insoles than she would ever admit had given way to smart leather shoes. Mrs Anna Royce had changed and not just in appearance. As she talked he sensed a deepening determination, a will not only to succeed but to excel.

'I wish to expand my business.' Anna watched for a reaction but saw none. 'I want bigger premises and they must give me access to the larger towns.'

'Have you thought of building your own? That way they would be tailor made to your requirements.'

Anna waited only long enough to exhale.

'The shops I want are already built. Tell me . . . have you heard of Ellis Hardware?'

A puzzled frown drew his brows together slightly and his hands were lowered to the desk.

'Yes, but . . .'

'I want them!' Anna intervened.

'Have you any idea of the business they are doing?'

Anna was prepared, she had guessed he would ask this.

'I am quite aware it could be better,' she answered levelly.

'But hardware!' John Harris sounded concerned. 'Forgive me, Mrs Royce, but is that really your line?'

Anna stared determinedly at the man on the other side of the shining desk.

'That is exactly what I want,' she stated flatly. 'Will the bank back me with a loan should my funds prove insufficient to cover the purchase?'

'You are very much in the black, Mrs Royce, a strong healthy balance, but . . .'

'I have no time for buts, Mr Harris.' Anna's eyes flashed like emeralds embedded in ice. 'Only answers. If you can't meet my requirements then I must place my business in other hands.'

Three months later she became sole owner of Ellis Hardware and the same day cancelled all orders to Rewcastle Mill. She had one more paper diamond and the biggest, most brilliant of all, had come one step nearer.

Buying the chain of hardware stores had taken up all her attention, or was that her excuse for not talking to Hester about more staff? Anna knew she had been putting off the moment but now she must face it. All the way to Birmingham the question gnawed at her. What will you do if Hester leaves? And when she finally walked into the shop, she had still found no answer.

'Well, I'm not pregnant!' Hester's pretty face was flushed. 'And I'm not leaving or likely to be yet, despite what Maggie Fellen thinks. Because they had a kid the minute the wedding ring went on their finger, they think everybody else is the same.'

'Maggie didn't mean it that way,' Anna soothed her friend's ruffled feelings. 'She only meant to point out that I should be prepared for any likelihood, such as your being away from the shop for a while.'

Spooning sugar into the tea she had poured, she gave the cup to Hester.

'You know . . . if you only went down with a cold for a few days I would be in a right mess. I already seem to have to be in a dozen different places at the same time.' She took her own tea, stirring it absently. 'Honestly, Hester! We are going to have to do something. Ellen is good, I know, but we couldn't expect her to have to manage alone.'

'I've been giving the same matter some thought, I must admit, Anna.' Hester sighed. 'I feel as you do about Ellen. She's quick and works well but . . .' Putting her cup on the table that separated them, Hester leaned forward.

'Look, Anna, I don't know how you will feel about this but what about taking on some young girls and giving them one evening a week staff training? I thought in addition you might offer them a small commission. That way they will learn the gentle art of selling more quickly, don't you agree?'

'Sounds a good idea.' Anna nodded.

'I've also been thinking about your porcelain. You can't show much of it here.'

'True!' she interrupted. 'But with buying Ellis Hardware, I don't want to take on another shop just yet. But there is another way of showing customers a wider range of what Gladwin's Pottery produces.'

'How?'

Anna pushed her cup aside.

'Why not a catalogue?' she asked. 'We could have very posh ones printed and place them discreetly on the tables. That way customers would be able to see the whole range: designs, colours, the lot. Then if they wanted anything we could take their orders here in the shop!' She sat back. 'What do you think?'

For a long moment Hester remained straight-faced then her mouth widened into a beaming smile.

'What do I think?' she said delightedly. 'I think you're a blooming genius, Mrs Royce!'

The catalogue proved an immediate success: it had a cover of silver card, with scarlet and gold royal arms topping those marvellously influential words 'By Appointment', and inside the first page showed a spray of pink and burgundy fuschias trailing tastefully from the top left-hand corner to the bottom right, enclosing an elegantly scripted 'Exclusive to Anna Royce'.

Every day brought a flood of orders as more and more people discovered her pretty china, and more of the newly rich steel magnates wanted what was in the homes of the gentry. All three of her potteries were working and still demand exceeded output, but Anna would not exchange quality for quantity. She must keep all her products absolutely perfect.

On that she was building her reputation. On that she would string her paper diamonds. On that rested the future of her daughter and of the son for whom she longed, the son who would never know her.

Chapter Thirteen

From the curtained alcove of her bedroom window Anna
watched her daughter in the garden below. At eleven years
old she was gangly as a young colt, all arms and legs, and
growing at a frightening rate.

It seemed only yesterday that Misty had been born,
only yesterday Edward had been taken from her, and
only a little more than yesterday since she had left her
son.

Her son! Anna leaned her head against the cool glass. Would
this longing for him ever leave her? Would she ever have the
courage to claim him?

She closed her eyes, seeing again the tiny crumpled face,
head covered in golden down.

It would not take courage to claim him; the courage had
come in leaving him in Wednesbury. They had been so close
to sending for him, Edward and herself, but he had died before
they could and now . . .

Anna opened her eyes, letting them fix on the tall chimney
stacks of the steel mill, a skyline so like the one of her
childhood.

Now she could not face up to what might happen if she
disrupted his life; could not take the risk of seeing nothing
but hatred in those pale blue eyes, of being condemned for
leaving him.

'I did leave you, my little love,' she murmured, her very
soul twisting with pain. 'I did leave you but I did it for you,

so you could live in peace. I love you, my son, my child . . . I love you so much and I always will.'

Lowering her glance to the garden she saw in her imagination a tall young lad with hair like corn silk, the picture only deepening the longing that was always within her.

He would be working by this time, always presuming there was work to be had in Wednesbury. Would he come bouncing in at night when his day's work was done, like the Cresswell twins did? Was he as happy as they and as healthy? And her father, what of him . . . was he still alive even? Anna's heart twisted, knowing she would never go back; she could not take the risk.

Yes, she had done what she could for her nameless son, but what about Misty? She deserved more than Coseley could provide. Stepping away from the window, Anna sighed. This was not going to be easy.

'But I don't want to go to school! I want to stay with you and Grammie.'

'I know you do, darling, but Grammie needs a life of her own too. She has looked after both of us for so long and running this house is not easy. We can't expect her to go on forever taking responsibility for us.'

What I really mean is, she can't go on taking responsibility for you, Anna thought guiltily, and it was happening more and more often. As business boomed she was called on more regularly to give directions or decisions, often leaving Misty with Maggie or the Cresswells.

'Try to understand, sweetheart, it's for your own good.'

It wasn't the whole truth and Anna looked to Maggie for support but the look on those well-loved features told her she was on her own.

'I do understand.' The golden hair, still like so much summer-morning mist, swirled about Misty's face. 'You want to get rid of me. I . . . I'm in the way here . . . a nuisance under your feet.'

'Oh, Misty, that's not so and you know it!' Anna tried to take her daughter in her arms but the child twisted away, her mouth tight. 'You could never be in the way, either of me or Grammie.'

'Then let me stay. You say the business is taking too much of your time so why not let me help? That's all I want, to help.'

From her chair against the fire Maggie Fellen watched the child she had nursed from birth, reading the pain of rejection in that small face as clearly as though it were a book in her hands; and watching too that older child who had come to her out of a dark, rain-torn night. It wasn't an easy decision Anna was making but it was one that had to be hers alone.

'And I want you to,' she was saying softly, 'that is part of the reason I want you to go to boarding school. I've seen your sketches, darling, they are good . . . very good. I want you to develop that talent, to learn presentation and design, experiment with colour and materials. None of which you can do here.'

That much at least was true. Misty had inherited Edward's eye for drawing and was already showing signs of Anna's own flair for design, and there was no school in Coseley that could take that talent and mould it. Anna took a breath and plunged on.

'Think of it, Misty. If you can learn those things, you can join the business. We could use a good packaging designer.'

'You really mean that? You . . . you're not pretending, are you, just to get me to agree to go away to school without a lot of fuss?'

Her cornflower blue eyes were no longer tearful and Anna breathed a silent prayer of thankfulness. Who could blame Misty if she did kick up a fuss? Certainly not a mother who knew the heartbreak of losing a parent.

'No, darling, I'm not pretending.' She smiled at her half-grown daughter. 'You do well at school, learn as much as

191

you can, and when you leave there will be a place for you in the business.'

'I suppose you knows what you be doing.'

Misty had gone to bed and now Maggie voiced her critical concern. 'Misty is your daughter after all.'

'You must agree it's for the best, Maggie?' Anna settled on the floor, her head resting against the knee of her old friend. 'She really hasn't anyone here she cares to be with other than the Cresswell twins, and they are getting a bit too grown up to drag a schoolgirl with them everywhere they go.'

'Mmm, I sees your point, Anna, and I goes along with what you said about girl needin' the kind of schoolin' that ain't to be got in Coseley. But what did you mean about me needin' more rest? I be as good as ever I was an' don't you go sayin' any different, Anna Royce.'

'You know I only said that so Misty wouldn't argue.' Anna pressed lovingly against Maggie's knee. 'You are as strong as ever you were, we both know that. I said it because I simply didn't know how else to persuade Misty.'

'Well, that didn't do it.' Maggie stroked a hand over the shining red-gold hair. 'It was your promising her a place wi' you did that. My question is, did you mean it? Do you intend doin' as you said? I love that child as I would one of my own an' I couldn't stomach seein' 'er disappointed.'

'Of course I meant it.' Anna looked up, surprised Maggie should harbour any doubts as to her sincerity. 'Misty's sketches are good. Given the right training she could well become a very competent designer, and if things continue as they are now we will need someone like that.'

Returning from the long journey to Kent where Misty had been entered into the Haworth School for Young Ladies, Anna climbed into the trap brought to pick her up from the station.

'Did little 'un settle all right?'

Anna tried to smile. Whatever was said to the carter one day was all over Coseley the next.

'Yes, she was already making new friends when I left.' It was a valiant lie but she needed to hear those words, to reassure herself that the tears flooding her daughter's eyes would be gone by now.

'I be glad to 'ear that, Mrs Royce.'

He hadn't believed her, the flat tone of his voice said so, and Anna was glad when he lapsed into silence. She had tried telling herself that boarding school would be best for Misty, but was it, or was she risking her daughter's happiness in order to lighten her own load?

It was late when the trap turned around and the carter called goodnight but Maggie was waiting, the letter in her hand.

'But why, Maggie?'

'Didn't John Harris tell you?'

'No!' Anna slumped into one of the upholstered wing armchairs that graced the tasteful sitting room, a bewildered look in her fine eyes. 'And his letter never mentioned it.'

'Can't say I blame 'im for not writing thing like that down. Letters 'ave ways of fallin' into wrong hands.'

'But selling the mill!'

She still could not take in what the manager of Wigmore Bank had told her. Jacob Rewcastle was selling up ... completely. She might once have danced around the room with glee at hearing it, but now ...

'I've bin expecting something like this,' Maggie said, her own expression as troubled as Anna's.

'But he's closing down completely ... the whole lot ... rolling mills, everything. Why, Maggie?'

'Money!' the older woman answered dourly. 'What else? Jacob Rewcastle 'as spent 'ard and fast since his son's death, spendin' on them fancy bits of is'n, spendin' too much trying to rebuild what's dead and gone. It 'ad to come,' she shook her grey-streaked head, 'an' now it's here.'

Anna closed her eyes, leaning back against the softness of the chair. Yes, it was here, and it was her fault. God! She hadn't meant for this to happen. Cancelling all Ellis Hardware contracts had been her way of hitting out at Jacob Rewcastle, but they were Rewcastle's major buyer. Without them he had found it hard to survive and now it seemed he wanted cash more than he wanted his mill.

'It'll butter no parsnips, you blamin' yourself.' With her usual insight Maggie went to the heart of Anna's worry. 'Jacob Rewcastle can put this on nobbut himself. A man like him,' she went on scathingly. ''Avin' a bit on the side 'as long been the prerogative of his sort, and I suppose as it'll go on that way, but to fall for the tongues of lying trollops! Still, you knows what folk say . . . there's no fool like an old fool.'

Wasn't there? Anna's thoughts leaped to Charles Lazenby. She wasn't so old but she had certainly been fooled. He had never tried to contact her since that night more than a year ago.

'It's his wife as I'm sorry for.' Maggie's voice cut through her thoughts. 'To lose an only child the way she did, then 'avin' the shame of a man who meks a fool of 'imself with every loose woman he can find. Tcchh! Jacob Rewcastle needs a boot up 'is arse an' even then I doubt it would knock sense to his head. Closin' mill—! Eee, who would 'ave thought?'

'What about Coseley? Rewcastle's Mill is the only employment here . . . what of the men and their families, how will they keep them?'

Maggie expelled a long, troubled breath, head moving slowly from side to side.

'It's going to be 'ard, Anna, 'ard on everybody, I'm thinkin'. There'll be tears in a good few houses down yon side when they learns of this.'

In bed Anna stared into the darkness. She hadn't wanted this. Her sole aim in buying Ellis Hardware and closing its doors against Jacob Rewcastle had been to pay him back for what he had done to her, to pay him back for taking

King's Choice; but she didn't want revenge at the expense of people who had shown her only kindness, had accepted her as one of their own. At last pearl-grey fingers of dawn played across her face, turning pink then yellow. She knew what she was going to do now but the knowledge took away none of her worry.

She would be in London for a week, all the time she could spare, and it had taken one of those precious days to find the shop. She was taking a hell of a risk, opening another shop at this time, but she needed a wider market and this could prove the most lucrative of all. The shop she had found was small but the location opposite St James's Park was excellent. Quite a bit of carriage trade passed along Birdcage Walk, either to the park or into Buckingham Palace Road. This meant her 'By Appointment' sign would be seen by the wealthy or those who served them.

Paying three guineas a week rent for three months in advance made Anna grimace. It was scandalously high, but that she supposed was London, a fact her own prices would reflect.

She had chosen well. The building could have been custom-built with its deep-set alcoves and graceful niches, and Anna used them to full advantage, displaying her porcelain there and on pretty, lace-draped tables that looked as if just laid for an intimate luncheon or afternoon tea.

'Phew!' Anna pushed a straying strand of hair upward, securing it beneath a tortoiseshell comb. 'I never thought we would be ready in time. You've been marvellous, Emma . . . thank you for all your hard work.'

Emma Sanders, born of money-conscious, middle-class parents then rejected by them for daring to fall in love with and marry a working man, was one of the girls Hester had taken on for staff training, and although that was just weeks ago, both Anna and Hester felt confident she could now handle the London shop alone.

'We are both very grateful to you, Mrs Royce.' Emma's face was beginning to lose the haunted look it had held and not all the colour in her cheeks was due to the hard work of setting up the last of the displays.

'William and I still cannot quite believe it . . . a place of our own. You needn't worry.' She smiled, suddenly transformed by the happiness that lit her violet eyes. 'William and I will make the shop work, I promise.'

'I know you will, Emma, but the rooms over the top are not big . . . are you sure you can manage?'

'We will be together, Mrs Royce.'

Anna didn't need to hear any more. Understanding completely what the girl meant, she turned away, checking yet again the elegant displays, nervously rearranging a beauty box here or a jug there.

She had chosen her site well. With two days to go before she must return to Coseley, her books were already filled with orders that would keep Gladwin's Pottery working for weeks ahead and the catalogues had been an enormous success. Her beauty boxes, too, craftily placed in the tiny boudoir alcove, had not gone unnoticed. Benjamin Freeth and the Cresswell boys would be delighted with the several dozen orders already placed.

Behind her the tiny bell William had fastened above the door tinkled. Anna collected her thoughts, with Emma already busy with a customer, she must attend to the one who had just entered the shop. Taking a last nervous breath she turned, the smile that had come automatically to her lips fading.

'You came to London after all!' he said quietly, giving a slight bow to an overdressed dowager dragging a vinegar-faced companion in her ample rear. 'I am so glad, Anna.'

'Are you, Mr Lazenby?'

'You know I am.' He smiled into her eyes. 'You must have

dinner with me tonight so that I may tell you how much I have missed you.'

The smile was the same, slow and disarming, lifting the corners of his mouth in a dangerous, deceptive curve. His eyes, slumbrous, hypnotic, would drown the unwary.

'Thank you, but I am too occupied with the shop.' Pin pricks of sweat touched her brow like warm mist; her palms felt moist. He had taken her by surprise. Somehow she had never thought he might come to the shop. In the rush of her decision to open up here, she had forgotten he too lived in London.

'Nonsense.' He stepped in front of her, trapping her against one wall. 'You have someone here with you. She can see to whatever needs seeing to.'

'I prefer to do that for myself.' She had been surprised, taken off guard, but now she was herself again. His eyes no longer seemed hypnotic as she stared coldly into them. 'If you will excuse me, I have customers waiting.'

'Anna, listen to me.' He moved as she did, blocking her way. 'I can do so much for you . . . this shop, your porcelain. I can help open doors you never even knew existed.'

Sunlight reaching through the bow-shaped windows touched his fair hair, turning it to bronze where it curled softly above his collar. It would be so easy to accept his offer. Beneath the starched high collar, her throat felt hot and dry and she had to draw a long breath.

'Your price is too high, Mr Lazenby,' she said unsteadily. 'My tableware must succeed on its own merits, I won't sell myself in order to promote it.'

'Charles!'

The petulant cry ringing across the salon was her means of escape and as he turned Anna took it.

'Come here, Charles . . . I want your opinion on this.'

Hands trembling, Anna tried to concentrate on the plump dowager and her dilemma over which dinner service she should choose but she could not close off the strident voice.

'The colours are well toned, Charles, don't you think, but is it right for Abbotts Ford?'

'I'm sure whatever you choose will be perfect.'

Anna heard the rustle of satin as the dowager moved to another alcove, Charles Lazenby could charm ducks from the water when he spoke like that. Desperately wanting to get away to the privacy of Emma's upstairs rooms, she could only nod and try to smile as her portly customer continually changed her mind.

'But it must be perfect for both of us, Charles, it must please us both for we will be using it . . . once we are married.'

The dowager lifted her feather-adorned head, smiling fatuously in the direction of the over-sweet sentence, but Anna refused to look up. If Charles hoped the news would shock her, he could hope again.

It was two years since he had followed her to Birmingham and she had refused to become his mistress. That was more than enough time to get himself engaged. That was not what galled her. It was the fact that in the face of his coming marriage he still wanted her to be his mistress. That was the pill that was too bitter to swallow.

Putting down a flower-sprigged sauce boat, Anna walked into the back room which served as a store room. If the dowager didn't buy her china because of being abandoned, then hard luck.

'It isn't what you think, Anna.'

His gentleness had the effect of petrol on a low flame. Every nerve ending flared with sudden all-consuming rage, destroying any last vestige of respect she might otherwise have held for him. Skirts rustling against the rough stone floor, Anna whirled round to face Charles Lazenby who had followed her into the store room.

'Anna, it isn't . . .'

'I don't think anything!' Her voice was cutting. 'I'm not interested in you, in what you do or who you do it with! In short, Mr Lazenby, I prefer not to be burdened with the wearisome task of having to make polite conversation with you.'

Breasts heaving with every breath, Anna studied the handsome features already indelibly printed on her mind, then so quietly she was only just audible added: 'If you are the gentleman you imply then you will not impose yourself upon me again.'

Less than four paces away Charles Lazenby's mouth tightened, his fine nostrils flaring with the effort of holding his temper in check. His eyes became cold. Anger clearly visible in their depths, he stared at her for a long moment. Then, with one tap of his silver-topped malacca cane against a gloved palm, said tersely, 'Your servant, Mrs Royce.'

'I don't believe this at all.' Anna read the neatly penned note again before handing it across the breakfast table to Emma. 'I think this is a ruse. Charles Lazenby is using his mother's name to get me to go to Beldon House. I don't think Lady Strathlyn wants to see me or my catalogue.'

Emma read the letter and handed it back to her.

'But why ... for what reason ... I mean, why use his mother's name?'

'Because he knows there is no way on God's earth he would get me to go anywhere to see him.' Yesterday had left Anna badly shaken. She could not take another encounter with Charles ... not yet.

'But if the note really is from Lady Strathlyn,' Emma said in concern, 'it would place the shop in jeopardy if you snubbed her. She is bound to have influential friends.'

You don't know how influential, Anna thought, folding the note back into its crested vellum envelope.

'Can't you excuse yourself? Say how busy you are with the shop being so newly opened.'

'Not if we wish to extend our clientele, Emma.'

'What if you were not here?' William folded his news-paper.

'But I am here, William!'

The strain of the last week, the threatened closure of Rewcastle's Mill and all that it entailed, rang in Anna's sharp reply. Lady Strathlyn had been very kind to her. How could she repay that with a deliberate lie?

'But if you were not in London, surely she could not hold it against you if someone else acted for you?' He answered with plain good sense.

'But as Anna said . . . she is here, William. It would be gross bad manners to pretend otherwise.' Emma placed a hand over that of her husband.

'She wouldn't be if she took the afternoon train home.' William looked from one quizzical face to the other. 'Simply send a catalogue and more samples . . . I could take those and a note from Emma. If she said you had returned to Coseley, leaving her with permission to open any letters not marked 'Private' and deal with matters arising from them, surely that would remove any suspicion of deliberate rudeness?'

'And get me off the hook,' Anna admitted. 'But can you two manage here?'

Smiling at William, Emma's eyes darkened to that lovely shade of violet. 'We can manage, Anna,' she said softly, 'we have each other.'

'Excuse me, ma'am.'

Anna turned from the window where her eyes had barely noted the passing countryside. A man, dark-haired and dark-eyed, smiled openly at her and for a fleeting second Anna felt she knew him.

'I . . . I know it's not polite to address a lady y'ain't been introduced to but there being nobody here to do that, I thought I'd just up and take the risk.'

Anna noted the clear complexion, the hair cut higher than the collar, shorter than the way Charles wore his, and the clothes. The dark worsted suit was more workmanlike than

fashionable but the wide honest smile more than made up
for that.

'Fact is, ma'am, I was wondering if you was taking this train
all the way to Birmingham?'

'Yes.' Anna was surprised at the question but answered
anyway. 'But I go on to Coseley.'

'Say now, if that ain't pure coincidence. I'm going to Coseley
too. My mam lives there . . . say, you might know her. Name
of Maggie . . . Maggie Fellen?'

Andrew! It was all she could do not to gasp . . . this man
was Andrew, Maggie's son. She looked into his grey eyes, so
much darker than his mother's, and some tiny imp of mischief
made her hold her tongue.

'Lived in Coseley all her life, has me mam,' he went on
when she did not speak. 'I went to America a few years
ago and she wasn't too pleased about that but I've done all
right and now I'm here to fetch her back to the States. She's
gonna live in comfort from now on. I've got this ranch in the
Mid-West and I've had a place built on it in case Mam wants
a house to herself. Independent is me mam, always was.'

'Does your mother know you want her to go and live with
you in America?' Anna was giving nothing away.

'Shucks no, ma'am.' The smile broke out again, like a lad
who had been given a threepenny bit. 'I have to break news
like that gently. She won't want to come first off, but she'll
change her mind. After all, there's nothing here for her.'

'Perhaps not,' Anna replied, resisting the temptation to smile,
'but the habits of a lifetime can be hard to break.'

'Ya only have to do it once, ma'am.' He grinned boyishly.
'Like most things, ah reckon, rest comes easy after that, and
I want me mam with me for what's left of her time.'

He was right. Anna felt her heart lurch. Habits could be
broken and family was family after all. Perhaps Maggie
would go with her son. It was too painful to think about
on top of everything else so with an effort she pushed the
prospect away.

'I wonder how she looks?' Andrew Fellen rambled on, unaware of the heartache he was causing in the smartly dressed woman sitting across the compartment from him. 'She always tried her best to look smart, did me mam, even though it could never have been easy for her after . . .'

He broke off in mid-sentence; Anna could have told him she knew his father had left when he was still young, but from the look that suddenly closed his face, felt it would be tantamount to interfering so said nothing.

For several minutes the rhythm of the train and the huff of the steam engine were the only sounds in their closed world, and then, as if he had come to some decision, Andrew began again.

'I didn't think life was too bad when I were a lad and me father worked at Rewcastle's Mill. On Sunday afternoons he would take me with him up on to the heath. Me mam would create at that, said we should both be in Chapel, but Father would have none of it. He said there was more to be learned by watching birds and looking at plants and creatures God had made, and he was right. I reckon I learned more from him than I could from any Bible-punching Baptist Minister.'

His face had softened as he talked of his father and the stony look had left his dark eyes, but the heartache he had talked away had settled in Anna, arousing memories of her own carefree childhood and the parents who had been her life, bringing back all the agony of their loss.

'Winter was good too in its own way.' Maggie's son did not see the pain, could not read the distress in those wide green eyes fixed on his.

'The fire was always way up the chimney and the kettle on the hob. Mam would make toast thick with dripping and a mug of tea with three spoons of sugar. When me dad came home from mill he would take hot plate from the oven, wrap it in cloth and put it in my bed. Then we would sit downstairs by the fire together and look through his book while me mam did her crochet.

It were all pictures of ships. Mad about ships were me dad.'

I know, Anna thought watching him, and I know the misery that madness brought your mother. But even so she smiled inwardly as the brogue of childhood slipped back into speech.

'Talk about ships from morning till night, would me dad, supposin' he could get anybody to listen. Mam said he were just plain daft. He'd far better find summat useful to occupy his spare time.' His lids half-closed, narrowing the dark eyes as he stared into the past. 'It seemed me mam never could understand that was his way of relaxing, that an hour with that book brought him a pleasure nothing else could give; and after sloggin' his guts out in that mill for twelve hours every day any man deserved all the pleasure he could get.'

Beyond the windows sheep and cattle browsed peacefully in soft meadows; in the distance a church spire reached a bony finger to the sky, reminding Anna sharply of the smoke-blackened Parish Church that dominated Wednesbury from its own green sloping hill.

'I suppose he stuck it as long as he could.' His voice was softer, the hindsight of maturity not quite masking the raw pain. 'Then one day he just walked out. I thought my world had ended but me mam never said one word and if I tried asking she shut me up sharpish.'

'Did your father ask her to go with him?'

'Never knew. Like I told you, me mam would have nowt said after me dad had gone.'

Shadows lengthening in the compartment touched his face, softening the line of features sharp cut as his mother's, concealing the sorrow in his eyes.

'I left school then. I were twelve and got a job in the mill . . .'

The door slid open and Andrew stopped speaking, turning his head towards the gathering night. Anna watched the uniformed conductor turn up the wick of the polished brass oil lamps fastened to the sides of the compartment, watched yellow flame spurt along the tall glass funnel as the wick caught the flaring life of the match he held to them, then smiled good evening as the attendant touched his cap to her. To Andrew Fellen she said nothing; respecting the silence of a man mourning lost years, lost love; feeling the twist of sympathy. She knew that pain, she had travelled the same path.

'I had to get a job.' He began to speak suddenly, the words rushing out of him like some long withheld torrent. 'I didn't want me mam breaking her back, killing herself in that lousy sweat shop of a mill for a few paltry shillings, like all the others in Roker Street. There were only two of us, we had no family of kids, so I reckoned we could manage on the bit old man Rewcastle paid young lads. And we did manage until . . .' He halted again, hands twisting viciously against each other and his mouth thinning, the strength of his emotions draining it white.

'Forgive me, ma'am.' He leaned his head against the white antimacassar of the seat. 'I've rattled on like a child, I beg your pardon.'

Anna smiled then turned her head to the darkened vista, knowing the value of silence.

Conversation had kept Charles from her mind but as Andrew took her hand, helping her down to the platform, the spectre of him rose vividly. He had taken her hand that way. Like Andrew he was so tall she had to tip back her head to look into his face. Waiting while Andrew brought her bag from the train, Anna looked past him, catching the dark silhouette etched black on the deep grey evening, a shadow that darted towards the engine, beginning to pull away.

'No!' Pushing Andrew aside, Anna flew along the platform, grabbing the shadow intent on throwing itself beneath the massive wheels.

'Leave off!' it screamed, struggling so violently Anna almost lost her hold.

'What the hell . . .' Andrew Fellen twisted the struggling figure into his firmer grip.

'Leave off . . . let me go, you bloody interferin' . . .'

Anna heard the thud of clog against bone as the shadow kicked out viciously, the grunt of anger and pain followed by a rattle of breath as Andrew's strong hands whipped it back and forth.

'Do you be knowin' you can get yourself killed arsin' about in front of a railroad train?' he shouted, anger restoring his native dialect in full.

''Course I bloody well knows.' The struggling stopped and the figure fell against his chest. 'Why else does think I be 'ere?'

Anna's hand flew to her throat as she tried to catch the night-veiled face. Who was it . . . who in Coseley was desperate enough to want to commit suicide?

'I'll take her.' She reached for the sobbing girl, feeling the bones beneath a pathetic covering of flesh.

'It's all right,' she soothed, guiding her towards the arched entrance that led on to the cobbled road. 'It's all right now.'

'Say, ma'am . . . where do we get a cab around here?'

Only then was Anna aware of the tall figure following behind.

'We don't,' she said.

'Then how in the hell is a guy supposed to get where he's goin'?'

The accent Anna presumed to be the gift of America returned but where once she had found it pleasant, it now grated.

'He walks!' she snapped irritably. 'The same as a woman.'

'What possessed you to do a daft thing like that?' Maggie handed a cup of cocoa to the girl, now bathed and dressed in one of Misty's nightgowns.

'I thought it best an' I still do.' Red-eyed defiance met Maggie's stony glare.

'Best!' Maggie shoved the cup into the girl's hand, noting the skin yellow against the white pillows of Misty's bed. 'Best . . . to throw yourself under railroad engine?'

'At least that way I get to kill meself, and it's only what me mam'll do any road when 'er finds out.'

'Finds out what?' Anna asked. Looking into those drowned eyes was like looking into those of her own daughter, so blue, and the child would be pretty had her face not been so thin, and puffy from crying.

'Finds out I be pregnant.' She began to wail all over again. 'Oh, me mam'll kill me, I knows 'er will!'

'What about lad as put you up the spout?' Maggie asked without preamble. 'Is 'e going to marry you?'

''E can't.' The wail sharpened and Anna removed the cup before the girl's trembling hands slopped cocoa on to the white sheet. ''E's no lad, an' besides 'e's married already. Oh, God!' Dropping her face into her hands, the girl sobbed. 'Oh, God, me mam . . . an' the neighbours, won't they just love this?'

Turning away Anna set the cup on the marble-topped dresser, hiding the agony that had leaped to her eyes. She knew what this child was going through and the ordeals yet to come.

'Who be your mam?' Maggie pushed a large cotton handkerchief into the girl's thin hands.

'Connie Stevens . . . me mam's Connie Stevens. We live down by cut side. 'Er'll not tek me back once 'er knows.'

Maggie's brow wrinkled into a frown. She knew the cutsiders, living in shacks thrown together from anything, overrun with kids and rats, dirt and filth everywhere. And she knew Connie Stevens; large, loud-mouthed and aggressive, more interested in the gin bottle than her large brood that swarmed the banks of the canal up against the mill, living on anything they could lay their thieving hands on. Why this one should want to return was beyond understanding until you remembered the alternative was the workhouse.

'Wipe your snotty nose an' get yourself off to sleep,' she said, gently covering the puny shoulders with the bedcovers. 'Mornin's soon enough to sort that out.'

'Wench was right.' Downstairs she told Anna what she knew of the folk who lived alongside the canal. 'Connie Stevens will kill 'er an' all but not on account of any neighbours. It'll be 'cos the kid will no longer be fetchin' in money for gin. Poor little thing, life's 'ard enough down there without this. But she's bin a bloody fool when all's said and done an' none to blame but 'erself.'

'It doesn't always happen that way,' Anna answered quietly, her own rape vivid in her mind. 'We musn't judge until we know.'

A loud bang at the door brought their glances together before Anna went to open it.

'I'm sorry.' She blushed as the man standing on the whitewashed step finished speaking. 'I meant to tell you but when I saw that girl try to throw herself under the train, it completely slipped my mind.'

'Then it's as well Mrs Cresswell still lives down there, isn't it?'

'Who is it, Anna?' Maggie emerged from the sitting room.

'A visitor, Maggie.' Anna smiled. 'For you.'

She was silent for a second, mouth opening and closing, the blood draining from her lined face. Andrew too stood silent and immobile.

'Mam . . . oh, Mam!' Then he was across the hall, gathering his mother into his arms, his face pressed against her grey-streaked hair.

'Oh, Mam!'

Closing the door, Anna walked upstairs.

Anna smoothed the bodice of her grey corded day suit and pushed a stray hair under the lime green hat. The curling feather gave it a jaunty air but didn't reflect her feelings. She had visited Wigmore's Bank often enough but today she was nervous. Pushing open the door, her footsteps seemed to echo on the tiled floor as they had seemed to do that first day almost ten years ago, and catching sight of the watchful Mr Burrows, her spine tingled. Entering the hushed confines of the manager's office, her mouth was dry but the palms of her hands felt moist with sweat.

'That's it in a nutshell. By taking over Ellis Hardware I have been the cause of Rewcastle Mill's closing and I had not reckoned on that.'

Anna twisted her fingers together awkwardly. This was worse than being in the dock but she couldn't back down; she would go through with it no matter how awful it felt.

John Harris watched her closely.

'Then what did you reckon on?' he asked quizzically.

'I thought he would just sell King's Choice.'

That he could believe. She wanted only what Jacob had taken from her.

'It never occurred to me he would just throw the whole lot up,' she rushed on. 'I feel responsible, it will be my fault if the people of Coseley lose their work.'

'So what is it you want to do?'

'I want the bank to extend my credit, I want to take over the mill.'

'You!' John Harris was clearly astonished. 'But you have cancelled the main outlet for their products.'

'What I have closed I can reopen.' Confidence returned, bringing Anna's chin up firmly. 'I can resume the sale of hardware through Ellis Hardware and that way no one will lose.'

'But hadn't you intended those shops to be new outlets for your porcelain?'

'Yes, but in the face of what has happened I have changed my mind. The money allocated to re-designing the interior of those shops will help buy the mill. For the present it will be more sensible to lease smaller premises to launch my tableware.'

'Then you still intend to carry on with your plans for widening your market?'

'Most definitely, Mr Harris. The purchase of Rewcastle Mill will not affect my decision on that. As you yourself said when I approached the bank concerning Ellis Hardware, my profit margins are very healthy, I can repay a loan with no problem. In fact, my only problem at the moment is, do I borrow money here or from some other bank?'

The following evening John Harris called on Anna at home.

'Mrs Royce,' he said formally. He had waited until she had written her name across the foot of a close-written document, agreeing to a loan of three thousand pounds. 'I think you should know the directors of the bank are friends of Jacob Rewcastle. Take my advice, tread carefully.'

'I don't want my name put forward as a prospective buyer, Reuben.' Anna sat in Reuben Fine's office in the centre of Birmingham. 'If Jacob Rewcastle got wind of it he would see every man in Coseley starve before he would sell. Can I put in an offer to buy using a different name, one which Jacob might not so easily recognise?'

Reuben thought for a moment. 'You kept the name Gladwin for your pottery, and Stoke-on-Trent is a fair distance from Coseley. It could be an even bet that Jacob will not know much of the town, or recognise the buyer, and given that should he want to sell badly enough he might not pay too much attention to the name. It is a risk, Anna, but if that is the way you want it then we can try.'

'It is the way I want it, Reuben.'

Pushing his spectacles back onto the bridge of his nose, Reuben looked at Anna. Her face was pale and there were dark shadows beneath her eyes. He guessed what was driving her, but the need was not only to recover King's Choice. He knew there was a need in her that went deeper than that; he had known since that night she had talked with Hester and himself about the possibility of acquiring another shop. The talk had drifted to the past and it was then she had told them of her rape and of the son she had in Wednesbury. That was the driving force behind all that Anna Royce did, the need to have both of her children with her.

'We can sort the business of the mill, Anna,' he said, looking at her through the thick lenses of his spectacles, 'but what about you? You are pushing yourself too hard, taking on too many commitments. You can't burn both ends of a candle and not expect it to go out.'

'I am all right, Reuben.' Anna's smile was deceptively bright. 'So long as I can keep the men in work. Get that mill for me.'

Chapter Fourteen

Jacob Rewcastle entered The Fighting Cocks public house, making his way to the back room where he regularly met his business associates.

Business! He clamped his teeth together hard, face thunderous. His business had gone downhill since the sale of Ellis Hardware; a great deal of his trade had been with them, and now he was about to lose the steel mill.

To whom? The question had puzzled him for days. Who in Coseley had the money to buy out Jacob Rewcastle?

'Evenin', Mr Rewcastle, sir.'

The landlord greeted him as he strode through the smoke-filled bar, packed with men in tattered jackets, their moleskin trousers held up with wide, heavy-buckled belts.

Nobody, that was who, Jacob answered his own question, ignoring the landlord. There was nobody hereabouts could find that kind of money. Like as not the mill would go to some bloke from Brummagem.

Yes, it would be bought by somebody in Birmingham. He didn't really mind being out of business. The eternal rat race of undercutting the next man, always having to watch the market for signs of a slump – no, he would not mind being out of that now he had no son to leave it to.

No son!

The thought struck him like a physical blow as it always did.

Philip was dead and all because of that bitch.

Opening the door, he was greeted by several men already seated in leather armchairs, brandy glasses at their elbows.

Letting the door swing to behind him, Jacob returned their greeting. These were the men who would help him take revenge on that Royce woman. With their help he would see the bitch in the workhouse where she belonged, her and her brat!

Removing his overcoat and tall black hat, Jacob accepted a glass of brandy, carrying it to his accustomed place beside the glowing coal fire.

He had been too soft on Edward Royce's wife, had only threatened to put her out of business up to this point, but now he would make that threat a reality. If Jacob Rewcastle had no business then Anna Royce would have none, and if he had no child to come after him then she would have none either.

That kid attended some boarding school. It wouldn't be too hard to get somebody to see to it that one afternoon she had an accident!

'Now then, Jacob,' a voice hailed him from a deep armchair. 'Be you still set on giving up the steel?'

'I am.' Jacob took a pull at his brandy, pressing his tongue against the roof of his mouth as the liquid burned his throat.

'Can't say I blame you,' the voice replied. 'I would do the same if I hadn't a son to leave it to.'

You bastard! Jacob's thoughts burned like the brandy. You never fail to rub it in, never fail to make some remark, but you ain't got the courage to come right out with it, say what you mean. Jacob Rewcastle hasn't got it in him to make another son.

But he must keep his thoughts to himself. At least until he had what he was looking for, and that was the help of these men in destroying Anna Royce.

But he had to tread warily, take care what reasons he gave for enlisting their aid. They were men of the world as he was, men who wouldn't think twice about tumbling a woman, but at the same time they would have no sympathy with a homosexual

nor with the father of one; it must not come out that Philip
had been of that tendency.

'But why put the woman out of business?'

The man who put the question fingered bushy side
whiskers, his eyes watching Jacob through the a haze of
cigar smoke.

'Ar, why bother?' another put it. 'She won't survive long
anyway. Business be for a man. Ain't no woman capable of
runnin' more'n a kitchen.'

'This one is,' Jacob said over the murmurs of assent. 'This
one has a head on her shoulders, and if she ain't stopped she's
likely to have all of Coseley in her pocket in a few years' time
– and that won't sit easy with a few in this room.'

'But what does she do? I mean, to be a threat the woman
has to have money, so where does it come from? After all,
she cannot manufacture the loot out of thin air, can she?'

Jacob turned a cold eye on the snappily dressed son of a
late colleague. She could make mincemeat out of you. For
all your public school way of talking, you ain't got a decent
brain cell in your head, he thought. Swallowing a little more
brandy, he drowned the desire to speak the thought aloud.

'She can do the next best thing,' he answered, swirling the
contents of his glass. 'How many in this room can pick plants
off the heath and turn 'em into face creams and sweet-smelling
lotions?'

'Is that what 'er business be, Jacob?'

'Some of it.' Jacob turned his glance to the older man. 'I'm
told as she also has considerable interests in some fancy china
place up along Stoke way. I tell you, that woman has her head
on right way round. Face paints and fancy china – the things
every woman wants, and every woman with money, and even
some without it, will have.'

Going to the table to replenish his glass from the several
bottles laid on it, he looked at each man in turn.

'You all of you have wives *and* them you passes off as
wives on the side. Tell me, which of those women has no

liking for fancy cups and saucers and pretty china doo-dads? Which of them don't put powder and paint on their faces, even if they don't own to it, eh? Which one of your wives would be content knowing the one next door had summat she hadn't got? None of 'em, and you know it. That woman has chosen her business well and it'll grow, my friends, it'll spread like ripples in a pool. And then her money will grow with it, and with that money she will *buy*. She will buy any business she can lay hands on, and like as not that business will be *yours*.'

'Be you certain that your warning don't 'ave no foundation in what 'appened to that lad o' your'n?'

The man who had first addressed him now spoke up again, his face partly hidden by the wing of his armchair.

Jacob's nerves tightened. That one was always on the bloody ball, there was no pulling the wool over his eyes.

'It does have a part in it,' he answered after another pull from his glass had settled his nerves. 'My lad lost his life protecting a whore, because that's what she be. Who else but a whore would be up on the heath alone? She was expecting the man who tumbled her, and spread her legs willing enough till my lad come across them. Then she starts to scream rape. Think on it, the lot of you. It was my son that time. Whose will it be next? Which of you will be like Jacob Rewcastle? Which of you will have no son to follow after you? Don't think it can't happen again 'cos it can, and it will – unless we drive that bitch out of Coseley!'

Outside The Fighting Cocks Jacob climbed into a hansom. It was late, but not too late for the establishment he was headed for.

'Railway Station.'

'Station it be, sir.'

The cabbie whipped up the tired-looking horse and Jacob leaned against the shadowed upholstery.

They had taken his warning, albeit only when he had wondered aloud how their wives would react to learning of some of the bawdy houses their husbands frequented. Soon Anna Royce would find herself back where she started. But that won't be the end, he vowed silently, it won't end till you're in the workhouse.

She had taken his son, killed him as surely as if she had put a gun to his head. Had she not been on the heath that day, Philip would not have died. He gave his life to save hers, Jacob told himself.

But in the darkness of the hansom cab he closed his eyes, trying to shut out the truth that could never be escaped for long. Philip had not given his life to protect Anna Royce, he had died as a result of his own jealousy; jealousy that Robert Daines, the man he was in love with, could want a woman.

No one had told Jacob so, not even the Royce woman. But she had not needed to. He had seen the way his son's feelings were directed, seen it from the earliest days of his boyhood. But that knowledge must remain his alone and while Anna Royce remained in Coseley, he could never be certain that it would.

'You are telling me the truth, Amy?'

Anna watched the girl struggling to fasten the threadbare dirty blue coat across her thin chest. Several times too small, it had already known many owners.

'Yes, Mrs Royce.'

Maggie shook her head at the whisper.

'I be going with you. That one is as sly as a cartload o' monkeys.'

'No, you stay here with Andrew, I can manage.' Anna knew the temper of the older woman. Fastening the last of the row of shiny bronze buttons that adorned her dove grey corded suit, she pushed a bronze-knobbed hatpin through the hat perched on top of her heavy folds of hair. She no longer looked like the drab widow who had visited Wigmore Bank years before.

'He'll deny everything, you knows that.'

'Yes, Maggie, but it won't stop me. I'm going to face him with this, he's not getting away with it.'

'You might try!' Maggie was abrupt with her. 'But you'll get nowt. It's 'er word against 'is'n an' there's no justice where there's money. That one could buy his way out even if wench 'ad means of bringin' 'im into court, which he knows nicely she 'asn't. Still . . . go if you must, but don't say you went without a tellin'.'

Amy Stevens close by her side, Anna walked from Woodgreen through the streets of Coseley, the sound of clogs loud on the cobbles as whole families went to Chapel. She hadn't been since Edward had died. Where was the love and mercy that allowed a child to be raped, and that could have saved her husband from death? No, she hadn't been to Chapel since that day and wouldn't be going today.

'Don't start snivelling again,' she said tartly to Amy as they followed a winding drive lined with glorious copper beech trees.

'Mrs Anna Royce to see Mr Rewcastle.' Her tone was still sharp as the footman opened the heavy oak door of Highfield House.

'The tradesman's entrance is at the rear, through the arch and to the left!' His features wrinkled disdainfully showing positive disgust when they reached Amy, trembling by Anna's side.

Stepping back, he began to swing the heavy door to but Anna was inside, dragging the girl in after her.

'You get smart with me and your rear will feel my foot – and not only through the arch and to the left but all round every inch of this stinking pile! Now move or I'll find Jacob Rewcastle for myself.'

'What is it, Newton . . . what is all that noise?' Halfway down the carpeted stairway stood Beatrice Rewcastle, her watery blue eyes taking in the scene below.

'Amy?' She took two steps down, skirts rustling with each movement. 'Where have you been?'

'I . . . I . . .' Visibly terrified, Amy tried to hide behind Anna.

'Well, wherever it was you are no longer needed in this house, and do not bother asking Cook for a reference – there will be none forthcoming. Don't think you can leave without any sort of explanation then creep back here a week later and expect me to keep you on. Newton!' She switched her watery glance to the smirking servant. 'Get these . . . people . . . out of here and see them off the grounds.'

A silken swish of her skirts and she had turned about, one foot already on the step above.

Anger at Jacob's treatment of the girl swept through Anna. Anger so strong it burned away her usual good manners.

'If Newton needs his legs to carry out his duties in this house then I suggest he keep his distance. One step nearer and I'll kick them from under him.' Anna's eyes sparked like lightning in her furious face. 'And as for Amy's job, that's not why she's returned to this mausoleum.'

'Just who *are* you?' Jacob's wife was unused to the lower classes speaking back to her or at least not with the cool authority with which Anna spoke.

'It's not who *I* am should worry you, Mrs Rewcastle, if that is who you are . . . and unless you want this maukin to hear what we've come about, and I think he would rather enjoy what I have to say, then you will send for your husband now.'

Beatrice Rewcastle blanched visibly, long thin fingers gripping the gleaming mahogany balustrade. For a moment she wrestled with Anna's revelation.

'What the bloody hell is all this?' A door was thrown back and Jacob Rewcastle strode into the hall. 'Newton, what the bloody . . .?' He coloured fiercely as he saw the visitors.

'What are you doing here?' he demanded.

'I think you know that already but I can tell you just the same.'

Anna met his furious glare, unflinching. There was a time she might have been as afraid of Jacob Rewcastle and his wife as Amy was now but hard knocks had long driven that sort of fear away.

'Amy tells me that you . . .'

'You bugger off!' Jacob barked at the black-coated Newton. 'And you, Beatrice, get yourself back upstairs.'

'But, Jacob, I . . .'

'Don't bloody Jacob me!' His voice ricocheted from the panelled walls like bullets. 'I told you to get back upstairs. This has nowt to do with you.'

His eye caught the movement of a black coat.

'I thought I told you to bugger off . . . stand there with your bloody earholes flapping and you're likely to get the buggers knocked off!'

Beatrice Rewcastle's face flushed a deep carmine red but she turned and walked back up the stairs as Newton vanished.

'Now then!' Jacob's piggy eyes returned to Anna. 'I don't entertain the likes of you in my house. If you have business with me then you can call at the mill . . . maybe I'll see you there. As for you,' the glance narrowed to slits as he turned to the pathetic figure of Amy, 'there's no work for you here or at the mill so get out, and if I see you here again I'll have you up at quarter sessions.'

'That would suit Amy admirably. I'm not certain the magistrate would be interested in what she had to tell him,' Anna was superbly cool, 'but even if he were not, there are those in these parts who no longer take the view that a man seducing a young girl on the grounds of being her employer and having a great deal of money is right or in any way acceptable. The magistrate may not take a serious view of what you have done to this girl but there are opinions other than his in Coseley, opinions which can be brought to bear where a magistrate cannot reach.'

Jacob felt the warning even through his rage. The bitch was right. There were those in Coseley and outside of it had a dose of religion, especially the women. Offend their finer feelings and he could kiss goodbye to any support from their husbands.

'As for myself, I'd prefer to conduct this business at the mill.

There are so many more listening ears and willing tongues up there. They will carry word of what you have done to this child to a far wider audience than we have here and will feast on this titbit for a long time to come.'

'What's that bloody lyin' slut been telling you?' Veins stood out like thick cords in his short neck and his voice dropped to a menacing hiss.

Anna read the danger in that bloodshot glare, the hostility curving the flaccid mouth, but at the same time recognised the fear behind both. Jacob Rewcastle was in no doubt of what had brought them here.

'There is always the possibility that Amy is lying, Jacob Rewcastle,' she said quietly, 'but we both know there are far greater liars. As for her being a slut, I don't think a man with the morals of a rutting dog is qualified to judge on that point.'

From the curve at the top of the stairs Beatrice heard a low curse, the door of her husband's study opening and closing, then remained straining to listen.

'I'll give you two minutes.' Inside the tobacco-stained room Jacob removed the heavy gold hunter from his waistcoat pocket. 'Afterwards you have a choice. Walk out or I'll throw you out, and enjoy doing it.'

'I'm sure you would.' Unperturbed, Anna faced him in the masculine, book-lined room. 'But then you enjoy mauling a woman, don't you, Jacob? With or without a reason.'

'You bloody bitch!'

'Amy is pregnant. She claims that you are the father of the child she is carrying!' Anna matched his snarl.

'What's that you say?' His lips remained still, words emerging through clenched teeth.

'You are the father of Amy's child ... what do you intend to do?'

Amy had stayed close to Anna during the rapid exchange. Now, as Jacob Rewcastle's anger flared a new, she turned her face into the other woman's shoulder, sobbing hysterically.

'Do!'

Beyond the closed door Beatrice had heard the accusation and waited for his reply.

'I'll tell you what I'm going to do. I'm going to wring her bloody neck. I know her sort, splaying her legs for any that fancies a ride then looking round for the best bet to hang the consequences on. She must have the clap up to her eyes, the bloody trollop. And you think I'd fancy that?'

'You would fancy anything in a skirt.' Anna wrapped one arm around the sobbing girl, her face a cold mask. 'The only difference being, you pay some trollops for their services . . . like a ruby necklace for a certain blonde.'

His angry exclamation carried to Beatrice whose fingers clawed into her brown bombazine skirts. She had guessed at the activities keeping him from the house until the early hours but while he was keeping his filth from her door she could accept it. Now . . . with a common servant, and her no more than a child . . . Her fingers curling closer into her rustling skirts, she turned away.

'How do you know about that?' Inside the room Jacob's face contorted with fresh fury.

'Let's just say I know.' Strangely, in the face of his anger Anna felt herself grow calmer. What few reservations she had harboured at the thought of confronting Coseley's wealthiest man had disappeared altogether. She no longer cared what he or his money could do.

'You took advantage of your position as Amy's employer,' she went on, watching the hatred play across the bloated features. 'You gave this child an ultimatum: either she consented to play your dirty little games or she was out of a job. You knew the terror such a prospect would hold, especially for a cutsider; they have little or no choice as it is with you refusing them work at the mill and God all else to do in Coseley.

'You knew if she went home and told her mother that the paltry few shillings she got for working her heart and soul out here would no longer be forthcoming, then her life would be hell. And like the vulture you are, you preyed on that.'

'And that dirty little whore told you that, I suppose.'

Moving to the fireplace, he turned to face them, legs spread, hands behind his back, arrogant, conceited and totally contemptuous.

'If she is a whore then it's you who made her one,' Anna retorted.

'I ain't a whore, Mrs Royce, truly I ain't. I ain't never bin wi' a lad . . . me mam would kill me.' Amy lifted her head, leaving a damp tear stain on the front of Anna's coat. 'I ain't never bin wi' anyone 'cept 'im an' . . . an' then it was only because 'e said as 'ow I couldn't work 'ere no more lessen I did!' Tears washed down her face. 'Oh, I daren't go 'ome, Mrs Royce. I daren't tell me mam.'

'Don't be frightened, Amy.' Anna still held one arm protectively about the girl. 'We will see your mam after we leave here.'

'Which is right now!' Jacob pulled the watch from his waistcoat pocket. 'Two minutes was what I told you and that time is up.' He flicked the gold hunter, sending it spinning into the slitted pocket. 'But I'll spare the time to tell you this. You'd do better to find yourself a man and spread your legs for him. It'll get you more in the long run than tryin' to hang that trollop's bastard on me.'

'That's all you think a woman capable of, isn't it?' Anna's glare was lacerating. 'Find yourself a husband and home then stay there. And if you can't, then let someone else's husband set you up in a cosy little place where you can spread your legs for *him*. That's what you wanted me to do, isn't it? And you deny you seduced this child! I told you once before, Jacob Rewcastle, and now I tell you again, you are nothing but a bastard.'

Maggie had said she would get nothing but she had needed to try, if only to let him know that others besides Amy knew what he had done. Walking home to the sound of church bells, Anna found herself wondering once again if there really was a God.

'She will be all right there. It has given her a job that will keep her and the baby, and Mary Cresswell will love having someone to fuss over, though I was surprised when your mother suggested Amy take on the front-room shop.'

'My mother was always a pushover for a hard luck story.' Andrew looked down at the woman walking beside him and couldn't help wondering what had brought her to Coseley and his mother's door.

'There are a good many have cause to be grateful to her, Andrew, myself among them.'

'Gee, Anna, I didn't mean . . .'

'I know you didn't, Andrew.'

'Me mam always said as 'ow I had a big mouth.' He grinned, adopting the speech of his youth again.

'Mmm, but a nice one.'

They walked in friendly silence on the heath, above the smoke of the mills, and Anna lifted her face to the sharp kiss of the wind. She hadn't walked on the heath since Philip Rewcastle had ended his life there.

'I used to play up here as a lad.' Andrew pushed his hands into his pockets. 'Over there against the Devil's Finger. My mother used to say it pointed the way to hell and that's where I would finish up if I fell over the edge. Want to take a look?'

'No!' Anna sat down, tucking the russet folds of her skirts beneath her. She did not want to peer into the blackness of that hole, to look into the place where two men had met their death.

'I've had enough walking for now, let's just sit and look at the view.'

'That's no view for you, Anna.' Andrew settled at her side. 'There are places on this earth would take your breath away and I want to show them to you.' He turned towards her, taking her hand in his, dark eyes aflame. 'I want you to come to America with me, Anna . . . I want you to be my wife.'

'Your wife!' She gasped. 'But you've only known me for two weeks.'

'Two weeks, two lifetimes . . . what the hell difference does it make? Anna, I love you. I've loved you since you spat like a scalded cat on that railway platform down there . . . I love you and I want you to marry me.'

Anna's eyes gazed across to the horizon. 'I love you and I want to marry you.' Andrew had said both . . . Charles had said neither.

'Please, Anna . . . say you will?'

At her side Andrew waited.

'You don't know about me, Andrew,' she said after a long interval. 'About my background.'

'And I don't want to know because it doesn't matter, it's you I love . . . you I care about, not your background.' He took her face in his hands, his eyes drowning in hers.

'Understand me, Anna, I love you. Nothing in the universe will alter that.' Holding her face, he lowered his mouth to hers in a fiery lingering kiss.

It was sweet as Edward's had been but there was no music in her head, no brilliant starburst against her closed lids. But Andrew wanted her for a wife, not a mistress, perhaps that was why she lifted her arms to his neck and returned his kiss.

'Why did you go to America?' she asked later when, taking her kisses to mean she would marry him, Andrew lay happily on his back, a long blade of grass between his teeth.

''Cos old man Rewcastle gave me the sack!' He squinted up into the sky. 'That son of his tried the old come on with me but I wasn't taking it as some had just because his father owned the mill and our lives with it. I told him I would break his hands off and stuff them up his arse if he tried anything again. His answer was: "There is only one letter's difference between hiring and firing, Andrew Fellen." I said the letter was "F" and that his old man could stick his fucking job, then I punched the living daylights out of him.'

Spitting the blade of grass away as if clearing a nasty taste from his mouth, Andrew sat up, his gaze ranging over the tall black chimneys and high imprisoning walls of the steel mill with its sentinel rows of terraced houses.

'That bloody family,' he muttered. 'They've a lot to answer for but I think the old man was more to blame, buying Philip his nancy boys . . .'

'Philip is dead, Andrew.' Anna glanced towards that awful place. 'He . . . he fell over Devil's Finger.'

'So Mam said.' His head turned, following her glance to where the ground cut steeply away. 'He didn't have much of a life, for all his father's money, and underneath his pansy ways I believe there was the makings of a man. After I'd knocked him half-daft, I told him if his old man took one step against my mam, I would kill him. Then, I remember, he stood up and glared at me. He had tiger-coloured eyes that seemed to glow, and he said, "Whatever else I might be, I am still a gentleman. I do not take revenge on women."'

'And that was when you left home?'

'What else could I do, Anna? There was nobody in Coseley or for miles around who would risk incurring Jacob Rewcastle's wrath by giving me a job, and I wasn't going to let me mam keep me.' Andrew jumped to his feet, his smile wide and stubborn. 'But I'm back now and I've got you. Let's go tell Mam the news.'

Why couldn't she smile? Why was there only emptiness where there should have been something, even if that something was not happiness? Walking beside him, Anna could not help remembering that other tall figure, the figure of Jacob Rewcastle's son.

'Beggin' yer pardon, Mr Rewcastle, sir, but I 'ardly thinks as 'ow the lady should be in foundry.'

'Who the bloody hell asked you?' Jacob Rewcastle turned

florid heavy jowls towards the man who spoke. 'You're bloody paid to puddle iron, not to think.'

'Jos is right, Mr Rewcastle.' Eli Curran, smart in a stiffly starched collar, came to Jos Ingles's side. ''Tis dangerous, men are just about to tip the basin.'

'That's you, ain't it, Curran?' Jacob peered through bloodshot eyes, swaying unsteadily. 'Why're you all dressed up in a monkey suit . . . have you been to a funeral or summat?' Laughing at his own unsavoury joke, he placed a hand beneath the arm of his woman friend. 'You'll like seeing this, my dear, it's like fireworks on Guy Fawkes Night.'

Eli felt the weight of being appointed foundry manager weigh heavily. He had never argued with Jacob Rewcastle before. Nobody had argued with Jacob Rewcastle before.

'I be sorry, Mr Rewcastle, but I must ask you to take the lady out of the foundry. We can't tip basin wi' 'er so close an' all.'

The cords in Jacob's neck bulged; rage deepened the colour already high in his face.

'Take the lady away, you say?' His bellow rang above the clang of rolling beds where ingots of red hot metal were rolled into long strips. 'It's not a lady who'll be leaving, Eli Curran, *you* will. You can pick your bloody tin up right now. You're finished at this mill, do you hear me? Finished.' He glared round wildly. 'And that goes for all the rest of you who want to say their piece. Now tip that bloody basin!'

Jos Ingles shrugged at the man standing on the other side of the crucible filled with molten metal. Jacob Rewcastle carried a lot of clout. It would be asking for trouble to cross him.

Raising the wooden poles that supported the crucible, the two men operating the tip began to pour, the molten metal giving off a shower of sparks as it ran into the moulds placed on the ground.

Jacob grabbed his companion out of the way of the showering sparks and stepped backward. Catching his heel in one of the narrow channels dug in the earth floor for draining any spilt metal, he lurched sideways. As he threw out his free arm in an attempt to arrest his fall, he fell against Jos Ingles sending him sprawling beneath a glowing stream of molten metal.

'What happened?' Crossing the mill yard Anna was in time to see the blackened, burned figure being carried into the shed beside the offices.

'Jacob Rewcastle, Mrs Royce, he brought a woman . . .'

'Tell me later!' she ordered. 'Get the doctor, Eli, and send a couple of the women to Molly Ingles. Tell them to stay with her till she's calm then one of them come to me here.'

Two minutes later, her whole body stiff with anger, Anna faced Jacob Rewcastle.

'What are you doing here?'

On his feet again he leered at her, the fumes of his breath blinding. 'Well, well! If it isn't Mrs Royce! You're like horse shit, woman, you're everywhere.'

Around her, faces pale beneath sweat-streaked dust, the men waited. Anna breathed deeply, her glance taking in the weeping girl before returning to Jacob.

'Horse shit, Mr Rewcastle, has at least one use,' she replied icily. 'And that makes it at least one hundred per cent up on you.'

With all the swiftness of a summer storm his drunken humour faded. Piggy eyes receding to nothingness, Jacob Rewcastle stared at the only woman who had ever defied him.

'I told you once before,' he grated, 'if you set foot on my property again, I'd have you whipped off.'

'So you did.' Anna held her ground. 'But this is no longer your property, you sold it some months ago.'

'What if I did!' Jacob's face turned a dark red.

'Then having sold it, you have no right to be here.'

'Rights!' Jacob laughed harshly. 'I have all the bloody rights I need, seeing the man who bought this mill be a good friend of mine.'

'That is not true.' Anna said as he glanced triumphantly at the girl he had brought with him. 'You have never been a friend of the owner of this mill.'

'Eh!' Jacob shipped back to her, anger turning his face to purple. 'How would you know?'

Anna felt the flick of her nerves. She had taken every precaution against his finding out just who it was had bought his mill, but now she no longer cared: she wanted him to know.

'Because you have never been a friend of mine.'

'Nor never bloody likely to be!' he spat. 'But I don't see how that has anything to do with it.'

'Then I will tell you,' Anna said calmly. 'I am the one who bought this mill. It belongs to me.'

'That's a lie!' Releasing the girl's arm he took a step forward. 'This mill was bought by Gladwin Pottery of Stoke-on-Trent.'

'Which also belongs to me.' Anna's voice was quiet. 'You should instruct whoever acts for you to look more carefully at any purchasers you may deal with in future. But now I am telling you what you told me, stay off my property.

'Eli,' she glanced quickly at her foundry manager, 'should Mr Rewcastle show his face here again you have my permission to throw him out. I will take the consequences should anyone bother to complain.'

The listening men didn't muffle the comments that brought an apoplectic gasp from their former employer.

'I should have trodden on you from the first, broken you together with your bits of bloody crockery!'

'But now it's too late, Jacob.' The sight of Jos Ingles's burned body stamped on to her mind, Anna no longer cared who heard. Her voice, cold and clear as a mountain stream, vibrated from the roof beams.

'It was my bits of crockery bought your mill and it's my bits of crockery paying these men their wages. You're finished, Jacob Rewcastle. Not only are you a nobody, you're a nothing.'

'You told me you would take more than my son,' he hissed, purple with rage.

'Philip was the one good thing that ever came out of you.' Anna was impervious to the hatred he spat at her. 'And though you spend money on a hundred like the woman standing at your side, you will never replace him. You would be better advised to look to the son you have.'

'Son!' Hatred and anger, a powerful admixture, brought Jacob a new clarity of mind. 'I've got no son, you've seen to that.'

Anna looked steadily at the man she despised.

'Amy Stevens was delivered of a child two nights ago,' she said quietly. 'The child was a son . . . your son.'

'I'll be back in two or three months, Anna, and then we'll be married.' Andrew gathered her into his arms. 'God, I wish I didn't have to leave but I have to return to the States to settle my affairs and sell the ranch.' He touched his lips to her hair, hand cradling her head. 'I love you, Anna,' he whispered. 'I love you . . . the days are going to be hellish dark until I see you again.'

Still his arms held her and Anna made no attempt to move, ignoring the stare of the station master-cum-porter-cum-ticket office attendant-cum-caretaker. The man who watched was all of those, in fact he was the only employee at Coseley Station as he had been on the night Anna had arrived. She had come on since that rainy night, that much he knew, but it hadn't changed her none. She was still the quiet wench she had been when Maggie Fellen had taken her in. Leastways with all except Jacob Rewcastle, and there was none in Coseley held that against her. No, this place was the better for her coming and if Maggie Fellen's lad could bring her happiness then there was none in Coseley would mind that. Picking up a broom, he shuffled away to the other end of the platform.

'Oh, Anna.' Andrew's arms tightened round her. 'The days are going to be so dark, so hellish dark.'

They would be dark for her too. Anna lifted her mouth to his goodbye kiss. But for a different reason. Andrew Fellen was a man who deserved the whole of a woman's love, the love a woman should hold for her husband, a love that held her heart and soul – and this was a love she couldn't give him. She closed her eyes, shutting out the cowardice that held her to an unspoken promise. Yes, the days ahead would be dark for her too, dark under the shadow of her own guilt.

Watching the train steam out of the station, and the figure waving until a curve in the track carried him from her sight, Anna felt that guilt settle heavier on her shoulders.

'You 'ave a visitor.'

Anna had walked slowly from the station, unwilling to go home, unwilling to face Maggie, convinced she must know the truth of her feelings for Andrew; she had that uncanny knack of knowing Anna's feelings almost as well as she knew them herself, and looking at those penetrating grey eyes now, Anna was convinced she knew it all.

'Visitor?' She slipped off her coat, letting Maggie take it from her. The last thing she wanted was a visitor. She wanted to be alone with Maggie, to sit with her and reason out the happenings of these last weeks, let Maggie's down-to-earth common sense sort out the tangle matters had taken.

'Ar, that's what I said.' Maggie folded the coat, nodding towards the sitting room. 'I've put 'im in there. I said as 'ow you'd gone to railway station but 'e said as 'e would wait.'

Removing her hat, Anna touched a nervous hand to her hair, her look questioning, but Maggie had already turned away. Smoothing her hand over the pale cream of her blouse and her green skirt, she breathed deeply, a feeling of sickness rising in her stomach.

Opening the door of the sitting room, her eyes flew to the man who stood at the fireplace and the sickness faded. Her visitor was not Jacob Rewcastle.

'Mr Harris.' Anna glanced behind her, not wanting to close

the door on Maggie, but seeing the hall empty she stepped forward, closing the door.

John Harris accepted the chair she indicated.

'I didn't wish to intrude, Mrs Royce, but I thought I ought to bring this in person.' Taking an envelope from the pocket of his black three-quarter-length coat, he held it out for Anna to take.

'There was no need for you to put yourself out, Mr Harris.' Anna felt she should smile but couldn't. 'I would have come to see you at the bank tomorrow.'

John Harris looked at her, unsmiling.

'I think when you read that you will understand why I had no wish to wait until tomorrow, Mrs Royce.'

Taking the envelope and tearing it open, Anna scanned the contents.

'I'm sorry.' John Harris stood up. 'If there is anything at all I can do . . .'

'Thank you.' She mouthed the words unconsciously, her mind stunned. She sat unmoving as the manager of Wigmore Bank let himself out, her eyes resting unseeing on the words of the letter he had just given her.

The bank had foreclosed.

They were calling in her loan.

Jacob Rewcastle had not called to see her but somehow she felt he was here in this room, and he was laughing.

Chapter Fifteen

Anna walked from the station into a street that had changed little in the years since she had seen it last.

One or two heads turned to look at the smartly dressed woman, a dark veil shrouding her hair and face, but as quickly turned away. Folk in Wednesbury were too busy earning a living to spend time gawking after a stranger.

Booking into The White Horse Hotel, she asked for a sixpenny runner to take a sealed letter to Polly Shipton.

'How . . . how did it happen, Polly?' she asked later greeting the woman who had delivered her son.

'It was suicide. 'E 'ung issself, Anna.'

'Oh my God!' Anna paced impotently about the room. 'But why, Polly, why?'

'Who knows the answer to that 'xceptin' the Almighty, me wench? P'raps 'e'd 'ad as much as he could tek.'

Like a wounded animal Anna didn't know whether to run or stay. It should not cause her this much pain . . . not after so long.

Turning to the window, she asked, 'Did he say anything . . . leave a note?'

''E said nothin' to anybody . . . the lad is as surprised as the rest on we. Knocked 'im sideways this 'as.'

The lad! Anna twisted her hands together. It must be her son Polly was talking about. Who else was there to be so upset at her father's suicide?

'How is he, Polly?' she asked quietly.

'A fine lad, Anna.' Behind her the old woman's voice carried obvious pride. 'Tall as 'is . . .'

'His father.' Anna finished the sentence. 'Did he know, Polly . . . about me?'

'No, me wench, Jos never 'ad the courage to tell 'im an' I thought as it was none of my business.'

'I see.' Anna's voice dropped to a whisper. 'And his name? What did my father name him?'

'Aaron . . . 'e were christened Aaron.' The old woman smiled. 'Learned 'is letters well 'e did at St Bart's until 'e were thirteen, then 'e left to set on for Joby 'Ampton. Jos didn't give much to that but said as 'ow lad 'ad a choice of 'is own.'

Anna's nails bit into her palms and her lips were white with tension but she knew she had to ask the question.

'And me, Polly?'

''E never spoke your name but 'e thought on you often, but what with the pain of what 'e did to you . . . I just 'ope as now 'e 'as found peace.'

'I . . . I can't see him, Polly.' Anna's hand trembled violently.

'I know, me wench.' Polly Shipton pulled the checked shawl closer round her thin shoulders. 'Anyway, Aaron 'ad 'im screwed down last night. Reckoned as there'd be none save 'imself an' me would be payin' respects.'

'When . . . when is it to . . .' Anna broke off, the words choking in her throat.

Crossing to the door, her crippled leg dragging heavily behind her, Polly looked back.

'Tomorrow mornin', eleven o'clock, at the Parish.'

It was time.

Anna sat on the edge of the bed in her small room in the hotel, as she had most of the night, reading over and over again the special delivery letter Polly Shipton had sent her.

'I thought as 'ow yer should know yer father died last night.' The words seared into her brain. Her father was dead, he had died without hearing her say she had forgiven him. But had she forgiven him? Could she forgive him? In her most secret heart Anna heard the words: Not yet . . . not yet. And now her father was dead, today would see the burying of him and she must be there. At least she could give him that.

'Will you be wantin' a carriage, Mrs Royce?'

Fat balding Harry Fletcher, who had been landlord of The White Horse when she was a child, danced attention on her as Anna walked down the polished wooden stairs to the lobby.

Inside she smiled acidly. Would he dance the same attention if he recognised the woman who had checked into his hotel last night as Jos Bradly's daughter? It was a safe bet Polly's tongue would tell him to mind his own business should he ask who it was had sent for her last night.

'I can send to Joby 'Ampton's for one, won't tek but ten minutes.'

Joby Hampton. Anna remembered the tall friendly man who owned the steel works that had employed many of the men of Wednesbury when the coal seams began to run out. His pride and passion had been his horses, trotters that drew his two-wheeled racing traps. Her father had driven many a race for Joby and sometimes in the evening he had gone to help exercise the horses. He had taken her with him then, swinging her squealing with delight into the trap when Joby had said she could ride with him.

'No, thank you.' Anna stood waiting as Harry Fletcher opened the door that gave on to Holyhead Road. 'I'll walk.'

A slight drizzle began to fall as she walked up along Lower High Street towards The Shambles. The last time she had walked these streets her heart was breaking. It was breaking still. People glanced as she passed but paid no more heed and Anna spoke to no one. There was no need. Every street in the tiny town was engraved on her heart. Passing The Pretty Bricks public house, nicknamed for the maroon-glazed tiles beneath its bottle-glass bay window, she walked halfway up steep Ethelfleda Terrace, stopping short of the house that had been her home. Below her the houses she had passed, all with closed curtains, pretended grief at the passing of Jos Bradly.

Hypocrites! Resentment flared in Anna. You tortured him with your lies about Mary Carter, accusing and backbiting, until you drove him mad.

It was you who raped me, every single one of you.

Standing half-hidden behind a tree, she drew little notice from the women grouped about the gate of the house: they were too engrossed in their morbid occupation to pay her much heed. From where she stood on the gentle swell of the hill Anna watched the wooden ladder placed against the bedroom window; watched as with the aid of ropes the rough coffin was lowered down then carried, not along the garden path and through the gate, but across the tiny garden where it was passed like some nameless parcel over the low wall.

It was a matter of yards to the lych gate but the men carrying her father's coffin did not carry it beneath its shelter but set it on the ground, leaving it there while Polly Shipton and the tall lad with hair the colour of Misty's followed the vicar into the church. He had been right, her son, there were only two to pay their respects.

Anna glanced over to where the group of women was dispersing. The show was over. Now they would gather like scavenging crows to pick over bits of her father's life. Alone in the rain, Anna kept her silent vigil, unable to walk the few yards to that lonely coffin; equally unable to turn and leave it.

They came at last from the church, her son and cripple Polly, followed by the vicar and four men who had doubtless been well paid to carry this particular coffin. Anna brushed the rain that clung like tears to her cheeks. Now finally her father would be taken to his rest in the churchyard. Trembling from head to foot, she watched the four men lift the coffin to their shoulders and carry it outside the wall of the churchyard to where a large hole gaped black beneath a huge oak tree. Of course. Anna bit her lip to stifle the cry in her throat. Her father would not lie in the sanctified ground of St Bartholomew's Parish Church. He was a suicide, he had suffered a suicide's funeral, yet still his punishment was not finished. His body had received no blessing, his grave would know no tombstone.

'Was I wrong, Polly?' Back at The White Horse Anna looked at the woman who had cared for her son. 'Should I have stayed?'

'Nay, wench.' Polly Shipton saw the anguish tearing at the woman who paced the room. The wench had always been pretty; now she was beautiful, with the creamy colouring and classic bone structure that had been her mother's and the proud bearing that was a legacy from her father. Oh, yes, he would have been proud of her, would Jos Bradly.

'You would never 'ave survived, not against the bitches as 'aunts this town.'

'But my son, Polly, I left him, I turned my back on him.'

'You left 'im, 'tis true.' Polly made no attempt at denial. 'But turned your back on 'im you never did. You sent money regular though it must 'ave been mortal 'ard on you . . . aye, wench, afore you asks Jos knew where it came from though 'e never commented . . . like I says, you 'ave nowt you should 'old against yourself. Go. Get you away back to where you 'ave made yourself a good 'ome. You 'ave a daughter you must think on an' it seems you 'ave a good friend in that Maggie Fellen.'

'As I have in you, Polly.' A thin smile touched Anna's mouth. 'I have a son too and I love him.' The smile faded. 'I loved him when I left him with you.'

'You went to the 'ouse?'

'Yes.' Anna stood at the window, looking out over the one decent street the town could boast. 'While you were at the graveside. I . . . I hadn't the courage to see . . .'

'Ar, wench,' Polly nodded, 'did 'e see you there?'

Anna could only nod.

'An' did you tell 'im?'

Anna turned from the window, tears coursing from her eyes.

'I couldn't, Polly. I hadn't the courage. I love him but I . . . I can't risk his hatred. Better he never knows me.'

'Ar, you 'ave your life an' lad 'as 'is. Best leave it that way.'

'But it sounds so heartless put that way.'

Polly Shipton pulled her checked shawl higher on to her shoulders.

'An' is it less 'eartless to tell 'im now? I tell you, Anna, lad's 'ad as much as 'e can 'old. Tell 'im if you will but not yet. 'E can't tek another blow like the one 'e 'as just been dealt.'

She was right. Anna watched her crippled friend limp to the door. Her son was tall and strong but it was the strength of youth. Tax it too hard and it would break.

'He will always be cared for, Polly,' she whispered, 'as long as I have a penny, it will be his.'

'You 'ave no need to tell me that, me wench.' Polly's lined face broke into a smile. 'Hasn't it always? But from now on you must see to some other road of gettin' it to 'im. I can no longer pass it off as comin' from 'is grandfather.'

'His grandfather?'

For a moment the question hung in the air then Polly answered.

'Ar, that's what Jos told 'im an' I saw no reason to change it.'

'Did . . . did he ever ask about me?' Anna asked tremulously. 'Did he ever ask about his mother?'

'Ar.' Polly Shipton gazed levelly at the daughter of the man they had buried less than an hour since. 'Ar, 'e asked about you all right. I told 'im you was dead.'

'But why didn't you discuss it with me first?'

Sitting in Hester's pretty sitting room, Anna looked at her solicitor.

'It all happened so quickly, Reuben. John Harris brought the bank's letter in the evening and next morning I got one telling me my father was dead. That drove all else from my mind.'

'Is there anything you can do, Reuben?' Hester was close to tears.

'Under the terms written here the loan can be called in any time.' Reuben tapped the document he was holding.

'It was a stupid risk to take in the first place, Anna, buying Rewcastle's Mill. You must have known that you were putting most of your eggs in one basket.'

'My only thought was of all those men losing their jobs.'

'But why, for what reason, should the bank act this way?'

Reuben Fine shook his head, peering at his wife over the spectacles he had taken to wearing. 'From what Anna says it sounds like collusion.' Someone, somewhere, had called in some favours and Anna was paying the price.

'But I still don't understand.'

'There's nothing to understand, Hester.' Anna had gone through the whys and wherefores a thousand times since opening that letter. 'It's my bet Jacob Rewcastle is at the back of this. It's my own fault, John Harris warned me the directors of Wigmore's Bank were friends of his.'

'But what does he get out of it?'

'Satisfaction!' Reuben glanced at his wife. 'Jealousy ... revenge ... spite. Each is a powerful motivator, but reasons we can discuss later. Right now we need to find a solution.'

'I've counted every last penny of cash.' Anna produced a list from her bag, handing it to Reuben. 'There are accounts yet to be paid but I can't guarantee the money will come in time and as things stand I'm short some three hundred pounds.'

'Seven days!' He blew down his nose. 'Whoever dreamed this up didn't give you much time.'

'That old swine would make sure they didn't,' Hester said, 'but we've got a bit put by, Anna, you can use that if it will help.'

'Thanks.' She patted her friend's hand. 'But I couldn't take what you and Reuben have worked hard for, I couldn't live with myself if I lost it. Besides,' she saw Hester's rueful look, 'it's not the end of the world. I've lost the mill but I still have the shops.'

I have failed you, Edward, Anna thought as the train carried her home from Birmingham. I tried to get King's Choice for you but I failed.

'It'll be none but 'im.' Maggie listened to the reason for Anna's new worry. 'I told you that Jacob Rewcastle was as sly as a cartload of monkeys. If 'e couldn't put one over on you one way, then 'e would find another.'

'Well, he has found one I can't fight, Maggie. Joby Timmins has gone through these figures with a fine-toothed comb and I have done the same, but I am still three hundred pounds short. Another month, Maggie, another month and I could have paid the lot.'

For several minutes more Anna gazed at the neatly entered columns of numbers, their totals emblazoned in red ink, then slammed the black bound ledger shut.

'He has won after all, Maggie,' she said resignedly, 'Jacob Rewcastle has won. In a week there will be no Bradly Engineering and King's Choice will be gone.'

'You tried your best, wench,' Maggie said softly. 'Nobody could have done more.'

'It was not enough though, was it?' Anna stared at the ledger.

'I knows this be more easy said than it be to do, Anna, but try to put it out of your mind. The mill has to go, and that be all there is to it, you have other ways of keeping a roof over your head, Rewcastle hasn't took the lot.'

'I don't mind losing the mill, but to lose it to him! What would Edward say?'

'He would tell you what I've told you already. It ain't through no fault of yours that the mill be going, he would see Jacob's hand in this as I see it. He's got his friends to put their heads together and they have come up with that letter. Foreclosing! That be a bit of conniving if ever I seen it.'

'Connivance or not,' Anna sighed, 'it has taken the mill out of my hands. I only hope it will not affect the workers.'

'We can only wait and see, wench. Won't do no good worryin'. What the Lord has set to happen will happen whether you worry or you don't. But the way I thinks is this: He has let you work too hard and too long only to take it from you now. My mother had a saying, "God is good, if He don't come, He sends." Something will turn up, wench. I be sure of it.'

'I wish I had your belief, Maggie.' Leaving the ledger on the table, Anna crossed to where the older woman sat and sank to her knees, resting her head in the wide lap. 'But not having that doesn't matter, as long as I have you.'

Maggie touched a hand to the red gold hair of the girl she loved as her own, remembering what Kate O'Keefe had said. But Anna was more than the daughter of her heart, she was the blood in her veins, and even when she was wed to Andrew she would not mean more.

Undressing for bed, Anna turned over events in her mind. She was in no doubt that Jacob Rewcastle's hand was behind the calling in of her loan. He would have called on his cronies, most probably holding some threat over their heads. Either that or it was the old pal's act, men closing ranks against a woman who dared to enter their world; a woman who had the audacity to presume she could hold her own in the field of heavy industry.

Pulling a brush through her hair, she stared at her reflection in the mirror of her dressing table. She was no longer the girl who had been driven from her home, a girl who had given up her son in the face of other people's spite.

He thinks I am dead.

The hand holding the brush fell to her lap and the gaze resting on the mirror no longer saw her own reflection but instead the tall figure that had followed her father's coffin, the over-large suit in no way diminishing her pride in the way he carried himself.

He was her son. The child she longed for in every waking moment, the child whose tiny body she seemed to feel against her own every time she lay down to sleep; the son she would never hold in her arms again yet whom she would hold in her heart forever.

'Aaron,' she whispered, 'don't hate me too much, my son. I left for your sake, not for my own, what I did, I did for you, for the sake of my child.'

'Maggie Fellen is a strong woman.' Doctor Merrow pulled on the chamois gloves that had long since passed their best and took up his black Gladstone bag from the hall table. 'But I've known the strongest horses to fall, Anna, and this last blow . . .'

The doctor who had brought Misty into the world shook his head slowly before going to the door.

'We all need courage to go on living sometimes but that woman is going to need more than most. Take care of her. We don't have too many of her kind.'

Anna held the door ajar, her own face pale and drawn. 'I've asked her so many times to have help, this house isn't Roker Street, but she would hear none of it, do you think that now I should insist?'

'No, Anna.' The doctor touched a hand to her arm, his smile gentle on a face lined before its time. 'This is the wrong time to impose any kind of change. She needs to do the things she's always done, she needs things to be as normal as possible. It's a bad business, Anna, but with the Lord's help and yours she'll pull through.'

She watched the doctor, his shabby collar turned up against the cold, climb into the small trap, take up the reins and urge the bay mare into a gentle trot, before she closed the door and returned to Maggie's bedroom. The woman she loved with all her heart was sleeping, the laudanum draught the doctor had given her doing its work. Anna gazed at the sleeping figure, so small and lost in the bed she had once shared with a man who had walked out on her. The passing of the many years since showed on her tired face. *WHY?* screamed Anna's heart. *WHY?* The old clock on the mantel chimed softly as she left the room. Going to the small room off the hall that she had turned into an office, she lifted the telephone, cranking the handle at the side.

'Good afternoon, Miss Grant, this is Anna Royce,' she told the headmistress of Haworth School for Young Ladies. 'My daughter has asked permission to spend the holiday with the Rothmans in Switzerland. Would you tell her, please, that if the invitation still stands, she may go?'

Replacing the ear piece on the hook, cutting off any questions, Anna walked into the sitting room. For a moment she stared around the room, so empty without Maggie, then crossing to the huge Christmas tree in the corner, began to strip it of its tinsel and delicate glass balls. Gathering the brightly wrapped presents, she pushed them into a cupboard under the stairs. There would be no celebration in this house. Picking up the yellow envelope from where Maggie had dropped it on the mahogany table beside the sofa, Anna held it for a minute: such a small envelope to carry so terrible a message. Screwing the envelope into a ball, she flung it into the fire. Maggie would have no need of it to remember what was written inside.

'Appendicitis' the shipping line had telegraphed. Andrew had developed appendicitis a week off the Azores. They had made all speed but had been too late. He had died on board.

'I should have known,' was all Maggie had said. 'I thought that this time Kate O'Keefe was wrong, but I should have known.'

'*One ye will see again in this life but once only.*' Again the Irish woman's prediction had proved true. And what of the words spoken to Anna Bradly? '*The man who will encircle yer heart is not in this land.*' Anna's mouth tightened. This was the end of the prediction. She had married Edward and he had died; she was to have married Andrew and he had died; Philip Rewcastle had taken his own life and that of Sir Robert Daines after becoming involved with her; her father had committed suicide because of her. But there would be no other. No other man would lose his life because of the jinx that was Anna Royce.

'Oh, how beautiful, you spoil me dreadfully!'

'They be nowhere near as beautiful as your eyes, my dear!' In a private room of the Birmingham Royal Hotel, Jacob Rewcastle fastened a necklace of sapphires about the neck of his latest paramour. His hot eyes lingered over the magnolia of her jutting breasts and his body quickened at the thought of what was to come. Young and pretty, she welcomed his embraces. She would give him what the girl Amy had claimed yet he did not believe. She would give him a son.

She would give him a son to replace the one that bitch had taken from him. He had thought to harm that daughter of hers. Pity the brat had been whisked off to some school or other before he could, but there would be other chances. Stroking a podgy hand over the taut young breast, Jacob smiled. He was not through with Anna Royce though his associates would see her finished in business. Tonight would see the start of a new beginning, a new son for Jacob Rewcastle.

'You must let me thank you properly, Jacob.'

She turned to him, her eyes meltingly soft. Slowly she removed the cravat from his throat then dropped her hands to the buttons of his waistcoat, expertly slipping them loose. Blood beat a throbbing rhythm against Jacob's temple, deepening his florid complexion. The girl was a fever in his blood. Pushing his hands away, she continued to touch and stroke, building the fires of passion as she stripped him.

The sheets of the bed were cool but the heat within him soared as Jacob watched the girl lift her arms, carrying her shift above her head; saw her free long slender legs from a pool of silken petticoats. He felt the breath snag in his throat as she shook her black hair loose, letting it fall in a cloud about her shoulders. Climbing into bed beside him, naked except for the sapphires about her neck, she pressed the cool column of her body against his.

'Put out the gas, my dear,' Jacob whispered hoarsely.

'Why?' The girl pushed herself to her knees, a pout on her red mouth. 'Does the sight of me not please you, Jacob?'

The beating in his temples intensifying, his eyes slid from the pretty childish features to the dark triangle at the base of her soft belly. He was so bloody lucky, finding a girl like this. Every minute with her was a pleasure, especially when those minutes were spent in bed. He closed his eyes, brain throbbing like a steam engine as she bent over him, brushing her nipples against his lips.

To hell with what society might think. Fingers clumsy with passion, Jacob grabbed a soft breast, sucking at it like a hungry infant. To hell with what anybody thought, he was going to make this girl his wife.

His mouth still clamped around his soft prize, he rolled her beneath him. She gave a cry as he penetrated her, as though receiving him for the first time, and the pleasure of it increased the pounding in his head. The pressure behind his eyes threatened to force them from their sockets with every thrust into that warm moistness. He had fixed that bitch Anna Royce and tonight he would fix the only other thing he wanted. Tonight he would fill this girl with his child.

'This is for my necklace, Jacob.'

Beneath him the velvet eyes smouldered, but his own closing against the pain of passion, Jacob missed their expression of loathing.

'You like this, don't you?' she whispered, contracting then releasing the muscles of her vagina, sucking at his bloated penis. 'Tell me you like it, Jacob.'

Jacob Rewcastle didn't answer. His lower jaw falling slackly, he choked in the back of his throat, dropping full on to the girl beneath him.

For a minute she lay listening to the sounds of Jacob fighting for breath then, heaving him away, rolled from the bed.

Replacing her clothes, tidying her hair carefully beneath a trim red bonnet, she looked again at Jacob, her mouth parting in a cold smile as his eyes begged for help.

'Not from me, you slimy bastard.' She laughed quietly. 'You'll get no help from me.'

Picking up first his jacket then his trousers, she removed every penny then closed the door behind her and walked from the hotel, nodding to the night porter as she went.

Chapter Sixteen

The long days of Christmas were over and though Anna was reluctant to leave Maggie she was glad to be free of the house. It had been hard letting Misty go to Switzerland – the time she had with her daughter was precious – but home had been no place for her this year.

Misty was growing up fast. Anna closed her eyes and saw in her mind the pretty smiling face, eyes blue as a cornflower and the pale blonde hair. Her daughter would be a beautiful woman. Opening her eyes, Anna stared out of the window of the train carrying her to London. The house had been so quiet, it would have been unfair on a young girl, so full of all the gaiety of life, to insist she come home for the holiday, a home heavy with sadness and fear, fear that Maggie might not recover from the death of her son. It might have been easier on them all if Maggie had cried, instead of this awful dry eyed quiet . . .

Across the compartment a man cleared his throat then noisily refolded his newspaper. Anna glanced across at him, then returned her gaze to the passing fields as he settled back to his reading.

Maggie had said almost nothing since receiving the telegram that had told her, so coldly and abruptly, of Andrew's death at sea, but Anna had heard her murmuring, 'One ye'll see once more.' The words of Kate's prophecy.

But Maggie was keeping her tears inside, Anna thought. Keeping them to shed in the long lonely hours of the night, as Anna kept hers. Allowing only the shadows to see her pain, to know the extent of her suffering.

Maggie had lost her son as Anna had lost hers. True, Aaron was not dead in the sense that Andrew Fellen was dead, but he was just as lost to her.

Don't tell the lad just yet, Mother Polly had warned. And she had not told him. She had left Wednesbury without telling her son who she was. That had been as painful as leaving him that first time.

In her lap her fingers clenched with the memory that had never truly left her. Could telling him have been worse than this, worse than the hurt that ripped through her every time she thought of him, every time she saw a mother with her son, every time she spoke of him in her prayers? And if he had turned his back on her, what then? Could she have stood the pain of that?

One day she might have to.

Watching the passing scenery her fingers curled even tighter, but the bite of her nails into her palm was nothing compared to the bite of the thoughts in her mind.

One day she would have to face that threat, for Aaron had the right to know his parentage.

Beatrice Rewcastle looked at the still figure of the man they had carried from that room in the Birmingham Royal. Doubtless he had gone there with some woman, one who had robbed him then left him to choke his life away.

'You should have died,' she murmured, 'why should you live when my son is dead?'

Jacob's right eyelid twitched then opened, leaving the left one closed, paralysed by the stroke that had taken all power of movement from the left side of his body.

He swallowed, but distaste returned as quickly as he tried to rid himself of it. His body might be half dead, but not his mind. Whatever had struck at him in that hotel room had not affected his brain, or his sight, he thought, gazing at the woman who stood at the bottom of the bed. He knew what he must do, and it was almost as galling as having to look at her!

'I want Brown,' he muttered. 'I want to see 'im. Tell 'im to come in the mornin'.'

'What for?' Beatrice asked.

'Mind your own bloody business!' His uncertain temper remained unaltered. Try to keep him as quiet as possible, the doctor had warned. He could suffer a second stroke at any time and that would certainly kill him; don't let him excite himself and he might pull through.

'Couldn't you see him next week?' Beatrice watched the purple patches on her husband's face. 'The doctor said you were to have complete rest and quiet.'

'Doctor! 'E's as bloody daft as you!' Jacob exploded. 'Send word to Brown to get 'is arse over 'ere in the mornin', and bloody well do it now!'

Lips tight, against the smile that so wanted to curve her thin mouth, Beatrice pulled the bell cord hanging beside the huge bed.

'Daisy,' she said as a maid answered her summons, 'tell Newton to send over to Lawyer Brown, he is to say that Mr Rewcastle would be obliged if he would call tomorrow.'

'Obliged!' The thunder was muted by twisted, half-closed lips but Jacob's one eye flashed brilliant with anger. 'Who said owt about bein' bloody obliged!' His heavy head lolled towards the maid standing nervously near the door. 'You tell Newton 'e is to say as Jacob Rewcastle 'as business with 'im an' 'e is to 'ave 'is arse over 'ere in the mornin' afore nine o'clock.'

'Yes, sir.' Not daring to look at her mistress, the girl scuttled from the room.

Beatrice folded her hands over her brown bombazine skirts. Her grey hair was parted along the centre and pulled severely over her ears into a tight bun on the nape of her thin neck, it only accentuated her rapier-honed features.

Jacob squinted at her, distaste thick in his mouth. She looked like a freshly sharpened pencil.

'You can bugger off,' he slurred. 'I can do wi'out your parsimonious face.'

'I agree I was never pretty, Jacob.' Beatrice didn't move. 'Never pretty enough to work you into the kind of filthy frenzy that has left you less than half a man.'

Struggling to lift himself, he dropped back in breathless defeat.

'Wha . . . what do you be knowin' of passion, you bloody vinegar-faced bitch? You who 'as always been too miserable to open your mouth, let alone your legs.'

'That didn't really bother you, Jacob,' she said acidly. 'You had my money. Enough to buy all the women you wanted.'

'An' enjoyed 'em all.' Jacob's twisted mouth screwed into a smile. Beatrice continued to smile also, a smile of satisfaction.

'But that is all over now, Jacob. You are crippled. Oh, not in your mind and that is good. You still have full control of that, and with it you can think of all these long hours you have left . . . to spend alone in that bed.'

'The devil take you, you bloody bitch!' He seethed, his right hand grasping fruitlessly at the bed cover. 'The devil take you!'

'Devil or God,' Beatrice returned calmly, 'I would willingly go with whichever put you there.'

Two hours later she held the letter Lawyer Brown had sent in return to her husband's message. She could guess why Jacob wanted to see him. She had heard of the birth of Amy Stevens' son.

Putting the letter on the tray which held a cup of mulled wine, she nodded to Newton to carry it upstairs. A smile on her narrow face, she turned into the sitting room. With that nod Beatrice Rewcastle had sentenced her husband to death. Who would know it was poison and not a second stroke had taken him to his grave?

• • •

Anna tried to relax in the hansom carrying her across the city to the shop she had set up in London. Everywhere was noise. The shouts of men loading wagons, the clang of trams and the clatter of horses' hooves. She should be used to the noise, after all she visited Birmingham regularly enough, but this . . . Anna leaned back in the carriage, even Birmingham was no match for this madness.

What would Maggie make of it? She smiled at the thought. She would probably use one of her favourite phrases, 'everybody rushing around like a man with his arse on fire looking for a bucket of water to put it out'.

Maggie. Anna's thoughts turned to the woman she had left behind in Coseley. She had always been so strong, always ready to push on when Anna herself had wanted to give in. It had been Maggie who had helped her when she had arrived penniless on her doorstep, Maggie who had been so understanding when she had told her of her son, and it was Maggie who had been there for her when Edward was killed.

Please God, take care of Maggie, Anna prayed silently as the hansom dropped her at the shop.

'I hope you approve, Anna.' Emma showed her the small tea room she and William had created from an almost derelict side building. 'We thought that if we served tea and cakes after the clients had browsed through the shop, they would probably look through the catalogue and order their purchases before leaving the premises. It seems to have worked rather well,' she added nervously.

'I think it's a marvellous idea. Thank you, Emma. No wonder the shop is so popular. Your William makes a lovely cup of tea.'

'He is wonderful, Anna.' Emma's nervousness faded and her violet eyes glowed with a soft secretive warmth that tugged at Anna's heart. 'He works all day unpacking deliveries, making up orders, brewing pots of tea – he has even learned to make cakes and scones. Then in the evening he takes out deliveries.

That was why we bought the hand cart, Anna. We tried to do without it because of the expense but . . .'

'It was the sensible thing to do, Emma,' she interrupted, 'as was this tea room. You and William have proved your worth and that is why I am putting you on a share basis. From now on, Emma, you take the same as Hester. Two per cent of what this shop makes is yours, over and above your salary.'

When Emma's tears of happiness had subsided, Anna continued, 'Did William take my apologies to Lady Strathlyn?'

'Yes, Anna, and Her Ladyship *had* asked you to call. She questioned William very closely.'

Then it had not been a ruse. Charles had not wanted to see her. Wrong again, Anna, she thought grimly. But then, you were wrong about Charles from the start.

'Whew!' Anna wiped the perspiration from her face. 'We are all going to have a cup of tea, and this time, William, *I* will make it.'

'It's beautiful, Anna, quite the loveliest yet.'

The three friends sat together in the salon which had taken the whole day to set out.

'Credit where it is due, Emma.' Anna sipped gratefully at the hot tea. 'I only design the china. It's Seth Gladwin who does the rest.'

She looked at the setting the three of them had created; unable to afford a huge dining table they had laid floor boards across piles of house bricks, covering the whole down to the floor with a flowing damask cloth William had found on the rag market and which Emma had boiled until it was white as new snow.

She had proved invaluable in so many ways: taking Anna to the Saturday night market in Petticoat Lane to find elegant wine glasses; refusing to pay more than tuppence each for the chairs the junk man wanted sixpence for, then rolling up her sleeves and helping scrub and polish them until they shone. She had folded napkins into white pleated fans and laid the King's Choice cutlery.

Edward would have been so proud. Tears trembled along Anna's lashes as Emma lit two four-branched candelabra that only that afternoon had been black with the dirt of ages. Pale translucent candlelight spilled in soft lemony pools, tinting the glasses and playing gently over the exquisite claret and gold china. Royal Edward, Anna's own design and choice of colour, brought into vivid, beautiful reality by Seth Gladwin's skilful hands. Emma was right: this was her most beautiful range of china yet.

'A gentleman to see me?' Anna wrapped the glistening folds of her wet hair into a towel. Something had happened at the shop. It must be William come to tell her for only he and Emma knew where she was staying. Reaching for a peignoir, she fastened it hurriedly. She had only left the shop an hour ago.

'Ask him to come up,' she said, tightening the towel about her head. William would understand her informality . . . nothing must go wrong with tomorrow's launch of Royal Edward.

'Yes, ma'am.' The blank-faced hotel maid bobbed a curtsy and two minutes later a knock sounded on the door.

'Come in, William,' Anna called from the bathroom, then stared in disbelief as she emerged.

'Hello, Anna!' said Charles softly, his eyes drinking in the flushed loveliness of her face.

'How . . . how did you know I was here?' The first stunning blow of surprise fading, Anna found her tongue. 'Did Emma tell you?'

'No.' The well-formed mouth curled to a smile. 'And I very much doubt if that worthy lady would tell me anything I asked her.'

'Then how?'

'I saw you walking along Queen Anne's Gate. It was an easy guess you would be staying at The Conway.'

'How very shrewd of you,' Anna returned acidly, 'and how thoughtless of me. I shall know better than use this hotel in future.'

'If I knew you were in London, Anna, I would visit every hotel until I found you.'

If he thought to flatter her, he had made a mistake. All the latent anger and misery of the months since Andrew's death, and the travesty of a funeral that had been accorded her father, suddenly broke through.

'And tell your wife what?' she blazed. 'Or have you got your seedy little life so well ordered you don't have to tell her anything? Perhaps she is so pleased to be Mrs Lazenby that she turns a blind eye to your excursions. Or could it be that, like myself, she is not interested in what you do?'

'My wife . . .'

'Don't bother to tell me she doesn't understand you, Charles.'

'Anna, I must talk to you.'

He stepped nearer and her chin came up defiantly.

'Why? Isn't she interested in listening to your lies either? And if all you have to talk about is some nice little house in the suburbs, you can save your breath, Charles. Now, please go. As you can see, I am not prepared for visitors, especially unwelcome ones.'

'What gives you the idea that I am married, Anna?' He asked it softly, no trace of rancour in his tone.

'Are you telling me you're not?' Eyes filled with scorn were fixed on him disbelievingly.

'I mean just that.'

He was cool, she had to give him that.

'Then the girl who was selecting china was your mistress! A bit young, I would have thought, even for you.'

He remained perfectly still, only his eyes hardening beneath the fall of fair hair still worn without pomade.

'The young lady I was escorting the last time you and I met was not my mistress, Anna, she was my sister.'

She felt the room revolve about her. His sister . . . and she had accused her of being little more than a high-class trollop!

'I . . . I'm sorry.' It was all she could say.

His smile returned, softening his eyes. He was so devastatingly good-looking, no woman could be blamed for becoming his mistress.

'I will accept your apology only if you accompany me to the theatre and then dine with me afterwards?'

Anna walked to the window, looking out over the darkened street.

'I can't,' she said. 'As you can see, I am not dressed for the theatre.'

'Then we will dine here, in this room!'

'No.' Anna turned sharply. 'That would not be proper.'

Charles Lazenby was naturally charming, and knew now to use that charm, but he was a fool if he really believed he could hoodwink Anna Royce.

'Wait for me downstairs.' She saw the smile curve his mouth again and her own lips tightened. Charles would get his apology . . . but that was all he would get.

Fastening the tiny pearl buttons of her cotton gloves, Anna gave herself a long look in the mirror. The cream grosgrain dress with its wide belt and fashionable hobble skirt, stopping short of her ankles, emphasised her slim body and accentuated the shining red-gold of her hair. Her skin was as soft and creamy as it had always been, and for all that she had suffered, not a line marred her face.

'You make a presentable picture, Anna Royce,' she whispered. 'Presentable enough for any man's mistress, but not acceptable enough for a wife.'

Turning, she picked up the cream silk chiffon scarf lying on the table and tucked it into her belt. At thirty-four years old she should have been at home with a husband and family instead of going for a picnic with a man who had no intention of ever offering her a legitimate position as his wife. Why did you say you would go? she asked herself for the umpteenth time. Why didn't you stick to your plans and say you were returning to Coseley this morning? But she hadn't, she had accepted Charles's invitation before he had left the hotel last night, and now she must go through with it.

She had reached the lobby when Charles came in. Dressed in a thigh-length belted slate grey coat, teamed with breeches and knee-length leather boots, he drew every eye as he slipped off his gauntlet gloves and raised her hand to his lips.

'You look very beautiful, Anna,' he said, eyes filled with admiration. 'Like some pale goddess who will suddenly melt away in a pearly mist – only I'm not going to let you melt away, now or ever. I thought we'd go somewhere along the river. The parks are always filled with people you simply have to stop and speak to, and I'm not ready to share you with anybody.'

He didn't smile as he looked down into her face and Anna did not blush as she once would have done. She had the measure of Charles Lazenby, she was under no illusions about him.

'Your coach, ma'am.' The seductive smile giving way to a delighted boyish grin, he stopped beside a green horseless carriage, its lacquered coachwork and huge brass headlamps gleaming in the morning light.

'I'm not riding in that!' Anna stepped emphatically backward.

'Why not?' His grin widening, Charles took her arm. 'It won't bite you. It is only a motor carriage.'

'Is that what you call it?' She cast a disparaging glance along the shining length of the vehicle. 'I saw one of these in Queen Anne's Gate. Noisy smelly things! I don't like them.'

'You haven't given them a chance. Come on, Anna, be fair. If you don't like it after you have given it a go, I will never ask you to ride in one again.'

Against her better judgement she climbed into the high leather seat, her hands gripping tight to the side.

'Relax,' Charles laughed, 'and I should fasten that pretty hat on with something. It can be breezy riding in this.'

'I prefer a hansom,' she grumbled, tying the chiffon scarf about her head. 'They are much more civilised.'

'But not half the fun.' Charles cranked the starting handle and the huge machine jerked into life.

'You'll see, Anna,' he called over the noise of the engine. 'By the time we get home you will love this asthmatic monster as much as I do.'

Don't count on it, she thought, every bone in her body jolting as they drove away. Give me an old cart any time.

The sound of a stone hitting water caused Anna to open her eyes. She watched concentric circles widen in the sun-sequinned river. Along the banks, huge trees dipped their branches in worship, and somewhere among their foliage birds sang a hymn to their creator.

'Sorry . . . did I wake you?'

'I wasn't asleep.' She sat up. 'I was thinking about the last time I went on a picnic . . . it seems so long ago.' Perhaps it was the magic of the moment, Anna could never decide why later, but easing her back against a tree trunk she told Charles of that Sunday school outing, of Peter and her paper diamond.

'Peter was right.' He turned to her as she finished speaking. 'You should have diamonds, Anna, but not paper ones.' He caught her hands, his eyes fathomless and serious. 'I want to give you those diamonds, Anna, I want to drown you in them.'

He had taken the moment, her lovely peaceful moment, and shattered it. Feeling she had lost something irreplaceable, Anna was overcome with rage. She had tried for so long to keep calm but now her angry reply sent the birds wheeling from the trees.

'How many more times do I have to say it? How many more times must you hear it before you will accept it? I will not be your mistress!'

Anger draining her, leaving her empty of any feeling at all, she walked to the edge of the river, staring into its depths.

'Why?' Charles asked, stamping a boot against the riverbank. 'Because of your business? How many paper diamonds does it take to make a string, for Christ's sake?'

'No, it is not because of my business.' Anna felt strangely calm, the anger of a moment before dissipated. He had made her a totally unacceptable offer, one that should preclude her ever speaking to him again, but deep down she had a feeling that beneath the arrogant self-assurance, Charles was a kind and caring man.

'Not my business,' she repeated, 'but my morals. I am not a whore and I will be no man's mistress.'

Charles Lazenby looked at the woman, her head held high, and admitted he had lost. He had thought to make Anna Royce his mistress but once again his gamble had not paid off.

'I beg your pardon, Anna.' He smiled sheepishly. 'My behaviour has been reprehensible, and I apologise. But with your beauty, you cannot condemn me for trying. Will you forgive me?'

'If I have your word you will never refer to it again?'

'You have it.' He gave a slight bow. 'But might I ask that we be friends, Anna?'

She smiled.

'No one can ever have too many of those,' she said, 'especially me.'

'Then as one friend to another, Anna, may I ask you once again to call me Charles?'

How many paper diamonds does it take to make a string? Charles's question echoed in her mind as he drove her to the railway station, but it was a question to which she found no answer. She had thought only to take back King's Choice but now she could not stop, the livelihood of too many others was tied in with her own. '*The lives of many will be bound to yer own . . .*' How true Kate O'Keefe's word were proving, but how much more must she do? Charles had been right to ask – how many more paper diamonds *would* it take? With sickening certainty Anna knew she had become caught in a web of her own making, chained by manacles strong as her lust for revenge.

'Would you prefer it if we came to the house?'

'I would appreciate it,' Anna answered Reuben's question.

'We could call around seven this evening, is that too late?'

'No, seven will be fine.'

'Seven it is then, Anna.'

I could have done without having to see anyone tonight, Anna thought, feeling the weariness that seemed at times to eat into her bones. But she had not wished to refuse Reuben's request she see this friend of his father's.

Hearing the quiet click that told her Reuben had hung up she replaced the telephone on the hook. He had said it was a matter of business.

More business. Anna leaned back in her chair. Why discuss more business when she was losing half of what she had? Why not give it all up? Paper diamonds. That was what Peter had said. But she would give them all and more besides, everything she had fought tooth and nail for, if only her son were with her. If she could only have both of the children she loved so much. That would be the brightest diamond of them all.

She had kept the promise to take back King's Choice, in doing so had acquired a few more paper diamonds, but she would trade them all for one smile from her son's proud young face.

'I love you Aaron,' she whispered, pushing up from her chair. 'You may never know it but I love you, my son.'

Reuben Fine arrived at seven on the dot, bringing with him an elderly man he introduced as Emanuel Goldberg.

'Such a name, sheesh!' The man shrugged his shoulders, blue eyes twinkling behind heavy framed spectacles. 'But my friends are good to me, they call me Manny. Maybe you will call me Manny, Mrs Royce?'

Feeling an instinctive liking for the short grey-haired man, Anna took the hand he held out to her.

'We might do a deal.' She smiled. 'I will trade Manny for Anna.'

'Sheesh, Reuben my boy!' The eyes holding Anna's twinkled like blue sequins. 'You say the woman is not Jewish . . . so where did she get such a head for business?'

Taking both of their coats, Anna hung them in the coat closet standing against one wall of the hall, then led the way into the sitting room.

'Will you take some tea?'

'No, my dear.' The old man replied smilingly. 'It was good of you to agree to see me, I should not take even more of your time.'

'It will take very little of my time to make tea.' Anna appreciated the thought behind his refusal and her smile was warm.

'Then I shall say yes, a little tea always helps the business of business.'

In the kitchen she collected china on a tray and brewed tea in a china pot, and all the while she could hear the voice of Jacob Rewcastle in her head. 'You've lost it after all, Anna Royce. You've lost the mill that was mine, and you'll lose that son of yours, the same as you took mine from me. You'll lose it all . . . you'll lose it all.'

'I hope Maggie is well.' Reuben got to his feet, taking the tray from Anna as she came back to the sitting room, then settled himself once more in a comfortable armchair, his small Gladstone bag at his feet.

'Yes,' Anna answered, glad that Maggie seemed, at last, able to come to terms with Andrew's death. 'She is over at the Cresswells'. She goes there once a week, she says it is the only real natter she gets to have any more.'

'She will get that all right.' Reuben smiled, taking off his spectacles and rubbing the lenses with his handkerchief. 'My mother-in-law can talk the wheels off a wagon.'

'Don't let her hear you saying that, Reuben.' Anna smiled across at him. 'Mary can have a sharp tongue as well as a busy one.'

'Don't worry, Anna, that is something I know well already, being her son-in-law entitles me to no exceptions.'

'She and Maggie are two of a kind,' Anna replied. 'They say what they mean, regardless of who is on the receiving end. But they are without price, both of them.'

Manny Goldberg kept his eyes on Anna while she and Reuben were talking. This was a strong woman, despite the marks of tiredness on her face. A woman of character and principles, one who, he felt, would not easily break a bargain once it was made.

Manny took the tea she poured for him. 'Anna,' he said. 'I asked Reuben to bring me here this evening. His father is my dearest friend, a man whose word I can depend on – and that word was that there was none better than Anna Royce with whom I could do business.'

'Business?'

'Let me explain.' Manny stirred sugar into his tea. 'I have shops in the Hague, Amsterdam, Rome and Zurich. Shops that sell only the finest.'

He looked up at her, eyes a little enlarged by the thick lenses of his spectacles.

'I wish to introduce a range of fine china into those shops, china of the highest quality, and my friend tells me you have such a product.'

'I think my china will match any you can find elsewhere.'

'It must not match.' He raised the delicate cup. 'It must surpass. The name Goldberg has a reputation in Europe for supplying only the best.'

Anna waited, watching the way in which he balanced the fragile cup in his hand, the way he held it to the light.

'This is one of yours?'

He smiled as she nodded. 'It is exquisite, truly exquisite. My friend the father of Reuben was correct in his advice – yours is the best I will find.'

Placing the cup and saucer on a table beside him, he looked at Anna.

'Can you supply these to Manny Goldberg?'

'I . . . I am sure we could,' Anna answered, surprised. 'Perhaps you would like a catalogue of our designs?'

'Oh, he's got one of those, Anna, Hester saw to that.' Reuben grinned.

'Yes, I have your catalogue, but I will need more for my shops. Customers like to be given a choice. And when they cannot say, "I like this better than I like that", they buy both. Sheesh!' He smiled, lifting his shoulders in a shrug. 'It's business.'

'Hester also showed him one of your beauty boxes.'

'She did, she did!' Manny Goldberg laughed, the spectacles sliding along his nose so that he was looking at her over them.

'She is a smart girl, that Hester, you have the best for a wife, Reuben my boy.' Pushing the spectacles back into place, he returned his gaze to Anna. 'The beauty boxes are made by Benjie Freeth, I understand? That is good. Every one will have the highest workmanship, be a thing of beauty in itself. Can you also supply these to me?'

Anna nodded again, hoping she was not taking on too much.

'Then I have a proposition to make and it is one I wish to put to you in the presence of your solicitor. It is this.' He pushed again at his spectacles. 'You agree to make Goldberg's the sole agent in Europe for Anna Royce products. In return I will pay ten thousand pounds for the franchise. After that we agree a separate price for your china, and another for beauty products.'

'You . . . you mean you are willing to pay ten thousand pounds to become the sole outlet for my products?' Anna choked with surprise at what he had just suggested. 'But I can't . . . I mean . . .'

'It is a good offer, Anna,' Reuben said.

'Is my proposal not acceptable? Does Manny Goldberg not offer enough money?'

'No, please, it isn't that!' Anna blushed at the thought of appearing greedy when it was the sheer magnitude of the offer that had caused her to protest. 'I am flattered you wish to sell my china through your shops, but . . . but I can't take all that money over and above what is paid for each product. It . . . it seems like . . . well, like robbery!'

Throwing back his head, the Jew laughed, setting his spectacles once more on his nose.

'Robbery?' he chuckled. 'Manny Goldberg doesn't get robbed. Being the only man in Europe to sell Anna Royce will make me money, make *both* of us money. When your products can be bought nowhere else then people will come to Manny Goldberg. So, Anna, what do you say? Do we have a deal?'

'It's nothing unusual, Anna,' Reuben said as she looked at him, a question in her eyes. 'A great deal of business is done on the same lines. A man wants something, then he has to pay for it.'

'It still seems a great deal of money to pay . . .'

'Money, sheesh!' The shoulders rose in the shrug that seemed second nature to the man. 'Manny Goldberg respects it as a man should respect his mother. Be assured, I do not throw it away. I expect to recoup it many times over. So, Anna Royce . . . are we agreed?'

At her smile the man rose to his feet, taking a package from the pocket of his coat and handing it to her.

'Reuben will make out an agreement. That is the ten

thousand.' Behind the thick lenses his eyes smiled at the look of astonishment that crossed her face. 'Manny Goldberg keeps his word.'

Anna shook the hand he offered. 'And I will keep mine,' she said, her throat thickening, 'I will keep mine.'

'*One way or another the Almighty will send what you be lookin' for.*'

Maggie's words of a few nights before stirred in her memory as she closed the door behind the departing men. The money Manny had given her would mean she could keep the mill and King's Choice, but more important, it would keep her son in her life.

'. . . the Almighty will send what you be lookin' for.'

It felt like a miracle but the whisper that slipped from her was not addressed to God.

'Thank you, Edward,' she murmured, 'thank you.'

Chapter Seventeen

'You knows your own business best, Anna, but I would 'ave thought it daft to keep running that place at such a loss.' Joby Timmins looked from the ledgers to her.

Reuben and John Harris had both virtually called her a fool for buying Joby Hampton's Wednesbury foundry. Now it seemed they'd been right.

'So what do I do, Joby?' she asked in a tired voice.

'Seems to me nobody knows steel trade like Eli Curran. Why don't you send 'im to this Wednesbury place? 'Appen he might find out why place is a millstone about your neck.'

She hadn't thought of that and thanked the clerk for a suggestion that might just bring a solution.

'Can I go too?' Misty asked when Anna told her and Maggie what she planned.

'What on earth for?' Anna looked at her daughter. At seventeen she was chic and sophisticated, the perfect product of a boarding school for young ladies; so very different from what Anna herself had been at that age. 'There is nothing you can do there, it's just a small steel foundry.'

'I know.' Misty perched on the arm of her mother's chair, one finger toying with her hair, 'but I want to know more about the business than designing packages for cosmetics.'

'Your designs are very good, darling. They are responsible for the popularity of Mistique.'

'I enjoyed that, Mother, the sketches and talking to the

263

printers and everything, but that doesn't mean I wouldn't enjoy seeing the inside of a foundry too.'

Anna smiled, trying to imagine her elegantly dressed daughter among sweating workmen stripped to the waist against the heat of the coal furnaces.

'You would have to wear something more durable than those.' She nodded towards Misty's pale blue calf shoes.

'That means I can go . . . yippee!' The girl danced excitedly round the sitting room until Maggie called for her to stop.

'You mind you do as Eli Curran tells you,' Maggie warned. 'It's no cake walk inside a rolling mill.'

'I will, Grammie.' Misty rested her golden head against one that had turned pure white soon after hearing of her son's death.

'Grammie is right,' Anna said in a tight tone, 'you do exactly as Eli says.'

Misty glanced at the clock on the wall of The White Horse dining room. She and Eli had eaten together this evening as they had every evening since they had been in Wednesbury, and she knew Eli would want to follow his usual pattern of going to his room, writing up a few notes for her mother then going on for a pint of beer. But this evening Misty had no intention of following her own usual pattern. Tonight she was not going to lie on her bed and read, going slowly out of her mind with boredom.

'I thought I would walk into the town, Eli.' She folded a heavy white napkin, paying it more attention than was warranted.

'Eh? You can't do that, wench! This 'ere is a strange town. You can't go gallivantin' about like you do in Coseley.'

'Why not?' She smiled, hiding iron determination behind a soft expression.

''Cos you never knows who might be about.'

Misty laughed, showing pretty white teeth. She had to play this one very smart.

'Oh, come on, Eli, there are no monsters lurking in the

bushes. In fact, I've seen precious few bushes around here at all.'

'You knows what I means, miss.' Eli was testy. He was responsible for Anna's girl. "Sides, there's nowt to this town 'ceptin' little 'ouses and factories so what does you want to go looking for?'

'The landlady here says there is a market on tonight. It goes on until after midnight. I must see it, Eli, the girls at school would never believe it.'

'If you must.' Displeasure adding to the lines already cutting across his brow, Eli pushed his empty plate away. 'Wait on five minutes till I write up fer your mam an' then I'll come wi' ye.'

'No, Eli.' His sharp glance told her she had been too quick. Leaning forward, she squeezed his hand in hers, voice pleading. 'I can't look at any womanish things I might find if you are there.' Eyelids lowered, she even managed a blush. 'I . . . I would be far too shy.'

She had a point, and Eli was itching to be away to The Turks Head pub, just a few yards along the street. He had struck up a friendship with some of the local men; one that was telling him far more than that manager up at the foundry.

'But I can't leave you to walk about place on your own.'

Misty's smile was inward, secretive. Eli was already halfway to where she wanted him.

'I know you want to take care of me, Eli, but the people here seem friendly enough and I won't stay out late, honestly.' She increased the pressure on his leathery hand, her blue glance wide and candid. 'Please, Eli . . . I want to see the market. We never have anything like it in Coseley and the staff of the Haworth School for Young Ladies would drop dead at the mention of the word!'

Eli grinned. He'd always liked this wench of Anna Royce's and having grown up with the Cresswell twins she could take her own part with the best of them, he reckoned.

'You mind what y'ave said then, young miss, an' mind you gets yourself back 'ere reasonable like.'

The smile she gave him was pretty, masking the thrill of triumph. She was learning more at that posh school than was on the curriculum.

The grey sky of evening assumed a scarlet cast as the iron foundry opened its blast furnace. Below the hill that held a grim stone church, market stalls nestled among the cluster of tiny terraced houses. But Misty wasn't interested in them.

Aaron lived on the hill close to the Parish Church he had told her when she had stopped to speak to him on the tour of the foundry with her mother, and she had learned enough from Eli to know this was the last opening of the furnaces for the day shift. Soon he must pass this spot to get home.

Touching the pale gold hair she had piled on to her head, she smoothed her sapphire velvet suit, glad she had brought it with her and confident the well-cut line enhanced her slender figure. She wanted to appear older, more mature. That way Aaron would take notice.

A slight breeze caught a blonde tendril, weaving it among her thick lashes, and she turned her head, letting the same breeze blow it off her face. It was then that she saw him, tall and broad, his long stride making easy work of walking up the steep hill.

'Good evening, Mr Bradly!' Misty smiled as he drew level.

'Good evening, Miss Royce.' Aaron hesitated, unsure whether or not to walk on. 'You shouldn't be up here all by yourself. It will be dark soon.'

'Oh, not for a while yet, Mr Bradly, and it is such a pleasant evening I thought I would try to see a little of Wednesbury before I have to return home.'

'Was there no one could see it with you? Do you have to be alone?'

'There is only Eli.' She liked the way he looked into her face, an open confident glance with none of the shiftiness she had seen in some of her mother's employees. 'And he was very busy. Besides,' she lied competently, 'I wouldn't have wanted to tire him further by asking him to walk with me, not after a long day's work.'

'Well, you can see all of Wednesbury from here.' Aaron pushed a hand into his hair, holding it against the breeze. 'What there is to see. I recommend you take a look and then return to The White Horse.'

He was walking away, leaving her standing.

'But there must be more than houses and factories?' Misty started after him, her attempts at worldly sophistication abandoned. 'There must be some pretty places to see, and I wouldn't be alone if *you* showed them to me.'

He stopped and turned, showing no surprise at her forwardness.

'You won't go until somebody does . . . that somebody had better be me, I suppose. Wait there.'

This time he did stride away and Misty felt a glow of triumph as she watched his broad upright figure.

'There is Hob's Hole.' Foundry grime washed away, burn-sprinkled trousers changed for neat dark worsted, a white open-throated shirt showing a little of his wide chest, Aaron walked her slowly down the hill. 'Folk go there sometimes to get away from all this. That's when they're not too bushed.'

'Bushed?'

'Yes,' he answered without looking at her. 'Tired. Worn out from grafting for a living.'

'And you go there?'

'I like it despite its name. It's a wide pool rather like a lake, I suppose. When the weather is hot the lads swim there after they've finished work.'

'And the girls?' Misty could not resist a mischievous smile as he threw her a quick glance.

'They don't swim, but quite a few of them go along for the view.'

'Is it such a pretty place?'

He roared with laughter then, blond head thrown back.

'I was teasing,' he said at last. 'They go to see the lads – they swim naked.'

Misty held his glance with sparkling eyes.

'I would still like to see Hob's Hole, with or without the vagaries of its view, Mr Bradly.'

'Then see it you will, and on your head be it if one of the men has decided on a dip.'

Taking her hand to help her over a low stile, Aaron kept it in his own as they crossed a broad meadow, the small tree-fringed lake that was Hob's Hole reflecting the crimson of the lowering sun. She would be gone soon, leaving his drab life drabber, but for the moment they were together.

Picking up a pebble, he sent it bouncing flat across the dark water, spreading circles in its wake. Hesitating only a moment, Misty selected a stone and skimmed it expertly after Aaron's.

'I learned to do that before I went to school,' she said, grinning.

Across the pool a man's low voice mingled with a woman's laughter and Aaron turned, taking Misty's hand.

'I'm on the first shift tomorrow,' he said, a hint of shyness in his voice. 'That means I shall be finished at two o'clock if you've a fancy for a walk?'

Her fingers twining in his, Misty smiled. 'I've a fancy.'

'I don't care for the way things are being run, Anna.' Eli Curran sat a little uncomfortably in Anna's finely furnished sitting room. He hadn't needed the two weeks they had stayed in Wednesbury to sort out the steel mill's problem or to realise that missis's daughter seemed reluctant to leave.

'What exactly do you think is wrong, Eli?'

'Steel,' he answered bluntly. 'It's nowt short o' rubbish, what's bein' turned out down theer. You can't be blamin' folk for not wantin' to buy the stuff. It's a wonder place 'as gone on as long as it 'as.'

'Why is that, Eli? It seemed to do all right when I was a . . . down there.'

Eli Curran caught the swift correction but his lined face gave no indication. Anna Royce had done all right by him and by Coseley and was entitled to her privacy.

'Seems since old gaffer went and works was sold to Bradly Engineering, that manager – what's 'is name? – seems to think it meks no matter 'ow much shit is in the pig iron he uses. Some young lad tried tellin' 'im it were no good but he were told to shut up or get out.'

'I see.' Anna rose. 'Thank you for going, Eli, I'm very grateful.'

Seeing him to the door, she closed it, leaning against the hard wood. Why was fate drawing her back to the one place she didn't want to be?

'I don't want to go,' she whispered into her hands. 'Please God, I don't want to go.'

'There just ain't the call there was a year or two ago.' The manager of the Wednesbury steel mill eyed the red-haired woman and the slip of a girl at her side. He remembered that one from a month or so gone, come here with that snipe-nosed bugger Curran who thought he knew everything.

'Isn't twelve months rather quick for the steel business to fall off as drastically as you say, Mr Dean?'

'It was fallin' off afore place was sold.' Samuel Dean didn't like being questioned, much less by some toffee-nosed bitch of a woman. What did she know about puddling iron?

''Course,' he went on, 'there was ways of cuttin' costs but Joby Hampton wouldn't 'ear of it.'

'Like what?' Across the dirt-packed floor two men heaved on the heavy link chain that lifted the iron door of the furnace. From where she stood Anna could feel some of the heat that ran hell a close second, but she didn't move back.

'Well, he 'ad no need of puttin' best quality pig iron into smeltin', he could 'ave used a lower grade.'

269

'Like you have been doing.' She said it quietly, her eyes on the sweating men shovelling coal into the red hot maw of the furnace.

'Is that what you would have done?'

Anna stopped, addressing her question to Aaron, the muscles of his arms and shirtless back rippling with the effort of pulling bars of glowing steel across the rolling beds, teasing them into ever more slender rods, feeling the same pride in him as she had felt watching him follow after her father's coffin.

'There can be no excuse for shoddy work.'

Transparent blue eyes lifted momentarily to her own and again she experienced a glow of pride. Her son was not afraid to speak his mind, neither did he make an effort to hide the fact he had overheard their conversation.

Directing his stare to the foundry manager, he added. 'It is a poor workman blames his tools.'

'My sentiments exactly.' Anna nodded. 'I hope you will continue to think that way once you replace Mr Dean, as manager of this foundry.'

Anna watched her son straighten in front of her, watched the surprise flare in his blue eyes.

'Eh!' Beside her, Samuel Dean's heavy face darkened. 'What's that yer say? What the bloody hell does yer think you're playing at?'

'I assure you I am not playing.'

Anna's voice was suddenly cold and hard as the bars of steel stored in the yard.

'And hell has nothing to do with it. *I* am giving you your tin, Mr Dean. I will not have men with your sly underhanded ways in my employ, and I will most certainly not have them in charge of my foundry. I will have the clerk make up your wages . . . you are finished at this foundry, as of now.'

Turning to leave she caught Misty's amazed expression and gave her a quick wink. If her daughter was going to learn then she must learn it all, especially how to kick a man's backside.

* * *

'You still look after him, Polly?' Anna sat in the tiny kitchen that was filled with so many memories.

'Ar, me wench, I do, much as 'e'll let me. Says it's too much for a woman my age to cook and clean. Huh!' She picked up a bucket, throwing a heap of coal onto the glowing fire. 'I told 'im I could do a day's work as good as 'im any day, cheeky young bugger! Mind you, Anna, I was glad enough when 'e said it would be easier for me if I moved in 'ere. That hill were gettin' to be a bit much.'

'He hasn't got himself a girl then?'

'Not courtin' strong if that's what you'm askin'.'

Polly picked up a small hand brush, sweeping the dust of the fire from the hearth. 'But I reckon 'e be sweet on some wench, he's bin maudlin' this last month or more.'

'Polly!' Taking the brush from the old woman's hand, Anna pressed her into the one chair the kitchen boasted.

'I've made some financial arrangements for . . . for Aaron.' She hesitated, still feeling the strangeness of speaking her son's name. 'When he is twenty-one he will come into quite a bit of money. Try to see for me that he spends it sensibly, doesn't squander it.'

'You need 'ave no fear on 'im doin' that, Anna. One thing Jos always told 'im was you look after the pennies, the pound will look after itself.'

He would say that, Anna thought, turning towards the door. Her father had not stinted her or her mother but had always tried to take care of his money.

'I don't know whether I will come to Wednesbury again, Polly,' she said, staring out towards the blackened walls of the Parish Church, 'but if I don't, you will always have my love and thanks for what you have done.'

Polly eased her body slightly, lifting the weight from her crippled leg, as she stood in the open doorway watching the woman in a smart green suit walk slowly past the wall of the churchyard to stand beneath the oak tree, looking at the bright flowers growing among the grass that covered a lonely grave.

'You've had a hard life, Anna Bradly,' she whispered into the soft air of the afternoon, 'an' I'm thinkin' there's more of the same yet to come.'

Chapter Eighteen

Spooning extra sugar into the pretty china cup, Anna stirred it vacantly, her mind miles away in Wednesbury.

She could not help. There was nothing she could do. All day the thought had plagued her, all day the worry of it had weighed on her like an iron bar, and all through the day she had found no solution.

The heat of the drink she was stirring travelled up the metal spoon, its sting bringing Anna back to the present. Taking up the cup and saucer, she carried it to Maggie's bedroom. Ordinarily she looked forward to this small ritual that had grown up since Maggie's illness; she valued the quiet minutes with the woman who meant so much to her.

'You looks done in, wench.'

Propped up on vast pillows, their frilled white slips starched stiff, Maggie took the cup of cocoa.

'You shouldn't 'ave bothered makin' this. You 'ave enough to do wi'out waiting on me.'

Anna smiled but the smile was tired.

'I like to do it, it's the only real time we seem to get to talk anymore.'

'That be the truth an' all.' Maggie patted the side of the bed. 'Sit you down for five minutes. I knows y'ave 'ad a long day but there be summat as needs to be said an' it won't improve wi' the keepin'.'

Anna shook her head.

'It will keep at least until tomorrow. You have had a long day too. You don't rest nearly enough.'

Maggie was right as always, it had been a long day and one that had added another worry to the list that seemed ever ready to plague her.

Maggie's eyes were faded but they had lost none of their keenness. Now they seemed to reach inside Anna's mind, to read the worry there.

'It might 'ave been a long day, wench,' she patted the bed again, 'but it'll be a damn' sight longer night if you don't tell me what it is be ailing you. There's a worry in you an' don't go denyin' it. We have shared the same house too long for you to go trying to pull the wool over my eyes. It ain't bad news about Misty, is it?'

'No.' Anna sat down on the bed, reaching a reassuring hand to her friend. 'Misty is fine. She is doing well at school, and every letter is filled with the new friends each year's intake brings and the madcap things they get up to. My only worry about her is that she may never want to leave school, never want to come home.'

'There be no real fear of that.' Maggie put her cup aside on the small night table beside her bed then put her hand over Anna's, holding it between both of her own. 'That one has her heart with her mother.'

For a few seconds neither said a word, only the ticking of Maggie's old clock audible. Then, with the foresight that always seemed to lead her to the heart of any trouble, Maggie spoke.

'If it ain't Misty that be worryin' you, an' I knows it ain't the business, not since you paid off them vultures at the bank, then it 'as to be the other one. It be your son, your lad. That be what's gnawin' at you. Tell me if I be wrong?'

But Anna could not tell Maggie she was wrong, though again she could not tell her she was right; she could not place her own worry on those frail shoulders which had been bent often enough on her account. Yet to tell her nothing at all would do as much harm. Maggie would, she knew, lie awake most of the night wondering.

'I think I am just overtired,' Anna said, knowing this would not satisfy Maggie.

'You be that all right, but there be more to it than tiredness. You 'ave a sadness about you that ain't no fault of workin' too hard. Won't you tell me what it be, Anna? Might be as together we can put things right.'

Anna looked at the lined hands that held her own. Maggie had helped so many times and in so many ways but this time there was nothing she could do. There was nothing either of them could do.

'Seems like lad will be leaving . . . he don't seem to have the heart he once had for his work.'

The words of Polly Shipton's letter ran through her mind as they had since it had arrived that morning.

'. . . and unless he should write, I won't be able to tell you for where.'

Her son would be gone from Wednesbury and she would lose the one tiny thread that held him to her. The thought sent a shudder through her and Maggie's hand tightened on hers.

'Tell me, wench,' she said softly. 'Don't shut me out now.'

'Oh, Maggie . . .' Anna drew a long sobbing breath. 'I don't want to lose him. I love him . . . I love him.'

It was too much. She had not meant to place her burdens on the other woman's shoulders but the sheer love in Maggie's voice had broken that resolve and slowly, between sobs, the story of Polly's letter came out.

'So you see,' she finished, 'I can't do anything to hold him there in Wednesbury, and I feel . . . I know . . . he would not come here to me. He is proud, Maggie, every line of his body tells you that. Too proud to accept a woman's charity.'

'Ar.' Maggie nodded. 'That I can believe. The folk of the Black Country 'ave little 'ceptin' pride, but that they 'ave in great measure. Your lad wouldn't take kindly to your sending for him now, but this I feel certain of – you won't lose 'im,

Anna. The love you 'ave always held for that lad of yours is too strong. A way *will* open, wench. God is good, 'e won't take away what you 'ave cherished all these years. One way or another the Almighty will send what you be lookin' for.'

God is good.

In her own room Anna felt the bitterness in her throat. Where was His goodness when she was being raped? And where His goodness when Edward was crushed to death beneath a machine? And where would it be when she lost her son?

'. . . he don't seem to have the heart he once had . . .'

The words Polly had written refused to leave her mind.

She knew the pain and loss he must still feel at losing Jos, but would leaving Wednesbury heal her son's pain?

Anna knew the answer. It was one she had learned so long before. Pain and longing, the sort of longing she had for Aaron, was not so easily left behind.

She had wanted to tell him. Wanted him to know she was his mother. But she had held back, telling herself it was for his sake she said nothing. But was it? Anna buried her face in her hands. Was it for Aaron she had said nothing, or was it because she could not face what she might see in his eyes?

'I can send money,' she whispered into the stillness as if answering some accusation, 'enough for him and for Mother Polly.'

But what of the foundry? Anna dropped her hands and stared into the shadows of her bedroom. She had made Aaron manager. But if he were no longer there did she still want it? Did she want the worry of another foundry? Did she want to be responsible for so many other lives?

What would happen if she closed it?

Anna let the thought hover in her mind.

What of the other men who worked there? Men she knew had nothing but the money they earned each week.

'Why should I care about them?' Anna flared, throwing back

the accusation. 'Did they care what happened to me? Did they care about what they did to my father? Did they care that their lies and torments drove him to take his own life?'

For all the truth of her protestations, Anna knew she *did* care about the people of Wednesbury. She did care about the hardship and suffering her closing the foundry would bring.

Across the years Maggie's words came back to her: '*Some will cry an' others will starve, it's nothing as 'asn't 'appened afore.*'

Some will starve.

In her lap, Anna's hands tightened into a ball. Where was the goodness of the Almighty in that?

'*It's yer back their fortunes will ride on . . .*'

She had seen the owning of Wednesbury foundry as a way of meeting with Aaron, of speaking with him, but to close it because he left . . .?

That was her only real reason and Anna knew it was not reason enough. Bringing hardship to others would not heal her pain, it would not soothe the hurt that came in the night. She might never see her son again if he left that town, but if he had decided his work was no longer what he wanted she could not force him to stay.

'What do I do, Edward?' she whispered. 'What do I do?'

'Where are you going?'

Anna looked up from the newspaper she was reading, seeing her daughter, already half way out of the door of their room at The White Horse.

'There's someone I want you to meet, mother.' Misty's eyes sparkled and her cheeks blushed to a soft pink. 'He . . .'

'He?' Anna's eyebrows rose. Her daughter's interest in the steel foundry had waned rather quickly she had noticed, and her excuses for going out alone in the evening had increased, but she had not thought there to be a 'he' at the root of it. A boy, here in Wednesbury? Surely not. Misty had not had time to make an acquaintance, much less find herself a boyfriend, even in the two weeks she was here with Eli.

'Yes, mother . . . he.' The colour in Misty's face deepened. 'There is a man I want you to meet. He . . . he will be waiting for me downstairs.'

Anna opened her mouth to speak but Misty was already gone, the door banging behind her. She had not referred to him as a boy but a man. And she *was* interested; a girl's eyes did not sparkle and her cheeks turn pink if she had no interest in the man she spoke of.

Anna tried to return to her newspaper, telling herself that, knowing her daughter, this could just be a flash in the pan.

'Mother!' Half an hour later Misty bounced back into the room. 'Mother, this is the man I told you about, he wants to ask your permission for us to become engaged.'

Told her about! The only thing she had heard about this man had been that he was waiting downstairs. Half smiling at her daughter's thoughtless impetuosity, Anna looked up.

He was holding Misty's hand. Their fingers were closely entwined. Anna's own fingers tightened on the newspaper, then slowly, as if held in some terrible nightmare, she lowered it, staring almost hypnotised at the pair standing proudly before her.

It wasn't true! This couldn't be happening! This could not be the man Misty had meant was waiting for her.

'. . . *I reckon 'e be sweet on some wench. He's been maudlin this last month or more . . .*'

Polly Shipton's word returned to her mind, sending her senses reeling.

But it couldn't be! She had got it wrong. Misty would have told her before now if the two of them had met when she was in Wednesbury with Eli Curran. But would she? She had not mentioned him during the whole of the past week.

But she must see! Anna stared at the couple laughing into each other's eyes; eyes so very blue, so very alike. Misty must see . . . the same eyes, the same hair . . . she must see the likeness.

'Mother.' Misty stepped towards her, pulling the man along with her. 'Mother, this is Aaron.'

'. . . *he wants to ask your permission for us to become engaged.*'

Misty's words ran wild in Anna's mind, tumbling over and over, banishing all rational thought, leaving only panic.

'Mother!' Misty bent towards her, anxiety replacing the happiness on her face. 'Mother, are you all right?'

'Yes . . . yes . . . I'm all right.'

Anna swallowed hard. She was not feeling all right, she felt as if she were drowning, but then how should she feel faced with this: her daughter and her son wanting to marry?

Not this! Oh, dear God, not this!

Somewhere in the vacuum that had once been her mind, Anna prayed.

At her side Misty reached again for the hand of the man she loved.

'Mother, Aaron and I want to become engaged.'

With a supreme effort Anna dragged herself from the hell that threatened to engulf her totally.

'Engaged? Is a week of knowing one another enough for a decision like this?'

'Oh, I have known Aaron for longer than a week,' Misty bubbled on, not giving him a chance to answer. 'We met the last time I came to Wednesbury and have written to each other several times since then.'

Written to each other? Anna wanted to scream at the ludicrousness of the statement. A couple of weeks of knowing someone, a few letters . . . and on the basis of that she planned to ruin three lives?

'Two weeks when you were here with Eli and a week here with me – I hardly think that a proper basis for an engagement.'

'But Aaron and I think it is. We know our own minds.' Misty's tone held a childish, petulant note.

Anna looked at her daughter, then for the first time since he had entered the room, her eyes met those of her son: those pale yet intensely blue eyes, the eyes of Jos Bradly.

'No, you do not.' She spoke quietly. 'You only think you do. You know nothing about each other.'

'We do!' Misty flashed. 'We know all we need to know.'

Do you? Anna felt her heart twist. Do you know all you need to? Do you know that Aaron is your half-brother?

Aloud she asked: 'And you, Aaron? Do you think three weeks and a few letters a sound basis for marriage?'

'It is a short time, Mrs Royce, I agree . . .'

He holds himself like my father, Anna thought as he answered. He even sounds as my father used to before . . .

'. . . but we do not wish to be married just yet, we simply wish to become engaged. That is all we ask.'

But you can't! Anna's brain screamed. Don't you see, you can't become engaged? Can't you see who you are?

'You may see that as asking very little,' she returned, her calm voice totally belying her feelings. 'But *I* see becoming engaged as a serious undertaking, one that requires a firmer foundation than a few meetings and a few letters. I'm sorry but I will not give my permission.'

'If your objection is because we have only known each other for a short time, Mrs Royce, then Misty and I will wait for a while.'

He held her eyes, though at his side the hand that was free clenched with tension.

'No, I don't want to wait!' Misty sounded like a child denied her own way. 'Why should we? We are both old enough to know our own minds so why shouldn't we become engaged now?'

'You might feel you know your own mind.' Anna switched her glance to her daughter, seeing the disappointment that pulled her mouth down at the sides. She tried to sound as gentle as her own terror and shame would permit. 'But in a month or so you may feel differently, you are still so very young.'

'Waiting will make *no* difference to the way we feel, will it, Aaron?'

'Waiting will not make a difference to the feelings I have for Misty, Mrs Royce, but if it will make a difference to the way you feel about our being together, then we will wait.'

'No!' Misty clung to his hand, tears running down her cheeks. 'No, Aaron, I don't want to wait!'

Releasing his fingers, he looked again at Anna.

'How long would you like us to wait?'

It wasn't a question of that. No matter how long they waited they could never be man and wife. So why not tell them so, why not tell them the truth of their birth? Anna knew she should, but also knew she could not.

'Make no attempt to see each other or to communicate for six months and then . . .'

'No! I won't . . . I won't . . . it's unfair! You're cruel, Mother, you have no feelings . . . you have no feelings!'

Running out of the room, Misty slammed into her own bedroom and Anna heard the key turn in the lock.

'Six months, Mrs Royce!'

Turning abruptly, Aaron walked out.

Anna looked down at the newspaper still held in her lap and realised only now the strength with which she had been gripping it. It had sent her fingers right through the pages.

'It's unfair' her daughter had said, and there was some truth in the words. The whole of life had been unfair to Anna Royce, but her daughter had been wrong to say she had no feelings.

With her heart splintered inside her, Anna knew just how wrong it was to say she had no feelings.

Chapter Nineteen

Anna let fall the designs for her new range of china. It was almost two months since she had refused Misty and Aaron permission to become engaged; two months in which her daughter had hardly spoken to her. She had thought that sheer youth would cause Misty's feelings for Aaron to change. She had never known the girl want anything for more than a few weeks. In Maggie's words, she changed her mind as often as a collier changed his shirt.

Not this time!

Anna leaned tiredly back in her chair.

She had tried so many ways to deflect Misty in these last few weeks: asking her to accompany a consignment of goods to the Goldberg shop in Rome; suggesting the cosmetics design department would welcome some help. But no matter what she said or asked, it met with the same polite but frosty refusal.

Determined to keep on trying, Anna looked across the room at the girl who sat idly thumbing a women's journal.

'Darling, would you take a look at these?' She held up the sketches. 'The shapes are so beautiful, I can't decide if they would benefit from being painted or if they should be left as they are.'

Rising from her chair, Misty dropped the journal on to a table.

'I am sure you *will* decide, Mother. You decide on everything else.'

Maggie looked up as the girl strode towards the door of the sitting room feeling her patience to be at an end. Maybe Anna hadn't done the right thing by both of her children in not telling them outright why they couldn't marry, but this kind of treatment of her mother had gone on long enough.

'Misty!' she called after the girl. 'Wait on a minute, I be wantin' to say summat.'

'Yes, Grammie?'

'Sit you down.' Maggie felt the familiar stir of her heart at the term Anna's daughter had addressed her by ever since she first learned to talk, but she would not let the love it roused deter her. It was high time the girl was made to recognise a few home truths.

'Now then . . .'

She stared at Misty, perched in front of her, and her grey eyes were hard.

'. . . don't you be thinkin' I be so old as not to remember what first love was like, or to think I don't know what I be talkin' of when I say denial comes 'ard.'

Opposite her, Misty's blue eyes clouded but Maggie resisted the urge to take her in her arms and tell her Grammie would make it all right, as she had so many times in the past. The child had felt her feet, had a taste, however brief, of the sweetness of life, and it could not be long before she had a taste of the sour, but in the meantime she must not be allowed to think she could go on hurting her mother.

'We none of us takes kindly to being told we can't 'ave what we believe to be our 'eart's desire, but that don't give we the right to snipe at them as has the saying of it.'

'Maggie . . .'

'Don't Maggie me, Anna!' The older woman's voice was sharp. 'I know what be goin' on an' I know what I be goin' to say, an' it be no use you tryin' to stop me.'

She turned a harsher look on Misty than the girl could ever remember seeing from her.

'You just remember, your mother has worked 'ard to keep

you ever since you was born, worked almost every hour God sent to give you as much as 'er could. You might not realise it but the love 'er 'olds for you be one no bond will break, an' it be that love that made 'er say no to you. No matter 'ow you might see it now that refusal was made for your own good, but whether you ever comes to see it that way or you don't, you won't carry on speakin' to your mother as y'ave been doin' this last couple of months.

'You try it again and it'll be Maggie Fellen you'll answer to, an' your smart arsin' will get you naught but a smack across the mouth. You want to be married, to take on the responsibilities of a woman? Then try actin' like one instead of comin' the spoilt child!'

Lying in bed, Anna watched moonlight creep through the clouds and play across the walls of her room.

Maggie had been sharp with Misty but even when the girl had run sobbing from the sitting room, she had been unrepentant.

'It needed sayin', Anna. You can't go on coddlin' the wench all 'er days. 'Er be growin' up Anna, 'er be growin' fast.'

Yes, Misty was growing fast, soon they would lose her to a husband – but not to Aaron. No matter how much Misty begged or pouted, she could never have Aaron.

But Maggie's chiding had not ended with Misty.

'You be wrong, Anna,' she had gone on. 'You be wrong in not tellin' them two children of your'n the truth of who they be.'

'I can't, Maggie . . . I can't! If I tell them, I will lose them both. They will turn their backs on me.'

The chill warning of the answer she received circled Anna's heart with a ribbon of fear.

'You be like to lose 'em to a worse fate than that of turning their back on their mother. They be like to 'ave the world turn its back on them. They be little more than children for all the fancy education y'ave given to the wench, an' the education a

285

'ard life 'as given to the lad. Young blood runs hot, Anna, hot an' fast. They two 'ave abided by what you asked up to now, but for how long will at last? You 'ave to tell 'em, wench, tell 'em afore they does summat you'll all 'ave cause to regret.'

How long would they go on? Anna watched the pale light play among the shadows. Misty was stubborn. It could just be she would go to Aaron, despite what he had said, go to Aaron and . . .

No! Above the sheets, Anna's fingers curled into her palms, pressing the nails into her flesh.

'You be like to lose 'em to a worse fate than that of turning their back on their mother.' The words echoed in her mind, heightening the fear of what Maggie had said. It was too dangerous to let things go on as they were. Misty had not lost interest as Anna had hoped, had prayed; her determination to marry Aaron seemed as strong as before.

'Now *you* as well as Misty must accept things can't be as you want them,' Anna whispered to the shadows. 'You must face the reality. You have to face them, protect them instead of yourself.'

Protecting herself! Anna closed her eyes, pressing the lids hard together as at last her mind allowed her to see the full truth of why she had not told her children of their relationship.

She had been protecting them but she had been protecting herself more; shielding herself from the horror she knew she would see in their eyes when she told them: shielding herself from their condemnation.

But in shielding herself she had left them open to much greater heartache. She had known the misery of rape. She must not allow them to know the misery of incest.

Waiting in her room at The White Horse, Anna tried to still her dancing nerves.

She had brought Misty with her to Wednesbury. She and Aaron deserved an explanation and she would give them it, born at the same time. That way they would at least have each other's support.

'You sent for me, Mrs Royce?'

Anna looked at the tall figure of her son, his white shirt open at the neck. Will his sleeves be rolled above the wrists beneath his jacket, as my father's always were? she thought.

'I asked you to come so that what I have to say can be heard by both of you.'

'We haven't changed our minds, Mother.' Misty stood at Aaron's side, her whole attitude defensive. 'We still want . . .'

'I know what you and Aaron want!' Anna interrupted, her tone sharp though it was not anger that coloured it. 'You and Aaron want to become engaged, but I am afraid that is impossible.'

'But why?'

She had thought a few weeks ago she would have no need to explain why, that the chameleon nature of youth would carry them both along to new desires.

'The time you stipulated is not up yet, Mrs Royce. You do not have to give us your decision yet.'

But I do . . . I do! Anna's heart screamed.

'I think she does.'

'No, Misty.' Aaron looked at the girl whose head was just level with his shoulder. 'Your mother stipulated six months and we will hold to that.'

'It would make no difference.' Anna met the eyes of her son, so like the eyes of the man who had fathered them both. He deserved that at least. Deserved to have her look him in the eyes when she told him the truth.

'Why?' The demand was Misty's. 'Because Aaron has nothing, is that it?'

Why was this happening to her? Anna felt the bitterness of years gone by rise like bile in her throat. Hadn't she been through enough?

'*There be tears in yer cup an' it's refusin' to be dried so they are . . . ye are not to be havin' an easy life . . . toil and tears are the price ye'll pay.*' Kate O'Keefe's words rang across the years, and still they were proving true.

'Why?' Misty demanded again. 'Is it because he hasn't the money Anna Royce has got?'

'I am not afraid of work, Mrs Royce.' The almost transparent blueness of his eyes met hers. 'I can make enough to keep us both. Maybe Misty won't have so many of the fine things she has now, but she will have enough.'

'Money does not enter into it.'

Even as she answered Anna felt detached, isolated, apart from the scene being played around her, only the sickening lurch of her heart telling her it was real.

'Then what does?' Misty snapped. 'If money is not the reason why Aaron and I can't become engaged, then what is?' Her cheeks taking on the red flush of anger, she glared at her mother. 'Or isn't there one? Tell us, Mother, *if you can.*'

Anna was silent for a few seconds, a silence in which she fought for the strength to say the words that would blight their lives and completely destroy her own.

She spoke at last, her voice dull and flat.

'I refused my permission for you to become engaged because nothing could ever come of it. You two can never marry . . . you are half-brother and sister.'

'That's a lie!' Misty gasped. 'A cruel, wicked lie!'

'I only wish it were,' Anna answered, agony in every word. 'But I am Aaron's mother, as I am yours.'

'It *is* a lie.' His face darkened. 'You are not my mother. She died soon after I was born.'

Anna was weary. It seemed all of a sudden that nothing mattered any more. The will that had kept her going through the years of unhappiness was suddenly sapped, drained by the bewilderment and shock on the faces of both her children.

She had done this to them, she was the one bringing that shock and unhappiness, she was the one breaking their hearts.

'Who was it who told you your mother died soon after you were born?' She forced herself to meet his eye. 'Was it crippled Polly Shipton or was it Jos Bradly?'

A new expression in his face, Aaron stepped towards her, the tense lines of his body holding a threat.

'What do you know of Jos Bradly?'

Anna swallowed, every part of her crying out to be free of this, free of the hurt in her son's eyes, of the horror on the face of her daughter.

'I know that he was your father . . . and mine.'

'No! No, that's not true, that's a filthy thing to say.' The strain of the last weeks broke in Misty and she rounded on Anna, her claws unsheathed. 'But you *would* say it, wouldn't you? You would say anything to prevent my marrying Aaron, stop the daughter of the wealthy Anna Royce, the expensively educated daughter of the self-made Anna Royce, throwing herself away on the son of a foundry worker! Well, you can keep your money, Mother, I want no more of it. And I want no more of *you*, either.'

'Misty, let me tell you . . .'

'No!' Misty's breasts rose and fell with the effort of breathing and her young face became a mask of scorn.

'Let *me* tell *you*. Let me tell you the real reason you refuse to allow me and Aaron to be together, why you really refuse to let us marry. You, my beautiful mother, my so clever and efficient mother, my so very hardworking and devoted mother. Oh, I remember all that Maggie said. You had your reasons for keeping Aaron and me apart, but did Maggie know it all? Did she know all of the truth or merely the bits you chose to tell her? Did she know about Charles Lazenby? Did she know that for all your looks, you could not inveigle him into marriage? Did you tell her he did not find you good enough to be his wife, and that what you can't have, your daughter won't either?'

Anna looked at her daughter, at her anger and her hurt.

'Misty, you don't know what you're saying.'

'Oh yes I do!' she replied scathingly. 'I know all about your furtive little trips to London, running off to the bed of your fancy man. You're no different from Amy Stevens, except she got pregnant and you didn't.'

Deep within Anna the fires began to stir, melting away the numbness. This was the child she had struggled for, worked day and night for so she would never know the bitterness of poverty. Her hands closing over the arms of the chair, she struggled to control a rising tide of resentment.

'That expensive education you spoke of does not seem to have done you much good,' she said quietly. 'You are still a little girl, Misty, a child with more mouth than sense.'

Aaron had not moved during the exchange between Anna and Misty and remained unmoving when the girl slammed out of the room.

'I don't believe you, Mrs Royce.' His eyes, intense and unblinking, were fixed on her own; his voice throbbed with anger.

'This is your way of keeping Misty and me apart. Keeping her from marrying a man who, to your way of thinking, has nothing. And it's a bloody dirty way, sullying the name of a man who can't answer for himself!'

At his sides Aaron's fingers curled and uncurled and his square jaw, so like that of the father he was defending, set in a grim line, so that his next words were squeezed out.

'My grandad would never have done what you accuse him of. If you say it once more, I'll make you sorry for it, woman or no woman.'

Only her fingers moving, clenching and unclenching on the arms of the chair, Anna knew she had to finish what she had started. She had to show him once and for all that he *was* her son and that Jos Bradly had indeed been his father.

'Did your father hang himself?' she asked.

It had taken him by surprise, her quiet question. She saw him recoil, surprise and something else, something close to despair, passing across his face.

'Did he tear some cloth into strips? And did he plait those strips together?'

She went on inexorably though her pain matched his own.

It would do no good to leave even the tiniest margin of doubt. He had to know it all.

'That cloth, Aaron,' she asked, her voice a little above a whisper, 'was it pale blue cotton with darker blue cornflower sprays all over?'

The fierceness of his anger giving way to uncertainty, Aaron's face paled.

'How . . . how did you know that? I burned that cloth . . . I burned it before anyone else saw him.'

Tears thickening her throat, Anna told him.

'I was wearing that dress the night he came home the worse for drink, the night he raped me, thinking I was Mary Carter.'

The last trace of colour drained from his face and his hands doubled into fists. Anna could see he was fighting to control the rage and misery burning in him. But she had been forced to tell him, to save both Misty and him from creating their own tragedy.

'That is a lie.' He spat out the words. 'A dirty, stinking, rotten lie, and I'm . . .'

'I think you should ask Polly Shipton about that.'

'I don't need to ask anybody!' he shouted down her interruption. 'I know my grandad. If he did rape you, which I won't ever believe, it would be because you teased and tormented him until he didn't know what he was doing . . . you are a whore, Anna Royce, *that* is what I believe. A dirty, disgusting whore . . .'

'Aaron!'

Anna's cry was of pure anguish but it did not halt the flow of words streaming from his mouth or dim the hatred in his eyes.

'. . . yes, Mrs Anna Royce, you are a whore, and one of the kind who enjoys seeing others suffer. You are one of the lowest kind of people, the sort not worth the talking to . . . and as for your job, try sticking it up your arse! I wouldn't work for you if hell fetched me!'

He had reached the door and was opening it before Anna spoke. Then, though her legs shook, she stood up and her voice was calm beyond her belief.

'Maybe hell will not fetch you yet, Aaron, but it will certainly come for many of the men you work with, to say nothing of their wives and children.'

Aaron swung to her, his blue eyes still molten with rage.

'What do you mean?'

Anna held the gaze. Inside she was crying to take him in her arms, to take both of her children and hold them, tell them it wasn't what they thought, she was as much a victim of fate as they were. But even to try to touch her son at this moment would send him over the edge of reason.

'What I mean is this,' she went on quietly, 'if you do not work for me then that is your choice, but go and you take every man in that steel mill with you. And think on this also, Aaron. The money that bought Joby Hampton's place was nothing. There is enough to buy most of Wednesbury, and mark me well – I *will* buy it, every stick and stone of the places that provide men with work, and I will close them, *all* of them. You leave Bradly Engineering and you take almost every man in this town with you, and that is *your* choice.'

Chapter Twenty

Locked in her room in The White Horse Misty watched the door handle turn and heard her mother's voice asking her to open the door, to let her just explain.

But there could be no explanation; there was nothing her mother could say to explain what she had done. Aaron was right. She had heard him shout that Anna Royce was a whore, and she was . . . she must be, and of what sort to lie with her own *father*?

Staring at the twisting handle Misty wrapped her arms about her chest, trying to still the trembling of her body. Her mother . . . with her own father!

'I don't want it to be true,' she sobbed quietly, 'I don't want it to be true . . . please, please, I don't want it to be true.'

But beneath the pain and horror she knew it *was* true. Why else would her mother have said so terrible a thing? Why sow the seeds of so dreadful a doubt? Certainly not because she could find no other way to prevent a daughter's marriage to a penniless steel worker, Anna Royce was too powerful for that.

'I hate you,' she whispered, her body shaking from head to foot. 'I hate you . . . I hate you.'

In her own bedroom Anna sank to the bed, staring unseeingly at the wall. Aaron had left with anger on his tongue and hatred in his eyes and Misty would not let her come near, would not answer when she called. Both of them . . . both of her children spurned her. Neither of them had asked how or why, seeing only their own pain, seeming to think she felt none.

But she could place no blame on them for that. What she had told them had snatched away more than a marriage, broken more than their dreams – it had broken their hearts.

'I didn't know,' she whispered. 'I never thought that when Misty came to Wednesbury that first time she would become involved with Aaron. I didn't think . . . Oh God!' She dropped her head into her hands, sobs wracking her. 'When will it end . . . when will it end?'

The note was under her door when Anna woke. She had lain sleepless until long after the first spears of dawn drove back the night.

Opening the slip of paper she looked at her daughter's extravagant hand. There was no heading. Anna felt a new twist of pain add to the pounding of the headache that was almost blinding her.

I will make my own way from here. I want nothing more from you and no more to do *with* you. You are no longer my mother. You are a despicable woman, one who cares for nothing and nobody save herself, and you deserve to suffer. I hope that the very worst life can throw at you hits you full in the face!

The unsigned note slid from Anna's fingers. She deserved to suffer? Despite the pain she suddenly wanted to laugh. She deserved to suffer! Didn't Anna Royce know what suffering was? Hadn't she known it since she was seventeen years old? And what had life left that had not already hit her full in the face?

'I don't know where 'er went.' Maggie ran a worried hand over her white hair. ''Er come back sayin' you was stoppin' a while longer to sort things out an' 'er was goin' back to school.'

'She didn't arrive, Maggie, I telephoned.'

'Eee, what would you do wi' 'em?' Maggie poured the all-healing tea, handing Anna a cup. 'Try not to worry, Anna. That wench of your'n might be young but 'er's got all 'er marbles. Take care of 'erself, will Misty. Give 'er a week or two an' 'er'll come 'ome. It was the shock of 'earin' you say you was the lad's mother. Give 'er time, an' like I says, she'll be 'ome.'

'I don't know, Maggie.' Anna touched a trembling hand to her mouth. 'I keep seeing the look on her face – so angry, so unhappy.'

''Course 'er was.' Maggie held on to her practical manner. Anna couldn't stand up to seeing how worried she really was. Misty was headstrong as she was pretty and there was no telling what she might do, but panicking would do none of them any good. 'It be about the only time as 'ow 'er ain't 'ad exactly what 'er wanted and it knocked 'er sideways. No child likes bein' told no, Anna, but this time it 'ad to be. 'Er knows deep down that you would deny 'er naught wi'out good reason an' when 'er temper 'as cooled down 'er will be 'ome, you can depend on it. But the other one! There's a different kettle of fish altogether. Strikes me 'e'll not come to terms wi' you as easy.'

In her mind Anna saw again the doubled fists and the hatred that darkened those pale eyes.

'He will never accept me, Maggie, even should he accept the truth of his birth.'

'You be wrong there, wench, of that I be convinced. From what you 'ave told me the lad 'as pride and 'e 'as 'ad a knock to that pride, a shock that will take some getting over, but 'e 'as a strength of character and a knowin' of what's right an' wrong that 'e gets from you, an' what you in your turn got from 'im as fathered you. That lad stood by them as 'e worked alongside of, same as you when you took on Rewcastle's Mill. Though you gave 'im a hard time, Anna. What you said was naught short of blackmail an' that ain't like you. Why did you say what you did? Why did you tell the lad you would put 'alf the men of that town out of work?'

Anna stared into the fire.

'Because I love him, Maggie, and I could think of no other way of keeping him. If he leaves Wednesbury I will have lost him for good and I couldn't bear the thought of that. I want him so much and that seemed the only way.'

'Even if he despises you for it?'

'Even so,' Anna answered softly. 'He is my son, the child I have never stopped aching for. I would rather have him with me, hating me, than lose him altogether.'

In the quietness of the sitting room, Maggie watched the shadows of despair play over the face of the woman she had laughed and cried with, the woman she loved as a daughter. What had she gone through in Wednesbury? What hell had opened up for her there?

'But whatever Aaron decides, I know he can take care of himself, he has grown up with the world howling at his back, but Misty . . .'

Anna hesitated, feeling the dread she had carried back to Coseley well up afresh.

'. . . She knows nothing of the world, she has always been so protected.'

'I've told you, Anna, that girl o' yours will take care of 'erself. 'er ain't the helpless little wench you seem to think 'er is. Give 'er time and 'er will be back, safe and sound and cheeky as ever.'

Anna looked up, the fear that haunted her showing dark in her eyes.

'Do you think she will have returned to Wednesbury? Do you think she might go back to Aaron, despite what I told them? Oh God, Maggie, what will I do if . . . if . . .?'

Maggie's hand stroked the red-gold head that bowed itself against her skirts, feeling her own heart breaking as Anna's was.

''Er won't go back there, me wench,' she soothed. 'Don't you go worryin' yourself wi' that thought.'

'But . . . but what if she didn't believe me?' Anna sobbed. 'What if she still believes the whole story was a lie?'

''Er'll 'ave believed it.' Maggie knew the comfort she was trying to give was grounded in sand, holding no foundation, but Anna needed something to hold on to. 'Anybody seein' the pain on your face would know you were tellin' no lie. And even if 'er didn't believe, I reckon that lad would, and should 'e not, 'e seems to 'ave enough backbone to pack 'er off back to 'er mother till things were sorted. Draw your strength from that, Anna. That son of yours won't touch Misty, not in the way you be feared of.'

Watching the dawn break over houses huddled like grey sparrows around the tall steel mill, Anna's mind still rocked with doubt and questions despite Maggie's assurance.

Had Misty returned to Wednesbury?

Had she and Aaron gone off together?

No, had that happened Polly Shipton would have told her. So where was her daughter? Tomorrow she must contact the police. For all Maggie's confidence, the thought of Misty alone terrified her.

And what of Aaron, what of her son? Would he place any value on her threat to put men out of work or would he see it as just that, a threat to be ignored? Would he stay on as manager of the steel mill or would he go?

Anna leaned her head against the cold glass of the window pane. Whichever way he chose, he had turned his back on her, as had Misty. She had lost both her children.

The letter had arrived the next morning. A cold informal missive in which Misty informed her that she had money she had not used from her allowance, that she was safe, and would Anna not attempt to have her brought back to Coseley?

That had been six months ago.

There had been other letters since. Letters as cold and distant as the first, but at least they had proved Misty was well and coping on her own as Maggie had predicted she would. But knowing that did not ease the heartbreak her leaving had caused. Yet knowing the terrible hurt her daughter had suffered, and the girl's own heartbreak, Anna had complied with her wish not to be brought home.

Perhaps Maggie would yet prove right. Anna stared into the heart of the living-room fire but none of its brightness penetrated the dark shadows of her despair, nor any of its heat warm the coldness that gripped her heart. Perhaps Misty's temper would cool, perhaps she would soon be home.

And what of Aaron? There had been no word in those six months, either from Polly Shipton or from the foundry, so he must still be there. She could so easily have found out but had made no move to enquire, done nothing that might possibly embarrass her son further, though she doubted he could ever now be brought to see her house as his home.

A knock at the door sent shudders of fear through Anna.

'Sit you still, I'll see who that be.'

But Anna was at the door before Maggie had finished speaking. Was it Misty come home or a message to say her son had left Wednesbury? Her hand shaking, she opened the door.

'Charles!'

Surprise mixed with an inexplicable feeling of relief as Anna stared at the tall figure of Charles Lazenby.

'You did write to me, didn't you?'

Charles looked at the woman whose blunt refusal of his advances had roused in him a respect he had rarely felt for one of her sex. Was it work that had circled those eyes with dark rings, taken all colour from her face and so much flesh from her bones, or was there something other than business troubling Anna Royce?

'Yes . . . yes, I did write.' Flustered by the sudden appearance of the man who had wanted her to be his mistress, she stumbled over the words. She had forgotten the letter she had written him months ago. 'But I ... I only wanted your advice.'

'That is all I am bringing!' He smiled down at her.

'Don't you think you should be lettin' man in, whoever 'e be?'

Behind her Maggie's voice was reassuring. The sight of Charles on her doorstep had thrown her. Stepping aside, she closed the door as Maggie appeared.

'Maggie,' she said, 'this is Charles Lazenby. Charles, meet my best and oldest friend, Maggie Fellen.'

Anna knew her friend stood on ceremony for no one, regardless of who they might be, so was not surprised by the blunt, 'Y'ad best come in, sittin' room be through 'ere.'

A smile touching his lips, Charles laid his gloves and cane on the hall table then followed Maggie.

'Your daughter is well, Anna?' Seeing the shadow flit across her pale face, he tactfully left further enquiries unspoken.

''Ow about a nice cup of tea?' Maggie asked the inevitable question. 'Or p'raps you prefer summat stronger?'

'A nice cup of tea would be most acceptable, thank you, Mrs Fellen.'

Waiting until she had left the room, he said quietly, 'Anna, I am asking no questions but I want you to know that should you feel you need my help, you have only to ask.'

Her smile was weak and left her mouth almost instantly but she said nothing. She knew he was referring to Misty but that problem was hers and hers alone.

'Your letter referred to the horseless carriage,' Charles continued, covering her silence. 'Are you thinking of going into that business?'

'I had thought of it.'

'But I seem to recall your telling me they were noisy, smelly things?'

Anna nodded.

'And you said they were the future, if I remember rightly.'

Waiting while the returning Maggie set the tea tray on a table beside one of the wing-backed armchairs, Charles accepted the cup she offered.

'Thank you, Mrs Fellen,' he said again, smiling at the older woman. 'Would you allow me to call you Maggie? I should like us to be friends.'

'Ar, lad, you do that.' Maggie returned his smile, a thing that had rarely happened since her son's death. 'If you be good enough for Anna, you be good enough for me.'

'I could ask no more, Maggie.' It was said with a warmth she knew was genuine.

His tea drunk, Charles returned his cup to the tray.

'So, Anna, you have thought of going into the horseless carriage trade? At least, your letter intimated as much.'

She had not thought much about it in these recent weeks but now her mind returned to the possibility.

'If you are still so sure that they are the future, then yes, I am interested.'

'They are, Anna, I am convinced of it. I have just returned from the Continent, which explains my delay in coming to see you and your receiving no reply to your letter. The motor carriage is creating quite a stir over there. At the moment they are merely a rich man's toy but soon they will be more than that. In twenty years or less they will have replaced many of the forms of transport we have today. The future is in engines, Anna, and the man who produces the best could hold tomorrow in his hand.'

'You seem very sure of that.'

'I am.' Charles leaned forward eagerly, his hair bright against the brocaded velvet of the chair. 'I am as sure of that as I am that day follows night.'

Maggie had sat silent through their talk. Now she stood up, taking the tea tray with her.

'Don't go, Maggie.' Anna put out a hand to her friend.

'Nay, wench,' she shook her head, 'I 'ave little understandin'' of 'orseless carriage an' less interest. Be it all same wi' you, I would rather be doin' summat useful.'

After Maggie had left the room Anna stood up, her hair fiery in the light of the lamps.

'Anna.' Charles came to stand beside her. 'Anna, asking you to become my mistress was a mistake, one of the biggest and most foolish of my life. It was an insult to you, and I apologise most profoundly.'

'Charles, it . . .'

'No, Anna. Hear me out please.' Reaching for her hand, he held it in both of his. 'There is something I have to say. I have wanted to say it for some time, but at the last moment my courage always failed me, I could not risk facing the anger I saw in your eyes when I asked you . . .'

'Charles, that is in the past,' Anna said gently.

'Yes.' He smiled ruefully. 'And it always will be there, a shadow between us. God, why did I ever say such a stupid thing?'

'Charles, that day, by the river, you promised you would not refer to that, ever again.'

'That is one more apology I must make, Anna.' His smile faded but he kept hold of her hand. He had been fool enough to offer to make this woman his mistress, an offer that had troubled him for many months before realising its cause. 'But I must tell you, my dear, I was wrong, terribly wrong, I did not recognise my feelings for what they were, but I know them now, Anna. I know that I love you and that I want you to be my wife.'

Charles loved her. He wanted her for his wife. A year ago she might have shouted for the sheer joy of it, but now? Now she felt a little sorry. Not for herself, but for Charles, knowing what her answer must do to him. She could not become his wife and carry on with her business, that she knew.

'You don't know what you are asking, Charles,' she said looking up at him.

'I know I love you, Anna, and that is all that matters.'

301

'No, no it is not, there is much more to it than that.'

'What more could there be, Anna?'

Pulling her hand free she turned away from him. 'The responsibility, Charles. A wife must be able to put her husband first in all things. To do that I would have to give up my business.'

'Damn your business!' Catching her by the shoulders he swung her back to face him. 'I can give you all the money you will ever need!'

'And that would be enough, would it?' She lifted her glance to his, her eyes moist. 'No, Charles, it would not. That is what I mean by responsibility. I could not abandon all those people who work for me, I am a part of them, a part that can never be Mrs Charles Lazenby.'

'Anna!' With one swift move he pulled her into his arms. 'You wanted me once, you can't deny it.'

'Yes, I wanted you, once,' she whispered against his shoulder, 'I would not be hypocritical enough to deny that. But wanting is not loving.'

Holding her there, against him, he was silent for a moment, then. 'Are you telling me you do not love me, Anna?'

Pushing free of his arms she looked at him. 'I am telling you I will not marry you.'

'But you could continue to run your business, and still be my wife.'

'No, Charles.' Anna shook her head. 'That would not work, you know it and I know it.'

'I love you, Anna.' He smiled, a soft, half apologetic smile. 'I am sorry I left things too late.'

'But never too late for friendship?'

'No, my dear. Never too late for that.'

'Then can I ask, will you come with me to Wednesbury?'

'To where?' He knew it was useless to press her further to marry him, he had had his chance months ago and had missed it.

'Wednesbury,' Anna replied. 'If I am to go into motor

carriage production, as no doubt you would advise, then I would value your opinion of the place I have in mind as a factory, and of the man I have a mind to put in charge.'

Leading the way back to the hall, Charles picked up his gloves and cane then turned to Anna, the smile he gave her hiding the hurt of her refusal.

'Wednesbury it is then, and thank you, Anna, for asking me.'

Watching him leave, Anna felt weary. She would go to Wednesbury even though she would rather stay here in Coseley until some word came of her daughter's return, but she knew she could not afford the luxury of isolation. People depended on her.

The string of paper diamonds hung heavy about her neck.

'Anna, allow me to present my very good friend, André Levassor.' Charles half turned to the man he had brought with him to Wednesbury. 'André . . .'

'No need for you to tell me, Charles.' Black eyes smiled into Anna's. 'Who but Anna Royce could have the beauty of Aphrodite and the hair of a Titian nymph? Who but the woman Charles talks of so often, yet described so ineptly; but then, I am being unfair to Charles, yours is the beauty only a poet could describe.'

'Give her a chance, you rogue.' Charles smiled. 'At least tell a lady your name before you try to charm her off her feet.'

'Forgive me.' The smile deepened turning his eyes to velvet darkness. 'I am André Levassor. *Enchanté*, Anna.' Taking her hand he raised it to his lips.

'You are interested in motor carriages?' It was not the most intelligent of questions, why else would he be here? Embarrassed, she drew her hand away.

'André comes to England whenever he can.' Charles guided her toward the door that led onto the street. 'That being when he can tear himself from the racing circuit.'

'You race horses?'

Holding the door for her to pass through, Charles laughed. 'Not horses, Anna, our M'sieur Levassor races motor carriages.'

'What!' Anna halted in midstride. 'But isn't that awfully dangerous?'

'It is fun.'

Climbing into the hansom, Anna kept her thoughts to herself. She would not call haring around in a motor carriage fun.

'This is the way Anna prefers to travel,' Charles said as they climbed in beside her. 'She reckons motors are "nasty, smelly things".'

'Then I shall agree with her.' André Levassor smiled. 'At least until I can change her mind.'

'That is my plan, Mr Bradly.'

The two men she had brought with her at her side, Anna walked the length of the steel foundry.

'Motor carriages!' The son who detested her glanced not at Anna, but from one to the other of the tall elegant men she had introduced, Charles Lazenby and André Levassor. 'The men here know nothing of building motor carriages.'

'Do you?' Anna steadfastly ignored his refusal to pay her any attention.

'Not the body work, no.' Still he did not look at her. 'But I think I know a fair bit about engines.'

'I see. And where did you learn about them?'

His look still not for her, Aaron returned, 'The man who owns the coal mine along Lea Brook has a car, and he often lets me work on the engine.'

'Car?' Anna raised a quizzical eyebrow.

Aaron turned a cold glance on her. Not once had he smiled at her, not once had he mentioned that awful night at The White Horse, and not once had he mentioned Misty.

'It is a Mistral.' He glanced at André. 'One of yours, I believe, sir.'

'*Oui*.' The Frenchman nodded. 'My grandfather is also crazy for the motor carriage. It was he who began the production of the Levassor engine.'

'It's one of the best, sir, the Mistral is a very good car.' He turned to Anna, the warmth vanishing from his eyes. 'It was brought over from the Continent, and though strictly the term for such a conveyance is "motor carriage", it tends to become shortened to car.'

That's me with my wrists slapped. Inwardly Anna smiled. Well, my lad, she thought, car or motor carriage, you are going to build them.

'And which Levassor engine does your friend's car have?' Charles broke in.

This time Aaron did smile as he answered and the light that leapt to those amazingly blue eyes tugged at Anna's soul. If only he looked at her with the same enthusiasm.

'Two cylinder, sir.'

'And its capacity?'

'Two and a half horse power. I believe it is their newest design.'

'Is he right, André?'

'He is indeed, Charles.' He switched to Aaron. 'You are very well acquainted with motor engines. Perhaps we can talk together, you might like to hear about my latest, the one I am putting in my racing machine.'

'You race motor cars, sir?' Aaron's eyes gleamed. 'That must be the most exciting thing in the world. Lord, what wouldn't I give to have a look at one of those engines. How many horse power do they have?'

Anna listened to her son, pride in him warming her. Polly Shipton had said he had learned well and it was obvious she had not tolerated any of the local slackness of speech, just as she had tolerated none with his mother. Mother . . . that was a title he would never afford Anna.

'Do you feel you could manage the engine side of the manufacture of motor carriages if someone else were brought in to organise the building of the coachwork?'

The question, put so abruptly, stopped her son in his tracks, so that for a moment he made no answer.

'I could have a real good try.' His shoulders straightened visibly, and this time he did face her, looking squarely into her eyes with none of the deference that was usual between workman and employer. 'And if I am no good, *you* may have the pleasure of telling me so.'

'He is a good man and an intelligent one.'

They were having dinner at The White Horse and Charles was speaking of Aaron. He had been impressed with the knowledge and the efficient way of dealing with the men under him that a man so young had shown.

'A bit young, I grant you, but he has a brain and a mind he is not afraid to use. I think you could do worse than put him in charge of your new motor carriage works, Anna.'

'Then you think this town is a good site for it?'

'As good as any other, I should think, given the work force.'

'There will be no shortage of that here,' she answered. 'But how do you think the foundry will convert into a motor carriage works?'

'Quite easily,' Charles sipped his brandy, 'though I think such a move would be inadvisable.'

'In what way?' she asked.

'Well, were I beginning such a venture, I would look to the future. Motor carriages are going to be a major part of that future, Anna. We are seeing the birth but the industry will grow, and that growth will need steel, lots of it. Yours won't be the only motor carriage works, and each one will be needing steel. That being so, you could find yourself facing delay if that need is not met. Maybe even forced out of production should you meet another Jacob Rewcastle.'

'But I have the steel mill in Coseley, I can always use that.'

'You can, of course.' Charles took a further sip at his brandy, savouring the warmth in his throat. 'But what of the industry that mill is already feeding? Will you discontinue that side of your business? Closing one in order to open another is not always good practice, Anna, to say nothing of the people it would put out of work.'

She nodded.

'You're right of course, Charles. I hadn't thought things through properly. I'm jumping in with both feet again and I haven't noticed the puddle of mud.'

'There need be no puddle, Anna. Leave Coseley mill as it is and let *this one* here in Wednesbury go on producing steel. It seems that young fellow in charge has the place very much back on its feet. If finances permit, I would go for building an entirely new place to house your motor carriage construction, somewhere in the vicinity. That way you will have your own guaranteed supply of steel.'

Anna pursed her lips, her thoughts moving rapidly.

'That makes sense, Charles. I could build here or in Darlaston. That is not too far, three miles at most, and from what I remember that town needs work as much as Wednesbury.'

'Whichever you choose, Anna, be sure there is room for component works.' This time it was André who spoke. 'Motor carriages have more bits and pieces to them than is obvious from looking at them.'

'I'm going to need help, M'sieur.' Anna smiled, hoping the form of address she had heard Charles use sounded the same coming from her. 'I have never done this sort of thing before, it has always been the straightforward buying of an established business.' She turned her glance to Charles. 'I don't know if I'll cope.'

'You'll cope, Anna, you always have, but if it would help, I could always look the area over with you?'

'And I am always willing to give advice on the building of your engines.'

'Whenever you are in England, that is.' Charles smiled at his friend.

'You know, Charles.' André picked up his glass, swirling the brandy around its sides. 'I think that might be more often than you think.'

'Thank you, both of you,' Anna said gratefully. 'But where do I find a coach builder to set the other side going? I need someone to train men to the work. Most of the men of this town have only ever known steel making.'

'I can arrange that, Anna, if you will allow.' Taking up his own glass, Charles leaned across the table, the light of the flickering gas lamps enhancing the blue of his eyes. 'To the success of your venture. And to you, Anna, may you be successful in all you do.'

'*Oui*, Anna.' André held his glass beside that of Charles. 'May you be as successful as you are beautiful.'

As she reached her own glass toward theirs, Charles caught the scent of violets, and again he felt a stab of regret. He had thought to seduce this woman, to use her for his own pleasure. But he was the one who had been seduced, ensnared by his own stupidity.

Touching her glass to each of theirs, Anna spoke softly.

'Charles. When you came to Coseley you said we could be friends, but after hearing what I am about to say you may wish to withdraw from that.'

Seeing the play of emotions on Anna's face, André Levassor rose to his feet. Whatever she was about to say to Charles was obviously going to need courage. 'I will leave you together, you will want privacy.'

'No, M'sieur Levassor!' Anna looked at him. The time for secrets was over. From now on she would hide nothing. 'You too were kind enough to offer your help, and you also must be given the chance to rescind that offer.' She glanced down at the glass still held in her hands. They had both offered their assistance. Inevitably that would mean them talking with Aaron, and in so doing they might accidentally learn of her relationship to him. She did not want that. She preferred to tell them herself.

'Charles, M'sieur Levassor.' Lifting her head she spoke clearly and without embarrassment. 'The young man you spoke with earlier today, Aaron Bradly. He is my son . . . my bastard son.'

'New places be doin' well, Anna.'

Spectacles perched on the end of his nose, Joby Timmins ran a practised eye over the monthly returns.

'Sovereign Motors was a right good move on your part. Growin' at a faster rate than anythin' I've ever known. But then, you always 'ad a good eye for business, wench.'

'It's what is known as the Midas touch.' Anna closed the heavy ledger and stood up, pressing her palms into her back, stretching her aching body. Charles had kept his word; he had helped her choose a site for her motor carriage works, and André Levassor had helped tremendously with the engine side of things. Anna had liked him. Liked his quick smile and easy personality.

'A what touch?' Joby went into the hall, picking up his flat cap from the table Maggie kept polished to a glassy shine.

'Never mind.' Anna's smile flashed as she opened the front door. 'It was good of you to come to the house, Joby, I couldn't get to the office.'

'Think no more on it, Anna. You pays me well for what I do.'

'Well, can I send you home in a Sovereign?' she teased, knowing the old man's feelings about motor carriages.

'Nay, wench, I'll walk. No disrespect to you but you can give me a good 'oss afore one o' them contraptions any day.'

'Good night then, Joby, and remember me to your son when next you write to him. You and your wife must be very proud of him, getting a place at grammar school. And King Edward's, no less. Tell him there's a place for him with me if he fancies it once he is finished there.'

'I will, Anna, and thanks, me wench.'

Watching until he turned out of sight around the end of the drive, Anna closed the door. Joby had spoken true about Sovereign Motors. In the two years since starting out at Wednesbury she had bought more factories, and each was now producing motor bodies and components. More paper diamonds adding to the weight about her neck. She did have that legendary Midas touch, everything she took on made money, so why did none of it make her happy?

She was halfway up the stairs when the front door swung back on its hinges and Misty threw herself into the house.

'Mother!' As if she had merely been away for a school term, she came tearing across the hall and up the stairs. 'Mother, it's so lovely to be home.'

Flinging both arms about Anna's neck, she hugged her rapturously. Then: 'Grammie! Where's Grammie? I simply have to see her.'

'In . . . in her room.' Flabbergasted, Anna watched the flying figure of her daughter disappear around the head of the stairs.

'Mrs Royce?'

Turning sharply, Anna almost missed her footing, having to grasp the mahogany banister to prevent herself from falling.

'I apologise if I startled you.'

From the well of the hall a man stood watching her. Dark hair parted down the centre was slicked to either side, carrying on to side whiskers that touched his jaw; on his top lip a moustache blossomed in a small curve. His eyes, bright and darting as a ferret's, ran over her with swift appreciation.

'Misty insisted I come with her. I hope I'm not intruding?'

He stepped forward and Anna knew a sudden insane desire to turn and run.

'Of course not.' She forced herself to move. 'Do come in, Mr . . .?'

'Saverry,' he answered. 'Edwin Saverry.'

It came back nimbly, as practised as the smile that

didn't reach his eyes, a smile that sent a shiver along her spine.

'You two have introduced yourselves ... good.' Misty sprinted down the stairs, grabbing Anna by the hand. 'Now come and let me get a good look at you.'

In the sitting room that Anna had vacated just minutes before Misty held both her hands, spreading her arms wide and looking her mother up and down.

'Doesn't she look just marvellous, Edwin ... didn't I tell you my mother was beautiful?'

'You did.' The quick ferret's glance swept over Anna, resting fractionally too long on her firm breasts before returning to her face. 'But your description did not do her justice, Misty.' The thin mouth curved into that same sickly smile. 'Your mother is not just beautiful ... she is very beautiful.'

'Isn't he charming, Mother?' Misty broke loose, crossing to Edwin Saverry and passing her arm through his.

Too charming! Anna pulled the bell rope beside the fireplace.

'She's new,' Misty said as the maid left to fetch the tea Anna requested.

'Yes.' Anna sat in one of the green wingback chairs, feeling those too bright eyes trace her every movement. 'Maggie isn't getting any younger and I don't like leaving her alone in the house when I'm away.'

Curling down on to the carpet, one arm resting on Edwin's knee where he sat opposite Anna, Misty lost some of the vivacity that had burst from her since she had run into the house.

'I didn't think Grammie looked well, Mother. Her hair is so white and I never saw her cry before, not ever.'

'She has had a great deal to contend with,' Anna said, still slightly amazed at how calmly she had taken Misty's sudden return. 'The news of Andrew's death almost killed her, and the last two years have proved a dreadful strain. You could at least have visited even had you not wanted to come home to stay.'

'I did intend to, Mother, honestly I did, but Paris was so very exciting. Something new to do every day, a new interest every minute, takes your mind away from mundane things. And I *did* write.' Misty dismissed her actions and her mother's mild reproof with the inconsequence of youth.

'So coming home to your family was mundane, and the worry you gave them of little importance!'

Anna could not hide the recrimination in her voice, and across her daughter's pale gold head Edwin Saverry looked swiftly at her.

'Misty got caught up with a young crowd on the Left Bank, Mrs Royce. I am afraid they give little thought to parents.'

'And you do?'

'Yes, Mother,' Misty answered for him. She turned an adoring look up to his face. 'It was Edwin who told me how selfishly I was behaving. It was he said we should come home.'

The maid carried a tray into the room and, placing it in front of Anna, asked if she should prepare something for them to eat. She left as Misty shook her head.

'We should come home?' Emphasis heavy on the first word, Anna resumed their conversation.

Misty gave Edwin the same infatuated glance.

'Yes, Edwin said we should both come. We are going to get engaged but he insisted we come and ask you first.'

Anna felt as though a heavy weight had descended on her. Two years ago it had been the same, only then her worry had been that her daughter's choice of a future husband had been her own half-brother. Now she had chosen instead a man who made Anna's flesh creep.

She looked at the girl whom she had last seen running in tears from that room in The White Horse Hotel. She wasn't weeping now; her face held a soft radiance, a glow of happiness that radiated from it like a beacon. Anna had seen that same look before, seen it when Misty had introduced her to Aaron. And she had seen it die when she'd said they could not marry.

She couldn't do that again, she could not destroy her daughter's happiness a second time.

'That was very thoughtful of you, Mr Saverry.'

Anna poured tea into paper thin cups, sparing herself from looking into his eyes, feeling her unwarranted dislike of the man harden with each moment. It was unfair, she told herself, unfair to harbour such feelings on so short an acquaintance, but telling herself so did not erase the dislike, or the feeling that Edwin Saverry was not a man to be trusted.

Picking up a cup, Anna held it out to him, and in doing so was forced to meet his pallid eyes.

'I would prefer a whisky, Mrs Royce.'

Anna withdrew the cup, grateful he had not taken it; grateful his fingers had not, even accidentally, touched her. Strange how the very sound of his voice turned her cold.

Jumping to her feet, Misty poured a straight whisky and handed it to him, pressing an adoring kiss to his almost languid hand.

Quailing inside Anna asked: 'How long have you known Misty, Mr Saverry?'

'Simply ages, Mother.' Misty danced round to the back of his chair, reaching her hands over the back of it and resting one on each of the man's shoulders. Her eyes, when she looked across at Anna, sparkled like blue diamonds. 'Long enough to know what we both want.'

I've heard those words before, Anna thought, looking at her daughter. The last two years might never have been. The joy in the young face was the same as it had been then, the eagerness matched that which she had shown in the Wednesbury hotel. Only the man was different.

Anna had so wanted this to happen. She had been convinced that with time Misty's feelings for Aaron would change. But this change was giving her no pleasure. She could feel no relief, no happiness for her child. Misty's first love had been doomed from the start. Why did she feel that this one was destined to follow the same path?

'Perhaps we have not known each other so long as your mother would wish?'

One limp hand lifted, fastening over the one that rested on his shoulder. The eyes that met Anna's were challenging. He was daring her to refuse permission.

'. . . in which case we must wait. A little while more will do no harm, my sweet.'

'Mother, please don't say that!'

Misty's look was one of pure pleading and Anna felt the weight at the pit of her stomach grow heavier still.

'Edwin and I love each other . . . I don't want to wait, I want to get married now.'

It was all the same: the impetuosity, the warmth of her feelings, even the words. It all seemed like a dream, some awful recurring nightmare. Except Anna knew this particular nightmare was real.

There was no point in prolonging this. She would not deny her daughter a second time, could not destroy the girl's happiness because of her own feeling of dislike for the man Misty had chosen.

Opposite her the pallid eyes of Edwin Saverry smiled at her. A cold sly smile, a smile of triumph.

Why? Anna asked herself as she held out her arms to her daughter. Why is this happening again?

'*Toil and tears*' . . . the words of so long ago drifted back. '*Toil and tears.*' Was fate about to deal her another blow?

Chapter Twenty-one

'Buy all the lovely things you want to, darling. I just wish I could come with you but I'm really tied up at the moment.'

'Don't worry.' Misty kissed her mother's cheek. 'Edwin is coming to Paris with me. He will keep an eye on me, though I shan't let him stop me buying the most fabulous trousseau a girl ever had.'

'I couldn't deny you anything, my sweet.'

Edwin Saverry's words were for Misty but his eyes bored into Anna's. He had been a guest in her house for a month and even though it meant losing Misty for a week or so, Anna couldn't help but feel glad he was leaving. There was something about her daughter's fiancé she disliked intensely.

Maggie had summed up the fears of both of them a few days after his arrival.

''E's no good, Anna. 'E'll bring naught to 'er heart but sorrow.' And in those words Anna heard the ring of truth.

'You'll be here when we get home?'

'Of course.' Anna touched a finger to her daughter's brow, smoothing away a frown. 'I'm going to London on Thursday but I will be home the following Tuesday, I told you that. Now stop worrying and go or you will miss the train, and that means a long wait for the next. We don't get so many through Coseley.'

It had been a long day. Business meetings with Reuben and John Harris had left her feeling tired. Charles had been right when he said motor carriages were the future, and the way her ventures were expanding she was holding a lot of tomorrow in her hand.

Stirring an extra spoon of sugar into Maggie's cocoa, she carried it up to her bedroom.

'They be gone then?' The frail figure in the wide bed smiled thinly. 'I could 'ave hoped for better but the days of choosin' for the young 'ave gone. They'll 'ave their own way, though the 'aving of it chokes 'em.'

'We could be wrong, Maggie. He might be good for her.' Anna heard the hopelessness in her own voice.

'Ar, an' pigs might fly!' Maggie retorted. 'But there be naught to be gained by moping so get you to your bed and leave matters to take their course. And think on this, Anna. At least mother and daughter be together again, so if things should go wrong, 'er will come 'ome to you.'

'But ought I to have told Misty how I feel about Edwin?'

'What, and 'ave 'er run away a second time, an' this time do summat rash? If you 'ad done that you might 'ave turned the girl's heart against you for good. No, you could do naught but what you be doin'. Let 'er make 'er own choice an' pray 'er won't be hurt by it.'

She would pray. In her own bedroom Anna slipped her nightdress over her head. She would pray but would the Almighty listen?

'. . . if things should go wrong, 'er will come 'ome to you.' Maggie's words in her mind, Anna slipped into bed.

But what of Aaron? He barely acknowledged her as an employer; he would never acknowledge her as a mother. No, her son would never turn to her.

Hovering between sleep and waking, Anna wasn't sure just when she became aware of the figure standing beside her bed.

'You're not asleep, Anna. But then, if you were it would be a pleasure to wake you . . . like this.'

The dark shape bent swiftly, clamping a moist mouth over hers. Caught in a vice of terror, her brain numbed, Anna lay still.

'I knew you wanted that.'

Edwin Saverry! Anna's heart lurched. Edwin here in her room? But he should be with Misty on their way to Paris. So where was Misty? Had she come back too? No, in the numbness of her mind Anna knew that had her daughter returned to the house, she would have come straight to her . . .

'I knew you wanted me,' Edwin whispered against her mouth, and just the knowledge of who had entered her room dissolved most of Anna's fear and her brain began to function.

She must not scream. That would wake Maggie. Maggie! Anna's fears took on a new twist. Edwin Saverry knew she was in the house and Anna felt he would not hesitate in harming even an old woman.

'Can't we have the light on?' She forced herself to stay calm, hoping the loathing coursing through her didn't show.

'Another kiss and then the lights.'

He caught her mouth in a hard kiss. One hand slipped under the sheet, finding the vee of her nightdress then beneath it the firm mound of her breast.

Revulsion rising in her like physical sickness, Anna twisted her mouth away.

'I . . . I always prefer to make love with the light on, Edwin.'

It was a risk but she had to take it. Edwin Saverry was slight in build but that gave no positive indication as to his strength. If he decided to try and take her now she might not be able to fight him off. Above her she heard the harsh intake of breath and as he moved to switch on the new electric light, Anna rolled from the bed.

'What the hell do you think you are doing?' she demanded as the room flooded with light. 'And where is Misty?'

'She's on the boat train for Paris.' He smiled, the same sly repulsive expression she had seen so often during his stay in this house. 'I told her there was something I had to take care of.'

'Then why are you back here?' It was a silly question in view of what had happened but it gave her time to think. The maid was not in the house, but then he would know that having lived here for a month; there was only Maggie, and Anna couldn't risk her being harmed.

'You know why I'm here. Because it's *you* I want.'

She hadn't reckoned on the speed with which he moved. Before the sentence was said he had closed the gap between them, his hands fixed on her like grappling hooks, his wet lips seeking hers.

'But Misty?' Anna twisted again, managing to avoid the onslaught.

'Misty!' One hand fastened in the silk of her nightdress, dragging it off her shoulder, then slid it down to her breast, squeezing and moulding.

'I don't want Misty,' he breathed thickly, 'I want you.'

The strength of him pressing against her forced her back on to the bed and in doing so brushed her against the rosewood cabinet that stood close beside it. In desperation Anna reached towards it, clutching the heavy cut-glass three-branched candlestick that stood on it. She brought it with all her force against the side of Edwin Saverry's head.

Was he dead?

Had she killed him?

'I don't care.' Anna's whole body trembled and her fingers convulsively gripped the candlestick. 'I don't care . . . I don't care.'

It seemed she travelled through eternity as she stood watching the still figure sprawled on her bedroom floor but at last he moved, moaning as he opened his eyes.

'Get out!' Anna hissed as he touched the cut oozing a trickle of blood from beneath his brilliantined hair. 'Get out now before I hit you again! I don't know what the hell you thought you would get by coming back to this house, but whatever it was, you are mistaken.'

Pushing himself to a sitting position, he pulled a handkerchief from the top pocket of his snuff-coloured jacket, wincing as he held it to his head.

Stepping back, a little afraid he might renew his attack despite the blow she had struck him and the candlestick she still held, Anna watched the bright crimson stain seep slowly into the perfectly laundered square.

'Maggie was right about you.' Her lips felt tight, unwilling to move. 'You're no good . . .'

'Maggie!' He spat the name viciously. 'That bloody old bitch!'

'A bloody old bitch she might be but she got your measure.' Anna glared. 'Now you had best leave before I call the police.'

He looked at her, a line of blood snaking down his cheek, undulating into his moustache.

That is what you are, Anna thought as he watched her, a slimy, no good snake.

'Why don't you do that?'

His pallid eyes gleamed in the light of the room, sending new tremors of fear through Anna. She had disliked this man from the moment of their first meeting. Now she despised him.

'Why don't you send for the police? By the time they get here I could be undressed and in your bed. Now wouldn't *that* make a nice little headline? Anna Royce of Sovereign Motors steals daughter's fiancé.'

'You could be in my bed or you could be dead!'

'I could be dead . . . but I won't be.'

He smiled again and Anna knew the true depth of her feelings for the man her daughter was about to marry; the real measure of her hatred.

'Don't be too sure of that.'

'Oh, but I am. You can't hurt that daughter of yours, can you? Not after what has gone on between you. Aren't I right, Anna?'

'You swine!' She raised the candlestick a little higher, every cell in her brain screaming at her to bring it down again, to strike him until that sly smile dropped from his face, until those pallid gleaming eyes were closed for good. 'You swine, I'd like to kill you!'

'But you won't.' Taking the handkerchief from the cut, he looked at the vivid stain then folded the cloth, reapplying it to the still bleeding wound.

'It is as well you don't want Misty because I would never give my consent now. I would never let her marry a swine like you.'

Edwin Saverry dabbed at his head, his bright ferret's eyes on Anna's pale face.

'I don't want her, that's true, but it doesn't mean I am not going to marry her. And you, my dear mother-in-law to be, can do nothing to prevent it. You see . . .' he screwed up the handkerchief savagely between his hands before stuffing it back into his pocket '. . . I would tell your daughter you planned this, that I came back here because you had begged me to, that you wanted me so badly it didn't matter I was engaged to her.'

'Misty would never believe that!' Anna gasped.

Climbing to his feet he swayed unsteadily, thrusting out an arm to steady himself. Still wary of what he might try, Anna lifted the heavy candlestick again.

'You think she wouldn't believe that of you?' At her movement his eyes darkened, narrowing to vicious slits. 'She wouldn't believe that of her darling mother? But I think she would. After all, she is only too familiar with your background . . . a bitch of a mother so in heat she gave herself to her own father . . . the half-brother she has in Wednesbury. Think about it, Anna, who do you really think she would believe?'

'Where did you hear that?' Anna could not believe Misty would tell him about Aaron. 'Misty would not . . .'

Straightening his jacket, running a hand over his slicked

down hair, Edwin Saverry looked at the woman he had tried to rape.

'Wouldn't she?' He smirked. 'Not tell the man she loves of the silly flirtation with a young man who turned out to be her half-brother? Not tell the man she is to marry of her mother's bastard son? You see, Anna, your daughter hasn't enough sense to know when to keep her mouth shut. She wanted to start our marriage off on the right foot, no secrets; so very right for a stable relationship between a man and his beloved wife, don't you think?'

Anna's arm fell to her side though her hand still gripped the candlestick.

'How much do you want?'

Loathing, disgust and fury fought within her as he smiled.

'Oh, you can't buy me off! I might not have got the particular cherry I wanted but I still have the tree.'

'What do you mean?'

The smirk on his face widened, showing teeth that were almost too white, and the small feral eyes gleamed with the warmth of ice.

'What do I mean? I mean your daughter. She's got nothing in her head, and nothing between her legs I can't get anywhere else – and much more enjoyably. In fact, all the stuck up little cow *has* got going for her is your money, and sooner or later the lot of it will be hers . . . and mine!'

'No . . . no, it won't! Neither my money nor my daughter will ever be yours. As soon as Misty returns from Paris I will tell her what you are and what you tried to do tonight, and when I do there will be no marriage.'

'And should you try that, you will find yourself once more without a daughter.'

His smile was gloating and revulsion spread through her, burning like a forest fire.

'If it means I have no daughter then so be it. I would rather that than have her married to you.'

*   *   *

'I still don't know if it's the right thing.' Anna sat in Hester's sitting room. 'The business is doing fine as it is, I really see no need to expand.'

'Why stand still, Anna, when you could bring employment to so many more people?' Reuben asked over his spectacles.

Bring employment to others. Anna sighed inwardly. She had done that on so many occasions, but what had it brought her other than a great deal of worry? Why enlarge on that? Why add to the burden?

'There's a lot to think of, Reuben.' She was still doubtful. 'The risk . . .'

'Where's the risk?' Hester intervened quickly. 'You heard what that woman said.'

Yes, she had heard. It was her visit to the shop in Queen Anne's Gate two months ago that had triggered the idea she had since discussed several times with Hester and Reuben. Two women had been buying her china.

'If we had this in the States –' one of them had been holding a Royal Edward plate, tracing the exquisite design with a finger '– there surely wouldn't be a house without it. Why, I tell you, when we get this home we are going to be the envy of Washington. There won't be one single woman wouldn't pay a fortune to have the same.'

Maybe Reuben was right, maybe new markets were to be had in America, but did she want to be the one to take them?

'Truth is, Anna,' Hester's toffee drop eyes looked concerned, 'you need a break after the business of Misty breaking off her engagement.'

It was true. Misty's marriage to Edwin Saverry would no longer take place. Anna could still feel the relief that had swept over her when Misty had returned only days after leaving. They had met up with friends when they got to Paris, she had said, and Edwin had drunk too much. She had been in the bedroom of the friend's house showing her the silk lingerie she had bought. Edwin was talking to the husband, his voice drifting in from the living room getting louder with every glass of wine. He boasted he had been back to see her bitch of a mother, told her that all her daughter had was money and that he would take that while taking his pleasures where he fancied. Misty had come home the following day.

Anna remembered expecting the girl to dissolve into floods of tears, but there had been none. It was better she found out now rather than after marrying Edwin Saverry, Misty had said. In her heart, Anna thanked God. Her daughter had grown up.

'Why not go to America, Anna?' Hester cut into her thoughts. 'Give yourself a holiday.'

'But I can't go toddling off to America.' She gave a thin laugh. 'The business won't run itself. I really ought not to have asked you to go, I don't know how I can manage without you, and Reuben has his practice.'

'We talked about that when you first mentioned a trip to America, Anna.' Reuben looked at her over heavy-rimmed spectacles. 'We both agreed a holiday was due to us and this is an opportunity that may never come again.'

'I wouldn't call it a holiday, Reuben,' she said. 'Going to sound out the prospects for a new market, especially in a foreign country, can't be any joy ride. In fact, I'm sure it would terrify me.'

'It might be a bit scary,' Hester agreed. 'But you would have Reuben and me with you. You really should come. If anyone deserves a few weeks off, you do.'

'Say you will come, Anna.' Reuben added his voice.

Her thoughts chaotic, Anna shook her head. Since Andrew died Maggie seemed so frail, hardly strong enough to stand up to life anymore. And Misty. How could she leave her daughter so soon after that awful business with Saverry? She had shown no real regret, no depth of emotion of any sort other than anger. But that did not mean she held none, and if they surfaced, Anna wanted to be close, not half way across the world.

'I will come next time.'

Hester guessed that the reason for Anna's refusal was to be with Misty.

'We understand.' Her quick glance silenced the suggestion Reuben had been about to make. 'You're right, Anna, there is always next time. And if America is as wonderful, or as shocking, as I hope, then we will take me mam and Maggie with us.'

A smile on her lips, Anna rose to leave.

'Now *that* would take some arranging. Maggie has not stopped complaining about Birmingham yet.'

Slipping her arms into the coat Reuben held for her, she did up the row of buttons that reached from waist to throat.

'Was Maggie not impressed?'

Anna slanted a glance at Reuben, knowing his question was tongue in cheek. 'Oh, Maggie was impressed. Said everyone was "haring about as though the devil were after them . . . forgot 'ow to walk, they 'ave."'

Reuben smiled at Anna's mimicry. 'We will compromise. We will take the ladies to London and if they enjoy that, then who knows? It could be: Stand back New York!'

Smoothing on her gloves Anna picked up her bag.

'You know what Maggie would say to that, don't you, Reuben? "Ar, an' pigs might fly!"'

Anna looked across at her daughter. She had sat for over an hour, her pencil resting on a paper in her lap. Anna had watched her closely since her return from Paris, dreading any signs of unhappiness, which, strangely, had not shown yet. Today's faraway mood was the first time Misty had been other than her old bubbly self.

'How are the new designs coming?'

'Mmm? Oh, all right. They are coming along.'

'Misty.' Anna decided to ask the question that plagued her. If it brought on a storm then perhaps it would be for the best, at least storms usually cleared away clouds. 'Do you have any regrets, at breaking your engagement?'

'Regrets!' Misty's head jerked upward, her eyes wide. 'That's the very last thing I feel. Believe me, Mother, I thank heaven every day that I found out about Edwin Saverry when I did. How on earth could I have let myself be taken in like that?'

'It happens,' Anna replied.

'But it wasn't as if I was not warned about him.' Misty let the pencil fall from her fingers. 'My friends tried to tell me what sort of man he was, but I wouldn't listen. I had to have my own way, just like before.'

Anna held out her arms, and as Misty came to her she folded them about the slight figure. 'Don't blame yourself for that.' She murmured against her daughter's hair. 'It was my fault, I should have told you about Aaron before.'

'I wish Aaron were with us.'

'So do I, dear, but he refuses to have anything to do with me.' Anna felt her heart tighten. Aaron would never own her.

'He will learn, one day,' Misty said, her head resting in Anna's lap. 'The same as I did, but I hope he doesn't learn with someone like Saverry. It was awful, Mother, listening to him bragging about what he had done.'

Anna sat quiet. Misty had given her a bare explanation of what had gone on in her friend's house, maybe now she was ready to tell more.

'He said he had told me he wanted to see an old friend before joining me in Paris.' Misty talked softly, but with no trace of sorrow in her voice. 'But that he had come back here, to this house. He said he had asked you for money, and I could guess *how* he asked. But it was clear, for all of his boasting, that his devious little plan came to nothing, he was too angry to have been successful. The next morning he came to my hotel. He tried to pretend his whole outburst had been intended as a joke. Huh!' Misty's shoulders shook. 'Some joke. The man must have a sick mind. When I told him our marriage was off he tried to threaten me with Aaron. He said he would tell the world of Anna Royce's bastard son, a son born of her own father, unless he were well paid to keep his mouth shut.'

Anna sat perfectly still. Edwin Saverry would do what he threatened. She did not care for herself, but what of Aaron? What would it do to him?

'I told him to go ahead,' Misty went on. 'But I advised him to spend whatever he got quickly. I reminded him I had lived on the Left Bank months before he came to Paris. I had friends there who knew the right people, people willing to do anything for the right amount of money. I told him that given your money and my connections he could very well be found one morning, floating face down in the Seine.'

'Misty!' Anna lifted her daughter's head to look into her face. 'Misty, you didn't.'

'I most certainly did.' Misty grinned. 'And given the look on his face, Edwin Saverry believed it.'

'A visitor for you, mum.'

Anna glanced to where the maid stood in the doorway.

'I've asked him to wait in the sitting room.'

'Tell him I will be there in a moment.' She would have liked more time alone with Misty but the girl was already on her feet.

'I will come with you.' Misty held out a hand. 'Whoever it is we will see him off together.'

'André!' Misty bounded across the sitting room. 'We were not told it was you. We came to see you off!'

'But you would not be so cruel to an old man.'

Anna watched the greeting between the two. André Levassor had called several times since that first meeting in Wednesbury, and each time Misty was happy to see him. And she, Anna, how did she feel?

'You do not mind, Anna? That I come uninvited?'

Glad her thoughts had been halted, Anna held out a hand.

'Since when do such good friends need an invitation? But

326

when you were here last you said you would be in Europe for several months.'

'*Oui*, that is true.' He took the chair Anna indicated. 'But I found myself with a few days to spare, so,' he shrugged his shoulders, 'I came to look at the designs Aaron has for a new motor engine.'

'You have seen Aaron?'

'*Oui*.' He answered Anna's question.

'And how is my obstinate brother?'

Anna caught her daughter's smile and felt a surge of warmth at her complete acceptance of their relationship.

'He is well.' André smiled, then looked at Anna. 'He is a very good designer of engines. I would suggest you go see for yourself, but not today, Anna. Today, I ask you spend with me.'

Anna felt the colour rise in her cheeks. 'I . . . I'm sorry, André, I have . . .'

'You have nothing to do that won't keep.' Misty cut short Anna's refusal. 'And if you are going to mention Grammie, then don't. She has promised to tell me all of the tricks I got up to with the Cresswell twins, and that is likely to take a week at least.'

'There, you see, Anna, you have no excuse. So, you will come?'

'I really should not have given in so easily,' Anna said as André drove the carriage he had hired for the day before coming to the house.

'Did you not want to come?'

'Yes.' Anna replied truthfully. 'Yes, André, I wanted to come.'

They had driven to a small inn where they had been served lunch by a red cheeked woman who smiled constantly, and now Anna knew she was happy not to have missed their day together.

Calling the horse to a halt, he jumped down from the carriage. 'I have something I must say to you, Anna.' He held up his arms, wanting to help her down. 'Tomorrow I must leave, but before I go . . .'

Circled by his arms as he helped her down, Anna felt suddenly nervous.

'Have you enjoyed our day together?' he asked, and when she nodded, 'That is all I ask, that you be happy with me.'

Gently, he turned her toward him and Anna felt herself being drawn into the depths of his dark eyes. 'You will always be happy with me, *chérie*, through all the long days and nights that are left to us. Come with me to South America and when the racing is over I shall take you to Bordeaux. You will love it there, Anna, the vineyards and the streams. But most of all, I want that you will love being my wife.'

'Your wife!' Anna gasped. 'It seems no more than yesterday we met.'

'Who knows when yesterday began?' he asked softly, taking her face between his hands. 'We have known each other for eternity Anna, you feel that, as I do.'

He kissed her then, his mouth tender yet firm and Anna realised with a sudden blinding clarity that she wanted him to kiss her. She wanted him to hold her, wanted to go with him to South America. She wanted to be his wife.

'We will marry in Bordeaux,' he said, when at last he released her mouth.

'No!' Anna pushed free of his arms. 'I can't marry you, André, I can't marry anyone.'

'Why? Because of your paper diamonds?' He laughed softly, pulling her back into the circle of his arms. 'That was an excuse, *chérie*. You refused to marry Charles not because of your business, but because, deep in your soul, you were waiting for me.'

Anna held her face against his shoulder. Maybe he knew already, maybe he had heard it from Aaron, but she must tell him herself.

'My business was not the real reason,' she said quietly. 'There is something more.'

One arm about her trembling body, one hand gently caressing the head buried in his shoulder, André Levassor listened, letting the hurt pour from her; listened as Anna whispered out her past; her father's raping her, her illegitimate son, and lastly her fear that any man who became involved with Anna Royce would die as a result.

'We do not need to fear the past, *ma chérie*,' he murmured as she stopped speaking. 'What we will have in our future together is all that is important . . . nothing else matters.'

Charles had said that and she had refuted it, but with André the words brought a sense of peace, a kind of rightness as though fate had at last given her life a benediction.

'There can be no more excuses, Anna.' His fingers brushed the silken folds of her hair. 'No running away from the truth. You belong to me, you always have done. I will not let you go. What happened long ago was not of your doing, it is over, *chérie*, and we need never speak of it again.'

Lifting her face, he kissed her gently and as Anna opened her eyes she saw behind his dark head a shooting star curve across the evening sky, a glittering moment of beauty, a scanty reflection racing over a dark earth before ebbing away into nothingness, leaving the sky darker for its passing. Was this an omen of what was to be for her? Was meeting André to be a brief moment, a brilliant starburst of happiness that would pass, leaving her life darker and emptier for his leaving?

His mouth closed again over her own and Anna pushed away the inner warning.

'This has to be, Anna.' His mouth touched her closed eyelids. 'We both know it. We have carried this love within us, waiting, searching for the one to whom it truly belonged. But now that search is ended. I love you, Anna, I love you and I want you to be my wife. Shhh.' He touched a finger against her lips as she made to speak. 'The past is gone, *chérie*. It is finished. It does not matter anymore. We have each other, Anna, and we have the future, that is enough.'

Standing there, the sweet smell of meadow grass in her

nostrils, the feel of André's arms about her, Anna knew she loved this man, loved him not with fierceness but with a gentle, calm love that filled her with a contentment she had not known before. On the breeze that touched her hair she seemed to hear the words of Kate O'Keefe.

'*Toil and tears . . . The lives of many will be bound with yer own. Ye will have the carryin' of them, for 'tis yer back their fortunes will ride upon. Ye will work all the days of yer life, but that life will prove to be a great one . . .*'

Toil she had had, building her life, and tears she had shed for a father she loved and a son who would not own her as his mother. And there were many whose lives and fortunes were tied to her own. She had come a long way from Ethelfleda Terrace, and from Roker Street. She had her paper diamonds. For all she knew, the toil, and maybe the tears, were not over yet, but Kate O'Keefe's prediction had proved true. Down to the very last words.

'*The man who will place a ring about yer heart is not of this land.*'

André Levassor was that man.

'No . . . no more!'

Her face drained of colour, Anna stared at the small buff-coloured envelope that held the wireless telegram.

'I won't . . . I won't let it happen again . . . oh, please God, not again!'

'Steady, me wench!' Seeing Anna tremble, Maggie dismissed the delivery boy then closed the door. 'Don't go gettin' yourself all riled up, Anna, you don't know what be in that envelope yet.'

It must not be them. Mouth clenched against the fear that was swallowing her, Anna allowed herself to be pushed into a chair.

It must not be Hester and Reuben. They were on their way to America, they were safe aboard that ship . . . they had to be safe. Oh, why had she agreed to their going? Why had she allowed herself to be talked into looking for new markets?

'You 'ave to open it, wench.'

At her elbow, Maggie held out the dull yellow envelope. Anna stared at it, her teeth clenched. If she did not open it then nothing would happen to Hester and Reuben, if she did not touch it then everything would be all right.

Maggie looked at the stricken face, seeing again that of a girl, no more than a child, who had come to her out of the rain; a girl she loved but could not protect from the blows it seemed life was determined to deal her.

'See 'ere, Anna,' she said gently, 'I knows what you be feelin', the fear that haunts your heart. But it be a fear that be groundless. No matter what you 'ave told yourself, you 'ad naught to do with Edward's death nor that of Philip Rewcastle an' his fancy friend. Same as the death of your father was none of your makin'. You can't be holding these things against yourself, just as you can't go through life thinking you be a jinx on any man who looks on you!'

'I let them go.' Anna seemed not to hear. 'I let Hester and Reuben go, I thought they would be safe . . .'

'Anna, stop mewlin' like a babby!'

Maggie's voice cut through her fear, sharp with anger, anger for the years of anguish and heartbreak she had watched her friend live through, anger that it was still not finished.

'You don't even know if that there telegram be about Hester and Reuben at all. You be buildin' walls wi'out bricks.'

'I thought they would be safe.' Anna's mouth trembled.

'Ar, I know you did, wench. And safe they will be.' Maggie's anger had not faded but was muted now by a softer tone. 'Like as not this 'ere telegram be to tell you they have arrived in America and be 'aving a rare old time, but you won't know 'less you opens it.'

Her hand shaking, Anna took the small envelope, drawing out the slip of paper it held. Slowly, having to force herself to look at the bold black print, she read the words then re-read them, unsure if the fresh flood of pain that surged through her was that of relief or of guilt.

The telegram was not from Hester and Reuben.

Anna sat in the train carrying her to Wednesbury. She had been so terrified for her friends that no other thought had surfaced in her mind. Turning to the window, she watched the spume of smoke from the engine drift like black foam over the passing fields.

The telegram had not been from Hester and Reuben, that had been the relief, but it had been from her son, and that was a cause of the pain.

Worry had pushed many things to the back of her mind, so far as to be almost forgotten.

The carriage wheels screamed against the brakes as the train pulled into a drab little station, the painted sign on the wall of a waiting room proclaiming it as Bilston. Anna pulled in her feet, tucking them beneath the slatted wooden seat as a large woman with several baskets struggled to manoeuvre herself from the carriage to the platform.

She could have travelled first-class with a lot more comfort. Anna watched a thin man in shabby jacket and trousers take the place the large woman had vacated. But for all her success in business, she still felt a trifle uneasy at what she saw as unnecessary spending on herself.

Hissing and spurting like some childhood monster, the train moved and Anna found herself listening to the clicking of its wheels. She had loved watching the trains pass along the track that ran through Wednesbury. As a child it had been a regular summer evening walk with her father when he had taken her to sit on the bank above the sidings of the Great Western Railway and sung little rhymes to match the rhythm of the trains going by. Then he had lifted her to his shoulders and carried her home along Dudley Street, stopping on the way to buy two ounces of Tigs Herbal from the sweet shop on the High Bullen.

So many things had been pushed to the back of her mind, hidden but not forgotten. She would never forget.

The train groaned again, juddering as it came to a stop once more.

'Be you wantin' Wednesbury, missus?'

Anna had not realised she was standing in the compartment doorway and murmured an apology to the thin man standing behind her, waiting to leave the train.

Glancing along the platform and beyond, Anna saw the grassy bank above the sidings. No, she would not forget.

'I had no intention of letting you know Polly was dead, but then I realised she would have wanted you to be told.'

Anna sat in the tiny back room of the house that had been her home for sixteen years. Everything was the same: the grate black-leaded to a silvery shine, the smoke-blackened kettle on the hob, a mat of clippings on the floor, the scrubbed table top white beneath the cloth of deep red chenille that had been her mother's treasure.

'I got your telegram yesterday evening.' Anna brought her thoughts away from the past. 'Was Polly ill, Aaron? Did she suffer at all?'

She caught the shudder her unconscious use of his name caused.

'Heart attack,' he returned coldly. 'But Doctor Shaw said she would have felt no pain. More like a door closing in her face, he reckoned.'

'Thank God!' Anna whispered. Then: 'Is there anything I can do?'

'Nothing!' He almost spat the word. 'I don't need your help. In fact, I don't need you for anything.'

'Aaron, please.' Anna's heart was in the cry. 'Can't we at least try to be friends?'

'Friends?' His laughter was harsh. 'We could have been so much more than that. Oh, I know the truth of what happened in this house, Polly told me. I know the getting of me was

333

not your fault, but you turned your back on me. At least he stayed.' He flung an arm towards the tiny window beyond which the oak tree stood outside the wall of the church. 'He had the courage to own me, didn't turn his back and bugger off without a thought.'

'Yes, he had the courage to stay,' Anna answered quietly. 'He had the courage to face the tongue wagging and the back biting of people we had always thought of as friends, and I did not. All of that is true but I never forgot . . .'

'Oh, yes.' Bitterness twisted the face that swung back to her, the translucent blue eyes darkening with pain. 'Polly told me about that as well. Conscience money. You thought that would cover everything, didn't you? Well, hear this. All the money in the world couldn't dry the tears of a child longing for its mother . . . money might be your universal salve, Mrs Anna Royce, but it doesn't cure all ills and it doesn't buy me. I'll take no more of it from you. I've told you before, I'll pay back every penny you ever sent to Polly Shipton. I don't want your money and I don't want you!'

Anna stood up. The unhappiness that had driven her from this house all those years ago was driving her still.

'The funeral,' she said quietly, 'I would like to be there if you have no objection?'

'Church and cemetery are open to everybody.' He turned his back dismissively.

That was a way of telling her there was no welcome for her in this house, not even to say a last goodbye to a valued friend. Swallowing the deliberate insult, together with what was left of her pride, Anna asked again. 'Would you mind telling me what time the service will be held?'

When he didn't answer she took the few steps that carried her from the little whitewashed room.

'Ten o'clock.' His words followed her through the closing door.

*   *   *

In the room she had taken at The White Horse Anna removed the jade velvet travelling suit and silk-trimmed hat that had drawn many questioning looks in that third-class railway compartment, then stood staring at the splash of colour against the plain buff bedspread. They were a far cry from a cornflower-strewn cotton frock. She had come a long way from Ethelfleda Terrace. She had her paper diamonds and knew the string that at times lay like a yoke about her neck would grow heavier yet.

'The lives of many will be bound to yer own. Ye will have the carrying of them.'

It was true. Anna continued to stare at the suit, green as that grassy bank of long ago. The lives tied to her own increased as her business prospered, but where was the happiness that should bring?

'Toil and tears, Kate,' she murmured into the silence of the room. 'You promised me toil and tears and I have had both. Your words were true, down to the very last one.'

She had consented to become André's wife. When he returned from racing in South America they would be married. She had once thought herself in love with Charles Lazenby.

After hanging her suit in the wardrobe, she crossed to the wash stand where she poured water from a plain heavy jug into a matching bowl.

But like her daughter's love for Edwin Saverry, her own had proved to be an infatuation, a mere illusion of love that had faded long before her meeting André.

Yes. Anna dried her face. She had come a long way since sitting on a bank watching trains pass by, and tears had followed her, almost every step of the way.

For a second time Anna stood waiting for a coffin to be carried from the house in which she had spent her childhood. This time there was no group of women, shawls drawn tightly about their heads, waiting at the gate for the coffin to pass by. This time there was no spectacle for them to gawp at, no suicide's coffin to be lowered from a bedroom window and passed over the garden wall. This was just the funeral of an old woman who had stood by Jos Bradly and reared his daughter's bastard child. But Anna knew that though she stood alone in the street, more than one pair of eyes watched her from behind piously closed curtains.

They would have guessed by now the identity of the woman dressed in a grey suit edged with black frogging, her auburn hair caught beneath a black veiled hat. She had stayed out of sight when her father was buried, but no more. From this day on they would all learn who it was held their town in her hands.

The door of the house opened and the plain coffin was carried out, its one simple wreath of white lilies telling Anna that even the house-to-house collection of pennies and tuppences, those contributions of friends and neighbours that customarily helped to bury one of their own, had been denied Polly Shipton; she had lived with the stigma of helping Jos Bradly and it was one she was to die with too. Aaron's tribute alone graced the wooden box that held her body.

His solitary figure, dressed in dark trousers and a coat that was too big, which Anna guessed had been bought as an unredeemed pledge from Thomas Bennet's pawn shop, followed it from the house, falling in behind the pall bearers who would carry it the few yards to the church.

Anna's hands tightened around the flowers she was carrying. Head held high, Aaron had not acknowledged her presence in any way. But she would not let his hostility deter her. Polly Shipton deserved her respect and no one would prevent her from paying it.

Following beneath the lych gate to the graveyard where the body of her father had not been allowed to rest, Anna paused, wanting to place her own posy of pink and white carnations beside the white lilies, yet not wanting to offend.

'I'll tek 'em, mum.' One of the bearers held out a work-grimed hand, and when Anna gratefully passed him the flowers, placed them on the coffin.

Walking slowly behind the son who ignored her still, Anna stepped into the church she had not entered since the day she had been churched, the day she had been made to pray for forgiveness for a sin that was none of her making. On one side of the altar steps a plaster virgin held her son whilst from the other a forgiving Christ held out his hand towards the box that held the body of the last friend Anna had in Wednesbury. Her eyes passed the painted figures, going to the high altar with its gleaming cross and chalice.

Where was her forgiveness? When would her dues be paid?

'. . . we are come together to give the soul of our friend Polly Shipton into the keeping of God . . .'

Polly Shipton had no friend in Wednesbury, Anna wanted to scream. Because she stuck by a man and raised his bastard child, the people of this town turned their back on her. She was a social outcast, as was the man their accusations and malicious talk drove to take his own life. Polly Shipton had no one but my son.

No one but her son. The voice of the priest droned on but Anna heard nothing save the sound of her own pain. Polly had cradled the child she had left, held him to her body in the night, soothed him when he cried, taken the flowers his tiny hands had picked, watched him grow and learn. Polly had known his love, and she his mother knew only his hatred.

'We thank God for the life of Polly Shipton . . .'

The change of voice recalled Anna to the service and she looked to where Aaron now stood at the lectern, the great Bible supported not on the outstretched wings of a brazen eagle as was customary but on the back of a fighting cock, the special gift to this church of a grateful King Charles II.

'. . . she lived not for herself but for others . . .'

Anna caught the break in his voice and fought to hold back her own tears. He was so tall, her son, his body showing muscular and strong even in the suit that hung from him. From the great east window a single shaft of sunlight touched his blond head, as if Polly herself were touching it for the last time.

'We have so much to thank her for ... we will not forget ...'

No, Anna watched Aaron's proud face, he would not forget how Mother Polly had loved and cared for him ... nor how his own mother had left him!

It was over. Polly's body had been lowered into her grave, set against the enclosing wall at the rear of the ancient, smoke-blackened church. Priest and bearers were gone and Anna stood alone, staring at the dark hole still waiting to be filled with earth. Polly Shipton had given up a lot for Anna Bradly; forgone the friendship of neighbours she had known for years, making herself as much an outcast as the man and boy she kept house for. Even the finding of a tinker trapped in a mine shaft up along Dangerfield Lane, and his deathbed confession to the murder of Mary Carter, had not eased Jos Bradly's burden. He had raped his own daughter and they would not forgive. Now Polly too was gone and with her the last vestige of loyalty Anna might still feel towards Wednesbury.

Anna walked slowly along the bank of the Tame, the gentle song of its water soothing her frayed nerves. There would be no train for Coseley until morning and she had no wish to sit in The White Horse nor yet to visit any part of the town. After today Wednesbury would hold nothing for Anna Royce.

Above her head birds called loudly, disturbed by her presence, while a lone butterfly fluttered from blossom to blossom in search of its kind.

But the butterfly wasn't orange. Anna sat down on the soft earth, drawing her knees up to her chin. No, there were no orange butterflies, no children laughing and calling, no Peter, just her and her memories.

'I've got them, Peter,' she murmured, 'my string of diamonds ... but the cost was too high.'

A leaf floating on the dark water carried Anna's gaze downstream. She and Peter had so often raced leaf boats during those Sunday school outings . . . had Aaron been a part of such outings, had he climbed trees or fished for tiddlers, had her son fallen into the stream? She would never know. She felt the pressure of dry sobs in her throat. There were so many things she would never know.

Cramped from sitting, Anna got to her feet, brushing grass from her skirts. There was one more thing she had to do before turning her back on Wednesbury for the last time.

Heads turned as she walked the familiar streets leading to Ethelfleda Terrace and the house close to the church, but this time it was no frightened girl they watched, her head bent and hidden by a shawl. This time it was Anna Royce, head held high and confident. A woman no other in this town would dare throw dirty insinuations at; a woman who could crush their lives as easily as they had crushed Jos Bradly's.

Pushing open a door she knew would not be locked, Anna stepped into the tiny whitewashed room, every inch of which was engraved on her heart. Aaron sat beside the fireplace, his head slumped in his hands. Anna's heart jolted, every instinct telling her to take him in her arms, to drive away his unhappiness with the force of the love she held for him, but she did not move.

'I know I am not welcome here.' He swung to face her, the full extent of his misery exposed for only a moment, then he was on his feet, the guard of anger dropping over his pale blue eyes, and Anna rushed on before he could say anything.

'My presence in this house is unwanted, but please remember this was my home before it was yours and what I have to say to you will be said inside these four walls.'

At his sides Aaron's fingers clenched into tight fists; his teeth clamped together as he fought the tide rising within him. She had no right here, this woman who claimed to be his mother, the woman who had turned her back on him.

'What my father did caused pain to both of us,' Anna went

on, aware of the emotions ripping him apart, aware her words could only heighten his pain, aware also that they must be said. 'But he wasn't responsible for his actions. My father was incapable of deliberately harming me and I am sure he never once harmed you. Joseph Bradly was a decent man driven to insanity by mindless fools and others who kept the lie alive, even after Mary Carter's killer was found. Men and women who fed the gossip and kindled the scandal to draw attention from their own dirty work.'

'But he stayed!' Aaron's answer was filled with quiet rage.

'Yes, he stayed.' Anna saw his fury but didn't flinch. If she backed down now the rest of her words would never be said. 'He stayed and I went. You think that was the coward's way out. Well, maybe it was, maybe I was wrong to do what I did, but if so, I did wrong for the right reasons.'

Beyond the tiny window evening shadows began to gather a purple veil about the black-spired church.

'Had I stayed then people would have said I was his whore – as some already had – and we would both have finished up being whipped from the town. How would my father have felt then? A daughter and a newborn child and nowhere to go. Well, perhaps you think I should have faced that, or at least have taken you with me. So think of this too. I had no idea where I would go or how I would live. I had no money, not even enough to buy you milk . . . when I left Wednesbury I had money for a railway ticket and nothing else besides.'

Anna saw his mouth soften but it was the softening of contempt.

'Yes, I know, Aaron.' She read his thoughts. 'Why didn't I come for you when I was earning? Don't think I didn't want to, but Coseley is no different from Wednesbury. They don't take kindly to women who have children out of wedlock, won't entertain it in their own, so what chance for me, a stranger?

'And later, once I *was* married?' Anna parried his next

question. 'Edward wanted to bring you to Coseley and was planning to do so, then he was killed and I was back where I started. Call what I have said explanation or excuse, whichever you choose, but it is the truth. And it is the truth when I say that never, for one moment, did I stop loving you, and never, for one moment, did I stop missing you. You are my child, Aaron. I love you and I miss you as I always will. You despise me for what I did to you, that is understandable, and when I leave this house you will never want to see me again. That too I understand. But it will not change the way I feel, it won't change the love I have for you. You are my son, Aaron, and I will thank God for that every day of my life.'

Anna followed the path that led from the lych gate to St Bartholomew's, turning aside before reaching the heavy door to step across the turf to a headstone set against the curtain wall.

Beyond the gate, partly hidden by the same tree that had sheltered Anna as she had watched her father's coffin lowered into an unmarked grave, Aaron watched the woman who was his mother. Why had he been stupid enough to send her word of Polly's death? Why hadn't he told her flatly to go back to where she came from? Why hadn't he told her he would never feel anything for her but hatred and contempt?

Across the churchyard Anna stooped, laying one red rose on the grave he knew held his grandmother. Aaron stepped further behind the tree, watching the graceful figure start down the path.

Why was he standing here? What was he waiting for? Hadn't this woman caused him enough pain already? He had guessed she would make one last call on her mother's grave before leaving, and despite himself had waited at the window of the house until he had seen her walk past. Then an urge stronger than his will had drawn him to the church, drawn him to the woman coming out through the lych gate, the woman he would not meet again after today. His eyes followed the grey-clad figure as she moved across the grassy hill towards a huge oak, its branches spreading a wide canopy over the unmarked grave of the man who had been his father and hers.

She could not know he lay there. Aaron remained still but his mind ran in circles. Polly might have written, telling her of her father's death. Yes, Polly might have written but she would not have told her of the place of his lying and Anna Royce had not followed his coffin. There was no way for her to know where that grave had been dug, yet she had gone straight to it and now, as he watched, sank to her knees.

Beneath the great spreading branches Anna touched the green earth with one hand.

'You did not mean to hurt me, Father,' she whispered. 'I have always known that. I could not come back, I was not as strong as you. But I never stopped loving you.'

Lifting the tiny bunch of cornflowers and buttercups she had picked from the open heath that lay to one side of the church steps, flowers she had so often picked with her father, Anna put them to her lips then placed them on the soft turf.

'You took good care of him, Father,' she said softly. 'You loved him as I love him.'

Tears too strong for her to hold spilled down her cheeks. Anna stood up. Spread out below the hill, Wednesbury sprawled beneath the pall of smoke from its foundries and tiny back room workshops, while beyond it stretched the heath where Mother Polly had taught her the art of using plants and flowers. She let her eyes rove, seeing one more time the playground of her childhood and the arena where her misery had begun, then glanced at the house that held so much of her heart and so many of her memories.

'Mrs Royce.' Aaron stepped from the shelter of the tree as she drew level. 'I . . . I was waiting for you.'

'Oh!' Anna halted, her head tilted back, forced to look up to reach those intense blue eyes. 'You have something you wish to say to me?'

The dark, over-large jacket hung loosely across his shoulders but to Anna that in no way detracted from the dignity of the young man who faced her; a dignity that was inborn, a dignity that was so much a part of him.

'Yes . . .' He hesitated only fractionally. 'I wanted to say thank you.'

'*You* wish to thank me? I see nothing you need thank me for.'

'Maybe you don't, but I do.'

Behind the wisp of grey veil that covered her face, Anna's eyes held surprise and admiration. Whatever her son had to say, it had taken a man's courage to bring him after her.

'Then perhaps you will tell me what I have done that warrants your thanks?'

She kept her voice cold, almost impersonal, fighting the urge to cry out for him to love her.

'For coming here,' he replied. 'For coming to Polly's funeral.'

All around them the afternoon sky leapt to brilliant crimson flame, silhouetting the church and the cluster of surrounding houses as the steel foundries opened their furnaces.

Anna gazed at the scene she had known from childhood.

'I did not have to come.' She spoke without looking at him. 'I came because I wanted to. Polly Shipton stood by me when nobody else in Wednesbury would. I was proud to follow at her funeral and I will always be proud to have been her friend.'

'You are the only one she had apart from me and him.' Aaron nodded towards the oak tree. 'You saw the turnout for yourself.'

'Yes, I saw. My only comfort is that she must have found it worthwhile. Rearing you, I mean.' She looked at him now. 'She must have loved you very much.'

Seeing his mouth tighten, herself feeling the emotion she knew he was fighting to hold in check, Anna resumed the walk down Church Hill, the walk that would take her away from her son.

'I don't care what your reason was for coming, I still thank you for it.'

Anna turned. A slight breeze caught her veil, and lifted it clear of her eyes.

'I believe André Levassor has been to see you recently?'

'Yes.' Aaron did not close the gap her few steps had placed between them. 'Yes, he has been several times since you were last here.'

Anna caught the fluttering tulle, folding it back across her hat.

'So I understand. Might I ask what you thought of him?'

'He didn't stay all that long either time he came, he always had something else on hand.'

Why was she standing here prolonging the agony? Why didn't she go, why add to the pain his walking away would bring? But she didn't go. Instead she asked, 'But even so, you must have formed some opinion of the man?'

There was still a space separating them but Anna realised the few feet of earth was not the only space between her and this man who was her son; a gulf too wide for him to bridge stretched between them.

'Yes,' Aaron answered. 'He seems a nice enough chap, no airs and graces, and he certainly knows a hell of a lot about motor carriage engines. A man could learn a lot from him. He says what he thinks, you know where you are with him.'

'Has Mr Levassor given any opinion on your handling of motor carriage engines?'

'Yes, he has,' Aaron answered bluntly.

'And?'

'He said I had a good working knowledge of engines and of the motor car as a whole.'

He still called it a motor car, Anna thought remembering the first time.

'Did he ask you to go and work for him?'

'He did not ask that, but he said if ever I wanted to leave off working for you, then I could go to him.'

André had asked her son to go to him and suddenly she knew why. He knew her dread of losing all contact with Aaron and if he worked for André she would at least receive the odd word of him.

'Aaron . . . Mr Bradly . . .'

Anna's glance passed to the tiny patch of blue and gold lying at the foot of the oak tree, and curled her fingers into her palms to stop their trembling as she looked back at her son.

'There is something I wish to tell you, but before I do I want you to know that André Levassor has asked me to become his wife!'

Aaron stared at the woman he had spent so many hours of his childhood dreaming about, so many hours listening to Mother Polly telling him of the courage it had taken for her to leave her child. And the woman had courage. That he had been forced to admit: she need never have returned, never have owned him as her son. But she had returned, bringing with her the power to destroy this town as it had destroyed her father. With a single stroke of a pen she could have taken away the livelihood of almost every man in Wednesbury, instead of which she had developed new industries, giving life to a town that had once driven her away.

'What's that to me?' he asked, stubbornly pushing his thoughts away.

Anna's head tilted backward as she looked up into his face, drawn with tight lines.

'You are my son.'

The simple statement hit him more forcefully than a blow and for one fleeting moment the longing showed in his eyes. 'And what answer did you give?' he asked, once more guarded and hostile.

Anna dug her nails into her palms. 'I accepted, Aaron,' she said as he turned away. 'I told you some time ago that should you leave my employ I would close not only my own business

345

in this town but many more beside. I want you to know that what I threatened no longer applies. You have my word no one will lose his job as a result of your leaving. If you wish to work for André Levassor or for anyone else then you are free to do so. But though you might remove yourself from my life you will never remove yourself from my heart. You are my son, Aaron, and I will never stop loving you. André and Misty want you as I want you, to be part of the family, but we understand you have to do what your heart tells you.'

Turning again to face her, Aaron met the eyes of the woman he had hated for so long. Now he knew why he was here, now he knew how to put into words the thoughts that had plagued him through a long, sleepless night. He stepped toward her, the rage and hate that had held him icebound for so long melting away. 'I much prefer to work with my family,' he said softly, 'and with my mother . . . if she still wants me.'

In the branches of the oak tree birds called softly to each other and the tiny splash of cornflowers and buttercups that lay beneath it seemed to gleam with a new radiance, 'She still wants you, Aaron . . .' Anna whispered softly, 'she still wants you.'

MEG HUTCHINSON

A HANDFULL OF SILVER

Banished from her father's sight and home since the age of four, wheelchair-bound Esther Kerral is horrified when Jos Kerral forces her into an arranged marriage with Morgan Cosmore, the son of a local factory owner. Both fathers hope the union will save their ailing businesses; little do they know that each is as bankrupt as the other.

But Morgan's inclinations have long lain in another, perverse, direction and poor Esther must struggle as best she can not only to survive a loveless marriage, but also to build up a business of her own in a man's world.

HODDER AND STOUGHTON PAPERBACKS

MEG HUTCHINSON

A PROMISE GIVEN

Reeling from her stepmother's accusation that she killed her beloved little brother, Rachel Cade is shocked to find that she is at the mercy of the village's evil Magistrate Bedworth, who sends her to the workhouse to await trial. There, Rachel fears her fate is sealed, but she has reckoned without the actions of handsome landowner Jared Lytton who comes to her rescue.

Despite being vindicated, Rachel is nonetheless forced to leave the village and life is a struggle until she meets the widow Beulah Thomas and her son William. Working on their farm, Rachel is treated with generosity and kindness and when William asks for her hand in marriage, she agrees. But Rachel cannot forget Jared Lytton, whose path seems destined to cross hers . . .

HODDER AND STOUGHTON PAPERBACKS

MEG HUTCHINSON

A LOVE FORBIDDEN

Robbed of marriage to the man she loved, Leah Bryce rears his daughter Miriam as her own. But her bitterness and desire for vengeance lead her to treat the girl with extreme cruelty, and when Miriam falls pregnant, Leah refuses to let her marry the father of her child.

Leah's son Ralph has always loved the girl he believes to be his sister, and fights to subdue feelings that are more than brotherly. When he discovers Miriam's seducer has no intention of standing by her, he takes a terrible revenge: Saul Marsh will leave no other woman pregnant.

But Miriam's trials are far from over. Her mother's hatred reaches new and evil heights – even on her deathbed she seeks to ruin the girl's happiness. Only when Leah's malign influence is removed for ever can Miriam overcome the horrors of her girlhood to find love and joy at last.

HODDER AND STOUGHTON PAPERBACKS

MEG HUTCHINSON

CHILD OF SIN

'I've no idea where the slut can go and I don't care. She's a no-good stinking little whore who don't 'ave sense enough to know when to keep 'er legs closed.'

Agnes Ridley has a cruel tongue and a heart of stone: when she discovers housemaid Lizzie Burton has fallen pregnant, she turns her out with only the clothes on her back. If it weren't for loyal Debbie, who follows her friend into exile, Lizzie would be friendless as well as destitute.

The girls are blessed when they meet big-hearted Sadie Trent, who takes them in and cherishes them like her own. But even Sadie cannot protect the girls from the vicious malice of Abe Turley, who is determined to take his pleasure – and then his revenge; and from sinister Fleur Masson, who hides an evil trade behind the respectable façade of a fashion house. After such tribulations, can there ever be true happiness for a child of sin?

HODDER AND STOUGHTON PAPERBACKS